Sara... ...nham was born in London in 1915. She m... ...y in her early thirties, shortly after the Second World War, and then to Austria where she remained for over fifty years. ... thrillers such as *Cold Dark Night, The Sto...* ... out.

Night Falls on the City is Gainham's n... international acclaim in 1967, and w... She later wrote two further novels set in Vien... *Private Worlds*. Gainham also reported regularly on central E... for the *Spectator, Encounter* and the *New Republic*. She died in Austria in 19...

Praise for Night Falls on the City

'A pleasure to read ... A compellingly intimate portrait of Vienna from the Anschluss to the end of the Second World War, which captures its atmosphere of fear, mistrust, corruption and ultimate collapse. There are no heroics; instead Sarah Gainham offers a scrupulously detailed story of individuals forced through barbarism into chaos'
Helen Dunmore

'*Night Falls on the City* really is an arresting book ... I don't think many books like this get written any more. The scope is huge; the eye for minute detail unfailing. The author asks the question directly: "What was one to do?" Why risk oneself for a stranger who is already beyond saving? Friend and neighbour fall to the same logic. Ultimately, the falseness of lives lived carefully saturates Vienna and Julia cries out for just one gesture of morality. It is a powerful book with a message that will always be timely'
William Brodrick

'*Night Falls on the City* is one of those rare novels of beauty and scope and ambition that brings to life a particular moment in history ... An important and courageous novel, it is timely that *Night Falls on the City* is now being restored to its rightful place on the bookshelf beside other classics of Second World War literature'
Kate Mosse

NIGHT FALLS ON THE CITY

Sarah Gainham

ABACUS

First published in Great Britain in 1967 by Wm Collins Sons & Co Ltd
This edition published in 2012 by Abacus

A CIP catalogue record for this book
is available from the British Library.

ISBN 978-0-349-00033-6

An Hachette UK Company
www.hachette.co.uk

www.littlebrown.co.uk

Foreword

Autumn had arrived in the city. The trees in the square in front of the Westbahnhof were already browning, dusty with the exhaustion of summer.

Book Three: August 1939–November 1940

*A*ll bar one of Sarah Gainham's dozen novels were set in central Europe, a region she came to know intimately after the Second World War. Born Rachel Stainer in London (she took her *nom de plume* from her maternal great-grandmother), she settled in Vienna in 1947. From the mid-fifties to mid-sixties, she was the central European correspondent for the *Spectator*, and her first novel, *Time Right Deadly* (1956) – and the four that followed – are thrillers drawing on her own experiences and knowledge. But it was with this, her fifth novel, that Gainham found her true voice.

Night Falls on the City is one of those rare novels of beauty and scope and ambition that both brings to life a particular moment in history, a particular society, while at the same time rejoicing in the minute details of everyday life, everyday emotions. The novel opens at the Burgtheater in Vienna in March 1938, on the eve of the Anschluss between Hitler's Germany and Austria. From the first lines we are plunged into the ancient city on the brink of Occupation. In spite of the rattlings of war, the 'blunt snouts of tanks' on the border, this is a world of chandeliers and glittering glass and champagne, a world the protagonists do not yet quite believe will be taken from them. The tone is naive, flecked through with disbelief and arrogance. By the time the novel closes – in May 1945 with the Russians entering Vienna – the guileless spirit of the opening pages has been replaced by one of despair, hopelessness, weariness after seven years of betrayal, occupation, brutality and horror. The consequences of living with tyranny, with fear and the slow death of hope, are clear: the scurrying about 'heads bent and eyes averted in what was . . . only an acted servility'.

It is a story about politics and the failure of politics; about love and betrayal; about passion for a person, for an idea, for faith. At the heart of the novel is Julia Homburg, a wealthy, strong-minded and celebrated actress with the theatre company. The story that follows explores how she – and the small group of artistic, naive, opportunistic people and servants who surround her – learns to adapt first to occupation, then to war, then finally to defeat. Julia's husband, Franz Wedeker, is a Socialist politician. More significantly, he is Jewish. In Book One (of five sections, each centered on a key moment of the Occupation), the sense of disbelief and the contempt the leading characters feel for the 'Reich Germans' and the SS – the impossibility of being in thrall to 'those people' – is evident; so too is their disingenuousness as the old world of liberal privilege crumbles.

Gainham is excellent at balancing real history with imagination and, without the effort being apparent, lays bare the background that makes it possible for the Nazis to enter Austria without a shot being fired: the rampant inflation, the terms of the Treaty of Versailles, mass unemployment, poverty, jealousy, an existing peasant class and servant class, the mood of the kind of young men who join the SA and SS with their 'bellies full of undigested resentment'. She is equally strong in describing the volatile atmosphere of the beer cellars and the mob violence in the poorer districts, the markets and the railway stations and the decimated Jewish quarter, as she is in bringing to life the comfortable drawing-rooms and country estates of the rich.

Of course, the contemporary reader has the advantage over the characters. We know, as we turn the page and then the next, how real is the threat and what is to come. We have the architecture of the story. There are, if you like, no surprises Gainham can spring on us. Yet it is a testament to her great skill that she writes some very harrowing scenes and succeeds in making us feel we are reading such horrors for the first time: the murder of an old Jewish scholar in front of his family and neighbours, the brutalising of a peasant woman in the market, the petty violences inflicted by boys in uniform drunk on power.

Gainham is without judgement – she is a novelist, not an historian – but the question the novel asks is implicit in every scene: how would we act in a similar situation and what might we do to survive? At what cost? The justifications for not engaging, the self-loathing, the thin line between acceptance and resignation, the compromises each is prepared to make: as Julia says, 'We're all rotten with lying.'

Though Julia is the leading lady, there is a cast of supporting characters. Franz, who – after a failed attempt to flee to Prague in March 1938 – lives hidden away, a broken man; their housekeeper, Fina, a devout Catholic whose only love is for Franz and for God; the actors and actresses of the Burgtheater company, some of whom actively welcome the Reich Germans, others of whom find a way of working with or around the new order; Georg Kerenyi, deposed editor of the *Wiener Unabbangige Zeitung*, who believes he can manipulate the new order; Julia's lover Ferdinand von Kasda – known as Nando; the unpleasant, weaseling, spiteful Pichlers, caretakers of the building in which Julia and Franz live.

In some ways, Vienna itself is one of the most important and enduring characters: 'the tempered grey stone, the steely sky and shadowed, blue-white snow'. Gainham's love for the city, its changing seasons, underpins the sense of loss and waste and destruction at the heart of the novel. Our sympathies are also for the city as it is, little by little, corrupted and compromised and destroyed. Throughout, the beauty of the architecture and art and theatre are there as counterbalances to the seeping ugliness of the Occupation.

When it was first published in 1967, *Night Falls on the City* was a worldwide success, especially in the United States, where it was in the top ten of the *New York Times* bestseller list for several months.

It is, without doubt, Gainham's masterpiece. An important and courageous novel, it is timely that *Night Falls on the City* is now being restored to its rightful place on the bookshelf beside other classics of Second World War literature.

Kate Mosse
2012

This book is for K.R.A.

List of characters in order of appearance

Julia Homburg-Wedeker (Julie)	an actress
Hans-Joachim Ostrovsky (Hansi)	a theatrical producer
Serafina Moosbauer (Fina)	the Wedekers' housekeeper
Dr Alois Pohaisky	a lawyer
Dr Franz Wedeker (Franzl)	a politician
Dr Georg Kerenyi (Georgy)	a newspaper editor
Fraülein Bracher	Kerenyi's secretary
Hella Schneider	an actress
Colton Barber	an American journalist
Dr Hanau	a politician
Dr Peter Krassny	a senior civil servant
Wilhelm Mundel (Willi)	an actor
Frau Lotte	a theatre dresser
Casimir Schoenherr	the Director of the Burgtheater
Ruth Wedliceny	a relative of Franz Wedeker's
Frau Wedliceny	Ruth's mother
Ruth's grandfather	a Talmudic scholar
Horst Winkler	an electrician and SA man
Ulrich Benda	an SA man who joins the SS
Luther	a policeman
Dr Moller	Julie's doctor
Maris Pantic	an actress

Friedrich Lehmann	an administrator appointed by NSDAP to the Burgtheater
Walter Harich	an actor
Weber	an accountant
Frau Schneider	Hella Schneider's mother
Sturmbannführer Blaschke	a German Gestapo policeman
Herr and Frau Pichler	the caretakers of the Wedekers' building
Margarete Pohaisky	Alois Pohaisky's wife
Ferdinand von Kasda (Nando)	a civil servant who joins the Army
Anita Silovsky	a young actress
Moosbauer	Fina's brother
Frau Kaestner	a charwoman
Helmut Korning	a Nazi civil servant
Otto and Christian Krassny	Peter Krassny's sons
Schultze	a German SS officer
Countess Kasda	Nando's mother
Lali (Anastasie)	Nando's sister
Jochen Thorn	a German actor
Oberführer Tenius	a Gestapo officer, quickly promoted
Corporal Berthold Luders	an Army driver
Malczewska	a Polish woman

BOOK ONE
March 1938

1

The unlit auditorium of the huge theatre was a constant presence of authority and grandeur, containing in its looming interior the promise and threat of the evening lights and chatter, of the public who were its loving judges. It stretched away from the sloping, half-lighted stage wholly present to the consciousness of the only two persons left standing on the stage; it nearly always was present to Julia Homburg and Hans-Joachim Ostrovsky. The two of them stood well back near an exit, like minor characters about to make a discreet withdrawal; but the stage was undecorated and as they stood there more of the lights went out, leaving them in half darkness. To reassure herself of its reality Julie half turned so that she could look into the dark and familiar body of the hall.

'But Hansi, I don't understand. What do you mean, will Franz stay in Prague? You know he's coming home to-day.'

'Julia,' he said quietly, using her correct name to indicate that he was serious. 'Julia, don't hedge. Haven't you seen this morning's papers?'

'No. No, I left home too early.' She spoke rapidly, too reasonably, untruthfully.

Everyone else had left and this was quite normal for the rehearsal had lasted well into the luncheon hour but it suddenly displeased Julie as if the disappearance of the others was directed against herself. That feeling, a warning to restrain herself, swam up from her schooldays, of misunderstanding and being misunderstood; as on the many occasions that her father said in his civil servant voice 'the child is overwrought – she had better go and do her school work until she can command herself.' And her mother's indifferent kindness, which yet always took her father's side, for the sake no doubt of peace and quiet. Immediately, without recognising the memory or the long process it formed part of, Julie became herself again and the sovereign calm which was her own achievement, returned to her.

'The plebiscite has been called off. You understand what that means, don't you? If Franz comes back to Vienna – though I can hardly think he would – he will have to leave again at once.'

'They really are coming then? Are you sure it's going to happen?'

'I wish I understood more about politics,' said Hansi angrily. 'And even more, I wish you had been with us in Berlin last summer. Then you'd know what I mean. Of course they are coming. I have to say it quite brutally. All the Socialist ex-deputies will be in danger of arrest in a few days' time. And Franz is Jewish too.'

'But the Party has been proscribed for years and he's never been threatened up to now ... But it will all be different if – when – they come. That's what you mean? I have to get used to the idea. Perhaps I had better telephone home and see if Fina has heard anything from him? I'm not sure what time ... if he hasn't caught the train, I mean ...'

'No, don't. I wouldn't telephone anything private for a day or so.'

Julie turned her head slightly, forehead forward and the dark eyes wide open, looking up at him under her brows, the rather big mouth still. He had seen her do it a thousand times; she had done it only an hour before, rehearsing the last act of *Doll's House*. It was the look of realisation of a fathomless emotion, the tiny movement of the head ducking down gave the eyes a frame from the noble brows and withdrew attention from the silent lips. For she said nothing; to an instruction of such unbelievable implication there was nothing to be said. Hansi gave her, and himself, a

2

moment before actually speaking the words heard that morning from the theatre's chief director. But she was too quick for him.

'Schoenherr said something to you this morning! I should have noticed – his being in the theatre on a Friday morning.'

'He's worried about the opening. *Doll's House* is due in just three weeks' time. Any break or confusion in the programme in the next months may cost us the theatre. We shall be watched like criminals for any sign of disaffection, sulkiness. I know Schoenherr is in some ways an old phoney, but he's right. We can't let them take over the theatre.'

'It will happen so quickly? Will they put in an administrator or something? But I still don't understand. Why me, particularly?'

He stammered a little. 'If Franz has to leave … I mean, when Franz has left. Or if he does not return here … Schoenherr is worried about your contract. The Nora couldn't be replaced now. You see?'

'My contract,' said Julie flatly, 'I see. Franzl would be gone, you mean, and I'd be here? Yes, I see now what you mean.'

Hansi, not looking at Julie's face, took one of her hands. The rings flashed in the slant of light as she gripped his fingers which were shorter than her own. He had stumpy, knobbly hands, not at all artistic, and he bit his fingers sometimes.

'I don't think you do see yet, Julie. You have to face this. It may be for a long time. It may be – for good.'

They spoke very quietly, using the second person singular of old friendship and familiarity. Since their first meeting at the academy as sixteen-year-olds their careers had risen parallel for seventeen years. The boy with the untidy flop of pale hair, a little awkward, apparently inexpressive, was surrounded now by all the pressures, talents and intrigues that form and contain a striking theatrical gift; a producer pushed forward over the shoulders of older and more established talents by the approval of the public. The rangy girl with loose dark hair, aggressive and uncertain, had grown into beauty and power, possessed of the jealous and critical love of an audience for which the theatre was almost a rival to the Church.

'But that's impossible!' He was not sure whether she meant it was literally impossible or whether she used the word, as she often did, to describe anything or anybody that did not in some way, suit her.

'This whole conversation is pretty impossible,' he agreed gloomily. 'We can't really be standing here saying such things. It's quite mad. But then, I imagine life is going to get madder and madder. At any rate until we get used to – to living with it.'

'I wish I had gone to Berlin, now.' Julie looked at him quickly and looked away again. She had missed the guest visit out of loyalty to Franz. She gave his hand a little shake as he made to release her and moved closer to him. 'It seems to have explained something to you but I still don't understand what.'

'Explain? No, on the contrary, it explained nothing. They have this new organisation for the theatre there now. Very orderly, lots of officials busy with everything. They don't seem to interfere much, but ... Then, too, half the people we used to know from the Deutsches Theater, the Piscator lot, Rheinhardt's people – half of them weren't there any more.'

Julie interrupted sharply. 'Jews, you mean?'

'Yes, Jews. Some have been gone for years, almost forgotten. Most are still around, not working, one doesn't see them. You remember Moisewitsch? You weren't in it, but you remember him producing *Dream Play* for us? I went to see him. Nobody had his address, but I found him. Of course, he's an old man, they won't do anything to him and he's teaching privately. But it gave me ... what I can't explain is that everything is terrifically organised, there's a rational explanation, it's orderly, practical. Much better organised than we are. But it's all got a mad feel. Everybody there feels it – it's not just me.'

Julie said vaguely, 'Yes, people have said things. Only I never took much notice. I suppose all the people who came to Vienna from there will be going away again now.' This reminded her and she dropped Hansi's hand and moved away, towards the wings. 'I must go home. I suppose there are things I should do. But I don't at all know what. I must think.'

'Shall I call you a taxi?'

'No, Hansi dear. I shall walk.'

4

At the outer door, in the sharp, cold, sunny air, they stopped again, pulling on gloves. Hansi took her elbow, moving away from the drowsing porter in his box. They walked from under the shelter of the huge curved building and across the wide roadway, glancing sideways for traffic. At the gate of the Volksgarten Hansi released her arm.

'What are you looking at?'

Julie was staring back at the theatre, disposed by the rules of baroque architecture in the space designed for it. The late nineteenth-century building, of pale stone with its green roof and massive decoration was, by the taste of the time, not beautiful. But it was handsome, impressive and above all, well designed for its purpose.

'I always like to look at it from here. Not for itself, but to contrast it with the Rathaus.'

Hansi looked past her, from the curve of the theatre's oblique façade to the leafless gardens across the Ring and the fabulous towers of the City Hall beyond. He laughed involuntarily.

'You are wonderful,' he said, delighted for a moment out of his depression. 'You know, I'd never noticed it.'

'But why is it?' she said. 'The theatre is imitation baroque and the Rathaus neo-Gothic. They ought to be equally horrid. So why does the theatre always give me a satisfied feeling and the Rathaus make me want to laugh?'

Hansi narrowed his eyes, assessing the two buildings by his expert internal measure for masses and space. 'I think ... yes.' He turned back to Julie, disposing of the problem with typical narrow clarity. 'First, space. The theatre sits in a space clearly designed for it, that it fits into. The Rathaus is imposed on the skyline, not fitted into a space. Then, derivation. The theatre derives straight from the late eighteenth century, it's a copy of Erlach's designs in feeling. The Rathaus takes a jump back for centuries to an ideal Middle Ages that we have no emotional contact with at all. Third, use. The theatre is practically designed for its purpose; the Rathaus, as everyone knows, is not. So it looks, and is, an anachronism.'

'Bravo, Hansi,' she said. 'Come after dinner to-night, can you?'

'Just a moment,' he said, his face changing. 'I've remembered something else. Schoenherr made some contacts last summer while we were in Berlin. It seems one of them is here now. A private visit for the moment, Schoenherr says. But it's clear he is one of the officials from the Chamber of Culture.'

'Chamber of Culture.' Julie gave a bubble of laughter.

'Awful, isn't it? Yes. Well, what I mean is, there are a lot of such chaps about. Not only in the theatre, one supposes. So you do understand, don't you, that you have to be a bit discreet and careful?'

'But Chamber of Culture! Such an expression!' She glanced at his averted face and stopped laughing. 'I'll try,' she said, quite humbly.

She had walked into the gardens when she turned and called back to him. 'Hansi! Do come to-night?'

'It will be latish,' he shouted back. 'I'm dining. About half past ten.'

She waved agreement and walked on. It was her daily exercise when she was working, through the Volksgarten across the wide space of the Heldenplatz round the jutting wing of the New Hofburg and across the Burggarten. Out into the busy street between Hotel Sacher and the Opera and down Walfischgasse into Schellinggasse to the big apartment on the fourth floor.

In the Burggarten she stopped and watched the water birds on the ornamental water fountain, cleaning their feathers busily on the peaked top of the low fountain in its winter wooden housing. Through the boning of the winter trees loomed the stolid bulk of the Palace, dark grey and gloomily reassuring. Its broad empty terrace, intended for great occasion, Imperial State occasions, produced like theatrical scenes, no longer had any purpose. Julie's view was loaded with childhood memory of the glory of the All-Highest House, the service of which had given her father's life its meaning, stiffened with the jewel-encrusted arthritis of six hundred years and to her the place was no historical monument – it was too near in time to be that – but seemed in its neglect to be forlorn, resentful, as if the stones could be aware of being robbed of meaning. How childish, she thought; Franz would call that anthropomorphism. He often used the word to her, always accusingly. You must not attach your subjective emotions to inanimate objects, he would say disapprovingly, and she would laugh at him. He would be there this afternoon.

A small man in a long frieze overcoat walked rapidly past her and then stopped to gaze as she was gazing. It was clear from the quick turn of his head that he recognised her; Julie was used to that and smiled for him. She was aware of him a few feet away, turning to take in the harmony of the library roof soaring over the palace hot-houses, the tall peak of the Augustine steeple austerely cutting the baroque; he lifted a sharp chin to take in the enormous hatchment with its crown presiding over the centre wing of the façade. Julie turned her head away from the passer-by to glance at the pretty equestrian statue in a frame of small bare trees, just to be glimpsed from here. She had never known just which archduke the statue commemorated. She strolled on and as she passed the small man, he said something in a half-tone which she did not quite hear, but she gave him again an absent smile and in a few moments was slipping through the traffic where the silence of the little park was as lost as the thrum of motors had been a minute before. There was nothing in the least symbolic about Julie's stopping to look at the palace from its garden. She often did; it was beautiful, familiar and melancholy and she loved it.

A face, familiar but unidentified, nodded as she passed the café windows of Sacher's. On the corner a knot of discussion surrounded the paper-sellers. Julie never looked at a newspaper; she took her news from her husband's political friends – and enemies – if at all. A tall man in English tweeds with a bad-tempered hawkish face disengaged himself from the group with the assurance of one who has always had authority. He shook out the newspaper he held, gripping it firmly at its edges with hands more used to horses than newsprint. It was thicker and of larger format than the Vienna papers, with deep headlines underlined in red. After two steps back towards the hotel entrance, he stopped, an expression of stupefied disgust and anger on his face as he took in what he was reading.

'But, really, it's perfectly …' he muttered, and stared straight into Julie's face as she stopped on the kerbstone, without seeing her. Behind Julie an exquisitely gentle voice said, 'I see you are reading my death-sentence, Graf?'

7

A soft, well-formed hand, as small as a woman's, twitched at the page held by the tall man. He was shorter by a head and shoulders than the man he spoke to. As if studying a new role Julie stared at the face between the black homburg hat and the dark grey silk stock fixed in old-fashioned folds by a black pearl; the face was the colour of undyed silk, its folds so clean-shaven they looked beardless and the amused eyes behind lenses were folded at the corners with age-old urbanity. The doorman was still bowing behind him.

'My dear Deutsch,' said the tall man in greeting. He frowned down at the shorter man, screwing up his eyes in unaccustomed effort of perception. 'This is going to be worse for you than for us.'

'It will be worse for us at first,' said the short man. 'Later it will be worse for everyone.'

'What are you – have you made your arrangements?'

'I believe my lawyers are competent. As for personal matters, I have already cancelled my Philharmonic subscription. And you?'

'I must get back to Styria at once. They will be running about like chickens with their heads cut off.'

The banker slid his right-hand glove through his left hand, looking down as if the gloves were important. Then he glanced up and gave the tall man a measured smile.

'I have occasionally had the pleasure of being asked for advice by you, Graf. If I might now offer some without being asked …?'

'Naturally, my dear fellow. Please.'

Still playing with the glove. 'It may be possible for you to come – with the aid of, let us say, discretion – to come to a working arrangement with the new order of affairs. I suggest that is your wisest course, the best chance of protecting your inheritance. For me, of course, it is different …'

Julie moved back from the kerb as a large black touring car with its hood down sighed to a stop immediately in front of her. Both men beside her bowed slightly to let her pass as she moved away. The shining doors swung open, their polished steel handles and the strip of metal inset in the coachwork glinting in the acid sunlight. Four men were getting out. They were all tall, with a long-necked upright stiffness of bearing, somewhat like that of professional soldiers. Their civilian clothes were noticeable as they bent their heads together, taking no notice of anyone about them. They walked together into the hotel, with long, self-absorbed strides. The man in the homburg had gone. The tall man stared after the newcomers, still holding his newspaper open. The doorman was bowing again.

At the corner of her own street others were standing about, listening like herself and talking to strangers. In their excitement their dialect was almost unintelligible, even to a born Viennese of the educated sort, nasal, high-pitched, slurred. A short thin man, cramped with want, leaned his unkempt head towards a stocky old man with bent shoulders and the near-sighted frown of a master artisan whose work is close and detailed. The little man had a drooping moustache which blew up and down absurdly with the force of his shouting.

'You've never been out of work,' he yelled. 'Years, I been out. My father worked there and his father, and what did they do? They sold out to some bank, years ago in the Inflation and never said a word. So then when Rothschild shut up his railway bank, they just shut the shop and retired. Did they care about us? You bet your life they didn't. I been out ever since. Ever since!'

'I never said things wasn't bad,' said the old artisan, trying to move away from the little man's waving hands. He coughed softly, as if to himself, inside. 'And I never said things might not get better now. Mayhap things will get better. And maybe not. I only said, what's it matter who they sold out to, Jews or Christians, that's all I said.'

' 'E's right, you know,' said a third man with assumed reasonableness. 'I've been out for two years after twenty-four years with Hacha in the Graben. They ain't Jews nor heathens. And what's more, they still ride in their motor. I see them. Takes off me 'at, I do, like I always did. "Grüss, Herr Director" same as always. Ah, if they knew what I was thinking, though, they wouldn't sleep easy. We'll be after them now, that lot!'

'Look at our house,' cried a fat, loose-built woman shaking a fist like a lump of mutton fat under their assembled noses. 'The professor only has his little flat now, where he used to own the whole house. The mortgages took it away from him. And him seventy-three and a professor twice over!'

The old artisan looked at her under shaggy brows. 'You still got yer job, ain't yer?' he said, and coughed again softly. 'And the professor's got his flat. How many flats can he live in, tell me that?' He turned to go, hunching his shoulders as he moved away. 'Mortgages,' he muttered. 'What do they think they are, mortgages?'

Julie followed his steps. He turned into a little pub in the cellar of the house next door to hers; a mouth-watering smell of vegetables and soup as he opened its door made Julie aware that she was starving hungry.

Frau Pichler slid her tortoise head out of the dark half-window in the hallway.

'It's all right, Frau Pichler. I have my key,' called Julie. But the woman came out to open the lift door in any case, for the wife of the house-owner.

'Have you heard anything, gnae' Frau?' she asked in her confidential whisper.

'Nothing I understand,' answered Julie, smiling deprecatingly, in spite of the irritation she always felt at Frau Pichler's conspiratorial manner. 'But it's a lovely day.'

'Ah, the weather, yes. But we're going to see some changes here, if you ask me.' Frau Pichler lifted her fat shoulders as if in regret, releasing the smell of sweat from the black stuff overall she always wore, day in, day out. A lifetime of small envies glinted in her sideways look as she sighed heavily and closed the heavy wrought-iron gates of the lift. Julie pressed the fourth-floor button. The lift gave its usual shudder and clang and rose slowly with a slight moan of effort, past the upper-ground-floor, the mezzanine, the first floor. At the fourth storey it gave the same clang and shudder as it stopped. The flat door opened and Fina's round face popped out before Julie had stepped out of the cage.

'Ah, there you are then,' she said with satisfaction and reproach. 'You are late for your lunch.' She came and pushed the brass knob at one side of the cage, clashed shut the sliding door and shut the outer gates. The lift clanged and shuddered and sank out of sight as Fina followed Julie into the apartment.

Julie sniffed hungrily. 'The soup smells good,' she said, throwing down her coat and woollen cap. 'What's to eat?'

'Fish. It's Friday.'

'Yes, but what fish?'

'Just fish.' Every Friday the same question and answer, for years, even on major fast-days when a particular fish was prescribed by custom. It was no truer to-day than any other Friday, for Julie heard the egg-beater in the whites of eggs as she went down the hall to the big living-room. They would have fish soufflé, it seemed. She leaned up against the square tall stove of porcelain tiles of an ugly mid-brown colour, and spread her cold hands sideways over the smooth bumps of its ornamented surface. The glowing warmth that never became too hot to touch was comforting. The whole room basked in an even warmth. It was a dark room. Book-shelves reached well over her head down one long wall and the narrower, end wall. The opposite long wall was broken by three long double-casement windows covered by curtains of coarse linen net, for the room looked over the street, across which were other casement windows just like theirs. Julie went down the room to her husband's desk where papers and writing materials were, for once, in order. As soon as Franz returned they would be disordered, used. Deliberately, with the consciousness of doing something forbidden, Julie opened the silver cigarette box and took out one of the fat, oval cigarettes, lit it inexpertly and blew out the scented smoke. Between two windows a tall vase of Meissen porcelain whose handles were bunches of snakes stood on the floor holding a mass of copper chrysanthemums with shaggy, curled petals. Holding the cigarette away from her, Julie went to them and began to pull them into a more becoming group. When Fina changed the water she stuck flowers back into their vases without arranging them, and it was an automatic act on coming into the room to rearrange whatever flowers were there. One of the soft round heads came to pieces and a shower of crisp, slender petals fell on to the carpet. Julie gathered them up and stood with them in her hand, smelling their aromatic, wintry odour. The carpet was worn in patches, in some places its oriental pattern worn half away. It had never been changed since Franz's grandfather had built the new block in his old age and furnished this apartment for his only son, Franz's father. Not for the first time in her life there, Julie considered buying a new carpet. She knew she would do nothing of the kind; at the most they would buy another beautiful rug to cover yet another patch.

Julie had never seen the grandfather, though there was a very bad portrait of him in the dining-room, done by some provincial painter in his middle years when he still travelled to and fro in Galicia on his various businesses. He must have been a rich man by then, but the whole family still lived in a muddled and insanitary three rooms in the Second District on the other side of the Danube Canal. The rest of the family had gone on living in the three rooms. The fine new apartment in the new block, like the Germanising of the Galician name, was for Franz's father. He was to carry on the businesses of the family in real offices with secretaries and clerks and bank accounts. But not a big bank, stuffed with the affairs of strangers; a small private bank whose interests were one's own and who knew what was happening to one's money.

Franz, then a child of seven or eight, was the point of all the change. Though his family wrongly assumed that he would remain a good Jew, Franz was to be no longer a nomad camping in the Imperial City, but a German citizen of Austria-Hungary and a university professor. At least a university professor, if not a privy councillor. Herr Hofrat! Herr Geheimrat! Perhaps even Herr Wirklicher Geheimrat! Well, that perhaps was too much to hope for, but Herr Hofrat – that was a possibility. Julie remembered with a slight shock that Franz's uncle, his father's elder brother, was still alive. He was the kind of scholar the family had wanted Franz not to be, and this wish had certainly been granted them. A Talmudic scholar who still wore a black kaftan and side curls under his low black hat. She had seen him only once, but recalled his murmuring voice through the open door of the one room out of three that was reserved to him as the scholar of the family. Franz wanted his blessing simply out of a powerful clan feeling, for religion had long ceased to mean much to the Socialist

Deputy, Franz Wedeker. The old man had continued his murmured ritual, not turning round and still less looking at the tall Gentile girl, whose scandalous and forbidden profession had to be hidden from the entire family. If they had known beforehand that she was an actress she would not even have crossed the threshold in a home where a holy scholar might be contaminated by one so nearly a scarlet woman. They married without a blessing. What Julie remembered about Franz's uncle was his deep, lilting voice and the long black-edged nails of one hand resting on the Book on his table; he was very foreign, very remote from Franz and his room smelled enclosed and mean as any hermit's cell must smell. Afterwards they laughed about it, and Franz told her stories of his childhood; the charm and generosity of his grandfather, the traveller's tales long drawn out by the old man, his uncle's greed over food and the ways he ill-used his wife.

Hearing a slight clatter from the next room, Julie dropped the chrysanthemum petals into Franz's wastepaper-basket and put out the cigarette which had in the meantime burned down. She went through a single door panelled in the long book-shelves, sat down at one side of the oval table and unfolded her stiff napkin.

'What time does Herr Doctor's train get in?' asked Fina as she lifted the lid of the soup tureen.

'About five,' Julie helped herself to vegetable soup. 'If . . . ' she dropped the heavy ladle back into the dish with a clumsy clatter.

'If what, gnae' Frau?' said Fina crossly. 'You'll break that dish, knocking it about like that.'

'If nothing. I had a bad rehearsal this morning. And don't be so familiar.'

They both laughed at this old joke. Fina covered the dish. 'I only mean if he's here for dinner I'll keep some soup for him. He likes vegetable soups.' She stood, hands folded, watching Julie eat. Then she said, 'Frau Nosy Pichler says we're all going to be Germans. Is that right?'

'We're Germans already, aren't we?'

'Well, you know how I mean. She says the Reich Germans are coming to-morrow to take us over and run this mess here, properly.'

'Did she now? Were those her words?' Fina nodded, pressing her lips together. Julie put down her soup spoon. 'Well, don't get arguing with the old beast or we shall have trouble with the laundry deliveries again.'

'I never argue. I've got too much to do,' Fina sniffed with conscious superiority as the valued employee of the house-owner.

'And if she asks any questions, just don't answer. Politely, though.'

Left alone with dessert, Julie peeled an orange and looked up at the portrait of her grandfather-in-law. The near-primitive painter had given the old man a squint. I suppose he owed you money and did that to your picture on purpose, Julie silently addressed the dark face. If you were here now, you'd know what to do; you must have been used to this sort of thing. As for me — contract — I don't even know its terms, never even looked at it. And I haven't the least idea what to do.

She left the orange on her plate and went into the living-room, wiping the water from her fingers with her napkin and dropping it carelessly on a little table. She leaned against a window-frame. She could see the street, out of focus through the glass of the double panes and squared by the mesh of the curtain. Before Easter Fina would haul the steps into the room and watch Frau Kaestner detach the curtains from their massive brass rings and clips, and make a great to-do over getting the windows and frames washed. She would complain about the chipped paintwork and they would agree that the whole room needed doing; one might have the paintwork white? The fresh set of curtains would have folds from the linen cupboard that took several days to hang out by their weight, and would give off the scent of soap and herbs — verbena and lavender — that Fina brought back each summer from her visit to her parents in the Lungau. But now they smelled of cigar smoke, brown coal, dust; they were slightly gritty to the touch. In the street below, a cart stood. Men made invisible by foreshortening under their black hoods went to and from the cart and a coal-chute almost level with the pavement. A policeman strolled up to see that the statutory warning to passers-by had been put out, looked through the black hole of the chute into the deep cellar and kicked the iron grille back against the house wall. He stood talking to a servant girl in a white apron with a jacket thrown over her shoulders, who stood holding the big padlock of the grille well away from her skirts as she waited for the coal heavers to finish. The sun had gone and the street was many shades of grey. It was still winter and in the frosty air outside the protecting glass the two massive horses stamped from one hoof to another. One lifted his head from his bag and shook his blondish mane, but his snort could not be heard, only seen by the steamy jets from his nostrils. Now is the winter of our discontent made – something – summer by ... where does that come from? They were not my lines. This time next month it will be spring. By then there will be people sitting along the benches in the Burggarten on the walk from the theatre. If I am rehearsing then; I shan't be. *Doll's House* is my last premiere this season. The man who stood beside her at the water this morning had said, 'After all, I'm Viennese too.' Odd, she hadn't heard what he said at the time but she was quite clear about it now. She recalled the thin poverty-grained face under the rather wide brim of his dark hat though she had not, at the time, been aware of looking at it. What can happen, after all? There are so many in Vienna, and so many of us are mixed. I probably have Jewish blood myself. Mother coming from Transylvania could easily have some in her family. They would have kept quiet about it when Father wanted to marry her, no doubt. That's impossible. I couldn't have Jewish blood. All the Viennese are anti-semitic, especially the Jews, as Franz often said. He was a bit anti-semitic himself, belonging to the German-National wing of his party. They can't proscribe the Socialists here, anyway, since it has already been done. Politics. Franz had wanted Germany and Austria to be joined in 1919; so had everyone else then; that was why he went into politics when he came back from the Italian front. I was twelve then, or was it thirteen? She remembered it; being hungry and not going out because of the riots and the convent being closed. Her father worried himself sick that he would no longer be addressed as Herr Geheimrat, and who was he to write reports to, now that the House, the All-Highest, was no more? His and his superior's claim to authority was surely gone with it? He need not have worried about the Herr Geheimrat at any rate, because everyone went on using their titles. And then he died, of influenza, the next spring.

The name on the side of the coal cart was Fridolin Schmitz. Fridolin. That was the name of her first love, an absurd name, like a boy in a play. They had not known there would be blood, and Fridolin was frightened of his landlady, an unseen gorgon, and his concern had made her angry so that she never spoke to him again; he had failed his interim exam and disappeared from the Academy. I suppose that cured me of curiosity, she thought; certainly it was after that she had begun to work hard and had not thought for some years after, of those actions and feelings, nor attached them to the boys she knew. She had thought of it as boring and knew it to be humiliating. Later there had been others, but she never understood what all the fuss was about until she knew Franz. Then the whole complex matter fused by some magic into certainty and reality. The feelings and actions became real from the inside.

The telephone jangled in the hall. She saw it was gone three o'clock as Fina answered.

'But Frau Homburg is resting,' protested Fina as Julie came out into the hall. Julie took the telephone from her and sat down beside its table, pulling the upright mouthpiece towards her so that it made the little squeak it always made on the polished surface. The wire to the earpiece was twisted as usual. It was Franz's lawyer.

'Yes, come here to me, Herr Doctor; I'd rather not go out in case ... ' Before she could explain he interrupted her. He would be with her in ten minutes. Julie did not replace the receiver, but idly unwound the line straight and listened to the humming of the wire. She was now aware that she was frightened; the worried voice, dehumanised by the telephone, had connected her directly with Hansi's words that morning.

He was there in less than ten minutes, so he must have telephoned from a coffee-house and not from his office. Fina took his hat and coat and he smoothed his bald patch as Julie asked after his wife and the younger son who would take his medical finals in three months' time.

Julie sat where she always sat, in a high-backed wing chair with dark velvet upholstery, where Franz had posed her in the early days so that now she always used it, both aware of the frame it made for the outline of her face, and indifferent to it. Pohaisky laid his narrow briefcase beside him on the corner of a wide couch covered by a silk prayer-rug. He was watching her, but not with his usual look of aesthetic pleasure. He was a deeply religious Catholic for whom all beauty comes from God.

'I won't waste words, gnae' Frau,' he said and patted his inner pocket, then laid his veined hand again on his knee.

'Do smoke, Doctor Alois. You know I don't mind.'

He was vain of his carefully groomed hands and made quite a business of selecting and lighting a long Balkan cigarette. He smiled his thanks.

'One is always conscious of your voice. That adds a perverse pleasure to smoking when one is here. But I had better come straight to business. You may guess why I am here?'

Julie did not at all know and shook her head. Pohaisky looked at the blue wreath of smoke.

'Is Franz coming back to-day?' he asked, his voice even more calm and measured than usual. 'He intended to, I know.'

'I have heard nothing. So I don't really know, though Hans Ostrovsky thinks he won't. But I think . . .'

'I think with you that he may, in fact, come home. Ostrovsky was in Berlin last year if I remember? Yes. That means, you see, that he has some real notion of what he is talking about. Whereas Franz, Franz has only theory, and the theory of the brotherhood of man is not going to help much in this situation.'

Although they were passionate opponents in politics, this was unexpectedly brutal. Pohaisky had taken care of the affairs of Julie's family and Franz had added his own business after they were married; and though they had become friends in a cautious way, they had never agreed about politics and never could have done. After 1934 they had not spoken for many months and were only reconciled on Julie's insistence.

'Your joint affairs are in order. It is only necessary for Franz to sign over everything he possesses to you. You must know what is happening in case I am not able to help you; it is by no means certain that I shall remain unmolested. I hate to burden you with tiresome business, but in your position it is likely you will be left in peace.'

'About my position – it isn't decided what I shall do.'

Pohaisky misunderstood her, perhaps intentionally.

'As a life member of the State theatre you will be treated as an asset of the people. They constantly use these Jacobin phrases, you know.'

This was what Hansi meant this morning and was afraid to say openly.

'You mean they will not allow me to go with Franzl?'

'My dear lady, they will not allow Franz to go. Still less will they let you go with him – or to him.'

Julie moved quickly in her chair and then laid the palms of her hands together between her knees so that her face was bent down and he could not see her expression.

'But it may be for a long time,' she quoted Hansi. 'It may be – for good.'

'For all of us.'

'But Franz is my husband. If he goes, I go.'

As she said the words, the absurdity of them struck her. Leave this city? For one of those she always preferred when she reached them and was always so glad to leave again, for home. Paris? Golden Rome? The immense weight of London's urbanity? Leave for – for the sake of language – Zurich, that town of insurance agents and bankers? Leave Vienna, the tempered grey stone, the steely sky and shadowed, blue-white snow? Leave the sentimental chestnuts and lilacs, the comically maddening people of the streets? The music, the theatre – the Burg, that inextricable knot of many knots of work and ambition. The long intrigues and the short alliances of cliques; familiar friends and even less dispensable enemies of fascinating and intimate cruelties and quarrels. Leave the many-headed unit of the public? Every evening to be seduced afresh. Lose the giant feeling of holding them in her hand on those rare evenings when the whole company, in a furore nobody understood, was welded into a power greater than its added parts that shifted the very stones of the foundations. To stop working – what people did who didn't work had always been mysterious. In other theatres she would always be a guest. The imperial mass in the lost imperial glory had a meaning for the city, even for those who rarely went within its doors, strong enough to rival the Church with its symbols – a meaning other cities could never understand. A solid richness of meaning in the quicksands of poverty and rootlessness. In Paris, in London, the public slipped over the surface, constantly amused, in constant fear of boredom; they had no understanding. They never stopped still long enough. How could one understand the theatre in languages where even their own great poets were invariably cut for length and where *Wallenstein* was not even translated because it was too long to play – seven hours? How give anything to an audience that allowed *Hamlet* to be cut – did not even know it was cut? An audience that thought of Oscar Wilde as frivolous, had never heard of Schnitzler, of Molnár? Did Hofmannsthal, that echo, exist in French – his singing idiom would be cut to pieces on the sharp edge of the language. Her language, her instrument. The voice Pohaisky was concerned about was quite different, she knew, when she spoke her excellent French, her careful English. And the nerve-memory connecting words, movements and meaning? It would never work in any other tongue.

'That may perhaps be considered later, Frau Julia. The immediate need is to regulate Franz's affairs. What is quite certain is that if he does return to-day, he will have to leave again at once. There is no alternative for Franz. The papers are here – I have them with me. They have been ready for some weeks, in fact ...'

'Some weeks?'

'Some weeks, yes. They are, however, dated three years back. When Franz was operated for appendicitis, you remember?' Pohaisky touched his flat case. 'The best course will be for me to leave the case here. If there is any discussion as to why I was here to-day, you will say you wished to check these instruments in the – ah – in view of the new circumstances. About which latter you will be well advised to make no comment. You know nothing of politics or State affairs and need to know nothing. I am advising you as your lawyer, you understand? But until the papers have in fact been signed by Franz and countersigned where necessary, by yourself, they must be hidden. Your cook, for instance, must not know they are here. Can you, by the way, trust Serafina?'

She lifted her head and stared blankly at him.

She said, 'She's been with Franz fifteen years. Long before we were married. Before his parents died.'

He spoke as if he spoke of the weather and did not look at her, 'A friend of mine in Stuttgart – we studied here and at Goettingen together – has been in prison for two years because of something his own son said of him.'

Julie clasped her hands together tightly and rose from her chair. She walked to the window against which she had been leaning when he telephoned, touched the curtain as if to lift it aside – the cart was gone – and then came back to her chair and sat down again.

'But all this is impossible,' she said helplessly.

'Yes, it is all quite mad. The papers have annotations clipped to them, so that you will both understand where signatures and initials have to be made. It will be quite clear to you. Just do as my notes instruct. Then detach all the notes and burn them in this stove here. Not in the kitchen and not just torn up. Make sure you take out all the notes from between the papers. That is important because the witnesses' signatures are already on the documents. My son-in-law and my confidential secretary signed them. You realise what I am saying, do you not, Frau Julia?'

'Good God,' she whispered. Then, abstractedly, 'Have you confessed all this? Oh, forgive me, I hardly know what I'm saying.'

He put his hand up to his brow. 'Yes. As soon as the papers are signed and the notes burned the whole matter is in order. Though of course papers of such importance would not be left about but kept under lock and key, it is no longer such a vital matter that nobody should know they are here. That is, of course, if Franz returns home. If he does not the procedure is different. You sign where indicated yourself, not forgetting initials where necessary. Then detach the notes and burn them. Hide the papers again. Telephone me on Monday. Simply say you would like to see me.

If he has signed them, they then exist legally and you will say on the telephone that you have now had time to read them through again and are reassured that everything is in order. I will then come and take them away quite openly. Have you understood? Can you repeat what you are to do?'

'I ring you up on Monday. If Franz has signed the papers I say I have read them and they are in order. If he does not come back, I just say I want to see you. In either case, I sign where I am directed to sign and destroy all your notes. Is that right?'

'Quite right. You understand, don't you, that you should sign now, but if Franz does not return and by some mischance the papers come to light, then you are as much in the conspiracy as we three already are?'

'Yes,' said Julie, 'that too is clear to me.'

'Good. Now, if Franz does not return, we must contrive to get the papers to him, and of course, back again. Since he went to Prague, we may take it he will still be there next week. Now, fortunately, one of your father's investments is in Brünn — the sawmill. My son-in-law will be able to go to Prague where he will sell the sawmill and get Franz's signatures. There will be a certain amount of confusion for a week or so, no doubt, and we shall be able to use that confusion. Besides, my son-in-law has taken the precaution, very noble of him, of joining the Party in order to protect our interests — as you know my politics are as suspect as poor Franz's ... Ah, where was I — yes, he goes quite frequently on business to Prague, and there is nothing unusual about you wanting to consolidate your property at this time.'

'But your son-in-law? I can't ask him to take such risks.'

'He himself suggested it. He has a number of other things to do in Prague and will be going there in any case. The risks are not so great as they seem; at least not at this moment. No doubt things will be tightened up, but not at once. And once the inward obstacles to committing such acts have been overcome ...' He sighed deeply and smiled at her. 'Every respectable lawyer in Vienna is engaged in such affairs at this moment, I assure you.'

Julie said quietly, 'Some day I will try to thank you. I won't ask a lot of stupid questions. I'll just take it for granted that all this is necessary. But one thing – you do know that I understand what it means to you to do such things. You do know that, Doctor Alois, don't you?'

She watched him select another of his fat cigarettes and saw that he was deeply moved; and this frightened her more than anything he had said.

After a moment he spoke again.

'Now, where are we going to hide these dangerous objects?'

They both looked round the long room, silently dismissing one after another the obvious places.

'I know,' said Julie at last. 'The bases of the book-shelves are hollow. We can put them in one of them.' She rose and went to the long, dark and heavy book-shelves built on the wall from the floor to a height of about two metres. They were deep enough to take two rows of large books, one behind the other, so that whole sets of histories, law books, literature, were ranged in blocks instead of single rows. The base-boards, of moulded and polished wood like wainscotting, were about twenty centimetres high all along the wall of books. Julie kicked one section lightly and it gave a woody, hollow boom. She kneeled down and began to remove the heavy books that stood on the lowest shelf. The shelves were laid on bronze pins movable to any height needed by the height of the books, which fitted into perpendicular rows of bronze-lined holes in the uprights of the cases. Pohaisky came over and took the books from her as she lifted them out, laying them neatly in the correct order behind himself on the carpet. When the section was clear Julie lifted the oak shelf out, and below was a hollow to the floor half a metre wide. She looked at her hands and brushed the dust off them. Pohaisky had his briefcase in his hand and was about to lay it in the space.

'Hadn't we better put the papers in something else?' said Julie, hesitantly. 'I mean, you came with the briefcase – hadn't you better go away with it? I certainly wouldn't like to trust our house caretaker, and still less his wife. She may just possibly have noticed you were carrying it?'

'You are quite right,' agreed Pohaisky, smiling painfully.

She got a big envelope from Franz's desk, already used. Their address was on it and postage marks and stamps. Pohaisky took a bundle of papers from his briefcase and slid them into the envelope. They laid the envelope in the dark, dusty hole and Pohaisky lifted back the heavy shelf. He got it back to front and lifted it out again to turn it round. Then they silently ranged the books back as they had been before. When they rose to their feet they did not look at each other. It was as if each of them had come unexpectedly upon some small, humiliating indecency in the other.

Pohaisky fished out of his waistcoat pocket a flat gold watch and flipped open its chased cover.

'It is four o'clock already,' he said. He wiped his dusty fingers on a large, perfectly clean handkerchief. Without saying any more, she reached him her hand and he bent his grey head and kissed it and went out. She could hear Fina asking after his grandchild, the son-in-law's baby, as he put on his coat and hat. Then the apartment door shut behind him with its familiar thud into the felted frame and the door opposite their door rattled faintly in the displaced air made by the heavy ironed front door shutting; tiny household sounds, instantly recognised, but so familiar as to go unheard at normal times.

Julie stood still for a moment or so by the book-case. Then she went into the hall as Fina came out of the kitchen.

'You've had no rest at all, gnae' Frau. Will you have tea or coffee?'

'Tea, I think, please. I couldn't rest, anyhow.' She went across into her bedroom and through into the bathroom. She washed her hands and dried them as carefully as she always did on one of the cold, slippery linen hand-towels with her initials on it. She had lived in that apartment for seven years and never consciously noticed before that the inter-curving blue and white tiles of the bathroom floor were just like those in her parents' home. This was not surprising, almost all the big town apartments of the period — the last twenty years of the last century — had similar tiles on kitchen and bathroom floors. Black and white or blue and white, shaped like formalised knucklebones and curving endlessly into each other.

She switched on the lamps in the living-room; the pools of

yellow light made its quiet less oppressive with the illusion of something alive. Yes, but this with Pohaisky – what was it all about? He had so taken it for granted that she understood why Franz's not inconsiderable property should become hers that Julie had taken it for granted too. On the writing-table lay that morning's papers, untouched. Julie read the first paragraphs of the lead story. Without some knowledge of what had gone before, it was almost meaningless. Bewildered by the details of Chancellor, plebiscite, Minister of the Interior, Julie threw the paper down and picked up the next one. This was the disguised organ of the proscribed Opposition, Franz's party. The main news article and the leader were both violently polemical; but against neither the Austrian Nazis nor the Reich Government; against the Austrian Government which, as she supposed vaguely, was trying to resist the Nazis. It was, it seemed, all a question of the destruction of the power of the working class by Dollfuss in 1934. For a short time Julie could not remember when Dollfuss had been murdered for the newspaper read as if he were still alive, and the tone as well as the matter seemed to have no connection with the events described in the government paper she had looked at before. She turned to the *Independent* and tried to understand its leading article. It was so carefully balanced that she read in each succeeding paragraph the reverse of the previous argument about some agreement made between the Austrian and the Reich governments in July 1936 and what Chancellor Schuschnigg had probably understood by it. Julie did not know it but while she was reading the Chancellor was actually resigning his office and the long shadow play was over. She laid down the papers, giving up hope of understanding what was happening by means of the printed word. There was a small wireless set in one corner of the book-shelves and she went and turned it on. A voice sang a kitschy song about love not being sin. The voice was deep and hoarse enough to be a man's voice, but Julie recognised it as the Swedish prophetess of sex who had become a living symbol of what had happened in the Reich. Zarah Leander, she thought, I wonder what her real name is – Pedersen, probably. The record ended and at once a news-reader began to speak, relaying a message to the populace from the

Archbishop of Vienna who counselled the people to be calm and to pray. What they were to pray for was not specified. There followed short news items. The frontier between Germany and Austria had been closed that morning, rail traffic between the two countries had ceased. This, said the news-reader, was causing a certain amount of confusion in rail communications and intending passengers were advised not to travel unless they urgently needed to do so. Massive troop movements were reported in Bavaria. General Keitel's name was mentioned and large figures of tanks. In reality the movements of troops to the border had been completed, and the tanks were already standing along the border on every road capable of carrying their weight, their blunt snouts menacing, the fingers of their guns pointing, their swaying antennae humming with the tension of waiting.

Julie left the wireless on and went out to the telephone. At first the East Station did not answer. When she did at last get the information clerk he could tell her nothing about the times of any train.

'But at least tell me if the trains are running between Prague and Vienna,' begged Julie. He rudely did not know, his voice rose with strain and cracked and Julie cut him off hastily with a jerky move of her finger on the earpiece fork. She looked up; Fina was standing in the kitchen door, a glass cloth with red checks in one hand, staring at her. Fina's round face was as rosy as ever, the hard round cheeks with their prominent bones shining in the electric light from the ceiling. The two women looked at each other in silence for a moment. Fina opened her mouth to say something and changed her mind. Julie found that the palms of her hands were wet. She pulled the address book across towards herself by its pencil cord and searched for the name of a fellow ex-deputy of Franz's who might be able to tell her what was happening. She rattled the fork and asked the operator for the number and waited while it rang and rang in uneven spasms. When the operator chipped in again, Julie gave her another number, of the 'secret' headquarters of the Socialist Party. Unobtainable, the number buzzed dully. This is impossible, argued Julie. The operator, who knew Julie, would find out. At last the number rang and instantly was answered from the other end. A harsh North German voice demanded who was calling. Without replying, the operator pulled her switch. Should she try another number? No, said Julie, leave it. The operator's voice dropped several tones. They were in a terrible muddle, she confided; a whole block of lines had been taken over and many others cut off. It was said Himmler was himself in the city; the airport was closed and the supervisor ... Julie never heard what happened to the supervisor for the line went dead. She rattled the fork again and again. The line was cut. At that moment the sighing moan of the lift rising could be heard. It gave its clang and shudder as it stopped. Julie stared at the apartment door, her finger still on the telephone fork. She found her teeth clenched and forced herself to relax her jaw muscles. Fina turned her head staring fixedly at the lock of the front door, chin stuck out, mouth slightly open. The small coil of tightly plaited hair made her look like the little wooden woman in a weather-house, emerging from her door to indicate rain. Brisk footsteps passed the door and then the thud of the door opposite could be heard, closing. Julie looked up at the hall clock in its sunburst. Even if the train were on time and even if Franz were on it, he could hardly have left the station yet. She got up stiffly and without speaking to Fina went down the hall to the living-room. The open half of the tall double door was swinging to behind her when she heard his key in the front door. The door opened, his voice was thanking Frau Pichler for helping him with his bag. She stood perfectly still; the flood of relief drained through her nerves, and as if every drop of essential energy went with it, she found her knees were shaking.

The frosty breath of outside air was still about him and he was half out of his overcoat as Julie reached him. He shook his fur-lined coat off into Fina's waiting arms and took Julie's hands; and the mysterious quality of their relationship was instantly re-established.

His hands, usually so firm and warm were hard and dry with the cold.

'Nice and warm, you are,' he said in his soft, gentle voice, and leaned his cheek against hers for a moment. They went into the living-room and stood close up against the stove, sipping kisses from each other's lips, their arms about each other. When Fina came in with coffee they took no notice of her and she put down the tray on the table it always occupied, picked up the napkin Julie had dropped after lunch, and went out again, shaking her head and laughing to herself.

As Julie went to pour out his coffee, Franz said, 'Pohaisky has been here!'

'You smelt his tobacco! He's a better judge of character than Hansi. He knew you'd come back. Hansi thought you wouldn't.' For a second it seemed as if they could shut the world out of their little world of simple, almost innocent eroticism. But something changed in his face, the sensitive mouth took on a resigned set, the thin, handsome features were suddenly drawn and he looked his forty-three years, and more.

'But why Pohaisky? To warn me – or you?'

'He – must we talk about it now?' His smile agreed to put it off, and he reached out to draw her towards him, but she said nervously, 'I suppose I'd better tell you, though. Pohaisky brought a lot of papers to sign. They are not supposed to be here. Even Fina mustn't know. Do you know about it?'

He rubbed his forehead and put down the coffee cup.

'I'd forgotten,' he said blankly. 'Yes, he did talk about ... some time ago ...'

'You have to sign them; I have to sign too, somewhere. He'll come and collect them on Monday, he said. Something about turning all your property over to me ... Franz, what is it all about?'

'Have you heard of the Nuremberg Laws? You must have a vague notion?'

'But of course,' she said impatiently, 'of course I've heard of them.'

Franz looked at the watch on his wrist.

'In about twenty-four hours from now those laws will be in force here. I shan't be capable of owning any property by then. If it is your property, it won't be sequestrated.'

'That's why it is supposed to have happened three years ago, then?'

'When I made a will. Yes, that's clever of Pohaisky, to think of that. Then there can be no question about it. It's very, very illegal though.'

'That's why they are so secret, the papers. The witnesses have already signed. Pohaisky was very upset – even though he has confessed it.'

'Poor Pohaisky.' Franz shook his head with the tolerant sympathy of an enlightened man at another's bondage to superstition.

'But Franzl, what are we going to do?'

'First, we must sign these papers. There's no sense in throwing good money into the sewers of the Third Reich. It can't last for long and then we can come back ...' He stopped abruptly and stared at Julie's face.

'What is it?' she said sharply.

'He expects you to stay here, then? Pohaisky?'

Julie sat down suddenly in Franz's chair by the writing-table.

'He – he seemed to think they would prevent me going. Hansi hinted as much this morning, too. There's a man from Berlin at the theatre already.'

'If you left they would confiscate *your* property, don't you see? Do you think Pohaisky knows something – more than he told you?'

'I don't know,' she said, bewildered. 'I think he would have told me anything that affected us.'

'I'd better telephone him at once!'

'No!' She put out a hand to stop him. 'Don't do that. It would put him in danger. And you, too.' Remembering, she added faintly, 'It's cut off.'

'The telephone? It can't be!'

'Yes, while I was actually talking to the operator.'

Franz looked around the room with incredulous eyes. 'My God,' he said, 'this is a pretty kettle of fish!' He used the English idiom; it gave his incomprehension a curiously affected, unreal tinge and Julie stared at him, not quite understanding what he meant, or what was happening.

'What else did Pohaisky say?' he asked urgently. 'Julie, you're not listening to me. What else did Pohaisky say?'

'He said – he said for you there was no alternative. You had to leave here again, at once. I said then I would go with you. He said

28

they wouldn't allow that. But, of course they wouldn't allow you to leave, either. It would mean going secretly.'

'Secretly!' Without noticing what he did, Franz picked up one of the newspapers, and now he sat down slowly and sat staring at the rumpled sheets quivering slightly in his clenched hand.

'Franzl, the wireless said the frontier to Bavaria was closed this morning. They will close the other frontier too, won't they?'

'But they are not here yet,' he said hoarsely.

'The telephone girl said Himmler himself was here ...'

'But in Germany they haven't stopped people leaving. If they have somewhere to go.'

'But Hansi said ...'

'What? What did Hansi say?'

'He – that all the Socialist ex-deputies would be arrested. And you are Jewish too.'

'That about puts it in a nutshell.'

'But Franzl, how can this have happened without us knowing? Did you know nothing about it at all?'

'Of course I knew,' he said dully. 'As you did. As everyone did. But I never quite believed it, I suppose.'

'It's my being away in Prague,' he said after a long pause. 'That is what makes it seem so sudden. I just didn't think it could happen so quickly.' The remark was quite meaningless for the papers of every European city were just as easy to get in Prague as they were in Vienna. Franz got up again and went over to the coffee tray. He poured out a fresh cup of coffee, stood holding it for a moment and put it down again.

'The first night,' he said. 'When is it? I forget.'

'You mean of *Doll's House*? Three weeks to-night. But that doesn't matter now.'

'That was what Hansi Ostrovsky was worried about?'

'My contract,' she said miserably.

'Of course. Obviously you can't leave before the play is a week or so old, or the whole theatre will be in trouble. Who under-studies Nora?'

'Hella Schneider. She's very good. She's going to play it some-times, in any case.'

'I'll wait for you in Prague,' he said. They smiled conspiratorially, at one in their desire to keep their intimate, their so fragile community intact. It was all unreal, and most unreal was the pretence that Julie would leave the theatre, her life for seventeen years since she first walked on to its uneven, sloping stage as a student of the Academy at sixteen. She remembered the occasion clearly, the crowd scenes, the smell of backstage, the cold wind that blew on one side of the stage, mysteriously, in winter. The dust and apparent confusion. Above all the slow sweep of the great curtains rising almost silently and the first consciousness of that warm, scented, quiet mass in the theatre on the curtain's other side. Not single people, and not a crowd; an audience. It was Grillparzer, *King Ottokar*, so the audience was serious; either young or elderly, unfashionable. Consciously, she stopped herself thinking of it, and when she looked up at Franz it did indeed disappear in the pain and understanding of his eyes.

'You must be tired and dirty,' she said, smiling lovingly. He disliked the promiscuity of trains, they offended his intense fastidiousness. Typically Viennese, he never noticed the muddle of newspapers, the dusty floor or the full ashtrays of the coffeehouse where he met his fellow oppositionists; it was strangeness he disliked, the dottle of one unknown traveller's pipe gave him thoughts of tuberculosis though he would sit for hours in committee with old Morawec, the Party Secretary from the 21st Bezirk coughing his soft, contained cough into his handkerchief; in a closed room full of smoke and their sliding, nasal artisans' dialect that he too affected in local meetings and committees.

'Come along, dreamer,' said Julie touching his greying hair where it grew in a curving slight wing from his temple. 'Have a bath and change your clothes. And tell me, how was it you were so early? The train can hardly have arrived by the time you were at home?'

'Kerenyi and I decided to get an early train instead. We were up at an unearthly hour to catch it. But coming from Krakov, of course, it was hours late. The Poles never had a train on time in my whole experience, I believe.' He followed her through a drawing-room big enough to be called a salon, which they rarely used; through his study and the bedroom into his narrow dressing-room.

'I often wonder what my father and mother did with all these rooms when they first lived here,' he said, coming back into the bedroom in a dressing-gown. Julie came in from the bathroom followed by the happy gush of water.

'Just as we do, I expect,' she said, laughing a little. She laid the big bath towel she carried in the middle hollow of the white porcelain stove to heat. 'They didn't use them. After living eight together in three rooms they must have felt pretty cold here for a bit. What made you think of it?'

'I never go through the drawing-room without thinking of mother's coffee parties. I thought them very grand, as a boy.'

'I expect they were very grand, too,' Julie looked through the doors standing open. She could see in the dusk the lights from the living-room lamps reflected in varied sparks off the cut drops of the chandeliers in the unlighted room.

Franz went over to Julie's dressing-table. A round bowl of Bohemian glass stood on it, full of dark violets. They were sunk, drowned, in the water that winked glassily between the soft little horns of the flowers. Air-bubbles clung like inverted dew-drops on the petals under the water. The fresh, sweet scent hung over the bowl. The outlines of purple blue and watery glass wavered and swam as his eyes filled with painful tears. Julie, behind him, passed her arms round his waist; leaning against his back, she slid her hand inside the fold of the dressing-gown against his naked breast.

2

$\mathcal{G}$eorg Kerenyi was a tall, sandy man with a big nose which he was in the habit of lifting and pointing in the air like a game dog scenting a hare in long grass. This big, jutting hook of a nose was so noticeable that his other features seemed unimpressive but in fact his eyes were shrewd and hard under their prominent brows. Though he had lived in Vienna for twenty years – he had become an Austrian in 1919 – he still had a strong Hungarian accent.

He ran up the short flight of stairs to his office two at a time and flung open the door, shouting to his secretary as he positively leaped inside the room. He hated sitting still and the hours on a slow train had filled him with a raging impatience that he had to rid himself of by some physical demonstration. The door slammed against the wall and swung back to close with a bang. From her typing-table his secretary rose, not with her usual nervous alacrity, but with a curiously sheepish air, as if she were not quite sure whether to rise or not. She was a tired-faced woman in her late thirties with the greyish complexion of chronic malnutrition. By Viennese standards she was not badly paid, but she had an elder brother seriously wounded in the War and a complaining old mother to keep. Kerenyi was never sure whether this handicap had prevented her ever getting a husband or the massive overdevelopment of her hips and backside, almost deformed in their largeness when contrasted with a meagre upper body and thin face. She moved now round her table with her waddling sideways walk, not quite looking at Kerenyi. He took no notice of this because she was neurotically shy, but an atmosphere in the office communicated itself to him at once.

'Herr Schmittgen came up to see you three times to-day, Herr Chief Editor,' she said, forcing the words out breathlessly. She was, he knew, a member of the forbidden Socialist Party and always used their formal, serious courtesies of speech. That she should have failed to greet him and ask about his journey was a sign of disturbance amounting to a major shock.

'What did he want?' said Kerenyi, emphasising the pronoun.

'He didn't say. The publisher wants to see you at his house this evening, too.'

'What time did Herr Keppler say? Didn't Schmittgen say anything at all?'

'He kept asking when you would be back. Oh, he did ask why you had gone to the Conference, to Prague. I didn't know what to say.'

'So you said nothing? I hope you have left me time to write my dispatch on this damned stupid socialist congress I've been wasting my time at.'

'Your appointment is for nine o'clock with the publisher,' she said, pressing her livid lips together to show her annoyance at his rallying manner. He always used it to her and she always found it humiliating.

'And otherwise, Fräulein Bracher? Everything quite normal?'

She stared, biting her underlip. Without any change of expression her mournful eyes became suffused with red. Kerenyi was ashamed, but his own raging anger and impatience made it impossible to apologise. He went behind his desk and stood looking through the pile of neatly opened letters on his blotter. He leaned over and turned the pages of his desk diary to see what appointments she had made for him in his absence. Then he picked up the pulls of purple-inked paper from a steel basket labelled REUTERS; after a hasty glance he threw them back again, having seen the last news on the machine downstairs in the newsroom before he came up.

'Why didn't we all join, long ago?' he said. Fräulein Bracher said nothing. Kerenyi walked across the room and looked out of the window, down into the darkling narrow street where the yellow blooms of lamps threw condensation rings on the outside windows. Motors flashed headlamps, the offices and flats opposite were alight in that early evening hour between business and home-going when every light is burning. As Kerenyi watched, a whole stream of light went out of the first floor as the Armenian carpet-dealer closed his business for the day.

'Winter is back,' said Kerenyi under his breath. 'It's begun to snow again.'

'Herr Kerenyi,' said Fräulein Bracher behind him in a quite different voice, 'what is going to happen to us?'

'That is what Keppler is going to tell me, I assume,' he said, turning from the window. He looked into her pinched face and said seriously, in a normal, human tone, 'You're an SP member, aren't you ... is that what is worrying you?'

She nodded, still biting at her underlip, and looked anywhere but at him.

'They won't bother with ordinary rank and file members, you know.' He watched her face closely. 'Most of the membership will join the NSDAP now, if one may judge by what happened in the Reich. I advise you to do just that; and keep quiet.'

'But — what will happen?' Her voice was quiet but desperate, she looked about at the office furnishings as if expecting them to show changes.

'To your job? I don't see why you shouldn't keep it. I mean,' he corrected himself, 'as far as I know, myself. Whatever happens to me the new editor will need a secretary who knows the ropes. I know you don't like Schmittgen, but he will need you far more than I do — he's never had responsibility yet. I don't want to say anything with certainty, because I just don't know. But life will have to go on, and offices will have to be staffed. Even if I am fired this evening — and I almost certainly will be — there is nothing as far as I know to prevent you keeping your job.'

'Join the NSDAP,' she muttered. 'What about my beliefs? You think it doesn't matter ...?'

'My dear girl,' he said, but not in the joking way she hated, 'it is the curse of our time that people believe in political sects. Neither socialism nor any other way of ordering affairs is worthy of being put in the centre of a man's belief; it is only a system of organisation as good or as bad as the brains that run it. It doesn't in the least matter whether the controlling interest in this paper is held by Herr Oskar Keppler, by a bank or by a political party — except that party papers are usually dull, but that's for other reasons. What matters is the men who run the paper, the quality of their brains — their hearts, too. These new people will fire me, but remember, if the paper had been bought up by the Fatherland Front, I should have been fired too. All political parties dislike the man who denies that *any one* of them has the truth.'

'You are so calm,' she said stubbornly. 'You must have known it was coming. Why didn't you do something? Arrange something? Instead of going off like that, just at the moment when ...'

'And just what do you suggest I should have done?' For a moment he returned to his humiliating, joking tone, and she flushed a patchy, unhealthy red. 'Yes. I knew it was coming. So did the Chancellor, so did the President. So did everybody in Vienna who knows anything about anything. None of us could do anything. Except make private plans which is what I have just advised you to do. If I knew what was going to happen here — in the office — I'd tell you. But if I say anything, it's a guess and may be misleading because I am not in the confidence of the NSDAP men here. All I know is Keppler will either be forced to sell out to a front man for the NSDAP or to join the Party — if he hasn't already done so — to keep his paper. One of the conditions would clearly be that I must go. Ever since the agreement of two years ago it has been clear that if we wanted to stay in business we had sooner or later to give up our independence as a newspaper. This is the final stage of something that's been coming for several years; it seems like a crisis because no one knew just how it could come — that's because Hitler & Co. play it by ear; they wait upon events and then use them. You ask me why I didn't change my tone towards them, if I knew. I ask myself that question all the time. I just didn't. The word "Independent" in our title means something to me, it seems. Something obstinate in my head stopped me conforming. We discover things about ourselves in moments of crisis, Fräulein Bracher. I thought for months of getting quietly in touch with the Party people. Somehow I always put it off, and now it's too late. Evidently I never meant to turn Nazi. But you are in the position of being able to appear to conform. You will type just as well, and keep the files as tidy. That, it seems to me, is the end of your personal responsibility here.'

He was half-sitting on the corner of his desk, his long legs thrust out in front of him, and his hands in his pockets. He watched her averted face for a little while, then pulled his feet in and stood up with a jerk. He went round his desk and sat in the swivel chair, reaching for a bulging despatch case on the other side of the table. Out of it he took a bundle of notes and newspaper cuttings and dropped them in a scramble on the blotter. He pulled a large block of scribbling paper towards him and selected a sharpened pencil from a blue pottery jar that stood, full of pencils, a ruler and a long, thin pair of paper-scissors beside his big diary.

In the top right-hand corner of the paper he scrawled the hieroglyph that signified the article was to appear under his signature. Then he sat looking at the blank paper. After a moment he drew a diagonal line with his pencil from bottom to top of the sheet of paper, tore off the sheet, crumpled it in his hand. He put the pencil back into its jar and turned in his chair to pull the big wastepaper-basket to him. With one bony muscular hand he swept the bundle of notes and cuttings and the sheet of blank paper into the basket. On top could be seen a column from the *New York Times*, and a square cutting in French. Kerenyi looked up at Fräulein Bracher.

'That is one analysis of the Congress of the European Federation of Social Democratic Parties that will never be written,' he said briskly.

Fräulein Bracher stared, not at him but at the papers in the basket. Her thin face worked angrily. She put up her ugly hands in front of her mouth and burst into the noisy weeping of exacerbated nerves. With clumsy haste, turning her hips as if moving an unwieldy load, she ran from the room and disappeared.

Kerenyi sat staring at his now empty blotter for a few moments; then he pulled a telephone towards him on a scissors-like swivel arm and connected himself with the switchboard operator.

'Order me a car, please, for eight-thirty, and tell the driver I want to go out to Hietzing and then back into the old city.'

He looked at his watch. He had two and a half hours. He pulled a small bunch of keys from his trousers pocket, selected a complicated steel one and went to a framed map of Europe which hung opposite his desk on the wall. He opened the map with an ordinary handle at the side as if it were the door of a cupboard, and unlocked the safe in the wall behind it.

From the several neat piles of folders Kerenyi took a heap bound in black with red spines. The last five years were numbered in white on the spines. Beginning at 1933, Kerenyi began to go through the files carefully. He was a methodical man for a journalist. The papers were the private personnel files of all the senior employees of the newspaper he edited. He left untouched official papers, contracts, salaries, income tax and such matters. Personal recommendations, character references, confidential notes on the private lives of his colleagues he removed one by one, considering each letter or report as he read it, and replacing some that seemed innocuous. Sometimes he took out a letter because of the name it was signed with – an old recommendation from the Chairman of the Co-operative Workers' Bank of Styria, recommending the newspaper's head accountant for his post, for instance, would hardly seem a recommendation to the new editor, and it was accordingly shoved into the waste-basket. Sometimes he removed a note because of its contents; in the file of a sub-editor who had left the paper a few months before was a complaint from the welfare section of his repeated advances to the apprentices in the printing shop – this too went into the basket. Kerenyi was familiar with the circumstances of the people he was dealing with and he did not need to read all the papers through, only to refresh his memory which retained with considerable accuracy the details of the lives and careers of his staff. He was finished with the files in less than two hours. There was an extra folder containing comments and receipts for payments to those odd informants and contacts which newspapers keep with porters in Ministries, house servants of famous people, back-stairs hangers-on of the political parties who live in part by the sale of information to the press. Kerenyi considered this folder for some time, chewing his upper lip; he was tempted to destroy it altogether, but rejected that idea – at least in part they must take their own chances, those marginal people. If he destroyed the lot it would be noticed, for all newspapers must have such contacts, and Kerenyi had no desire to give the Party a handle for interrogating him. He knew quite well that the thought of avoiding at least one interrogation was the outcome of an unreal desire to ignore the approach of catastrophe. Natural enough, perhaps, but dangerous at a time when a calculating presence of mind was his only armour against the mistake that might precipitate him into the outer dark.

The last folder was his own. He removed one or two highly personal letters from his employer and some lawyers' documents about a lawsuit. He wondered wryly if Keppler was having the consideration to do as much in his own private files for his chief editor.

When he had finished to his own satisfaction he put the whole pile of folders back neatly where they had come from and ran his finger over the other papers in the safe to remind himself what they were. Then he opened his personal cash box and took out what money there was, with the cashier's slips for expenses. The cash was, of course, correct and the bank account up to date. It was not difficult for Fräulein Bracher to keep his personal accounts since he spent almost every groschen he earned and had no private means.

Kerenyi stretched back in his swivel chair and yawned widely. His stomach gave a warning grumble that reminded him he had not eaten for many hours since hot sausages and beer in the gloomy pre-dawn of the station in Prague. He looked at his watch. The printing-shift canteen would be open.

All the papers from the personnel files he pushed down into the waste-basket. Swinging it in his hand he went out, leaving his door open in the usual signal that he was somewhere about in the building. The paternoster rising in a ceaseless succession of boxes gave him the momentary depression it always did give him. Somewhere in his boyhood a steel engraving of prisoners on a treadmill had been transferred in his memory to this jerky procession of little cells, carrying preoccupied human beings about errands that were anything but mysterious except at the moments they spent in the moving boxes. On the other side of the shaft Kerenyi stepped into one of the downward moving boxes and was lowered to the cellars. Hollow echoes in dark corridors lined with closed doors, the smell of concrete, coke dust, and for some reason the raw wood of crates, engulfed him down there. Above his head the steady thrum of the rotary printers was a deep tremor through the building. The old fireman had a stooping gait as if he constantly negotiated the low galleries of a mine; in fact it was the result of a war injury to his back which also entitled him to a modest but permanent position on the staff he had first joined more than thirty years before. Normally he would see Kerenyi perhaps two or three times in a year: at Christmas; the staff outing to an *Heurigen* on St Elisabeth's Day; the First of May.

'Good evening, Herr Pittermann,' said Kerenyi formally. 'If you would be so good, I'd like one of the furnaces opened.'

The old man opened his mouth to object. Then he looked downwards and saw the basket full of papers. He lifted his grave eyes to Kerenyi's face and turned down the corners of his wrinkled mouth, considering. He nodded slightly, saying nothing. Kerenyi followed him as he shuffled down the corridor into increasing warmth where the two big central-heating furnaces hummed gently to themselves. Taking a long steel hook the old man opened the coke door high up in the side of one of them, almost level with his own head. Kerenyi lifted the basket and poured out the papers into the dull surface of coke. The old man turned a key and there was a whoosh of heat and light. The door fell back and the old man locked it with a practised gesture. Kerenyi looked about him in the dusty light of the powerful electric bulb. It was very tidy, with coke stacks against two walls and the space round the furnaces swept clean. A police notice of fire regulations was prominently displayed, washed according to regulations once a week so that it was always readable. One of the rules was against throwing rubbish or paper into the furnaces. Kerenyi's eyes came back to the old man who watched him, still holding the long hook. He smiled.

'Thank you, Herr Pittermann,' he said. 'Good evening to you.'

'Good evening, Herr Chief Editor,' said the old man. As Kerenyi walked back down the echoing corridor he heard the steel hook returned to its nail where it swung to and fro with a grinding ring against the bricks of the wall.

The newsroom was brilliantly lighted, full of clattering machines and talk as it always was at this hour. A woman in a smart hat typed fast in one corner, smoking all the time, with her head tilted.

Kerenyi came over to her and she looked up and nodded at him. He raised his eyebrows and tipped his chin at her packet of cigarettes; she nodded again and went on typing. Kerenyi took a cigarette and lit it, throwing the match into an ashtray already full of ash and butts.

'A good film?' he asked.

'Horrible,' she said, 'but of course a good notice.'

He turned away, conscious of sour anger at a cynicism so like his own. The desk of the night editor was empty, tidy. The chief sub said anxiously, 'I didn't know you were back, Herr Kerenyi.' They shook hands.

'I don't know that I am, officially,' said Kerenyi. 'Herr Silbermann not here, I see.'

'No. He – perhaps he is ill?'

'I doubt it. No fool, Herr Silbermann.' The chatter of the tape machines covered their voices. The sub-editor pulled his tie away from his collar. He was sweating, but that meant nothing, he always was.

'Do you know where?' he asked in a cautious undertone.

'I think Zurich,' said Kerenyi and threw away his cigarette half-smoked. Two reporters watched them covertly.

'Can you get the paper out?' asked the editor. 'Not that it matters to-night. There's plenty of stuff to fill it. Do you need any help?'

'It's all right,' said the sub. 'Shall I use the long feature on the

Everest expedition instead of your article about the European Federation at Prague?'

'Ah, Fräulein Bracher told you, did she? Yes. Use that. Is it set up?'

'Been set for days, waiting for space.'

Kerenyi looked round the big room, and shoved his hands in his pockets. 'There's just one thing,' he said. 'Tell everybody that I've done as I said I would and cleared the files of any personal matter that might be ... But be careful with Schmittgen. Is he back?'

'Herr Schmittgen is in Linz,' said the sub. One of the telephones on the night editor's desk rang. 'That will be him now.' He leaned over the desk and picked up the instrument, a new and modern one.

A high crackle of sound broke from the black receiver almost before it was answered. Kerenyi could hear the words quite clearly. After a few exchanges the sub had the call switched to the stenographers' desk to be taken down for copy.

'How shall I handle his stuff, Herr Kerenyi?'

'Print it,' said Kerenyi, shrugging his rather high shoulders cheerfully. 'Print the lot. Schmittgen is a very good reporter. I should not be surprised if he's editor by to-morrow night.'

They had nothing to discuss; it had all been endlessly discussed and all the speculations were meaningless now that it was happening. One of the two reporters had gone out, the other sat at a typing-table with his back to them.

'I'm going to see Herr Keppler after I've had something to eat in the canteen. By to-morrow we shall all know more.' The two men shook hands again and said good night. Kerenyi started away down the room, but the sub-editor caught him up. 'Shall we see you ...' He stopped. Kerenyi looked coolly at him, twisting his mouth a little, as if he had not taken in what was said. He was, in fact, thinking of the scene in this room about ten years ago when the old editor-in-chief retired and the owner and two or three political persons of consequence and the editors of all the other Vienna papers had come to present the old man with a silver box and to greet him, Kerenyi, the young newcomer who was taking over the paper. The speeches and wine and photographs had taken up more than two hours. Kerenyi remembered the old man's silky white beard and his own impatience to get rid of the old fool and get on with the task of making the *Independent* a paper of his own.

Kerenyi did not answer the sub. They looked at each other for a moment and Kerenyi went out. As he passed the reporters' table he said good night to the young man hardly out of his teens. The boy half rose from his chair. He had the embarrassed and swaggering air of the very young. Kerenyi glanced sideways and then stopped. He put out a bony finger and touched the boy's lapel. There was a small enamel button there, a white ground in a black ring and a red swastika.

'Something new, eh?' He nodded at the boy, thoughtfully. The young man half raised his arm, and let it fall again. In a voice strangled with embarrassment he muttered, 'Heil Hitler!' Then, looking after Kerenyi's back, he cleared his throat and said the words again, very loudly, 'Heil Hitler!'

Kerenyi did not talk much to the taxi driver, contrary to his usual practice. On the long splashing drive out to the villa of the paper's owner and publisher, he thought of the compositors in the night canteen. The half-hearted snow, falling soft and wet, of late winter, made the varying surface of the streets dangerous. They skidded wildly coming out of the Schoenbrunner Strasse, recently macadamed, on to cobbles. A tram slewed jerkily round the wide curve of its rails and its driver leaned out of his dark cabin to let the taxi man have his opinion of taxis and the weather in hoarse Ottakinger dialect. The first car of the tram was crowded, the windows breathed over mistily. Only the curved sweeps of glass cleared by coat sleeves showed the figures inside between streams of condensation. The taxi swung in a dizzy turn. For a timeless moment Kerenyi stared from his darkness into the vivid lighted expanse of tram window. A girl's face gazed blindly at him framed in the hood of her dark coat; the face was thin and wan with weariness. Mournful dark eyes stared and pale lips opened to speak a soundless word to herself. Before the face could be fully seen the taxi was past as the empty second car of the tram clanged by. One huddled man, his head sunk in his shoulders, sat alone in it. The young girl's face stayed printed on Kerenyi's retina as the taxi sped across the wide dark space of trees and gates before the Palace.

It returned now as the car took him back from Keppler's house into the city, a fading image whose essential look remained so that he would recognise that face again if he ever saw it. The roads were almost empty now. Even the narrow streets of the inner city lacked the normal traffic of theatres and restaurants, the hurrying passers-by, the standing whores, the taxi drivers. On the corner of Kaerntnerstrasse and the Opera the newspaper vendor was alone in his shining oilskins, stamping his thick boots. They had made a slight detour to buy the early editions of the next day's paper and the driver leaned out and beckoned to the man who came over and handed Kerenyi his own paper and the chief government paper. It was twenty-five minutes to eleven. The taxi turned and a moment later Kerenyi got out in the Schellinggasse, gave the man his usual tip and signed the bill held out to him. The man waited while Kerenyi rang the caretaker's bell, and as the side door was opened from the inside he put the old Daimler into gear and drove off. The taxi's whine faded round the corner into the Ring, and the street was empty and very still. It had stopped snowing, a sharp, cold little wind flicked Kerenyi's coat, the street lamps swayed slightly as if it were four in the morning. Kerenyi's heels rang on the patterned black and white stones of the hall floor as he crossed to the lift to the rattle of locks behind him. The caretaker shuffled after in carpet slippers, waistcoat hanging open over a collarless shirt, a thick woollen shawl round his shoulders. Coins tinkled, the lift gave its moan of effort and rose. Below, the caretaker pushed the time-switch and all the staircase lights came on.

'Ah, here is Georgy at last, scenting the air as usual.' The long living-room seemed, as he came into it, to be full of people. Julie was stretching out her hands to welcome him. From the skilful lightness of her tone Kerenyi could gauge the tension of the atmosphere. Kerenyi kissed both hands, bending his sandy head deeply and wondering for the hundredth time as he did so what it would be like to be in bed with a woman of such conquering

43

beauty. It was an academic question, for though he was devoted to Julie he was not attracted to her physically and supposed he would be afraid of her; a situation he was not used to and would not have enjoyed.

'You know everybody, don't you? Hella Schneider, Hansi, Colton Barber, Dr Hanau, Dr Krassny?'

Kerenyi nodded to his American colleague and the others, and bowed to the only man present he had never met.

'We have not had the pleasure of meeting,' said the man she addressed as Krassny to Julie.

'Dr Peter Krassny, Sektionschef in the Chancellor's Office – Dr Georg Kerenyi, Editor of the *Wiener Unabhängige Zeitung*.'

'Of course, I have often heard of you,' said both men together as they shook hands. The chance duplication gave them both the disguise of laughing, but both were thinking – what is he doing here? Neither of the theatre nor a Social Democrat and this is hardly the moment for displaying one's unorthodox friendships. The American newspaper correspondent moved away to talk to Franz and Hanau, another ex-Socialist member of Parliament, who were sitting, their heads bent to each other, by Franz's writing table, where Kerenyi joined them.

'Come and listen, Georgy,' said Franz, catching Kerenyi's wrist. 'You simply won't believe it.' Frau Schneider came by and kissed Georgy's forehead lightly.

'It's quite true, you do sniff the air,' she cried. 'A most impressive nose you have, Georgy. A real journalist's nose. So tell us, what is happening?'

'Yes, we have rather been waiting for your arrival,' Hanau's voice was thin and precise, a lawyer's voice; he wore pince-nez spectacles and had a trick of sniffing, slightly but constantly.

'Barber can probably tell you more than I can,' said Kerenyi, but before either of them could answer Hella's question Hansi Ostrovsky called her over to decide an argument as to the exact words used by Princess Tekla in the third act of *The Death of Wallenstein* when she hears that her lover is dead. A loud and laughing debate began on the other side of the room, and at least for a moment, the political situation was forgotten.

'Tell us your story, Dr Hanau,' said the American in his strongly accented German. He was a tall and serious man, younger than the other three and his seriousness had an air of bewilderment to it, as if he did not credit what was going on about him.

'I assure you it is true – every word,' said Hanau, answering Georgy who had asked him what it was he would never believe. 'Dr Wedeker is to be asked to resign from the non-existent Party because of his final speech at the Prague Conference.'

Kerenyi glanced at Franz, whose look showed that he was in two minds as to whether Hanau's joking pleased him.

'You did go a bit far, Franzl; I thought so at the time,' he said and turned to Hanau. 'But surely, surely, nobody can be so mad as to worry about Franz's views as to the sacredness of every word Marx ever said at this moment?'

'Ah!' cried Hanau, delighted, and hitched his chair a little closer to shut out the laughter of the group at the other end of the room. 'It is not so much that dear Dr Wedeker attacked the omniscience of Karl Marx. We have become used to that! Or even that he expressed the supposition that some adaptation of Marx's theories might be going on inside the Soviet Union, whether in the form of inner-Party discussions or of general practice in the realities of Russian experience. No, no, it is much more serious than even those heresies. Wedeker went much further. I am astonished that you did not notice it while you were listening to the speech, Dr Kerenyi!' Hanau sniffed and flashed his lenses at Georgy who laughed.

'Quite right, my dear Hanau,' he said. 'I did not listen with both ears to every word of the speech. Tell me what I missed.'

Slowly, with that air of slight pompousness of a licensed joker who likes to stage a joke elaborately, Hanau drew a sheaf of cyclo-styled papers from his pocket, unfolded it, smoothed out the corner where the staple had made a ridge and began to read aloud, rapidly. At first he flew over the words half to himself. Then he came to the passage he sought and read more slowly, aloud and clearly, savouring each word. He glanced up at Kerenyi and the foreigner in turn, to make sure he had their whole attention, without the flow of his words being interrupted.

'Wedeker then said, "What is needed is a deep psychological alteration, not in our thinking, for we do too much thinking, but in our attitude, our instinctive attitude, to the world. We must—"'

'I don't remember anything like this in your speech, Franz,' said Kerenyi, interrupting with a tight grin.

'Wait a bit,' said Hanau waving the papers at Kerenyi. 'Wait until I've read to the end. "We must alter, not outwardly but from inside our own minds, the state of affairs in which socialism consists of an opposition to something. That is, in dialectical terms, socialism as the antithesis to the possessing and ruling class and its ideology. It is not a philosophy of its own, so to speak, but a reaction to a former, established and power-holding philosophy. Everything we do is an answer to what is done by our opponents – we accept their existence as the prior condition of our own existence. We do not desire their disappearance, for a vacuum would force us to fill it with our own long-demanded power. We consist almost without exception of masochists who love their wounds, their hardships, but who cannot envisage winning the struggle. It was not by chance ..."' Hanau paused weightily, raising his eyebrows at Kerenyi and Barber warningly. He sniffed twice and continued reading. "'... not by chance that the key to the workers' firearms arsenal was lost on 11th March, 1934. It was inevitable that it should be mislaid; for otherwise we might have been able to defend ourselves effectively."'

Hanau looked up, triumphant, and Kerenyi could feel the glee rising like a tide in him; a hundred years of life would not be enough to contain this man's pleasure at the folly of his fellow men.

'I don't quite see what ...' began Barber.

'Of course, the point is, I did not say any of this in a speech. I said it at supper after the final meeting of the Congress,' Franz explained. 'It was supposed to be a private occasion, but someone was making notes.'

'Verbatim!' cried Hanau.

'You will never be forgiven that – the bit about the arsenal key,' said Kerenyi. 'I wish I had been there, to see their faces when you said it.'

'I don't regret any of it,' said Franz heatedly. 'It needed saying for our own sakes.'

'For your own sakes?' echoed Barber, simply unable to understand what he heard.

Kerenyi turned to him. 'You will never make them practical,' he said. 'And it's no good trying.' He spoke brutally to compensate for a creature inside himself that wanted to scream and weep and beat on the walls with its fists.

The American stood up and put his hands in the pockets of his jacket. He hesitated for a moment. Then he said quietly, 'I know this is none of my business, Dr Wedeker, but I wouldn't have an easy conscience if I didn't say it. I've seen these Nazis in Germany, and you don't seem to understand what they are like. You haven't any time to discuss ideologies now. *They* will be here by the morning. And you have just that much time to make your escape.' He was staring fixedly in his embarrassment at the marble inkstand on the desk, but he glanced quickly now at Hanau. 'Both of you,' he said in an expressionless voice. 'There's a train for Prague just after nine in the morning. I have to go there to meet my editor. I just hope I shall see you both on that train.' He took his hands out of his pockets and made a stiff little movement of his head. 'And now I think I'd better say good night. I still have to pack my grip.'

He stood there for a moment, in the shocked silence. After he had gone, Kerenyi got up and went to join the other group where, as he came up, Hella Schneider caused an outburst of gusty laughter, the origin of which he did not hear.

As he sat down on the arm of Hella's chair, they turned their faces towards him, always glad to change once again the subject of conversation.

In spite of the rage inside him, Kerenyi felt obscurely the need to preserve the absurd, sociable atmosphere, as much for his own sake as to give Franz and Hanau time to recover from Colton Barber's outburst.

'The new film is a great success, I understand without surprise,' he said to Hella. He smiled into her round, sparkling blonde face. She was a year or so younger than Julie and of a rounded prettiness; one of those women who give an impression of a gay plumpness while in fact having fashionably slim figures. Where Julie was tall, almost commandingly so, Hella was small in stature, and the contrast between her roundness of line and feature, and Julie's sparely elegant, slightly aquiline face was often noted by critics and theatregoers. Kerenyi glanced up at Julie, standing with a decanter in her hand and was struck, as always when he looked at her from another woman, with the extraordinary strength and calm – hardly feminine in comparison with the overt sexiness of Hella – given to her face by the over-large dark eyes with their firmly marked brows and straight, wide stare. She was looking over at Franz, a look at once tender and anxious; she caught Kerenyi's sharp look, her face changed instantly to an awareness of social presence, and she turned her dark head gracefully towards him, offering him more brandy with a lift of the fine brows. He held out his glass. Hella was prattling in answer to Kerenyi's sarcastic remark.

'How unkind to tease me,' she was saying with a little pout of her full underlip, in a brisk tone of pleasure, 'as a matter of fact, quite in confidence, I was staggered at the amount they paid me. You know, Director Schoenherr almost forced me to accept the part. He offered to release me for two months to make the wretched thing, and when I said I should have to think it over, he telephoned the *Völkische Beobachter* personally – from Vienna – and told them I had accepted. I was furious; we practically had a stand-up row. But just the same, the wages of sin may be death but the wages of artistic dishonour seem to be a fat bank balance!'

They all knew that the film, under review as Kerenyi left the newsroom of his newspaper, was a vulgar distortion of the life of a poet whose work they all valued. It had been made as a placatory demonstration of national – that is, German – feeling towards the rising tide of power that was about to flood over them all.

'Of course, it is the most awful nonsense,' went on Hella, 'but quite effective in its vulgar way, I think.'

'A pity its grand opening performance will be pushed off the front pages by other events,' said Hansi Ostrovsky, unable as always, to hide his feelings, in a moment of irritation. He said it to pay Hella out for the lie about her release from the theatre to make the film, which she had forced on Schoenherr at the threat of a scandal.

'If it takes place at all,' said Kerenyi, and pointed his arched nose at Krassny. 'Don't you agree that the gala performance will be cancelled, Herr Doctor?'

Challenged so openly for an opinion, the civil servant looked embarrassed. He fidgeted with the gleaming cuff of his white shirt which showed well below his sleeve, and when he answered his voice was, like his whole manner, studied almost to caricature. He had the slightly nasal drawl that survived only in those upper-class Viennese not forced by the need to deal with new and unfamiliar situations in the last years to jettison their class mannerisms. Trained before the War, he was a survival of those families – like Julie's family – produced only in the capital cities of great powers, whose profound but silent self-satisfaction grows from their indispensable control of administration and whose rewards are not normally counted in figures.

'I am not, you understand, in the protocol department,' he said at last, 'so that I am not aware of any alterations to such arrangements that may have been made.' He stopped and swallowed, and then smiled painfully at Kerenyi. 'As a matter of fact, I am in a twi-light state of unofficial suspension, I believe. Being a member of the Chancellor's personal staff. Ah – perhaps suspension is too strong a word – nothing has been said; there has hardly been time. But since this afternoon, my office has been occupied by a young man, a clerk from the archive section. I have the impression, how-ever, though I may be wrong, that his tenure of the chair will be temporary.'

'We may take it that this young man appeared in your office in Party uniform to-day?' asked Franz who had come over with Hanau to join the group.

'He did indeed,' answered Krassny bleakly. 'SA khaki shirt with armband and top boots. Which he proceeded to put up on my table while swinging on the back legs of his chair and playing with a paper-knife. I imagine he had seen such a scene in some film or other. A curious sight it was, when one remembers that the table was first used by a *chef de cabinet* to Josef II.'

'The local Party boys are in great form at the moment, thinking they are going to take over the government at any second,' said Kerenyi.

'I see you don't think they will do so?' asked Hansi Ostrovsky.

'Of course not. The key positions will all be held by Reich Germans a week from now in every ministry in Vienna. Old Austrian Party members will be rewarded with jobs in Germany itself, where they can do no harm.'

Krassny's reference to past glories produced a response from Hella Schneider of sentimental nostalgia. 'This is the end of a whole history,' she pronounced in her theatre voice, repeating something said at dinner that evening. Hanau looked round, delighted at this, and his eyes meeting Julie's they exchanged minute smiles.

'My dear Hella, imperial history ended in Galicia in 1915,' said Franz.

'Imperial history ended then,' agreed Krassny, 'six hundred years of Habsburg history; but the enforced Anschluss of Germany with Austria is the end of a concept that began with Charlemagne.'

'On the contrary, my dear Doctor,' Kerenyi interposed with noticeable energy, 'the Nazis seem to me to be carrying out Charlemagne's work!'

Krassny, startled, looked at Kerenyi with the undisguised hostility of a man looking at one who disturbs his life-long illusions.

'Charlemagne's concept was not one of violence,' he said stiffly, 'but was based on the unity of Christendom.'

'Oh, come now,' interrupted Hansi Ostrovsky, his voice high with irritation. 'We are talking like first-year students.' Kerenyi guessed from his tone that he had been listening to this talk all evening at dinner, in other rooms with other people all trying to theorise out of existence the fact of their own impotence, or their own half-conscious acquiescence. 'Hitler is the heir of Napoleon and he deals in power, as Charlemagne did, and all other conquerors.'

'Napoleon was at last defeated, we should remember,' said Franz. 'He was part of the long historical purpose of the French to keep central Europe weak and divided. In 1919 when the successor states were established under French protection, the political vacuum of central Europe was completed, as the French have desired ever since they were a nation. That Germany was united at all under the hegemony of Prussia was the direct result of French policy. By disrupting unity in southern Germany for generations, they ensured that it would be imposed by a State far enough to the East to be not easily controlled by France. French encouragement of nationalism and her alliance, with panslavism through Russia did the rest. And after the last war, by pressure of England and America, France succeeded in wrecking any chance of a unified Germany-Austria as a stable, social-democratic State. She would have succeeded in selling the Entente the idea of dismemberment of Bismarck's Reich, if the victory of Bolshevism in Russia had not frightened them into some sort of sense.'

'But really, Franz, I don't think we can leave out our own internal quarrels, which made any sort of Danube federation impossible at the time.' Kerenyi found himself drawn, as so often, into the unreal debate on the past, always in terms of someone else's responsibility.

'We do not know,' cried Franz passionately. 'We never had a chance to try. The French had their ideas about Poland and Czechoslovakia all worked out for Wilson's ear in terms of self-determination and so-called democracy which they knew would touch his schoolmaster's mind.'

'There is a gap in your argument, Franz,' said Hanau. 'German unity could never have been achieved at all, if the major nation of Europe was so implacably against it.'

'Don't make it more involved than ever, Hanau,' protested Kerenyi. 'You know perfectly well that the industrialisation of Germany brought unity with it. Once coal and iron became the dominant factors of politics ...'

'Your pragmatism, Kerenyi!' said Hanau, much enjoying the argument. 'You explain every phenomenon of politics with economics. I sometimes suspect you of a streak of Marxism, in spite of your denials.'

'I don't see any point in your argument at all,' interrupted Julie. 'What does it matter now, why it happened?'

'You are right, Julie,' said Hansi. 'Charlemagne and St Germain.

What do they matter now? Hitler is unifying Europe, or conquering Europe. And Dr Krassny's argument is not valid, either, for so far there has been no force; no shot has been fired. And does anyone believe it will stop with Austria?'

'You make it sound as if it were a good thing, Hansi,' objected Hella. 'Do you really want those thugs back here who murdered poor little Dollfuss?'

'A good thing? No, I think it is the end of everything. But one thing is certain – talking about it does no good.'

'Oh, no, Hansi,' said Julie's clear voice behind his shoulder. 'I don't believe in your end of everything. We shall survive. That is our business, to survive.'

She did not see Kerenyi's sharp glance at her, nor the frowning look exchanged between him and Hansi. Unobtrusively, Hansi moved his position so that he was next to Kerenyi, and, choosing a moment when the voices rose in argument again, he spoke in an undertone.

'Listen, Kerenyi. I tried to tell her this morning what this Nazi business means for Franz. She hasn't grasped it, and neither has he. You will have to talk to him.'

'Leave it to me,' said Kerenyi in a grim undertone. He leaned forward to a cigarette box open on the table to disguise their exchange. 'I'll speak to Franz.'

'We are at this moment quite impotent,' Krassny was saying, 'but that will change when the world understands what is happening.'

'The world,' said Hanau, smiling and sniffing, 'the world will protest. Perhaps even angrily. And in a few months' time the world will say that because seven million Austro-Germans made no attempt to fight eighty million Reich Germans, we wanted the Anschluss.'

'Georgy,' called Hella. 'You were going to tell me what is happening, hours ago. What is the latest?'

'The Chancellor was still discussing affairs with the President when I left the office,' answered Kerenyi. 'I imagine they must both have resigned by now, since they are not in a position to change their attitude of hostility to the Nazis. The border to Bavaria is closed, in theory. But whether the Wehrmacht is already over the border I don't know.'

'And your paper?' asked Hanau. 'What does your publisher – what's his name, Keppler – what does he mean to do?'

'He has agreed to join the NSDAP at the last moment, in order to keep the paper. A man called Schmittgen is taking over.'

'You mean Keppler has fired you, Georgy?' cried Franz. 'But that is really monstrous!'

'My dear chap,' Kerenyi shook his head. 'He had no alternative. And in fact he has behaved with extreme courage. He managed to get me transferred to the literary editorship as a condition of his joining the Party. It was the most he could do, and I'm grateful to him.'

'Literary editor,' murmured Hanau. 'There was a time when that post was more important than any other kind of editor.'

'About fifty years ago,' said Kerenyi savagely. 'But at least I shan't starve.'

'I suppose in that case,' Krassny said, 'it is no good asking you to telephone the paper and find out the latest news, Herr Doctor?'

'I imagine I can still do that,' said Kerenyi. 'I'll go and call the newsroom, if I may?' He looked sideways at Julie.

'Of course, Georgy,' Julie smiled assent. 'Oh, but you can't. I'm sorry. The telephone was cut off this afternoon. I'd forgotten.'

'Cut off? Are you sure?'

'Why didn't you tell us this before?' cried Hansi. 'Don't you understand what it means?'

'I didn't think of it.' Julie was bewildered, 'What does it mean, then? I was just talking to the operator and the line went dead ...'

'Do you mean she cut you off?' persisted Kerenyi.

'No, no, we were talking. It was cut off somewhere else. It wasn't the operator.'

By some chance of conversation, everybody seemed to have stopped talking at the same moment. Kerenyi had been bending over the high back of a chair, and he straightened up now, sharply. In the silence he said coldly, 'What was the girl telling you when you were cut off?'

'She was apologising because she couldn't get the number I

wanted, she said something about the muddle they were in. A lot of lines were being taken over, or something ...' Julie's voice trailed off nervously.

'Himmler and Heydrich were in Vienna by then,' said Kerenyi. 'The first thing they would do would be to cut off all the telephones on their list of wanted men, so that nobody could get in touch with their friends. To-morrow the arrests will begin.'

'Himmler!' Hella's voice rose like a schoolgirl's on hearing a naughty word, and she giggled.

Krassny had risen to his feet, and turned to Julie.

'I must get off home,' he said, 'I hadn't realised how late it was.'

'I must go too, Hansi,' said Hella. 'Shall we get a taxi?'

'I'm coming,' answered Hansi, and glanced sideways at Kerenyi, who nodded slightly.

It seemed that suddenly everyone was going, and in the bustle of getting coats and hats from the carved cupboard in the hall it was not noticed that Kerenyi stayed in the living-room. Franz and Julie came back into the room, holding hands, to find him reading the leader in the government paper he had brought in with him – the last time it was to appear. He was standing by Franz's table and put down the newspaper as they came in.

Franz was always pale and his features fine drawn, but he looked now, in the overhead lamplight that seemed harsh in the empty room, haggard and grey. His face was empty and Kerenyi realised that he was stunned by a disaster he had succeeded for too long in banning from his mind.

'Franz,' said Georgy, 'you are going to take Colton Barber's advice, aren't you? You are leaving in the morning?'

'In the morning,' said Julie quickly, breathlessly. 'There's a good train to Prague about nine o'clock.'

'Barber said he would be on that train, you remember? It would be some sort of protection to you perhaps, if you were travelling with a well-known American journalist. Even Himmler has to take some sort of notice of what Barber's newspaper prints. Because we don't know if the Czech frontier has been closed or not, and I can't think of any way of finding out now without giving the game away. We can only hope it is still open to-morrow.'

'I will go on that train, Georgy. I've already said so.'

'I don't feel much confidence about it, I tell you frankly. There was a train back this evening you could have caught; but I found you here entertaining friends as if nothing had happened. You promise me you will go?'

'Of course,' said Franz, his voice cold with resignation. Kerenyi's mouth was pulled crooked by a curious grimace that might have been anger as he turned to Julie.

'Julie, you are not going to attempt to go with Franz, I hope?'

Julie moved her hands defensively, but said nothing. Kerenyi went on in a voice of rigid distaste. 'You would inevitably be recognised. They would stop you and that would mean Franz's instant arrest either at the station or on the border. You do understand that?'

Julie looked quickly at her husband. He was staring at the floor.

'Is that true, Franzl?'

'I hadn't thought of it like that ... but yes, I suppose it is possible. Like all the opposition, I am on the police lists. That is, if you were recognised, and your face is so much better known than mine.'

'I have a rehearsal in the morning; half Vienna would know by eleven o'clock if I weren't here.'

'You didn't tell me that,' said Franz helplessly.

'I hadn't thought of it until this moment.'

'Franz,' said Kerenyi again. Julie opened her lips to speak and he nodded impatiently. 'I know, and I'm going, now. But I've known Franzl since the University. We were on the Isonzo together. I have to say this. Franzl, these people are not relying on the Fatherland Front lists. They have their own lists and their own methods. It isn't like the half-hearted fooling about that has been going on here for the last four years. Franz, I beg you, for God's sake don't think – don't make the terrible mistake of thinking you can play with these people ...'

'Oh, Georgy, please!' cried Julie in a voice of terror.

'If they lay their hands on you,' went on Kerenyi slowly, measuring his words one by one as if there were only so much meaning in the world and he must make this use of his share of it. 'If these men lay hands on you, you will disappear from the world, and time, and life. You will never have existed.'

Julie went to her husband and put her arms around his bent shoulders, pressing him against her with her hands on his back. They were exactly the same height, and Franz leaned his head against Julie's and closed his eyes.

Kerenyi went out. He took his hat and coat and the bunch of spare keys that always hung beside the apartment door. He let himself out, as he had often done before, locked the iron-bound door behind him, ran down the winding stairs and crossed the cold hall. He unlocked the side door in the heavy front doors and stood with his head bent for a moment, listening to the still, midnight house. Then he pulled the door open and stepped outside into the lighted street, empty and shining in the light of the street lamps. He locked the door behind him twice and pushed the keys back through the letter-box marked HAUSBESORGER.

There was not a soul to be seen. The Schwarzenberg Strasse was as empty as if it were just before dawn. A single cab waited on the corner rank, its driver huddled over the wheel asleep. Kerenyi woke the man, who from his breath had been drinking, with some difficulty. On the whole drive to his flat in the 8th District Kerenyi saw only three human beings, apart from a standing policeman here and there.

3

During the whole morning Julie was aware of people being kind to her. Not, she knew, out of nervousness because she was accepted as professionally well balanced. Her lack of 'temperament' was the chief reason for her popularity with her fellow artists; she was not of those actresses who crowd other figures on the stage, have trouble managing bulky costumes and drop properties at awkward moments of other actors' lines. Her faults lay in the other directions; she was slow to learn, slow to feel the relationships of parts to each other, the comparative weights of complex impacts which must balance each other; cautious and afraid of intuition. Hansi Ostrovsky complained that she thought too much in a new part.

But on Saturday morning he did not complain once, and her stage partner was so considerate with her difficulties in the subtle curtain scene in which Nora, for the first time acting as a human being and not as a reflection of a man's idea of her, turns aside her husband's lovemaking, that the real woman began to feel herself as manipulated as the female object in the play.

Drinking the familiar bad coffee as they rested, Julie avoided thinking of the early morning, the smell of strong hot coffee in the bedroom, the confusion of packing. Neither she nor Franz had slept much and her whole body felt dry and obscurely bruised, both heavy and empty, wooden with exhaustion and of a dizzy blankness as if she had a bad hangover.

'*Olympia* to-morrow night,' said Hansi.

'Thank goodness,' she sighed, 'it's something I know backwards.'

'Good old Molnár,' contributed her rehearsal partner. 'All charm, if not much else, and the public always loves it.'

The actor who played the doomed doctor in *Doll's House* put down his coffee mug. 'It's one of the plays one always feels one should write a fifth act for. Why don't you write a pastiche act for *Olympia*, Hansi?'

'I haven't the talent,' said Hansi Ostrovsky. 'I could only write kitsch. But you're right, Willy. Somebody ought to write another act for the Burgtheater party piece next winter. It's a good idea.'

'Why don't you ask Kerenyi?' suggested Julie. 'He's quite a poet, you know.'

'I believe I will ask Georgy. I've been looking for an idea for next year. And it will give poor old Georgy something to occupy himself with.'

Julie turned her head away and they all looked at her.

'Let's go back to work, shall we?' Hansi's tone was an apology for having clumsily reminded her of the vacancy of Franz's life now gathering timelessness and emptiness on the Prague train.

Later her stage 'husband' asked her if she was doing anything that evening. 'If you would like company, I mean ...?'

'You look all in,' said Willy Mundel. 'Don't you listen to Ostrovsky and his warnings about pill taking. Have a couple of my sleeping tablets and sleep a bit of your life away. It's the infallible cure.'

'Crude oaf, you,' Hansi pretended to be jovial and it did not suit him.

They moved away in a group as Julie's dresser came on to the echoing stage.

'Willy,' called Julie as the dresser held out her coat.

'I'm sorry,' he mumbled. 'I didn't mean to ...'

'You're perfectly right,' she said briskly. 'Have you got the pills with you? Give me a couple.'

She knew he had the box of pills. He was famous for his hypochondria and carried a variety of panaceas about him. Out of his baggy pockets he pulled three little boxes, and from one

58

took two small white tablets. He looked at them in his big, unhealthily soft palm, and then looked shyly at Julie.

'They're strong,' he said. 'You'll only need one. Take the second if you wake up. You see?'

He was carefully holding the little tin so that the label was hidden from her and she smiled when she noticed this. He shrugged defensively.

'Not that you could get them without a prescription,' he said. 'Now remember, only one at a time. You never do take anything, I know, so two would give you a stinking hangover.'

Julie dropped the tablets loose into the pocket of her beaver coat.

'I promise,' she said, suddenly sounding gay. '*Servus*, Willy.'

'There is a taxi waiting, gnae' Frau,' said the dresser with heavy disapproval.

Julie patted her fat arms. 'You're only cross because you didn't think of it,' she said. 'And what are you doing in the theatre this morning, anyway, Frau Lotte?'

'I had some work to catch up with,' said the woman evasively, but she smiled then, a little reluctantly.

It's all so stupidly false, thought Julie angrily in the grinding taxi. They are only worried about keeping me on the job. And I'm as false as they are. She was aware that this was unjust; that the old character actor's apparent tactlessness showed as much real sensibility as Hansi's careful gentleness, and that her dresser really cared for her, and had come that morning to reassure her. She stared out of the grimy window, indulging her unreasonableness as long as she could; and already afraid of the loneliness that awaited her.

There was a vague drift about the crowd in the Ring, against the normal movement away from the inner city for the week-end. The mob was gathering, that mob which is moved mysteriously to collect in any great event. Here and there Julie could see couples and groups of young men in light brown uniform with heavy leather belts and knee boots. They were never alone; they showed in groups an experimental toughness, as yet only of manner. Around the newspaper kiosks milled unsettled knots of dark-coated citizens. The weather was of a cold, dusky grey.

Far away, in the remote calm of the Salzburg uplands meagre snow fell on the ominous blunt tanks skirting the steely gleam of winter lakes on winding, unmilitary roads. The unresisted progress, at first lonely, was greeted with more and more waving and welcoming cries the farther they penetrated towards Linz and past Linz towards Vienna. As the inevitability of their unused force slid deeper and deeper into consciousness there was more and more show of concurrence in what nobody could hinder. And everywhere were the groups of brown-clad young men, organised and excited; drawing as it were by a reflection off the tanks constantly more and more waverers to themselves. They were about to inherit, where the meek were abdicating, this earth which they felt to be theirs.

They had been visited by Director Schoenherr at the rehearsal this morning; apart from the unusualness of his appearing at all on a Saturday, he was accompanied by a tall man with anxious eyes, smooth hair and a rather exaggerated air of conciliation whose speech had the sharp accents of Hamburg. For a moment they brought in the atmosphere of an inspection at the Academy – no, rather Mother Superior talking round one of the trustees at school. Remembering her telephone call to Pohaisky from the porter's lodge – the telephone at the apartment was still dead – Julie stumbled in her words and stopped speaking. With murmured apologies the two men at once withdrew.

When Julie reached home, Fina popped out to the waiting lift even more sharply than usual.

'Herr Doctor Pohaisky is waiting,' she said in a cross whisper. 'You didn't say he would be coming before lunch.'

'I don't think I knew,' said Julie, and saw that Fina's blackcurrant eyes were red-ringed. As she let Fina take her coat she sighed heavily, and sat down by the dead telephone to change her outdoor shoes for the high-heeled slippers Fina handed to her. She looked up at Fina, and shook her head helplessly and Fina nodded, pressing her lips together so that they almost disappeared in her round, apple-hard, shiny face.

The papers were locked in the middle drawer of Franz's writing-table. They had, unbelievably, almost forgotten them, and Franz finally signed them between packing and drinking coffee, at seven that morning. While he was still leaning over the table signing the last page where the witnesses' names were already scrawled and stamped, Fina hauled the heavy trunk out of the room.

Pohaisky was not five minutes checking the papers. He replaced them in the briefcase used for them before.

'Was there,' he asked carefully, 'any particular reason for calling me this morning instead of on Monday?'

Julie put a dismayed hand up to her mouth. 'Oh, good heavens, I was supposed to leave it until Monday! No, there was no reason at all. I'm terribly sorry – have I caused you trouble, Herr Doctor? I simply ... I must have been so frantic to get rid of the wretched things ... I simply forgot it was still only Saturday. I am more than sorry – really ...'

'It does not matter,' he said, sedate as always. 'I only asked you to make sure nothing had happened that I ought to know of. You burned all the notes?'

She had burned them; held them in her hand while Franz said good-bye, unreal, unbelieved; and then burned them in the bedroom stove.

He had turned to go when he remembered something.

'You will almost certainly suffer the attentions of the police – perhaps several calls – in the next day or so. Just tell the truth. Franz has left for Prague; you don't know his address there or how long he will stay. Tell the cook what to say. They will ask her too. Can you remember that?'

'Yes, I can remember that.' Her heart failed her and she turned her head away. 'I don't seem to be very good at this sort of thing. I'm sorry I worried you.'

'No, now,' he said gently. 'Don't play the little woman for my benefit, Frau Julia. You would be very much miscast. And as for being good at this sort of thing – I've no doubt we shall improve with practice.'

He made no attempt to say anything comforting, ignoring the signs of her distress. Julie smiled unwillingly.

'Doctor Alois, you are always good for me.'

She went with him to the door this time.

'I shall be at ten o'clock Mass to-morrow. Shall we see you there?'

'Yes,' she said. 'Yes. At St Anna's?'

She did not often go to Mass, neglecting her duties except on the great festivals of the year.

'My wife will be happy to see you.'

As Fina removed her plate at table, she said abruptly, 'What does Herr Doctor think he's at, going to Mass at ten? He always goes at seven. I see him every Sunday at St Anna's.'

'I wondered that myself. Perhaps he is going twice to-morrow?'

Fina sniffed. 'You don't know what to believe, you really don't. Oh, I know what you mean; he's going to pray for Austria. But on the other hand everyone is saying what a good thing it is for us all. What with the out-of-works and everything. After all, we are German, you said so yourself, gnae' Frau. And Doctor Franz is always on about the Germans being all united together.'

'But, Fina, it's all quite different from what Doctor Franz wanted. Don't you see—' her voice shook in spite of herself. 'Don't you see – Doctor Franz is a Jew?'

'He's not a Jew to me,' cried Fina angrily, slamming the fruit dish on the polished surface of the table. 'I put him in my prayers every night and morning and Sundays too. What you ought to have done is got him properly baptised,' she went on triumphantly. 'Once his parents were gone, that was your duty, plain as plain.'

They had been over that a hundred times in the last years. Julie put up a hand to her aching head. 'But he doesn't believe,' she pleaded. 'I couldn't ask him to do something he doesn't believe in, for my sake, could I?'

'Ah,' Fina's voice was dark with meaning. 'Grace often comes after conversion. Save the soul first, and argue after, that's what I say.'

'But Fina, listen to me; listen for once. It wouldn't make the slightest difference to these Nazis if Franz were twenty times baptised. They think – it has nothing to do with religion for them – they don't like the Church much, either. They think it's something to do with blood – race, they call it. And they'll be after the priests soon, you'll see.'

'Ah, well, that's where you're wrong, gnae' Frau. You should go to the Holy Mass more regularly. The Cardinal broadcast this morning, and I turned on the wireless to hear him. "Keep calm and orderly," he said, in that beautiful, saintly voice.' And here Fina crossed herself. "Render unto Cæsar," he said. Now the Cardinal must know, mustn't he? You don't set yourself up to know more than he does, now do you?'

'But you see, the Cardinal is thinking of us; he's not thinking of all the thousands of Jewish Viennese. It's different for them. It was impossible for Doctor Franz to stay here – how can that be good? They would have arrested him and he would have ...' She stopped, unable to go on.

'And now he's gone,' muttered Fina, ducking her chin into her neck. 'And who's going to take care of his clothes and his food now, I'd like to know ...' She gave a harsh sob like a hiccup and began to cry noisily as she stamped out of the room. Julie could hear her banging the pans and bowls in the kitchen as if she were knocking the heads of the ungodly together for their own good.

On the writing-table in the living-room, beside the still untouched letters addressed to Franz, lay her morning's post. And a large, heavy white envelope with the Austrian State Crest on its flap. Julie broke it open and took out the gold-embossed card which invited her to an evening reception on Monday, 14th March, in the State Apartments of the New Hofburg. It had been delivered by hand. Among the post was a note in Director Schoenherr's own handwriting, informing her that an invitation to the reception for the Führer was being sent to her and that he was looking forward with great personal pleasure to seeing her on that occasion.

Julie switched on the little wireless set. It was playing traditional Austrian march music, but she left it playing in case a new announcement should follow. That was why she did not hear the door-bell when it rang, nor notice the door open slightly so that a thin young girl could slip into the room. The girl came up close to her with a sliding gait, as if she were trying to efface her presence, edging one shoulder forward with a submissive bend of her neck.

'Oh, Jesus-Maria! You startled the life out of me, Ruth.'

'I'm sorry,' the girl almost cringed. 'Fräulein Serafina said not to knock in case you had gone to lie down ...'

Julie used the familiar '*du*' but the girl addressed her as if she were a stranger. She was. They had met not more than half a dozen times in as many years. It was the granddaughter of the Talmudic scholar whom Julie had met on that one occasion before her marriage. She had forgotten them again since that thought the previous day, before Franz returned. Now she realised with a guilty shock that neither she nor Franz had considered their position.

'Uncle Franz is not here, then?' asked the girl, casting down her eyes and fidgeting with the pocket of her dark brown dress. It was of an ugly colour and depressingly cut, high in the collar and with long sleeves. Since her early childhood this granddaughter had been dedicated as companion and servant to her distinguished relative and had probably never in her life had any thought that was not of his comfort or of her duty towards him.

'No. He – he left this morning ... Your grandfather?'

'He is at home,' Ruth said unnecessarily, for the old man almost never left his room. 'He doesn't know I am out.'

'Of course, it's the Sabbath ...' It was, Julie knew vaguely, almost incredible that Ruth should have undertaken a visit or anything else, on the Sabbath.

'But I had to come. It was the only chance I had, while Grandfather's room is locked, to-day. I wanted to see Uncle Franz ...'

The soft, submissive voice trailed into silence.

'What to do?' Julie finished for her. 'My dear, as if we knew. As if anybody knew.'

Julie pressed the girl's shoulder slightly to indicate that she should sit down, and sat down herself in her own chair. The girl sat on the extreme edge of the chair, her ankles neatly together, and folded her beautiful hands into each other.

Ruth was silent. She turned her head from Julie to look timidly round the room and Julie watched abstractedly the movement of the long, thin throat, balanced by a loose knot of dark hair in the nape of the neck, already pinned up as if the child were grown up.

The thin, oval curve of the cheek was unbearably pathetic, not because she seemed to Julie a lost creature but because she had been sacrificed to that self-righteous, gloomy and severe old man and shut up away from her own youth in isolation and stifling puritanism. Her thoughts on flight, Julie asked the first question that came to mind. Through her own uncomprehended misery, she had to force herself to concentrate on the dilemma of these defenceless strangers.

'Have you and your grandfather got passports, Ruth?'

It was clear from Ruth's wondering stare that she had not followed Julie's thought.

'Passports?' she said. 'Only our identity papers.'

'How — is he?'

'He doesn't know anything,' the girl said. 'We've managed to keep it from him and he knows nothing about it. What is happening, Frau Julie? Do you know?'

'They are moving into Vienna now. A few hours from now and they'll be everywhere.'

'The local boys have been — they've often done it before, of course — but they've been singing outside the house all day to-day. I had to slip out of the courtyard door into the next street.' The child's unnatural self-control gave way and she gave a little sob, and put up her handkerchief to her mouth.

'Nazi boys, you mean?'

'I suppose so, yes. They sing dirty songs and — shout things.'

'I didn't know that had been going on.'

'Oh, yes, for some time now, but not like to-day. Now they have uniforms and stand openly in the street. They know it's a Jewish house, you see. The caretaker said he can't be responsible ... I think he's one of them, himself.'

Nobody had thought to transfer that property, thought Julie, and was pierced by the thought of this pale child's shivering courage, coming alone through the hostile streets.

'Who owns the house?' she asked.

'Grandfather, I think. We get the rents, I know. The caretaker said — it wouldn't be ours any more. That's what we live on. What are we going to do, Aunt Julia ...' She sobbed again, once, and the long hands twisted together; but the voice did not rise, maintaining its soft, tremulous tone.

'That at any rate you don't have to worry about. There's plenty of money. Franz arranged all that before he went, so they can't get at it.'

The girl bent her head, still trying to hide her tears. 'My mother is very frightened,' she said softly. 'One of the local boys pulled her hat off yesterday and her wig came off. At the fish-shop.' Julie shuddered but Ruth seemed quite calm again. 'Mother doesn't know where we shall get our food if the kosher shops are closed.' She lifted her eyes for a second to Julie's face. 'I don't know how I'm going to tell Grandfather that,' she said.

Julie looked at the dark hair. 'You — you don't wear a wig, do you, Ruth?' she said stupidly.

'Oh no,' said the girl, shocked. 'I am not married.' She stole another glance at Julie and quickly looked down again. 'Lots of women don't do it any more. We're very old-fashioned. Everyone says so.'

'It's a horrible custom,' said Julie with quite unnecessary violence. Then, 'I'm sorry, Ruth.'

'It's Grandfather,' said the girl simply. 'Nobody does it any more.' She giggled softly, the tears still standing in her eyes, and Julie was reminded of the nuns at school who giggled just like that at some tiny joke they thought of as worldly. 'He's making up for Uncle Franz all the time — you know?'

'Ruth — don't mind me being so direct, will you? Do you need money now?'

'Oh, no, thank you. We had this month's rents only last week. I only came because — Mother was so frightened yesterday. I thought Uncle Franz could come over, perhaps, and explain to her. She keeps crying, you see. I'm afraid Grandfather will notice — hear her.'

'Do you think you ought to move out of Vienna? What do you think?'

'He's ninety-three, you see,' said the girl.

'What did your mother say — when she sent you for Franz, I mean?'

There was a silence. 'Well – just to know what we should do; that was all.' Another silence, then in a burst. 'She didn't say anything. I came on my own. She doesn't speak, only cries all the time.'

'There's just you and your mother there – with your grandfather, I mean?'

'That's all. Aunt Hanna went to Cologne when she got married and Uncle Josef is in America.'

'I can't think anybody is going to bother you, you know, Ruth. I mean, an old scholar of ninety-three and two women. Surely nobody . . .'

'That's what I told Mother.' Ruth began to weep again, but after a moment succeeded in speaking again in a trembling voice, 'But she doesn't listen to me, of course. I thought Uncle Franz would know more what's happening; these new laws they have now, and all that.'

Silence again. Then, as if someone had made a comment, Julie said, 'Franz had to leave; he would have been arrested if he'd stayed another day. They have already cut the telephone line here.'

'Of course, being so well known, Uncle Franz,' Ruth agreed submissively. She ran an experimental finger over the carved armrest of her chair. 'I know it's a frightful nerve, Aunt Julie, to ask you. But – I suppose you couldn't come over and just have a word with Mother? I mean, that she shouldn't worry about the money and what the caretaker said and all that?'

'I don't know about the caretaker – I'm afraid that may be true,' said Julie dubiously. 'But certainly there's no need to worry about money. Franz's lawyers have tied all that up in some clever fashion.' Ruth's head was still bent and averted. 'But of course, I'll come with you. We'll get a taxi. Ah, here's Fina with coffee. Let's have a cup of coffee before we go, shall we?'

The girl turned her face to Julie now. The dark eyes were glistening and enlarged with tears of fear, gratitude and humiliation. Julie thought with grieved surprise, she would be quite pretty if she had a chance, poor little soul.

'Those *Kipferln* are all right,' said Fina aggressively, as she put down the coffee tray. 'Nothing in them but fresh butter and flour and sugar. And vanilla.'

67

'Thank you, Serafina,' said Julie in a tone to convey that Fina had gone too far this time. Fina sniffed and moved her right hand; but at the look in Julie's eye she decided not to cross herself there and then, and went out, shutting the door with deliberation.

'Fina is a superstitious peasant,' said Julie, who knew Fina hated to be reminded of Franz's family and their religion. 'But her *Kipferln* are delicious. Have some.'

Ruth accepted one of the little half-moons of pale shortbread and nibbled at it with fifteen-year-old pleasure at doing something forbidden.

'Mm, they are good,' she said, flushing slightly and lifted her upper lip in a timid smile which showed small even teeth.

The taxi took them down Kaerntnerstrasse and Rotenthurmstrasse where vague crowds drifted to and fro, quite different from the sub-urban clerks and their wives who normally went window-shopping on a Saturday afternoon. These were slum-dwellers from the ten-ements of Simmering and Ottakring, looking for trouble. Here and there the stocky, respectable figure of an industrial artisan pointed a contrast. Those lower-middle-class young men who were there were in the khaki uniforms and had left their girls at home; they carried within them their bellies full of undigested resentment, for they were the sons of thousands of small civil servants who had run a multilingual empire; the shopmen who served prosperously a heavy superstructure of Court, nobility and gentry; and their places in the world were gone. Their pallid faces and meagre physiques were compensated suddenly by a new, aggressive self-assertiveness which was meant to look like self-confidence; and in their twos and threes they held the middle of the pavements so that other people walked round them and gave them room.

On the other side of the canal bridge, in the Jewish quarter of the 2nd Bezirk they were both more numerous and more aggres-sive. On a corner of the Taborstrasse, outside a shabby beer-house, a whole crowd was being harangued by an SA officer from a wooden chair held steady under his weight by two underlings.

'I would like you to wait for me,' said Julie to the taxi driver. The man looked into his driving mirror and humped his shoulders.

'Don't know as I want to stick around here for long,' he said gruffly. He was looking at the crowd round the SA officer, Julie knew, but she did not turn her head.

'Please wait for me,' she said and opened her handbag. 'Will you?' She offered him a fifty-schilling note.

'How long will you be gone, then?' asked the man uncertainly. 'You don't want to be about here yourself, y'know, gnae' Frau. It isn't healthy.'

'Twenty minutes. Half an hour. Not more.'

The driver looked ahead up to the wide road.

'All right, then. I'll park around that corner. But I don't want my cab smashed up; if they start any rough stuff, I drive off. All right?'

'Very well,' said Julie. 'I won't be long.'

Ruth kept close to Julie, glancing quickly first to one side and then the other, while they were speaking. When Julie went towards the big house doors she followed closely, keeping her head bent. They were in an octagonal court, surrounded by a winding stair with pretty iron railings. At each floor an open runway ran round the octagon. Under the first curved flight of stairs the entrance to the back courtyard made an arch. In the middle of the court were grouped the tidy tall dust-bins with their hinged lids.

To the right, in front of the glass door of the lodge stood the caretaker with two other men. He was small, round, elderly, so typical of Viennese caretakers that one could hardly see him as a human being. Here, off the Taborstrasse he wore a collarless shirt and open waistcoat all day. There was a smell of goulasch cooking, as inevitable as the caretaker's appearance.

'Good day, Herr Lubasch,' murmured Ruth automatically, as they passed by to mount the stairs to the second floor. Julie hardly glanced at the group by the caretaker's door. Now, as she came under the dingy light from the high well, she saw that the two men with Lubasch wore the brown blouse and breeches, the black knee-boots, the armband with the hooked device. They lounged, shoulders against the door frame, big hands on the heavy buckles of their leather belts. They straightened themselves as the two women crossed the small courtyard, with a shove of the shoulder against the lintel to push themselves upright. Like their clothing, their manner was formalised, and their movements too had the stiffness of a prescribed procedure, almost a ritual in which they must move in concert, using certain postures of the head and arms, certain steps, a certain tone of voice. Now the taller of the two moved forward, swinging his wide shoulders a little in a swagger, setting down his heavy boots loudly on the stone floor of the yard so that the metal tips of heel and toe rang.

'Here *is* the pig of a Jewess,' he said quietly over his shoulder to the other men. His voice was measured, steady, as if he were making an effort to control himself; under the play-acting was an unsureness very clear to Julie's expert ear. He had the coarse tone of the street-corner yob and spoke a thick dialect of back alleys. Julie gave him a fleeting half-smile passing as if she had not heard his words, and slipped a hand through Ruth's bent arm, feeling the child's shudder of fear through every nerve. The young man reacted by hesitating. His step faltered. He was forcing himself on in his first public appearance in a role which had seemed so easy, so laudable in smoky meeting halls. The other man gave a whinnying laugh from behind him, which could have been admiration for the determination of his comrade, or contempt at his momentary hesitation, but which was taken by the younger man to be contempt. Jabbed by the fear of making a fool of himself, the young man took another clumsy step forward and grasped for Julie's arm, which slipped, as if by chance away from his hand, and the two women were past the foot of the curving stair and out of his reach.

'You missed the whores that time, Horst,' yelled the other man with another crow of laughter, and slapped his big hand against his thigh loudly. The coarse insult excited him, he felt a jerk of male violence in loins often too timid to buy a woman on a Saturday night who might laugh at his urgent efforts. He slid a hand into his pocket and felt, amazed, the assurance of manhood.

'Come on!' he screamed, 'let's get after them.'

Julie and Ruth were at the turn of the second flight of stairs as the iron-shod boots clanged on the first steps upward. The apartment door was opened a crack by trembling hands and slammed shut again as Horst's head topped the railings. As the two heavy bodies collided together, bumping into each other clumsily against the shut door, they could hear the grind of a key turning inside, the rattle of a shot bolt that was failure. They were shut out.

'Open the door!' yelled the second man wildly, pounding with his fists against the faded paint of the panel. 'Open up! Open up!'

The phrase became instantly in his mind a reference, not to the shut door, but to all soft darkness and enfolding warmth which he was going to dominate in liberated strength. From the floor above a woman leaned over the iron railing and screamed stridently in the very accents of his childhood's harshness and hard-handed ferocity.

'What are you up to there, you louts! Get out of here and leave us in peace!'

'Ulrich. Wait a bit,' said Horst, gasping with the run up the stairs and with excited fear. 'Our orders ... We weren't supposed to start ... '

Ulrich threw off the younger man's hands as if it were the restraint of that termagant he had never dared defy in his childhood.

'You going to let those kosher sows get away with that?' he yelled, thrusting his spittled mouth into the boy's face. 'You run off home to Dad; I'll take care of them, once and for all!'

'What yer gonner do?' stammered the caretaker behind them, trying to push himself forward between the straining bodies. He did not himself know whether he wanted to preserve order or to watch the fun. The woman from the floor above came down the stairs halfway and stood watching them, one worn hand up to her mouth and the other clutching a wooden spoon against her soiled apron where it still ran with the food she had been stirring. The smell of the food and the odour of a brown-coal fire came with her; anger, and the excitement of a row in the house showing in her plain, respectable face.

Inside the door of the flat Julie and Ruth leaned against the wall, trying to catch their breath.

'They've been there for more than an hour,' whispered Ruth's mother. She was not much older than Julie and looked sixty;

unhealthy fat and the finicking bustle of the housewife for whom nothing exists outside her home, making her even older than the dark, shapeless clothes and the shawl over her head. Fresh, unending tears welled up in the puffed eyes already washed colourless with weeping. Her shaking hands grasped frantically at her daughter's sleeve. But it was Julie she looked at and spoke to; Julie who was the outside world that would save her. 'What are they going to do?' she quavered.

The little hall they stood in was crammed with furniture. Above the cupboards there was hardly a centimetre of the wall not covered with small dark-framed pictures. She pulled Ruth and Julie with her, into the living-room where an improbable luxury of oriental carpets, damask wall hangings, heavy velvet curtains and carved rococo furniture made a riot of old-fashioned domesticity.

'Break the door down, by the sound of it,' said Julie half to herself, pulling herself together with the stringent irony that she at once saw to be no irony but the simple and horrible truth. The front door was in fact already shaking to the echoing thud of heavy boots.

'The telephone — where is it?'

The other woman pointed with an uncontrollably shaking hand to the far side of the crowded room where an open door led into that typically Viennese half-room, a narrow slip of space called a *Kabinet*. On a three-legged gilt table stood the telephone. No directory. Julie pulled out the pile of magazines and newspapers on the under-shelf of the table with such force that the unstable thing almost fell over. No directory. She looked quickly around. She had no idea in the world how to get the police. She dialled, without thinking what she did, the unlisted number of the producer's office at the theatre. Like a miracle, Hansi Ostrovsky's voice answered at the first shrill of the bell. It happened as things do happen at a moment of crisis; it simply was so and she felt neither surprise nor gratitude.

'Hansi,' she said, her voice not shaking. 'I'm in the Novaragasse. Get the police and come at once.'

'What number? What are you doing? Julie!'

'Seventy-seven. At once. At once, do you hear?'

At the splintering crash from outside Julie dropped the black telephone and ran back into the living-room. The instrument swung, clacking, against the frail leg of the table.

One panel of the front door was splintered. A further hail of booted blows knocked a jagged hole in the wood. Ruth and her mother stood together in the middle of the living-room, Ruth holding her mother with all her little strength from collapsing to the carpet.

At the other side of the hall the closed door opened. A figure of ghostly thin tallness, yellow bony face agape with outrage, stood in the doorway. Long hands with overgrown nails clutched each other with an atavistic knowledge of what was afoot not shared by the unbelieving anger of the ancient features. The prayer shawl shifted as the old man moved his head. A terrifying sight, he was like one risen from the grave, his thin greyish beard and side-curls shaking with the palsy of great age, his yellow nose cutting the face like a scimitar. He fixed his clouded eyes on the ragged gap in the door.

A coarse, reddish hand groped through the opening, upwards for the handle, the lock.

The key was in the lock.

With infinite care, gloating, cautious, the rough hand moved round the iron key and slowly grasped it. It ground the lock back, twice. Very slowly the bolt drew out of its socket and swung down on its chain with a thin clattering sound. Outside the door was an awed silence. Inside, even breathing seemed to be suspended in an eternal icy moment of helplessness. Slowly, as if indecisively, the door opened inwards.

The man called Ulrich took a long stride forward, but the door between himself and the old man hid that figure from him and he had his eyes fixed on the women. Horst crowded after his older friend. At the door of the living-room they stopped, startled by the contrast of the rich furnishings with the poorness of the outer appearance of the house. Ulrich stared round the room, narrowing his pale eyes; he went to the nearest wall and rubbed his hand over the damask-covered wall. It made a tiny rasping noise in the total stillness within the room.

'Silk!' he said hoarsely, and this seemed to impress him with some special significance. He nodded his head several times, pressing his lips together as if calculating the cost of such a wall covering.

'You see,' he turned to Horst almost with admiration. 'It's true they have everything. Hidden away as if they were as poor as church mice – and inside everything, like this.' His voice was measured, solemn. It was clear that all his Party teaching with its crazy inverted logic had been proved finally to be true. Here was the evidence under his hand. He turned his whole tall body slowly round, taking in everything. Finally he swung the broken door to see past it, and his eyes met the eyes of the old man standing silently there, swaying slightly with his age and the shock of this sudden apparition. Ulrich recoiled a step, crowding Horst back behind him.

'God, look at that!' His square face turned a greyish white as his starting eyes went over the unlikely figure in its pathetic dignity which to him was a living symbol of his own hatred. The old man stretched out his yellow hands towards the two intruders. His beard trembled; he muttered something unintelligible. Then, at the look in the eyes that stared into his, he began to pray aloud in a high, quavering voice, the beautiful rhythmic Hebrew prayers to which he had dedicated his life.

From grey, Ulrich's features flushed a congested red; a thick vein in the middle of his forehead came up and throbbed visibly. Horst put a trembling hand on his arm.

'Wait a bit, Ulrich,' he said in a strained, anxious voice.

There was a moment of silence. Suddenly Ruth's mother gave a trembling wail of broken nerves. Out of her senses with terror and desperation, she tore herself from Ruth's grip and flung her soft weight on the brown figure. Her whole body clung against Ulrich, trying helplessly to beat at him with soft, pudgy hands, to pull his hair, to scratch his engorged face. For an instant he felt the soft, yielding heaviness of her flesh, loosely chubby, female. A shot of power drove through his belly as he caught the fat arm trying to hit him and with one contemptuous shove of shoulder and knee threw her away from him as her nails made a slight ineffectual scratch on his cheek-bone. As she fell way from him, staggering backwards, he felt and saw the quivering swell of her big breasts under the loose black cloth of her dress stretched taut by wide-flung arms. For an instant Ulrich had the impression of the arms opened for him, the big nipples rigid with helpless submission to his conquering maleness.

'You wait a bit,' he said softly and the spittle appeared again on his stretched mouth. He took two steps towards the old man, dragging his eyes away from the woman, caught the prayer shawl and phylacteries together with one hand and tore them off. The ancient figure staggered and would have fallen but for the wall that supported him. The thin voice gave a gasping moan of anguish. Ulrich's hard hand had his beard and pulled the victim forward by it, a wavering step at every jerk of the fist. As the macabre pair, joined as if in some sinister dance, reached the apartment door the woman from the floor above screamed wildly.

'Police! Help! He's going to kill him!'

There was a babble of cries. Julie's voice rose like a silver trumpet in furious commands that nobody heeded. Ruth's endless screaming drowned her mother's moans. The caretaker rushed into the room, shouting hoarsely for quiet. Horst shoved past the caretaker, not knowing whether he meant to rescue the old man or, in his wild excitement, to help to torture him. He simply felt the uncontrollable anger and pleasure of a boy at the hunting of an animal that cannot defend itself. At the head of the winding stairs Ulrich turned round, still grasping the thin yellow-white beard, so that the old man was backing on to the downward stair. Stiffly jerking, the figure before him seemed to fold together as the knees collapsed. The old body was no more than a clutter of dry bones as it fell. Even before the bony head struck the stone step the heart had given up the struggle and Ulrich distinctly saw the liverish whites of the faded eyes turn upwards as the toothless mouth opened in a last cry.

The fall of the body must have made some sound but it seemed noiseless to the accompaniment of screams from behind Ulrich; the nerve-tearing cries filled the two men with an unbearable, straining excitement that was more than half a fear at all costs to be hidden. Horst felt sickness rise, saw as if a picture had formed before his reeling sight, the dusty half-closed curtain of the confessional box, himself as an urchin kneeling and the wobbly voice of the priest questioning him and complaining of rheumatism in the same breath. Clutching the iron railing he shook off the memory and turned his eyes wildly to Ulrich for guidance. Ulrich was turning towards him; for a moment the two men's eyes locked over the stretched bundle of sour clothing, full of the awe of death. The body had fallen grotesquely, uncannily defying the law of gravity by spreading itself down over the top steps, one foot touching Ulrich's boot with a carpet slipper and the bared head with its thin, disordered hairs tipped backwards so that the pointed beard stuck up in the air, and the open jaws made a black hole behind the beard, the elongated slits of the nostrils above it, the eyes invisible. Horst stared down, glared back at Ulrich, wildly searching for an explanation. Then he saw with a sensation of gratitude that the other foot had caught in the iron railings and was twisted over sideways. It was no dreadful miracle of revenge on Judah, then, but a simple and brutal accident. The old man had caught his foot weakly in the railing, and the long, twisted foot in its heavy woollen sock held his body from slipping backwards down the stairs. Horst leaned over the railing and saw the second slipper on the landing below. He just had time to see a shadowy figure peering from the door beneath, when the door shut quickly and locks could be heard closing. Though the terrible reality of the old man's death was still there, at least the world returned to its familiar moorings. Together they had discovered something crucial; a barrier, up to that moment absolute, was now seen never to have been there – death was not only possible but could be caused by their own personal actions. It was a mechanical event, and the constant repetition of beer-hall cries of 'Death to the Jews' was simply true. Before their onslaught the enemy dissolved into a dead old body. He was no longer there, he had escaped; the bewilderment of an excitement that no longer had any object ebbed into gratitude in Horst's mind that the death was an accident; Ulrich felt his rage increase and well up into a new and more frantic need to prove his sensation of power on some other object that should not so easily escape before it could give him best. Ulrich drew away from the top of the stairs, crouching a little, his light eyes still fixed on Horst. Into their isolation penetrated anew the cries of the women and the shouting of the caretaker. As if at a signal they both threw up their heads, and Ulrich, closely followed by Horst, turned from the stairhead and tore back into the apartment. Ulrich was not even aware of Julie and the woman from upstairs holding the wildly struggling Ruth between them, though he almost collided with the group. With the instinct of women to save the young they were dragging the distracted girl, her face streaming with tears, towards the upper stairs. Catching an unbelieving glimpse of the figure stretched out over the downward stair, Julie covered the eyes of the frantic girl with one hand and the two women together turned her away from the sight, into the rough embrace of the neighbour's hard arm.

'Get her upstairs,' gasped Julie. 'Lock her in. Can you?'

'Leave her to me,' said the older woman, and with a movement practised on many squirming children she gripped the straining thin body round the waist and practically carried Ruth up the stairs, her feet dragging on every step. She shouted at the half-conscious girl to behave herself, to do as she was told, as if in anger with an urchin in a tantrum.

At the narrow neck of the hall Julie paused, looking helplessly round for Ruth's mother. A feeling of total unreality gripped her. The two brownshirts strained outward, at the living-room window. It was wide open, both casements. One pane of glass, shattered, crunched dryly under their boots. The caretaker plucked at Ulrich's sleeve, trying to get at the window, to see out.

Ulrich wheeled away from the window. In his headlong passage across the crowded room he threw over a table and a large vase crashed to the floor, pouring water over his breeches, the mass of flowers breaking apart around his boots. He swung against Julie, knocking her out of his way. As she fell back against a book-shelf she caught the wide stare of his pale eyes which did not see her; they were fixed on something only he could see. She caught herself with a twisting effort, holding on to the carved edge of the shelf. The iron clatter of heavy boots rushed down the stairs. The other man gripped her arm as she reached the window, pulling her round to face him.

'I was trying to stop her,' he yelled. 'I was trying to hold her. She jumped!' His frantic eyes begged for belief. Julie pulled herself free of his clutching hands, reeling against the open window-frame which jabbed painfully between her shoulder blades.

'You murderer!' she screamed, and realised with horror that her voice was a hoarse whisper. She forced herself to look once, down from the window to the pavement below, and then covered her face with her hands. Her shaking knees folded beneath her so that she kneeled in the shattered glass covering the carpet. She found herself wondering stupidly what the broken glass was doing here.

Ulrich tore open the house door and rushed out into the street; the caretaker hobbling after him. A small group had already gathered round the figure lying on the pavement. They fell back before him as he pushed his way through. Her wide skirts were flung up over her shoulders, half hiding her face. From nose and mouth dark blood ran and from the back of the head over the pavement stones. The plump legs and arms were spread wide. He took in the woollen stockings rolled over garters above her fat knees. Her white petticoat had an edge of linen lace. The body was quivering and jerking with little snuffling moans. Ulrich felt the glorious uprush of strength in his whole body. He glared round at the gaping strangers and they drew away from him without his even having to command them; drew back before the power of his look. As he stood by the figure he heard from somewhere the words 'she isn't dead'. He lifted one heavy boot and kicked strongly at the fat body and a dark, grazing mark appeared at once on the white exposed flesh of her thigh. There was a muffled, confused noise behind him that he hardly heard. He shifted his stance and kicked again, feeling an irresistible force that sank into the weak softness at every kick, until an effortless, gushing thrilling pleasure possessed his whole body, and he staggered away, drunk with glory through the terrified people who cowered away from his masterful tread. He could hear their voices like distant music. The tall buildings seemed to reel and bow; the stone pavement swayed under his boots.

By the time the police got there Ulrich was gone.

They were carrying the dead old man down the stairs as Hans-Joachim Ostrovsky jumped out of his car with two officials from the Police President's office. They stopped in their tracks, staring in unbelief at the uniformed local men staggering under a burden not heavy but unwieldy. With haggard faces the three men pulled off their hats and watched the macabre procession as the body was lowered to a waiting stretcher and covered with a cloth. The crowd round the dead woman hid her from them and a second stretcher had already claimed her body before they came downstairs again surrounding Julie. At the door to the street she recalled something and turned to go back; the three men tried to persuade her into the waiting car. She looked at them contemptuously and said coldly, 'I have to know if the child is all right.'

One of the policemen turned back into the house and ran up the stairs. The other two men and Julie waited silently until he came back. Someone in the crowd had recognised Julia Homburg and a clamour of voices surrounded the little group, but she stood there enclosed in silence until the police officer made his report. Then she bent her head slightly and allowed Ostrovsky to take her arm and lead her to the car.

4

'*You* must admit, it's a monstrous situation,' said Ostrovksy. 'Have the police no control over these hooligans at all? Or aren't they trying?'

The younger of the two policemen moved indignantly at this aspersion, his stiff leather belt creaking, but his superior did not immediately answer.

'There is a certain amount of confusion ...' he said at last, not with embarrassment but in a considered tone, meaning something other than what he said.

'Confusion! There was a "certain amount of confusion" in 1934. But at least then it was armed men killing each other, and that's bad enough, all over the city. But throwing old men and women downstairs — out of windows — you call that confusion? It's barbarism. I thought only the Cossacks did such things. And when a well-known personality like Frau Homburg gets beaten up ... Don't you realise, man, she's a public figure?'

Hansi stopped, perceiving the discrepancy between the two events. Yet it was the insult to a member of the Burgtheater that angered him, and though he recognised the inhumanity of his choice of ground for anger this only made him angrier with a bewildered feeling that he — that nobody — ought to be put in such a situation.

The senior of the two officials got up from a brocaded chair too low for his strong, heavy person and crossed to the window nearest him. He looked out into the street, but it was only a gesture to cover his own unease. They sat in Julie's drawing-room, finished in the style of Maria Theresia at great cost with elegant uselessness. The room was not only a display of wealth, it was a claim to equality, an assertion of citizenship. The central chandelier that clinked slightly and musically at the police official's heavy tread was an announcement that to this family such things as Cossacks did could no longer happen. When he came back the policeman took another chair, a straight one, and leaned his elbow on a marble-topped table where there stood a little box inlaid with lapis lazuli which he moved carefully out of his way. He pulled his thick chin and throat with a jerk against his tight collar. Every time he moved he put a gloved hand to his hip holster, nervous that the ungainly thing might scratch something.

'I will certainly make a report – a protest- – on your behalf, about what happened to Frau Homburg,' he said. 'If you wish it.'

There was a silence. From the next room but one they could hear the deep rumble of the doctor's voice saying something to Fina who then left the bedroom, and could be heard crossing the hall with her stumping tread. Hansi bent his head to listen, and then turned himself in his chair to face the policeman.

'Are you suggesting that it would be better to do no such thing?' he asked, astounded.

There was no answer.

'And the two murders?' asked Ostrovsky. He stared round the room with a feeling he had had once in the mountains when his companion's foot slipped at a crucial moment of a difficult traverse.

The policeman opened his lips cautiously to reply. His colleague made a slight movement of one hand, twitching on the knee of his breeches and the older man looked across at him.

'You say Dr Wedeker has left?' he then said slowly.

'He left this morning for Prague and is not expected to return.'

'I see.' He looked again at his junior. 'Is there something you want to say, Herr Luther?'

'I was – ah – considering the survivor of this unhappy affair,' said the other man nervously. 'Supposing she wished to join her – uncle is it?'

'Some sort of uncle,' agreed Ostrovsky impatiently. 'I'm not sure of the exact relationship.'

'Herr Luther means,' interrupted the senior official, 'the girl can't stay long where she is. And to draw the attention of the State Police who are now in charge, to a large extent, of the city, to a Jewish relative of Wedeker's would be unwise. To say the least.'

'I see,' said Ostrovsky.

'I merely wanted to suggest ...' began the junior official, still more nervously ...

'All right,' said Ostrovsky roughly. 'I've grasped it. I don't need it in letters a foot high to be able to see it.'

'From Frau Homburg's point of view too, the best thing would be for us to report Dr Wedeker's departure without any fuss, from private sources of information.'

'If you can persuade Frau Homburg of that.'

'Frau Homburg need not know.'

Ostrovsky took out his handkerchief and wiped his forehead. He was listening all the time to the sounds from the next room but one.

'Unfortunately,' he said with heavy irony, 'Frau Homburg is not a complete idiot. Nor is she likely to forget the existence of this unhappy girl – or the other two.'

Luther intervened again, this time without permission from his superior.

'Then she will readily grasp the implications of what happened this afternoon,' he said quietly.

The conversation was interrupted by the entrance of the doctor. Hansi turned his head sharply as he heard the door open, and all three men stood up to greet the newcomer, who made no move to shake hands to introduce himself.

'She will be all right,' said the doctor to Ostrovsky. He was a rather fat man with a blunt, square face and an irritable manner. 'I've given her a draught to calm her. There's nothing wrong but a few bruises. And shock, of course.' He looked for the first time at the two policemen and closed his mouth firmly. Then he said, 'Of course, her nerves and health are excellent. If she feels like it, she can even play to-morrow. She seems worried about that. Well,

I'll be off now.' He nodded brusquely to the room in general and turned to go.

'Oh, I forgot. I wanted to ring up in the morning to find out how she is. But I gather from the cook that the telephone is out of order. So I'll look in before lunch.' He glanced at Ostrovsky. 'Don't worry, she'll be all right. Constitution of a horse.'

'It's good of you,' said Hansi in an oppressive voice. 'I'll see you out, Herr Doctor.'

Out in the hall, pulling on his gloves the doctor said coldly, 'I shan't make any record of this visit.'

'Thank you. I was just going to ...'

'They're friends of mine,' said the doctor angrily. 'Where's Wedeker?'

'In Prague,' said Hansi. Fina opened the front door.

Hansi went, and tapped on Julie's door; when she answered he went in. The curtains were half drawn and he stood for a moment until he could see the arrangement of the furniture, and then went and sat on a chair drawn up to the bed.

'How's the voice?' he asked softly.

'I think it's all right,' she said. 'It probably just failed for a moment. It was ...'

'Do you want to talk about it?' he said, half fearful and half curious.

'No,' she said, and a strong shudder went through her that he could feel through his knee touching the bed frame. 'It keeps going on, over and over again, like after an accident. You know?'

'Yes, I know. If only I'd known you were going.' He chided her gently.

'But you'd have stopped me,' she said reasonably. 'I did think of it. I mean I did think of what I was doing. But the child – it seemed so cowardly. And I never dreamed ... And then Franzl and I hadn't even thought of them. I felt badly about that. He'll be in Prague by now.' She shuddered again at the thought that Franz might have been there, and stretched out a hand to Hansi which he took with a restrained feeling of fear that he would find her altered by touching her hand. But her hand was her hand, and though the fingertips were cold and trembled her

83

grasp was strong as ever. Reassured, he said, 'I must go, and let you rest now.'

'No, just a moment, Hansi. I want to ... Are those policemen still there?'

'Yes, but ...'

'I wish I hadn't told you to bring them. I didn't realise they could do nothing. And now they will be making reports and fussing. And we don't want any fuss, or Ruth will be in trouble too.'

He was so relieved that he almost laughed aloud. She was his good level-headed Julie with her solid common-sense, still. How stupid of him to fear that she would not see things as they were; she always thought of everything in practical terms.

'I wanted to tell you that before this stuff the doctor gave me took effect. I'm so sleepy already.' Her speech was slower than usual. 'He said I must stay in bed to-morrow. But of course I shan't. And don't suggest changing the performance. I shall be all right.' He had to lean down to hear her now, her voice was slurred, getting smaller and slower. 'On Monday I can do something about Ruth; that woman will hide her until then.'

'You'll be horribly stiff to-morrow, you know. Are you sure?'

'The theatre will be half empty in any case,' she murmured.

She really thinks of everything, he thought, now a little chilled by her presence of mind. He leaned nearer and saw that her eyes were closed. He remembered her saying the night before that her business was to survive. Very gently he released her hand and it slid slackly over the cover.

In the Taborstrasse beer-house, in the dirty and neglected public room, with its unwashed board floor and thin, food-spotted table cloths, Ulrich sat alone in a corner drinking one glass of raw wine after another from thick glasses. His light eyes were clouded and beginning to redden, but still full of the recollection of glory, the discovery of the secret of happiness and power. Horst had cleared off, he thought contemptuously; probably gone home. Not tough enough for the real man's world of the SA. He, Ulrich, had proved himself now. To-morrow he would report to the Party office. For to-day perhaps, better keep away, just in case the police misunderstood their duty and tried to create trouble for him. He grinned to himself, thinking of an imaginary underfed and under-paid policeman asking timidly for him at Party Headquarters in the 10th District, while he sat here, not a hundred metres from the house in the Taborstrasse, quietly resting and enjoying his wine. To-morrow was time enough to report; and on Monday there would be work for him to do. No nonsense about the police by then. One of the men on the Party Housing List would have Ulrich to thank for that fine room with its silken hangings and rich furniture; he felt proud of that. A fine glow of generosity filled him; such a flat was not his style; he was glad for some com-rade to get it. He, Ulrich, would rather live a real man's life with other men together; hard and active in barracks where the minor problems of living were all taken care of by the Party. The SA was fine for a time; but from now on it would only be on the fringe of the real work. The Party was already recruiting for the SS, he knew. He saw himself with his rakish black cap at an angle, the proud death's-head badge, the tight black tunic and the revolver in its black holster. He shouted for another glass of wine. Life was going to be different from now on; now that he had discovered the secret. No foreman was ever going to fire him again. He grinned up at the slight elderly woman bringing his wine and banged his doubled fist on the table. Her dragged mouth twitched obse-quiously and she put the glass down quickly and moved back behind the zinc counter.

Upstairs in the now quiet house at 77, the woman from the third floor looked out of her door. There was nobody on the stairs. She went quickly to the public water-tap on the landing and drew a big white enamel jug full of water. She looked over the railing to the floors below, where every door was firmly closed, and she knew, double locked. Leaning right over she peered down at the door of the Rabbi's apartment – he had not been a rabbi but the neigh-bours had always called him that. The door was closed but a gaping hole showed in the panel, and even from that awkward angle she could see the slit of the lock edge strained away from its frame. She went inside again, her lips working together.

She thrust a handful of split wood into the ashy fire of the cooking stove and stirred them in the embers. When they crackled up she put the black kettle on with a little water. In the stone bowl she smashed cinnamon and cloves together with the heavy pestle and tipped them carefully into a tall glass. A spoonful of thick honey went after the spices. When the kettle boiled she poured the glass one-third full. Then she pulled out a dark green bottle from the rough cupboard and filled the glass to the top with harsh red wine. She held the obscure bottle to the light to see how much was left. Enough for the old man's supper glass. She took the glass and went into the only other room, which was filled with three beds. On the largest bed, covered by the feather quilt in its clean and shabby cover of checked cotton, Ruth lay still. Her head moved when she heard the older woman, who sat down on the next bed and leaned over her. She stroked the girl's tear-stained and quivering face with her big hand, hard and rough as a man's. The long fine hair was matted with tears in a disorderly tangle on the delicate neck. The woman pulled the hair gently out from behind Ruth's loosely lolling head and quickly and skilfully plaited it into a tidy pigtail. She looked into the girl's unseeing eyes and spoke softly, in her slurring dialect, as if she were talking to a sick child.

'Here, now; come on, then; you'll feel better if you sleep. Come on, now, drink it up, it's good for you. Just an hour or so sleep, it'll do you good. There's a good girl, now, come on.' She supported Ruth's head with one hand and offered her the steaming glass with the other. Docilely, the girl drank a mouthful of the unfamiliar potion. The honey and spices softened the coarse red wine. It was hot and comforting and after the strangeness of the first sip, pleasant. Ruth drank about a third of the glass; then the woman took a big sip herself and Ruth drank some more; and so they finished the big glass together. The woman sat there, quietly stroking the girl's thin face until the shadowy eyelids drooped and the last shaking sobs slackened into the deep breathing of shocked slumber. Then she covered the unmoving body with the thick quilt and creaked softly out of the room.

5

*I*n the streets the restless crowds drew to and fro, pulled by obscure and baleful forces. Everyone knew that Hitler was in Linz. Rumours crept like fire, with the rustling of whisper. Hitler was much exercised over the many tank breakdowns in the Wehrmacht columns; the stories of tanks breaking down was a slander spread by the Jews and the Socialists; Hitler had visited his mother's grave and wept there that his triumph could no longer honour her. Hitler was ransacking Linz and the surrounding suburbs for evidence of his boyhood failures, at school, among the neighbours of his parents, in the records office where his neglect to register for military service was disgracefully recorded. Hitler had sworn that Vienna should be, not only the capital of the Reich, but of all Europe. Hitler was ill, having collapsed with the joy of his return to his homeland. Hitler would be in Vienna that night – at the latest on Sunday morning.

On the massive buildings wide strips of bunting appeared with mind-stilling repetitions. 'We thank our Leader' and 'Home to the Reich' over and over again. A little man with a club foot and the typical sallow darkness of the Rhinelander sniggered angrily at the innocence of the Viennese Party organisers. Of course the Leader would not arrive on a Sunday. Where would the fickle crowds be, if left to decide for themselves? A working day was essential for the entry when freedom from work could be proclaimed at the right moment and shops and offices closed, their inmates massed in the streets under the watchful eyes of the Party and each other. Spontaneously, of course, with flags in their hands they would greet their Leader and kinsman. Sunday? Sunday belonged to Rome. The Party would deal with Rome in its own time.

The arrests began. There were various lists. Official lists of politicians, journalists, bankers, of whom some needed warnings and some, of whom no complaisance could be hoped, other methods. All the lists were secret for secrecy is a weapon of great power. The murmur of fear from those who do not quite know is louder in the end than a shriek of pain. But some lists were more secret than others and there was a list so secret that only three or four men knew whose names were on it, and only one man knew why they were there. Neither those who tracked the obscure creatures down nor those who collected and 'dealt' with them knew why they had their orders. There was a scribbler of scurrilities with an obsession about the characteristics of the blonde and dark races of mankind whom a gaunt youth had once visited with his coat collar turned up to hide the missing shirt, and borrowed money to eat. There was an ancient lavatory attendant whose name had taken months to discover; she had been a whore in a filthy cellar brothel before the First World War; rotten with the disease she had given for a few heller to that same gaunt youth, she died quite quickly and neither her executioners nor herself ever knew why. There was a meagre old workman who had lived most of his life wretchedly in doss-houses; in one of them, years before, he had beaten up a boy whose ranting absurdities interfered with him reading a newspaper picked up on a bench in the Prater.

On Sunday the weather was fine and cold and before noon crowds were gathered all over the inner city. The tension of uncertainty and impatience, increased by the lack of their normal midday meal, turned the crowds at some places and some times into a wild mob. There were repeated incidents between the brown-clad men and workmen in the streets; between the brown-clad men and middle-class citizens who were sometimes Jews and sometimes only looked Jewish or foreign. A thickset mechanic lay stretched on the pavement not two minutes' walk from the

Archbishop's Palace with his head kicked in after he had drawn a red flag from his pocket and insanely shouted for the workers of the world to unite. Sometimes the crowd drew away from the violence in its midst. Sometimes, inflamed by a mysterious passion mingled of impatience, fear of its own actions and the maddening helplessness of a chance victim, the crowd joined the brown-clad men and became a many-handed animal. A single gasp of fear could drive a hundred fists and boots towards a pallid face. Sometimes a look of contempt from one among them would quiet them, and they drew apart, ashamed and glad to be spared from the act they had seemed driven to commit only a second before.

Fräulein Bracher meant to go to a friend on Sunday afternoon; it was not until she saw the crowd running across the narrow street that it occurred to her it would be better to return to her crowded little flat where her mother groaned and sighed. The thought had no sooner entered her head when she saw, with a feeling of detached bewilderment, a man who turned the corner where the crowd had passed a moment before and came walking towards her. Though he walked briskly, he did not seem to be hurried. He was a rather short man wearing a pince-nez. Why is he coming away from the others, she thought vaguely; from round the corner she could hear a confused noise of voices. Suddenly, above the voices a loud, startled cry rang out and at once there was silence. The man was level with Fräulein Bracher now; he turned his head in the direction of the loud cry. His head came back towards Fräulein Bracher, who had stopped walking at the sound of the cry. He stopped too.

'They've got her, then,' he remarked conversationally. His face worked; he gave two little sniffs that reminded her of a school-teacher she had had as a child. He looked up, past her shoulder. Then he turned as if to go back the way he had come. Round the corner Fräulein Bracher saw a tall man coming, doing up the buckle of his heavy leather belt. She could not understand why his belt should have been undone. She looked over her shoulder and saw two more of the men in brown shirts coming down the street towards them.

'I suppose all these doors are locked,' said the man, and sniffed again. He went to the nearest house door and shook the iron handle, but his guess was right; it was locked.

The two men were near them, now. Fräulein Bracher moved back into the slight shelter formed by the arch of the house door to let them go by. The man who had adjusted his belt was near them now too and she saw that he had dark sweat patches under his arms on his shirt and this disgusted her. It was a cold day and he wore no coat; how could he be warm enough to sweat, she thought.

As the three men came within a metre or so of each other they all flung up their right arms in front of them and shouted with loud, vibrant voices.

'Heil Hitler!'

The man with the pince-nez looked quickly from the single man to his two comrades and then at Fräulein Bracher.

'Greet the Führer!' shouted the single man. Fräulein Bracher stared at him.

'What did you say?' she said stupidly. 'Oh, Heil Hitler!' She flung up her hand in a small gesture of helplessness.

'You there! Heil Hitler!' the single man said, sticking out his jaw at the short man. The man addressed drew himself up but he was still much shorter than any of the other three men.

He said quietly, and very clearly:

'To the devil with your Hitler.'

Then he glanced round as if someone else had said it and Fräulein Bracher saw his eyes full of fear.

She did not really see which of the men it was who boxed the small man's ear, but all three men seemed to move at once and she heard the dull slap the open hand made. It was a strong blow and the man with the pince-nez was felled by it. He fell sideways and as his head hit the edge of the kerbstone Fräulein Bracher distinctly heard its rather hollow bump.

One of the three men was just about to kick the prostrate body, when another of them put out his hand to stop him and bent down by the injured man's head. As he rose again, he said hurriedly: 'We'd better get out of here.'

They all looked at each other and then back at the crossing where a few minutes before the crowd had run and then had come that loud cry. Then they walked, all together and very quickly back up the street, away from the fallen man, Fräulein Bracher and the crowd round the corner.

When they had disappeared Fräulein Bracher ventured out of the doorway and stood by the fallen man who lay there quite quiet and still. She made a movement as if to bend down and touch his head, but changed her mind. Then she began to run, lumbering awkwardly with her heavy hips, towards the crossing. The crowd, which had seemed so many people not five minutes before was gone and there was nobody to be seen. Fräulein Bracher pressed her hands together; she began to hiccup frightened dry sobs without tears. Though she had lived in the district all her life she found she could not remember where the police station was. She walked a little way, then stopped. Then she turned and went as quickly as she could back to her home, by a different route.

To this Vienna, utterly changed as it seemed to him, Colton Barber returned late on Sunday evening. The city, in the twenty-four hours he had unwillingly been absent from his real work, had degenerated into slumminess, the people of the streets become a gang of staggering louts. The wide street before the station was littered with torn paper, in itself a strange sight in a place of such civic pride, such enjoyment of its own urban beauty. The whole-sale distribution of propaganda leaflets was accompanied by its aural equivalent and the station loudspeakers relayed martial-sounding music. From a large tavern across the way came the roar of a coarse song and two men with a woman, arms linked, reeled in the roadway in a drunken dance. A street lamp in front of the cab rank was smashed and there were unmistakable signs near Barber's feet as he signalled a taxi, of vomit, so that he could not put his bag down. There was unusually little traffic but many people about. The inside of the car stank and Barber had to fight the desire to tell the man to stop and let him out, for then he would be in the disorder of the streets again.

There was a crowd outside the Hotel Bristol when they drove

up and to Barber's tired eyes it looked threatening, watching the coming and going with avid looks and appearing to sway to and fro across the pavements and the inner roadway as if it were one shapeless creature and not a group of separate beings. Inside, the familiar porter was anxious, hasty; he muttered something about Barber's room reservation and the reporter guessed rightly that the hotel was overfull of Party members and the accommodation insufficient. He knew that the Führer's staff had taken over the Hotel Imperial just across the Ring altogether, but he knew too that American newspaper correspondents were not going to be evicted no matter who else had to go. He pushed his way impatiently through the crowd of uniforms to the lift and reached his own room with an almost desperate sensation of needing to be alone.

As he shut the inner door and closed out the sound of voices in the corridor, the telephone began its refined and luxurious buzzing. It was a while before Barber could identify his caller for he had expected it to be the cable office with a message from his newspaper. But it was a woman's voice hysterical and broken with tears. Finally he managed to interrupt her.

'Listen to me! Frau Hanau!' he cried, shouting down the stream of explanations. 'Listen – don't on any account try to come here. The streets are full of wandering thugs and this hotel is full of Party officials. And there is absolutely nothing I can do for you in any case. I most strongly advise you not to go to the police, either. Are you there? No, *not* go to the police, I said. No, don't argue, listen to me. Have you a passport – a valid one? That's excellent. Then wait until the banks open on Tuesday morning – they'll be closed to-morrow – and take everything you can lay your hands on in the way of money and papers and then leave at once. Yes, of course I am serious. Of course it's terrible, I know that. You asked me for advice and I'm giving you the only advice worth having. Leave, leave, leave. D'you hear? Where? Prague – Budapest – yes, Laibach, if you have a sister there. But leave as quickly and quietly as you can. I wouldn't even sleep in your own flat after to-night. Go to a hotel to-morrow, a small one out in the suburbs somewhere. Yes, I know you live in a suburb, I mean another place, where you are not known, you understand? No, I don't think anything will happen to-night. The Führer will be here in the morning and everyone is very busy. Your home? Oh, you mean the furniture – God, I don't know what you should do with it all! Lock it up and perhaps you can get a lawyer from Laibach and do something from there. No, I wouldn't advise you to wait and try to move the furniture out properly. I certainly would not. Hallo! Hallo! Frau Hanau! ...'

'She's cut off,' he said aloud to the humming telephone. 'Why on earth did she pick on me to call up? I hardly know her. I suppose I'm the only foreigner she knows.'

He sat down, still in his coat, and put his head in his hands. After a few minutes he got up and poured himself a long whisky. They had forgotten, in the confusion, to put the ice in his room and he disliked whisky without ice. He ought to be working but could not direct his thoughts. The paper would have to have its news tonight from the agencies and if he was rebuked by the deputy foreign editor, as he would be, he would say his train was delayed. The thought of the train drove Frau Hanau and her news out of his mind. It was not his return journey he thought of, but the one to Prague.

He caught the train in a mood of intense irritation that his foreign editor had chosen just this week-end to summon him, when he should have been observing events in Vienna or going the other way to Linz to watch the Germans thrust through Austria. Barber had suggested postponing the visit of his editor, who was a prominent member of a New York Zionist society and refused to enter either of the two European cities where at that time everything was happening. That his, Barber's, forecast of German haste to forestall the Austrian plebiscite had been correct had annoyed his editor a good deal; more than the proposal to put off the journey, for editors do not like to be proved wrong. And he was aware, too, of having given an impression of vagueness, of absence of mind, perhaps even of feeling he ought to be elsewhere. He tried to explain his manner by recounting the train journey but his editor did not want what he called personal anecdotes, he wanted political analysis. This misunderstanding would normally worry

Barber, who was a conscientious young man, and it worried him now when he thought about it. But the scene in the train, then and now, kept driving it out of his mind.

The train stopped at a small station and Barber, looking up from a newspaper, just failed to see the signboard as it slid past his window. It was evidently not yet the frontier but the thought of the frontier reminded him with a sharp shock that Wedeker was supposed to be on this train. Disturbed at having forgotten what last night he had known to be much more important than his own enforced trip, Barber took his overnight bag and his typewriter and went hastily to look for Wedeker before the train should reach the border. He did not have far to search for there was only one first-class coach on the half-empty train, and Wedeker was alone in its last compartment. He was reading and looked so normal that Barber for a moment accepted the normality of the situation as real. But Barber had lived for years in Berlin and been present when the Nuremberg Laws were promulgated. Like everyone else at that time, he did not take these crazy laws very seriously and viewed them as a legalised form of plunder of fortunes and jobs for Party members – a cheap way for the Party to pay off old stalwarts. It was Wedeker's political record that worried him, knowing as he did what happened to his fellows in Germany; his companion's religion, or former religion, was only an added misfortune.

However, the two men greeted each other with the reserve of some embarrassment; Wedeker appeared to find the whole affair rather exaggerated and unnecessary, and to feel, although of course he did not say so, that Barber and his remarks were partly responsible for his undignified position. Both of them knew this line well, Wedeker having made the same journey only a few days before. It was not very long before the train stopped again for the customs team to board it and ride with it over the frontier which was their practice. It was clear to Barber that Wedeker was now nervous, but not more than nervous; he seemed still not to have realised that something fundamental had changed in his relationship with the outside world. Barber began to feel a fool at being so much more afraid than the man who ought to be afraid. Yet he knew, and Wedeker did not.

So after a few minutes in which the only sounds on the stopped train were the slight hissing of steam from the engine and the distant slam of a compartment door, Barber got up and went out into the corridor. From the long window he saw two men standing together on the platform. They wore the – to him – familiar uniform of the political police, and one of them carried a sheaf of papers in his hand which were ruffled at one side by the breeze but at the other were weighted by the small photographs attached to them with staples; the other man carried a briefcase. There was nothing in the least dramatic about them. A few moments later, while Barber was still trying to make up his mind how serious the position was, he heard the approach of booted feet from the next corridor and a second later the first member of the border guard appeared, holding in his hands a couple of passports. He was followed by his colleague, who carried the usual stamp, but behind them both Barber could see a stout man in the different uniform still half obscured by the diagonal turn of the corridor where it passed between the carriages. A curious feeling went through the journalist, as if he had not known before that such a man was bound to be there. He prevented himself from making a hasty movement, and threw his burning cigarette through the top of the window which was slightly open, as if that were his purpose in standing there. Then he turned slowly, trying to move like a man bored by a familiar hold-up in his journey, and re-opened the door to his compartment where Wedeker sat. He closed the door behind him and said, very quietly:

'You must get out of the train instantly. Do not speak. Just go.'

Wedeker, who had been staring out of the window, his hands nervously holding the side curtain, turned his head. He looked astounded and was about to speak, but Barber made a movement so threatening that in one instant of time Wedeker understood what no words of warning could ever have convinced him of. Barber, just inside the door, could hear voices in the first compartment between themselves and the customs men, but only two or three travellers in them. The platform ran only on one side of the rail, and on the other, the side on which Wedeker sat, there was a slight embankment with a cindery surface sloping down into a field with leafless willow bushes and rank grass growing high. As the two men stared at each other the train began, very slowly, to roll on its way.

Wedeker still did not move. His well-proportioned narrow head was turned rigidly towards Barber, and the fineness of his features, the unconscious elegance of his clothes and his whole appearance made the predicament of both men absurd to Barber as well as sinister. He took one long step forward, grasped the heavy door handle and turned it, holding on to the luggage rack for support against its pull with his free hand, his long arm stretched to its full extent. He was jolted by the pull of the opened door and his expression was one of anger and fear. In front of his eyes Wedeker's face changed in the instant of his standing up, a change so terrible that Barber never forgot it, though the next instant he pulled the heavy door shut again on an empty compartment and never saw Wedeker again.

Two minutes later the customs official opened his compartment door and wished him good day, and Barber, grunting his answer to disguise his still-short breath, put down his newspaper and reached for the case on the seat opposite to pull out his passport.

They did not even ask where the passenger was whose black Homburg hat and leather suitcase were on the rack. Perhaps they thought those objects belonged to Barber.

His foreign editor kept him up half the night, talking. The whole time Barber was only half concentrating on their conversation, the rest of his mind debating without coming to any conclusion the question as to whether he had needlessly forced Wedeker out of the train. He knew, yes; but what he accepted in Germany as observation, as objective fact, was preposterous when connected with a man of Wedeker's professional and personal eminence. It so happened that no close acquaintance of Barber's had been molested in Germany itself. The revolution of street-corner louts was there under a firm surface control by the time he came into it; and it represented in Germany, in any case, the end rather than the overture to a long-drawn-out public brutality and rioting, a bewildering contrast with the improvisation of the

Austrian situation. Barber had the feeling, the painful feeling, of having perhaps made a fool of himself, of having dramatised the moment; he dreaded that Wedeker would reappear in his normal setting and demonstrate this.

Until Frau Hanau's terrified voice on the telephone proved him right, this detail had worried him almost as much as the question of what had happened to Wedeker after his departure from the train. Barber had been too much concerned with the control of the door to see more than that Wedeker had at once lost his footing and rolled down the embankment.

He thought now of telling Wedeker's wife what had happened, but knew that her telephone was cut off. He discovered too a strong reluctance to talk about it, and especially to Julia Homburg. His own feeling of anxiety and guilt, like that felt after a suicide, that if only a slightly greater effort had been made a life could have been saved, combined with a growing anger with all Wedeker's and Hanau's friends who had not taken their predicament seriously. It had been left to himself, a stranger, who ought not to have been saddled with such decisions, to do anything at all. His thoughts concentrated on this resentment against Wedeker's friends and wife and so irritated him that after a little while he pushed aside his almost untouched drink and reached for the telephone to call, late as it was, his colleagues and get himself back into his own world.

6

When Julia Homburg awoke on Sunday morning she did not at once think of her husband or of what had happened the day before. She wondered where she was. The apartment was silent. Julie slid out of bed and padded over to a window to draw back the curtains. As she moved she was aware of a deep interior unease and giddiness before being conscious of bruises and stiffness. She rang her bell and then saw from the little travelling clock in its heavy glass case that it was just before eight o'clock. Where was her coffee ...? Then she remembered it was Sunday and Fina would not be back from Mass until a few minutes past the hour. Ah, Franz was gone. The thought brought with it a soft rush of physical desire for him, and as she tried unsuccessfully to put the reality of his distant body out of her mind she thought for the first time – this is going to be worse than I thought. She lay down again and pressed her hands flat on the bed and thought with unbelief that he had only been gone for a day. Tears rose helplessly; she was unaccustomed to weeping and choked on the tears; her head swam dizzily, nausea rose and expelled the other feeling. She did not notice Fina's quiet closing of the apartment door or her entry into the room.

Fina opened the curtains of the second window and brought the coffee to Julie's bedside. She was just going to speak when she checked herself, leaning over the bed and staring down at Julie at first astonished and then obscurely angered and stirred.

'Gnae' Frau, your coffee's ready,' she said loudly.

'I don't want it,' gasped Julie. 'Go away.'

Fina went away and stood thinking slowly in the hall. Then she propped open the door and went across the landing to the opposite apartment and knocked with her knuckles. The servant opened and Fina was allowed in to telephone the doctor, very quietly so that the people of the house should not be disturbed on a Sunday morning.

When the doctor came she said, 'There's nothing wrong really, Herr Doctor. But you said to call if ...' She turned her round head away so that he looked at the knob of her plaited hair. She was not aware that what made her call the doctor was a desire to interfere with Julie's grief, but she was aware of feeling uncomfortable. He looked at her closely for a moment and shrugged invisibly.

'I'm all right,' said Julie crossly. 'Fina was silly to get you out like this.'

'I told her to,' he snapped. He dropped her wrist. 'It's the sedative I gave you makes you feel wretched. It has that effect on some patients – undermines the inhibitions, like alcohol.'

'Well, why did you give it to me, then?' Julie was recovering her spirits. 'Now I feel awful. Can I go to the theatre to-night?'

The doctor smiled slightly. 'Probably better not. If you'll give me the address of that young man from the theatre, I'll get in touch with him.'

'Hansi Ostrovsky? Oh, no, don't do that ...'

'He'll be relieved, I expect,' said the doctor brusquely. 'This town is no place for you – or any other respectable woman – to be about in, to-day. They are probably closing the theatres, anyway.'

She lay back. 'You've seen the papers? Was there anything about ...?'

'Not a word. There won't be either.'

'Fina will get you some coffee. I can't believe such a thing could be hidden. It's impossible. There was quite a big crowd, dozens of people.'

'I'll drink a cup of coffee if you will. Is that the bell, that cord? They won't need to hide it; it's not even unlawful. It's happening all over the city, one way or another. Not quite so violently, perhaps, but outrages of one kind or another.'

'There must be something. People will protest — riot. They must do. Nobody could stand such things, happening in front of their eyes like that.'

Fina knocked and came in. Julie gestured at the coffee pot and Fina laid a red hand on the side of the pot. It was almost cold. She picked it up.

'A cup for the doctor, too, please Fina.' As the door closed, 'Is there nothing we can do, then?'

The doctor got up and, as he did so, he rubbed at the heavy lines in his forehead.

'Nothing. Nothing at all. If enough public men protest it will stop happening in public, that is all. There is nothing we can do, except survive.'

'Thank God Franz is safe away from here. Kerenyi was right. I thought he was exaggerating — journalists do.'

'Nobody is going to have to exaggerate this. Whoever Kerenyi is, you should be grateful to him if he persuaded Doctor Wedeker to leave at once.'

There was a silence. Then Julie said suddenly, 'I can't leave now. There are professional reasons. But I can't stay for much longer with things like this . . .'

'If you are thinking that, please don't tell me about it. I have four sons and a daughter, two of them still at school. I can't afford to lose my practice.' The doctor's voice was so stern that Julie was startled out of her self-absorption for a moment.

'It quite shocked me,' she said to Kerenyi later that day as they sat in the long living-room in the dusk of an early evening on which helplessness and despair had settled, without emphasis, like a fine but perceptible dust. 'I was glad Franz and I have no children.'

Kerenyi moved uneasily and looked from Julie across at his long-familiar lover, grateful when she spoke and saved him the necessity.

'What is going to become of that girl, Julie? What did you say her name was?'

'Ruth? I don't know. I shall get a motor car and drive her down to my mother's house. You know, that was very odd, too. Hansi and the police arriving so quickly. And I discovered today from Hansi that one of them was the police chief for the 2nd District. Of course, one is always ready to believe how important one is, but it really was a little slick, don't you think so, Maris? I mean, almost as if they expected trouble?'

Maris Pantic turned her fine-boned dark face dominated by large, melancholy and anxious eyes, to look at Kerenyi and then again at Julie. She was thin and nervous, a talented but unlucky actress who lived too much in an inward world of overwrought emotions ever to be a great success in her profession. Up to now Kerenyi's position had ensured parts for her.

'You don't mean the whole outrage was planned, surely?' asked Kerenyi hastily.

'Oh, no. No, no. I mean, perhaps some kind of trouble was expected in general; if anyone should get involved who could cause trouble – the press or diplomats, you know the sort of thing I mean – then the police were ready to intervene. No more than that. Perhaps because of Franz they might keep a special eye on me. On his family too, perhaps.'

'Perhaps they thought Franz might have gone there?' said Maris.

Maris had an unlucky knack of saying the very thing, without in the least meaning to be malicious, indeed usually out of a too thin-skinned perception, that should not be said. Kerenyi frowned at her quickly, but it was too late, the words were out.

'You mean, those men could have been waiting for ...' Julie half rose, her eyes dilated. She gave an ugly little gasp, her lips opened for a cry that did not come. She half turned, gripping the arm of her chair with a strained hand; but Franz was not there to restore the reeling world to sanity. Julie sat back, the effort to command herself visible to Kerenyi and Maris, who sat silent. Between her brows a little line appeared and the planes of her face were suddenly sharpened, almost gaunt.

'Julie, I'm so sorry,' Maris was almost in tears, 'I thought you meant ...'

'It's all right. I don't know why it so frightened me – Franz never went there from one year's end to another. They couldn't possibly have expected him – or me – to be there.'

'I think it much more likely that when you called Hansi at his office he simply called the police. As you say, trouble was probably expected. And I rather fancy Schoenherr would already have made some sort of general claim for protection of all theatre members. He is certainly desperately worried about anything happening that could endanger the Burg. After all, there are a number of members or connections of the Burg who are not entirely Aryan – to use the new word.'

'Of course, that was how it was, Georgy.' Julie looked at him quickly and looked away again. 'And the telephone was put on again this morning. I didn't even notice it; Fina noticed that Hansi was able to ring me up. Since then it has been normal again.'

Kerenyi refilled the glasses of the two women from the thin green wine bottle, and then replenished his own glass.

'Schoenherr made some contacts last summer when they were in Berlin,' said Julie slowly. 'With the Reich Chamber of Culture, you know? I dare say Hansi did so, too ...'

'But you don't think Hansi is ... he couldn't be—' Maris, warned by one disaster, managed not to finish the sentence.

'No, I'm sure Hansi is all right,' interrupted Kerenyi. 'But just the same ... Julie, I mean nothing more than what I say, you understand. But you have to remember that Hansi Ostrovsky is obsessed with the theatre – even more than Schoenherr. I think I would just not mention to Hansi anything you mean to do about this girl, Ruth. I only mean ...'

'That he would put the theatre – me, as he would think – before her safety?'

There was another silence. They all three stared at their wine glasses without drinking.

'Secrecy,' began Julie suddenly. 'Do you think I could ask Pohaisky about Ruth? You know his son-in-law is his partner and he goes quite often to Prague. I wonder if they could arrange somehow for the child to get out to Franzl there?'

'Pohaisky is a good man,' said Kerenyi slowly, pointing his nose inquisitively at the corner of the ceiling as he considered the question. 'But he's such a pious chap. Do you think he'd want to take such risks over a little Jewish girl, Julie? I can see him hiding priests, perhaps, but ...'

'He was willing to take a frightful risk over Franz's ...' Julie stopped abruptly, a cold shock of fear made her hands clammy. They were both looking at her. My God, what am I saying, she thought, unbelievingly. Pohaisky's life, his whole family – he trusted me completely, and two days later I'm talking about it.

'This is impossible,' she said distractedly. 'It's a nightmare ...' She felt her brow wet with a cold damp under the edge of her hair and put up a shaking hand to push the hair away. 'That beastly stuff the doctor gave me to calm me ... it's made me quite ill. I can't think why doctors use these drugs when they know the effect they have.'

'A good thing all the theatres have been closed to-night,' said Maris, watching her anxiously. 'I suppose because of all these dreadful crowds wandering about. But it's a good thing for you, really ...'

'It isn't the mobs the Party is afraid of,' said Kerenyi grimly. 'They like the mobs. It's any protest against the mobs they are worried about. The mob does their work for them, and looks spontaneous, don't you see?'

'I suppose the police will have told them – the Gestapo, I mean. About Franzl being gone?' She had spoken of him several times quite easily but now, perhaps because of the word 'gone', she felt a stab of deep anguish, like a physical pain.

'Must you really go to Graz, Julie?' asked Maris, and Julie knew how much she was giving herself away.

She said sharply, 'I must get the girl away from here.' She forced a smile. 'It won't be more than four or five hours, then she's safe in the country.' Maris is trying to be kind and sensible, she thought. And she must be worried herself. What bad luck the Josefstadt company have just produced *Liebelei*. It must have cost a packet, and now they'll have to take it off. Probably Maris doesn't even know Schnitzler was ... As if he had been following her train of thought from another starting point, which he had, in fact, been doing, Kerenyi spoke slowly into the silence.

'I heard to-day that various efforts are being made to persuade

Professor Freud to go to England before his position here gets impossible.'

'Various efforts? How do you mean?'

'Friends from England and America. The British Ambassador is said to have written to him already.'

'Of course, they will let him go?' Maris stressed slightly the subject of the question in a fashion that made it sound as if she referred not to the eminence of the great doctor but to the certainty of 'their' understanding that their interests demanded reasonable behaviour in this case.

'I imagine so. Though they have good reason to hate and fear Freud quite apart from their crazy "race" theories. Nobody in the world could be more inimical to their ideas; more undermining to their influence. And he's supposed to have made some kind of an analysis of Hitler from his speeches. At least, the story is circulating that he has, and that it's so funny that anybody might hate him for such a joke.'

'That's a very Viennese story, Georgy,' said Julie. 'Mild. Apt. And inwardly destructive to the very person it seems to praise.'

Kerenyi laughed his sudden snort of laughter, lifting his big nose.

'Exactly. The two-fold attack on Freud's real greatness that their own second-rateness can't bear and never could. It reduces him to the level of a parlour game for Sunday afternoon coffee. And at the same time a sly attack on the hollow overbearingness of these dreadful newcomers.'

'Poor old man,' murmured Maris, not understanding them. 'How sad that he has to leave his home at his age.' She caught her breath and glanced sideways at Julie and then, beseechingly, at Kerenyi.

'He always hated Vienna,' said Kerenyi slowly. 'Calls it his life-long prison.'

'I wonder if everyone is as ambivalent about their homes as the Viennese?' asked Julie. 'He could have left here a hundred times, after all.'

'Oh, dear, speaking of leaving,' Maris looked self-consciously at her watch. 'I'm supposed to be going to Hella's for an hour.' She looked across at Julie. 'I wouldn't have said I'd go, but I didn't know we were coming to you.'

'Hella Schneider?' Georgy stared at Maris. 'She won't want me there, you know.'

'Oh, Georgy, don't say that. And she particularly asked me to bring Julie with us.'

'I think I won't go out, you know,' said Julie with an abstraction that did not alter the finality of her refusal.

'Oh, but Julie! She did so want you to come.'

'I can't pretend I was too ill to play to-night and then go out, can I?' said Julie reasonably. 'And if I go out to-night I shall have to turn up to-morrow at their reception at the Hofburg.'

'Have you noticed,' asked Georgy, putting out his cigarette, 'that we've already started saying "they" all the time? Well, Maris, if you really want to go to Hella's, I'll take you there.'

When they were outside, walking to the corner of the Ring, to get a cab, he said, 'Dearest, you are a silly child. Why did you say you didn't know we were going to Julie's and then immediately contradict yourself by saying Hella particularly wanted her to come?'

'But what do you mean, Georgy? I didn't say ...'

'Hella could not have asked you to bring Julie on with you if you hadn't said you were seeing her, now, could she?'

'Oh, Georgy, you're always so involved. But I'm sure Julie wouldn't notice, even if I did say it. Goodness, what an egotist Julie is!'

In the cab, aware that she had displeased him, she leaned against him in a special way, hugging his arm with both hers to pull him against her body. But when he said again, outside Hella's house door, that he would not be welcome there in his new disfavour, she did not insist. He went on to his own flat, cold and untidy because his daily cleaner had not been to work, it being Sunday. Everything to light the tall stove in his study had been left ready, and he stuffed the paper and the thin sticks into the dead ashes, and filled the stove with chunky logs until it roared like a sleepy animal. From a cupboard he took a full bottle of *barack*. Then he looked at a pile of galleys lying in the general chaos of his desk and put it away again. He worked for an hour or more, fast and angrily. Then he ordered the papers on his desk for the next day, and went and got the bottle of *barack* out again and sat down in a big leather chair with springs comfortably loose, drinking steadily and smoking one cigarette after another, throwing the ends into a pewter plate beside him on the table where the bottle stood. He did not think of Maris, nor of Julie, nor did he read. He drank himself into a mild stupor and then went to bed in the next room in the unmade bed which smelt of Maris's scent from the night before. Drink, however – even *barack* – is no substitute for work and he awoke about five in the morning and lay there staring into the dark of the stuffy room. This, he knew, was going to be the pattern of his life, with never enough to do. It was not bad enough yet for him to force himself to some other and unfamiliar work; neither had the long habit of a definite job that had to be done been broken; it was the beginning of a new life which he had not yet clearly envisaged.

Hella looked past Maris as she came in, not knowing whether relief at not seeing Kerenyi was greater than annoyance that Julie, too, had not come.

'I did so want Herr Lehmann to meet Julie,' she said. 'But you must come and be introduced, Maris. Come along.' The condescension shrank Maris's self-confidence to a thin twitter of resentful nerves, though she was quite aware that Hella's phrase meant she had promised the strange German to produce the beautiful Julia Homburg for him. Tall, he had a long head, fair hair and pointed features; he spoke too with pointed clearness and sharp Hamburg sibilants, expressing himself too clearly and in too clear a voice for the other guests, who neither needed nor wanted to make themselves quite clear. To be clear is to be boring, provincial, unaesthetic; besides it is more difficult to withdraw from a position openly expressed, and definition restricts the fluidity and complexity of everything that is neither real nor unreal but simply is.

'I don't think I saw you yesterday when I was at the Burgtheater?' He was eager to be liked and promised himself much from the pleasant duty of reforming the corrupted Viennese theatre into a healthy Germanism. Hella Schneider bored him already with her directness; she was too like the women he knew in Hamburg and Berlin, and what Hella thought of as her greatest asset was too simple for his taste; too simply German. He felt a distinct pleasure at the delicate, worried, Slav lines of Maris's face and figure; her wistful, cringing smile was subtly intriguing, reassuring.

'You would have to come to the Josefstadt to see me, I am afraid,' she said, and her slow voice, deep and a little trembling, delighted him with exactly the atmosphere he had expected in Vienna.

'Another reason to go there.' He bowed for the third time and laughed, 'Of course, unofficially – I know the Josefstadt is not part of my field of study. But please tell me about it. The company, what you are playing, I want to know everything, to compare everything. I am a terrible bureaucrat; you will find that out, I'm afraid, so I tell you openly to begin with.'

Three times Hella drew Lehmann away to meet new arrivals; and three times he returned as quickly as he could to Maris. Her unsureness was what his own self-distrust needed. Supremely conceited, secretly convinced both of his superiority and his inferiority, he was the Roman among the Greeks, who had protection to give, subsidies, the favours of government. These people, in the person of Maris Pantic, represented the tenacious weakness of oldness, acceptance of what is, the patina of a mysterious order that had survived barbarians before and would survive them again, laughing quietly at them and at itself. Half ignorant and half self-deceiving Lehmann expanded suddenly into the happiness he had promised himself from Vienna, and had never believed he would get; happy, he became the kind, good and decent soul he knew himself to be. Maris, startled by her unexpected success, was ravished by gratitude that somebody of importance should find her so unmistakably wonderful. They were both unaware of the essential falseness of their comfort and pleasure.

The parents of Maris Pantic had come to the Imperial city in the train of a Croatian nobleman twenty-five years before when the multinational state was just tottering to its inevitable crash; she herself had gone back to a village of almost medieval backwardness and squalor during the starvation time of her childhood. It was just because she was an outsider that she had consciously absorbed, imitated and now reflected the manners and attitudes of her home; as a converted Catholic is better able to express his belief articulately than a believer of many generations for whom all is wordlessly taken for granted.

Presently Hansi Ostrovsky arrived with a whole group of actors and actresses, all of whom should have been acting that evening but for the closing of the theatres. The unexpected evening-off, with its taste of holiday, added to the intense expectation and tension brought in from the city streets by every new arrival. Willy Mundel, the elderly actor who was to play the Doctor in *Doll's House* with Julie came over at once to Maris.

'You saw Julie to-day, Maris? How is she?'

'Not well,' said Maris. 'The doctor gave her some draught to quiet her nerves yesterday, and it made her quite ill. At least, that was what she said, but I suppose really, it was ...'

'Poor Julie. She must be feeling like hell. But Franz got away to Prague?'

'Franz? Oh, yes, he went on Saturday morning. But that wasn't why the doctor had to give Julie ...' Maris stopped and looked at Lehmann, aware of danger.

Walter Harich, a well-known heroic actor, had come in with Hansi and now came over to them, glancing with curiosity at Lehmann, whom he had not met and whose identity he showed no interest in. He was a very tall, big man of striking presence and great physical beauty, who worried much about his waistline.

'What do you mean, Maris?' he asked. 'Julie was in perfect health two days ago.' He put a boom into his magnificent voice and turned his profile towards the stranger, lifting his chin.

'Oh, stop playing Egmont, Wally,' said Hella irritably, aware that the threads of her party were sliding out of her own hands.

'But what *do* you mean?' Mundel touched Maris's thin wrist. 'Is Julie really ill, then?'

'But don't you know?' Maris was plaintive, trapped in unwelcome notice. 'About Saturday afternoon?' Behind Lehmann a small, dark man, one of the administrative staff of the Burgtheater, leaned against the tall back of a chair.

'I know nothing about Saturday afternoon. What happened?'

'What has our Julie been getting up to?' demanded Harich, and then frowned down at the theatre accountant, aware that in the presence of strangers the tone of flippancy which they normally used about each other was out of place. Mundel, who had the advantage of knowing who Lehmann was, would have given a good deal never to have started the conversation. He was acutely aware of the accountant's eyes on the back of his neck, and of what they had all noticed, that this accountant who had only come to the Burg six months before, was constantly with Lehmann on his visits about the city. In the back of Mundel's mind was the four months' sick leave he had taken in the past fifteen months. Not all together; but seeing the contained face of the accountant he was uneasily certain that the odd days and weeks had all been carefully added together. He recalled with horrible clarity the occasion he called off a performance as Polonius at two hours' notice just before Christmas; and the edge to Schoenherr's cosy voice when he suggested 'a different kind of doctor'. Like many drunks, he did not drink much among colleagues and friends, indeed much at all except when the fit was on him; so he was able to persuade himself during his periods of normality that the people he worked with and saw every day 'did not know'.

'It was natural enough,' Maris was saying reluctantly. 'It was Franz's family, after all. She went to try and help them and there was some sort of a dreadful scene.'

'You mean a brawl with those ...' Harich caught himself up.

'Oh, worse. There was an old grandfather and a middle-aged woman — some sort of an aunt, I think. They were both killed.'

'Killed?' cried a woman's voice sharply. 'Maris, you're exaggerating!'

'Oh, no. Julie saw it all. One of them was thrown down the stairs and the other — the aunt, I think — jumped out of the window.'

'Revolting.'

'Monstrous.'

'I don't believe it.'

Hansi Ostrovsky glanced at Hella. She was staring at Maris, shocked out of social manners.

'I simply don't believe such things happen in a civilised city,' said Hella breathlessly. 'You must have misunderstood, Maris ...' She turned to Lehmann for confirmation. He twitched at his hand-kerchief pocket and then smoothed the sides of his perfectly neat hair. Before he could answer Hella, a short fat woman with fashionably tortured hair dyed black and a face that was an inextricable mass of wrinkles, came into the room and signalled to her daughter. Hella made a gesture of rejection, and then changed her mind. In the spreading silence of the room she crossed to her mother, who caught her arm and whispered.

'Hanau!' they heard Hella say clearly. 'It can't be true! I was talking to him only two days ago!'

'What about Hanau?' called Harich. Hella turned a stunned face to the group. 'He's dead,' she stammered and burst into tears. Hansi Ostrovsky jumped to his feet and hurried to her. He put one arm round her shoulders and drew her out of the room.

Lehmann rose alertly to his feet and raised one hand.

'Let us not lose our sense of proportion,' he began and then, firmly, 'one or two disgraceful outrages have occurred. The lower elements in a community get out of hand at moments like these. The atmosphere of historical change affects them like a thunderstorm – great events which inspire cultured persons bring out also the lowest passions of the mob. There is always the danger at moments of fate that the mob will attempt to take over. We learn that from the lessons of the French Revolution. But the Führer is aware of the danger; the Party will maintain control of the situation here as it did in 1933. That was a perfectly bloodless revolution; there was no violence in Germany then!' His voice had run away with him and he became breathless and paused for a moment to restrain himself. 'Naturally, here in Vienna where foreign elements have been able to infiltrate into the German nation, there is a danger of isolated acts of violence and revenge against personal enemies as well as against the enemies of Germany. But

Germans do not behave like barbarians; these rowdies will very quickly be brought under control. Believe me.' He looked round the circle of watching faces and his voice rose a tone. 'The Jews are strangling the life of the German people; but they will be treated with a dignity that is worthy of Germany if not of themselves. They will be enabled to lead their own lives in their own way; but in a way that prevents them poisoning Germany.'

Hella and Hansi had come back into the room and rejoined the circle.

Lehmann's voice took on a pleading note. 'These things are no concern of ours, except where we must grieve for personal friends. There are bullies and hooligans everywhere – such things happen at every country fair when the crowd gets drunk and excited. But order will be – has already been – restored.'

A kind of ripple went through his hearers; he had them now, Lehmann knew. He had struck just the right note, detached outrage from themselves, enabled everyone there to feel that such things were in a different world from their own familiar city. He caught Maris's frightened eyes and smiled reassuringly into them. She gulped and smiled waveringly back at him and a little thrill of pride and tenderness touched his heart. He turned his tall body and made a cupping gesture with his hands, inviting them all to return to their own affairs. Then he sat down again and leaned forward to speak to Maris in an undertone.

There was a moment of bewilderment, silence, knowledge of the trick they were allowing to be played. Then a rising stream of talk began to wash reality away as they returned with guilty gratitude to their private world. They did not want to believe that violence and death were among them; and if they had to know of it, they wanted it to be taken care of reassuringly, out of sight; horror belongs, if at all, somewhere else.

'They are different, after all.'

' ... to be among their own people. They are exclusive – always were, you know.'

Maris was trembling a little and Lehmann could feel it. 'Julie had no idea, I'm sure,' she said in her deep, wavering voice. 'I shouldn't have talked about it. After all, Franz ... '

'She married him years ago. Long before anything ...' Mundel intervened but neither of the two was listening.

'Don't upset yourself,' murmured Lehmann tenderly, gazing down into her raised face, made shadowy by a pallor from which the big eyes stared with mysterious pain. His large well-cared-for hand hovered for a moment over hers which lay inertly on the table. 'We are living through a moment of transition, but for us, to whom the theatre is everything, all this does not exist. Others take care of hard necessities for us; we are privileged to be the bearers of culture.'

Maris had the distinct impression of his hand as if she could feel it; it would be warm, dry, firm-fleshed but cushioned over the bones. There was an uncertainty in his grey eyes deeper than the unsureness of how to manage this personal moment; he knew as well as she did that what he talked was nonsense; nonsense they were both required to believe. She felt too that his choice of the word transition meant something other than its meaning in this context; it was meant for her, personally. She gazed up into Lehmann's regular, pleasant face, trying to guess what it was he wanted from her and failing so completely that her eyes filled with helpless tears of frustration that she should let this unlooked-for good fortune slip out of stupidity. Lehmann felt himself deeply moved by the tears in her eyes; his large hand now actually touched hers for a second, clasping it gently and feeling the delicate little bones, so thin and nervous, with a protective joy. Then he sat back in his chair smiling an inward smile.

'I know just what you are feeling,' he murmured. 'But you need not fear for your friend. You have not done her any harm by what you said. On the contrary, you have explained very well what her position is. You see, it is well known, this fascination – this "hate–love" – between German blood and Jewish blood. Everywhere there are sound patriots who say that their own Jewish friends are different. I do not, nobody else does, hold it against Frau Homburg that she tried to help her husband's family. On the contrary, her loyalty is a noble and a valuable emotion. Only in the past it has been misdirected by the cunning of the Jews. All that will change now that healthier winds blow through Vienna.'

Hearing his absurd words with half her attention, Maris listened to the voice speaking the words. It was quite different when he spoke these phrases from its slight hesitancy in personal talk. He spoke then with the assurance given by belonging to a large and powerful community; he pattered off his phrases as phrases of hell and damnation are pattered by Christians, believing they believe but not feeling any actuality. The phrases were the creed required of believers and were no more actual than a lake of fire and brimstone.

Willy Mundel moved away from them, answering a call from a group of fellow actors on the other side of the room who had already picked up cards and were preparing to play poker. Now the theatre accountant moved too, making a nervous movement of the head to Maris as he went which she did not even see.

One of the men shuffled the cards expertly and dealt very fast; it was clear they had often played together. Mundel pulled a fistful of small money out of his pocket and began to arrange it with care into little piles of coins of the same denomination in front of him.

'Willy and his luck ritual,' said someone.

'At least Willy never talks politics,' said the dealer meaningly. They began to play, seriously, not speaking except as the game required.

Ostrovsky sat with Hella near the stove in another circle of actors. Nobody took any notice of Frau Schneider. The layer of make-up over her mass of wrinkles, once a face like her daughter's, made her visage even more expressionless than it was by nature; she too had been an actress. She said nothing and worked ceaselessly at a square of dark embroidery, never lifting her eyes from it except to look about the room quickly to see that everyone had something in his glass or cup.

The theatre accountant wavered a little beside the card-players. When one of them looked up without saying anything, he went away. He sat down finally beside Frau Schneider.

Dealing a new hand, one of the card-players said under his breath, 'Can't think why Hella asked that man. She never has before.'

'He follows people about like a dog,' said Willy Mundel in the same tone, picking up his cards and squinting at them mistrustfully round a thread of cigarette smoke.

'Dog is just the word,' said Harich. 'He listens to everything, trotting about, wagging his tail and pretending to be friendly.'

'He's not a bad chap, though,' said Willy nervously. 'I'm getting horrible cards to-night.'

'Ha! When Willy says that, he is going to win. Concentration is needed.'

They settled down again to play.

Frau Schneider laid down her work and came over to their table. She seemed to know by instinct which was probably long knowledge of their habits, when their glasses would need filling, and she filled them without speaking. They nodded and smiled their thanks and went on playing.

'But Hansi,' said Hella smiling protestingly, 'it isn't that I don't like Julie. I do, you know I do. I only meant that she would find it very hard to live without Franz. After all, there's no secret about the fact that she was having a lot of affairs before she married.'

'Franz made her happy,' said someone else, 'but I don't see how a woman of her energy is going to live alone for long.'

'That's true,' agreed Hansi Ostrovsky. 'But,' he added stubbornly, 'not the way you mean it. Julie adores Franzl.'

'Of course, of course. But I see what Hella means. Julie has a strong, even violent nature, which has been tamed by happiness. Take away happiness and what is to become of the violence?'

'Sometimes I think Hansi is in love with Julie,' said Hella pretending to tease with a beguiling sideways smile. 'She is the only person he ever speaks sentimentally about.'

'I'm not in love with Julie and never have been. I admire her talent but as you say, there is something a bit violent in her nature that is intimidating.' Hansi looked down at his ugly hands and suddenly remembered Julie taking hold of one of them in the theatre when he spoke to her first about Franz having to go away. He flexed his fingers and made a knuckle crack, causing Hella to frown. 'Besides, there's something unfeminine about her practicality.'

Hella laughed aloud, throwing back her pretty chin and showing even, strong, small teeth. She was angered by her decisive loss of Lehmann's interest and at having lost control of her nerves at the shock of the news about Hanau. The consciousness that Hansi was pleased that Lehmann paid her no attention because he would be able to continue their loose and convenient relationship irritated her and at the same time sharply increased her sexual interest in him.

'Julie and Franz never had any real relationship together,' she said thoughtfully. 'Except physical love, I mean. Speaking as the survivor of two shipwrecks, I consider myself an expert on professional marriages. What ruins them is the impossibility of having a domestic relation with someone who is bound to be a rival in the theatre, and involved in the same complications there. The reason Julie's marriage was happy was simply that she had nothing in common with Franz except sleeping together. Neither of them have any money troubles – he's rich and she's taken care of by the Burg. And their professional lives were miles apart.'

'That's true. I doubt if she even knows what the name of his party means – meant, I should say.'

'You think the marriage will just quietly fade out, then?' asked a woman who had not yet spoken.

'If this goes on . . . ' Hella stopped herself. 'I mean, in time, yes.'

'One gathers from Germany' – the man who doubted if Julie could live alone helped himself to a cigarette from the box on the table in front of Frau Schneider – 'that a semi-official suggestion is made about divorces. Is that right, Hansi?'

'I think it's made openly, officially,' Hansi clipped his lips together.

'Good God!'

'Hella, my dear,' said Frau Schneider in a harsh, croaking whisper of a voice. 'I wouldn't . . . '

Everyone looked at her. There was silence. Then they all began to talk at once as if at a prompter's cue, about the cancellation of the premiere of Hella's film, set originally for that evening.

The accountant leaned over the low table between himself and

Hella's mother. 'I'm sorry to hear you have such a bad cold, gnae' Frau,' he said confidentially.

Frau Schneider looked at him; she had not met him before. Under the wrinkled lids her eyes were coldly impassive. 'I haven't got a cold,' she croaked. 'My voice is always like this.' Then she returned to her embroidery, leaving him in a transport of embarrassment to fidget with clothing, spectacles, the box of matches on the table.

Julie herself was alone all evening for the first time since her schooldays. Not that she had ever been alone at the convent; no one was ever alone there. But at home, before her father died, she was isolated and much alone; curiously, after her father died and her mother married again she had not felt alone. Loneliness was connected with the detachment of her father's nature and with her own room in the big apartment. She was required to come in to be formally inspected by the guests at chill receptions, being dressed and having her hair done for a ten-minute appearance after which she returned to her room again. The guests discussed endlessly the disaster of the War, shifting obliquely with expressions of loyalty over the unspoken questions of the monarchy and never mentioning the shortages of food for that would have reflected on the hospitality of their host who allowed them to pass the evening in near-hunger out of a stiff-necked pride in his own uprightness. Julie thought of poverty as having begun at her father's death but it was in fact a result of the War for almost everything he owned was invested in war loans and industrial shares which disappeared overnight as the huge shrivelled fruit of the State fell to dust leaving only the tiny kernel. Between the days in November when the Dual Monarchy and the Army dissolved and the day in April when he died after months of helpless, weeping idleness spent wandering up and down the cold apartment, there was little memory. Had she been at the convent? She supposed not — like every other institution it was suspended. She remembered her father weeping; her mother had not wept. She remembered her mother coming with food after unexplained absences. But there was no series of events, no time span. The only incident she could remember – the weeping was a condition of life, not an event – was a conversation between her mother and her father's friend. He used new words and said her father had always been hopelessly neurotic; as she came in her mother spoke hastily of the epidemic of 'influenza' which was carrying off many hundreds of victims in the starving city. The next afternoon – was it? – her father was in bed, still weeping.

Later she and her mother were at the house in the wooded hills near Graz that belonged, so luckily, to her new stepfather, and after that there was no more hunger. Even when she was back at the convent food had been delivered to her; she was forbidden to share the food parcels and the nuns kept the contents, doling out portions of butter and preserved meats. The girls who had food sent to them felt guilty and were sure the nuns kept at least half of their parcels. This was quite untrue. The nuns were starving, but the adolescents needed some outlet for their own feeling of being disliked by the majority of the girls, who were also starving. But Julie remembered the hunger; no human being ever forgets being hungry.

Her mind went back to the weeping man in the cold elegant rooms. She remembered another event now. It was after the turn of the year and grippingly cold; but she opened the tall windows and her father, coming in, joined her staring down in the bitter wind into the grey street. There was a scattered group of men and women running below them, disorganised, ragged, dissolving into single figures and then grouping together again, foreshortened to their sight, as something happened at the end of the street out of their view. Then the crowd was backing off down the street again. Its fringes frayed off single figures. The centre was a struggling knot full of hoarse yells, waved fists. There was a crisp, high shout of warning from a voice practised in authority, and a clatter of hooves, metallic on the cobbles. From the unseen horseman came a single shot and after a confused moment another crisp shout, then a volley of rifle-fire, shattering her hearing in the narrow high-housed street and echoing away, across and across. One figure, a woman in long full skirts of dark cloth, keeled slowly over, very slowly, her shawl falling first and the figure twisting down to lie bundled across the shawl. The crowd was gone, the clatter of hooves gone; the aproned figure was alone. Hours later they discovered that the woman, who had seemed so anonymous, was their cook.

Until the previous afternoon that was the nearest she had ever been to actual violence. There was much civil violence in the city in the years between, and even minor military operations in 1934, but Julie was never involved. Then and yesterday, she was an onlooker, drawn in as audience to a chaotic drama that had as yet neither plot nor meaning. In the weariness of her emotions, not having eaten much since Franz left and drinking without noticing it more wine and strong coffee than she would normally have consumed in a week, she imagined a connection between witnessing, unwillingly, what had happened yesterday and her own work; that of one delegated by the community to interpret the essence of life and humanity through the works of great artists. Not self-appointed as the lonely artists of more westerly cities are, but appointed by the community. She was not in the least aware of this feeling as a 'literary' notion – it seemed quite natural to one of her profession and upbringing.

Bewildered by the feeling of being left alone and by the strange thought that she had some duty – not to act, though she was aware that she must act, and quickly, to get Ruth Wedliceny out of Vienna – but in some way to witness, to record if only in her own mind, the previous day's crimes, Julie wandered through the interconnecting rooms and back again to her chair. She sat down and picked up a book. Then, at once, she had to walk again through the rooms and back again. As she stood by her chair, not quite knowing what she meant to do, the thought transfixed her that she was behaving like her father so long ago; except that she did not weep. It was not her nature to examine herself nor did her career allow much time for introspection; but she was suddenly aware that proof of her real moral substance had never been made – she had gone with Ruth yesterday without thinking further than that Hansi or Director Schoenherr would have stopped her. For the first time she asked herself, *as if it were possible that she too might be threatened*, what she would do, how she would behave, if she were afraid. Nothing had ever happened to her that would show whether she had this mysterious quality, courage, which she thought of as some static part of character that would remain constant.

The clock struck a thin wiry chime; she did not notice how many times, and looked at the gold-ornamented clock-face on the desk to see the time. But whatever it was, it did not go into her mind and she had no more idea how late or early it was after looking than she had had before. After the small whirr that accompanied the striking died away Julie became aware of the silent house, and felt the night draw out, going on for a very long but unspecified time that might be for ever, or might be the instants of drowsing and awakening that was all she had known of sleeping in the years of her marriage. She thought, then, of the little pills given her by Willy Mundel and went out to the hall cupboard where she found them in the pocket of her beaver coat. 'Sleep a bit of your life away.' Willy must have known she would not sleep to-night ... how had he known? What desert did Mundel live in that he could see the reflection of emptiness in her face ...? I must remember to thank him, she thought, knowing she would forget it again, and took one of the pills with the last of the wine.

Long before she awoke she was dreaming, knowing she was asleep, that all the lights were on in her room and she could hear a voice saying – 'she's hard to wake.'

Another voice:

'She must have taken something.'

'She never takes anything.' That was Fina, her voice furred with sleep and the unsteadiness of being suddenly awakened, overlaid by bewilderment and indignation.

'Well, she did to-night, all right.'

Fina's angry and frightened voice, 'But you can't ... don't you know who she is?'

'What do you mean, who she is?'

'Ach, take no notice of her. Don't you know by now, servants always talk like that of their masters ... Increases their self-importance.'

The sensation of struggling to wake and not being able to; that too in the dreaming. A hard, strong grip on her shoulder, shaking firmly, without brutality. Then a rush of chill as the silken down cover was ripped off the bed and an exclamation of outrage from Fina.

'Secret State Police! Wake up! No use pretending!'

The long figure leaning over the bed was enormously drawn up, slanted upwards, over her, touching the ceiling almost, and the peaked official cap ballooned hugely and disappeared as he stood upright again, and tough greenish cloth filled her microscopic view. Brilliant light flooded in as the shadowing figure withdrew and she opened her eyes. It was a man in uniform leaning over the bed, the now cold bed. As the uniform took a step back the folds of its breeches were replaced by polished boots. Julie put up shivering hands, crossing them over her breast and holding on to her own shoulders. She did not see Fina handing her her velvet dressing-gown, but took it automatically, struggling into the wide sleeves and pulling it around her she wrapped the slippery silk folds over her legs and feet.

Julie put up a hand to a head that began suddenly to ache and an enormous yawn cracked her jaw and brought tears into her eyes. She was awake enough to speak now.

'What on earth . . . ?'

'Secret State Police.'

The other man, who spoke, was not in uniform. He was much smaller than the uniformed one, now seen to be very tall, though not almost touching the ceiling.

'Turn the top light out, Fina.'

'Leave the light alone.' No expression in the voice, not even authority. Julie stared at the man blankly.

'All right,' she said at last, 'leave the light alone.'

Becoming aware of indignity, Julie slid her feet to the floor over the edge of the wide bed – she had been sleeping on one side of it, being used to another body beside hers – and stood up. She staggered slightly, took the three steps to the nearest chair and sat down.

'I'm still dopey,' she said to nobody. Nobody answered her.

'Where is Wedeker?'

'What?'

'Wedeker. Where is he?'

'You mean, my husband?' Franzl! 'He went to Prague.'

'When?'

'Yesterday, in the morning. There was a train at nine-something.'

'Yesterday? You mean Saturday?'

She stared at the meaningless question, the meaningless face.

'Yes, Saturday. Oh, I see, it's Monday morning, you mean. You are being a bit too exact for me, at this time of night, you know.' She slid into Viennese dialect, ironically, as she would have done with a customs official being awkward, and was aware of making a mistake.

'You are under the impression that this is funny?' No expression at all in the voice. 'Can you prove Wedeker took the Prague train?'

Julie stared. 'Prove it? Of course I can't prove it.' She yawned again and found she wanted to laugh. Then she became aware of discomfort and stood up.

'Stay where you are. Sit down.'

'But I want to go to the bathroom,' she said reasonably.

'Stay where you are.' Julie sat down.

'If you don't believe me,' she said, 'search the place.'

The small man did not smile, with derision or anything else. He looked carefully to see if she were making fun of him. Then he tipped his head slightly and the tall man in uniform went out of the room. His boots, which creaked, made a muffled stamping. The sounds of drawers, cupboards, doors, being opened and shut receded as he went away from the bedroom. He neither slammed them open and shut nor made any attempt to avoid making a noise. The house was solidly and heavily built and normally well insulated against domestic noise, but after a few minutes Julie could hear faint sounds of movement in the flat below them. Presently someone knocked from below. Julie looked at the small man, but he either did not hear or took no notice. After about fifteen minutes — she thought — the tall man in uniform came back into the bedroom. Methodically he opened the wardrobe doors, and stuck a long arm inside, sweeping it laterally through the hanging garments. After closing the doors he opened each of the long and deep drawers of a big chest of drawers, looked at the other drawers in the room to check that they were too small to hide a man. Then he went out into the side hall and into the bathroom and then the lavatory. Then he came in again and shook his head at his superior.

'It's a warren of a place, but nobody here.'

'You can go to the lavatory now,' said the man in civilian clothes. 'Do not close the door.'

Julie considered this for a moment, then she got up and went out. The tall man followed her, waited by the door, which she left unlatched, and followed her back. When Julie put her hand on the bathroom door handle, he shook his head and she desisted. She sat down again in the chair she had occupied before.

'Your papers,' said the small man.

'I'll get your handbag, gnae' Frau,' said Fina, speaking for the first time since Julie woke.

'Get the papers yourself.'

Julie got the handbag she had used on Saturday afternoon from a whole row of bags in one of the long drawers. She took from it her thin leather pocket book and offered it to the small man.

'Take the money out first,' he said.

She took out the currency notes and offered it again.

He took it now, and went through her personal identity card, and then her pass to the Burgtheater, which entitled her to certain vague, unwritten privileges somewhat similar to those enjoyed by foreign diplomats. Reading this, he shot one look at Fina, having evidently recalled her protest earlier on. Though he was certainly no Austrian he had enough knowledge of local customs to grasp what the pass signified. He returned the two cards to their place and looked in the other side of the folder, then he handed the wallet back to its owner.

Once again, he tipped his head at the man in uniform. This man now sprang to attention and saluted smartly. The small man put on the grey felt hat which he had laid upside down on the corner of Julie's dressing-table. He quietly pulled on his gloves. The man in uniform opened the bedroom door for him. They heard the felted thud of the apartment door falling shut, and the faint rattle the bunch of keys in the lock made. Fina came over to

Julie and put out her hand, which Julie took. Fina was shaking with a coarse shudder.

'It's all right, Fina,' said Julie automatically as she felt this shudder. 'What's the time?'

'It must be gone four.'

'We had better have some coffee. We shan't sleep now.'

'I'll make tea. Then perhaps you'll sleep again, later.'

'Very well. Make tea.'

Fina went out, shapeless in her dark woollen dressing-gown. Her hair hung between her shoulders in a tight plait. Julie sat in the bright room, staring at the bed. They had not searched the whole house. Or had they – she would not have heard, evidently? When the tea came, she drank it greedily; her throat was quite dry. Fina had brought herself a cup and stood beside Julie's chair, drinking the hot tea with noisy, wet gulps. She stood as peasants do, but as she had long ceased to do, on one foot, the other stuck out well away from the weight of her body, almost at a right angle and resting on its heel. Neither of them said anything.

When she had finished the tea, Julie stood up and put an arm round Fina's shoulders and kissed her cheek. Fina took the cups. Thinking of the long, slender, full line of Julie's body in the rosy silk night-dress she had often ironed, she shook her head.

'Looking at you like that,' she said.

Julie got back into bed and pulled her book towards her from the night-table. In a few moments she was dead asleep in the soft blur of light from the bedside lamp. It was ten o'clock when she woke to the telephone's shrilling. Fina answered and Julie could hear her explaining. It was evidently the neighbours below, complaining of the noise in the night.

'It was the Gestapo,' said Fina in the hall, using the vernacular for the dread name of the Geheime Staatspolizei for the first time. Her voice had a note almost of pride that they had been singled out for this earnest of misfortune. After a long pause, she said, 'I will tell Frau Homburg what you say, but I don't see what we can do about it. If I hadn't let them in, they would have broken the door down, I dare say.'

7

'*I* just dropped by to tell you all the news,' said Hansi as he came into the room. He rubbed his cold hands together and went at once to the stove. He looked round the room and to his sharp eye an air of something going to pieces was at once visible in it. The tall chrysanthemums were drooping, their petals browning at the tips; they looked as if the water must smell in their vase; three cigarette ends and a used cup on the coffee tray – a perfectly commonplace sight in that much-used room – looked sordid instead of homely. Newspapers lay on the carpet by Julie's chair; she herself wore her dressing-gown and had not brushed her hair.

'Julie!' his voice took on a feminine, nagging note. 'What on earth are you doing, not dressed at this time?'

'Resting,' she said simply, but with that stubborn, over-reasonable tone in her voice he was used to when she had a work-block with a new part.

'Been smoking, too, I see.'

'Smoking, yes. A very small defiance. Childish, too!'

He was aware that to be brutal with her would be cruel, might be dangerous to her shaken self-confidence, and might change the delicate relationship to each other that was the basis of their successful work together. An obscure fear that she might commit some less small act of defiance drove his nervous energy from those considerations into the opposite – a desire to interfere. He saw in time that in her state of inertia she was unlikely to undertake anything requiring decision from herself. If he could keep outside stimulus away from her for a day or so, she would return to herself by virtue of her practical, energetic and sanguine temperament. He swallowed his fears with a small sigh that escaped him like a smothered yawn – he too was in a febrile state of nervous anticipation which had an element of frustration in it because he knew only too well that neither he nor anyone he could influence was now in charge of those actions, large and small, which were in process of making a new fundament for all their lives.

'Unlike you, dear Hansi,' she said slowly, 'I can't quite accept all this – yet. No doubt that's a subjective attitude caused by finding myself married to a Jew. Of course, I had always thought I was married to a man . . .'

'Not sarcasm, Julie, please. That's not worthy of you.' He took a cigarette, she took one too; he lit them both with disapproval. 'I've got to have a drink,' he sighed. Julie moved her hand in the direction of the glass-fronted cupboard where he knew the brandy, slivovitz, vermouth and other drinks were housed. He went over and poured himself brandy.

'I'll have one too,' said Julie behind him, and as he turned quickly back towards her and drew breath to say something she added in a sharp, shrewish tone, 'Brandy. Neat.' He brought the two little glasses brimming with the golden spirit and they drank them silently.

'I don't accept it, you know,' he said quietly, determined to deal at least with that bit of her mind's furniture before it could become a settled fact. 'I am resigned to it; it is all inevitable. I've known that since the summer.'

'Since you were in Berlin.'

'Since I was in Berlin. But apart from that – look at the map, my dear. Just look at the map.'

'I know,' she sighed wearily. 'Eighty million – seven million – the whole of history – Hitler's homeland – yes, yes, I know.' She coughed on the cigarette and put it out. 'The strange thing is that we didn't all know it was inevitable – since it now so clearly is.'

'I dare say everybody did – except intellectual Vienna. That would be why there has been no fighting – not a shot fired.'

'Is everything quiet now?'

'Except for the organised welcome – rejoicings – whatever you'd call them. There are supposed to be a lot of arrests going on. I haven't heard about anybody I know, though.' He did not mention Hanau.

'Oh, yes, I didn't tell you. The Gestapo were here in the night. They didn't stay long; just searched the place and left again.'

'God,' he said. Then, 'Did they frighten you?'

'Fina was frightened. Dr Pohaisky warned me, but I forgot to say anything to her.'

'Perhaps they'll leave you alone now ...'

'I haven't heard from Georgy, have you?'

'No. He's bound to be bothered, I imagine. But Keppler had it all fixed up about the paper; they won't do anything to Kerenyi if he accepts the situation.'

'What else can he do?' she said listlessly. The question of whether or not Julie was going to accept the situation lay about in the room unanswered, even unformulated, but more real than any of the hard physical objects which to their rational minds were the real things there.

At that moment Kerenyi himself entered an office in the newly requisitioned headquarters of the State Police, where there were signs of a hasty take-over to be seen; in the corridors the filing-cabinets of the former occupiers still stood, members of the former staffs went hastily to and fro with a particular air of nervous conciliation, collecting their employers' property with a haste to be gone from this unlucky place only controlled by the fear of earning dread disapproval by showing it.

The man behind the desk was a short man with a fat neck and close-cropped hair of a nondescript blond colour and singularly stubby, ugly, coarse features. The uniformed Viennese policeman who had shown Kerenyi in, announced his name and shut the door behind him as he went out. Without speaking, the official opened a blue folder on his desk and ran a short finger down a typed list.

'Kerenyi,' he checked, in a strong Berlin accent. 'Chief Editor of the *Viennese Independent*. Right?'

'That's right,' said Kerenyi. 'Until last Friday, that is.'

'So? and now?'

'The owner kept me on as literary editor.'

The official began to sort through some loose papers and letters that lay to one side of his blotter, found the one he sought and nodded.

'Good,' he said with the satisfaction of a civil servant finding his papers in order. 'Now. Tell me about yourself. Sit down. Here, put your hat over there. We aren't properly organised yet.' His tone was quite normal, civil, abrupt with the customary abruptness of a Prussian policeman, but nothing more. It was at once obvious to Kerenyi that he was a professional policeman, though he wore regulation SS uniform whose rank badges were as yet unfamiliar.

'What do you want to know?' asked Kerenyi, more bewildered by the normality of the man than he would have been, he thought, by the expected brutality.

'Place of birth, education, family. All that stuff. I have it here, of course. Just checking my files.'

A civilian came silently in by the door behind him, and facing Kerenyi, laid a folder in front of his chief and went out again.

'Born Hatvan, Hungary. March 21st. 1896. After elementary school there my parents moved to Budapest, where I went to the Central Gymnasium. Then University there. I studied Modern Languages, History. Then I went to Prague for a year and took Law ...'

'Law?' said the official sharply. 'I haven't got anything about Law.'

'I didn't finish the course. Perhaps that's why? Then I came to Vienna University and finally took my degree here in European Literature and History after the War. As you will know, it was then possible to ...'

'I know all that. Go on.'

'The War interrupted my studies. I was nearly a year on the Galician front ...'

'Captured once, weren't you? At ... where's that war record ... ah ...'

'Berdicheff in the Ukraine. Yes, but I escaped. They weren't too well organised, the front was pretty movable at that time.'

'Yes. And then?'

'The rest of the War I was in the Alps and on the Adige. Oh, I got married on leave in '17.'

'In Budapest?'

'Yes. I was only in Budapest a month or so after the War. Then I came here and became an Austrian citizen in 1919.'

'Why?'

'My wife had run off with ...' Kerenyi stopped and considered.

'Go on.' The official looked up and saw Kerenyi's expression; a slight grimace crossed his ugly face and Kerenyi's face relaxed into a grin.

'Yes, she ran off with one of your chaps. A Berliner. Handsome chap.'

'You met him then?'

'I saw him once. Over the divorce.' Something so irresistible now occurred to Kerenyi that he began to smile in spite of himself.

'What is it?'

Kerenyi looked across at his interlocutor and his native cantankerousness overruled discretion.

'My wife was Jewish,' he said. The official looked sternly at him. Then, without warning, he began to laugh aloud, a laugh that made Kerenyi laugh too. He saw when the official laughed that he had a distinct Slav cast of countenance. But why not, he thought, the Prussians were originally a Slav tribe and they must be so mixed up with the Poles after all these hundreds of years that there's no telling them apart. And this thought, in the office of a protector of the Teutonic 'race', made him smile again.

'So you divorced her? She stayed in Berlin?'

'I believe so. No, she divorced me.' In answer to the raised eyebrows of the man behind the desk, he shrugged and said, 'Why not? Once she was gone it didn't matter much, and her new chap wanted it like that. He was a von Teckertdorff, you see.'

'Yes,' A hasty turning over of papers. 'Did you know they are now in America? New York.'

'Really? It's a mad world.' The official looked at him sternly again. 'It's a quotation – from Shakespeare.'

'Hm. Go on.'

'Then I stayed here. I went to work for the *Wiener Neue Presse*. After five and a half years I went to the *Independent* as assistant editor. And when old man Kowalski retired they made me editor and finally editor-in-chief — or responsible editor as you say.'

'Hm. You are a close friend of Franz Wedeker, I understand?'

'We were on the Isonzo together and met again when I first came here. No, we were at the University, too.'

Silence. Kerenyi waited for the next question. The official pushed a paper-knife from his blotter and lined it neatly between the edge of the blotter and the inkwell.

'And now?' he said at last. His tone remained civil, even friendly. But the atmosphere had changed slightly.

'Now? Wedeker is in Prague. He left on Saturday morning by the nine o'clock train.'

'He left,' said the policeman evenly. 'But he is not in Prague.' Kerenyi's pulses seemed to stop for a second. He had the feeling of a band round his temples, at once hot and cold. He said nothing.

'You know where he is?'

'No,' said Kerenyi abruptly, his voice strained.

'We should know if he had arrived in Prague. He hasn't. Where is he?'

'I don't know.'

The official leaned back slightly in his wooden chair and laid his forearms neatly along the arm-rests.

'Listen,' he said. 'We need to know where Wedeker is.' As Kerenyi was about to say something, the official raised his left hand slightly and dropped it back over the end of the arm-rest. 'Now listen to me. I like you. So I tell you this, quite frankly. I am a policeman. I transferred to the State Police a year ago from the criminal police. I do a certain kind of work. There are other officers here who do another kind of work. Do you get me? Yet others again who do still other work. As long as you are in my files, nothing of the sort of thing you expected when you came in here will happen to you. That will only be the case as long as it is policy. I do my job. I have nothing to say about policy.'

He stopped speaking and waited.

'I honestly don't know where Wedeker is.' Kerenyi looked up from his folded hands and stared at the official, hesitating.

'What is it?' said the man.

'I – it sounds idiotic … may I smoke?'

'Do. I think there's an ashtray here somewhere. Yes, here it is. What was it you were going to say?'

'I was going to ask you something.'

'Go on, then.'

'It's rather personal. All right. I was going to ask you why you transferred?'

The official looked at Kerenyi. He answered quietly with no sign of annoyance either at the personal nature of the question or at its implication.

'The pay and allowances are considerably higher.'

'I see. Excuse me.' Kerenyi lit one of his harsh black cigarettes and blew out smoke.

'If you knew where Wedeker was, would you tell me?'

Kerenyi looked at him thoughtfully. He could feel an inward shudder but nothing of it showed.

'I don't know,' he said slowly, and looked at his hands again. The cigarette was perfectly steady in his fingers and the smoke rose no more erratically than it normally did.

The door behind the official opened to the sound of the clash of boots stamping to attention. A very tall and graceful man entered, he ducked his head slightly, unnecessarily, at the entrance, and flicked ash from a cigarette on to the floor. The official rose and Kerenyi rose after him. The tall man smiled, and clapped the official on the shoulder familiarly. He looked over his shoulder and reached down to turn the papers in Kerenyi's file over with a long, well-shaped finger, and then looked directly at Kerenyi with a pair of brilliant, shining eyes set very close together in a strikingly handsome, gay face. He had a long nose but it was not the nose that made him look Jewish; something in his gay, self-confident air did that, a deep ingrained self-confidence with none of the self-searching of the true Protestant North German.

'Ah, Kerenyi, yes. I wanted to have a look at the famous editor of the *Independent*.' He smiled at Kerenyi, showing perfect teeth and Kerenyi saw that the eyes were a shadowy haunting grey-blue, almost violet. 'Or should I say, the ex-editor?'

Kerenyi bowed slightly, finding no answer. The tall man took a step past the desk and putting out his elegant hand he tapped Kerenyi lightly on his lapel. 'You're a good fellow,' he said briskly, 'I used to read your stuff. Shan't read it now, though. I'm no literary boy – too much to do for reading *belles lettres* and stuff.' His charm was so powerful that Kerenyi found himself liking the man, though he knew perfectly well who he was. 'Yes, you ought to be on our side, a clever chap like you; you must know we're going to win. And the prizes – Ha! – the world won't be big enough to hold us in a few years' time.' He looked about for an ashtray and thanked with his smile the official, who picked it up and offered it; he stubbed out his cigarette. 'Think it over; be on the side of history as the Marxists say.' He nodded at Kerenyi, clapped the official once more on the shoulder, crossed the room to the door by which Kerenyi had entered with a graceful springing step, and went out. At the door he ducked his head slightly again; his close-fitting tunic was of perfect elegance, the breeches and boots stunning. He left behind a scent of masculine cologne water, crisply aromatic.

Kerenyi looked at the official, who was staring down at his blotter, having reseated himself. There was a look of deep consideration on the ugly face, the look of one who adjusts an opinion to fit a new circumstance. His eyes were grave, almost respectful, when he looked at Kerenyi but to Kerenyi it was no good omen to have been singled out for notice by Heydrich in this fashion. Then he nodded, rather slowly.

'You can go now,' he said. 'If I need you I know where to find you. If you hear anything ... well we shall know, you know. Consider what I told you.' He did not refer by as much as a muscle moved to the man who had come and gone.

'You mean—' Kerenyi stared, not believing his ears. 'You mean, I can go?'

'Yes, go,' said the official, more sharply than he had spoken yet. 'Go and write your bit of book reviewing or whatever it is.'

Utterly bewildered, Kerenyi did as he was told, for once without argument. He had reached the outside door and was fishing in his pocket for the printed pass issued on his arrival, when a Viennese policeman in uniform tapped him on the arm.

'Your pass has not been countersigned,' he said. 'Return to the office of the Sturmbannführer.' Kerenyi knew that this was a police trick to inspire fear often used in Russia and Germany, and did not necessarily mean disaster; but he felt the constricting band round his forehead again as he turned and accompanied the man back through the corridors and up the stairs he had just traversed.

'Come in,' called the now familiar voice, and just as before the policeman closed the door after him and went away.

The official, still seated behind his desk, held out a thick hand for the printed slip of precious paper. He signed it quickly and then looked up at Kerenyi, holding the paper on his blotter with his left hand.

'My name is Blaschke,' he said. 'You will remember it? Or do you want to note it down?'

'I shall remember it,' said Kerenyi, feeling surprise at hearing his own voice.

'Good,' said the official. 'You'll be able to leave the building now.' He held out the slip of paper and Kerenyi heard himself saying, 'Good afternoon.' Going circumspectly down the corridor and controlling with a conscious effort his still-not-valid rush of joyful relief, Kerenyi made a mental note that his guess as to the policeman's Slav origins had been correct, for all Prussian names ending with 'schke' or 'au' are germanisations of Slav names. He reached the head of the main stairs – he had been on the first floor – and at that moment four uniformed men slammed open a door opposite. They ranged themselves quickly across the end of the corridor, one of them pushing Kerenyi roughly back without looking at him. Out of the door came two more tall uniformed men half dragging, half carrying a third man between them. He seemed to be a small man. The two men carted him to the head of the stairs and gave him, both together, a strong push. The small man swung round with the force of their push, staggered wildly, catching with one hand at the stair-rail, and then stumbled down the stairs, losing his balance completely halfway down and falling to the bottom on the clean stone floor of the entrance. His glasses fell off as he staggered. One of the men who had been holding him put out a heavy, booted foot and solemnly crushed the spectacles; he looked round at his comrades and grinned. Then he saw Kerenyi staring.

'What are you staring at?' he yelled.

'Where's your pass?' said one of the other men sharply. Kerenyi produced the slip of paper and the man scrutinised the signature.

'All right. Get out,' he said coldly and sharply.

As Kerenyi started down the stairs one of the two men above him gave a slight shove, not enough to cause him to lose his balance, but enough to make him rush down the stairs. The man at the bottom was pulling himself into a sitting position. He groped with his hands about him, obviously for his glasses. One eye was rapidly changing colour and a smear of blood showed on his chin where a blow on the mouth had cut his lip. Kerenyi hesitated for a second, he could feel the men at the head of the stairs watching him; then he walked past the seated man, closing his eyes for an instant with a sensation of deep shame. Outside, he found his knees were shaking; he went into the first coffee-house he came to and ordered black coffee and cognac. With a sensation of moral horror at his own depravity he recognised that the anger he felt mingled with his shame was directed at the injured man for being the cause of his own shame. He thought of Franz.

Julie said, smiling at Hansi's own smile of ironical complicity, 'I'm glad that Hella didn't succeed with this Lehmann, then. But Georgy won't like it much if it turns out to be Maris – they've been together for years, now.'

'It may not go so far,' said Hansi, 'I must go. I have various things to do before this absurd reception this evening. You won't go out, my dear, will you? Not this evening?'

'Oh, no,' she said, her listlessness returning. 'I shall stay here. Don't worry about me so much, Hansi. I shan't have any more escapades. But – you might find out that Ruth is all right, can you? Discreetly? These people she is with won't have a telephone.'

'Of course. I'll let you know. But she'll be all right, I think.'

'For the time being,' said Julie.

The silence settled back after Hansi went, as if it had become the natural state in that room which had always been so full of chatter, laughter, comings and goings, and work. Only when Julie was learning a new role or when Franz had a particularly involved theoretical argument to put on paper, had the room been silent if they were in it. Now the unnatural silence of the Inner City, cordoned off in its encircling Ring, seemed to penetrate the thick house walls, creeping in gradually as cold creeps in when in times of famine houses are not heated and the weather slowly invades them. The police cordons and SS troops remained in their stations after the official entry, for the Führer was in the Hotel Imperial on the Ring, a few metres distant from where Julie sat, and the reception of the coming evening was an affair of the most rigid and complex security arrangements. Not, as always in cities, to ensure the smooth passage of official traffic on State occasions, but to ensure the safety of this strange and demonic figure against a populace supposed to be feeling nothing but joy at his advent.

Kerenyi found no taxi when he left the coffee-house, so he walked back to his flat across the city a distance of something over two kilometres, and was asked five separate times for his papers on the way, twice by police cordons and three times by patrols of troops. On each occasion a typed list of many pages was consulted before he could go on. The first patrol of troops he met had a copy of the list which must have been a fifth carbon copy – it was so smudged and pale. Later these lists were printed but at first, because the entire operation had been put forward for several weeks to prevent the holding of the threatened Austrian plebiscite, they were of a somewhat provisional sort. The sergeant was reluctant to let Kerenyi go on, and it occurred to the journalist to tell him that he had just left Gestapo headquarters and to give the name of Sturmbannführer Blaschke as a reference. Instantly the man returned his papers and saluted civilly. This taught Kerenyi a very important lesson about living with tyranny: if you have been released by the Secret Police without arrest then you are in order. This attitude of mind quickly becomes habitual – if you have been granted a visa, a pass, a permit to live, then you must have been through the security machine and are therefore privileged in the passive sense of simply being allowed to be there at all.

When, in his own flat he considered this curious fact, he saw what it implied: that all who were at that time being summoned to the State Police, as distinct from being arrested out of hand, and who left their headquarters unharmed and 'free' were considered as possible collaborators. Heydrich's joking words were the simple fact – he was expected now to declare himself for the new order. It never for one instant occurred to Kerenyi that he might genuinely adopt the creed of the new masters even in the limited sense that Lehmann, for instance, accepted it and most other intelligent and creative people were to accept it; that is, simply as the only way of continuing to do their own work. What came into Kerenyi's mind was the idea that he might superficially connive at the new order so that he could in fact, in some way that was still unknown, work against it. Kerenyi was much too experienced and intelligent not to see the immense dangers of such an attitude. Nevertheless he began to think seriously, even in those first hours of the possibility of secret opposition which could only be possible to him as a man of the public world, if he were accepted by those whom he thought of automatically and unconditionally, of their very nature as his enemies. He had no clear idea of how anything of the sort could be done. But what was perfectly clear from the start – apart from the dangerousness of the idea – was that alone, nothing could be achieved. Kerenyi knew that this idea came into his head as a reaction to his shame at rejecting the fallen man at the foot of the stairs. He was quite aware, practical man of affairs as he was, that any show of helpfulness to that man would have terrified its recipient as much as it would have angered the men watching from the head of the stairs and have endangered himself. What troubled Kerenyi was that he had not thought of the incident in those terms at the time or acted on pragmatic grounds which would have reassured him as to his own cool-headedness, but had acted out of naked fear.

Later in the evening, Maris came unannounced and talked

135

amusingly and openly about Lehmann and the party of the previous evening. How much interest he had shown, how she had not realised that *Liebelei* might have to come off; but how that did not matter because there was a play of Gerhard Hauptmann's that Lehmann was keen to see produced at the Josefstadt and she had been promised a part. This told Kerenyi that he was about to lose her. When they later went to bed she showed such a clinging lovingness and such inventiveness in pleasing him that he knew something was on her conscience, that she was thinking of Lehmann. To his surprise Kerenyi felt neither pain nor anger at this; his jealousy made him even more vigorous than usual, but he found himself thinking that if the new situation developed he might find some way to use it.

8

*J*ulie rang the bell a second time, and had already gone out into the hall to call Fina when she appeared from the kitchen, having obviously come from her own room beyond it. She was dressed in her heavy overcoat and boots for the street and it was clear from the embarrassed way she ducked her head and did not look at Julie that she had meant to go out without telling her employer.

'But Fina, do you think it's wise to go out to-night?' said Julie, vaguely astonished that Fina should even want to do so. 'Herr Ostrovsky said it would be best to stay at home ...'

'I just want to have a look, that's all. I shan't be long, and I'll take my keys.'

'But there will be huge crowds ... Well, of course, go if you want to ... But won't you be frightened if you get stuck in a crowd? You may not be able to get out again very easily.'

'Oh, I shall be all right, gnae' Frau, don't you worry,' said Fina with good-humoured contempt for the upper-class prejudice against crowds. 'Will *you* be all right, that's much more to the point?'

'Of course. I shall stay here.'

'Yes, but ... you don't think they'll come again to-night? I mean, if they do, if you think they might, I'll stay in.'

'Oh, that. No, I don't suppose they will come again. And if they do it will be much later and you'll be back. You go, then. I shall go to bed soon. I only wanted a glass of wine.'

'I'll open you a fresh bottle.'

'Please. The same wine.' Julie wandered back into the silent room. When Fina came in with the wine, she felt the stove, looked at Julie and then laid two more brown-coal briquettes carefully on the soft, powdery glow inside it, which would burn, now, until morning.

'You're sure you don't mind?' she said, shifting from one stoutly booted foot to the other.

'Of course not. I hope you're not being unwise, that's all.' Offended by Julie's obvious indifference to her own disguised excitement Fina withdrew. As she clumped down the circling stairs she addressed Julie in her head, arguing from the newspaper read that lunch-time, that it was an historic occasion, though she did not know what the phrase meant very clearly. All very well for you, she thought, you have excitements every day. And yet she was worried by the knowledge that she ought not to feel excited by something that had caused Dr Franz to leave home as he had. Still, determined on her outing, she struck out across the criss-cross of the inner city towards the Hofburg where the great reception was to be, and in the excitement of the growing crowd all going in the same direction and the novelty of being asked for her papers by stalwart soldiers in black as she thought of the SS troops, with their strange accents that did not sound like German at all to Fina, she soon forgot the discomfort of the thought about Dr Franz having to leave home.

In the Kohlmarkt the crowds were thick, one could hardly move through. She made her way slowly, with much elbowing and back-chat, right round the Schaufflergasse, skirting the Hofburg, and then even more slowly through a dense mass of human beings nearly all standing still by now, across the Heldenplatz. She was not satisfied until she was within clear sight of the immense doors of the New Hofburg and the flights of windows brilliantly lit up, where, she thought with wonder and resentment at her absence, Julie ought to be.

Large motor cars arrived every moment, sweeping past with an effect of silence against the susurrus of the vast concourse of waiting people. They deposited their passengers at the open doors and swept away again down the long-disused approach. Far away the metallic voices of loudspeakers controlling the parking by numbers could be heard echoing. Along the roadway the black-uniformed troops in their darkly gleaming steel helmets stood shoulder to shoulder, the lights of the palace throwing little lights here and there off their bayonets and polished accoutrements to the rattle and gleam of harness from their mounted officers. Presently from the direction of the Ring the formations of Party members and SA began to march in, carrying flaming torches and with bands, singing their thumping songs in unison to the stamping of their boots. The sound of many hundreds of voices was exhilarating. The huge crowd, docile and wondering, stirred and murmured, moved internally by currents as of water. At the deep, masculine noise of their voices, especially when they shouted one of their ferocious slogans after singing some marching song, Fina, like every woman in the vast crowd, felt a deep stabbing thrill through her belly. She knew quite well there was something wicked about what she felt, for it gave her carnal thoughts, so it must be wrong. Yet she enjoyed the feeling, and it came over and over again and she began to be shaken by a subterranean current, both in herself and coming from every side in the crowd. The men in the crowd, who out-numbered the women by a large number, were stirred not only by their own excitement, but by aggressiveness and resentment communicated to them by the sexual excitement of the women as well as by the noise, the smoking, flamy torches with their pungent smell, the stamp of rhythmic marching and the streaming banners headed by the glinting eagles of the Reich. When the SA units shouted from open throats *Deutschland. Erwache!* and *Heim! ins! Reich!* every man listening felt the need to know he was as good a man as they were, with their uniforms and banners. Now and then a single voice specially chosen for its quality would cry out, like a bass trumpet on the still air of a pause in the noise, *Tod allen Feinden!* Another would answer in the same wild, brazen tone *Juda! Verrecke!* And then the crowd would give a deep groan, offered a target for its increasing aggressiveness and excitement.

By the time, hours later, that a single figure appeared on the high balcony above the huge doors, the crowd was no longer a mass of human beings, but a single, many-bodied creature of demonic force. Against the lights from inside, the single man, dwarfed by the huge pillars, left alone by the group attending him, which withdrew out of sight of the crowd, stood stiffly, leaning jerkily against the support of the stone balustrade, one arm rising and falling in the rigid, hypnotic gesture already familiar from films. A deathly silence fell, the catching of a great breath. Into the silence rang the wild, harsh, ecstatic voice, speaking recognisably their own dialect, yelling with strained throat meaningless words of exhortation and triumph; a harsh cry of victory and promises of more victory. That single figure, possessed and ravished by its own power, glared over the many-headed monster of the crowd, far away over the statue of Prince Eugen towards the trees of the park and the rounded white Burgtheater, seeing nothing but the silent hosts of his forefathers, horned helmets, spears and shields brandished in their hands, a wild, silent jubilation rising from their ranks as they rode across the clouded sky to victory after unassailable victory, shaking their tattered banners in the face of a trembling world.

When his voice ceased there was a moment of perfect stillness, and then a single solid, frantic cry broke out, going on and on for minutes, until it gradually died away in ragged hoarseness. The figure raised a jerking arm again; once again. The windows behind parted and he disappeared while the crowd roared wildly again.

For an unmeasured time the crowd tossed and roared in itself. Gradually, however, it began to move in clumps and streams, each clump drawing fringes with it, like ice-floes on the bosom of the wide, swift Danube in late winter.

The movement, as irresistible as water's flow, drew Fina back across the level space of the Heldenplatz, almost imperceptibly at first, and then faster as the mass thinned and broke apart. She found herself almost running at last, hard by the gates of the Volksgarten. Panting and full of a trembling excitement she felt her sturdy body pinned against the railings just inside the park. She squirmed and the group of which she was part disintegrated into twos and threes. She was in the grip of a single man who was pulling at her clothes. Without thinking in the least what she was doing, she pulled the unknown body with her into the wintry bushes, and they stumbled together to the ground, she pulling more frantically at her restricting skirts than the man himself did. Almost instantly the pent-up frantic tension expanded into a sensation of unbelievable pleasure and swam away into perfect peace and joy. She lay for some time, half-conscious; it was the cold that brought her to; the man was not there. Fina climbed stiffly and slowly to her feet, shakily ordered her clothing and pulled her head-shawl straight. She was already determined to ignore what had happened. By the time she reached home it had never happened, and therefore there was no need to think of it or to confess it the following Friday before the Sacrament on Sunday. It simply was not. She had been bumped into and knocked over by the crowd; by the next morning she believed this completely and never consciously gave it another thought.

All over the city people shuddered behind closed shutters as they heard from outside the waves of that sea of excitement ebbing, in running feet, shouting voices, loud colloquies of groups, the staggering tramp of drunken men, the shrill laughter of women lost for the moment to shame or pity. Not only those of Jewish faith shuddered, but many native Viennese, priest and lay, Christian, humanist, atheist; all who knew human nature well enough to recognise the accents of what it was already old-fashioned to call Evil, but for which no one of those who understood needed to find a new name. The old city had seen many horrors in its long history. But one thing always characterised it from its earliest days when the Celts lived in Europe; it was always a meeting place of many kinds of men – not the capital city of a single nation, but of a multinational State. Its essential nature was of the centre of many ways; it existed only as the focal point of many peoples, many tongues; xenophobia was of its nature impossible to it. Those other peoples might hate Vienna or think they did, but Vienna could not of its intrinsic being hate them for she was made up of them. With the artificial culture of xenophobia in this most urbane of all European cities, the spiritual Balkanisation of Europe was complete.

9

A slight sound penetrated Julie's imperfect concentration on her book. She thought it was in the street, from the crowds roaming the city; an echo of Fina's moment of history. For Julie too had read the paper for once, and marvelled naïvely at its altered tone. A police truck rushed up the street under her windows, its horns wailing on the familiar double note. Then there was silence again. In the silence came the shuffling sound and after a moment Julie found herself listening intently for it. The third time she recognised it as being inside the house. She went out into the hall, but all was quiet. My nerves are on edge, she thought but dismissed the idea at once. She had no nerves, everyone said so. After a moment she took a step back into the living-room; stepping off the rug her high heels clicked sharply on the hardwood floor. At once, as if at a signal, there was a small tap outside the door. It was so discreet she hardly heard it, but at the same time she was waiting for it, and felt as she heard it that she had known it would come.

The events of the last two days might have sharpened her perceptions, but they had not yet succeeded in making Julie cautious. With a lack of caution that the still peasant Fina would never have displayed even before there was any need for forethought, Julie went down the hall and picked up her key-ring lying where it always lay on the telephone-table. As Julie pulled open the door it did occur to her that she was being unwise, and the dark hollow of the door recess and landing, empty and cold, increased the feeling. The shadow in the other half of the double door was deep and it was with a subtler perception than sight that Julie became aware there was someone there.

Defying herself to feel fear, Julie stepped out from the door, feeling sideways with an outstretched hand for the time-switch on the far side of the deep recess. Only when the protecting arm was moved from the blur of a face could she really tell that there was a human being standing there.

'No light,' said an urgent whisper. 'Turn the hall light out. I can't be seen.'

'But what . . .'

'Quickly!' There was a febrile irritation in the voice. The figure slipped inside the door as soon as Julie had stepped back and switched off the ceiling lights. From the deflected glow out of the living-room, she watched the door close, the key turned. When the long dirty fingers fumbled for the chain, Julie said, whispering, 'Not the chain. Fina is out.'

He turned swiftly, as if accusingly.

'Fina? Where's she gone? What is she doing out to-night, of all nights?'

'She wanted . . .' The last shred of reality ebbed into absurdity and Julie stopped speaking. She switched the light back on.

'What has happened?' she whispered. 'Franzl, what have they done to you!'

There was nothing visibly wrong with him. He was tired, even exhausted; unshaven, dirty as if he had been climbing through a coal dump; but no more tired, no more unshaven than she had seen him many times after a long and difficult climb in the mountains. He was simply entirely altered, a different being. From the staring cunning of his look something animal looked out, frightening in its fear.

'What happened?' she whispered again, and hearing herself whisper, raised her voice to something like normal. 'What happened?'

'Shh!' He turned sharply to look at the locked door. 'Not so loud!' He made no move to come into the apartment, or to take off his heavy coat. They stood staring helplessly for a moment. Then Julie said:

'You must be hungry. Come into the kitchen. Wait, I'll pull the curtains.'

Franz looked round the square room, with its scrubbed familiar smell of a thousand meals, to make sure they were alone, and closed the door to the hall. As he moved to the scoured table his shoes left dark, damp marks on the white tile floor. He sat down in the chair where Fina always sat and leaned his head on his hand, his elbow on the table. Julie went to the larder, for eggs and butter. The door swung closed with a thud and Franz jumped up and round, crouching back against the table.

'It's all right,' Julie said hastily, 'that door always does that. There's no one there.'

Franz gave a little groan and subsided again on to the chair. Julie went to the refrigerator; she was blinded by sudden tears of pity and anger and a kind of shame, and shook her head impatiently to clear the tears. There was ham in the ice-box and a covered jar of soup ready for the next day.

'Shall I heat the soup?' she asked helplessly.

'No, give me some ham and eggs. I could use a drink, though.'

'I'll get it – what . . . ?'

'Cognac?' As she ran to fetch the bottle she thought for a moment that it was foolish to drink brandy on an empty stomach; for some reason that reminded her of the men who had been there last night and she had to lean for a moment against the door to steady herself. She forgot glasses, so they drank out of two coarse tumblers from the kitchen cupboard. The spirit brought a trace of life back into Franz's face. He watched her movements as she broke the eggs into foaming butter, sliding them to one side to make room in the pan for the pink slices of ham with an unpractised gesture that would, in the normal world, have made him laugh. Filling the kettle to make coffee, Julie fumbled and dropped the lid which rattled and rang as it rolled across the tiles. They stared at it as if the little noise would bring the house about their ears.

'This is crazy,' she muttered, 'it doesn't matter if somebody does hear.'

He stared round at her as if he could not understand her words. When the food was put in front of him, he ate at once, breaking the bread into the plate and bending forward over the soft eggs which ran off his fork. He started when the refrigerator motor started up with its muffled hum.

The coffee was strong and sweet, almost too hot to sip.

'More?' she said, and he nodded and pushed his cup towards her. 'Franzl – can't you tell me? Please tell me what happened?'

He stared wildly for a moment, remembering.

'They were coming down the train corridor,' he said at last. 'I had to jump out. That's where I ...' He looked down at his clothes. 'Just before the border, so the train was going slowly. There was only one other man in the carriage – that American journalist. What was his name? I heard several people moving down the corridor, opening and shutting doors. I thought it was the customs people. Then this man got up and looked out of the compartment door. He popped his head back in and said "Gestapo".'

'Yes ...' said Julie, prompting him after a long pause.

'I just didn't know what to do. This chap – this American – said, "You'll have to jump for it. Quick. I'll shut the door after you and they won't know." There was nothing I could do. I just had to jump.'

Jumping out of trains. It only happened in the sort of adventure stories one read – yes, one read on journeys translated from the English or American originals. But Franz? Gentle, thoughtful, indolent Franz? He must do such things in real life?

'I rolled over and over,' Franz was saying. 'It felt like cinders. If there'd happened to be a telegraph pole just at that point ... I lost my hat, of course ...'

'And your luggage,' said Julie. And then, 'As if that mattered.' She wanted to weep and forced herself into control with the feeling that weakness on her part would make things worse for Franz. In her relationship with her husband she had never before acted with calculation, or not consciously; now, as often when rational calculation, even for the best of reasons, enters an emotional relationship, she calculated falsely. Her quietness seemed to Franz hard, considered.

More than his nerves were stretched to unbearable tension; his whole character was in crisis. The haste, the danger and the loss of a whole life and all it contained, these were destructive. But the indignity of what was happening to him made himself unreal and alienated him from the world about him. The humiliation of being treated like a parcel, an object and at that an object of little value was unbearable; if Julie had collapsed into uncontrolled grief his reaction might have been a healthy anger against the world and the madmen who seemed to have taken over running the world. She seemed to accept his situation and his fear and anguish were driven back into himself; he was utterly isolated in his humiliation and the instant when Julie might have shared his lostness passed. Just because she recognised his danger even more clearly than Franz himself did, and was dominated by the thought that one of the two of them must keep control of their situation, she remained outwardly calm when the only thing that could have helped Franz would have been for her to lose her head.

Would the two Gestapo men or others like them come back again, that was the question. Should she tell Franz about the visitation of the night before? The great reception going on at this moment must engage the attention of every policeman for miles around. It was extremely unlikely that any operations would be undertaken inside the old city until to-morrow at the earliest. And from the Gestapo official's manner when he saw Julie's identity papers, Julie supposed that she would not in future, or not at once, be treated with the indignity and hatred accorded to enemies.

These thoughts issued in words as soon as Julie reached the conclusion that the Gestapo would not come back again that night.

'Dearest, I'll turn on your bath,' she said, gathering the soiled things together on the bare white wood of the table.

Franz started when she spoke and then held up his hands, inspecting them in a dazed quiet.

'Perhaps I had better ...' Then his voice became defensive, with the note of febrile irritation she had heard as he told her to be quiet in the hall. 'Yes, of course, I must get cleaned up at once! But – my luggage? I've got nothing to ...' He gazed round the kitchen as if washing and shaving things were hidden there somewhere in a mean and shaming trick against him.

'I didn't mean it like that, you silly. You'll feel better after a bath – you always do. There's a spare razor in the bathroom cupboard somewhere . . .' Julie heard in her voice a rallying note, like a nurse with a nervous patient. She repeated her actions of three days before, turning the gush of hot water on, pouring in her own bath oil whose scent gave Franz pleasure, gathering up the big bath towel to warm in the middle of the stove. It was like a recurring dream that subtly alters into a nightmare. She was aware that she must tell him about the visit from the Gestapo; not only because he had the right to know, but to explain her own manner. But she knew she could not; it was beyond her to deal another blow to his self-command.

'You haven't told me yet how you got back to Vienna,' she asked him when he was lying in the water, eyes closed against the light reflected in the wall-tiles.

Franz sighed deeply and opened his eyes. 'I walked a long way, I'm not sure where the place was. I must have gone a long way, on a side road somehow – I'd lost my sense of direction, I suppose. I rested in some woods by the side of the road for a time where it was a bit sheltered. I didn't dare go to an inn – I wasn't even sure I was not going towards the border. It was dark by that time, you see?'

'Yes. And then?' After a long pause.

'Just after dawn, I came to some village. There was a little shop open early, and I got milk and bread. Then I saw a Post bus, it was going to Retz, so I got on that. From Retz I got a slow local train and got off at Stockerau, of all places. You know that restaurant where we used to go . . .?' He looked at her now, puzzled at his own lack of memory. 'Didn't dare go there, of course, but there is another place right in the village where the peasants go. Dirty little place, but I got something to eat. I knew they wouldn't know me there. I rested there a bit. I could hold up the paper and pretend to be reading. Then I walked again. I didn't dare take a bus again – I could hear the locals talking about the police cordon. I thought of waiting and getting a lift on one of their carts. But I didn't dare. The rest of the way I was dodging police cars and patrols.'

'But how did you get over the river?' Julie said fearfully.

'Early this morning when everybody was going to work, I got on the tram on the far side – I could see there were no police on the tram. Then I got off a couple of stops after the bridge, and walked the rest down back streets. The canal bridge was easy, you can see across quite well. I walked over the Schwedenbrücke. There was a patrol this side, at Schwedenplatz, but I dodged down to the canal embankment and walked along. A lot of other people were avoiding the patrol too, so it was ...' A long silence again. 'I was hanging about here for hours. I hoped I might see you or Fina.'

Painful guilt and shame brought tears to Julie's eyes. How was it possible she had not felt he was there? How could Franz have to hang about all day, lurking round his own home like a criminal afraid to show his face?

'But how – how did you get into the house? Frau Pichler ... Franz, she didn't see you?'

He looked up at her again, hardly taking in her agitation; a little smile crossed his lips, for the first time he looked normal.

'I climbed the wall – you know, the low bit of the back court-yard where the next house doesn't quite meet ours? I did it often when I was a boy. As soon as it was dark. I couldn't wait because of the doors being locked ...'

The courtyard doors as well as the outer house-door were all regularly locked at eight in the evening by the Pichlers.

'What's that?' asked Franz suddenly, raising himself in the bath. They both listened intently.

'Someone using the lift, that's all.'

'Perhaps it's someone coming here?'

Julie looked at her wrist-watch and shook her head.

'I didn't ask anybody and nobody is likely to come without tele-phoning to-night.' The lift had gone up to the top floor.

'Fina will be back presently,' said Julie. 'I'll say nothing to her until morning. We don't want a great fuss now ...'

In the bedroom there was only one deeply shaded bedside light on, the curtains drawn against the night. It was a haven of calm, of warm luxury, of safety. In the half-light, Franz went across to the big dressing-table. The violets in the glass bowl were gone; instead of their soft voluptuousness and fragrance a jar of peasant stonework stood there, filled with stiff little wild daffodils. They seemed cold and meaningless, and Franz turned away quickly from them.

Filled now with an aching, sleepy lassitude, Franz lay down on their bed and drew the down quilt up to his throat. It was deliciously warm in the room, the windows closed and curtained shut out the world; insanity retreated. The two previous nights receded into a distance only dreamed and the familiar bed with its soft light was reality. When Julie slid into bed beside him he did not even start awake. His body was relaxed, his breathing deep; Julie lay beside him, not daring to put her arms round him. For a little while she dozed, half awake and half asleep. Then some slight sound roused her. Perhaps Fina returned with cautious quietness; or a shout blown up from one of the many groups scattered off by the huge crowd at the Heldenplatz and now draining away to every part of the city. She was not conscious of the sound's identity, it just woke her. She lay there, still and rigid, worrying silently that the Gestapo men would come back. The light burned rosily, faint sounds penetrated from time to time from outside to sharpen Julie's attention, to mark the passing of the long night. A long time later one of the outward sounds half roused Franz from his exhausted slumber and he turned towards her. He folded his arms about her body, drawing her against him. Her lips were against the corner of his eye where the laughter lines made a favourite kissing place. But almost at once he was deeply asleep again, the weight of his slack body on her shoulder so that her arm was soon numb.

As soon as she fell into a half-sleep Franz began to dream, muttering and twisting against her body. She was able to move her arm, to soothe him with her hands. She began to think of the old man and his daughter and the granddaughter, Ruth. Franz jerked and moaned, using her body as a pillow for his exhausted, unintelligible anguish. In the short intervals that she slept she dreamed of the old man and the two louts shouting and beating on the door; the door had become the door of her own home; and not the old scholar but Franz cowered behind it, helpless to save himself or even to understand what was happening.

When Fina came in at eight, Franz was instantly, rigidly, awake from his deadened sleep, awake and aware now that even here he could not count on safety. He was out of the bed before the door was well open, swinging round as if the room were strange to him and he must locate a place to hide in it. Then he took in Fina's face, gaping stupidly, gripping the coffee tray, and he began to shake all over with relief. Julie was out of bed and took the tray from Fina before she dropped it.

'Don't scream, Fina,' she said quickly. 'It's all right. Just don't make a noise, whatever you do!'

Fina moved slowly forward, sticking her hands out awkwardly before her as if feeling her way. When she came within touching distance of Franz, she gave a slight moan and put her arms round him, feeling his shoulders and arms, touching his head, ears, cheeks. Tears coursed down her round face. Franz put up his hands to her shoulders and they stood together, patting each other to make sure they were real. Julie, holding the tray, found that she was weeping too – at their emotion, for a dazed strangeness was all she herself could feel.

The door-bell rang. They all jumped.

'It's the post,' gasped Fina in a choking voice; and sure enough they heard the slide and rustle of letters being pushed into the letter-box.

'We must get him away from here,' said Julie, and set down the coffee tray on its usual table. She turned for her dressing-gown and became aware of wearing the same night-dress she had worn when the Gestapo men came. She spoke to Fina, not to Franz, and it was Fina who answered.

'No, no,' she cried, her tears stopping as suddenly as they had started, at this fresh threat. 'No, now he's back here, he must stay with us. We can look after him somehow ...'

'Fina, be sensible. He can't stay – he simply can't. Those men, they will come again. And Frau Pichler, you know we can't trust her!' Julie looked from one obstinate face to the other, as if she were trying to commit this outrage herself, not simply putting into words the arbitrary cruelty of the outer world.

'Franz,' she pleaded. 'We have to be reasonable. Fina, you're forgetting everything that has happened in the last few days ...'

Fina's face showed the red patches of her cheeks suddenly clearly outlined; it was the only way she could change colour. For a frightful instant she imagined that Julie knew and was speaking of the night before, of what was only a thought in her own mind. She clutched at Franz, whose accomplice she had been in boyhood escapades when she was first in Vienna, a fifteen-year-old peasant girl fresh from the pastures of her upland home and a thirteen-year-old schoolboy. All the difficulties of learning city ways, of cooking, of manners; all the hidden fears and resentments at finding herself working for a foreign, heathen household; all the restriction of the air, the narrowness and breathlessness of the town; everything she unconsciously suffered in transition from childhood to grown-up life was compensated for by the boy who shared her youth.

The narrow bonds of a superstitious earth-bound religion far different from the enlightened Catholicism of western cities would have prevented her, even if she had been capable of abstract thinking, from ever knowing that she hated her brutal father and coarse brothers. At home, daily cuffings and unending labour. Here, new fears and at first something very like slavery, for she was sent to Vienna without her consent and for years sent her wages home. But always one point of light and joy. The dark, quick boy with the narrow delicate face and the gift of learning who turned, without Fina ever seeing any change, into the slender, handsome, cultured man of middle age. He taught her to speak her own language properly, to read easily, not to be afraid of the traffic. It was Franz who discovered about her wages and persuaded his father to intervene. It was Franz who took her to the Circus and the Prater. He went to Mass with her, if only because, she knew, he loved the music. She never had a lover, never thought of marrying. He was her only idol.

Somewhere deep inside Fina's mind the strange feelings of the previous night became confused with Franz's return. Obscurely she transferred the two things into each other. Franz returned was a reassurance that those sinful moments were wiped out, had really never happened. At the same time, the duty and the need to care for him were a penance; she was forgiven but she must prove her worthiness of him, or of what gave her forgiveness and with which he was inextricably mixed in her mind.

'Franz, listen to me. Fina doesn't know quite what happened. But your uncle ... And your cousin too ...'

Julie found it for a moment quite impossible to put into words the incredible fact of their death.

She closed her eyes. 'It was quick, thank God, but they are both dead. The child is with neighbours. Something will have to be done about her, too. But you see – Franz, you must see – it is quite impossible for you to stay here.'

Franz sat down suddenly on the edge of the bed. He said nothing. There was a long silence, until Fina spoke slowly.

'Then you must go to my home.' She turned quickly to Julie. 'Not to my parents'. My brother's married and their place is right out of the village. He's all right, my brother. He'll be all right there. And I can go and see him there.'

For a moment Julie did not grasp what Fina had instantly seen. She herself must on no account be seen anywhere near where Franz was. His own face and figure were well known in Vienna; but Julie's person had become her husband's death warrant. If she had been only an actress at the Burg the peasants would not recognise her. But she had made films too. Her face was familiar in every farmyard in Austria, for films are to the country girls their one sophisticated outing.

Next day at about noon while the house was full of comings and goings so that nobody would notice them, and slipping quickly down the stairs, they made their way out of the back door and took a taxi to the station. Fina showed an unexpected talent for conspiracy, stumping down the stairs with as much noise as she could make, and shouting to the invisible Frau Pichler as she went through the back courtyard, while Franz moved silently along by the wall. They sat in the rackety old taxi side by side,

Fina perched well forward on her seat, and Franz put his hand out for her to hold. In the meantime, Julie took another car, under the eyes of a police agent watching the house door. She drove to her dressmaker and was fitted for a new spring suit. Then she went to the hairdresser. These services were a familiar weekly routine, quite natural, and she thought of nothing while her dark hair was being washed and the elderly, weakly handsome hairdresser chattered obsequiously and did the things he always did and tied the net over her head. When the hot scented air began to rush round her head she closed her eyes as she always did.

Then the thoughts began. She had not talked to Franz or persuaded him to talk to her. No sooner was he there than he was gone again; it seemed that he might perhaps never have been there at all. How could it happen that they had not talked — they always did talk, interminably; familiar words, phrases, endearments of that long conversation which is marriage recurred to Julie's mind, disembodied by the one night and morning when none of them had been said. None of those half-sentences that did not need to be ended had been started. The hands of the manicurist took possession of her own hands, elaborately polite, over-gentle, intimate, doing things to her as if she no longer had any say of her own in anything.

'And was gnae' Frau out last night? The crowds ...'

Words of bitter irony rushed into Julie's throat; she remembered Franz and dissembled.

'No, I stayed in,' she smiled with her lips. 'I wasn't quite well, somehow. Was it very ... exciting?'

The girl was talking away, her head bent over Julie's hand; in the rush of hot air inside the dryer half the words were lost. Crowds, music, such a crush, my boy-friend, couldn't really see much; every sentence larded with the overblown courtesies due to the esteemed and famous customer, to Frau Julia Homburg. A cold, hateful misery tightened Julie's throat, and inside the angry and contemptuous misery she could feel a sensation as if something were draining out of her heart, the physical organ; not blood, but the essential fluid and lymph of life itself, draining away. She always got on well with those who served her, never before had she felt this dislike and contempt for their automatic flatteries; but now they seemed false and cruel, meant to deceive, to cover up not self-interest but an active malevolence.

Hands drew away the hot helmet over her head. A thin, lined, ascetic face leaned close to her and whispered words against her padded ear.

'They have arrested Alois. Hsh! I just wanted to warn you . . .'

The face was already retreating.

'Wait! Frau Pohaisky!'

Reluctantly the thin woman returned, the weary and reddened eyes glancing quickly from side to side.

'Why?' whispered Julie quickly. 'Can we do anything?'

'Not because of business,' Pohaisky's wife shook her head. 'Subversive activities, they said.'

'But where — when did it happen?'

'Last night. I don't know where. Don't try to do anything. They warned me not to.'

The two women, so different that they could hardly be said to inhabit the same world, looked for a moment into each other's eyes. Julie looked sideways at the manicurist bending her head, pretending not to overhear. Frau Pohaisky knew that Julie would find out something among her influential acquaintances and admirers; Julie herself did not formulate this thought at all. She was remembering not having excused herself to the Pohaiskys for not going to Mass on Sunday morning as she had promised. With her free hand, Julie touched Frau Pohaisky's hand, and the grey, well-bred figure slipped away down the bustling, scented shop.

And I sit here. They are probably dragging them — she formed no names even in her mind, out of superstitious fear of drawing the attention of malign fate to what she must hide — off the train at this very moment. I ought to have gone with him, not let her go. It seemed to Julie then as if she were sitting there in luxury only in order to avoid hardship and danger; to avoid the unpro-tected suffering that looked out of Frau Pohaisky's eyes. And all the time the manicurist handled her hands softly, massaging them before painting the long oval nails.

A week after Fina returned, having safely installed Franz with her brother, Julie heard again from Frau Pohaisky with a formal invitation to luncheon. Formality was a way of ridding the meetings of friends from the all-pervading air of caution that now overtook a largely informal society – at least that part of it shared by Julie. For the moment, at any rate, it was better to know exactly who was coming into one's house; until it was clear where everyone stood; the days when friends brought their casual acquaintances with them simply because they seemed amusing, were over.

Of the four guests present the only one known to her was Krassny whom she had not seen since the evening before Franz's disastrous departure for Prague. He bowed over her hand, and they murmured the usual courtesies, but Krassny did not ask after her husband; it was understood that the subject was taboo.

Julie was the last comer and as soon as they had been introduced they went in to table.

'I know who you are, of course,' her neighbour opened the conversation, 'so it's only fair that you should know who I am. A sort of nephew. My mother's a cousin – a step-cousin, rather – of our hostess. I am not allowed to call her Aunt, however. But I think that makes me respectable, don't you agree?'

'Just,' agreed Julie. 'What do you do apart from being a sort of nephew?' He overtopped her easily, and bent his head respectfully towards her before taking up his soup-spoon. He was rather fair, with greenish eyes, she could see, and he looked young – as it seemed to Julie, younger than herself. To a foreigner he would probably have seemed a handsome young man with a gay, almost schoolboyish manner; but he was a so identifiable type of Austrian that to Julie he made little impression of a separate personality.

'I am a civil servant. Not a very good one, nor a high-up one like Krassny. But my people were always soldiers, so brains are not our speciality. It's the purest chance that I'm not a soldier myself. I didn't like the modern uniforms. Such luck, now that everyone talks war. Civil servants never get killed in wars.'

'Do you always talk like an upside-down hussar in a Molnár play? Or is that just your party piece?'

He sighed. 'It's become a habit. I was at the University in England for two years and got used to the idea that Vienna was a place in an operetta. Since then I find it works like a charm. But not with you – I'm sorry about that. I might have known better than to try anything so amateurish on a real live professional.'

'You're quite right – I can't stand amateur theatricals. But tell me, is Dr Krassny still a civil servant? I thought he was suspended?'

'Oh, no, indeed. That was only the excitement of the moment. He was reinstated the very next day, so our hostess tells me. In time to go to the great reception and give it, with some others, naturally, an air of correctness.'

'And everyone is talking war, are they? Not to me, or at any rate, not so far.'

'It's our Viennese provincialism, that's all. We think we are the centre of the world and if anything happens to us, that must precipitate enormous happenings.'

Julie glanced up from her food to acknowledge this local joke, and saw that Krassny was watching her and listening across the table to what they said. There was no reason at all why he should not listen; it was the events of the previous weeks that caused the feeling of uncertainty and distrust she had. But she attached this feeling, perhaps because it was the first time she felt it in a social situation, to Krassny and it remained with her so that years later the sight of Krassny's face or even his name pronounced by someone else, could reproduce in her an unease that in itself soon became so normal that she took it quite for granted. It became, in fact, the atmosphere of ordinary living.

'There was a von Kasda at school with me,' Julie said, to change the subject. 'Would that have been your sister?'

'I expect so. There's a horde of them, all over the place.'

'You mean, there are two or three?'

'Four in fact.' He grinned sideways at her and they both laughed again. The laughter sounded out of place; this dark, impressive apartment with its devotional air was always a little oppressive to Julie. She and Franz had made good-natured jokes about the all-pervading air of religion at the Pohaiskys' which Franz had pretended to find strange in a lawyer's household. It was the only table at which grace was normally said before every meal where Julie was a frequent guest. At the thought of Franz and the past,

Julie's face changed a little, and the young man beside her wondered what he had said that did not please her. But her other neighbour spoke and she turned dutifully to talk to him. He was saying something in a measured deep voice about looking forward to the new production, now imminent and much advertised, of *Doll's House* and went on in rolling periods, saying he had had the pleasure of watching Julie act many times, and recounting some of them. Krassny opposite talked to an elderly woman who might be, and in fact was, the wife of Julie's neighbour. Coming late she had not caught the name when introduced to them, but she remembered now that Frau Pohaisky said 'my brother-in-law' and 'my sister-in-law'.

As they rose from the table the old parlour-maid whispered to Julie that a telephone call had come for her during the meal and she was asked to call the theatre. At once the feeling of uncertainty and distrust came back but it was only the time of a fitting that had to be changed. Fina had passed on the information as to her whereabouts; Julie asked about this, a question that would not have occurred to her a week or so before.

'No, it is by no means as simple as that,' Krassny was saying as she came into the drawing-room. He stopped courteously as Frau Pohaisky rose and took Julie down the room where the brother of four sisters sat with his coffee. Krassny's expression as they left him with the brother and sister-in-law conveyed that it must be some frivolous feminine matter that caused his hostess to abandon his intellectual conversation. They could hear his voice continue and compete for influence over the room with the other man.

'My brother-in-law has been retired before the pensionable age,' explained Frau Pohaisky with the slightest suspicion of irony, affectionate and melancholy irony, in her voice. 'He was thought to be too K and K evidently, and found himself with a Party Order and his full pension from one day to the next.'

'The Party Order must have annoyed him as much as the — ah — termination of his judgeship?' guessed Kasda. They spoke in the normal undertone of social conversation so that nothing of what they said could be heard outside their group.

'He did not dare refuse that, but he has appealed against his retirement on the ground that it is unconstitutional. His appointment was for life.'

'That won't help him much from what I've heard,' Julie answered Margarete Pohaisky. She drank coffee, strong and black, from a tiny cup so delicate that the dark liquid could be seen through the porcelain.

'The appeal court bench will push his papers to and fro for a few months,' said Kasda, 'so that neither they nor himself can get into trouble over it.'

'He hasn't the least idea, poor chap, how useless, even how dangerous, such a gesture could be,' Frau Pohaisky shook her head. 'We, unfortunately, know already just how impotent we are. I find myself envying those who don't yet know.'

At this opening Julie raised her eyebrows slightly to question the propriety of speaking before Kasda and Frau Pohaisky answered with a movement just as unnoticeable, that it was safe.

'I've been asking about, very discreetly,' said Julie. 'I gather it will take some time, even to start any inquiries. But when things have settled down, as everybody is saying, I believe I can move one or two people to see what they can do.'

'Alois was still in Austria a week ago,' said Kasda, putting down his cup, 'but I think he was about to be moved then. I dare not ask openly, having a family interest.'

'You must be very cautious,' Frau Pohaisky warned both of them. 'They told me to do nothing or it would be bad for Alois. Good God, what times we live in!'

'This man from Hamburg who has been put into the theatre seems disposed to do anything he can for us.' Julie and Kasda accepted more coffee and she waited until the maid was gone to the other group. 'Maris Pantic has become very friendly with him – you wouldn't know her, Margarete – and she introduced me. He made it clear at once that he has both the power and the will to keep us as happy as possible. That was what he said.'

'I expect he can, too,' agreed Margarete Pohaisky. 'Of course these new people want to keep all forms of cultural life going intact, to cover their other activities.'

More experienced people could have told her that the new people did not particularly want to cover their activities, for the spreading of vague fear was a part of their method. What they needed was an appearance of enthusiastic acceptance and continuity for which public and cultural life was of the first importance.

'But I'm afraid it may be a long business,' Julie warned her. 'Don't count on anything, Margarete, will you?'

'I only wish I could do as much for you,' answered Frau Pohaisky, and laid her thin hand for a moment over Julie's. Julie frowned quickly and looked away, shaking her head, but Frau Pohaisky went on.

'You've heard nothing, then?'

Julie pressed her lips together and shook her head again with the assumed look of one determined not to give in to grief. Long experience of the frivolity of society, as much as the presence of Kasda, a stranger, made her dissemble even with Frau Pohaisky. Her daily dealings with colleagues had taught her years ago that any secret, to be kept, must be known either to everyone or to no one at all. Nobody but herself and Fina must ever suspect that Franz had returned; as Fina said on her arrival back from Mauterndorf, what people don't know they can't talk about. Her own thoughtlessness in speaking of Alois Pohaisky himself to Maris and Kerenyi had shown her, too, how hard it is for those untrained in conspiracy to watch their tongues all the time. A stubborn silence was the only safety, even if it had to be maintained for months.

'I expect his letters are being confiscated at the Czech border,' she said now for Kasda's benefit. 'I may not hear for a long time, I suppose.'

After a moment they all began to talk about trivial matters in a tone of lightness that at least two of the three of them were far from feeling, but which confirmed Dr Krassny in his notion that they must be talking casual gossip. The other group were quite loudly discussing politics in an indiscreetly frank way, but Krassny and the ex-judge still thought themselves the serious persons there. Presently Kasda got up and Krassny left with him; they walked away together and this meeting had important consequences for von Kasda for later. When Krassny needed someone for an appointment whom he could trust because he was of his own kind, he thought of young Kasda.

BOOK TWO

June 1939

1

*O*nce the public outrages were stopped after the first few days of the new order, and the wave of arrests was over, anyone who disappeared did so secretly, silently. They were not many, for the original arrest lists were fairly comprehensive, and were swamped in the general reorganisation and excitement of change. Both the excesses and the public protests caused by them seemed to belong to that short upheaval when with efficient speed all the professions were affiliated to the organisations of the Reich. Trades unions became National Socialist organs, new faces and new rules were substituted for former habits. The new rules were often simpler than the old ones so that people could easily approve of them. The ambitious joined the Party, the way to preferment; at that time this step was no more than deferring to stupid or vulgar superiors is to the ambitious in every city of the civilised world. Georg Kerenyi entered the Chamber of Journalism without whose approval he could not write, and applied for membership of the Party. It was not his fault that he did not, in fact, join the NSDAP; nobody wanted the responsibility of sponsoring a man with his reputation for opposition and his irony of manner.

During that year Julie heard from Franz only by enclosures in Fina's letters from her brother. These enclosures were dry, affected and artificial as any message must be that may be read by strangers. They were few, for it was dangerous although letters were rarely opened inside the country except on specific suspicions. If Franz Wedeker was still sought, it was not inside Austria. Three weeks after Franz left Vienna, Julie was able to travel to Graz to see her mother and took with her a new servant girl for the household: Ruth, frightened, silent and docile. Domestic service was one of the few jobs the girl could be registered for, and it was impossible to leave her in her new home without a pretext, a minor with no apparent means.

In the first months, Julie suffered, waiting for letters, longing for the chance to visit Franz which did not come. As the loss of physical love was dulled she became harder, less tolerant, more nervous without knowing why.

For pampered, highly cultivated people physical love is the only contact with human or animal reality. Those who are never ill and have no children, both of which states tie humans to their physical nature, have only this strong and slender contact with their roots. Julie lost this contact and her whole life was drawn into the interpretation of reality, the theatre; she became noticeably more polished, and though her time was as filled as it always had been with invitations, compliments and activity, it was also colder, more considered. There was a moment every evening when she reached her hand to be kissed and then was alone. In the happy years men had constantly made unwelcome advances to Julia Homburg; gradually now there grew up an unspoken and uncomprehended barrier only increased by her beauty, which produced awe instead of a desire to disturb its calm. At first she deliberately isolated herself for fear of saying something indiscreet that could endanger Franz. Reserve became habit and finally Franz and his safety were only a background to a loneliness that hardened and froze from week to week.

Late one evening in June several of the company left the Akademietheater after the performance to go to a party given by Friedrich Lehmann. He had quite been adopted by now. They tolerated him because he protected them from a more rigorous rule from Berlin by his presence; they also laughed at him. Those of the company who had mean natures were malicious and sarcastic to Lehmann, the generous were grateful to him and even showed their gratitude sometimes. Julie belonged by turns to both these factions; she shared the covert resentment at his protectiveness but her common-sense made her grateful too.

'Summer is really here at last,' Lehmann greeted them as they trooped up the curved stairway of his pretty little town house, a small rococo palace he had found in the 8th District and renovated. It was in fact very warm for almost the first time that season.

'He would have to say it,' muttered Willy Mundel behind Julie.

'Oh, look, everything's open. How lovely!' cried Julie, to cover this remark which echoed louder than it should have in the panelled doorway. Mundel had been drinking during the last act.

All the windows were open to the dark, scented evening. The still and heavy air which would soon be crowded with the scents of women and cigarette smoke and the odour of wine was filled with lime and syringa scents from the walled garden. Well inside the candle-lit room, not quite playing hostess, Maris Pantic was standing talking to the Director of the Burg.

Casimir Schoenherr took Julie's hand in both his soft, cushiony ones and patted it familiarly.

'You get more beautiful,' he said indulgently, as if this were an endearing weakness of Julie's. He cultivated an intimate fatherly manner with all actresses. Nobody had ever been known to succeed in using him through a greater intimacy than he showed to every woman, so that there was a general belief supported by nothing but a number of apocryphal stories, that he was impotent. 'See the garden with me from the big window.' He slipped a fat arm around Julie's waist and led her flirtatiously towards the shadowy bay.

'What is it, Maris?' asked Hansi Ostrovsky, passing her to go to the table with a champagne glass.

'I'm afraid he's going to tackle her here and now about the divorce,' Maris whispered, turning her slight dark neck towards the pair in the window.

'Of course he won't. He's not a complete fool,' Hansi said. But his brows came down in a look of anxiety and he moved towards the bay. The two were talking about the moonlight, which was indeed lovely and tranquil on the trees, but Hansi began to talk about the performance that evening at the Burgtheater.

'They ought to change that bit in the first act,' he said to Schoenherr after a remark or two about the lovely evening. 'The page has twice got in Hella's way by stumbling with the staff he carries.'

Schoenherr had been at that evening's performance at the Akademie, the smaller house of the Burg company, and had not seen the incident Hansi was speaking of.

'Why?' he asked with surprise, smiling at Hella. 'Who plays the page?'

The apparently meaningless question showed, as Schoenherr was fond of showing, that he knew every scrap of gossip that went on in his 'menagerie' as he often called the company to their faces.

Hella dimpled softly at him, looking prettily confused, 'It's quite clear you know who plays him,' she said, 'you wicked old thing.'

Schoenherr's heavy creases dissolved and reassembled as he laughed. He was short, and though his shrewd old eyes could look straight into Hella's, had to look up at Julie.

'She shouldn't trifle with young girls' affections, should she, Julie?' he asked.

'On the contrary,' replied Julie, willingly playing their game, out of habit. 'It will do Anita Silovsky good. Though I agree with Hansi that the page doesn't have much point just there. I don't see why he – or she – shouldn't stand still, a little farther downstage, instead of moving about.'

'But the movement makes a break in the tension just there,' objected Hansi. He agreed with what Julie said and they all knew it, but the producer of that play was his rival and therefore could not be openly attacked.

'That's exactly it, Hansi,' said Julie quickly, knowing what was wanted of her. 'It does break the tension and that's what's wrong with it. Hella's next line is absolutely crucial to the character and she brings it out just right, very quietly. If she bellowed the line, the business with the staff would increase the effect of disquiet. But the effect is created by the audience getting Hella's meaning just a second later. Don't you see? That's why the movement is out of place.' She smiled at Schoenherr. 'It's what you always call over-producing.'

'I'll come and have a look next time it's played,' promised the director.

At the other end of the room someone switched on a lamp and Hella's mother, with Willy Mundel, and Weber, the chief account-ant who had been new to the Burg a year ago but was by now a familiar figure to them all, busied themselves at a square table to play cards.

'Your turn to cut, Frau Schneider,' said Willy. He swallowed his large brandy quickly. Near the door, Maris was greeting Georg Kerenyi, whom she had not seen for some months. She flushed deeply as he took her hand, which trembled a little, and looked up imploringly into his ironical smile.

'Well, my dear?' he said and then, bored with the idea of teas-ing her, he dropped her hand without kissing it, smiled again briefly and turned to greet his host who had come up.

'My dear fellow,' said Lehmann cordially. 'I'm glad you could come.'

'I've never seen the inside of the house before,' said Kerenyi, nodding his nose at the room. 'You've certainly done a job with it. I'd noticed the house being done up and wondered who had bought it.'

'You live near here, then?' asked Lehmann, pleased. 'It was a horrible mess. This ceiling had to be completely redone. Dry rot, you know. But oddly enough most of the panelling was all right.'

They turned up their heads to view the ceiling.

'Come and look at the next room,' offered the proud owner. 'That's very pretty, I think.'

They all three strolled across the room and through a little oval sitting-room.

'Verr-y nice!' said Kerenyi, pushing his lower lip out and nod-ding to express high approval. 'Your wife will be delighted when she arrives,' he could not resist adding. It was a standing joke that Frau Lehmann was always coming from her Hamburg home and never got to Vienna.

'Yes. Yes, indeed.' Lehmann was nervous and smiled, passing a large smooth hand over his glossy pale hair. He glanced sideways at Maris behind Kerenyi's back.

'We . . . I thought of making this a little dining-room,' he said. 'Don't you think so, Maris?'

His self-conscious manner as he asked Maris's opinion when they all knew that he had bought and renovated the house entirely at her wish almost made Kerenyi laugh aloud. The point having been made that Kerenyi was, though just an acquaintance, accepted and welcomed by the representative of the Party, they all three returned to the larger room and Kerenyi went up to Julie.

'Ah, Kerenyi,' said Schoenherr graciously. 'That was a most amusing pastiche you did on Molnár. I haven't seen you since, to tell you – I thought it very good.' The others looked at each other with covert amusement. It was nearly six months since Kerenyi's fifth act to *Olympia* had been a success at the Burgtheater winter ball, but the director wished to show Kerenyi that he did not really belong.

'It's going to be published, didn't you say, Georgy?' asked Hansi, offering him his cigarette case.

'Zsolnay is bringing it out with a couple of other bits and pieces,' agreed Georgy. 'May I dedicate them to you, Julie?'

'I should love you to,' Julie smiled sweetly at him. 'It's your turn now to be shown the garden, though. Come and look.'

They moved to the window. In the garden the trees rustled softly, bathed in the bland moonlight which made the dark under the foliage black. The perfume of a mass of syringa welled up to them; a nightingale faltered two experimental trills. Behind them the room was full of babble. Then the glad song of the bird poured suddenly from its tiny throat in a long cadence. Julie leaned against the window-frame; she was filled with a dreadful yearning for love by the amorous warm scented night and her brows twitched down in the sharp little frown that was becoming habitual with her, as if at a sudden twinge of pain. Kerenyi stood beside her staring out at the darkness. He muttered something under his breath and she roused herself and looked at him.

'What did you say?'

'I said what hell life is,' he repeated loudly, and turned away abruptly into the room.

Julie stood, the night pouring over her, and felt a sickening weariness at the thought of returning to the bustle of pleasure behind her. Everything she did and said appeared suddenly artificial; her little manoeuvre in Hansi's cause looked now like a trick against the other producer rather than an act of loyalty to her own friend. Her throat swelled and she had a sensation of panic, feeling herself about to weep, as she heard the slight stir of someone who stood beside her. She waited a moment until the tears dried in her eyes and she could command herself before she turned; but whoever it was had gone again as quietly as he came.

Julie left Lehmann's party early, and after she went out they discussed her as people always do discuss those who are known to be unhappy.

'Is she not well?' asked Hella Schneider in an undertone meant to be heard. 'I thought she looked—'

'There's nothing the matter with Julie,' said Hansi Ostrovsky in what was meant to be a decisive tone that would stop a discussion; but he said it rather too quickly and it sounded querulous as if he were complaining about an accusation.

'She's miserable,' said Kerenyi, shrugging his shoulders. He pointed his big nose at a very young girl near him and added, 'Come and dance, Anita.' The sound of soft music could be heard from the oval room.

'Her face is changing, though, you can say what you like,' said Hella defiantly.

She spoke loudly enough to be sure both Hansi and Kerenyi would hear her as they moved away. 'She needs a lover.'

As she spoke she looked at Maris, who flushed and slipped her hand under Lehmann's arm. He patted her hand, looking down at her fluffy head as she pulled him towards the dancing and away from Hella. Maris was unsure of her influence over Lehmann still, but she continued to feed his need to feel strong by her weakness. She had been offered three new parts for next season; but although Hella had only one new part in the last months, she and everyone else continued to consider Maris her inferior and Hella was convinced as always of her own success. She began to talk now to a young man she had not met before, about her last film.

He was a charming young man and Hella did not notice that, though he smiled and flirted with her, making compliments about her film success, he constantly glanced over her shoulders to the door where Julie had disappeared, expecting her to come in again. But Julie did not come back; he should have taken the chance while she stood at the window but something in her still reserve had stopped him speaking to her.

Maris and Lehmann danced slowly; he stroked her upper arm, feeling intense pleasure from its thinness. Through her silk dress — she always wore loose clothes which made her seem even more fragile than she was — he could feel her slack little breasts and narrow thighs when he pressed her body against his own big, solid frame. He longed for the party to be over, in spite of his pride in his newly decorated house and in being host to such a gay company of well-known people.

As Julie let herself in to the silent apartment in Schellinggasse, she saw a line of light under the kitchen door and a moment later heard a man's voice speak.

Fina was in her woollen dressing-gown, with her black plait of hair over one shoulder. Behind her a chair scraped and a big broad man dressed in leather breeches and a peasant jacket with black bordering could be seen lumbering to his feet. On the kitchen table was his black pointed felt hat with a broad green band and a badger's brush at the back.

'It's my brother, gnae' Frau,' said Fina. The big man did not know what to do with his enormous brown hands.

'What is it?' said Julie sharply, the little twitch of her brows coming and going that gave her face what Hella Schneider had once called a fierce look. Then holding out her hand, 'Good evening, Herr Moosbauer. How are you?'

'It's the Herr Doctor,' said the big peasant without waiting for formalities. 'He's all right in himself,' he added hastily. 'But they've quartered a whole regiment near us. Training manoeuvre they call it.' He looked at his sister for help, pulled out a crumpled coloured handkerchief, looked at it, and pushed it back in his breeches pocket.

Julie came forward into the harsh white light of the kitchen. 'But does that matter?' she asked vaguely. A half-empty glass with foam clinging inside it stood on the scrubbed table. 'Has Fina given you something to eat? I hope she has. You've had a long journey.'

She could hardly take her eyes off his spade-like hands but moved them quickly, fearing to embarrass him. She looked at his lapel and was fascinated to see there the little emblem of a Party member.

'I didn't know you were a member of the Party,' she said.

'Of course. I have to be. No knowing what wouldn't have happened by now, if I hadn't been in with 'em.' He had a deep reverberating voice and Julie felt sure he sang in the church choir. She seated herself by the table on one of the four hard chairs, and moved her hand, but neither of the others sat down.

'I don't quite understand ...' she began.

'The Wehrmacht have taken over the land ...' began Fina impatiently.

'Not the Wehrmacht,' corrected her brother in his deep voice. 'They'd be all right, I make no doubt. These are SS troops. A sergeant is to be billeted on us — I don't like the look of him. Benda, his name is. Ulrich Benda from Vienna here. He wants to move in next week.'

Ulrich — thought Julie and a faint unpleasant memory stirred that she could not place at once. Then she remembered.

'Has he got queer light eyes?' she asked apparently inconsequentially. Moosbauer stared at her, then remembered his manners and shifted his gaze uneasily.

'Yes, he has,' he agreed. 'It's his eyes I don't like. Do you know him then, gnae' Frau?'

'I saw a man called Ulrich once,' said Julie and the sharp little frown showed again. She was conscious of a headache. She said to Fina, 'We must get Franz away from this Ulrich!'

There was a silence. Fina pushed with the toe of her felt slipper at a slight unevenness in the tiling of the floor.

'Herr Doctor will have to come back here,' she said. Julie parted her lips to say something. Instead she moved her hand again at the empty chairs standing askew by the table.

'Do sit down,' she said irritably. 'Drink your beer, Herr Moosbauer.' They scraped chairs as they reluctantly sat down. 'Wouldn't it be better to get him over the Tyrol border. He could go to Switzerland.'

'Nothing has happened here for months now,' said Fina, loudly and obstinately.

'I must think,' pleaded Julie, putting up a hand to her head.

'One of their officers was round to-day, asking all manner of questions,' said Moosbauer. 'I wouldn't have come frightening you like this if I hadn't thought it was serious.' He sounded defensive. Julie began to protest her complete confidence in him, which was indeed true for he was not only making a handsome profit out of Franz but discovery would mean utter ruin to him. The least that would happen if Franz was caught on his property would be the loss of farm and land that had belonged to his wife's fathers for time out of mind. Even if he wanted to, he could not denounce Franz now, for too many local people had seen the stranger and an anonymous denunciation would be just as dangerous as if he turned the fugitive in himself openly.

'I'll come back with you, to-morrow,' said Fina in a bullying tone meant for Julie's ears. 'You can drive us in the truck to – to Baden, or somewhere. We can get a bus into the town from there.' She turned to her mistress. 'Yes, that's the best thing.'

There was a long silence. Moosbauer looked helplessly at his beer but did not venture to drink it.

'Yes,' whispered Julie at last. 'We shall have to risk it.'

She stood later, staring out of the living-room window with a long glass of brandy and water in her hand – she needed it for her sleeping pill, for to-morrow there was a dress-rehearsal and she could not risk a possible sleepless night – and relived the dark, dewy softness of Lehmann's garden and the bird's song. Now idealised, the almost childishly erotic happiness of her life with Franz was equated in her mind with the nearly palpable scent of syringa and the trilling of the nightingale's call. If only we could go back and live like that, she thought, if only people would leave us alone.

A sound roused her from her reverie; it was Fina going into the narrow dressing-room to get Franz's boot-jack without which her brother could not take off his boots; the discreet sound of doors opening and closing and slippered steps to and fro broke her dream. She found herself wondering why she had never thought before of getting Franz over the border into south Tyrol and from there into Switzerland. Yes, but we ought to have done it ages ago, she thought indignantly. Why did it not occur to us? Now it's too late.

It was no more too late now than it had been a year ago. Franz acquiesced then in Fina's plan and went to her brother's, and there had never been a moment when another plan offered itself to remove him over the border, where the Italian authorities would allow him into Switzerland or where he could take a ship. Franz had never expressed a desire to leave his homeland; Fina was concerned to keep him in her own family circle, if not at home. Julie had gone on from day to day, accepting what was done and acting only when it was clear she must. Now, when it was obvious that she and Fina were acting for Franz — Julie had not even asked whether Franz knew of Moosbauer's journey but had taken it, without evidence, for granted — it occurred to her to wonder at her husband's passivity. He never had enforced his will, it was true, but in the past he did not need to. Perhaps he, too, accepted what was done? The assumption that he made decisions just because he was a man, was evidently not correct. Did anyone make decisions? Pohaisky became a lawyer because his father founded a law firm; had Franz gone into politics because nothing more interesting offered in the restricted life of the shrunken post-war country and because he had the money to do as he pleased? Had Kerenyi, leaving the no-longer-existing army with Franz, gone into journalism for the same reason inverted — he could make politics only through publicity, having no money? Their politics were singularly ineffective; in fact, a means of passing the time? These astonishing heresies led to yet another idea. It was Fina who had just made the decision that Franz was to come back to Vienna; she, Julie, had only agreed to it. Was she dependent on Fina, then? Were they both – were millions of people, dependent on those who simply did things in moments of crisis, not stopping to reason but deciding on what seemed obvious to a limited view? That Fina was Julie's dependant was a fixed fact. But Julie could not work without Fina, and Fina made decisions for her and for Franz, it seemed.

It would be better for Franz to cross the border than to return to Vienna. But Julie could not appear in the village near Mauterndorf without risking recognition. Moreover, she had a dress-rehearsal in the morning and she could not leave Vienna without it being noticed – the less real influence on their own affairs the public had, the more they concerned themselves with trivialities and the formal rebuke Julie would receive at cutting a dress-rehearsal would certainly appear in the theatrical columns of the Vienna papers. Franz would not leave of his own free will; and she could not persuade him unless he came back – was brought back – to the city she could not leave.

The sleeping pill – months ago Dr Moller had prescribed the same tablets once so guiltily offered by Willy Mundel – began to work, making Julie dizzy. She slept without taking her thoughts any further towards considering the personal implication of Franz's return to Vienna.

2

And the following day Julie had no time for anything but work. The apartment seemed strange at night, with Fina away; this reminded Julie that when Franz arrived in the evening next day, she would be at the theatre. It seemed all wrong, but there was nothing to be done about it except buy flowers and leave messages, inadequate messages, in the hall and the living-room.

An interior excitement began which made her impatient to leave as the last curtain fell, but she did not understand the sly jokes Director Schoenherr made on the subject of this impatience and its possible private source until she was in the taxi when his ludicrous rightness – and wrongness – made her laugh to herself.

The twitch of the curtain over the inside window of the care-taker's lodge – did they never go to bed? – brought anxiety; had Fina managed so that Frau Pichler saw nothing?

The hall was silent, it seemed chill too. Somehow, Julie expected Fina and Franz to be awaiting her there. Instead there was only a suitcase in the hall. It was not cold, but she shivered with tight nerves and the impulse, strong as she unlocked the door, to run down the hall, disappeared.

The lamps were lit; the room empty. Impatience, already mixed with anxiety, became incomprehension; and now slid instanta-neously into dismay. She closed the door of the long room with a new caution produced by that twitch of a curtain. After a moment's pause, Franz stepped out from the shadow in the far end of the book-cases where the lamp was not switched on. In spite of a deep tan and country clothes with their air of health, this was the man waiting in the dark hall a year and more before, hunted and afraid. The Franz of happy memories, the dreaming and illusions of the last months, the impatience of the last hour were gone for ever. No lover was here inspired by the song of nightingales and the scent of syringa; a fugitive, mistrustful, withdrawn, watched her from a safe corner.

This was not the Franz of Julie's memory, but the Franz of the one event she did not want to recall, the event that had, she recognised by remembering the look in his face, changed him. What had been easy for her to overlook, forget, had changed him not for that day but for ever. This was a man who jumped from a train on to a cindery bank, lost his hat, dared not go to a restaurant known for years; crept back into his native city by stealth. For over a year of peace and safety that event had worked in his mind. Isolated in the windy uplands in the deep activity of 'doing nothing' as the peasants called it, far away from the crowded streets and the abrupt hurried contact of a million eyes, indifferent and probably hostile, there had been peace to think.

Yesterday, while Julie occupied herself with the dress-rehearsal, was a day of blue brilliance, underfoot the thick-growing flowers of the late Alpine spring, the huge granite shoulder of the bald mountain top rearing up into a sky of infinity, where wisps of cloudy white swung off the rocks to emphasise the endless openness overhead.

Not until Fina arrived with Moosbauer was the invasion of the last week admitted. That a billeting party of the SS were in the village, Franz knew, but he rarely went to the village. Moosbauer had acted fast; Franz was gone before there could be any trouble. His return to the city completed a circle begun the year before.

Words stumbled. The stumbling was immediately understood to be a permanent barrier. The forgotten event was the only reality and this stab, like a wound from a thin blade, slid into Julie's being leaving only a mark that could have been a mere scratch. The shock was so complete that the very notion of a physical embrace, or indeed any contact of emotion, never became real. The continuous conversation of marriage was dead.

At breakfast, the outside world of the city from which they could never again free themselves, crowded in insistently, enforcing continual action, continual defence.

Fina was talking to the old cleaning woman who came five days a week, and then were heard the sounds of her working in the drawing-room. This woman, a real child of the Vienna slums, had worked for them for several years, engaged and paid by Fina out of the housekeeping money, entirely Fina's concern. While Franz was bathing, Julie went to talk to Fina about household matters. It was only when Frau Kaestner came sidling in her accustomed fashion, with exaggerated humility, into the room, that it occurred to either of them that she must not see Franz. The thought struck both of them at the same instant, and they exchanged startled looks in which for the first time the whole complex problem of Franz's presence was recognised. The cleaner was murmuring something to Fina, dropping her eyes and making a little bob when Julie said good morning; and on being given some cleaning material she asked for, sidling out again, keeping her back to the wall so that she did not turn away from Julie, as if Julie were royalty. For the first time Julie was conscious that she did not like Frau Kaestner and her humble, sly way of moving.

Julie followed her out and looked about to make sure Franz had left nothing lying about. While Frau Kaestner was having her breakfast in the kitchen, Fina came and tapped on the door to say that Franz had better go to the living-room which was finished and where the woman would not need to go again. She herself was going to do the shopping. Julie was in all morning, she had letters to write, a précis of a film script to read; Franz went through letters, some of them months old, which referred to his former life. They were from friends and colleagues in other countries, asking after him, offering advice, some of it good advice; one from Colton Barber even offered practical help if he needed it. All wanted to know where he was. He read through the copies of Julie's answers too, admiring her practical good sense and the neat way she misled the inquirers without actually lying to them.

In the meantime, Frau Kaestner cleared up in the bedroom and the bathroom. She heard Fina return from marketing and carried a vase of flowers into the kitchen, to change their water.

'You're a close one,' she said.

'What do you mean?'

'Well, you might have told a body she had a man here . . .'

'A man? What are you talking about?' Fina was clumsily angry with fear.

'Oh, go on with you . . . why shouldn't she have a man, poor soul. Alone all this time, I've often felt sorry for her. 'Tisn't natural.'

'You mind your own business,' said Fina churlishly. 'There isn't any man been here, and don't you forget it.'

'All right, all right, I shan't talk. No need to lose your temper.' Frau Kaestner pulled the flowers straight in the stonework jar and turned to go, half offended and half laughing at Fina's modesty, as she took it to be. 'Just the same,' she chuckled with a lewd look as she opened the door, 'I know there's been a man 'ere.' Fina was bending over at the refrigerator with the door open so that her face was invisible; she did not answer.

When Frau Kaestner was finished for the day and was pulling on her shabby old coat, given her by Fina herself a year before and much too big for her meagre frame, Fina came in red and frowning.

'I'm missing some butter,' she said loudly. 'I want to have a look in your bag. And you've been at the drinks again. I can smell your breath.'

'Well, you are in a state to-day, aren't you,' Frau Kaestner began and then saw by Fina's face that a joke would not work. 'You never said anything before about . . .' she began whining, picking up her bulky cloth handbag with both hands and clutching it. 'It was only the drop left in the bottom of the bottle. Why shouldn't I finish it off? You're not that poor here . . . go on, don't be horrid. Don't tell on me.'

'I want to see in your bag,' repeated Fina, breathing hard. The poor old face working with anxiety and the knobbly work-worn hands clutching the pathetic bag only increased her anger. They stared at each other, then Fina put out a hard hand and twitched the bag away from Frau Kaestner.

'You can't touch my property,' cried the little woman, her lips trembling with fear and anger. 'It's an insult to a decent working woman, that's what it is. I'll have the law on you if you as much as touch it . . .'

She had begun to cry now, snivelling and wailing; of course, the butter was in the bag, hastily wrapped up in a piece of torn newspaper. Fina knew Frau Kaestner was in the habit of helping herself to scraps of food. She was too scared to take more than a handful of beans or the butter left on a dish and the petty thieving had never reached a stage where Fina would think of getting rid of a quiet and clean scrubwoman where her successor might need watching with real valuables.

'I've suspected you for some time,' said Fina, working herself into a rage, 'I'm responsible for everything in the house and I'm not going to have you picking and thieving and getting me into trouble. It'll be her clothes or the silver next! I know your sort!'

'I'll go to the Labour Exchange and complain of you,' shrilled Frau Kaestner. She sniffed loudly and wiped her nose with her soap-softened, work-distorted fingers. 'Anybody'd think a spoonful of butter would break the bank to hear you go on. She's rich enough, isn't she? I wouldn't touch anything valuable, you know that, I'm not a thief and you can't go calling me one.'

'You'll get another job easy enough,' said Fina brutally, determined to get this danger out of the way. 'I'll see she gives you a character. But you can't stay here. So there it is, and I'll pay you for the week. But you go at once and I don't want to see or hear of you again. We'll send you a reference in the post. Now you come on out of here before I get in trouble with your row. Hear you all over the house, I shouldn't wonder.' She produced her battered leather purse with the household money from her apron pocket and began counting out a week's money. Frau Kaestner watched her. The thought of getting a week's money for nothing mollified her outraged feelings and it occurred to her that she would go to the little wineshop next door in the cellar and have a glass of raw wine to soothe her dignity. Fina pushed the money towards her on the kitchen table. 'This extra is your insurance money and don't you forget to pay it and drink the lot,' she said with all the contempt of the trusted servant for the casual labour of the slums.

In the dark little cellar tavern Frau Kaestner sat for half an hour leaning her elbows on the bare table. She had a big glass of the cheapest wine, and was making it last as long as she could. The tall fat man who owned the place came and sat with her, drawing on a rank cigarette. There was no one else there. It smelt comfortingly of spilled wine and garlic sausage and was cosily dirty.

'Well, how's your fine lady?' asked the fat old man.

'She's sacked me. I've lost my job. And all for a bit of butter you could hardly see.'

'Ah, they're mean as dirt when they've got money,' he said wisely.

'But I'll get my own back on them. I'm not finished with them yet.'

'Go on with you,' said the man, 'you'll get another job. Things ain't as bad now as they used to be.' He knew it was the wine talking.

'I'll go to the papers,' she muttered darkly, 'and tell them about her fancy man. They'll pay me for what I know.' The man got up to serve a workman and left Frau Kaestner to brood on her idle words that were no sooner said than they became an idea. Why shouldn't she actually go to a newspaper? They printed bits of gossip about famous people ... she began to imagine having a vaguely large sum of money. But she didn't know anything about newspapers, how to set about it or where to go. Then she remembered that her son, whom she had not seen for several years since he went to Germany to work, once had a job driving a delivery van for the *Unabhängige*. She knew where their block of offices was.

If her weekly ticket on the tram, paid for by Fina, had not still been valid and if her way home had not led almost directly past the newspaper block, she would never have had the resolution to try it. But by the time the wine was finished her courage was high enough to make the effort. Instead of going all the way to her usual stop, she got off the tram round the corner from the big red block and went boldly up to the door-keeper sitting in his glass box.

'Yes, you'll want the fourth floor,' he said when she told him she wanted to see somebody about the theatre. Frau Kaestner was already regretting her errand, but she did not like to turn back then, under his eye, so she walked on into the building. The paternosters slipping quietly up and down frightened her; the fourth floor was a long way upstairs. She was tired by the time she reached it. There was a chair in the long corridor and she sat down for a moment to catch her breath, but got up again hastily as she heard somebody coming. It was a tall man with a big curved nose and reddish hair.

'Are you looking for somebody?' he asked, noticing her quick movement. He smiled at the meagre little woman clutching her big untidy bag.

'Yes ... I ... No, no thanks. I'm just going.'

'Don't be shy,' he said. 'Tell me what it's about and I'll tell you where to go.' He supposed she must have strayed from the staff-welfare office, some cleaner wanting a certificate for treatment of an obscure female ailment.

She was afraid not to answer him, he had such an air of authority as if he knew everything that went on about here, as indeed he did. Intimidated by the largeness of the building, still out of breath and tired by the stairs, she told the truth instead of prevaricating and got herself still deeper into what she would now have been only too glad to be safely out of.

'I want to see the theatre department,' she said with an aggressiveness, that made it sound important to herself but was pathetic to Kerenyi.

'The theatre man is not here. Come in to my room and tell me about it. I'll pass it on to the theatre critic when he comes back.'

She followed him reluctantly into the door next to the chair she had rested on. There was a card stuck into a brass frame beside the door and though she did not have time to read the name DR G. KERENYI she could read in larger letters on the door above it LITERARY EDITOR. She could not know that it was simple boredom that had made Kerenyi speak to, or even see her in the first place, and imagined some official note in his invitation.

He indicated a chair on the outer side of a big flat writing-table and seated himself in the swivel chair behind the table, picking up a pencil to play with. He caught sight of an unfinished piece of work lying on his blotter, and pushed it impatiently aside. He was irritable with himself for asking this odd little body into his room; he had her placed now and could guess from her defensive and aggrieved manner that she had just been sacked since that is the usual reason for cleaners and washer-women coming to newspaper offices and using the words Frau Kaestner now used.

'I've got some important information about a — about somebody important.' Obscurity to the poor and ignorant always appears serious and respectable, since official pronouncements are always to them obscure.

'Somebody in the theatre world, I suppose that would be?'

'Yes,' she said, settling her bag more comfortably on her lap. 'An actress.'

'Well, out with it then,' he said idly. 'I know them all. Tell me something I don't know.'

'I want to be paid,' she brought out desperately. 'How much will you ...'

He waved the pencil he was playing with. 'I can't know if it's worth anything to us until I know what it is.'

'She's got a lover there in the house.'

'Hardly news. Who hasn't!'

'Not this one. Never since her husband went. I know. I made the beds.'

'Since her husband went?' He was so startled that he repeated her words. There was only one actress that could mean; of any one of twenty others she would have said since she separated from or divorced or left her husband.

'Who is it?'

'I didn't see him, but he's there. I could hear a man's voice.'

'I didn't mean who was the man. Who is the actress you are talking about?'

'If I tell you that you'll be as wise as I am,' she said with what she believed to be cunning.

'And if you don't tell me, I am not interested.' Kerenyi spoke with indifference.

Frau Kaestner leaned forwards in her chair. 'If I tell you will you pay me?'

He shrugged his big shoulders. 'You've been misinformed,' he said, showing his disgust. 'We don't use this sort of gossip. This is a serious newspaper.' He saw this was a mistake. If it was indeed Julie she was talking about and he sent her away she might go to one of the popular evening papers. 'But tell me and we'll see about paying.'

She shifted uneasily forward on the edge of the chair and lifted her shoulders. 'It's Julia Homburg,' she muttered half frightened and half pleased at referring to her employer without a title; and shrilly, 'but I want to be paid for it. I know the papers pay for information — I used to work at the Theater an der Wien, so I know.' It was a lie; her sister had once been a cleaner at the operetta theatre, many years before.

She watched the man, who considered her, as it were, past his big nose as if she were an object of no interest.

'How do I know you are telling me the truth?' he asked idly.

'I've worked there three years.' She stopped herself saying she had just been fired. 'I can describe the apartment. If you know all these people, you'll know where they live, won't you?'

'What's the name of Frau Homburg's cook?'

'Fina,' she said triumphantly.

'And the address?'

'Schellinggasse. They have a big flat on the second floor. When she's home she always uses the big room with all the books, that's where they were this morning, talking away; I could hear them.' She paused, aware that sitting in a room with books was no proof of immorality, only of eccentricity. 'He was in the bathroom a long time and then he went back into the bedroom and then I heard them in the living-room. That's what she calls the big room, though it's more of a library, really.'

It was obvious she knew what she was talking about. Kerenyi reached into his trouser pocket where he carried money loose and produced a hundred-mark note.

'Here,' he said. 'That's what it is worth.' Frau Kaestner had day-dreamed of a huge sum of money, but a hundred marks was to her, when it was actually held before her eyes, a very large sum indeed. She earned less than a mark an hour for working hard at menial tasks that others thought beneath them. She put out a shaky hand. The note was twitched away, out of reach.

'You understand, don't you,' said Kerenyi in a new, coldly professional voice that made him sound to Frau Kaestner 'like a doctor' as she would have put it, 'this is useless if anybody else knows it? It's just between ourselves. You understand?'

'Yes, I understand,' she said sullenly, staring at the note, afraid he would think of putting her off with less.

'All right, then. Here, take it. If you have anything else to tell, come straight to me. Don't go anywhere else. Understand?'

She nodded, never taking her eyes off the money. As she took it she made a little bob, as she had done when Julie spoke to her. She began to thank him incoherently, shuffling towards the doorway and asking permission to leave. He nodded at her and she closed the door very quietly and scuttled off down the stairs before he could change his mind and reverse her unbelievable stroke of luck.

Kerenyi sat playing with his pencil. Once he put out a hand to the telephone and drew it back. As he picked up the pencil again, something struck him. A casual pick-up from some party would not have stayed all night with Julie to be seen by the servants. He was fairly sure that Julie was not having a serious love affair, or even an unserious one, for he must have heard or seen some sign of intimacy. A man who stayed all night, whom Fina was allowed to know about? Kerenyi suddenly felt as if his head had gone quite cold.

3

'*I*'m very glad you didn't say anything to her at my party, but we'll have to broach the matter to her somehow; and soon.'

Lehmann took two paces away from Schoenherr's chair and that brought him to the window, where he turned and faced the director again. He could see that Schoenherr was about to make a suggestion which, he knew in advance, would make him uncomfortable, even unhappy.

'I think you really are the one person who can say it to her,' he added quickly.

The two men were in Lehmann's handsome office. It was clear they spoke of something already discussed without result between them.

'If the Minister hadn't actually mentioned it, we could shelve it again. But, unfortunately this is the only case in the company that hasn't solved itself. I mean, Frau Schneider's second husband — she's been divorced five years so that can't be taken as evidence of our zeal. Pellman and Klein have both left Vienna, and Frau Ungar is already retired. Frau Schneider — the mother, I mean — her husband is dead. Thank goodness he wasn't Hella's father. The only case left, which makes it so noticeable, is Frau Homburg's.' Lehmann had said all this before on his return from a duty visit in Berlin, and had listened several times to Schoenherr saying the same things.

'You don't think it is something a woman could handle more

easily?' Schoenherr turned in his chair to face Lehmann who paced to and fro. His fat body was uncomfortable, twisted as it was, and the creases of his face took on a deeper melancholy. 'Hella's mother, now; or Maris?'

'I don't think ... Maris would be too ... And I don't know that Frau Schneider would be willing.'

'She'd do it if I asked her to, I think,' said Schoenherr. He supposed that Lehmann knew what he was speaking of, but a look of inquiry made him explain. 'I arranged her teaching job at the Academy — after her voice went, you know. That was years before your time. I believe she would be glad — willing, at any rate — to do something for me in return.'

He stared in front of him, envisaging this idea in action, pushing out his under lip.

'She'd have to do it as if it were an indiscretion; as if it just popped out. They have never been intimate.'

'Then how would Frau Schneider bring it up?'

'Oh, they meet often, like all of us,' said Schoenherr vaguely. He did not like discussing his methods of controlling his 'menagerie'.

'Well, if she would do it ... How soon do you think ...?'

'Mm. A day or so, I suppose.'

'Or Ostrovsky? Wouldn't he be ...'

'Oh, no, not Ostrovsky,' said Schoenherr, sounding quite shocked. He shook his head decisively. 'Oh, on no account Ostrovsky.'

'Well, let's give it a couple of days to see if Frau Schneider can manage it discreetly. If not, one of us will have to tackle it.' Lehmann meant that Schoenherr would have to tackle it. He nodded at his desk where on top of the litter of papers a confidential memorandum from the Ministry of Culture lay. 'I can avoid answering that for a day or so. Let's say until the end of the week, shall we?'

Schoenherr, who never believed in wasting time, went straight from this conference to Frau Schneider's home near the Academy of Arts where she lived with her divorced daughter Hella. That evening Frau Schneider asked her daughter where 'everybody' would be on the next day. She did not explain why she wanted to know for she was too much indebted to Direktor Schoenherr and too much attuned to his ways of working to betray his confidence by as much as a hint and she knew her daughter's egoism too well to fear curiosity. The result, followed up by several telephone calls, was that Julie found herself greeted by Frau Schneider as she sat in the café at Sacher's having a quick luncheon by herself between a morning rehearsal and an afternoon fitting. This was a departure from the usual for Julie rarely ate outside her home at midday when she was working. And it was not only that she had to see an electrical dealer before her fitting; the change in Franz and the deep disappointment and bewilderment Julie felt at this change made her want to stay away from home even at the cost of her afternoon rest.

Frau Schneider greeted Julie with as much pleased surprise as if she had not already walked through all the public rooms of the hotel looking for the younger woman.

'I didn't expect to find you here!' she began. 'But I suppose you aren't playing to-night?'

'Yes, I am,' replied Julie, 'but I had a lot of things to see to in the town so I thought I would give myself a change.'

'I just ran into that little accountant man,' said Frau Schneider, signalling to the waiter with a gloved hand. None of the theatre people ever referred to this man, who had come to the Burg just before Lehmann came a year ago, by his name, which was Weber. He was by now a familiar figure and often to be seen at Frau Schneider's little evening parties but the habit of not including him as one of themselves had continued from his first appearance in their circle. 'Oddly enough, he was talking about you.' Frau Schneider talked on in her hoarse whisper of a voice, recounting as if it were gossip from a man she had not, in fact, seen for ten days, that Direktor Schoenherr and Lehmann had heard from the Ministry of the Interior; that the Party was certain Franz Wedeker was still alive although all trace of him was lost. It was believed that he had changed his name at once on his arrival in Prague a year and more ago. 'But of course,' she interrupted herself, 'you must know all this better than I do ...'

Julie said nothing, wondering at the deviousness of the Party machine and waiting for the point of this conversation which came, as she knew it would, after a pause.

'They'll insist on you divorcing him now,' said Frau Schneider, apparently concerned only with pouring cream into a cup of chocolate. But she was forced to look up at Julie's face.

'Divorce him?' Julie stared blankly into the shrewd indifferent eyes enfolded in a mass of wrinkles. She recovered herself. 'How can I divorce him when nobody knows where he is?' she said. Frau Schneider looked her over, bleakly.

'Well, you know best about that,' she said. Clearly nobody believed in Julie's ignorance of her husband's whereabouts, as she might have known they would not. But equally, she was aware, nothing could be proved; there had been no letters to intercept, no messages except through Fina, and Fina had not been interrogated, or searched on journeys to her home. Since the two Gestapo agents had come, late at night, and searched the flat, nothing had been heard of the police either officially or by the roundabout means that were used to control prominent persons who, while not being open opponents of the Party, might be considered to have reason not to love National Socialism.

'Do you *know* I'm going to be asked to divorce Franz?' asked Julie bluntly, and stared directly into eyes that showed curiosity without in the least losing their look of indifference. 'I've heard nothing myself.'

'You are being asked now,' said Frau Schneider calmly. 'Schoenherr asked me to have a word with you to avoid the Party coming directly into it. You know how he and Lehmann try to avoid anybody putting a finger into their theatrical pie ...' There was a silence. Then, 'What shall I tell Schoenherr, when he asks me?'

'Tell ...? Oh, tell him I'm thinking it over ... yes, thinking it over.'

'The new laws make it easy for you. It's quite automatic, I believe.'

'I have things to do; I must go.'

Without attempting to conceal her anger, Julie gathered up her bag and gloves and left, so that the waiter had to run after her with her bill. Outside on the pavement she stood for a few moments to collect herself, recall what it was she had wanted so urgently to do. Then she walked across to the Graben to Hawelka's and bought a big American vacuum cleaner and an electric floor-polisher so that Fina could do the housework without help.

'There will have to be several more wall plugs installed,' she said to the dealer. 'Will you send a man to fix them?'

'Certainly, gnae' Frau. In the next day or so. Will there be somebody at home?'

'Oh, yes, my housekeeper is always there ...' Somebody at home? She changed her mind hastily. 'Well, perhaps I had better be there myself. Can you give me an exact time?'

The man went to consult a work book and returned at once. 'I can come to-morrow,' he said. 'I will come myself with the electrician – you'll want to know how much it is all going to cost. There may be a good deal of work. For instance, if any of the rooms are panelled, gnae' Frau?'

'Yes, two of them are panelled. Come in the morning, can you?'

It was arranged that the dealer should come with his workman at ten o'clock.

So it was almost evening by the time Julie came into the living-room where Franz was walking up and down. He stopped in his stride and wheeled round, speaking at once as if he had only awaited her entry to say aloud what he had been saying in his mind.

'If only I had not been in the open all the time in the last year. There isn't even a tree to be seen from the windows here!'

He breathed fast and heavily, his eyes fixed on a spot past her shoulder. His thin, handsome face was taut, its healthy tan in cruel contrast to a strain that pulled his mouth into what was almost a grimace. Julie did not at once grasp what he meant; for hours she had been thinking of the danger of Frau Kaestner having seen something of her conversation with Frau Schneider, as well as of her professional affairs. She knew that what Frau Schneider told her was Schoenherr's way of letting her know what had to be done; he had arranged for Frau Schneider to be the messenger because Frau Schneider was near enough to the centre of their world, not a dangerous outsider with nothing to lose by gossip.

This intimate understanding of her own professional world and the people in it was, however, as far as Julie's intuition reached. She was not an imaginative woman and in her relationship with Franz it had always been the man whose insight and consideration had guided them. Now, Franz's whole concern was inevitably for himself. An instinctive reversal of their former roles which might have been achieved by Julie's need of his love was prevented by the change in him, and at this moment Julie had no feeling of her husband's predicament. The imaginative reach and sympathy needed for such a consciousness on her part were made unlikely, not only by the unconscious resentment she felt at the change in Franz, but even more by the pressing urgency of making detailed and complicated arrangements in the everyday world.

These arrangements on which their lives depended – and of this Julie was aware with a strong awareness that accepted her own responsibility as the only person capable of making them – were of that minute and minor sort which are normally considered superficial. She was worrying about the delivery of the electrical equipment, its installation and the attendant difficulty of hiding Franz during the morning. More than anything she was worrying about the complex difficulties of divorcing a husband she was not only living with in the same house but who must be hidden from the whole world as well; the always threatening possibility of publicity over the divorce was more real to her than the misery of the man for whose sake she must arrange it. There was no confusion in her mind about the need to her own life to preserve her career for this knowledge did not conflict with the need to protect Franz; the two necessities were parts of the same necessity. But the achievement of them involved ignoring the psychic needs of Franz. This is a situation repeated millions of times in marriage, where the husband is concerned with the outside world and his position in it to the exclusion of the emotional needs of his wife; no more than most women did Julie now consider what was not essential to their survival; as far as she went in that direction was the decision in her own mind not to tell either Franz or Fina anything of her conversation with Frau Schneider and that was largely out of expedience rather than consideration for Franz's feelings.

'When will my trunk be here?' Franz was asking her. 'Nearly all the books I need are in it. If only I could get back to work, it might be easier ...'

'I shall have to hire a car to get them,' Julie said and frowned in concentration. 'To-morrow is no good. But I can go the next day in the afternoon, I think.' She had crossed to the big desk and was running a finger over the page of her appointment book, making the stones in her rings wink.

'Why not to-morrow?' His voice had a complaining, querulous tone that she would have found quite new if she had noticed it. 'You have no rehearsal noted for to-morrow.'

'The electricians are coming. We have to have more plugs in the wall so that Fina can use the electric sweeper.'

Franz stared at her in astonishment and, with a sensation of bitterness that was almost hatred, turned away from Julie who cared more for electric plugs than that he should have the comfort of being able to work.

'I'm not quite sure where you'd better sit while they are here, to-morrow,' Julie said, unable to keep a note of irritation out of her voice. 'They will be going to and fro in all the rooms for an hour or so, I suppose.'

'Perhaps I'd better sit in the kitchen then,' he answered bitterly. 'Or Fina might lend me her room.'

'You see, Franzl,' Julie explained, forcing gentleness into a voice that sounded strident to herself, 'if Fina is to do all the housework she has to have electric cleaners and things.'

'But what's the matter with Frau Kaestner ... Oh! I see ...'

'Hadn't you realised that?' she asked a little wearily. 'You know, Franz, I wonder – I know it sounds dreadful – but I wonder if I'd not better start trying to get you out to France or England. People are leaving. There is a regular office for emigration. If you grew a moustache and dyed your hair, perhaps? I am sure I can get you false papers ...'

'It sounds absurd. And there is apparently no sign that they are going to put these filthy Nuremberg Laws into force except where property is involved, or one of the professions.' His voice rose. 'It can't last long now. All this talk about Poland ... it must lead to war. It must. The French and British will never allow ...' He moved a long, slightly trembling hand to indicate the day's newspapers spread on the desk. 'You don't care about such things, of course. But up to now all Hitler's tricks have concerned German groups and the consolidation of the Germans in one state. If he moves into Poland – and all this polemic against the Poles can mean nothing else – that means war. And I'm quite sure, at the real threat of war his power will collapse.'

'Yes, I remember that argument. Everyone said the same thing at the move into Prague!'

'No, no,' he said eagerly. 'You don't understand. On the other side of Warsaw is the Soviet Union. They – the Russians – think of Poland as theirs, only lost for the moment by the Brest-Litovsk Treaty. They wouldn't ...'

'But Franz, all Vienna believed that Russian panslavism would never allow the Germans into Prague. It will be the same with Poland, if Hitler has the nerve to move. But in any case – if it isn't going to last long, wouldn't it be better for you to be safe until it's over?'

'I should be caught. It's impossible for me to get out.'

'Will you agree to let me try to arrange it? I am fairly sure I can ...'

'The moment you begin making inquiries they'll know whom you are thinking of. Besides, the journey here exhausted me. You don't know what it's like. I have to have a rest. I'll think about it. We don't have to do anything at once.'

'You see, it isn't these Nuremberg Laws I'm worrying about, Franz. Everyone knows they were just passed to keep the Party madmen happy and to collect Jewish fortunes for the state – and, of course, to remove competition in the professions. They won't ever be taken any further now – even Georgy Kerenyi says so. But all the prominent politicians have been taken away. Catholics and Socialists alike. Anyone who had any influence, like poor Alois Pohaisky, they're all shut up in a camp near Weimar. Everyone knows. It's an open secret.'

'Pohaisky! It just shows what political idiots these National Socialists are! Imagine troubling with a vague romantic like

Pohaisky with his Order of St Nepomuk! Building a bridge between Church and Proletariat! It's the most pathetic rubbish!'

'Surely, the point is, Pohaisky is in a camp? Whether his Order had any sense to it really doesn't matter much, it seems to me.'

'Exactly. It's a good deal better for me to be shut up here than to be shut up in a camp. I don't want any more risks. We've been wildly lucky so far – first getting to Mauterndorf and then back here.'

Julie was silent. It was true. She picked up a film script she had already decided to refuse, and began to read it through again. When the door-bell rang they both jumped.

It was the delivery of the electric carpet sweeper, the polisher and a modern electric iron.

'I shall never learn to use all this stuff,' said Fina, shaking her head at the long and bulky packages.

'The man is coming to-morrow to demonstrate them and fix the plugs,' Julie encouraged her. 'You'll soon get used to them.'

'I could manage without all these things,' muttered Fina crossly. 'And you ought to be resting.'

Julie went and lay down, but could not rest. She felt unutterably exhausted and distressed at the change in their relationship. She wanted him now, not in some unspecified future, to give him comfort and get it again from him. The rejection could not be final. She knew she was beautiful and trusted her beauty to perform the magic it had never failed to perform with Franz.

Under her self-persuasion she was aware that something fundamental had changed in Franz, but she did not yet admit this thought to herself, and neither did she admit her own resentment. She got up; she must bathe and go to the theatre. In the long wardrobe mirror she watched herself. Yes, she thought, I am a beautiful woman. But a sensation of desolating waste and regret belied the hopefulness of her conscious thoughts.

Julie had only left the house a few minutes when the door-bell rang again. Franz went to the closed door of the living-room where he could hear into the hall. He stood flat against the right-hand leaf of the double door, his head turned against the wood to catch what was said.

'Ah, Herr Doctor,' Fina said. 'Gnae' Frau has just gone out – to the theatre. It's a long play to-night and she had to go early.'

'What a pity.' It was Kerenyi's voice. 'But I'll write a note if I may.' There were sounds of him entering the hall, the door being closed. A pause, while he wrote.

'Give it to Frau Homburg when she comes in, will you, Fräulein Fina? Been investing in some new household equipment, I see. That will make life easier for you.'

'We had to get rid of the cleaner, Herr Doctor. She was thieving. They're all the same.'

The scrape of the chair by the telephone-table on the parquet. He was going again. Franz felt an impulse to go out and speak to Kerenyi so strong it seemed for a second irresistible, to establish contact again with a friend of his own world. Before his hesitation could be overcome he heard the door opening, a few more words and then the door shutting. Fina's stolid footsteps, faster than usual, came up to the door and she came in without knocking. They stood quietly, very close together. Fina bent her head, listening for the clash of the lift door.

'Are you all right, Herr Doctor?' She was whispering.

'I'm all right, Fina.' Franz touched her hand. He received a deep sensation of protection and comfort from her solid presence.

'We shall have to arrange somewhere for you to go when people come.' She was talking half to herself as she often did, going about her work.

When the electricians were due next day, Franz himself suggested that he should go with a book to Fina's little room, and sat there quite peacefully reading and smoking and making notes. Even after seventeen years there was something of the close, stuffy peasant atmosphere to Fina's room. The crucifix with a little jar of flowers under it, the narrow bed with a plain white cover, and the window looking out on the courtyard hung with thick curtains over net curtains and a row of plants along the sill between the double windows.

He had been reading for over a year for a history of the Turkish invasions that was to be more than a chronicle of battles in Hungary and the Styrian March, a record of Emperors and intrigues; it was the study of the moral strengths of the two religions and cultures that interested Franz.

When the workman was gone and Fina called him out for lunch, Franz felt as he had when returning to Vienna – as if he returned to an alien, an imprisoning convention from the liberty of his thoughts. The habits of day-to-day political life, the balance of interests, the struggle of internal party discussion, the writing of letters and making of arrangements had always bored him; he lacked the drive of self-importance and still more the love of power that makes a successful politician put up with his life of bondage.

Franz had not thought of the machinery of his career as bondage; it was only when he was forcibly freed of it that he saw it as it was; a year of liberty had shown him his real vocation. The shock of his personal disaster not only isolated him from his own kind, it released him from all the obligations of a career essentially a matter of co-operation with others, and drove him to examine the springs of men's joint actions, rather than the means by which those actions are achieved in the outer world. Was the society of Central Europe in the fifteenth and sixteenth centuries simply a matter of organisation superior to the organisation of the Balkan countries where the Turkish armies succeeded in establishing their arid domination? Did the Habsburgs succeed because they headed a strong government apparatus, an efficient military organisation? Or was the outcome of the long struggle determined by a deeper cause; the vitality of the society itself? The two opposing religions he saw now as products of the general society, not as the mainsprings of their respective cultures, but as one aspect of each of them. Society produced and maintained the mythical figures that mirrored its own essential nature; men believed that their religion bore the culture of their society but it seemed to Franz a growing certainty that something far deeper rooted in an organic society of men produced their religion as well as their arts, peaceful and warlike, their trading and their superficial conventions. That the Balkan countries were overrun not because they lacked a native organisation strong enough to throw back the alien society whose overflow of energy arising from a social and cultural aridity, drove them northward and westward, but because they lacked some confident social cohesion which would have induced them – perhaps unwillingly, a choice between evils – to accept organisation from a larger society which would in its turn have dominated them but would have left them their own character and religion to develop within the larger framework, instead of plunging themselves into the rigid stony waste of the Moslem world. Superficially, the Greeks, the Magyars and South Slavs did not and could not know how disastrous the fatalism, the absolute conservatism, of the Ottomans must be for them. The conventional view that their Christianity was too superficial to dominate their minds into organising its protection was obviously not true, for Christianity, though corrupted even more than in Western Europe, had largely survived in the Turkish domains in Europe. They had lacked the corporate vitality to make a judgment, to decide to resist in the company of stronger allies. And they lacked it up to the present day, for the financial domination of absentee capital that seeped in after the withering away of the Turkish Empire, though a life-long belief of Franz's socialism as the cause of division and poverty in the south-east, was in fact a very recent factor.

Franz was a quarter of an hour late for lunch; he was writing a list of books that Julie must order for him. Irritably he thought of various means of studying the State Archives and dismissed them as impracticable or dangerous or both. He hardly spoke at the meal, and ate little. Julie thought he was humiliated by being shut up in Fina's room and took care to be as quiet and calm as she could. Her thoughts kept returning unwillingly to a little incident with the electrician.

They had needed to install a wall plug at the stove end of the living-room among other places. This meant removing books and shelves from one of the book-cases. The workman decided where he had best install the plug and then began pulling out the books and laying them on the floor. When he lifted out the shelves Julie saw there was a large yellowish envelope laying in the hollow between the lowest shelf and the floor. For a moment she attached the envelope to nothing, then with a cold shock she remembered the day Pohaisky came to give her the legal papers. She must have taken them out of that envelope – she remembered taking it from the desk for the papers rather than use Pohaisky's briefcase – and afterwards dropped it back empty into the hiding-place without thinking what she was doing.

The electrician picked up the envelope and turned it over curiously. There were the stamps, the franking mark of the post office, the name and address of Herr Dr Franz Wedeker.

She reached out a hand for the envelope.

'It's probably been there for years,' she said, she hoped idly.

The man looked at the postmark. 'A year last March, gnae' Frau,' he said. There was no meaning in his interest, simply the curiosity of a man whose job is dull except when it takes him into the homes of rich people. Because she had once nearly committed an indiscretion with Maris Pantic and Georg Kerenyi over Pohaisky and those papers Julie was nervous of the subject and though she knew that it was the lawyer's politico-religious views that had sent him to Buchenwald, she felt guilt as if her own lack of thought had helped condemn him.

'It probably got blown from the desk one day while the windows were open,' she said quickly. 'That happens a lot. The gap between the panel and the floor is rather large.'

'That was it for sure,' said the man and gave her the envelope. She looked inside; it was, of course, empty. She tore it up and threw it into the wastepaper-basket beside the desk, shocked to find her hands trembling. As with Frau Schneider's conversation, she said nothing of this meaningless little incident to Franz. His silence and preoccupation released her from the duty of talking, about that or any of the concerns of the day. The work was finished just at one o'clock and Julie heard Fina suggest to the electrician that he should share her meal; they could be heard chatting together and laughing in the kitchen.

Fina thought of this hospitality as a stroke of cunning; even if Frau Pichler in her glassed-in spying-window or anybody else remarked on Frau Kaestner's disappearance the perfect naturalness of their behaviour would disarm suspicion. But it was the unusual hospitality that caused the trouble, for the electrician talked about it when he went to visit his sister and brother-in-law that evening to admire their baby, his godson.

'Not a bit snobby, and she's just as beautiful close up as on the screen. I've never seen her on the stage.'

'I saw her once,' said his sister. 'We were taken at school to the Burgtheater the year I left.'

'And the cook too, a very nice person, you couldn't ask to be nicer treated.' He smiled affectionately up at his plump sister who leaned over to put a dish of cut sausage and some pickled cucumbers and paprikas on the table. 'Those rich people aren't nearly as fussy as you are about the house, though. Dust everywhere. They don't seem to notice. The book-shelves hadn't been cleaned for an age, you could see that.'

And he repeated the little incident with the envelope.

'What was the name, did you say?' asked his brother-in-law. 'I thought you said this was Julia Homburg's apartment?'

'I expect she has a stage name,' said his wife with the assurance of one who has experience of these matters, having been taken to the theatre while at school. 'They all have, these actresses. Go on, do, and tell us what she said, and everything. What did she have on?'

'I don't remember her dress,' said her brother. 'Only sort of how she looked.'

'Well, how did she look? Though I suppose it's all make-up?'

'She didn't look made up.' He hesitated, unable to express his feeling. 'She looked ... her face ... well, when you look at her you have the feeling she couldn't possibly be any different.'

'Still, it's funny about the name being different. I wish you could remember what it was.'

'He's hopeless,' said the sister, 'never remembers anything.'

'I remember very well,' protested her brother, helping himself to more sausage. His brother-in-law poured out beer. 'I know – it was Weker or Weder or something like that. I just can't quite recall – wasn't she married to a Member of Parliament or something?'

His brother-in-law looked up from a well-filled plate. 'Wedeker, you mean. He disappeared. Of course, I remember now. How long ago did you say?'

'Last March, a year. Yes, that was the name, all right. I remember him, too. He was . . . ' The electrician cut off his reminiscence because he had been a member of the Socialist Youth Movement before joining the NSDAP and did not want to remind either himself or his brother-in-law of this piece of youthful misjudgment.

'Last March, eh?' The brother-in-law began to pick his teeth. 'Those were the days, last year. My God, do you remember what it was like eighteen months ago? You and me, we were both out of work and I couldn't get married, remember?'

The electrician laughed slyly at his sister, who blushed brightly.

'Yes, the whole thing happened just right for you two, didn't it? In three weeks we both had jobs and you two got married – only just in time too.' They all laughed with happy embarrassment and as if at a signal the baby gave a hearty wail from the other room. His mother put a hand to her full breast and said, 'I'd better give his majesty his supper, too. You two will be all right for a minute, will you?'

'We don't do so much Party work as we used to,' said the electrician to his brother-in-law. 'One time we were always out with the SA.'

'Well, a lot of that stopped when the Reich Party took over here. It's really more of a ceremonial duty now, SA.' He was senior in the movement to his wife's brother and his voice took on a pompous and didactic note. 'You see, the SA had already passed its most active stage in the old Reich when the Führer came to power. It was of use to the Führer in the unofficial stages of the struggle for power, when a professional force like the SS was not feasible. In Austria this stage of the struggle lasted in some respects until after the country returned to the Reich. That is, the struggle was still partially unofficial.' It was clear from his use of unfamiliar and high-sounding words which he mispronounced that he was repeating a party lecture word for word. Now he reverted to his normal tone. 'Besides, we were out of work like half of Austria in those days. It gave us something to do – free meals and all.'

'Yes,' said the electrician reflectively, 'there's no doubt things have improved. I was out of work over a year when I finished my apprenticeship – remember? And less than three months after the return to the Reich, I had a steady job. It was a good thing for Austria, there's no doubt.' Still, his repetition seemed to show some doubt of which he himself was perhaps not aware.

'Mind you,' said his brother-in-law, not listening and following his own line of conversation, 'if the Führer needed us, we'd be ready for anything. I'd get back into uniform to-morrow.' His wife came into the room carrying a fat baby of about five months old that crowed and clutched like all healthy babies, but like the only baby in the world to its three elders.

'Yes, well, let's hope it doesn't come to that.' The two young men looked quickly at each other, a quite new and anxious look in their faces.

'Come to what?' said the mother, a little sharply, bouncing the fat baby in her arms.

'Nothing, we were just talking. Here, give him to me ...' The father took his son and sat him up in the crook of his arm as he had been taught to do by his mother-in-law, supporting the rolling head.

The baby clutched his finger in its little fist, and its uncle leaned over and touched the fluff of hair on its head. On both their faces was the serious expression of men who are occupied with the real business of life though both of them firmly believed that their political conversation was of far more importance than playing with a baby.

'Still, it's funny about Wedeker's name coming up,' said the father. 'You remember we were offered a flat over the river in the 2nd District when we got married?'

His wife nodded abstractedly. 'I didn't want to live so far away from Mother,' she said. 'But it was a nice flat. All that lovely furniture.'

'Better to buy your own, like you did,' said the electrician quickly, pushing out of his mind the memory of proposing his fellow SA man and future brother-in-law for the suddenly emptied flat in the 2nd District. The local Party office had been quite willing, but the young pair politely refused the apartment. The strained, defensive note came back into the electrician's voice that was noticeable when he talked of his days with the Sturm Abteilungen and he spoke as if he were forced to, against his will.

'That's what made me remember Wedeker. The house where the flat was, that belonged to Wedeker's family. His money and everything was made over to his wife some years before, and she owns the house now. I'd forgotten it, but I remember when I said the name, hearing about it in the Party office at the time.'

'He was a sharp one all right,' said the other man with admiring envy. 'What became of Wedeker, then?'

'He disappeared. Skipped in time. He knew what time of day it was.' He changed the subject he had started himself before they could ask more questions. 'Drink up, now. Let's have another glass of beer and a hand of cards.'

An hour later, the electrician stood up and stretched.

'Time I went,' he said.

'I'll walk down with you, Horst, and get a breath of air,' said his brother-in-law. As they went down the stairs:

'Do you ever see that man Ulrich we used to drill with?' asked Horst uneasily. 'He was a queer bird.'

His brother-in-law glanced sideways in the light of the street lamp and clearly knew what Horst meant by his comment.

'He joined up in the regular SS,' he said, 'but I rather avoid him when I see him at Party meetings. There's something about his eyes ...'

'I avoid him, too,' agreed Horst eagerly, glad of corroboration. 'Ever since ...'

'Since?'

'Since the Anschluss. He seemed to me a bit crazy then.'

'Well, I'll turn back now, I think. Until Sunday, then?'

Horst raised a lazy hand and walked on. On the walk from the corner of the road to his mother's flat, he thought again of that Saturday afternoon over a year ago when he had acquired a claim on the flat near the Taborstrasse. It seemed to him now that he ought to assert his confidence, his belief, in the Party doctrines. The feeling of anxiety he had when he thought of that afternoon and still more the fear that his family should ever hear of it made it seem important to reaffirm that he was a good Nazi.

The next day on his way from work he went into the Party office for their sub-district and told the secretary of the little incident with the envelope in Frau Homburg's apartment.

'You were quite right,' said the secretary encouragingly. 'Quite right to come and tell me. I will make a report.'

'Well, it doesn't seem to be important,' said Horst Winkler. 'But I know we're supposed to report anything that seems queer.'

'Quite right,' repeated the secretary. He was a man who loved organising and made reports on the minutest details of insignificant events. Every sheet of neat paper in the files increased his own importance to himself. 'You should persuade your brother-in-law to join the Party. Make an application. I'll see that it is favourably considered.' He smiled briskly, with good-natured condescension, dismissing his junior member, who evaded wounding his vanity by telling him his brother-in-law was already a member of the NSDAP. New members also added to his importance.

Even then it would not have mattered, but ten days later the district office of the Party instituted an inspection tour of the sub-district offices. It was one of those routine affairs that Party officials liked to undertake for the same reason that the secretary of the sub-section liked to make excessively detailed reports; it increased their importance. It was called keeping in touch with the rank and file of the Party. On that inspection everything in this particular sub-section was so completely in order that the District Secretary felt he must be especially careful and circumspect, and he read through the copies of recent reports, the originals of which were already filed in his own office but which he had not read. Among them was the report on Wedeker and his envelope which was, of course, quite meaningless. But the name was on a list that the District Secretary kept locked in his safe, so he made copious notes with a great air of knowing more than he did; and, frowning with self-importance, congratulated the sub-section secretary on his vigilance and the perfection of his filing system. He went back to his district office and read the original and then made a fresh report, coming from himself naturally, in even more pompous and incomprehensible German, which he forwarded with a covering memo and marked SECRET MATTER OF STATE SECURITY to the Ministry of the Interior.

The Vienna Ministry of the Interior was by now a section of the Reich Ministry of the Interior and State Security. Vienna was a locality, but a locality with some administrative autonomy; and though a copy of the district report was sent automatically to Berlin where it was filed unread like a thousand others, the responsibility for acting on it or not rested with the Vienna ministry.

4

*I*n the reorganisation of the Austrian civil service that followed the merging of Austria in the German Reich, Peter Krassny had lost his position on the personal staff of the Austrian Chancellor, an office that ceased to exist. For some months he was moved from one department to another, sometimes at his own wish, sometimes at that of others. He was not a Party member and did not become one; but belonged to that upper circle of public servants by right of birth and training which exists in all states where public administration has been stable for many generations.

The new German chiefs of departments often wished to remove such men from their own new field of responsibility out of jealousy or suspicion – just as they often removed the old secret Party members who knew the inner workings of the Austrian Party machine before the Nazis were in power in Vienna. These were in the main easy to get rid of; they were promoted, but into Germany, Prague, the Foreign Service, seconded to inter-ministerial or military liaison. Krassny and his fellows were more difficult to deal with. They not only managed the obsolete machinery of state administration with a confidence and efficiency that left their new masters in the dark, but their colleagues were concerned to retain them, to protect their positions and to circumvent the efforts of new chiefs to root out the old methods of doing things and institute their own. So that when a departmental head asked for Krassny's transfer, some friend of his arranged that another department should need his services. In this way, after some time, he became the assistant chief of the department which maintained internal order in the city, a highly responsible and necessary post that needed considerable knowledge and experience and a skill in dealing with local officials which no stranger from Germany could have.

A few days after Horst Winkler's sub-district secretary had his meticulous report copied by the District Secretary, the renewed report was one of the matters to be considered at a meeting of departmental officials at which Krassny presided.

'What's next?' he asked his personal assistant, seated to his left at a large table where ten men were gathered with papers and notepads before them. 'If there's nothing more for the Chief Inspector, we can release him.'

The young man he spoke to was reading a scribbled list of the subjects of their meeting. He looked at his chief and shook his head.

'I think we've dealt with all the police matters,' he said.

A tall and burly man, the only one there in uniform in which he looked very smart, rose, pulling out his handkerchief and wiping his face and neck. 'I'll get along, then,' he said, and went round the table to shake hands with his colleagues.

'It is hot in here this morning,' said Krassny as if agreeing with a complaint. 'Let's have some more windows open, Kasda, shall we?'

His junior went gratefully to the windows and opened them all. All. A slight breeze came in and modified the stifling sunlight of the room. The men at the table shifted and eased their overheated bodies. Kasda surreptitiously undid the top button of his shirt behind his formal tie.

'This report from the 15th District Party Secretary,' said Kasda briskly, smiling sideways at his chief.

'Read it, read it, then,' a thin cross-looking old civil servant said in a precise high voice.

Ferdinand von Kasda read the report with exaggerated care and a solemn voice from beginning to end which took seven minutes.

A small man in grey sighed as he finished. 'The things these half-educated apes do to the language!' he muttered.

'I don't believe I caught the sense of it myself,' said Krassny with a circumspect smile. 'Have you, Nando?'

'As far as I could make out after a careful study, it rests on a bit of idle gossip and has absolutely no meaning at all.' He raised his eyebrows and turned his curly head to one side of the table and the other, asking other opinions. 'An electrician removed a panel to fit a new plug and found an empty envelope which had been there for at least ...' he looked back at the first page of the typed report '... at least fifteen months. I have looked back in the files at the relevant documents and the addressee of this envelope (if the whole story is not a fabrication, that is) was in Vienna until the actual week-end of the Anschluss. He then went to Prague and has not been heard of since. Recent reports from another source show that he probably changed his name and papers on arrival in Prague and disappeared.'

'I suggest the whole thing is simply the story of a workman who wanted to talk about an important customer and get himself some notice.'

'Why should he do that particularly in this case?' asked another man. 'It sounds to me as if there's something missing from the report. In spite of its length and prolixity.'

'Who lives in the apartment now?' asked the small man in grey. 'The wife of the ex-Deputy, Franz Wedeker. She owns all his property it seems.'

'Seems to be no mystery. Why shouldn't Frau Wedeker have an old envelope addressed to her late husband? And I can't see why it should gain the electrician any prestige to tell this stupid tale.'

Before anyone could answer him the cross old man spoke again.

'When you say "another source", Kasda, I take it you mean the Secret State Police?'

'No, sir. In fact that report came from an SS Intelligence source in Prague.'

'All this duplication,' snapped the old man, crosser than ever. 'Those amateurs playing at spies in the SS have absolutely no idea. No idea at all.'

'I agree one can't place much reliance on their stuff as a rule,' agreed Krassny slowly.

'The fact is,' said the small man, 'they don't know what happened to Wedeker and neither do we. But while we are prepared to forget him, they cover themselves against possible queries by inventing some plausible tale.'

'I really can't see how the electrician gained any prestige from this bit of gossip,' plaintively persisted the man in grey.

'I think you may have forgotten,' Krassny said carefully, 'Wedeker's wife is Julia Homburg.'

'Ah, yes. The Party wishes her to divorce her husband in his absence,' said a man at the end of the table who had not yet spoken. 'I understand – from a private bit of talk – that she has not yet agreed to do so.'

'What I still don't understand, is what the whole thing is supposed to mean,' said the old civil servant. 'I fail to see why Frau Wedeker-Homburg should not leave her husband's envelope lying about if she wishes. It probably got pushed under the panel and nobody noticed it.'

'How often does one remove panelling, after all?'

'It was the panelling of wall book-shelves,' said Kasda in his tone of assumed solemnity. It was clear that he thought the whole matter funny as well as meaningless, though he did not smile.

'Presumably the implication is that something was hidden in the envelope?' asked the man at the end of the table who had spoken of Julie's possible divorce.

'It is specifically said to have been empty,' snapped the old man in a still more disagreeable voice.

'Ah, yes, so it was.' Everyone at the table now looked at the man at the end of it.

'Some action had better be taken on the report,' said Krassny considering. 'Though it is difficult to see what, on the strength of this.' He put out a finger and touched the report lying in front of Kasda.

Kasda glanced at the man at the end of the table. 'How would it be if I had a chat – I happen to have the honour of her acquaintance, though slight – with Frau Homburg?'

'We'd better do something of that sort,' said the irritable old man. 'Ask her a few questions and then we can close the matter. Something like that, eh, Krassny?'

Krassny did not say that he too knew Julia Homburg. He nodded.

'You might have a word with her about the divorce at the same time,' hinted the Party representative.

'That is, after all, exclusively a Party affair,' objected Krassny.

'Might be a good idea to slip in a friendly hint, though,' said the small man, doodling on his notepad. 'I mean,' he added with determination, 'I mean for her own sake, not for any other reason.'

'On the whole I am against our taking a hand in purely Party matters,' said Krassny slowly. He looked up the table at the man sitting at the end. 'It causes duplication and therefore, confusion. If the Party wish Frau Homburg to divorce her husband, they will no doubt tell her so.'

'She has already been approached,' said the man at the end of the table, his voice slightly louder. 'I think it would be a good idea for Kasda to mention the matter – in passing, as it were.'

'She has already been approached, you say?' asked Kasda dubiously. He was by no means inclined to take up the subject of her private life with a woman he had met only once and had made his suggestion of speaking to Julie out of a youthful impulse to claim her acquaintance. 'I thought you said it was a bit of gossip?'

'It was a piece of gossip that she has not yet agreed to divorce him. Not that the matter is afoot. That I know officially.' The man at the end of the table looked challengingly at Krassny. But Krassny had made his protest and did not mean to expose himself by insisting on it. Instead he spoke to Kasda.

'What do you think of saying to Frau Homburg – or Frau Wedeker – about this absurd envelope?'

'I shall have to think it out,' said von Kasda, and laughed slightly. 'There's so little in it, I shall have to be careful not to make an ass of myself. I'll think of something suitably vague.'

'There is no point in discussing this any further,' the old man with the disagreeable manner said suddenly. 'I have a great deal to do to-day, if no one else has. I suggest we get on to more serious business.'

Von Kasda took up his scribbled list of matters for discussion and ticked off one of the items. He turned to his chief and nodded at a file lying on Krassny's blotter.

'Then, there is a complaint from the Rathaus. The head of the Street-cleaning Department says ...'

The meeting proceeded as such meetings do, dealing with the matters of real concern and idle things of no moment with equal seriousness and at equal length. Every man at the table played his own hand according to his nature, his circumstances and his ambitions. The agent of the Party and perhaps of the Gestapo who sat at the end of the table took an interest only in matters that could further his ambition to rise to power within the Party. The old civil servant with his irritable temper and his memories of times when the backstairs gossip of little people was dealt with by discreet agents of the police and not brought out in the light of day in this undignified and inefficient manner, was concerned only to maintain himself until his imminent retirement should be due. Others wished to ingratiate themselves with the Party's agent, still others to baulk him if they could without endangering themselves, out of a local patriotism that resented strangers in their midst. Krassny himself was determined to maintain his position in the civil service for what he still thought of as a temporary interruption of his career. And von Kasda was determined to keep out of the armed services in the inevitable trouble that was coming, to remain a civilian and in Vienna where his own life could be lived as little touched as might be by the immense changes of the times.

Peter Krassny and Ferdinand von Kasda took their midday meal that day as they did every day when they had no other engagement, in the Kaffee Kaisergarten. As he did every day the brisk little old waiter flicked non-existent specks from the brilliant table linen, adjusted the folded napkin at the place set facing the entrance and bowed twice.

'*Grüss Gott, Herr Sektionschef!*' he intoned. '*Grüss Gott, Herr Doktor!*' They always sat at the same table, the last one by the window.

Between each table was a screen of highly polished mahogany with engraved and frosted glass panels. Strangers were unnoticeably led towards the other side of the long and narrow room, to sit under the tall, mahogany-framed mirrors. Krassny seated himself facing the door and Kasda with his back to the screen and the room.

The waiter, crooning ritual phrases, said aloud, 'Tuesday, Herr Sektionschef?'

'Ah, Tuesday. Good.' Krassny looked up at the old man and frowned while smiling. 'But last week it was a bit stringy. I hope it's tender to-day?'

The waiter did not stop murmuring to himself, but shook his head at the same time to indicate that he understood that this remark, too, was ritual.

As soon as they finished their soup, in silence, a dish of the beef cooked in the soup appeared, sliced rather thick. They ate the beef with creamed spinach and chopped potato browned slightly in butter. With it they drank tall glasses of draught beer. The beef was very good, velvety, delicate in flavour. Krassny was always given the same cut. Halfway through the beef Krassny spoke for the first time.

'Very good to-day, Waiter. I shan't complain next Tuesday.' He would and they all knew it. The waiter bowed, hovering and murmuring.

'There's something in that business, though, Nando,' went on Krassny without pausing. He could have been referring to several of the matters discussed at that morning's meeting but Kasda knew which one he meant.

'No, really? You think so?' Kasda showed surprise, which was genuine. 'Not just a workman showing off about the Homburg ménage?'

'Oh, that, yes,' Krassny put down his knife and fork. 'Nando, I've asked you before not to use names. Please try to remember.' He did not look up at the waiter who was doing something by the next table with his back towards them. 'Naturally, the envelope was nonsense. But there's something in it, just the same. You know, it's a very curious thing. I've noticed it several times in the last few months.'

By 'the last few months' he meant the year and more since the National Socialists took over in Vienna.

'Noticed what, sir?'

'That sort of thing – absurd bit of gossip – quite meaningless in itself – it seems to attach itself to those who have something not quite in order.'

'But isn't it that one naturally notices such things when they concern people whom one knows to have something ... not necessarily something to hide, but something as you say, not quite in order. I mean, if we hadn't all known about the case,' he remembered this time not to mention a name, 'we should simply have dismissed it as the idiocy it is?'

'One might suppose so. I should have thought so myself. But I've wondered recently whether people don't attract notice by some atmosphere they give off ... Nothing they do or say, you understand. But something in the air about them caused by a half-conscious nervousness ...'

'It seems awfully unlikely in this case. Such a very accomplished dissembler, don't you agree?'

'You're improving, Nando,' Krassny looked up and smiled briefly. 'I shall make you secretive, yet, given time.'

Von Kasda made a little grimace which clearly showed that he hoped this not to be true.

'You have shaken my theory a little. But would she be dissembling in that place – her own living-room – and with that person?'

'I just don't know enough about the profession, you know.' Von Kasda grinned at his chief, a sweet grin with both vanity and shyness in it that made him seem a boy far younger than his years. 'I shall have to do a little research on the subject and let you know my conclusions.'

'Yes. One just doesn't know how much they carry their professional talents into private life, does one?'

Kasda finished his meal and patted his mouth with his napkin. He reached for his beer and drank the rest of it. 'But look here. Even supposing there is something in what you say about her giving off some subtle atmosphere of nervousness or caution. Don't you think this electrician was intrigued by the meaningless envelope just because he would expect that particular woman to be exciting – dramatic – something of the sort?' Krassny did not reply and Kasda went on. 'And anyway, supposing she was startled to see the envelope – it may have been annoyance with the servant for leaving things about?'

'Maybe. Maybe.' Krassny put his knife and fork neatly together. 'Are you going to have anything else?'

The word *'Kirschenstrudel'* emerged from the waiter's undertone monologue.

'Yes, please, *Kirschenstrudel* and coffee for me,' said Kasda with the pleasurable surprise of one who gets an unexpected bonus of luck.

'Yes, you're right,' went on Krassny after a long pause. 'It's as simple as that. Besides, if any atmosphere was picked up by this electrician, it was certainly that she knows – I suppose we may take it for granted that she does know – where her husband is, and the sight of his name on that envelope reminded her suddenly of it.'

'It's very odd he just dropped out of sight like that. Most of the émigrés are known about.'

'Most of them who are able to, make themselves as noticeable as they can. To read some of the stuff in the foreign press about Vienna now one would hardly recognise the place. The Minister called it the greatest propaganda action in history, the other day.'

'Do you think it really is all Communist propaganda?' asked Kasda. 'All this flood of hatred and fear?'

'I don't myself think so, though a good deal of it is inspired by left-wing writers. Especially in Paris. My own opinion is that it is mainly caused by the Jewish question.'

Krassny watched von Kasda eat his strudel with the mild envy of one whose liver does not allow him to eat sweetmeats.

'As for the subject of our conversation just dropping out of sight. I suppose it was all planned carefully in advance, and he is sitting in some University somewhere writing another *History of Socialism* – the international variety, of course.'

'Almost certainly,' said Krassny. Then he remembered as if it were yesterday the Wedekers' living-room on the night he was last there. He recalled the conversation and the atmosphere and knew quite certainly that Wedeker's flight was not planned in advance, or even considered. There is definitely something odd about this business, he thought rather uneasily. He looked down the long room, in search of some relief from the vagrant memory that so disturbed his peace of mind and found it in the person of Georg Kerenyi walking up the room, who lifted a hand in greeting at Krassny's nod. It was unusual to see Kerenyi here at this time of day – he could no longer afford to eat regularly at the more expensive places. As soon as Kerenyi spoke, with his accustomed ironical and indifferent tone, Krassny knew that something was wrong.

They chatted for a few minutes casually; then Kerenyi looked round the eating and drinking men in the room, his eyes passing coolly over bent heads, balding or with greying hair, the occasional uniform, the look of responsibility and solidity which characterised the habitués of this eating-place.

'I was looking for somebody, but he seems not to be here,' he said mendaciously, not even trying to give his excuse the appearance of truthfulness. The hovering waiter had now been signalled from three tables down. Kerenyi dropped his voice and, still looking about him, said very quietly, 'I must see you about something important.'

Krassny and von Kasda looked up at his tall frame with surprise. The big nose jutted out of the face looming over them, the frowning eyes looked down into the room, saw someone and nodded a greeting. Kerenyi leaned over the table to put a matchstick in the ashtray, and pulled on his cigarette.

Krassny knew that whatever Kerenyi wanted to talk to him about, it must be something to do with his official life for they hardly knew each other. 'I'd better not come to your office,' continued Kerenyi. 'Might get you into trouble. What would you prefer me to do?'

'Come and see me,' said Krassny, looking up at him. 'I shall be at home by six o'clock. Here's the address.' He slipped two fingers into a waistcoat pocket and withdrew his card which he laid before Kerenyi on the table for a moment before putting it back where it came from. Kerenyi nodded idly, narrowing his eyes against the cigarette smoke. 'Ostrovsky and Barber have just come in, after all,' he said and turned away. He went down the room, said something and laid his hand on the back of a chair, and at the answer, drew out the chair and seated himself.

'That was pretty cool,' said von Kasda.

'Do you know him?'

'I met him the other night for the first time – at Friedrich Lehmann's party for his new house.'

'Is that where you met ...' Krassny was himself about to commit an indiscretion, and recognised Kasda's humorously raised eyebrows by laughing slightly. They strolled out together into the Ring. Once in the open air Krassny spoke more freely.

'Was it where you met Frau Homburg?' he asked. He was teasing his junior mildly, referring to the younger man's vanity in claiming acquaintance with the actress that morning.

'No, as a matter of fact, it wasn't. Though she was briefly there, I did not speak to her. She seemed very subdued, I thought. I met her some time ago at lunch with my cousin, Alois Pohaisky's wife, and you were there.'

Krassny turned his mouth down at the name. 'I'd forgotten,' he said. 'As for Kerenyi – a lot of people come to see me over one thing or another.'

They turned another corner and were within a few metres of the entrance to the beautiful seventeenth-century house which contained Krassny's department. The manner of both men changed consciously as they went into the big doorway crowned by the splendid hatchment of its one-time owners, and von Kasda dropped very slightly behind Krassny.

'I suppose I owe you an explanation,' Kerenyi said, as a gesture towards the conventions rather than a genuine apology, but Krassny recognised by it that Kerenyi really did not know how to begin what he had to say and by this sign knew that the matter must be serious and perhaps dangerous.

'Go on,' he said calmly, pushing a box of cigarettes towards his self-invited guest. They sat in his small study and from the next room could be heard the clear voices of his two sons repeating their Greek preparation to each other for tomorrow's school.

Kerenyi considered.

'I'd better begin at the beginning,' he said slowly. 'Immediately after the joining of Austria to the Reich I was sent for by the Gestapo. It was, of course, not unexpected. In fact, I expected much worse.' He stopped and rubbed his nose with the hand holding his cigarette. 'They seemed to take it for granted that I would be "reasonable" and as you know I did not disappoint them. What they were interested in was the whereabouts of Franz Wedeker. They knew he was a friend of mine since our University days. I did not know where he was and they believed me. That is, I thought he had gone to Prague.' He stopped again, frowned and corrected himself. 'I mean, that he had returned to Prague.'

'I remember very clearly,' said Krassny. 'Poor Hanau – and the American, the one we saw to-day.'

'Apparently the complete disappearance of Franz in Prague has them worried. They checked with me once or twice in the past year. I never knew anything.' He looked across at Krassny with a painful grin. 'I was by no means certain what I should do if anything came up about Franz. I hoped for a long time I should hear from Barber or by some roundabout means that he was safely in London – or more probably in Oxford – he had academic contacts there. He might have gone as far as America. Then I could tell the Gestapo what I knew, without ...'

'Exactly,' said Krassny.

'That's one reason I keep in touch with Barber, but he knows nothing; he tells me he tried to find out and failed too. I heard nothing. As far as I know, neither did his wife. I doubt if anything material could change in her life without my knowing – sooner or later and probably sooner. Yesterday I had a telephone call from the same man at Gestapo headquarters. As you see, they are still handling me with kid gloves. No midnight visits – so far. This man – Blaschke is his name and he seems to be a professional policeman rather than one of their more ...'

'Quite. I know Blaschke. You don't have to explain.'

'I went to see him this morning. He was civil. I even like him.

He said that the search for Franz still goes on; it has been stepped up, in fact.'

He stopped again but Krassny did not help him. There was a silence. Kerenyi sighed and went on.

'Your department must have a pretty good idea of what is actually known about Franz. I need to know how much is known.'

'You are saying that you know something of Wedeker's whereabouts? And . . . ?'

'I know nothing of his whereabouts. But if I know how much is officially known I can continue to persuade Blaschke of my ignorance.'

'My department is by no means in the confidence of the Secret State Police,' said Krassny sarcastically.

Each man was aware that the other was lying by implication, knew that this lying was necessary and that they must continue, perhaps for many years, with this so vulnerable method of half-truths and unspoken implications.

'You are asking me,' Krassny went on with an appearance of blunt openness, 'to betray State secrets in order to preserve your safety. What makes you think I would do such a thing? And for a man I hardly know?'

'Yes,' said Kerenyi, putting out his cigarette. 'That's about it.'

'The waiters at the Kaisergarten are not reliable, as, of course, you know.' Krassny got up, walked across the room and back and sat down again. 'It is an unfortunate coincidence that von Kasda and myself were actually discussing the Wedeker-Homburg household just before you came up to speak to me. In a veiled fashion, naturally, but I am not sure we were not understood. Kasda is still young and has an unfortunately open nature.'

'So the matter *is* being stepped up?'

'Not as far as I am aware. Some idiotic piece of tradesman's gossip was reported to the Party. You know how such things occur in government departments. The files are brought out and two or three people reread them. Inter-departmental notes are circulated. But nothing new is known about Wedeker. Nothing, that is, in my department. I don't know what the Gestapo have on their files of course. I don't believe it is much more than we have. But what I have just told you is more or less what Kasda and I were saying at lunch to-day. That is, practically nothing. It's just that a question is shaken up afresh by some small stimulus — like this piece of gossip.'

'Your remark about the Kaisergarten waiters means that my speaking to you and Kasda may come to the ears of the Gestapo?'

'It is possible. You know that yourself. If anything of the sort does happen, you will not expect me to protect you, I hope?'

'I expect nothing from you for myself,' said Kerenyi.

A spasm of irritation showed in Krassny's face.

'You talk like the foreign press,' he said sharply. 'It is beginning to be taken for granted that anyone of Jewish religion has some special claim to the sympathy and protection of the entire world.'

'You will hardly deny that they need it?'

'And poor Pohaisky? The Jehovah's Witnesses? Heaven knows they disgust me with their absurd enthusiasm. But a large family of them were removed from their home two days ago and sent to some horrible camp because the young man refused his conscription papers. Twenty law-abiding and useful citizens. But the foreign press does nothing for them. Half these other people I am constantly being asked to help are not nearly so deserving.'

'I suppose the Jehovah's Witnesses have no foreign friends,' said Kerenyi, returning to his usual tone.

'Exactly. And I don't find the subject amusing. About a third of the Jews in trouble since I have been in my present office were stateless and had made no attempt to put their papers in order or to get Austrian citizenship. They moved here when the Imperial frontiers were still open and then could not get back into Galicia, after the war, so they made use of us here, making one shift or another. I don't for a moment underwrite anything the National Socialists are doing, robbing them of their money if they have any and ill-treating them. But they always made themselves separate; they wanted to be different.'

Krassny stopped talking, aware that he was exposing his impotent irritation to this almost complete stranger whom he did not even like. Kerenyi, who knew that Krassny had done whatever he could to moderate the Nazis' behaviour since he had been in a position to do so, understood quite well the resentment that made him speak as he did against the very people he had often exposed himself to help. He said something of the sort, assuming an even more casual tone than was normal to him to lessen Krassny's embarrassment.

'Why should they have worried about papers, after all?' he asked reasonably. 'Thousands of Christian citizens of the Empire didn't either but we don't notice that because they are not being persecuted and can get their registrations and the rest of it made up retrospectively. I might easily have neglected to become an Austrian citizen myself, but it was simpler to return to the University as a citizen, so I became one. I didn't mean what I said personally. It is well known that you have helped a lot of people with their papers.'

'I've done nothing for the Jews at all,' disowned Krassny, now thoroughly out of temper. 'Except for a couple of personal acquaintances whom I helped with their emigration papers. Anything I have done in my official capacity was simply to maintain decency and order in Vienna as far as it was my business; that's my job.' He stood up and continued angrily as if someone were accusing him of some personal indecency. 'I didn't vote for these repulsive Nuremberg Laws. To read the *New York Times* yesterday one might suppose we were all personally responsible for men like Franz Wedeker leaving here, or for Buchenwald where an old friend of mine is being ill-treated every day – a good Catholic ...' He drew out his handkerchief to blow his nose with a loud trumpeting noise. 'You must excuse me. I am overworked and tired. I hardly know which way to turn with these new regulations and ... every day something fresh and impossible!'

The young voices in the next room had ceased and when Krassny stopped speaking there was silence.

Kerenyi stood up to go. They said nothing as they took the two steps to the door. Then Krassny said quietly, with his head bent as if to examine something on the carpet, 'If I hear anything dangerous about Wedeker, I'll try to let you know – in time.' His voice rose again angrily, 'Though God alone knows how!' He touched Kerenyi's elbow.

The Krassnys lived in the 3rd District, and Kerenyi went across into the Stadt park and walked about among the scented trees and the beds of brilliant roses, his disarranged thoughts disturbed still more by the brass band playing light music from the bandstand. It was dusk when he came out of the gardens and the roses were only present in their clouds of perfume. As he passed the Akademietheater the audience were strolling up and down on the pavements to get a breath of air in the interval, and Kerenyi saw from the playbills that Julia Homburg was playing that evening. On an impulse he went back to the stage door and showed the doorkeeper his press pass. Julie was in her dressing-room and made a sign to her dresser who left the room.

Kerenyi only stayed long enough to let Julie know that the authorities were once again interested in the whereabouts of her husband, but seemed to know nothing definite. He said nothing of Frau Kaestner's visit to his office, or of his own observation of the new cleaning equipment in Julie's apartment.

5

*T*he season had the feeling of being already over. Cast, audience, the building itself had an atmosphere of the past tense. The players were already half gone to their summer hiding-places, the audience only filling in time before their holidays.

'It's your last night, Julie, isn't it?' said someone. 'You'll be off to your mountain fastness in a day or two.'

'Here's Hansi,' said Julie to change the conversation; she tried not to think of that moment, which filled her with blank dismay. The usual rooms in her remote inn in the Dolomites had been reserved since last year. For six years she had spent a month or more there in the summer.

'Are you going to Rapallo, Hansi?'

'Oh, yes,' he said. 'My mother is expecting me.' He turned slightly to exclude the group and said to Julie, 'Come along, Julie, and get changed. We'll have supper at the Stadtkrug, shall we?'

'Isn't it too hot to-night?' she said. She only said it to say something and when he looked dubious and opened his lips to offer another place with an open terrace or a garden, she said hastily, 'No, let's go there. The food is always good.'

The Stadtkrug Restaurant was in the town and she could be home sooner. If they went out of the city she would not be back for hours.

That Julie should be given supper by Hansi on her last night of the season was habit, but this was the first time their supper was for the two of them alone.

'Georgy came in for a moment, just to say hallo,' she said as they went down the crowded passage. 'I won't be ten minutes, Hansi.'

Hansi went to the telephone in the stage manager's office and tried at several places to get hold of Kerenyi, without analysing why he felt he wanted someone else to be at the supper table and cursing himself for not thinking of making up a party before it was too late. Georg Kerenyi was not to be found at any of his usual places. He was in fact sitting not five minutes away from the theatre, drinking steadily and gloomily by himself.

'This place seems to have changed a good deal rather suddenly.' Hansi and Julie seated themselves at a corner table in the inner room of the Stadtkrug Restaurant.

'Yes, it seems to have become very popular.' In the middle of the room, not large and with a low ceiling, stood a grand piano where a favourite chansonnier sang dialect songs in a crooning undertone, vamping softly the tunes of the old songs he made new words for.

'He's not as amusing as he was,' said Julie, having listened to a few lines.

'Is anything?' Hansi gave in suddenly to his real mood. 'He has to remember a whole list of things he daren't sing about nowadays.'

Involuntarily she looked over her shoulder. The gesture was already called the 'German look'.

The restaurant was crowded, safest of places for indiscretions in the murmur of voices, the rattle of silver and glass, the passing of waiters and the elderly 'girls' who helped them. On the piano stood a huge glass vase filled with many-coloured gladioli. Two large tables on the far side of the pianist were crowded with young Luftwaffe officers with pretty young girls. Both parties were noisy and very gay.

'I see that American correspondent is in town,' said Julie, glancing at a distant table where Colton Barber sat with a woman Julie did not know. 'Yes,' said Hansi, 'I had lunch with him the other day. He's become absolutely fanatical – one can hardly talk to him.'

'I haven't seen him since ...' Julie stopped, for the last time Barber had been in her company was the night before Franz went back to Prague and she had not heard from him again; this struck her now as sinister in the heightened realisation of danger induced by Kerenyi's hasty warning. Strange, he had never let her know he had seen Franz on the Prague train, not even when he wrote and asked for Franz's new address. She could not know that Colton Barber had assembled herself, Hansi and Kerenyi into a larger group of unidentified guilty ones responsible for the terrible moment in the train when Wedeker was flung into the hostile world outside. And Barber was right; nobody had tried very hard to persuade Franz that he must leave in time, and least of all Kerenyi who was with him in Prague when the news came that meant his exile. She shook her shoulders slightly to push away the memory of Franz's return, changed into a hunted creature, the change that issued in the quiet and uneventful ruin of their relationship. She said, inconsequently, the first thing that came into her mind.

'They say Göring himself comes here when he's in Vienna.'

One of the young officers caught the edge of the elaborate silk shawl draped across the piano on which the heavy vase stood. A waiter hurried across and bent forward anxiously to dissuade the boy who, unsure himself of his prank, desisted at once. The waiter twisted the shawl up over the piano, readjusting the position of the vase, shifted by the young man's pulling. Julie went back to the big menu card with its bewildering variety of dishes.

'I never can choose, Hansi,' she said. 'You order.'

He ordered a meal he knew she liked and champagne, but the champagne was more like a gesture of desperation than of close-of-season celebration. Several persons at neighbouring tables had by now recognised Julie but convention kept their curiosity within discreet glances and whispers.

'How's Hella?' asked Julie, picking up her fork.

'I think she's all right. But I haven't seen her since Lehmann's dreadful party, you know. She only sees Party members now.'

'You always were a cynical beast,' she said, pretending to laugh.

'Hella wants money and lots of it, and hates me for trying to keep her away from films. She's so terrible before a camera.'

Julie considered this. 'It's her round face,' she said at last.

Hansi recalled what Hella had said of Julie's face at that party and looked at her, so close to him, and so familiar. It was true. The broad and noble brow, the dominant eyes, remained as harmonious as they would always be. But the face was thinner, the cheekbones cut sharply; the mouth, once so tranquil, was getting a set look. And something was happening to the expression in her extraordinary, dark and luminous eyes. She was and would be for many years the most beautiful woman Hansi knew, but Hella was right; no matter what anyone said, Julie's face was changing.

Hansi lifted his glass. 'Here's to a wonderful new season next year.'

As he spoke, a new party came in of four people. Elderly, solid with well-being and at home in the world, they seated themselves at the only free table, clearly reserved for them. They talked earnestly and quietly together. One of the men leaned forward over the table to emphasise some point he was making. The other man evidently demurred, for the first put a thick white hand in the pocket of his dinner jacket and drew out a cutting from a newspaper. As he smoothed it out and passed it to the man opposite the heading could be clearly seen, *Le Temps*.

'If I'd managed to get hold of Kerenyi, we'd know what they are talking about,' said Hansi. 'Something must have happened.'

'Don't try to find out,' said Julie. 'Something happens every day and every day it's worse.' They watched the four people talk for a few moments. Then Julie said, 'They don't seem much disturbed. It can't be so very bad this time.'

The waiter told them as he changed their plates. The Franco-Russian treaty talks had broken down and the breach seemed to be final. The four people at the other table were trying to decide whether that removed the peril of war, as one of the men thought, or only postponed it, as the other believed.

'If the Russians haven't succeeded in getting the French to come in with them, it will be all right, you'll see.'

'You mean without the French Army the Russians won't stand up to the Wehrmacht? That means no war, doesn't it, Hansi?'

'It looks as if it might – to me,' he said. 'But politics are by no means my strong suit.'

'Can he really get away with it?'

'Poland? Why not – he's got away with everything so far. Why not the Corridor – it always was an injustice, hopelessly unworkable.'

'He' was always Hitler, as 'they' were always the Party.

'How far will they go?' she asked. She had never been in Poland, or Prussia and had no clear notion of geography.

'Oh, Danzig and the Corridor, I imagine,' he said. The main course came, chicken in champagne sauce with rice.

'Why *can't* you make salads properly?' said Hansi as one of the black-clad 'girls' put down two glass dishes with shredded lettuce in watery dressing. 'You know perfectly well I never eat Viennese salads. Bring a bowl of dry lettuce, not all torn to shreds, and some oil and lemon juice; I'll do it myself.' There was a flurry and the two glass dishes disappeared. 'Disgusting stuff,' he said and the querulous tone of his voice recalled Franz, who now had his books. A shudder moved inside Julie; she ought to have called it off and gone home at once; she was not quite sure whether it was caution about appearances that made her come out after what Kerenyi had said to her or a cowardly desire to stay away from home.

Finally the salad was right; it really was much better than the dripping limp mess usually served and had a crisp, nutty taste.

'You see, they can produce decent salad if you insist,' Hansi said. 'Julie, you will go through this absurd form of a divorce, won't you? They'll leave you in peace then. You know it means nothing.'

'So that's what the champagne was for!'

'Don't be a fool,' he said sharply.

'I'm sorry, Hansi, dear,' she said at last. 'That was childish. Would they really leave me in peace? I mean – if I do, they won't start on me to join the Party?'

'They haven't made any of us join. Lehmann tries to be reasonable. He knows quite well what the form is.'

'It's just – I can't bring myself to do it.'

'I never thought you were such a bourgeoise,' he said. 'What does it matter? You're just as married ...'

'Or just as not married,' Julie said.

'I would never have mentioned it if ...'

'If what?' she said sharply, feeling the inward shudder of fear again.

'Lehmann is bothered about it. Old Schoenherr was dead against him coming to me about it – he thought I'd get mad. I did, too. But if they mean business ...' He looked at her covertly. 'I don't want to lose you,' he said.

The little frown twitched her brows together and gave her the fierce look. It was precisely the wrong thing to say at that moment. Schoenherr had known very well what he was doing when he rejected Lehmann's suggestion that Hansi should talk to Julie about divorce. His possessive, yet impersonal feeling for Julie made him blind to everything about her that was not professional.

'There are limits to what I'm prepared to do for my job,' she said evenly.

'I've never heard you call it a job before,' he said, shocked but not realising his own mistake.

'We make far too much of this *théâtre mystique*, Hansi. It isn't the whole world, and there is something false about trying to make it the whole world. I mean – talking as if it were the most important thing on earth, more important than any other consideration, reduces its real importance somehow.'

'I don't know what you mean,' he said miserably. 'It is the most important thing – to me.'

'Well, it isn't. "The theatre" – who said it, I can't remember? – "the theatre is meant to illumine life, not to replace it."' Hansi could not help knowing that Julie had indeed replaced life with what she now brusquely termed her job, for the last year, and to him her change of attitude was almost frightening. He attributed it to the question of the divorce which only now he saw as humiliating to her as well as painful.

'I shouldn't have spoken of it so lightly,' he said. 'I don't mean it lightly. I only thought it would be easier to discuss ... I'm sorry.' He stopped, seeing by her face that this apology sounded even more frivolous than his former tone. 'I'm afraid we rather get pushed by our desire not to seem bourgeois into mixing up a real situation with marriage as a social institution. I didn't mean for a moment to speak of you and Franz in such a wounding way; I only meant the legal fact of marriage doesn't seem to me so important as the relationship itself — nor, I must admit, as your career.'

Julie was surprised herself at her anger and at the coldness of her anger, for such a tone was quite usual with the whole circle in which she lived; she herself often made flippant and cynical remarks about marriage — other people's marriage.

'By "we" I expect you mean the people who have all been discussing my marriage. Certainly you can't mean you and myself; or if you do I absolutely disassociate myself from your "we". You have picked up this vulgar attitude from Hella, I suppose. She's a bitch at heart, after all.'

Hansi was too dismayed by the turn of the conversation, which a more perceptive man would have foreseen and avoided, to defend Hella even if he had a mind to. He remained silent and Julie went on.

'It doesn't seem to have occurred to any of "us" that this thing is a tragedy to me, and it doesn't seem to have occurred to you either what effect my divorcing him would have on Franz.' She hurried on as Hansi put out a hand to try to stop her saying what must deeply hurt both of them. 'I had a revolting conversation with that horrible woman Frau Schneider about it. Schoenherr put her up to it, of course: he must have thought she would be careful how she said it to me. But naturally, she took the opportunity to be as hateful as she could — which is pretty hateful. Now you. I would never have believed you'd let yourself be used against me like this ...'

He stared down at his hands, gripping his fork and knife as if they were struggling to get away from him. 'It's because we are such old friends — because I really am your friend, that I said anything about it at all,' he said, stubbornly and miserably.

She made a confused movement, as if to rise from the table, and he dropped his knife and laid a hand on her shaking arm.

'Julie. For God's sake, let's stop this. Don't let's say things we can never un-say. I should never have spoken. I beg you to forgive me and ...'

He was actually gripping her arm now. They were both too socially adroit to have raised their voices, but a woman at the next table was looking curiously at them and turned to whisper something to her companion. Suddenly, perhaps because of the pressure on her arm, Julie saw, as if he had appeared across the table from her, as clearly as if he were real, Franz's face with that blanched stare of fear that estranged him from her; the look of the change in him.

Anger and pride faded out of her mind. It was no use struggling. If Franz were really in England or America she could afford to be proud and angry; he was here and she could afford nothing but to conform to necessity. As Hansi released his grip Julie looked with calm face, smiling slightly round the vivid, busy room. Every human being in that room, the servants with jobs to lose, the guests who had positions and bank balances; all of them with lives and loves to protect, they were all antagonists. Even a momentary sight of the hidden man if it were not reported would put them in the same danger he was in himself. There were over a million souls in Vienna, Julie supposed, and only two of them could be trusted to protect Franz Wedeker. And if the least of accidental ills came to herself or Fina, an illness, a traffic accident, a minor brush with the police, he was lost. The vagueness of these thoughts was only momentary; immediately Julie's essentially pragmatic mind moved to actual facts and considerations. I must have a look at Fina's papers – and my own, she thought. If we got into a tangle over her health insurance as we did – when was it – a couple of years ago? And since Pohaisky went I've never checked with his son-in-law about my income tax payments ... and Franz's passport. I must destroy that. I don't even know where it is. We must arrange a hiding-place for him and signals between ourselves. Food stocks – I must buy tins and bottled stuff in case he gets locked in the house alone by some chance. We must organise. The bathroom, he must never bathe when Fina and I aren't there in case someone hears the water ...

'What are you laughing at!' Hansi looked from her face, now quite normal, about the room to find a cause for her broad smile.

'I was thinking of Frau Schneider and her lost voice,' she lied. 'You're quite right, Hansi. What do these people matter to me, after all?'

'I just don't understand you, sometimes,' he said, laughing and shaking his head. 'Only a moment ago you were spitting with rage at Frau Schneider; now she makes you laugh!'

'End-of-season nerves. We are all rather tired, I expect.'

They talked shop. They ate peaches and drank the rest of their champagne. The Luftwaffe officers were noisier and gayer than before and the other guests, more normal to this old-fashioned and solidly reputed restaurant, were stimulated to gaiety by the sound of the healthy, confident, joyful voices of the young. The coffee seemed to take a long time, but at last she was free to rise, to draw about her shoulders the light wrap Hansi held for her, to brave the room with her sovereign and public smile and to leave them all the poorer of her presence.

In the car it was only three minutes to her house door, so Julie said what Hansi wanted her to say at once.

'Can you find a lawyer when we all get back? I don't know anybody. Someone discreet? It mustn't get into the papers.'

'I'll arrange it,' he said, trying to keep relief out of his voice. He knew that Lehmann had already approached an elderly and unsuccessful lawyer at the wrong end of the Mariahilferstrasse. 'All you have to do is sign a paper. Everything else will be automatic and nobody but the Party need know.'

They had reached the house and she was fishing for her keys in her elegant handbag.

'My dear,' she said while he was holding the car door open for her, 'have a wonderful time in Rapallo. Remember me to your mother, won't you?'

He realised for the first time that she meant to end the evening here and now and assumed that this was because she did not want to discuss details of an autumn divorce. But Hansi wanted, with his dogged caution, to pursue his success – as he thought it – in persuading Julie to agree at least in general, to fall in with the wishes of the Party.

'I'll invite myself for a last drink, if that's all right?' he said, pushing the door of his open car shut behind him. 'After all, I shan't see you for two months. I want to talk about next season — you know, before any formal conference, so that I know what you want to do.'

'Oh, Hansi, yes, there was something. We must decide what to do about the continuation of *Doll's House* into next season. I'm very dissatisfied with the idea of—'

Hansi, putting one hand under her elbow to lead her and reaching with the other for her house keys, knew at once what she was going to say.

'I know. Matty is too old to take over the sister's part,' he agreed. 'But it is only for the first few performances until the Number Two group gets back from their tour in the middle of October. I wanted to put off playing *Doll's House* altogether until they got back, but Schoenherr can't wait. It always draws such big houses and he has to account for the costs of the production in October. That means he has to use it and have the figures to show for the audit.'

They were by now inside the big house doors and Hansi turned to lock the postern. The preoccupation with work had taken their minds away from more immediate concerns. So he was startled when Julie stopped dead by the lift doors. He saw the curtain over the inner window to the caretaker's lodge move slightly as the lights went on. Julie stood stock still.

'Hansi, I'm really awfully tired. Perhaps we could meet to-morrow and go all over this?'

'But I thought you had so much to do to-morrow?' he said bewildered. 'But of course if you'd rather ...' His eyes followed hers to the curtained window, and the absurd notion that she was concerned with what the caretaker could think of his by no means infrequent visits to Julie's home, crossed Hansi's mind. He had been one of the few who constantly came to see Julie at home in the last year during which, as it seemed quite naturally, the informal hospitality taken for granted at the Wedeker household had stopped. An embarrassment quite common between professional men and women but not to them, was for a moment present. They had rid themselves both of sexual curiosity and sexual interest in each other years before in a fleeting love affair, and the return of this embarrassment was painful to both of them.

'What a clown I am, when you must be worn out,' Hansi recovered himself almost without a pause. 'I'll telephone in the morning.'

Later, sitting over a solitary drink in a coffee-house, Hansi decided that Julie's sudden change of mind must have been caused by the remembrance of a late appointment with another man, that evening, but he could not think who this might be.

The apartment was dark and silent, only the small table lamp in the living-room, always left burning until Julie turned it out on her way to bed, shed a slight glow through the half-open door into the hall. When Julie went into her bedroom to get ready for bed she saw that the dressing-room door was closed. Of course, she thought, of course ... The desolate sensation of waste and loss filled her again as she undressed and lay down. The dark world was vast, threatening, and she was alone. In spite of the two people bound to her in a desperate compact, in spite of successful talent, in spite of being always sure of a hundred companions and an endless supply of new ones eager for acquaintance, in spite of beauty, she was alone. Just as in her childhood; at school she was admired and envied, in the street strangers tried to approach her; but at home she was rejected by the cold egotism of her father, the preoccupations of her mother. The nuns had chided her – they chided everyone for some fault or other, only the individual children did not see that for each some special fault was chosen to be rooted out – for self-pity. Julie had been sorry for herself as a child, and that her unhappiness was a fault had added to the unhappiness but had done nothing to cure the fault since it never seemed to occur to any of the nuns that she had reason to be unhappy.

Memories of childhood and girlhood slipped in interchanging visions of coming sleep, into memories of soft caresses, meaningless, unrelated to deeper emotions, at that time dominated by the over-stimulus of religious exercises, caresses of her own and the other girls as they discovered their bodies. The innocent, gentle, purely physical and amoral lovemaking they indulged themselves in, in spite of or perhaps because of the prurient watchfulness of the nuns, their amorous curiosity only increased by hinted warnings and homilies of purity, had a sweetness and pleasantness entirely appropriate to the bodily ripeness and emotional infancy of their state. Memories and dreams merged into sleep.

The electrician beat wildly on the book-case with his long and heavy screw-driver and shouted at some invisible 'Ulrich' that the new wall plugs were to be moved ... The noise rose, a battering of fists and boots on a door like bursting fireworks, spattering splinters over the piano player who sang on in his dialect; Hansi was pulling at the silken scarf that lay over the piano, he was pulling at her shoulder ...

'What is it?' cried Julie and knew before the words had formed themselves what it was. Franz was shaking her shoulder and the lights were on. The pummelling and battering at the front door seemed to shake the house, seemed to shake inside Julie with the hammering of her heart, with the hammering of Franz's heart.

'Where shall I go?' cried Franz. 'What shall I do?' His terror confused Julie and infected her with a fear such as she had never dreamed of. They stared round the room with dilated eyes, their breath coming in gasps of horror. She could not think, impotent despair numbed her, her brain was numb with terror, her arm hurt numbly under Franz's gripping fingers. .

'Not in the hall,' she gasped. 'Through the other way.' She was out of bed as Franz turned back towards the dressing-room door, now gaping open.

They ran into the dressing-room. It offered nothing but the blank faces of tall cupboards, mirrors reflecting their indecision. From the hall, distantly, came Fina's voice, shouting with anger and fear shrill questions through the thick, ironed door. Franz opened the dressing-room door into the corridor that connected it with the bathroom opposite, to the right the rest of the apartment, to the left the spare room.

'The spare room,' he said, whispering, stumbling forwards.

'But there's no way out of there,' she whispered back, fresh terror rising like a sour gush in her throat so that she could hardly breathe.

He was already inside the dark, stuffy, unused room.

'No light,' he whispered. 'I know – the gap behind the stove. It's right against the wardrobe on one side. And the door opens towards it, so it doesn't notice.'

'It's too narrow,' she cried in an agony of haste.

'Sideways,' he gasped, and groaned with an anguish of humiliation and haste as he flattened his body against the wall and forced himself into the thirty centimetres or so of space between the porcelain stove and the wall. He was forced to stand on tiptoe like a dancer and to turn his head flat towards the wall. With trembling hands Julie pushed at him, stuffing the edges of his dressing-gown after his frame into the impossibly unyielding, smooth back wall of the stove.

'The dust,' she whispered, remembering professional caution. 'You'll sneeze. Blow your nose. Have you got a handkerchief?' His answer was lost. He could not move in any case.

She did not wait, but ran back into the dressing-room to pull the pillows flat and the light summer cover smooth with frantic movements before she turned off the light and left the window wide open, as she might well always leave it, to the soft night.

As Julie came out into the hall, pulling her dressing-gown, a new one of dark rose-colour for Franz's homecoming, about her, they were already in the apartment. This time there was a whole group of them and all in the now feared and hated grey uniforms. Afterwards neither Julie nor Fina could recall how many they were, but they seemed to fill the hallway. They were big, well-grown men of the long-boned North-German stamp; the actress's eye assessed at once the audience she was playing to, histrionic display of brutality reversed by corrupted sentimentality. The sort of men who would be put off by a cuddly child or a pretty animal; I must get a spaniel, she thought, apparently irrelevantly but with instinctive shrewdness. Her own sovereign presence was the last thing to oppose to such men, it could only increase their intransigence.

With a transfer so fast that nobody but perhaps Kerenyi or Hansi would have noticed it, Julie put up her hands and pulled her hair forward, the face crumpling from pride and anger to a cringing, half-sleepy bewilderment and fear that the real Julie would never have exposed. Her voice stammered and wept; she was overplaying but a long-schooled experience restrained her from attempted artistry; nothing could be too cravenly female for the unstable arrogance of these men, and she let the sash of her richly silken robe fall exposing a body veiled but not obscured by the thin silk of her nightdress, and caught it again with a flinching modesty that would have had any one of them at her feet if the others had not been there.

In a couple of sobbing sentences she had them all in the living-room. (She must give the bed in the dressing-room time to cool from Franz's body.) Half the diva of legend demanding explanations, half the shrinking but submissive female creature, she asked first one and then the other for answers, avoiding the officer in charge of the operation for she must keep them in the room at least for a few minutes, not allow them to disperse in the apartment. By the time the young officer in his SS uniform had asserted his right to answer questions – his right to ask them had been abrogated in the first moment of her appearance – several precious minutes had passed.

'But are you mad?' she cried. 'I'm divorcing him. It's all arranged; but days ago arranged. Your orders must be out of date. Who sent you – no, no, I shan't make a complaint; I know you have to obey orders. Even if it means waking me out of – but what is the time, it must be ...' Her eyes sought the young officer's with the suggestion that to be wakened out of sleep by him, if it had been by him alone, would have been ... Beer and brandy seemed to have been conjured on a silver tray.

'No, I can't. You know, you frightened me so much. No, really ...'

Then, 'Fina, perhaps a glass of wine ...' To the young officer, 'You would rather drink wine, wouldn't you?'

Miraculously, Julie herself hardly believed it, the stamping and muttering men, pouring their beer into long glasses and tossing the little tots of schnapps back into their throats with sighs of pleasure, were crowding out of the room. She did not dare protest, or show anxiety; but the first impression was true, they were filing out, they were clattering down the winding stairs. Only two remained by the door, and the young officer within. The door was closed, two tall black-clad men standing beside it, watched in their turn by Fina. If only she has the wit to get them into the kitchen, thought Julie, returning from the living-room door to where the young man sat, in her own high-backed chair, self-consciously playing with his heavily cut Bohemian wine glass.

'You know, you're sitting in my chair,' she said with sickening playfulness. 'No, no, stay there. You look rather well in the frame. You know we actresses always think in settings. I rather like your dark uniform and your blond head against the green velvet.' She picked up her glass and drank, looking at him over the rim of the glass. 'In fact, I'm rather sorry we aren't alone ...' As he moved hastily, uneasily, she went on, 'But perhaps it's just as well you are escorted. Have you been here long, in Vienna?'

'Three weeks,' he almost whispered, and cleared his throat. The words suddenly came out in a rush. 'I always wanted to come here. I studied the history of the Holy Roman Empire at school and I always wanted ...' his voice faded. 'You are so beautiful,' he said.

'It's a fascinating city,' she said. 'At least so they tell me. The Viennese don't see it, of course ...' She looked over the rim of her glass at him again. 'I'm very Viennese, you know ... Tell me, what's your name?'

He rose instantly to his feet in one movement, and drew the heels of his well-polished boots together. 'Schultze,' he said seriously, 'Ernst.' It was all she could do not to laugh.

'Excuse me, please, gnädige Frau. I should have introduced myself before this.'

'It's all right,' she said. 'These are informal times, and living alone – as I do, you know – one gets out of old habits of formal manners.'

'Revolutionary times,' he agreed eagerly. 'But Vienna, we are here to protect her. You don't know – you said just now the Viennese don't feel this passion for our history ... you can't know, you who are German history, how we long to restore and protect the ancient glory of the Empire. You mustn't feel – I know a lot of people do – that we are strangers.' He smiled shyly at her. 'We are really in the direct line of Charlemagne, you know ...' It was not the idiocy of his own nonsense that stopped him but the knowledge that his thoughts were on a quite different path. It occurred to Julie to ask how he had ever got into such a doubtful set as the Gestapo auxiliary guard, but she stifled the thought. Idealism, she thought, good God, what that word means to Germans.

Julie moved from her chair to reach the wine bottle. She passed her hand, long, slender, glittering with rings, in front of him and poured out, first in his glass and then in her own, a little wine.

'I'm not being mean,' she said, smiling, 'but we must make it last. I don't often have someone to talk to. And certainly not at this hour of the night.'

'You feel, then, that when the wine is drunk we have nothing more to say?'

She smiled, the great lady unaware who admits her own humanity.

'At any rate, no excuse for saying it,' she said.

At this moment she was perfectly aware that she could get rid of this boy at the price of a few more empty aphorisms and a slight weariness in the morning. As everyone does who lives in public, she calculated what she had drunk – a bottle of champagne with Hansi Ostrovsky, and after that an enormous shock. She was now embarked on a further bottle of wine of which the result must be tipsiness.

He interrupted her calculation. 'Frau Homburg, may I tell you something?'

'Of course,' she said, 'why not?'

'I fixed this job to-night. The Sturmbannführer cancelled it, and after he had gone off duty I put it on the list again.'

'That was very naughty of you,' said Julie, 'won't you get into trouble?'

'I probably will,' he said. 'But it's been worth it. I wanted to see you, you see ...'

'You should be ashamed, waking me up like that, just to talk to me. Why didn't you simply come to see me?'

'I'd have been scared. You never would have seen me — I mean it wouldn't have been like this ...'

The boy became aware that someone — it was Fina — was moving about in the hall. His immediate embarrassment made Julie aware that she must dismiss him now or risk making herself vulgar in his eyes. The idealism that misled him into the organised nihilism of the SS would judge her harshly if she allowed her ruse of war to become another kind of manipulation and the moment Julie thought of this it seemed incredible that she could even for a moment have thought of taking this further.

She sighed aloud and drank the little wine in her glass.

'The world is too much with us,' she said. 'What very banal things one does say in the middle of the night.'

'It's wonderful that you are so human,' he said, gazing at her with the adoring greed of a thousand standing-room students. He rose slowly, pulled down his taut tunic, and became a very junior SS officer again, reaching for his cap with its *Totenkopf* badge and bringing his heels sharply together when it was tucked under his arm.

'Gnae' Frau,' he said, using the local expression self-consciously and hesitated. She knew what he was failing to bring out. It was always the same thing that standing-space youngsters wanted to say.

'Give me your name and address,' she said. 'Here, there is a pencil on the desk. No, wait a moment.'

She could not risk his approaching the desk which might well be covered with papers and notes in Franz's hand. She got the pencil and a little block used for telephone messages and gave it to him. He wrote his name and the address of his barracks over the impression left by Franz writing upon the leaf last torn off.

'I'll see that you get seats for the very first premiere next season,' she said. She held out her hand and the boy bent his blond head to kiss it, hardly daring to hold it on his own brown hard paw, still not quite formed to its adult shape and calloused by weapons practice. Hands were always more immediate and real to Julie than faces that carried masks. For the instant that her own hand lay on his she felt a terrible pity for him, so young and unknowing.

Franz was so stiff and cramped that he almost fell into Fina's stout arms when they managed at last to shuffle him out of the hiding place. They brought him into the living-room and sat him in his arm-chair. Fina kneeled, rubbing his stiffened feet while Julie gave him brandy to restore the congealed blood-stream.

'First thing to-morrow, Fina – I mean to-day – we must get this whole thing organised,' said Julie. 'We must leave nothing to chance like this again.' She looked up at Franz, whose sad face began to lose its deathly pallor under the country brown.

'You know how it happened?' she asked. 'He wanted to see me. Imagine, the Sturmbannführer had cancelled my name and address from the list of calls they were to make; that idiot of a boy put it back on because he wanted to see me.'

'Why were we on the list at all?' asked Fina, rubbing away at Franz's left foot and ankle. 'That's more to the point, gnae' Frau.'

'I didn't dare ask him. He wouldn't have known in any case.' She considered, frowning, and went on. 'That thrice-damned electrician. There was something about him, I'm sure he was a Gestapo spy. I had a feeling at the time, when he was here that something was wrong about him. His voice or something, he reminded me of something . . . ' She shook her head, puzzled at the vagrant memory, and moved restlessly about the room. Outside the slow dawn crept through the windows. Franz said something in a low voice to Fina and she stopped her massage and stood up, reluctantly.

'We dare not go back to bed,' said Julie. 'We had better give up to-night for lost and start on to-morrow.' Franz closed his eyes and lay back in his chair, exhausted and spent. The two women left him and went to the kitchen where Fina busied herself making coffee and boiling eggs. Julie ranged restlessly about, frowning unconsciously that little twitching frown. She looked at the apartment she had always taken for granted as if it were a battlefield, trying to work out a hiding-place that nobody would find, to see her home with the view of a strange policeman.

When the whole house was built this apartment had been

designed for the owner, and was both bigger than any other flat in the house and differently laid out. Even if the search for Franz Wedeker became so pin-pointed that the lay-out of the flats above and below the Wedeker home was examined, it would not help the searchers much, for the muddled, uneven shapes of the other two flats on the same floor had been laid out after the main apartment was planned, to fit in with its needs. Julie's slight tipsiness was now quite gone and she was suddenly struck by this fact as if it were new to her. She began to examine the shape and sequence of the rooms and as soon as she viewed them with this fresh perception the solution became clear.

The flight of rooms on the street front were useless to their purpose. From living-room, through drawing-room, study, main bedroom, dressing-room, they all connected with each other. The end spare room was only to be reached from a narrow corridor between the bedroom and dressing-room on the street side and the bathroom on the other, looking into a narrow air shaft whose windows were frosted. Next to the living-room, at right angles to the street, was the dining-room. Its only window overlooked a second courtyard. Next to that came the kitchen with a window on the same courtyard as the dining-room. Past the kitchen was the hall cloakroom and lavatory and past that a narrow corridor again, running along the far side of the inner courtyard, a hollow square. That corridor window looked into the dining-room. It led to Fina's and another room full of household ladders and empty boxes stacked in dust and disorder. Its door was across the narrow corridor. The fourth side of the inner courtyard belonged to the next-door flat, occupied by an elderly widow. Fina's and the window of the box-room looked out over the big centre court where a plane tree grew, the rubbish bins stood and the rail for beating carpets. The two nearer arms of that courtyard were occupied by the other 'front' apartments; on the far side the small flats of the 'back-house', all showing into the main court. The only thing against the use of the box-room, therefore, was that it looked across at the flat opposite, a single-room apartment in the back-house. Otherwise, if the door of the box-room could be covered by a cupboard the room was completely cut off and the only danger was that someone should search at the same time the next-door flat of the widow and also look up from the court-yard to wonder which of the two flats that window belonged to. Julie had been in the widow's flat once and knew it was such a cramped little oddly shaped affair that such a consideration was exceedingly unlikely.

Julie was unaware of the succession of small incidents that led from the sacking of Frau Kaestner to Kerenyi's hasty warning to her that evening earlier. But the extraordinary chance of a boy of nineteen's naïve arrogance in simply forcing himself on her atten-tion by using the cancelled order for a search – and why cancelled, Julie now asked herself – was enough to show upon what small accidents Franz's safety must be based.

Breakfast was ready and the coffee unbearably appetising. While they ate and drank at the kitchen table Julie explained her plan.

'The junk will have to be cleared out,' she said. 'It will have to go into the spare room and be thrown away bit by bit, or we shall attract attention. The wardrobe from the spare room can be moved up against the door and we shall have to get the back panel of the wardrobe to move somehow, so that we can go through the wardrobe into the room door as if it were a double door. You see how I mean, Franz?'

'I see how you mean, but how are we to make a door in the back panel of the wardrobe? Otherwise it seems a perfect idea. If the wardrobe will fit into the space, that is.'

They went to measure the piece of furniture in question. It would fit the space with a few centimetres to spare on each side, but was too high for the lower ceiling of the back corridor. Fina kneeled down and examined the solid round feet of the cupboard.

'If we can get the feet off and have it standing on the floor it will go in the space,' she said. 'Standing direct on the floor will be better, anyway. Nobody will be able to look under it and see the bottom of the room door, then.'

'But who is going to do the work?' said Franz.

Fina stacked the plates and carried them to the sink.

'My brother.'

'He'll never agree,' said Julie.

'He'll have to. He's in so deep now he can't refuse. He can come up to Vienna for a few days to visit me while you are away in the mountains, gnae' Frau.'

'Oh, but I was thinking of not going away …' Julie began. 'I can't just leave …'

'You'll have to go,' said Franz sharply, staring at her. 'It would be unheard of for you to be in town in August.' He looked for a naked moment into her eyes and saw that he had spoken too quickly, too urgently. 'So many people would know you were here,' he added, his voice fading with the weight of his recognition that he longed for her to go away and that she had seen his longing.

'I see,' she said. 'Yes, no doubt you are right.' She got up from the table and left the room.

6

'The Lord God is on our side,' announced Fina some hours later. She had ceased in the last months to quote the Cardinal of Vienna, and so had a number of other simple people; not because the Cardinal could have done anything but what he did, but because his doing it so quickly and apparently whole-heartedly had made it possible to blame him for the harm in what nobody could have prevented; it never occurred to anyone, how-ever, to praise the Cardinal for any of the benefits they received from the embodiment of their country into a larger one – for the drop in unemployment or increasing trade.

The evidence of God's willingness to help was a circular announcing precautions to be taken against air-raids which included the clearing of inflammable rubbish from lofts and box-rooms, the storing of preserved foods, and other such preparations familiar at that time in every country in Europe.

'God has a rather curious notion of help,' remarked Julie dryly. 'But it does come at the right moment, I must admit.'

'We shall be exemplary citizens and clear out all that junk,' said Franz. 'And what's more, it solves the problem of book-shelves. We can buy some shelves to store food.' The question of hous-ing the books in the new room exercised them, for though there was plenty of other furniture and to spare, there were no book-shelves that could be moved.

All three of them felt a sudden return of hopefulness; they

were almost gay, as if this chance piece of luck were an augury of good fortune. Only Julie noticed that a long section of the new regulations concerned the fitting out of the cellars as bunkers to which all the people living in the house must retire at the air-raid warning signal on penalty of fines and even imprisonment. That bridge could be crossed when and if they came to it, and the memory of the conversation with Hansi the night before helped to make it seem hopefully academic.

There was also, in the post, a note in a strange hand signed by Ferdinand von Kasda, asking Julie to spare him a few minutes of her valuable time; might he call on her, or would she prefer to call on him? She would prefer to call on him and she telephoned and said so later when she was dealing with routine matters of bills and the note to the theatre booking clerk asking for tickets to be sent on some suitable occasion to the young SS officer of the night before whose name Julie forgot as soon as the note was written.

As she wrote the appointment into her diary on the desk she wondered what von Kasda could want with her; she remembered him as a flippant, rather good-looking young man related to Pohaisky's wife. Since she did not know what department of government he worked in and the address on his note gave simply the street number of the building in the inner city a few minutes from her own home where Kasda's office was, the invitation did not worry her. People whose lives are full of varied engagements are not even curious about such things; she thought it was one of those discreet pre-invitation probes to find out if some dull duty such as the opening of a charity show will be favourably viewed.

Julie was busy in the next two days, not only because there was much to do for Franz before she went away as it was tacitly decided she would do after the breakfast-table conversation, but because she needed to fill the time with all manner of details to avoid thinking of what was really in her mind. The shock of the abortive Gestapo raid issued in an intense irritation of the nerves that could only be assuaged by activity; while Franz and Fina busied themselves with his hiding-place, Julie bustled about the city doing odd jobs for herself that could better have been done for her by others.

She was a few minutes late for her appointment with von Kasda. Her taxi drove into the entrance of the building and she followed the clerk who came to escort her up to the second floor without knowing where she was.

So that the conversation between von Kasda and Julie began at cross purposes and was bound to issue in misunderstanding.

'From the outside this house looks quite as it always must have done,' said Julie as von Kasda relieved her of a parcel of books she was carrying. 'One wouldn't know it was an office at all.' She looked round the room, making a slightly wry face, 'though I must say you look official enough in here. Tell me, what do you do all day?'

'Shuffle papers mostly. Everything important – you understand I mean everything officially important; I don't imply that anything we do here can be important to anyone outside the official machine – but everything important in my sense is done either by those over me or those under me. I am just a stool-sitter. Or rather, a between-stool-sitter.'

'So you can't have any important business with me? That, I suppose, must be good news.'

'On the contrary, anything, even the slightest thing, to do with you must be important. But there, we begin to get our terms of reference mixed. Moreover, business with you is important to me in any case, because I've been trying to meet you again for months and months and months.'

'That is obviously not true,' said Julie, laughing in spite of herself at his nonsense. 'All you had to do was to telephone – or turn up on any one of a dozen occasions.'

'Oh, I did that. Twice I went to the theatre, only I couldn't get up the courage to go backstage. I even paid for my ticket. And I spent days of official time and dozens of official groschen – ah, sorry, they are pfennige now, aren't they – making telephone calls to get invited to a housewarming where I was sure you would be.'

'And?'

'Courage failed again. You were looking out of the window. It was a marvellous evening. I didn't feel I had the least chance of living up to it. So I went away and consoled myself with a blonde.'

'That must have been Lehmann's party. I remember ...'

'It's useless to ask me who the blonde was. Since I've already committed myself to the ill-bred opinion that she was the sort of woman one could have no fear of not living up to, I clearly can't tell you who she was ...'

'It's enough that you didn't like her. Now tell me what you wanted to see me about. And before you do, I must tell you that I shall be away for six weeks, so if it's any sort of invitation, I can't.'

'Oh, no, not an invitation. I wouldn't dare. Semi-official. As a matter of fact, it's such nonsense that I can hardly get it out.'

Something about his smiling embarrassment gave Julie a little jolt of shocked surprise. He reached out a long arm and pulled a bundle of papers towards him from a side table. He picked up the wrong set and rose to his feet to see which of the neatly ordered covers was the one he wanted. Julie looked at him for the first time carefully, aware from a change in the atmosphere that he was going to say something unpleasant.

He was a tall and graceful man and about her own age, though his affectation of presenting himself as a cadet as well as his bonny, open face made him seem younger. His faintly impudent air implying a flattering prestige in his view of her, as if he were a boy taking liberties that he knew would not be allowed to an equal, was deceptive, she saw.

'Here we are,' he said, his smile now noticeably nervous. He was wondering how he could have been such a fool as to volunteer for this unneeded duty; and though his protestations were much exaggerated – a frivolous exaggeration was the only possible way to express his half-nervous admiration – there was enough truth in his story of trying to become more nearly acquainted with Julie for him to regret allowing his vanity to push him into what seemed an opportunity but was proving its opposite.

'You mustn't take it seriously,' he began weakly. 'And please forgive me in advance, won't you? If I hadn't seen you, it would have been that Party horror. He's begun to take everything into his hands in the department ...'

'Perhaps you'd better tell me what you are talking about, don't you think?' said Julie. 'You forget I don't know what department you are talking about.'

'Oh, dear,' he muttered, 'worse and worse. Well, here goes. It's about the electrician. You remember having some work done by Hawelka, the electrical firm?'

Julie did not answer because she was stifled by the return of the dreadful fear that gripped her the other night at the sound of the battering on the door and the sight, misty before her sleepy eyes, of Franz's painfully agitated face. Von Kasda thought her silence was caused by anger and astonishment and he hurried on to get his explanation over as quickly as he could. The first few sentences went unheard by his listener; it appeared obvious that everything was now known, and the horror of this thought was mingled with a craven terror of what would happen, in that case, to herself. She stared with blank eyes and face apparently calm at Kasda, not taking in a word of what he said. It was incredible that this man, whose sisters had been at the same school as herself, who belonged so completely to her world, should have accepted the job of acting for the Gestapo and condemning her, or trapping her into condemning herself, into the chaos of outer darkness.

'Needless to say, I – we, that is my chief and myself – are quite sure the whole thing is nonsense ...' Still she said nothing, but he could feel the silent desperation behind her blank look and was afraid of it. 'We know, that is, we don't know, we just feel sure, that Doctor Wedeker is living under a new name in England or America. You mustn't feel ... please don't feel that you are expected to say anything ...' He was going far past what he ought to say, far past what was safe, but her silence drew the words from him. 'I mean, it's obvious that this stupid envelope may – certainly was – just dropped somehow, in any case it has no meaning at all. The date-stamp along – this busybody even noticed that. March last year – before ...'

'You mean – you mean it is simply this workman finding that old envelope?' Julie looked straight into his face, not believing that this tale was all he had to say – it was clearly a trap. They, 'they' again, knew something. But not enough to move against her. That was why the Gestapo raid was cancelled; it was thought better to

243

be careful, to make sure of more evidence. How nearly that blond boy in the SS uniform had come to gaining himself promotion. Now, when his disobedience came out he would be disciplined instead, for giving her warning. And this man sitting behind his desk, pretending friendliness, had orders to trap her by the claim on their common background, and the suggestion of his personal admiration.

Everyone who engages in conspiracy goes through the first stage of finding it easy, makes a mistake and goes to the opposite extreme, seeing hostile intrigue and danger in everything. This happens inevitably, changing character and relationships, killing generosity and spontaneity, putting every man's hand against his neighbour. The survivors are those who adapt themselves to moral savagery; this is called survival of the fittest. Society arranges for the wrong people to survive and for the wrong reasons.

'It can't be that workman and his absurd envelope,' said Julie. 'That would be crazy – meaningless – it must be something else.'

'But of course it's meaningless,' cried Ferdinand, throwing up his hands. 'Utterly meaningless. This electrician, for some unknown reason – probably a desire to show off – reported the incident, if it can even be called that, to his district Party secretary. All these local Party men want to increase their power by interfering. That is what they are doing in the Party – it gives them the chance to mind other people's business. The Party secretary, pursuing his little ambitions, made a report. I think it went through several hands.' He turned over the papers in his folder, checking the stages of the story. 'Yes, several hands. When it got as far as the Ministry of the Interior, we had to discuss it. Not because there is anything in it or because anyone thought there might be. But because the Party channels are all duplicated. The Party man in this depart-ment – I mentioned him just now, you remember? If the department does not pursue it as a matter of civil service proce-dure, and the Party man does on his Party duplicate line, as it were, then we shall be disciplined.' He stopped and looked up at her still face. 'I am being wildly indiscreet. If you turn this into a tale for a boring half-hour, I shall be in trouble.'

She must not protest the meaninglessness of the whole matter again. That would imply that she knew there was more in it than the envelope. That indeed, was the trap.

'I do see now what you mean when you say nothing you do here is important,' said Julie and laughed slightly. 'If this is the sort of thing you spend your official life doing!'

As she said the words, two things occurred to her quick wits. The first, that she must use this man who knew what was going on. He could keep her informed, if she was clever with him. The second, Franz's actual whereabouts were still a mystery to these people. If they knew he was in his own home, the raid would not have been cancelled and he must have been found the other night.

'It's all so bewildering,' she went on. 'You know the Party wants me to divorce my husband? It damages the prestige of the theatre, it seems, for one of its members to be married to a world-respected scholar like my husband ...'

'Even Professor Freud was not safe ...' he said, shrugging his shoulders. 'God knows what would have become of him if he hadn't left for England when he did.'

'Yes, but I'm not speaking generally. I mean, I was assured only two days ago that if I gave in over what they call this matter of form, I should not be exposed in future to this sort of thing. It's only a day or so since I agreed to this outrage; now already I'm in trouble again, it seems.'

'I didn't know that,' he said quickly. 'I mean that the divorce was settled?'

'It can't be arranged until the new law term in the autumn but it's all agreed upon. Apparently no sort of assurance means any-thing; they do these things, as they say, so discreetly — that's supposed to be for my sake, of course — that afterwards one has no means of holding them to their promises. I am beginning to think there's no alternative to ...'

'You see,' he said anxiously, shifting uneasily in his chair, 'it's this duplication I spoke of. The Party does one thing; we try to modify it, or take matters out of Party hands; then Heydrich's pri-vate spy-net takes a hand without anybody else knowing. The Gestapo itself is quite independent of the Party, everything. Certainly of us.'

'But what on earth has Heydrich of all people to do with me?'

'Your husband went to Prague. Some bright boy of Heydrich's has been searching for him there. They feel it as a reflection on their competence that they can't find anything . . . you see?'

'See? See what? I can't see anything but a tangle of nonsense.'

But she did see. She saw that by some means evidence of Franz's death must be arranged. Only by satisfying this mad machine could she protect his life, which with every day of private sorrow and public entanglement became more precious. It was ceasing to be the man himself who must be saved; without being aware of it Julie was changing the living man into a symbol of what must be rescued, what had value in the senseless tangle of intrigue and struggle that enmeshed her. What it was that must be saved she did not analyse; her whole cast of mind was practical, the abstractions of Franz's and Kerenyi's thought were mysterious, to be respected without understanding. But only by being dead could Franz be saved. This clear, limited objective was something she could deal with.

Von Kasda went on speaking but she did not hear him.

'. . . where you can be reached.' He finished.

'You mean during the holidays?' Julie's brows twitched together. 'I've been to the same place for six years and I'm going there again in two days' time. Surely there is no question of my being stopped?'

'Oh, no!' he said, shocked. This is how they keep a watch on me, Julie thought.

'Shall I give you the address, or go direct to the Party? You'll have to tell me what to do. Do I report to the District Secretary or something of that sort? Or is it enough if you know?' Her sarcastic tone stabbed his vanity painfully.

'Of course you don't have to report your address to anybody. Most certainly not to me. You can't really think . . .'

'I have no idea what to think,' said Julie decisively. 'At any rate I shall give you the address. 'It's Gasthof Pfaundler, near Dirnhorn, about thirty kilometres from Meran. The Italian name is . . .'

'Please,' he said. 'Listen, please. I know I deserve your suspicions.

I can understand that to you it seems ... But honestly, Krassny and I thought it was better to deal with the stupid business ourselves, rather than let the Party ... don't you see that?'

'It seems to me that the Party will act independently of you in any case, so that the whole thing will be gone through at least twice again. Always in my own interests, naturally. But perhaps you'd see that "they" know I didn't try to be secretive? It's a tiny little place, right off the main road, and everybody round about has known me for ages.'

She stopped, touched by his obvious misery. He couldn't help it after all; and if she were to use him she must retain his friendship.

'Let's forget it,' she said, briskly, and began to pull on a glove. 'Where are you going for your holiday?'

'Venice,' he said miserably. 'Or rather, Lido. I need some sun.'

'Motoring?'

'Yes.'

'But you'll be coming back through the mountains, then? Come and see Dirnhorn on your way back. It's well worth a detour as Baedeker says.'

He watched her odd little resigned smile as she pulled on the second glove with great attention to its fit.

'Do you mean it?' he said.

'Of course. I love the mountains, don't you? Various friends always drop in on their journeys. A couple of days' walking will refresh you. One gets so dazed by the sun and the sea ...'

Julie stood up and he rose with her. At the door she held out her hand and he took it.

'Your books,' he said. 'You ought not to carry such a heavy parcel.' They were books for Franz.

'It's only two minutes from here.' He was still holding her gloved hand, looking down at it unhappily.

'I'd do anything to undo this,' he said. She freed her hand, and then patted his, left in the air.

'Let's forget it. One should always forget unpleasant things.'

'I wish to God I'd got out of here,' he muttered, looking round the trim, official room.

'That would be silly. I remember you saying at the Pohaiskys' you didn't want to be dragged into the Wehrmacht.'

'You remember that? I thought you'd forgotten my existence.'

'Oh, no,' she lied easily. 'I didn't quite forget you. So! I shall see you at Dirnhorn? You will come through on your way back?'

'If you really mean it? May I really?'

Julie had no sooner gone than Kasda went through to Krassny's room and, tapping once on the door, went in.

'I've seen Frau Homburg,' he said. 'It was pretty uncomfortable.'

'I can imagine.'

'She's agreed to divorce her husband; did you know?'

'No, I didn't. But I'm glad, for her sake. It will save her a lot of trouble.'

'She doesn't seem to think so,' Kasda said gloomily. 'She seems to be going through a regular persecution.'

'That's why I'm glad for her sake. Listen, Nando, my leave starts to-morrow. Before I go I want to warn you. You'll be gone when I get back. Now don't forget this, it's important, and I shan't be able to say it again, probably. You know there's a lot of secret wiring going on in various offices just now?'

'No, really? Is there? You mean, they will wire our rooms for sound while we are gone?'

'I think it's possible. Some offices have had their electric wiring "renewed" recently, while the occupants were away. We have to assume the worst. When we come back, we must assume that everything said can be overheard. You understand?'

'Understand?' Kasda shook his head. 'I understand nothing any more. But nothing.' Krassny noticed that the younger man's usual detached and flippant tone was missing, the smile with which he announced his unconcern with the madness of the world had disappeared.

Fina did not pop out of the kitchen as Julie went in; she did that less since Franz had returned. Now she had Franz to chat to she did not need her conversations with Julie, and though they were often irritating, especially when Fina talked about religion, the smile of someone always glad to see her was missing.

Julie was just about to call Fina as she always did on entering – the old habit of calling for Franz had been sternly dropped as one of the new security rules – when she heard a sound that seemed to turn the blood inside her deathly cold. There were voices coming from the living-room, from behind the closed doors. Her knees gave under her and she sat down at the little telephone-table. Not again to-day, she prayed; please God, give me time. Had Fina already been arrested? Was Franz being interrogated behind those doors? The voices were men's voices, that much she could hear. Or had both Franz and Fina already disappeared and were those voices waiting for herself?

One voice was louder now, and heavy steps approached the double doors from inside the room. Julie had no time to examine the feeling of familiarity before the door opened; it was Kerenyi.

'It's all right – it's Julie,' called Kerenyi over his shoulder, and only then saw that she was chalky and shaking with fear.

'Julie! My dear – you heard our voices!' Julie bent her head forward until it touched the shiny dark surface of the table. It seemed for a moment as if the world withdrew to an immense roaring distance and the blackish gleam of the wood rose like the swell of dark waters, shimmering up towards her inner reality. For an instant of time she knew the horror of losing oneself; it was a moment she never forgot.

It was Kerenyi who helped her to her feet.

'I thought it was the police again!' she said at last, not looking at Franz. 'They were here the other night.'

'I know. Franz told me. But I'd guessed from what Blaschke said that they were looking for him again.'

'Blaschke?' she asked sharply. 'Ah, that policeman! Then they do know something?'

'Blaschke doesn't. If he knew Franz were here the search the other night would have been success ... they would have found Franz then.'

'Yes. Yes. It really is just the envelope.' She frowned impatiently as Kerenyi tried to interrupt. 'When the electrician came, he found an old envelope with Franz's name on it – here, behind the books. The fool reported it. I've just been questioned about it. That was why I ... Listen, Georgy, how did you know Franz was here? How did you get in here?'

'I suppose I'd better tell you. I didn't want to worry you with it. Your charwoman. She heard a man's voice and thought she would get her own back on you for being sacked, by selling a bit of gossip to a newspaper. By a stroke of luck, she came to us and I saw her. When Blaschke sent for me I thought she'd been to the police too. But she would be too scared to do that – people are so afraid of the Gestapo, it must interfere with their work sometimes.'

'You don't think she will go to the police? My God, if she does ...'

'No,' he comforted her. 'She's much too scared. She wouldn't have the courage.'

'But Georgy, you can't come here again. It's far too dangerous. The caretaker or someone will see you.'

She could see from her husband's face how he longed for Kerenyi's company, the relief of a friend he could talk to, but the danger was too great to risk.

'Wait,' said Kerenyi. 'I'm cleverer than you think. When I was here the other day, the day I left a note for you, I told the old black beetle in the caretaker's lodge that I wanted someone in the back-house. There really is an old Frenchwoman living there, a former governess, I can use her as an excuse. She does translations and types manuscripts. I can go in and out to see her – and you. Why shouldn't I come to see you?'

'And when I'm not at home? Besides, have you any translating to do?'

'Certainly. I've always had an ambition to translate Albert Vandal's book on Tilsit, the treaty between Alexander and Napoleon – there's only a very bad German translation, you know. She can help me.'

'But how did you think of all this?'

'It wasn't done in a moment, my dear. I've been working on it for a week now. Ever since I knew Franz was here. And the book will take time – years perhaps.'

'It does make it easier to go away ...' Julie frowned thought-fully. 'I was thinking of staying here, but if I know you are keeping an eye on things—' She looked quickly at Kerenyi, knowing his sharp eyes would see her real reason for going, that she was not wanted here. 'It is more dangerous for me not to go with so many people to notice it than to leave Fina to deal with …'

'Of course, there's that problem too,' agreed Kerenyi. He glanced quickly at Franz and she knew with a stab of jealousy that Franz had talked to him about this, too. 'I'm sure it would be a frightful risk for you to change your arrangements. It will only be for this summer, in any case.'

'What do you mean?' said Franz sharply.

Kerenyi stared. 'Well, of course there is going to be war. Next year no one will go away for the summer. That problem at least will have solved itself.'

'But Georgy, I thought the news was better!'

'There will be war,' said Kerenyi. 'Don't let's even discuss that.'

'You obviously know something,' said Franz. 'Tell us.'

'A friend of mine, First Secretary at the French Embassy in Bucharest, returned to Paris last week and I saw him when he stopped in Vienna. The French talks with the Soviets are being taken up again. Paris is trying to get the Rumanians to allow the Russians to pass through Rumanian territory if "necessary" to get at the Reich. That's the point on which the negotiations stick. The Rumanians won't agree; and the Russians won't help the French unless they do agree. Of course, the Rumanians are right – the Red Army would occupy the country.'

'I see,' said Julie blankly. 'But I didn't know the Reich was threatening Rumania. I thought it was Poland?'

'My dear girl,' sighed Kerenyi. 'You will never understand politics. It is Poland. But if the Russians insist with Rumania which is not, at the moment, in danger of a German invasion, how much more must they be insisting with Poland. And how much more determinedly will the Poles resist the French plan than the half-wits in Bucharest.'

'So the French won't succeed in making a Russian mutual aid pact?' asked Franz.

'But Hansi said only the other evening that reduced the danger of war!'

'Hansi is a political idiot. Remember your history lessons. Who divided Poland in Maria Theresia's day?'

'Austria, Prussia and Russia,' said Julie automatically. 'And Maria Theresia said—'

'Good God,' Franz interrupted her. 'Georgy, you don't think that's possible?'

'Inevitable, if the Poles don't let the Red Army through their country. They won't and can't agree. And the Russians have no more forgotten Brest-Litovsk and Riga than the Germans have forgotten Versailles.'

'But if there's no danger of the Russians moving against Hitler, surely the Germans will take back Danzig and the Corridor and that will be the end of it.'

'The British have contracted to protect the Poles.'

'Now who's being a political idiot,' cried Franz derisively. 'The British! They won't fight! For the American-French artificial Poland? They have far too much sense! Their guarantee was a gesture, nothing more. There is no way they can reach Poland!'

'Well, let's hope so. The only hope for peace is to sacrifice Poland. But I see the foreign Press and you don't. I don't feel too happy about the attitude of the English. Of course, they can't help the Poles and they must know that, but their tone has changed alarmingly in the last few weeks. They made the treaty with Poland to warn Hitler. If it doesn't succeed and he attacks Poland, they – the English – may feel bound to go to war. Even if they don't, the Russians will move into Eastern Poland as soon as the Germans attack in the West. That could mean war, too, don't forget. If they have not already agreed between themselves!'

'In any event, there's nothing we can do,' said Julie. 'What interests me far more than all this, Georgy, is how you got into the flat when Fina was out?'

Kerenyi smiled at her. 'I rang the bell and Fina didn't answer, but I had the feeling there was somebody listening inside the door. I knew Franz was here, you see, or anyway I was almost certain. So I wrote on a page of my notebook and pushed it under the door. As soon as he knew it was me, Franz opened the door.'

'Show me,' said Julie to Franz. He put a hand in his side pocket and pulled out a torn scrap of paper, on which she read: *Franz, it is Georgy. I know you are there. Open the door. There is no one else here.*

Julie sat looking at the crumpled scrap of paper.

'I know I am a political idiot,' she said slowly, 'and you both know far more than I do. But at least I'm sensible about practical things. Don't you see that this is just what a Gestapo agent would write if he had Georgy in a dungeon somewhere and was coming to get you?'

'But I know Georgy's writing,' protested Franz.

'It isn't at all like his normal writing. Couldn't be, scrawled with a pencil up against the door in the half-dark out in the hallway.'

The two men looked sheepishly at each other like schoolboys caught smoking.

Julie tore the scrap of paper into a dozen pieces and went out to the lavatory, where they heard her flush the scraps away.

When she came back they saw her eyes were full of tears. She turned to Franz and said, her voice cold but shaking, 'If you have no respect for your own life, you might at least think of Fina and me.'

'She's quite right, you know,' said Kerenyi at last.

'But it need not happen again,' said Franz pleadingly, and his friend could hear the whole weight of his terrible loneliness behind the words.

'We must make a signal that only I use,' said Kerenyi. 'If I'm always careful that the caretakers don't see me I can come up often.'

'But, my dear chap, you can have a key,' said Franz. 'That will be the simplest way and I'm sure we have a spare.' Kerenyi knew Franz very well, but this remark reduced him to an astonished silence. Franz really saw this small but crucial problem as simple. Although Kerenyi had already told him he was being interrogated by the Gestapo, it never crossed Franz's mind that Kerenyi could betray him and the constant possibility of a mishap that could lead the police to him without them suspecting anything until too late was not, apparently, real to him. And it was this simplicity in Franz, his unworldly goodness that made him so irreplaceably valuable.

There was silence until Kerenyi returned to a subject much on his mind.

'You know, if one tries to be objective about this Nazi system, one begins to see a pattern in their methods.'

'You mean the Gestapo man?'

'No, not Blaschke. He is just a policeman, the old-fashioned kind using normal police methods. But the others there are entirely different. Blaschke keeps me under control for a definite purpose – to find you. Probably he would prefer to keep Julie under his official eye; but he is forbidden to do that by cultural policy. So I'm the next best means of contact.'

'It's quite typical of these apes that they have an awe of culture,' Franz interposed. 'That seems to be the difference between them and the Russian Secret Police, to whom nothing is sacred.'

'I think that's only a difference of several hundred years of education, not of purpose. Still less of method. Russian society is still, after all, in a semi-barbarous condition, whereas the Nazis took over a cultural society of a thousand years. But that's not what I meant. Blaschke's purpose is a limited and definite one and his methods are suited to it, ordinary police interrogation and investigation. It's the others who are new and interesting. *Their* purpose is simply control for its own sake. At first I thought they knocked suspects about down there on the Kai because they didn't know how to interrogate – some of them are incredibly low-class, stupid fellows, slum louts who managed to slip into safe jobs through the SA. But when I'd been there two or three times I saw that the methods they use are deliberate policy.'

'Police brutality is, after all, nothing new, Georg.'

'These are not policemen in the usual sense of the word. For one thing there are far too many of them. Then, they operate a good deal, if not mainly, on the reports of their amateur Party spies.'

'But all security police use local informers. The Imperial State Police, for instance, used the caretakers. Julie is sure the Pichlers here work for the police.'

'No, you've got it wrong. The Pichlers – if they report – do so to the block-leader. He reports to the sub-district and so on, up to Party secretary. One of their levers is the self-importance of little men. The other is fear. That is the point. Where everyone can read, everyone must be controlled. Consider: industry and administration depend on millions of more or less literate workers so every mechanic can be a saboteur, every file clerk a subversive. In the end, every citizen is watching himself and every other.'

'And you think this will become a constant factor of life?'

'It must as long as rulers have ends opposed to the wishes of the vast majority – which are always, as Machiavelli said, for as little oppression as possible.'

'But my dear Georgy, that's always been the case.'

'Not in a mechanised society. Formerly whole masses of people could be ignored by the police except in moments of great upheaval or famine. Now nobody can be ignored – everyone can literally throw a spanner in the works. Mechanical society gives everyone a little power – not political power, but the power to interrupt at least his own little job by being careless, stubborn, lazy. As far as it reaches, propaganda tries to convince everybody that he is happy; where that does not reach, mutual spying takes over. The mechanised society is new and the power of a typist to put pressure on her rulers has to be answered by universal policing. Either the rulers must act as mechanics want them to act or they must use force on the mechanics.'

'You no longer believe, then, that feeling – nationalist or patriotic perhaps – moves people, ordinary people?'

'Of course. But – only as far as they are tolerably comfortable. As soon as they become uncomfortable enough, people begin to grumble. The grumbling takes the form of unconscious slackness. The slackness is, in a complex machine, sabotage.'

'This is an interesting idea, Georgy. You mean mechanisation, which I agree is something quite new in its modern mass form, must bring police-state methods with it. Is that it?'

'Pleasant prospect, eh?'

'Then, according to you Western Europe will not resist Hitler because they are not forced. But you can't be including the English?'

'We don't know how far ordinary people there know what is happening. But I would guess, more discreet coercion – I would judge from the newspapers I read that it takes the form there of a complete misrepresentation of the real balance of powers in Europe – is being used than we know.'

'That's the Goebbels line,' Franz rejected this with a shake of the head. 'That I can't believe.'

'One can't disbelieve something just because one does not like it, or those who say it. What is happening here is only more intense, more sudden than what will happen everywhere as the pressures increase. This is the disease of modern man. In the name of co-operation, co-ordination, orderliness, every single human being is to be isolated from every other by mutual fear.'

'That is true now, for some of us. I suppose, then, you see people like myself as only the first, isolated victims.' They were both silent. At last Franz said slowly, 'That whole societies of individuals submit to this horror of loneliness without a sense of outrage, means that we are all – already – deadly sick.

'How else could a man of Hitler's type, as I understand it, demonic, irrational, obsessive, control half of Europe? He says himself he moves with the certainty of a sleep-walker and that's only another way of saying he doesn't know what he is doing until he does it. He in person is the chaos inside us all – that is why he interprets this chaos to people who would – in their normal state – find him absurd and revolting.

'The horror of loneliness; we know it already in Russia in its mass form – the great purges when members of families denounce each other to ensure their own, or their children's safety. This control you talk of then, is based on what must be the deepest fear of human beings – to be alone, driven out, isolated from their own kind. People will do anything to avoid that and that is precisely what happens … Freud has it all wrong. What dominates human beings is this fear of being left alone and it comes from the long helplessness of human childhood when to be abandoned means death. Listen, Georgy, that is the sure instinct of madmen, that they have picked on this fear – what else are these camps but places where men cease to exist, never were? You said that to me, once, I remember.'

Franz rose from his chair by pushing himself up with his arms and went to the window; and Kerenyi saw how he wavered in his step and had to support himself with a shaky hand on the window-frame, without, however, moving the sheltering curtains.

'Poets have been warning us for generations; Goethe felt it coming even so long ago. And Nietzsche – we assume he approved of his supermen but I wonder now – was it not the terror of his own prophecy that drove him mad? The dreams of Kafka, they too are coming true. Prophets are always called mad by those who are so diseased that they can't recognise their own faces.'

BOOK THREE

August 1939–November 1940

1

here were two letters. One in Fina's scrabbled script, and one from Frau Pohaisky to let Julie know that her husband had been sent home 'and is well'. It was August now, and in the four weeks away from home, three letters had arrived from Fina, partly dictated by Franz; the arrival of each one produced in Julie a sensation of sharp relief; but she was depressed that day, as she had been when the two previous letters came. She would go out, she decided, standing on the wooden balcony of her room and tapping the opened letters on the balustrade. Better get out in the sunlit upland meadows. Julie picked up her bathing suit from the rail where it hung drying and took a towel.

The daughter of the house was in the hall, writing in an order book.

'Dorli, I shall be gone all day,' Julie told her.

'I wish I could come with you and have a swim,' said Dorli. 'Don't freeze to death in that cold water, now.' The two women were dressed alike in the peasant dress that everyone wore in the country; one head bleached by sun and wind and the other stubbornly dark, but faces equally tanned; they talked as equals, for the obsequiousness of Vienna did not reach to the mountains. 'Leave the letters here,' added the girl, 'I'll put them upstairs when I go up.'

Julie went out round the back of the little pinewood house and up the long slope of the alpine meadow. After a few minutes she could see down the valley far below. On its slopes men and women with their horses, bullocks and wains were collecting the highest crops, the last to ripen. Through the belt of dark conifers it was chill and always slightly damp, but the sunlight at the other side was the hotter in contrast, blazing off the empty, silent crag of the mountain above her head. It was over an hour's walk to the little lake, still, black, icy cold, where no one ever came. It was too far for the peasants and there was nothing there to tempt them. The peasant boys and girls swam down in the valley where the river water was warm. Julie knew the local people believed the lake to have malign properties and she had been warned, years before, about swimming there; but for herself and Franz its sinister reputation had been a welcome protection against intrusion. She dived and swam for a few minutes before the icy grip of the water drove her out to lie in the hot sun, on the mossy odorous short turf where a thousand tiny plants clung in the thin soil to provide a carpet of multi-coloured flowers in the mountain spring.

Presently she dressed again and walked on round the shoulder of treeless pasture skirting a sheer rise of rock that jagged up to the peak. The peasants called it Old Man's Tooth, and farther on round the shoulder there was a little mountain rest-hut where she knew she could get dark bread with cheesy butter and honey to eat.

It was empty to-day, and the elderly retired schoolteacher who spent his summers there as warden for the Alpine Federation was alone.

'What happened to the soldiers?' she asked as he sat down opposite her on the other bench. She dribbled honey over the thick chunk of bread and ate greedily, setting her bare elbows on the rough planks of the table. 'Have they finished their training?'

He was a scrawny, tall man, prim and self-righteous in manner.

'They left yesterday,' he said, pursing his mouth in that unconscious envy of youth that issues as disapproval in those who wasted their own years of bounty. He came from North Tyrol and was, like Julie, technically a foreigner here in this still entirely German region that was yet part of Italy. 'But their training was not finished. Or so I gathered from their sergeant.'

Julie was silent, she knew that he wanted to explain to her and would do so. After a sufficient pause the schoolmaster said solemnly:

'The sergeant, of course, should not have told me so. But he did say that the unit was to return to its base immediately.'

'Recalled, then?' she said blankly.

'Recalled. The sergeant supposed they were to be regrouped.'

Julie looked round at the glowing midday silence of the rocks where the squad of half-naked youngsters were climbing a few days before. Bleached to tow and burnt dark red by the mountain sun, they usually did their training climbs and marches, against regulations, without uniforms and without most of their equipment. The only record left of them now was the group of yellowed patches on the turf where their tents had stood.

'They won't get a chance for a training course like this again in a hurry,' said the schoolmaster with what sounded like satisfaction. 'Poland, I dare say.' He was well-informed. He went down to the valley twice a week to read the local paper and get his mail.

'Poland? Alpine Scouts — what would they do in Poland?'

The schoolteacher looked at Julie with his head on one side and smiled condescendingly.

'There is going to be war,' he said at last. 'To-day is the second of August — it can't be more than a week or so at most before the campaign for Danzig begins.'

'But the Russians . . . ?' asked Julie.

'The Führer no doubt has the whole matter well in hand. It is well known that the Russians are very weak. Especially in leadership since the purges took nearly all their competent staff officers . . .' He glanced up over Julie's shoulder. 'Someone coming,' he said.

Julie looked over her shoulder and saw a tall man dressed for the mountains in leather breeches, checked shirt and heavy boots. As he approached she saw it was von Kasda.

'Ah, it's a friend from Vienna,' she said. 'He will have the latest news, perhaps.'

'I came, you see,' he called before he came up to them. He greeted the schoolmaster courteously and turned to Julie.

261

'You have a marvellous tan,' she said. 'Have you any news of the war?'

'Is there a war? Not that I've heard.'

'Have you seen to-day's papers?' asked the schoolmaster, not wanting to give up his forecast of disaster.

'To-day's and yesterday's,' answered Kasda cheerfully. 'There's nothing about war in the Italian papers.'

'Ach, the Italian press. They pretend nothing is happening. Fighting is hardly their strong point.'

'No, indeed,' agreed Kasda, 'it's one of the things I so like about Italians.'

'Well, I can't sit here chattering,' cried the schoolmaster, jumping up, 'there's work to be done.' He took the plate from in front of Julie and disappeared into the rest-hut with the air of a man returning to the serious business of life.

'Silly old goat,' muttered Julie at his back. 'Then there really is no news of trouble?'

'Of course, all the time, but no war. The Lido was wonderful; I wish you had been there. I'm this colour almost all over.'

'My lake will be a change for you. It's like ice, even in this sun.'

Kasda groaned theatrically. 'Return to German puritanism, I suppose. As you see, I brought clothes that would fit into the landscape.'

As they went away, calling farewells to the silent hut, Julie said, 'Have you noticed that we are all becoming nationalist? I mean, either pro or anti, but nationalist-minded?'

'Yes, I have, and I'd rather not think about it. And most particularly, I'd rather not think about wars.'

'Then we agree on that. Let's not.'

'I do hope you don't mind me taking you at your word, as I did, and coming to see you?'

'No, I'm delighted. I was very bored with my own company.'

'So was I,' he said. He had quite lost his awe of Julie; it seemed their holiday disguises gave them the equality of the mountain people. He had been thinking of Julie during the fortnight he lay on the beach and unconsciously took an advance in their friendship for granted that only existed in his imagination. But she

262

seemed to take it for granted too and they both quite naturally dropped their defensive, flirtatious tone to each other.

They talked about Venice, that most absurd and lovely of anachronisms. And about Trieste, and hunting in Slovenia, and about the Dalmatian coast where she had never been. She discovered that Kasda had a grandfather still alive in Croatia at some immense and uncounted age.

'He lives in a funny little house in the forest ... everybody else has died but him and an old huntsman, and they live there together in happy filth. I'm waiting for him to die so that I can go and live there.'

They sat for a long time by the little lake, and watched the still dark water. On this side it was held in a basin of rock and ran on the far side, where Julie never went, into a reedy swamp from which a stream trickled through the meadows and later fell over the edge of a steep drop in a veil of mist.

From the top of the peak, puffs of white cloud formed in the blue emptiness. The late afternoon was gold and green, very still.

'I was asleep,' said Julie, sitting up suddenly.

'Yes, for half an hour. I've been watching you and the hawk up there. He's asleep too, I imagine.'

'A hawk? Or an eagle?' She shaded her eyes with her hand to stare up at the creature swinging almost motionless between earth and heaven.

'Rather small for a mountain eagle, but it may be a young one,' he said lazily. They looked down from the sky at the same moment, looked dazed with light into each other's faces, and smiled. They rose together without a word and started off down the sloping Alm towards the strip of woodland. Julie shivered a little under the dark trees and they hurried their steps. It was evening by the time they reached the inn.

'So you found her,' called the innkeeper. 'A glorious day!'

They ate with appetite on the terrace, as the small wooden extension to the dining-room was called, though it hardly amounted to such dignity. It was a moonless night, the dark sky filled with the flash and glitter of mountain stars to which their candles offered no rivalry.

'I've never seen such a night ... not even here in the mountains!'

The stout peasant girl came and took their plates, returning in a moment with a mountain of creamy fluff on a flat dish.

'Miss Dorli said to say, she just felt like making it,' she announced.

Kasda sighed with pleasure as he attacked the airy mountain of *Salzburger Nockerl*. 'My favourite pudding. She must have known by instinct.'

'Mine too. It was always my birthday treat.'

'When?'

'April 10th.'

'But so is mine! What an astounding thing!' Kasda laughed with pleasure. 'That makes us almost relations, don't you agree?'

'I shall start calling you Ferdinand – at once.'

'Nando, please. Nobody ever calls me Ferdinand. Only emperors and archdukes are called that.'

They sat until late; neither would have been able to explain what it was they talked about so pleasantly and easily. Instinct made them want to find out about each other and they exchanged scraps of memory from childhood and youth, to identify each other and fill in the shadows of background. Dorli and the stout peasant girl in the kitchen finished clearing up, turned off the lights and went to bed with the feeling that something pleasant was happening. The only lights left burning were the candles on the table in their glass wind-protectors and the hall-light and inn-sign that burned all night. Dorli was quite unconscious of furthering a love affair though she did everything she could to do so. She was a pious, even a bigoted Catholic; but an instinct older than the Church could reach told her that it was a waste of life and sweetness for a still-young woman to live alone, and that this pleasant bonny man with his long slender legs and graceful movements would renew Julie's life for her. No one at the inn knew what had happened to Julie's husband, but they knew that in some way the relationship was dead; perhaps they thought that Franz was dead, he had not been mentioned since the autumn of two years before and they may have assumed Julie's loneliness and the hardening they felt in her to be widowhood and were simply glad that this state was to be altered as they accepted it was to be. Before it was clear to either Julie or Nando, Dorli and her father saw that he was in love with her.

It was days before Julie realised that Nando meant to stay here in the mountains with her for the rest of his year's leave. He stayed for more than a fortnight and they went out every day walking the surrounding country and Nando fished for trout in the mountain streams. They went down to the valley and danced at the big tourist Gasthof on Saturday evening. It was full of English and American tourists, Italian families and local peasant couples who tasted the life of the outside world, as they supposed, while the tourists thought themselves to be sharing the simplicity of the mountain folk. They were all pleased with the deception, particularly the foreigners. Only simple people with no interest in politics and little knowledge of the world stayed so late in the dangerous part of Europe, which everyone from Land's End to the Iron Gates who read the eager, angry newspapers in every language knew was about to go to war. There can never have been a war so publicised before it happened, or one that was so certainly awaited. Julie and Nando never mentioned the news; when they heard the hectoring tone of the newsreader from Innsbruck on the innkeeper's wireless – he listened to the news every evening – they closed the door or went away. But, like every other thinking man and woman in all of Europe on each side of the lines already clearly drawn, they knew that it was coming and soon.

They were concerned entirely with their own feelings of discovering each other, exploring each other. Discovery slipped naturally into physical love; the moments when their eyes met and smiled became moments of hands touching, the laughter of shared pleasures extended into nights of whispered happiness, detached from the world and ordinary life. The distance from Vienna of their sanctuary made it easy to forget the interview that led to Nando's presence in the mountains, and Julie's gratitude for release from the tightening bonds of coldness matched Nando's gratitude to her for his marvellous luck, as he felt it to be.

But his holiday was over before Julie's and the day came when he climbed into his sports car in the afternoon and drove away towards the mountain pass that took him to Austria and Vienna and back to his office.

They had succeeded so well in shutting themselves off from the news that when, on Wednesday of the next week, the innkeeper ran hastily into the hall and told Julie that Russia and Germany had signed a pact of friendship, it was as much a shock to her as if she had really known nothing about it at all. She recalled then what Franz and Kerenyi had said weeks before and recognised this news was the black sign of coming disaster, while the innkeeper was still trying to persuade himself that the news was of peace.

'Don't you see,' she said sharply, the quick vertical frown showing between her eyebrows, 'they have agreed on what is to happen to Poland.'

They stared at each other, and heard the single bell of the little church halfway down the side of the valley as it began to toll.

'Listen,' Julie turned her head, 'He knows what it means.' By 'he' she meant the priest.

Dorli came out of the kitchen wiping her hands on a coarse towel.

'Has someone died, Father?' she asked. She looked from the face of her father to that of the guest and turned back into the kitchen, crossing herself. 'We'd better go down,' she muttered. 'I'll take the things off the fire.'

The little whitewashed church was crowded with people in their working clothes, smelling of sweat and the beasts they tended. The women pulled their black scarves up over their hair and sighed heavily, kneeling and rising. The men stood stolidly, heads bent while the priest prayed for a peace that was already gone. The young men at the back of the church, crammed together under the deep arch of the organ-loft hung with primitive votive pictures commemorating escapes from accident and death in the mountains, shifted uneasily about, like cattle that feel a storm coming. Their crude boots scraped on the stone flags; it was for them the prayers were meant, the young who would be sacrificed.

Afterwards Julie walked on down the hillside to the nearest house with a telephone, and ordered a car from Merano to fetch her in the morning.

When she passed the church again on her way back she could see the priest standing in the porch talking to the unofficial Nazi Party secretary for the district, who was waving his arms and shouting protests. She heard the words — 'provocation ... war-mongering ... the Führer ...' On a sudden impulse she turned in at the churchyard gate and went up the path, pushing close past the angry man and nodding at the priest as she went inside the church again and stayed there ostentatiously long, sitting in the back pew with her head bent on her hand as if she were praying, though in fact she thought of to-morrow's journey and what she would find in Vienna.

Autumn had arrived in the city. The trees in the square in front of the Westbahnhof were already browning, dusty with the exhaustion of summer. Everyone was ill-tempered, including the passengers on the night-train from Innsbruck. No one was there to meet her, and though Julie knew that Fina never left the house any more unless to go to Church or the shops, this made her anxious. She pushed the thought away as the surly old porter trotted off with her luggage to find a taxi, an old motor that smelt mysteriously of straw and the urine of horses. It was not far. Her scratchy impatience made it seem further, but when the taxi stopped by the familiar doors she felt nothing but a deep reluctance. The side door was ajar and Frau Pichler stood there talking with a shopman carrying a basket. She left the man and jogged forward, crying greetings to Julie in her hoarse, obsequious voice.

'Are you well?' asked Julie, smelling with disfavour the familiar release of sweat, envy and the fats of a thousand pots of goulasch stewing eternally in the close little porter's lodge. Inside the black and white hall, sure enough, the smell of yet another goulasch in the half-dark. And the moan of the lift bringing Fina down at Frau Pichler's ring.

Julie embraced Fina, and saw Frau Pichler register the familiarity. Fina began to cry a little.

'I've missed you, gnae' Frau,' she said and sniffed. She looked a little sallow and puffy from staying indoors all that summer.

'What are you staring at, eh?' she said sharply to the taxi driver. 'Put the bags in the lift. Don't stand there gawping!'

'I'll come up with you and help,' said the man, who had been rude to Julie and now grinned companionably at Fina and understood her perfectly. 'They'm heavy, they are.'

He put the bags down in the apartment doorway and Fina paid him from her big housekeeping purse, pulling it out of the skirt pocket under her apron as if she expected him to make a grab for it. She gave him half the tip Julie would have given, and he was twice as pleased with it. The living-room was empty. Not until Fina had locked the flat door did she hear a door close quietly somewhere in the big apartment and a moment later Franz appeared in the dining-room doorway. He looked thinner, paler. His absent-minded look was very noticeable, and he hovered for a moment in the door as if uncertain whether or not to enter the room.

They did not embrace. 'I've missed you terribly,' they both said at the same moment and both lied. 'What a splendid tan you have,' said Franz, and there was no envy in his tone. With relief and pain, Julie saw that Franz had adapted himself already to his confinement as he adapted himself eighteen months before to a country existence in the Lungau. He began at once to talk of the work he was doing and the day's news. The mountains and Julie's holiday were unreal to him; his scholar's mind was focused on its own content. I ought to be glad for him, Julie thought; I am glad for him. Then why do I feel angry, as if someone had injured him?

She was at once back in the confines of their triple conspiracy, and saw that Franz and Fina had evolved a clear system of life in the weeks she had been away. Fina was protective and possessive, she seemed to know instantly when Franz moved from one room to another though he wore new carpet slippers that made no sound except for a tiny slithering on the parquet. They had developed a curious sense of each other's presence so that when the door-bell rang she seemed to know whether or not she might safely open to whatever stranger waited there, without even looking to see where Franz was. In fact, he was almost always in the secret room. He took Julie through the wardrobe across the end of the passage with a naïve pleasure at the cunning of the device, and showed her the shelves that Fina's brother had built all round the room. The shelves went right up to the ceiling except for the thickly curtained window and the door. The space, narrow before, was now tiny and crammed with books, with a thick carpet on the floor, a small writing-table and a chair with arm-rests. The bed folded up against the wall; not to take space from the book-shelves, it had been fitted under the window by neatly sawing off the feet.

'Fina's idea,' said Franz. 'The carpentering took nearly a week.'

'Where did you find the carpet?' asked Julie and then saw that it was one from the drawing-room, folded double to fit. 'It's really turned out very well.'

'He's as safe here as he would be abroad somewhere with nobody to look after him,' said Fina. Julie saw they had discussed the future and decided, probably without saying so, that any plans Julie might come back with for Franz's escape from his captivity should be scotched from the first. They had worked it all out, or at least they had worked out everything that concerned life inside the apartment. Going back into the living-room, Julie saw that many of Franz's book were gone into the new room, leaving gaps in the book-shelves. They will have to be filled, she thought; they didn't think of that because nobody has been using this room while I was away. It had always been the focus of their domestic life, but now it would become Julie's room alone.

In fact, Julie had come back with a half-formed idea of getting Franz across the Styrian march into Slovenia. This idea came from Nando's remarks about his grandfather's little house; but she did not think of Nando now and was quite startled when the tele-phone rang in the hall and she heard his light, easy voice say, 'I knew you would be on this morning's train ... how are you?'

'Yes, I thought I had better get back — after the news ...'

'Forgive me for not meeting the train,' his voice said. 'We are flooded with extra work and I couldn't get away ...'

He took it for granted then, she thought, and this surprised her for she had hardly given him a thought since the moment when the innkeeper rushed into the hall with the news of that so misnamed treaty of friendship. He took it for granted that it would go on when I got back. And she knew and accepted that it would go on and that this too was now a part of her life and could no more be just ended than her responsibility for Franz could be ended. And in the moment that Julie accepted this entry of Nando into her real life, she recognised that she was in love with him. And just as she completely forgot the scene in Nando's office before she left for the mountains, so it never occurred to Julie that she was doing something that could cost Franz, Fina and herself their lives. She hardly knew Ferdinand von Kasda and what she knew of him was that he was a gay and irresponsible young man who appeared to take nothing very seriously. She herself did not take life, except for her work, very seriously, nor was life, up to the year before, a serious matter. If some solemn person had pointed out to her that she had a duty to think of Franz first, she would not have known what he was talking about for it never once entered her mind that Franz did not come first. She now valued Franz more and not less; the less they understood each other and the further they seemed to move from each other in spirit and body in their claustrophobic box-like world, the more precious was his being to her and at the same time the more essential to her a life outside the apartment where he was. It was only when her physical loneliness was removed and the resentment she naturally and unconsciously felt against Franz because of that loneliness was gone, that she really began to love Franz as a human being.

Without knowing why, all the three persons in the apartment recognised that they were easier and calmer together than before Julie went away. They did not examine this, any of them, for the terrible events that now crowded in from the outside world left no time or energy for introspection.

The war began.

2

The first premiere of the season was always marked by a reception after the theatre; and though there had been some discussion of the propriety of receptions, in which those who wished to appear patrio tic and earnest had expressed doubts, the other party carried the day and the reception was held as usual. Director Schoenherr settled the matter, neatly as was his habit, by pointing out that the campaign in Poland was the greatest feat of arms for centuries (he carefully did not commit himself to a comparison) and a matter for general rejoicing. And if one or two cynical whispers were heard as to the disparity in the strength of the armies involved, these were treated as jokes.

Julie arrived from the theatre attended by Walter Harich and Willy Mundel at Lehmann's rococo house to find everyone torn between curiosity and malicious laughter. Frau Lehmann had arrived unexpectedly from Hamburg.

'May I present my wife,' Lehmann bowed towards a tall, serious, handsome blonde who might have been his sister and who stood beside him with her gloved hands folded in front of her waist as if she had been planted into the floor. She wore a dark, rich dress of some metallic silk that gleamed.

'Ah, Frau Homburg! I have heard of you. Delighted!' The woman inclined her head and moved a hand to touch Julie's. 'Herr Harich. Herr Mundel. Are you performers too?'

'Heaven!' chuckled Mundel into Julie's ear. 'Who is she imitating? The delicious condescension!'

They were, of course, looking round already for Maris, who stood in a far corner with her back to the entrance with a group of men in black uniforms.

Hansi ran up the stairs and followed them past their 'hostess'. 'How long before someone tells her?' he asked. 'Anyone taking bets?'

'What a bad psychologist you are, Hansi,' answered Mundel. 'After five minutes she won't have a single champion in the place.'

'She is a supporter of Himmler's idea of an Order of German Noblewomen. They are going to found a new race of superior beings. She has three children already and plans to breed at least ten – all superior.'

'Then she must have come to get another,' pointed out Harich. 'Since her husband doesn't go to Hamburg.'

'Did you know she was here, Hansi?' asked Julie. 'You might have told us.'

'There was no time. She came in a special flight – with Heydrich from Berlin.'

'These terrible aeroplanes,' said Mundel, 'nobody is safe for a moment. They ruin social relations.'

Julie moved away from them as Nando came in, and walked across the room towards him. Neither of them made any attempt to hide their relationship from their friends, and now went everywhere together.

Hansi joined them. 'Something frightful has happened,' he said to Julie. 'Just as I was leaving to come here.'

'Not yet,' said Nando, watching Lehmann's narrow blond head over the heads of the others, 'but it will.'

'No, I'm serious. Julie, that damned lawyer. I told Schoenherr we should get a good man, not that back-street shyster. Now he has gone through all sorts of unnecessary rigmarole about establishing the whereabouts of poor Franz.'

'I thought that was all finished,' said Julie. The laughter died in her face and she looked suddenly older and tired. The frown twitched between her arched brows and she put up a hand to her forehead as if at a sudden headache.

'It should have been. He didn't say a word to me or Schoenherr, knowing he'd made a mess of it. Now he finds that Franz — forgive me Julie — has been declared deceased by the Emigration Board.'

'But that was wound up months ago,' objected Nando.

'Apparently, it's being started up again in some new form. There is to be planned emigration to somewhere in Poland as soon as the civil authorities take over from the Wehrmacht there. They've made up a lot of new lists of everyone registered with the Jewish Community. So now the whole proceeding has to begin again from the beginning.'

'Julie, angel — you'd better sit down.'

'I'm all right,' she said irritably. 'What does this mean, Hansi?'

'It means you can't get a divorce, I'm afraid. Or not yet.'

'But do I need to, if . . . ?'

'It's safer,' Hansi glanced at her out of the corner of his eyes.

'Safer?' she cried sharply, 'how safer?' I must control myself, she thought desperately. He doesn't know anything; it means nothing.

'The Emigration Board has no legal status; what they say doesn't really count; they just write off any name they can't trace as suicide and treat the person as already emigrated.'

'That's crazy,' interrupted Nando again. 'That means they equate emigration with death . . . That can't be so, Hansi. There's a mistake somewhere.'

'No. It's a device they use, apparently, to enable the property of illegal emigrants or suicides to be sequestrated.'

'That doesn't come into the question in this case, though,' argued Julie. 'The property was transferred to me before it all started.'

'It was?' said Hansi, startled. 'I didn't know that.'

'It never occurred to me to say anything about it. The Emigration Board or whatever it calls itself can't take a penny off me.'

'We must get the name taken off that list,' said Hansi. 'They'll follow it up for years; we'll have endless trouble with them. We shall have to prove your claim – all sorts of difficulties will arise. Oh, God … if only we knew where he was!'

She went so white that Nando put out an arm to hold her.

There was a silence.

'You and Schoenherr have made a fine mess of things,' said Julie at last. 'I shall go to Pohaisky's son-in-law to-morrow and do it myself.'

'We only wanted to save you the embarrassment,' begged Hansi. 'And you know you didn't want to have anything to do with it all.'

'Well, I see I shall have to. And I think I'll go now.'

'I'll take you,' said Nando and they left Hansi standing there.

In the car she suddenly clutched Nando's wrist, so that he swung the wheel sharply and skidded on tram lines.

'I can't go to the Pohaiskys',' she cried. 'I'll have to find some-body else …'

Nando straightened the car and turned a corner.

'We must go to your place,' she said. 'I can't go home like this … I mean, not yet …'

'Really, I like Ostrovsky, you know. But he has a most extraor-dinary lack of tact. Imagine coming out with such a piece of news at this time of night …'

'Hansi is famous for his awkwardness,' said Julie wearily. They went towards the lift, and gave the car keys to the porter to garage the car which could not be left in the narrow street.

Once inside Nando's little flat, Julie seemed to collapse inside herself and sat suddenly in an arm-chair as if she could no longer hold herself up. He kneeled beside her and took her limp hand which was cold.

'Why can't you go to the Pohaiskys'?' he asked gently. 'They know you – they'll understand without all the explanations …'

He pressed the back of her hand against his forehead and then his cheek, feeling a tenderness for her he had never felt for anyone before and a sensation of the loss of his freedom, for her sudden weakness demanded something of him. They had not discussed the subject of her divorce since the conversation in his office. It occurred to Nando, that if Julie were free … He did not push the thought to its conclusion.

There was a silence. Julie turned her hand and stroked his springing hair.

'Have you seen Alois Pohaisky since he came back?' she said at last.

'No. Have you? As a matter of fact, he's at my mother's house in the country, but I haven't been there for months.'

'I saw her. Frau Pohaisky. She sent a note round and we met at Sacher's. I can't add to their difficulties with anything so sordid as this divorce business.'

He remembered something. He got up and put two sofa cushions over the telephone, and then turned on his wireless and found music. It was *The Merry Widow*.

'I still haven't got used to being careful,' he said. 'Though my chief — Krassny, you know? — warned me, months ago ... Are you playing to-morrow?'

'Yes ... the Archduchess in *Egmont* with Harich. Why, darling?'

'I thought if you weren't I'd get up some champagne ...?'

'What a good idea! Let's anyway ... I can sleep late.'

He took the cushions away from the telephone again and called the café. Five minutes later the waiter knocked on the door, brought in two bottles, one in an ice-bucket and a second which he put into the refrigerator without being told; greeted Julie with the greatest respect and left again, closing the door after him. Turning from the foaming bottle with two glasses in his hands, Nando found Julie laughing helplessly.

'It's so absurd,' she gasped, 'so crazy. We don't bother to hide from the waiter, yet we cover the phone so that nobody can hear what we say to each other ...'

'I've known that waiter since I left the *Gymnasium*,' protested Nando, and began to laugh himself. She stretched out her hands to him and he pulled her to her feet. They danced a few steps to Lehar's lovely music and then drank to each other.

'You are so exactly right for me,' she said, still laughing. 'I couldn't bear my life without you.'

'And you are the most beautiful, heavenly, glorious ordinary girl. I adore you. Come and dance again.'

Presently he said, 'I thought to-night's performance very bad ... am I right?'

'First nights ... mine are always fearsome. Can't judge by a first night. She was better than I'd have been.' Julie referred to the leading actress.

'I remember the first time I ever saw you. You were ...'

'Don't tell me. Let me guess. Helena in *Midsummer Night's*?'

'Wrong. How you sentimentalise yourself. It was years before you played Helena. Do you remember the Akademie putting on Coward's *Private Lives*?'

'Heavens! The second wife. Yes, of course. But that was ... seven ... eight years ago?'

'I felt romantically sorry for you. But then you became so starry, so successful, that I couldn't see you as human any more.'

'I hadn't thought of it, but it must have been rather odd ... was it a shock to find me out – just a woman – tell me, was it?'

'I had a dreamlike feeling for about two days. Then the picture shifted and you were just you!'

It was after two o'clock when Nando set Julie down in the Schellinggasse and left his motor running while he opened the door for her.

'I hate to leave you,' he said quietly, 'even for an hour ...' They did not often use endearments, except as a sort of exaggeration, almost as a joke. He turned, but Julie pulled him back, and putting up her hands to his face, kissed him again. In the gleam of the street lamp, he saw that her eyes were filled with tears as she pushed him gently away. In the flat, she went, as she always did now when she came back late, and listened at the door behind the wardrobe in the corridor, to hear Franz breathing.

Director Schoenherr telephoned early the next morning, while Lehmann and his wife were still at breakfast in their dressing-gowns.

'I'm sorry to trouble you,' the breathy, elderly voice said. 'An absurd thing has happened over Frau Homburg's divorce. She is very much upset and I shall have great trouble persuading her that this sort of harassment is not being done on purpose. Yes, it has all fallen through. No, no fault of the lawyer's; not at all. The Board of Jewish Emigration intervened. Really, I might say they have interfered. I understood we were to be spared this sort of sordid affair. Yes, Julie is very angry, very angry indeed. You know her, she is not the sort of woman who easily gets upset, but I must say I rather agree with her in this matter ... I will tell you exactly. The emigration office is trying to get hold of her husband's property, but that is quite improper, quite out of the question. I gave Julie my personal word that if she agreed to divorce her husband, this sort of thing should not happen ... Well, if we could get the name taken off their lists? I am afraid it is all a frightful bore for you, just when your charming wife is here, too. Not a good moment; if such a thing had to happen at all, it might have come when you were not so delightfully busy. Yes, the property is entirely Julie's. Certainly, I will send a porter round to you at once, with all the relevant facts. Yes, yes, I know how busy you are; everything on a sheet of paper and I can get the birth certificate and marriage certificate copies from her lawyer. You will? I know I can rely on you to act quickly ... I want to be able to tell Julie. Forgive me if I have been a little impetuous; I know you have much on your mind. You will go yourself? That is all I could ask, many thanks, many thanks. I shall tell Julie at once. My compliments to your beautiful wife, and the box is entirely at her disposal for as long as she wants it ... Yes, yes, of course, the opera too, naturally.'

The director pushed the hook of the telephone with his short, fat forefinger that always shook a little from his high blood pressure. He dialled Julie's number and the telephone rang by her bed.

'Oh God,' she sighed. 'Of course, the very morning after I was out so late.'

'You bad child,' the coy gallantry of his normal manner did not suit the hour of day. 'I thought you went to bed early. Well, it will be all right. As soon as that foolish fellow Ostrovsky told me what had happened I got hold of Lehmann. It just happens to be the perfect moment; with his huge wife here he can't afford to refuse me anything. And she has great influence. If this awful little Gestapo man at the emigration office causes any trouble ... Just the mention of her father's name and all doors open. Now listen, my dear child, do not do anything, nothing at all. You understand? Leave it all to Papa Schoenherr – he'll arrange everything. And this time, he'll do it himself, no nonsense this time. So don't worry your lovely head. I must go now, I have things to do.'

The next call was made with a voice and manner so different they might have belonged to a different man.

'Doctor Vogel? What d'you mean, he is not ready? Call him to the telephone at once – at once, d'you hear. Director Schoenherr … Vogel? You took long enough getting to the phone – where were you? Hmm. Now listen, and try not to make a botch of it, this time. I want the papers of the Homburg-Wedeker divorce over here in half an hour. And don't leave half the stuff lying in your desk. I can't help what you have to do in Court. Get over here.'

Later that morning, Lehmann, having excused himself from a shopping tour with his wife to whom he explained that nothing ever got done properly without him, entered the crowded premises of the Board of Emigration and was conducted to the room of the colonel in charge.

He waited for a few minutes in the ante-room, standing by the tall window and looking out at the broad boulevard where a long queue of people waited and the usual bustle of a workday went past the silent straggling line. Somehow Lehmann found it difficult to look away from the waiting people, and yet to look at them gave him a constrained and anxious sensation that he did not attempt to explain to himself. At the rattle of the door handle, he turned into the room. Three men came out of the inside office. They were elderly, bearded; they wore dark formal clothes of a vaguely clerical style and carried low-crowned, broad-brimmed black hats in their hands. They were quiet, dignified; they turned to say good-day to the man inside the office and their voices were a little obsequious, slightly relieved. The voice of the man inside the room who spoke to them, was businesslike and civil, somewhat condescending but no more so than, perhaps, it would be if the man speaking were the owner of a large undertaking doing business with a small firm. To Lehmann, who knew who these three men must be, this very civility had an unpleasant tone which moved him to irritation.

'Come in, come in, Herr Doctor Lehmann. Very pleased to make your acquaintance. Please have a seat ... now, what can I do for you?' There was a slight emphasis on the last word that connected Lehmann somehow with the three men who had just left.

'You seem to get on very well with them,' he commented, unaware of a note of resentment in his voice.

'Yes, yes, we have done business in the past and we always got along very well. Then it was a matter of negotiation. Their community members paid up and we issued emigration permits. The State was the winner. Now, of course, it will be simpler.'

'My wife told me something of it. As you probably know, she was on the special flight with General Heydrich ... Ah, you came on that flight too?'

'Yes, I have the honour of your wife's acquaintance. Hmm. Very slightly.'

'Somehow I had the impression you had been in Vienna for some time?'

'I was, but the Emigration Board – it was to have been closed but now it is to be extended. We were able to persuade our masters that an organisation already in existence and working well was better than a complete new start.'

The man behind the desk was rather short and thin, with a sharp-featured, indoors face. He leaned forward to offer Lehmann a cigarette from his own crumpled packet and then turned over some papers lying on his blotter with the air of a man who politely gives up time otherwise filled with much more important things. He was one of those administrators who are always hurried, always overdriven with work; inventing difficulties in order to make life uncomfortable and his own role more important.

'Yes, yes, we have to expand our organisations in a hurry. The Führer wishes the entire Reich to be freed from their presence.' The identity of those from whom the Reich was to be freed was not stated, as if the word were an obscenity. The self-importance he attached to his office was combined with a curious air of personal humility. 'When something has to be done in a hurry,' he said, smiling deprecatingly, 'then we civil servants become very important, all of a sudden. Nobody takes into account the amount of work and organisation such a large deportation requires; we've always managed and I suppose we shall have to go on managing. Yes, the idea of a reserve in Poland, that was easy, anyone could have thought of that. I even thought of it myself, long before it was practical policy.' He stopped and coughed. 'Not, of course, that I was not certain that the campaign would be fast and successful. I mean, before the Polish campaign started – in fact I thought of a Jewish Reserve when the Foreign Minister first went to Moscow. Long, long before it was public knowledge that we should achieve a *modus vivendi* with the Soviets. And now, it all falls on my shoulders and everything has to be done at once.'

He leaned back in his chair, and waved a thin hand.

'But all that dull stuff does not interest you, Herr Doctor. You are concerned with pleasanter business.'

'Not at the moment, I fear,' said Lehmann stiffly. 'Let me explain as briefly as I can.' He pulled the papers out of his crocodile-skin briefcase which he laid on the desk. It only took a few minutes to read the notes made by Schoenherr and explain what he wanted.

'The only thing that concerns me,' remarked the man behind the desk with a brisk air of cutting short a matter really beneath his interest, 'the only thing is the legal transfer of the property.' He leaned back and his chair creaked. He noticed this and added. 'I never have time even to get my office properly furnished, as you see.'

'I have a sworn copy of the transfer here,' said Lehmann, and opened his briefcase again, pushing some papers on the desk a little to one side, at which the SS officer frowned. After a slight fumble, Lehmann found the right papers and pulled them out.

'Ah, just a moment, the clip has come off. There are several sheets, I see.'

'Hm. He must have been a rich man, this Wedeker.'

'I believe so, yes,' said Lehmann with distaste.

The SS colonel pushed a button and almost at once the door flew open and a tall, wide-shouldered SS trooper entered and stood rigidly at attention just inside. He had a face that could have been carved with a hatchet by an unskilful artisan from some very hard, intractable wood. His eyes were light in colour.

'Ulrich, take these papers down to the archives and tell Schmidt to get out the relevant entry in our lists. At once.'

'Yes, sir!' The man raised his arm sharply, dropped it back, took two paces forward and shot out his arm again, to take the proffered papers.

'I take it you would like to wait?'

'It would be better,' answered Lehmann.

'You will excuse me? I must read these letters through ...'

Lehmann sat silent for about ten minutes, when the door flew open again, making him jump, and the tall trooper stamped in, made his grotesque salute with a loud clap of his booted heels, and laid a folder on his desk.

'All right, Ulrich, thanks.' The man went out. 'Noisy fellow, and stupid. But a faithful servant.'

Lehmann smiled briefly. The SS colonel frowned at his reserved manner.

'We need such men,' he said. 'He's being promoted – going to Poland to help set up the Reserve at Lodz. Now, where are we with these details? Ah, yes. Yes.' He took up a pen and slid it down the typed sheets. Yes, here we are. Disappeared without trace, March 1938. In Prague immediately prior to his disappearance ... yes. And here we have the property transfer, signed and sealed by the notary public. It seems to be all right. Can I keep this copy?'

He glanced up sharply for permission, and then slipped the sworn copy into a folder and scrawled something on it. Then he laid down the typed list flat on his desk and, using a ruler to guide his pen, neatly crossed through the relevant entry three times. 'Quite obliterated now,' he said with satisfaction. 'One less for me to worry about. Pity about all that property, but I quite understand, quite understand.' He stood up and edged round the desk with quick, fussy steps. 'Your business to take care of cultural affairs, while I have less amusing responsibilities. Frau Wedeker will receive notification by the post, a matter of form, just a matter of form.'

'Frau Homburg, please,' said Lehmann coldly.

'Ah, changed the name, has she? Well, can't blame her for that, can we? Very well, Homburg it is. Good morning to you. Very pleased. Good morning.'

The man Ulrich was in the corridor and jumped to his exaggerated salute again as Lehmann passed him with averted head. Outside the queue was even longer. The people stood very quietly, talking little and in undertones. Lehmann made himself look at one of their faces. They look just like anyone else, he thought angrily. And why don't I feel disgust at them ...? Vienna is corrupting me, too. He crossed the street away from the queue and during a formal luncheon to which he accompanied his wife he excelled himself in his arguments – of course the planned emigrations were discussed with General Heydrich and his staff – as to how much better it would be in the long run for these people themselves, that they should have their own town and a life of their own.

He inquired, too, of General Heydrich's aide-de-camp what the queue outside the Emigration Board was waiting for. He learned that these were persons with claims to foreign passports, or who already had emigration certificates and had failed to use them at once and now needed to buy exit permits as well.

'Amazing how these scum find the money when they are up against it,' said the young man, laughing. 'They've all got fortunes hidden in their mattresses – or they sell a few of their pictures or jewels when their precious skins are at stake.'

'Skins at stake?' said Lehmann sharply. 'I thought they were going to a whole town cleared for them, in Poland.'

'Well, they are,' said the aide-de-camp, and then his face changed a little and he looked closely at Lehmann; after a moment he made some excuse to move away. 'Who is this Lehmann fellow?' he asked a fellow officer who had been in Vienna for over a year.

'He's the Burgtheater administrator – nice chap. Understands nothing but plays and actors. They give the best parties in Vienna, he and Frau Pantic.' The man stationed in Vienna, with all the condescension of one who has managed to arrange himself the ideal posting, drew the aide away and began to explain to him about Maris and the house, and the two stood laughing and talking together, looking across the room at the unconscious, statuesque figure of Frau Lehmann.

'I thought for a moment he must be an outsider,' said the aide-de-camp. 'He's a real innocent, that's plain.'

'Not a bit,' replied the other. 'Don't underestimate Lehmann. If he were an innocent he'd never have married the girl he did marry. He knows what the form is, all right. He's got this culture job and he naturally prefers not to know about these other matters. Quite right, too; that's what he gets paid for.'

What Lehmann got paid for, however, was presented to him after the formal luncheon, with its cold salmon and choice Moselle wine, and its roast suckling-pig with a good claret, followed by blissful Viennese sweetmeats and champagne. At four o'clock in the afternoon, with a slight buzzing in his ears, Lehmann entered his private office to find it full of angry people. He went to his desk and looked about him. When he saw Hella Schneider there with the others and no Schoenherr, he knew he had trouble on his hands. They had got rid of Schoenherr on some pretext, he saw; and Hella's presence told him that this was a concerted uprising, for only the closed ranks of her colleagues would induce Hella to show solidarity with them – authority was precious to Hella, but without her colleagues she could not work at all. Walter Harich was evidently spokesman.

'I'm not going to make a speech,' he began. There was a rustle of ironic clapping for Harich had unconsciously taken up a histrionic stance, the posture he assumed for the last speech in *Egmont* that he was to play that evening. He raised both his hands in the air and everyone was quiet.

'Now – it's like this. We don't – we've decided that – we don't give a damn for the Jews.' He pronounced this word with savagery, putting into it all the special quality he knew it had for Lehmann and his Nazi connections. With this word and the way he pronounced it, the actor pushed away from the group in the room and on to Lehmann, the outside world they wished to reject. 'I, for my part, can't tell the difference between a kosher rabbi and a good Christian, and I don't suppose you can either – left to yourself. The point is this. The courtyard of my home is full of weeping, screaming people. They've been collected there from the whole district around, and they've been there without lavatories or food or water for nearly a day now. My two kids can look out of the window and see them pissing in the corners. I left my wife in hysterics. And when Mundel walked through the Hofburg to come to the theatre, he found the whole Riding School filled with the same filthy sight. Hundreds of riff-raff crowded together, smashing the building up and fouling the floors. It's disgusting – filthy. If you have to put them somewhere, put them in the prisons, out of sight. Mundel says there are two men hanging from the central chandelier, dead. God only knows how they got up there to hang themselves … I …'

Harich stopped, stunned by what he was saying. He reached behind him for a chair and sat down, shaking. He looked up and round at the familiar faces and said, 'No. I can't. I can't go on.' A thick sob rose in his throat and he put his head in his hands.

There was silence. Lehmann tried to collect some thought, some coherent argument. The only thing that occurred to him was that Maris was not there and he felt a fugitive relief at that. But two others of the Josefstadt company were present and Lehmann recognised several faces from the Opera company as well. The ring-leaders are from my theatre, he thought, and a cold sensation of fear touched him. I shall be blamed if there's a scandal.

He became aware that someone was pulling at his arm while the whole group was watching him. Willy Mundel was beside him, swaying on his feet, his eyes red-rimmed, his mouth slobbering. He swayed so much that he had to take a step forward to hold himself upright; there was a strong smell of brandy.

'I'm resigning, Lehmann,' he said thickly. 'I'm getting out. Now.'

'You can't do that, Willy,' said Julie's voice, though Lehmann did not see Julie. 'You're on to-night.'

Willy Mundel was quiet for a moment, trying to manage his legs. Then he gripped hold of Lehmann's sleeve as if he would pull the man apart and shouted at the top of his powerful voice.

'I'm leaving,' he yelled. 'Leaving now. I'd rather go with the Jews to Poland than play in *Egmont* to-night.' He was a heavy man and shook Lehmann to and fro so that the administrator staggered, his mouth open to say something though no words came. 'Do you know what *Egmont* is about, you pipsqueak you? Do you? Have you ever listened to Goethe's words? And if you ever listened to them, could you understand them? No, and that's why I'm going.' He ended triumphantly, as if bringing his argument to a logical conclusion, shook Lehmann by the arm once more and let him go with a gesture of throwing something away. Using his arms as if he were swimming, he made his way through the expostulating and arguing crowd and threw the door open.

'Good-bye,' he shouted, as if he wanted to be heard in Graz. 'Good-bye. I'll take Goethe and you can have the theatre for your plaything.' He staggered through the door. 'You can use it to cover your foulness, but without my help.' He went out and flung the door shut behind him with a crash that made the chandelier chatter.

'Oh, God,' cried Julie. 'Now what are we going to do?' It did not occur to anyone to run after Mundel and bring him back. The finality of his going was accepted at once.

'Who will play Oranien to-night?' asked Lehmann stupidly. Hansi Ostrovsky came forward through the press of people and without answering the question, went to the table and picked up the telephone to call an understudy. Lehmann sat down in his own desk-chair and stared at the blotter before him. He realised now that he had drunk too much at luncheon and the strong black coffee had not sobered him. The blotter reminded Lehmann of something, but what he saw was confused with the line of people, standing outside the emigration office and with Harich's words. He could hear Hansi Ostrovsky's voice talking to someone called Toni, and who Toni could be worried him. I'm ill, he thought, I can't cope with this.

'There's nothing I can do,' he said suddenly, and propped his aching head on one hand. 'I'm as helpless as you are.' He saw a pen in front of him, and wondered disconnectedly where the ruler was. Julie, he thought, yes, that was it.

'Julie,' he muttered. 'I got the name taken off the list. I did that, anyway.' He remembered the man behind the desk and gave a violent shudder, his brow felt cold and sweat broke out on it.

'He really is ill,' said somebody.

'I got the name taken off the list,' said Lehmann again. 'Is Julie there?' He could see her now, leaning over him, the frown between her brows very sharp and her face livid and stiff with self-control. For an instant he saw the bone structure of her face, as if it were naked of flesh and the eyes alone were alive, glowing darkly from their arched sockets. She said in a whisper, 'What did you say?'

'Wedeker's name. It's off the list. I saw him rule it through myself.'

'But the others?' asked someone.

'They've taken my hairdresser,' said Hella Schneider's voice, boring into him.

Julie pulled herself upright, holding on to the edge of the table.

'Oh, Franz,' she whispered. 'What have we done to you ... we've all gone mad ...' She began to laugh wildly, theatrically, and flung out her arms. 'That's the only way to save anyone,' she cried through her laughter. 'We have to kill them off, officially. Get the name ruled through ... Get the ...'

She swayed and Ostrovsky caught her as she fell.

'Now look what you've done,' he said savagely to Lehmann. They laid her in the arm-chair, and Hella began to slap her hands gently. Someone ran out to get the dresser, and someone else to get water.

A girl ran back with a glass of water and Schoenherr collided with her at the door, spattering the water on the broad bosom of his dark suit. He flicked impatiently at the spreading stain, clicking his tongue against his teeth, and went at once to Julie.

'Fainted,' he said in his breathy voice. 'Dear God in Heaven, what are we coming to ...' He stood upright with some difficulty, looking old and stiff, and stared round him at the angry faces and at Lehmann's bent head. 'Now, what is going on here? Why did somebody tell me I was wanted in the wardrobe store?' Julie's dresser knocked and came in; it was clear she had been told why she was wanted for she went at once to Julie and uncapped a smelling-bottle. Julie moved at once, jerking her head away from the ammonia, and coughing.

'Somebody tell me at once what this is all about ...' Schoenherr said, not dropping his manner of a governess chiding unruly children.

Under his stern eye half a dozen voices began reluctantly telling their story, interrupting and contradicting each other.

'Now, now,' Schoenherr said at last, when he grasped what they were talking about. 'Now, now, children, all that is not our business. Our business is to produce plays and act them. Nothing else. So let's all get back to work.' He turned sharply on the dresser, who was stroking Julie's hand, as if it were all her doing. 'Get Frau Homburg to her room and see that she gets a good rest.'

Obediently, the woman put an arm round Julie and when the girl who had brought the water came forward to help, waved her angrily away.

'I'm all right,' said Julie, looking about her vaguely, 'I can walk by myself. Lotte, you take my bag.' They went out without looking at Lehmann whose head was still in his hands.

'No, wait a minute. That's not quite good enough.' Harich turned from the window and came back into the room, facing Schoenherr. 'Willy is right. We are conniving at all this filth, covering it up with "German culture". That's all wrong. We've got to have our say over this.' There was a murmur of assent. 'It's not the Jews, not at all. I told him that. It's our children seeing such things. It's the Riding School, the Hofburg being used for such purposes. I don't understand all this talk about the Jews, but I see there is nothing we can do. And perhaps they really will be better off all together; after all, there's talk about bringing the Baltic Germans back into the Reich and the Volga Germans — I don't suppose they want to move either. And I know the papers say these people are being provided with proper trains and taken care of. That's all very well but they aren't being taken care of here, that's all I say.' He ended weakly, feeling that his disavowal of concern with the victims had fatally weakened his position. But to his surprise there was a chorus of support for what he said. Lehmann lifted his head wearily from his hands and stood up.

'If I say I agree with you all, I put my own head in a noose,' he said. 'But I say it, just the same. It was the Führer's personal order that the people in the Old City should be taken to the Riding School. It's an open secret what the Führer thinks of the Habsburgs and their decadent Empire. In order to express the evil connection between these two non-German — anti-German — ideas, he wished the Habsburg Riding School with all its empty magnificence and all its

Spanish, non-German ceremonial memories, to be used to house these strange creatures in our midst . . .' Lehmann had slipped back into the habitual talk of the drawing-room National Socialist and not because anyone said anything to contradict him, but out of his own uneasy feelings, he felt now the falseness of all he was saying and the truth of Willy Mundel's attitude. 'Mundel is a drunk,' he broke out angrily, after a silent pause. 'Surely we can't take what he says seriously . . . ?' He looked around their stubborn faces; he had alienated them again by criticising their friend. He said brokenly, 'I've put myself in your hands . . .'

Schoenherr bustled forward to the desk.

'We are all conscious of the protection you have been to us,' he wheezed, in the urgency of the moment forgetting tact. 'None of us would wish for a moment to involve you in any . . .' He looked round the room at his 'children' and the creases of his broad face made a grimace that could have been a smile. 'There is nothing we can do.'

The brutal truth in this admission was shared by everyone in the room. They could rid themselves of their guilty anger but there was nothing they could do.

Goethe's poetic drama of liberty was played that night to a full but sullen house. For an audience to rise and leave in silence from a performance in the Burgtheater is considered an especial honour to the players, but on this occasion there was morose weight in the atmosphere. The public did not intend a demonstration, it was the emotions of the players, stimulated by Mundel's words and emphasised by his absence, that communicated themselves. That is what the theatre is for, to induce understanding by demonstration. Harich never spoke the familiar lines of *Egmont* with such authority and he, together with Julie playing the Regent, dominated so easily the substitute Oranien, the guest who played Klare, that Alba's son made his name that night in the contrast played to him by Harich. He was the man in the claws of power who cannot act, is impotent. At the end the house rose and stood still long after the doors were open, facing the lowered curtains. *Egmont* was quietly dropped from the repertory and was not played again for years.

3

'*I* haven't enough petrol left this month to drive down,' said Nando's voice on the telephone. 'Will you mind taking the train? They will meet us at Enns ...'

'No, of course not,' replied Julie. 'What time? Good, I'll meet you at the Westbahnhof, then, on Saturday morning.'

Nando was there before her, walking idly up and down the platform. Julie recognised him from the barrier by his long-legged gait, toes a little turned in, and by the boyish way he moved his head. In spite of the tiredness that seemed to have reached the marrow of her bones, she quickened her pace to the train, backed up round the curve by an old steam engine. The sharp tang of frost was in the opal mists of an autumn morning already shot with sunlight. It was going to be fine. There was a smell of leaves burning even on the concrete platform, strewn here and there with paper bags, cigarette ends, the detritus of a city no longer kept clean. There was no porter and Julie carried her own bag for the week-end.

He hurried towards her when he turned in his strolling and saw her. She could see as he approached that his usual delighted smile was not showing. He took her bag, touching her elbow to lead her forward. Their greeting did not need words and neither of them spoke. The old wooden carriage presented them with a first-class compartment just in front of them. As they climbed in Nando looked about him with disgust.

'Don't they clean the trains any more?' he said irritably. 'It looks as if it had been used as a troop train.' He kicked an empty sandwich paper under the seat and let down the far window. The train was almost empty, they could be alone. The stale smell was almost visible, wreathing out into the cleaner air outside.

Julie sat down gratefully in the corner and sighed. The upholstery was dusty and coal blacks lay along the window-sills.

'One doesn't notice how shabby everything gets,' she murmured, 'and then suddenly something reminds one that trains used to be clean.'

Nando gave her a brief, sardonic smile, not needing to answer the question, for they both knew all the new trains had long been transferred to the war machine. An old man brought back from retirement went past, slamming the carriage doors and almost at once the train started with a jerk and rolled forward. So small is Vienna that even before Nando finished one cigarette they were among the Vienna Woods.

'Has something happened?' he said, his voice strained.

'Bad news,' answered Julie calmly, and closed her eyes, leaning back in the corner. He could see the drained exhaustion of her face; the skin usually firm and dewy was grained and dry, the hollows of her eyes dark and below the fine cheekbones were drawn shadowy inward curves. He had not noticed before how thin she had become lately. She spoke quietly with her eyes closed.

'The Slovenian frontier has been closed. There is someone at my mother's house near Graz who can't stay there any longer. Where the house is ... is now a military area.' She opened her eyes and saw Nando's bonny face, made for laughing, freeze into horrified shock, and for a moment was bewildered. In her sleepless state of exhaustion she had spoken without thinking and it took her a moment of conscious effort to place the cause of Nando's shock. Then she knew and felt a sensation inside her as if a fist had slammed against her heart.

'No,' she whispered, and closed her eyes again, 'not him. Someone else.'

There was a long silence.

'If it isn't ... isn't him ...?' He was not quite sure what he meant to say, but Julie understood him.

'I am responsible for her,' she said, not arguing but just stating the fact, putting it outside argument.

After a moment she opened her eyes again and touched the window-ledge with a long, gloved finger.

'You're right,' she said, 'the train is filthy. I thought the war was supposed to be over, after the French armistice?' Her voice sounded querulous as if it were his fault that the conquest of Paris had not ended the war, and with it the growing sordidness of their lives.

'It'll be even worse now,' he said. 'This morning's High Command communiqué – I mean yesterday's in this morning's paper – says the air war over England has been temporarily suspended to allow for regrouping and consolidation. I suppose that means they want to invade ...'

'I thought England was going to ask for an armistice as well?'

'Evidently that hope has been given up now.'

His voice sounded so helpless and despairing that she realised at last through the mist of her tiredness that there was something more wrong with Nando than a distant piece of war news.

'What's it, Nando?' she said in a different voice.

He looked at her, hesitating. 'They've co-ordinated all the police, security and internal affairs people. Under Himmler. I shall be forced to wear uniform sometimes from now on,' he hinted. 'On official occasions, you know. You mustn't mind. It's only a formality.'

'Uniform? What uniform?'

He did not answer and she seemed to forget the question which, indeed did not interest her, and seemed frivolous compared with her own despairing plotting.

A month before, the peasant woman who supplied Fina with butter and eggs for high prices without ration coupons had stopped coming, so that the problem of making the rations of two people enough for three was now serious. Fina and Julie did not dare to inquire about the woman, or go to her Burgenland village. The thought that she could have been arrested kept Julie awake of nights. For if arrested she might give the police the addresses of her purchasers out of a very natural desire that they too should suffer. On the other hand a decree, published a week before the peasant came for the last time, threatened the death penalty for black marketeering in foodstuffs. Perhaps this had scared the woman off. They could not know. Julie's many friends gave her presents, no longer of flowers or chocolates in big gilded boxes with wide silk bows, but of poultry and game, butter from their own farms, wine from their own vineyards. That too would stop, she supposed, if this war went on. And then the moment would arrive when they – she and Fina – would have to explain to Franz about the shortage of food. She dreaded that far more than the problems of managing the increasingly repetitive menus. He would break into one of his febrile angers or worse still, weep quietly with humiliation.

This summer, after his old sentimental enemy France fell to the lightning thrusts of the Panzers, they had lived through a bad few weeks. Franz seemed unable to replace the vision of a France that dominated European politics with the France that made craven peace with her enemy. He had not been able to work for his anxious questioning. It was for Julie academic and theoretical, nothing to do with living here and now; and it seemed to her at times as if Franz were inventing his distress which, surely, could not be real. She did not understand when she heard Georgy and Franz discussing the book he was writing, that this breakdown in French national consciousness had a bearing on everything Franz was thinking; this strange new fact of European history – the moral collapse of the 'nation par excellence' – reached backward in the time to the subject that filled his mind, modifying its whole theme. Even Georg Kerenyi had not been able, in his cautious, quiet visits, to discuss the questions out of Franz's mind, get rid of them. Only Fina with her stolid acceptance that the Herr Doctor naturally took quite other things seriously than those things that exercised ordinary mortals, was able to comfort him. She did not need to understand his preoccupations and took for granted that they were of a higher order than hers or Julie's.

Julie knew that when Franz could not sleep, which was very often, Fina sat beside his bed for hours, stroking his hand, and would fall asleep upright on the hard chair she brought in from the kitchen for she would not use the Herr Doctor's chair. It no longer seemed strange to Julie that she herself was shut out of the little room where Franz lived, by an unspoken agreement.

And now – Ruth. Unconsciously, Julie sighed.

'I suppose it will be safest for her to be in Vienna,' she said thinking aloud, 'a big town is easier to get lost in than a country place. But of course, she can't come to the flat with me ... That's the problem, really.'

'Good God, I should hope not,' he cried. 'Julie, must you feel yourself obliged ...'

She cut him short, shaking her head. 'I don't mean I wouldn't have her ...' She stopped, a slow little smile caught the side of her mouth. 'Better if you know nothing about it,' she said tenderly. He smiled back at her anxiously.

'If only you would marry me,' he said, 'I could stop your quixotic ideas.' He had never mentioned marriage before and she stared at him stupidly.

'But I couldn't marry you!' she cried.

'But why not? Have you never thought of it?'

'But how can I ...?' she said bewildered. Through the mist of sleeplessness, by what had become second nature, she slid back into the hateful habit of lying to Nando, to everyone. 'Your family would be horrified. You couldn't do such a thing to them – a divorced woman. Besides, I don't think these German divorce laws are legal anywhere else, you know. I'm really only half divorced. When this is all over ...'

'My dear,' he said in a low voice, 'my dearest, I'm afraid it isn't going to be over.'

She stared at him, unbelieving.

'I'm afraid they are going to win,' he said.

The train ran into a country station and they both glanced up at the name-boards.

'St Pölten already,' he said. A man in hunting tweeds carrying a guncase came in and they were unable to go on talking. Julie dozed a little, they hardly spoke. One no longer talked either to strangers, or in front of them. That too had become a fixed habit, almost second nature.

At Enns the trap was waiting.

'We still have a couple of horses, thank goodness,' said Nando as he helped her up. 'I'll drive, Loisl. Have you anything to do in the town?'

The old groom drew a crumpled sheet of paper out of his pocket, on which were written several commissions in a large, clear hand so that he could read them easily.

'The Gräfin has several wishes,' he consulted the paper with the seriousness of a man to whom the knack of reading and writing are signs of a higher life. 'If Graf Nando would drive the gnädige Frau, I could stay and come out on the carrier's bus. Frau Gräfin suggested that might be best, so that the gnädige Frau does not get cold in the open trap, you see?'

He stood by the high driving seat looking up and wrinkling his faded blue eyes at Nando, who was already sliding the reins through his fingers.

'All right, then, Loisl,' said Nando cheerfully, not able to remain gloomy in the face of the old man's loving solemnity. Loisl took off his shapeless old hat and held it against his green Loden cape to see them off. Nando turned and waved as they clopped out of the station yard. The old man stood still, holding his hat against his chest until they disappeared. Then he sighed heavily, shook his square-boned peasant's head with its sparse grey hair and replaced the hat so that he could consult his paper again.

Out of the town, back over the river, and on to the gravel country road. The sun shone clearly and the woods were full of autumn colours. In the distance mountains could be seen, early snow sparkling on the peaks. Some shreds of the mists of early morning were still caught in the half-leaved trees of the forests, and late dahlias bloomed with coarse cheer in cottage gardens. Here and there a woman, bent over a tub or handling some farm implement, straightened up to watch them pass and greeted Nando with the harsh, masculine voices of the country folk. The men they saw were old or very young. Children shouted and laughed, running in flocks near the cottages.

With every trotting jingle of the bay mare's hoofs and harness Nando felt more carefree. He turned to look down at Julie, tweed collar turned up and the big, fur-lined rug wrapped round her legs, and saw that she, too, was feeling better. Presently she took off her felt hat and the fresh breezy air stirred her dark hair. She put up her face to the sun and murmured, 'It's quite warm now.'

They reached the low gate to the park, white-painted once, but almost bare now along the top and by the handle. A small girl carrying a pail much too heavy for her set down her burden and opened the gate for them. She was too shy to answer Nando's greeting and shook her head speechlessly, her round cheeks going a fiery red. She picked up the pail and staggered off with it, up the lane they had come by, short pigtails sticking out on either side of her round little head. The estate road was smoother than the public road, overgrown with moss and grass. The steady clop of the horse's hoofs took on a muffled sound and her trot became brisker.

It was a pretty house, in the staid country style, painted the usual dun yellow with green shutters. Like the park gate, the paintwork had not been renewed for many years, but instead of seeming melancholy, this unconcern with outward style, or the lack of money to keep it up, only increased the remote, sheltered and unworldly aspect of the house. To its right stretched formal gardens, beyond them kitchen gardens with neat rows and espaliered fruit trees, half hiding a long barn and another, smaller house. Behind, the ground rose steeply to a considerable hill, and atop the hill towered the blackened stones of a ruined wall, overgrown now with magnificent trees and creepers.

To the left of the house was a grove of tall beeches and on that side the pasture came almost up to the house itself, only divided from it by a ha-ha. The main windows faced south-west and looking over her shoulder Julie could see that their view must be of the distant mountains.

'What a heavenly place,' she called up to Nando on the box and he turned to laugh a welcome and point up at the hill with its ruin.

'All that remains of the ancestral castle,' he cried, his voice vibrating with the pleasure of being here with her.

Their arrival was heard before they crunched on to the clean gravel sweep, and the doors opened. An elderly manservant came out followed by a fat old woman in a white apron. Then a young girl and a boy perhaps a year her elder, in leather breeches and the short jacket of rough grey cloth bound in green, of the district.

They both began to laugh and wave, shouting greetings to Nando before the mare pulled up gently and he jumped down from the box. The young people fell upon Nando with loud cries and laughter before their social duties to the guest could interfere with the greetings. Julie sat in the trap, laughing down at them until Nando could free himself. The two young people were at once formal and shy. The boy bowed and the girl curtsied, touching her hand quickly as if she were made of porcelain and might break.

'My youngest sister, Lali,' Nando indicated the girl. 'Her name's Anastasie, so we call her Lali. This is Otto Krassny. They live just over the castle hill there.'

'Sektionschef Peter Krassny's son?' Julie asked him, surprised. 'I didn't know he lived down here too.'

'The house was let for years, but they came down when the war began,' Nando answered for the boy, who murmured something and looked at Lali for help.

'Mother's waiting,' said the girl. 'Come on, Otto, help Hannes with the bags.'

'He's not usually shy at all,' she said looking with bold, gay eyes like her brother's into Julie's face. 'But of course, we're all so terribly impressed with you, it makes us all act like clowns.' Her voice had a clear, still childish ring, that made Julie want to laugh with joy and relief. So she did laugh, and they all began to laugh with her, including the two servants.

'This is Frau Klara,' said Nando, putting his long arm round the shoulders of the woman in the white apron and kissing her smartly on her soft, withered cheek.

They were just inside the doors, in the dusk of the hall when heavy steps approached and a tall, big woman dressed in the same rough grey cloth came from the back of the house towards them.

'Well, there you are,' she said in a deep voice, enfolding her son in capable arms. 'And this is Frau Homburg. How do you do? We are very happy you could come down. Did my boy escort you properly?'

She had a weather-beaten hard face and to shake hands with Julie took off a heavy leather glove like a man's.

Julie could see at once that this was a family run by its women. 'Luncheon is almost ready. You will just have time for Frau Klara to show you up.'

The room allotted to Julie looked out at the mountains, away over the green slope of pasture, the multitude of russet and yellow trees, a single mass of forest on the other side of the pasture. Where it ended, as if a curved line were drawn round the deep green grassland, it was like the edge of a sea.

'I really understand how medieval poets felt about the great forests,' said Julie as they sat at the long dining table and soup was served to them from a huge tureen by the elderly manservant. 'How mysterious the woods are in autumn.'

Young Otto Krassny leaned forward a little. 'They are just like a sea from up here, the woods,' he said. 'Or so I think sometimes.' He blushed redly at having said something so intimate.

'No, not at all like the sea,' contradicted Lali, and glanced from Otto to Julie with her bold, charming look. 'But really as if there were dragons perhaps ... No, not dragons, but woodcutters' huts and old women who live by gathering herbs, like in the fairy stories.'

'Well, there are woodcutters' huts and women who live by gathering herbs,' pointed out her mother. She cut her liver dumpling briskly in two with her spoon, and chopped one half quickly into the soup to eat it before the delicate mixture could disintegrate. They all ate with the appetite of people who spent their vigorous lives in the open air. Julie, infected by their gusto, found an appetite for the first time for months, and ate up her soup as quickly as the others.

'But I don't mean it like that, Mamma. Not like real woodcutters, but strange woodcutters.'

'Yes, strange woodcutters. But it is like a sea, the forest.' Otto laid down his spoon neatly. 'Not THE sea. But a mass of its own, contained in itself, somehow.'

'You're a poet, Otto,' teased Nando and his tone was so

confident of their understanding that they all laughed happily, Otto as well.

'He's quite right,' said Julie. 'That's just what I felt, and that about old women — and charcoal-burners, perhaps.'

'You're all beyond me,' said the Countess. 'All I know is we have an order for timber-cutting that will be the ruin of us. And no arguments about whether we can supply it or what it will do to the forest. Just so many square metres.'

'But we can't cut much,' said Nando with dismay.

'I have put in an appeal,' said his mother comfortably.

The elderly servant, about to lay down a large silver platter, gave a loud snort at this point. Only Nando took notice of this and grinned up at the old man. His mother frowned disapprovingly at him, and he muttered under his breath, 'Just the same, he's right.'

'We must all make sacrifices in war-time,' said the Countess. It was clear from everyone's expression that this was a statement often made, from the recognition that something of the sort had to be said, not because it was meant. It did not occur to any of the country people that sacrifices would or could in fact be demanded of them. By 'sacrifices' the Countess meant that they would live on the produce of their own land and give up the riding horses; this had already happened during the Countess's youth in the First World War. Then all the young men had been called up to the armies of the Dual Monarchy, but this could not happen again now because the defeat had so impoverished the Kasda family and every other family of country gentry like them that there were no young men on the estate and most of the land was leased to peasant farmers.

Towards the end of the meal old Hannes asked Nando 'whether the Herr Graf wished horses to be saddled for the afternoon?'

'Oh, yes, we must go out,' said Lali at once. 'Let us all go.'

But Julie excused herself for she now felt the sleepiness that evaded her at night, coming down like a soft cloud and she knew she must sleep deeply as she had not slept for weeks. The others, talking and laughing merrily together, went out and Julie was left for a moment with her hostess.

'You are very much overtired, I can see,' said the stout Countess bluntly. 'Vienna can't be much of a place to live nowadays.'

Julie sighed. 'No,' she said, 'my poor Vienna.'

'Before you go up though, I must just explain to you about Alois Pohaisky. You know he has been living here since – since he came home?'

'Yes, I know.' A feeling of dread came over Julie.

'He lives over at the farm-house but he comes over most evenings to share our food and a glass of wine with us. It will do him good to see you; he is one of your greatest admirers, you know.'

'I understand you,' replied Julie in a quiet, oppressed voice. 'I shall not show any signs of noticing any – alteration there may be in Dr Alois.'

The Countess examined her big hands with their neatly round-cut nails; she glanced up at Julie's face, but they said nothing more. Then the older woman got up and Julie rose too. 'You go up now, and have a rest. I hope everything you need is in your room?' She smiled suddenly, a slightly condescending smile. 'I'm sure your toilet necessities are much more elaborate than mine. You must ask for anything you want.'

'Thank you. I'm sure I shall need nothing you haven't thought of already.' Julie smiled suddenly, and the Countess was surprised at the illumination, the intimacy, of her smile. The face which had seemed to the countrywoman quite ordinary, now showed its true loveliness; even the contours seemed to be altered. Without knowing why this smile and the change it made in Julie's face affected her, the Countess felt sad and sympathetic.

'Yes,' she said, 'these are bad times for all of us. It is much worse for you and my boy and all the others who must stay on in Vienna.' She stopped on her move to the door. 'I tried hard to persuade him to marry a year or so ago and come and take over here. Now I'm very glad I did not succeed. He would already have been called up.'

The significance of this remark, coming from one of an old military family, only struck Julie as she was taking off her rings before lying down. It is not our war, she thought, even this woman who clearly never thinks of politics, realises that ... A wood dove warbled outside the windows, in the farmyard a cock crowed. The soft hushing of the breeze in the beech grove was audible in the afternoon stillness, and Julie's thoughts began to slide, weave into each other and expand into dreamy fantasy as she fell almost at once into a deep slumber.

'We sit in Father's room in the evening.' Lali tapped gently on the door and came in, as she said, to help Julie, but really to watch this famous and strange creature dress. 'That is, it's meant to be called the library, but all the books are military histories and explorations and such stuff that we haven't opened for – oh, as long as I remember. They just stand there, smelling of mould.' This was an exaggeration, the books Julie found did not smell, but they really had stood for a generation untouched. 'They belonged to Grandfather; he wrote some stuffy history about some campaign or other ... Father didn't read them, either. You know he was badly wounded in the other war, did you?' Julie shook her head. 'He couldn't walk very easily, they set his hip all wrong or something. Of course, he was old when I was born. Mother's much younger, she always ran the place.'

'It's after seven,' said Julie, reaching for her little watch. 'Oughtn't we to go down?'

'No hurry, really. Your clothes are lovely. So simple. I only have these sorts of country things.' She looked disparagingly down at her pleated skirt and plain cardigan of light blue with the single string of pearls.

'You look awfully well in them, just the same,' said Julie.

She herself wore a black dress from Paris bought the spring before the war started, and a brooch on her shoulder of alexandrines and small diamonds given her by Franz years before. The girl kept looking at this twist of finest goldsmith's work.

'It looks so simple, as if it couldn't be any other way,' she said putting out a finger and not quite touching the pretty thing. 'Did you buy it in Paris or Rome?'

'No, it was made in Vienna ...' Julie paused and then added, 'It was designed by my husband.'

'Oh,' said the girl, in a shocked voice. 'I'm so sorry ... I shouldn't have ...'

'My dear, how could you know?' Julie wondered how much this child knew. The reference to Franz depressed her suddenly, and by a transference from one victim to the other, she wished almost passionately that she did not have to face Pohaisky.

The library was a big room, dark in the corners. A cheerful fire burned on logs in the open grate of stonework. The piled ash under the fire glowed as the crackling sparks fell down. A big old spaniel growled or snored, but did not move from the hearth where he lay curled with his chin over his back paws. If the room smelled of anything except the faint odour of the oil lamps, it was of the dog.

'No electricity in here,' said Nando rising from reading the local paper. From another door at the other end of the room the Countess came in still talking over her shoulder. Then Julie saw that there was someone sitting in the chair by which the spaniel slept. She knew who this must be and at once went towards him, glad of the restrained light for her heart beat uncomfortably and though she knew nothing showed in her face, still she could feel its stiffness.

'Here is Frau Homburg at last, then, Alois,' said Nando's mother loudly. She bent over the high-backed chair and Julie heard the leather creak.

'Doctor Alois.' He was struggling to rise. 'Please, please don't get up. I shall sit here beside you.'

'My dear Frau Julie,' the voice was the same, only smaller, hushed with the exhaustion of a long illness. 'How good of you to come.' She could see his face now and it seemed the same, but the hair was quite white. 'They gave me rheumatism, you see,' said the exhausted voice. 'But how are you? You look more beautiful than ever.' This observation, which Pohaisky would never have made before, gave Julie a shock. A few minutes later, Otto's father with his mother were announced by the old manservant. Frau Klara brought in a tall dumb-waiter on large wheels with plates, knives, napkins and glasses on its lower shelf and a variety of breads, cheeses and home-cured meats and sausages above, together with several bottles of red wine from Rust in the Burgenland.

'It's the only vineyard we own,' said Nando, pouring out for Julie. 'It used to run over into the Pannonian plain so that it was in Hungary and we sold most of it.' He was very careful to maintain a neutral and respectful tone to Julie and to avoid addressing her directly so that he was not bound to say 'you' to her. This necessity made his manner constrained and formal, and it was clear that everyone noticed this and that Lali and Otto found it very amusing; they had in fact already decided that Nando cherished a romantic and hopeless passion for the guest. The talk was of the countryside and its doings, and of farming, until Frau Krassny mentioned a friend whose home was near Graz. Julie turned on her low stool, to see Krassny's face which gave her, as it always did, a slight remembered feeling of unease she could no longer place but which merged into that general watchfulness with which anyone official must be treated.

'Herr Doctor, is it true that the Slovenian frontier has been closed?' she asked.

He considered before he replied. 'Yes,' he said slowly. 'It is true, I'm afraid.' He frowned then, a little. 'But how did you hear of it?'

'My mother lives near the frontier and she writes that they must all carry new passes to go to and fro.'

'Why would that be?' asked the Countess whose masculinity stopped at local affairs.

'Fresh Balkan adventures?' suggested Nando.

'There have been Russian movements on their Rumanian border in the last few months,' said Krassny thoughtfully. 'The closing of our border may have something to do with that ...?'

'But in that case, the Wehrmacht would have closed the Hungarian border area too,' objected Nando at once.

Krassny hesitated again before he answered. Then he said cautiously, 'Probably rather more confidence is felt in the Hungarian Army's ability to defend itself — in case of need — than that of Rumania or Yugoslavia.'

The exhausted voice from the big chair intervened.

'If the Russians are going to move, they will move towards the south-east, not towards Hungary. Their goal would be the Bosphorus. As always.'

'Nothing to do with Russian movements,' said Nando with unusual sharpness. 'The Führer means to move into the Balkans. The Italians have forced his hand. What else can all these negotiations with the Yugoslavs mean?' He got up and moved uneasily about the big room. 'Not that any of us knows what is really happening.'

'Sit down, Nando,' said his mother comfortably. 'You make me uneasy, traipsing about the place.'

Frau Krassny, a quiet little woman who had hardly spoken, now glanced at Julie sideways with a defensive, nervous look, almost of dislike. She seemed to resent Julie addressing her husband directly, or perhaps she felt slighted that her husband had known this famous woman for some years while she had never been invited to meet her.

'Tell me, Nando,' she said, using the familiar form of address to him, 'is Clothilde coming over to-morrow? I meant to ring up, but I forgot.'

'Tilde? I don't think so. I mean, I haven't heard.'

'No, Tilly is busy to-morrow . . .' began Lali hastily, evidently having some reason to cut off the subject.

'I talked to Tilde's father to-day,' said the Countess in her comfortable, booming voice. 'You know, Nando, about that wretched bull . . .? They aren't going out this week-end. I asked them to supper to-morrow, but the boy's had his call-up papers, did you know?' She turned to Frau Krassny, saw too late why Lali had tried to kill the subject, and unable to retreat, went on talking. 'He's leaving next week.'

Frau Krassny went pale and gave a little gasp. Her husband took her hand and patted it with his free one.

Lali looked imploringly round at Julie, her brother, her mother. Suddenly her charming round face with its sparkling eyes looked like that of a child threatened with some punishment it does not understand.

'It's all right, my dear,' said Krassny to his wife. 'Clothilde's brother failed his university entrance, that's why he is being called up at once.'

The whole atmosphere of the company had changed from a family gathering to that of a court-room where something terrible is about to be decided.

'No,' said Frau Krassny, with a cold angry look at her husband, 'no, they will call Otto up too. I know it.'

'If the others are going, I shall have to go anyway,' Otto said, too loudly, in a forced voice as if he were choking on a chunk of food.

'They will all have to go,' said Pohaisky's hushed voice suddenly. 'All. All.' And quite loudly, in an almost normal voice, 'We are being punished for something – some sin we do not know we have committed. Or perhaps some fault committed by others, that we must expiate.' He sighed deeply and was silent. The silence lasted for almost a minute.

'Yes, we live in terrible times,' said the Countess at last. In such an ordinary voice it sounded like a social phrase rather than an answer to Pohaisky, and the commonplace in a moment of fear and reality formed a lifeline back to normality. And as always, the very young people were not able to understand that the expression of reality must be avoided at all costs if people are to carry on with their lives at all, and both of them spoke at once.

'But, Mother, will Otto be able to go to the University?'

'I shall have to volunteer, if all my school chaps are called up ...'

'I'm sure nobody need volunteer for anything, Otto,' intervened Julie, her voice clear and high. 'I know a man in Vienna who has volunteered three times and they just lose his papers each time. He isn't due yet to be called up, so they just get in a muddle with him – you see? When are you going to the University? Next month? You must come and see me. You're going to Vienna, of course? Nando, he must come and see both of us, and we'll take him to the theatre.'

Everyone began to speak at once, and the young people felt that they were being put in their places and ignored as not grown-up, but the moment had passed and the family circle returned in place of that feeling of something terrible about to be decided.

'The man must be cracked, to volunteer three times,' said Nando, 'who is he?'

'A friend of my cook's,' said Julie, who had invented the volunteer on the spur of the moment, and laughed now at the way Nando almost caught her out. She saw from Nando's look that he knew this and felt a close intimacy with him as if they were bound together by more than physical fellowship, as if they two knew something about the outside world, from which they were momentarily so far away, that nobody else here knew.

She looked at Krassny, and saw him frowning at Nando thoughtfully. He was weighing in his mind whether or not he should make some remark about the indiscretion of the family conversation. Krassny knew from the inside how much the failure to reduce British air cover to impotence spread fear and questioning among the National Socialists, even in Vienna, far from the seat of power. He knew that the failure to free the Atlantic flank, seemingly so completely in Germany's hands after the victory in France, must result in ever more wild and desperate measures outwards from the Reich and inwardly inside it to still the underswell of doubt and unbelief that was everywhere to be felt.

Krassny was having a week's holiday with his family in the country – nobody had had any summer rest this year – and did not know of the new co-ordination of the police and the Ministry of the Interior with the German police, the Gestapo and the SS. Such orders and new arrangements were always introduced with extreme discretion so that the general public only became aware of them gradually, if at all.

Otto Krassny, sitting with Lali in a comradeship of youth against the conspiracy of the grown-ups to ignore 'the truth' and feeling scorn at the pusillanimity of their elders, had picked up the local newspaper. They bent their heads together over the page of jokes and puzzles in the week-end edition. This pursuit did not last them long, for the standard of public joking had gone down heavily, like all other standards, and there was nothing amusing to take their attention. Otto turned the page and they began to read, desultorily, the general news.

'Father,' said Otto, looking up, 'here's a bit about a colleague of yours. Isn't he? Ministerialrat Helmut Korning?'

This was the man who always sat in on departmental conferences and intervened only when some directive of the Party was concerned.

'What about Korning?' Krassny looked across at Nando, who glanced up at the name. Nando had had a slight brush with the Party representative after the affair of the envelope in Julie's flat more than a year ago, and they had been quietly on bad terms ever since.

'It says here he's been made Obergruppenführer. Appointment to be backdated to last June.'

'You see, we can't leave the Ministry for a day without something going wrong,' joked Nando, sliding with irony over the dangerous subject.

'But Nando, that's an SS rank!' objected his mother.

'I thought you were a civil servant,' said Lali, puzzled.

'An honorary rank, I suppose.' Krassny got up and went to read over his son's shoulder the announcement in the 'Official Notices' column.

'"In pursuance of the rearrangement of the Reich Ministry of the Interior",' he read in an undertone. 'Have you heard anything about this, Nando?'

'Oh, it's one of their changes without an alteration. Just different names for the same things, that's all.' Nando could not hide his unease; he gave Otto a look of intense irritation so unlike him that everyone noticed it. 'We had a directive yesterday, but it's only a matter of form.'

'Peter, does this mean you are joining the SS?' asked Frau Krassny. 'It can't mean that, surely?'

'Only formally,' said Nando, unable to lie about something bound to be known in a matter of days. That he should be forced to discuss it on this occasion, the first time Julie was in his beloved home; that this week-end, looked forward to with longing, should be overcast by this shadow seemed to Nando so bitterly unfair and – now that it had happened – so inevitable, that he was filled with anger and despair. Nothing was safe from the black corruption summed up in the initials SS. Even here it was creeping in on them, on the easy decency of centuries spent without want and without riches, in the service of the state and the cultivation of their modest possessions.

Nando felt this contrast between past and present in the form of an arrogant contempt for these new people who, as he would have said, were 'awful'. But under his superficial dislike of their vulgarity the traditions of generations of responsibility and the respect it had always brought his family told him more clearly than any argument what a blot it was that their name should now carry a title of the barbarian elite. He would have thought it snobbish and ridiculous to say such a thing. The revolution of his childhood and the distress and confusion of the years of the Republic, the conflicts and resentments of the students during his university days, had disillusioned him with the attitudes of his class besides filling him for life with a profound dislike and contempt for politics and politicians.

But here, sheltered in this house, was a prisoner of the SS, crippled with the hardships of his imprisonment, a living evidence of the dark that waited just outside their view, creeping nearer with every day of the extended war, waiting to engulf them all. He had never liked Pohaisky, and thought him a prig, a religious enthusiast whose exaltations were affected. But Pohaisky also gave him a feeling of awe and he recognised that this man lived his life on a higher plane of meaning than Nando would ever reach. It was part of the hideous injustice of the world that just this man was here to point the moral of Nando's position.

Julie was not sleepy now, and she opened the wide windows as far as they would go. The cool night air throbbed into the room, there was no frost and threads of mist lay over the woods in the white glare of moonlight. It was a hunter's moon, everything black or silvery white, the pastures over the ha-ha gleaming mysteriously with a heavy dew. From the beech grove came a soft sighing noise and somewhere an owl hooted constantly. Far away the mountain tops shimmered, their outlines invisible, only the reflection of the moon off the snow showing in the clear colourless sky.

Nando made no sound as he came in, but she instantly knew he was there and turned towards him.

'Should you have come?' she whispered. I don't want ... '

He made a sound that might have been a smothered laugh. 'Nobody sleeps on this side,' he said softly. Julie knew that he must have visited this guest room in the past for other feminine guests, and felt a prick of jealousy at his knowledge that they could not be heard.

'I have thought of you being here so often,' he said, and leaned a tall shoulder on the window-timber. Julie sat facing him on the broad window-sill, leaning against the frame. Dimly she could see their reflected faces in the dark glass opened into the room, repeated in the double window by the indirect sheen of moonlight.

'What do you think,' he said after a silence, 'ought I to volunteer for the Wehrmacht, or should I let things stay as they are?'

'Get me something for my shoulders,' she said, 'there's my coat hanging in the closet.' By the time he came back and put the tweed coat about her shoulders, she had made up her mind.

'Leave things alone,' she said. 'Not only because I don't want to lose you ... You're the last man here. Why should you go to war for them – it must be over soon, surely.' She waited but he said nothing. 'This Clothilde,' she said suddenly. 'The one whose brother has been called up. Does your mother want you to marry her?'

'She thinks it would be a good idea,' he said uneasily. 'Their land is next to ours. And they are a very prolific family. That's what Mother thinks of.'

'This is not the only son, then? The one who's called up?'

'He has four brothers and a sister – that's Clothilde. Two in the Luftwaffe, one in the Alpine Scouts and one whose eyes are bad, so he does the farming.'

'Lali had better marry the farming brother, then,' she said. 'You could hyphen the names ... '

'Lali will marry Otto Krassny in a year or so. If ... ' He stopped. 'They've always been together, since they were born, almost.'

'So. Then you will have to marry this Clothilde and have five sons to be killed in the next war.'

Nando kissed her hand and held it up against the bosom of his dressing-gown.

'Don't mind Mother,' he said. 'She thinks only of breeding. I can't marry anybody but you. You know that.' He looked at her reflected face in the glass like dark water. 'Look ... We belong together, we are caught in the glass ... You've never taken me quite seriously, have you?'

She laughed a little, irritably. 'I find I take you seriously enough, when I think of you marrying,' she said.

'Then the solution is for me to marry you. Besides ...' he stopped, feeling that what he was about to say would sound childish to Julie. 'Besides, I don't like deceiving *them*.'

'Yes. In the welter of deceit, there must be one place where one can still be open.' Unconsciously a deep bitterness spoke out of Julie's tone and without any explanation Nando became aware that this bitterness had nothing to do with Julie's previous irritation; it came from some other source. A thought came into his mind and he asked a question he had often before been on the point of asking.

'Julie? Why do you never let me come to your home? I've always wanted to bring you here, where I'm at home. But you never once have asked me to your home ...'

She said breathlessly, too quickly, 'It isn't my home in the sense you mean. It's just the place where I live. And it's full of ...' The falseness of her tone, taken aback by the sudden challenge, was offensive and he let her hand fall. He looked, not this time in the dark glass but direct at her shadowed face and saw a deep mournfulness in the droop of the lips. She looked up suddenly and they stared at each other, nakedly. The shadow of what had always lain between them, what he had never formulated simply because it had been there from the very beginning of their relationship, was in that moment alive. Nando did not suddenly know something about Julie's life, but he felt something new about Julie herself, a shadow on her spirit, a block between them like a door marked ENTRY FORBIDDEN. Such secrets can never be hidden in an intimate relationship, they creep into consciousness by some other route than any open communication, and there is no moment that can be looked back upon and labelled the moment at which something was first known. But from then on, Nando knew something not discovered but now acknowledged between them. The question about the door to her home, always closed to him so that it was a long time before he noticed that he never went there; this question, he now felt obscurely, was dangerous.

Julie, head against the window-frame, contemplated the shadowy reflection in the panes, of the moon, the small cloud quite still in the empty heaven and Nando's unclear features. The question about her own home reminded her of Ruth Wedliceny and where she should live. It was equally necessary to find the child some sure refuge in case a military patrol found her at Graz and started up the whole search for her uncle again; and to find that refuge in a way that could not be connected in the future with Julie's direct agency. Had the girl been no family connection, there were several people known to Julie in Vienna who would hide her, at least for a time. But all of them would connect her in their minds with Franz, sooner or later. It had to be somebody who would not connect Ruth Wedliceny with Julie at all – or who was so deep in their secret that a new risk could make no difference. There was only one person outside the Schellinggasse whom that condition fitted.

'Kerenyi,' said Julie aloud.

Nando seemed not to have heard her. He stared out at the landscape, lost in a profound depressive dream where the moon in the clear sky and the familiar outlines of pasture and woods were no longer a refuge from the daytime world of Vienna duties and encroaching involvement, no longer a beloved permanence to which one might return as to another self. He felt now that he would not come back here again, as long as this war lasted; this place should be spared. He considered again the possibility of volunteering for the army – there were enough old friends of his father's still serving to make his path easy, release him from his civilian 'reserved' status. But he knew he would not do it, and Julie's face, floating dimly on the foreground of the landscape was the main reason. Perhaps her ignorant belief that the war would soon be over was right ... perhaps his questioning would soon prove unneeded. After another winter cooped up on their misty island, the British would be ready to make terms – and Hitler ready to offer them. Then, with peace, he could quietly transfer to another branch of the civil administration – perhaps the Ministry of Agriculture.

Nando moved close to Julie and took her hands again, kissing them. He drew her to her feet, covering her face with kisses, but under his passionate love and desire for her was a deep feeling of helplessness and resentment against the fate surrounding and driving them, that they could never for a moment forget.

'How easy it would be, just to end it,' he murmured, his mouth against her hair with its familiar scent.

'Don't say that,' she begged. 'It makes me unhappy – you've had this mood before, and then things get better ...'

'No,' he said, 'nothing gets better – only worse. We just manage to ignore it sometimes.' He drew her away from the open windows into the dark room.

Later he dreamed uneasily that Kerenyi with his big nose very prominent was trying to wake him, and saying in his ear, 'You are dragging them all down with you, dragging them to ruin, dragging them to ruin.' He woke, sweating, with the sensation that there had been more to the dream than he now remembered, something he ought to recall; he could not sleep again, and lay silent until the first birdsong told him dawn was about to break. Then he went quietly to his own room, the room of his childhood, the holiday room of his schooldays, where there was no feeling of belonging any more. It was cold in the grey, vaporous dawn. Ever since he and Julie first kissed each other in the hot meadow by the lake he had imagined taking her to his home. This was their first whole night together since the first nights in the little inn in the uplands. He walked through the woods to the village, just stirring, and back again but could not rid himself of the helpless, trapped feeling of misery.

They all went out after breakfast, with the horses, and did not return until time for the midday meal.

'It's so warm to-day,' called the Countess to them as they dismounted. Otto and Lali took their horses' reins to go to the stables. 'We are going to eat on the terrace. It will probably be the last time this year.'

Alone for a moment, Nando handed her a glass with Campari and soda.

'No ice – but we may as well enjoy the advantages of having to have the Italians on our side.' He quoted wryly a current Vienna joke.

'It reminds me of the mountains,' she said. 'D'you remember?'

'I remember,' he answered. 'How I wish we could go back ...'

'You say that as if you thought we never could ... No, Nando, tell me – tell me why you're so depressed. Surely the war will soon be over? And then things are bound to be better?'

'You mean they will win? Yes, as I said yesterday, that's just what I'm afraid of. The English may stay there posturing as heroes from the safety of their island, but that won't make any difference. The war will be over.'

'That's what you were thinking of all morning, then? All through the lovely countryside? Though I don't know what you mean about the English – they will have to agree to peace, won't they?'

'What difference does it make?' he said, impatiently. 'They can't get at the Germans and we can't get at them, or the Wehrmacht would have invaded by now. What matters is that "they" dominate the Continent. England doesn't matter. In five years from now the Balkans and Hungary will be just as much under German influence as we are. There's no need of war to achieve that. Probably Italy too. They will be running things everywhere.'

Julie stared at him. For literally the first time she realised that the conditions of her life could go on like this with Franz precariously hidden for ever, until they died or some chance betrayed him to his enemies. Unconsciously she had clung to the thought that the end of the war would free him. Until this moment she relied blindly on the temporariness of this growing nightmare of deceit and caution. She walked slowly over to the railing of the terrace feeling all at once the weight of her riding boots, and gazed ahead of her at the trunks of the coppery tawny beech trees, elephant grey, smooth and tall, with drifts of fallen crisp leaves at their feet. Every now and then a freshly fallen leaf twisted down in the warm sun, and birds sang. Immediately in front of the terrace, growing in the garden below, a tangle of pale michaelmas daisies bloomed, over which a late pollen-drunk bee mused in the sun.

A curious sensation as if everything in her became immensely heavy and solid like granite, encased her; she could feel her fingers holding the narrow glass as if they were huge and heavy. Through the stone separating her from other people, she heard voices behind her, and knew the Countess must have come out on to the terrace.

'A lovely view,' she said, turning, the habit of years dictating social behaviour.

The Countess smiled at Julie and her broad face set in the smile while a frown incongruously appeared at the same time on her brow. 'But are you ill?' she said.

At this moment Lali's gay voice interrupted from the garden where she and Otto ran up from the stables at the back of the house.

'Frau Homburg! Do settle an argument! Otto is sure actors don't work all the time – sort of, in bursts. And I think you work every day. Tell us which is right, can you please? Otto always thinks he knows everything!'

'Don't bother Frau Homburg,' called her mother. 'She's trying to drink her *apéritif* in peace.'

'Oh, please,' said Julie. 'I'm all right. It was just for a moment ...' She turned back to the balustrade of the terrace and leaned over, glad of the interruption that returned the world to its normal dimensions.

'You're both right,' she called down, now hardly having to force laughter, their faces were so brilliantly real. 'Which is lucky! Sometimes we work every day like bank clerks; sometimes when a new production is almost ready we work day and night. Sometimes we don't work for days on end.'

The Countess and Nando, without knowing what it was about, joined in the conspiracy to push the dark away as the two young people began to pull themselves up by a method they clearly often used, to the terrace.

'Do you have to rehearse plays you have acted in before?' asked the Countess. 'Or does everybody remember the words?'

'Most actors remember the words of a play, once they have learned and played them. But the cast is usually different, so we do have to rehearse to fit in with new players. Sometimes a different producer, too, everyone has different ideas of a play. People move differently, speak faster or slower. All sorts of things like that.'

'Have you got a favourite part?' asked Nando. 'I've always meant to ask ...' He had used the familiar form, but no one seemed to notice it.

'I don't believe I have,' said Julie slowly, considering. 'It's a question people often ask. I enjoyed *The Importance of Being Earnest* very much – we had a lot of fun with that and the public loved it. That always makes a difference. But I love playing Hedda Gabler too, and that's never a popular part. Some of Shaw's plays – *Major Barbara*, I enjoyed. I never played in *Pygmalion*, but I should like it. That's a heavenly part.'

'You were very good as Nora in the *Doll's House*,' said the Countess. 'I saw you in that – what, two years ago?'

'It's a terrific part,' agreed Julie, but she felt a sinking of vitality again at the thought of Nora. The day when Hansi Ostrovsky warned her of the imminent arrival of the Germans came back to her and she had a visual memory of the ornamental water in the Burggarten, the birds fluttering on the cover of the fountain, the bare trees and a small man who said something to her, his face half turned away. A meagre little man, what was it he said ...?

4

$\mathcal{N}$ando took her directly to the theatre from the train for a rehearsal, and from there she had a luncheon consultation with Hansi Ostrovsky and Schoenherr. She did not telephone the apartment, and there was no message from Fina at the theatre for her. Up to a few months before, Julie had been in the habit of ringing up the flat if she were away from home for more than an hour or so. But one day, as she did this in Hansi's office, Hella Schneider came in.

'Has Fina run off with a soldier?' asked Hella as Julie turned away from the telephone on the desk. Her voice, as always, had the teasing note of an intimate who is no friend. 'You're always ringing up at home – anyone would think you had a houseful of children to worry about . . .'

For an instant Julie had found no answer. Then she laughed and agreed that it was a silly habit. But from then on, Fina had instructions to do the telephoning if she needed anything, and Julie always left her a list of numbers at which she could be reached.

Yet she knew at once that something was wrong. She knew it when Herr Pichler opened the lift doors for her and put in her week-end case.

'Shall I come up to carry your case, gnae' Frau?' he asked, eyeing her without quite looking at her as he always did.

'No, no, Fina can manage,' said Julie automatically, already in her mind talking to Fina and Franz.

'Ah!' he said as if she had answered a question. 'Then she is there? I haven't seen her for a day or so. I thought she must be away.'

And the hall was empty, no Fina to open the door as she heard Julie's key. This was a shock, and in her mind she told herself that she must be ready to meet it when it came — the moment that must come. People who live under a steady strain prepare themselves constantly for the shock of disaster; but often for the wrong disaster.

Julie went into the passage that led to Franz's secret room, just as Fina came out of her own room.

'He is ill,' she said abruptly, in the secretive undertone she now always used when they spoke of Franz.

'Why didn't you telephone me?' whispered Julie. 'What is it?'

'Herr Doctor didn't want me to. Don't go in to him. He doesn't want ... It's something he ate.' Julie had put her hand to the handle of the cupboard that masked Franz's room. Now she took it away again.

'But I must see him,' she said.

Fina's hand on her arm drew her out of hearing distance of the door, back into the main hall.

'He feels wretched,' she said obstinately. 'He said he couldn't see you until the spots were gone from his face. We had fish soup on Friday. Nothing's ever fresh any more ...' She began to cry with the angry look of her peasant stubbornness.

'Don't cry, Fina. Please, love, don't cry,' said Julie automatically. She glanced at the door through which they might be heard. 'Come in the living-room. It isn't your fault, the fish. Were you ill too?' She knew Fina had not telephoned the Kasda house in order to be able to blame Julie for her neglect of Franz.

'I was a bit sick.' Fina sat down slackly on the edge of a chair and rested her head on her hand, her elbow on the edge of Franz's tidy desk. 'Only for an hour or so. But he goes on being sick and groaning, and the spots came out on his face. He's getting weak.' She looked at Julie for the first time, panic in her eyes, reddened with little veins, in the round face that no longer had the apple-shiny colour of health. Her hard muscular face and body had softened and loosened with the lack of the open air, and she now had a yellow look. In the last eighteen months Fina had become a middle-aged woman, almost old. Julie noticed she was wearing her white cooking apron, and it was not very clean. Little strands of black hair had escaped the tight-plaited knob and hung on her neck. She had obviously not undressed for days. Her hands, accustomed to constant activity, moved all the time. Julie looked round the room, which was dusty, not touched since she went away. Oh, God, she thought drearily, Nando was right. It would be easier to give up and end it all. Even as the thought passed through her mind, her natural energy was working out what she must do. I must tell the doctor I'm not well, she thought. But when I say it's Franz he'll leave again at once. He warned me once not to try to involve him ... he has a family, he said so. Now how ...?

'Yes,' she said aloud. 'Now listen, Fina. I shall call Doctor Moller ... No, no, wait a minute, I've thought it out. He'll come and you must go down and meet him. So that Pichler sees him. You understand? Then he can't refuse to look after Franz. He's in it then, with us, and he'll have to keep quiet.'

'That's blackmail,' said Fina flatly. She glanced up at the considering expression on Julie's face and said hastily, 'All right. That's what we'll do. Now don't you start worrying about me, because I'm perfectly all right.'

'I'll come and help you with Franz's room. We'll change the bed and clear up his room and make him comfortable. Then you can have a bath and change while I sit with him. The doctor won't come until after his surgery.' She looked at her watch. 'I'll call him now and ask him to come after eight o'clock.'

'Yes, that's right, after eight. Then I can make the door an excuse to go down and wait for him. They close it now earlier sometimes.' Fina stopped speaking and sat staring abstractedly at Julie. She knew, and Julie knew she knew, that that considering look had been a threat; an empty threat for Julie could no more do without Fina than Fina could leave her master. 'I couldn't go to Mass yesterday,' said Fina suddenly, and began to cry again.

'Go to-morrow morning. I'll sit with Franz and get breakfast. But now we must ...' Julie was already going towards the door and

Fina got up at once to follow her. 'Have you given him anything —
to bring it up?'

'Salt and water. It wasn't any good. He was sick in any case. And
castor-oil. But the poison is too strong for those things. There
were some mussels in the market, Friday, and I put a handful in
the soup. It must have been one of them, or I would have been
worse off than I was.'

Julie was already telephoning. She put back the receiver.

'About a quarter past eight, he said.' Fina was standing in the
doorway, watching her.

'You're always so calm,' muttered Fina. 'I'm afraid!'

'So am I,' said Julie. She looked into Fina's reddened eyes, and
saw that Fina's fear was different from her own. Fina was afraid
Franz was going to die. For an instant, Julie felt panic that stirred
her nerves and intelligence, like the poison in Franz's body, so that
she could not think and everything outside herself and inside too
seemed to be coming loose and flying round and round like a
whirlpool at the bottom of a waterfall. She caught at the doorpost
and at Fina's hand. Her grip was so violent that Fina gave a little
moan of pain, and this brought Julie back to herself.

'Don't give way, Fina,' she said sharply, speaking to herself as
well. 'Get hot water. I'll get clean sheets and towels.'

'Better to leave him be,' muttered Fina, but she sighed and went
obediently to the bathroom to draw hot water.

Franz did not move as Julie opened his door. Was he too ill to
care she wondered, or had he become so used to his hideout that
he trusted it? His head, turned towards the wall, remained still.
One long hand, its spare elegance bony now and yellow, lay open
upwards on the blanket; it was utterly defenceless, the curving fingers had neither strength nor will to defend him. She could hear
his shallow breath, rustling; he gave a groan of weariness. The air
was foul and close. Like most healthy and practical people, Julie
was afraid of illness and normally felt a scorn for anyone ill, as if
they could help it if they wanted to.

Now, she bent down by the low bed, and feeling herself still too
tall, kneeled beside it. She touched his outspread hand, a little fearfully, forcing an extreme gentleness. He turned his head, without

a start, and opened his eyes. He saw who it was, and made an effort to turn towards her. A little smile filled the sad eyes, his parched lips parted and he smiled with an expression of such pity and tenderness, such understanding, that her heart filled with joy and gratitude.

'My beautiful girl,' he whispered. 'I was dreaming of you, and there you are.'

Julie hid her tears by taking his hand and kissing it. She put up a finger and stroked the damp streaks of greying hair from his high brow; not even noticing that the source of the smell in the room was in his sick breath.

'It's all right,' she said with love. 'We'll soon have you better.'

'No,' he whispered. 'Let me die in peace.'

'Don't say that,' she cried with an agonised sensation of panic again. 'Don't leave me, Franzl. You couldn't do that to me.'

'You will force me to survive,' he whispered, the loving little smile touching his lips again. 'You never would give me any peace.'

'Don't try to talk. We're going to make you more comfortable, and then I'll sit with you.' Still on her knees, she turned towards Fina, carrying a bowl and a jug of hot water. 'I don't see any spots on his face,' she said. In fact there were none, only the skin was disfigured with darkish blotches.

Together they pulled the bed out from the wall to move around it, and washed the sick man. Then they changed his clothing and the bed linen. Once he began to retch weakly, but the fit passed. Julie cleaned his haggard face with her face lotion, and he managed to rinse his mouth. Then she brushed his hair smooth with her soft brush, holding her free hand under his neck and head. The touch of his damp skin, the thinning hair, the coarse feel of the growing beard in his cheeks and chin, all renewed her possessive love. She felt sharp jealousy that there were things he would not let her do for him, and left the room only reluctantly until Fina had finished. She went into her own room and found a big shawl of soft wool to wrap round him, and a spray bottle of aromatic water to spray the room. When Fina called her, Julie leaned across the bed and opened the windows wide – they were small enough in any case and had clearly been closed for days.

'He'll catch cold,' objected Fina, making a move towards the windows.

'No, leave them. It's a fine evening, the air will do him good.' Julie's voice was sharp. She folded the shawl about his thin shoulders, feeling the fine bones, and then sat down beside the bed and took his hand.

She was still sitting there when the door-bell rang from the downstairs hall and dragged her from her reverie. Franz hardly seemed to notice it. But he stirred and murmured something when she pulled her hand gently from his and stood up. It was almost dark in the little room, only the reflected lights from the other rooms facing on the courtyard, and the faint glow of the city about them, lightened the dark through the open window. Neither of them had noticed it was dusk.

Julie screwed up her eyes against the hard light in the hall, as Fina opened the door and came in, followed by the familiar square figure of Dr Moller; she saw that Pichler had come up in the lift with them and wondered how Fina had managed that.

'You're up?' asked the doctor, with his normal abruptness. 'I thought you were ill?' He looked at her sharply, as they shook hands. 'You don't look yourself, I must say. Overtired, eh?'

'I am perfectly well,' said Julie, making her voice clear and hard. 'I am not your patient, Doctor.' She made no move to take him into the living-room.

'What do you mean?' Moller said angrily. It was clear that his sharp wits had warned him – or perhaps he remembered that conversation, over two years before? The doctor was not given time to consider what it was he suspected or why; Julie knew instinctively that the way to deal with this man was by simple direct attack.

'My husband is ill,' she said in the same clear, hard voice, as if he were slightly deaf and an enemy. 'No – don't go, Doctor. Remember the porter has seen you arrive. Franz is very ill, and if anything happens ... the whole story will come out and you, too, will be involved.'

'Not if I leave at once,' he said, and turned to the door. Fina had slipped away into her own room. The door was double-locked. It was clear the doctor knew this the moment he put his hand on the door handle.

'I shall go straight from here to the police,' he said.

'I shall tell them you have been supplying me with drugs without prescriptions,' said Julie with calm, but with a feeling of surprise at herself.

'No good,' he replied. 'My books are in order.'

'Then you're the only doctor in Vienna who can say that,' she countered instantly. She knew by his angry hesitation that she had caught him. 'Or perhaps I'll tell the police you have procured me an abortion,' she went on consideringly. 'Your family would love that, wouldn't they? I remember how concerned with the welfare of your family you were ...'

'You are an abominable woman,' he said loudly, looking about the hall for help.

'Yes,' said Julie simply. 'And you are going to help me.'

'I've closed his window and drawn the curtains,' said Fina from the kitchen door behind them. The doctor whirled round.

'You—' he stopped whatever he was going to say. Something in the fixed look of Fina's reddened eyes warned him that she would go even further than Julie, if goaded.

'You'll pay for this,' he turned to Julie again and spoke through closed teeth, his voice shaking with fear and anger.

'Send me a double bill,' said Julie laconically. 'But spare me the histrionics.' She swaggered a little and turned on a wide smile as if she were overacting the *Beggar's Opera*. She had the sensation of enjoying her own vulgarity; the doctor was staring at her as if he had never really seen her before; Fina was staring too. She could feel the sharp glower of the frown between her brows and the feral menace of clenched teeth bared in what might pass as a smile.

'If you please, Herr Doctor,' she said mockingly, and gestured to the narrow corridor. Beaten, he put down his hat on the hall table, and laid his gloves beside it.

Fina had warned Franz, but it was still a shock to him to see a stranger; he had seen nobody but the two women and Georg Kerenyi for many months now. His body seemed to shrink together, trying to draw itself away into the bed, and his long hands made a despairing gesture of pushing something away.

'It's all right, Franzl,' said Julie, going quickly to him; taking his hand gently in hers, she kneeled beside the bed. The time when she hardly came into this room and she and Franz spoke to each other like strangers seemed never to have been. The doctor was speaking to Fina but Julie was aware that he was looking at herself with blank astonishment.

The examination seemed to take a long time. Julie had told the doctor on the telephone that she had eaten something that disagreed with her so he had brought appropriate drugs with him in his bag. He gave Franz an injection, and wrote prescriptions, repeating instructions several times to Fina so that she should not forget.

'He was over the worst before I came,' the doctor turned to Julie and spoke with cold hostility, looking past her face.

'Let me have a look at those prescriptions, will you?' Julie held out her hand. 'It's just occurred to me— Yes, you've made them out for my name. That won't do, the chemist may see me, and I'm playing to-morrow night. You'll have to make them for Fina, here. And Fina, remember when you go out for a day or so, not to go near the chemist, in case he sees you.'

When they were in the hall again, the doctor, still not looking at Julie, began to talk about possible damage done to Franz's liver by the attack of food poisoning and the need for his diet to be carefully watched.

Suddenly they both heard the sound of a key pushed into the door from the outside. Julie whirled round, staring aghast at the keyhole, and then her face cleared.

'Kerenyi!' she said in an undertone. 'Go in there.' She pushed the doctor firmly into the hall lavatory as the key rattled, saw his hat and gloves lying on the hall table and hastily threw them in after their owner.

'Georgy!' she said breathlessly. 'Just the very man I wanted to see. I was just about to telephone you.' She almost pushed Kerenyi down the hall to the living-room.

'Where's Franz?' asked Kerenyi, looking about the long room.

'You know, it isn't good for him to spend all his time in that little room ...'

'I know, but he's been ill – you didn't know either, evidently. I was away for the week-end and came back to find Fina in a panic and Franz ill with fish poisoning. I was just getting rid of the doctor, when you came in.'

'The doctor?' he said with horror. 'My God, he'll talk!'

'He might have done, but he can't now. He'd be in trouble, too. He was here nearly an hour and wrote three prescriptions. The first time he wrote them, he made them out for me. I made him write them again, for Fina, on the excuse that too many people would know I wasn't really ill. I kept both sets. So if he thinks of going to the police to turn Franz in, I have the evidence that he was writing prescriptions for *someone else*.'

'You'll have to give up one set to the chemist,' objected Kerenyi.

'Chemists always return prescriptions. Surely you know that?' said Julie impatiently.

'I'm never ill,' said Kerenyi in excuse, and they both smiled. 'What have you done with the unfortunate doctor, if one may ask?'

'He's in the lavatory. I must go and let him out. Don't come out into the hall.'

Fina was already letting the doctor out, and he went without saying good-bye to Julie.

'It's all right,' said Fina after he had been heard going down the stairs. 'He said he would come the day after to-morrow again, but on no account to ring him up.'

The two women stared at each other for a moment, then they both began to laugh foolishly. Julie put her arms around Fina's shoulders and hugged her.

'Go and see if Franz is asleep,' she said, reverting to their usual undertone. 'I have to talk to Kerenyi about something, but he'll want to see Franz afterwards.'

Going back to the living-room Julie thought of the key opening the door.

'Georgy, the apartment key you have ... I hope you don't carry it on your own key-ring?'

He did not understand for a moment, and then he laughed.

'You really think of everything. You mean, in case I should be searched or something? No, I have a hiding-place for it in my flat, and only take it with me when I'm coming here.'

'Now listen, Georgy. I heard from my mother on Saturday. The border near them has been closed and everyone in the area has to carry a special pass. That means Ruth Wedliceny has to leave there. By the end of this week I have to find somewhere for her to go.'

'Can't she go over the border?' he asked.

'She's a complete infant,' said Julie. 'Never goes out alone, afraid of everything. How would she live, in Italy or Yugoslavia?'

'But you can't take care of every stray Jew, Julie. What do you mean to do with her? You can't possibly have her here ...' He stopped, looked up at Julie — he was seated and she stood by the window — then he rose and came over to her. He shoved his hands into his trousers pockets and stood in front of Julie, scowling at her thoughtfully. 'What you mean is that I'm to have her?'

'Yes,' she said simply.

'It's impossible. She'd be found at once. Dozens of people go in and out of my flat every week — the cleaning woman, the caretaker with coal every day, colleagues and friends, the copy boy from the paper — it's absolutely out of the question.'

'There's no one else. Don't you see — if she's picked up somewhere it will bring up the whole affair of Franz's disappearance again? We've got to do something about her. You know the Gestapo and the SS have the lists of the whole Jewish community. Franz isn't on them, but she is. If those deportations to Poland are started up again, she'll be picked up through the Rations Office or something ... one never knows with these madmen. The deportations did stop months ago, it's true, but they keep on with their wild threats about clearing out the Jews and such nonsense.'

'She's got a Jewish registration, then?'

'Of course. She's registered as Mother's servant — supposed to be doing rough work in the farmyard. They don't know she lives in the house with Mother — she's meant to be out in the loft over the barn, watching the pigs or some idiocy.'

'If we could get the name changed,' he said thoughtfully, 'it might be easier. That awful Galician name ...' Kerenyi turned about and walked to and fro in the long room, frowning at the carpet and wrinkling the bridge of his prominent nose.

'Wait a minute, Georgy. That's a good idea. You remember when Franzl was taken off the property list at the Emigration Board? I seem to remember Lehmann saying there were a lot of people there with foreign passports, or married to foreigners, who were about to get out still – if they paid up.'

'But nobody has been able to emigrate for ages now,' Kerenyi objected. 'She can only leave the country now by slipping over the border.'

'Yes, yes, I know that. But with foreign connections, they get some sort of privileges. How would it be if we found some tattered foreigner to marry Ruth? We could bribe him by promising him her inheritance after the war's over.'

'Anybody who would do that would want to be paid now. And you can't transfer much from your bank without it being known.'

'I could give him some contract, or something. Or perhaps some of my jewellery, for the time being. Yes, Georgy, listen. There are a lot of Yugoslav labourers in Styria and Carinthia. My stepfather would know – he probably employs some of them.'

'But there isn't time, Julie! You said yourself they have to register for these new frontier passes by the end of this week.' Georgy sat down on Franz's desk-chair and clutched his forehead in his big hands. 'It's no good. I'll have to take her in. Then we'll have to think of something – it's quite a good idea to marry her to a foreigner, if we can find one. But for that we need time. Does she look very Jewish? Could she pass, for a few weeks?'

'She looks like a Rumanian, or a Slovene perhaps. Thin little dark thing. No, I don't think she looks very semitic, as far as I can remember. I haven't seen her for two years, and she may have changed a lot, between fifteen and seventeen.'

'Christ, she's that young? I'd thought of passing her off as a girlfriend for the neighbours ...'

'You still can. She didn't ever look young, poor kid.'

'That's the only way I could explain her not registering her address with me, d'you see ... the caretaker is bound to ask about it.'

'And then we could find someone to marry her and change her name, with any luck.'

'Franz has had so much luck,' said Kerenyi grimly. 'It must be running out.'

'Don't say that, Georgy,' said Julie sharply. 'It frightens me.'

He laughed his short bark of a laugh, lifting his nose towards the darkened ceiling. He was angry with her for pushing this wretched girl on to him.

'Frightens you? My dear girl, you don't know the meaning of the word.'

Astonished, Julie stared at him. He meant it; he really believed she was not afraid. She remembered the whirling sensation of panic when the thought of Franz dying struck her, and the frightful night when the young SS men came to search the apartment – when was it? So long ago ... more than a year ago.

'It's the thing about you that always astonishes me, your courage,' said Georgy, feeling for cigarettes in his side pocket. 'I never understand how you can be a good actress – and there's no doubt you are a good actress – with so little inner disharmony. I mean, you seem never to have to struggle with yourself, never to do any soul-searching. There's no introspection in you; you don't need it for you always know what you are doing and, what's more, how to go about doing it.'

'You're talking like an amateur,' Julie said coldly. 'It's only the hangers-on in the theatre who go in for temperament. Except for publicity and to bully producers. Women like Maris are constantly torturing themselves because they know they are no good. Maris has to use personality – temperament, or what you will, to get parts. She'd never get them on her own merits, she gets them on her back, and you know that as well as I do. That's what the constant self-tormenting and worrying is all about; not about the problems of acting – she knows less than nothing about those problems.'

Georgy was looking at her through the thin veil of his cigarette smoke, and Julie saw in his look of assessment how cruel and vicious her remarks seemed to him. Like all men at bottom, even Georgy is vain and sentimental, she thought with resignation. He probably believes to this day that Maris loved him for himself while she lived with him.

'Have you ever seen that policeman again?' she asked abruptly, not connecting clearly the memory of Blaschke with her thoughts of Maris.

'Blaschke? What made you think of him? Ah, yes, it was just about the same time as my break with Maris. Yes, I see him, about once every two months. Krassny advised me to keep in touch with him voluntarily. He's no longer interested in Franz, though. Asks me questions about the paper, as a rule. I always answer — more or less, answer — his questions. I have the feeling sometimes that he is keeping me on ice for reasons of his own rather than using me as a source of information.'

'Because of Franz, you mean?' questioned Julie quickly.

'N-no,' he said slowly. 'I don't think so. I'm not sure what I mean. But I'll tell you what; Lehmann gives me the same impression. As if they were storing up good-conduct reports ...'

'But that's absurd, Georgy. Why should they? Nobody could ever be more sure of their power than these Nazis. And now the war is won, they must be even surer of themselves than before when they still had to fight.'

'The war isn't won yet. I don't think they are sure of anything; least of all their own power.'

'But of course the war is won. In a few weeks even the British will give in. I don't believe all this talk of the war being extended. The Germans would be mad not to end it as soon as the English ask for peace.'

'And if the British don't ask for peace?'

'What can they do? They are isolated. They will see reason, you'll see.'

Georgy bent his head for a moment. Then he got up jerkily, and walked down the room and back.

'God forbid,' he said softly. 'They are our only—'

'Well, my dear,' cut in Julie briskly. 'I'm sure you're right. You know all about those larger issues. But how are we going to get this girl to Vienna from the frontier before the end of the week? That's what is bothering me. Trains are out, of course. And I am playing to-morrow night and Friday. On Thursday I have a rehearsal. And next week-end there's a revival first night for this season's new cast of *Lear*. You know it had to be recast because of Mundel's retirement and there's a new German Lear. It hasn't been played for two seasons, it still needs a lot of work. This couldn't have happened at a worse time. I shall be busy every moment.'

Georgy stood with his head bent, the end of his cigarette hanging from the corner of his lip. He pulled it off, abstractedly, touched the sore spot where it had stuck and said 'damn' under his breath.

'I could go to Graz for a day,' he said reluctantly. 'I'll take the office car if I can get a petrol voucher.'

'Can you do that? You mean, visit the theatre there? A good idea.'

She was seated now in her usual high-backed chair. Her long hands on its arms appeared to be at rest, but when he looked closely, Georgy saw that the relaxed grace of their curve, the fingers glittering with rings, that almost boneless, fluid look her hands used to have had given place to the controlled tensity of will-power. He moved his eyes up to her romantic face and saw that the serene half-smiling passivity, for which her look was famous, was now held by a trick of nervous control. The chin was almost rigid, the tiny nerves above the cheekbones held deliberately the muscles controlling the expression of the eyes. Not, as formerly, effortlessly exposing a natural calm of expression; the calm passive look was acted. This will ruin her work, Georgy thought, and instantly a savage hot sensation of rage shook him so that he had to turn away and feel for a fresh cigarette to hide his expression. They are destroying her. Everything is being destroyed. She is right about Maris — the only things that are not being pulled into the whirlpool and torn to pieces are the things and people that mean nothing in any case. He spoke harshly.

'Leave the girl to me. I'll get her here and let you know when it's over. I'll borrow Fräulein Bracher's identity card. No, Bracher can come with me and borrow a card from some friend of hers.

Three is easier than two alone. We can pass her off as a typist from the Graz office being transferred. There are several jobs I can do at Graz. I'll look at the theatre and opera programmes when I get home and see which day will be best to go. Since I shall have to write something, I mean.'

'I can leave her to you, then? Georgy, it's very good of you ...' Julie leaned her forehead for a second on her raised hand and let the hand fall again in a familiar gesture. The little frown came and went between her brows. 'Don't think I don't appreciate all you do ... Did I tell you, Alois Pohaisky was with us at the week-end?'

'I knew he was at Kasda's mother's place. How is he?'

'Terrible. Crippled with rheumatism and turned into a religious fanatic.'

'He always was pretty cracked on that subject. God, the Nepomuk society! How was it that the only causes we had to oppose these barbarians with were such unrealities as the Order of St Nepomuk? What was it they wanted to do – build a bridge between Church and Politics? I remember poor little Dollfuss at their public meetings. Not a speech under forty minutes and most of them going on for an hour or more. All about the Occident, and Christendom, and humanity losing its way.'

'They were right about that part of it,' said Julie and laughed suddenly. 'Yet he's impressive in an uncanny way, you know, Georgy. Impressive enough to upset me thoroughly, anyway.' She stopped, thinking of Nando who seemed very far away. She was aware now of a submerged irritation at Nando's unhappiness; she needed him to be unaffected by the pressures on herself, to remain frivolous, unserious. He was no use as a refuge where she could laugh without bitterness if he talked of ending it all and clung to her in the night like a drowning child. It was superficiality she needed from Nando, and even as she felt the momentary unsureness and irritation she shrugged mentally, thinking it would not last longer than Pohaisky's presence. It had been a mistake to go where poor Dr Alois could upset them. Nando would recover his balance.

Kerenyi was looking at his watch and said now, 'It's pretty late. I'd better leave Franzl in peace for to-night ... don't you think?'

'I expect he's asleep,' she said vaguely, pulling her divided thoughts back to the present. 'The injection poor old Moller gave him must have been a sedative, I suppose ...' She rose from her chair. 'I'm sorry you came in vain to see him to-night. Though for me it was a stroke of luck — I was just wondering whether I had better get a taxi and go to your place to see you, rather than tele-phone.'

'Good thing I didn't walk into the doctor. No need to frighten the poor fellow more than is necessary, after all. I won't be able to see Franz for a day or so, I expect — as things are. Tell him, won't you, that I came?'

'Of course, Georgy. Good night, my dear. Goodness, I am tired.'

He bent over her hand. 'Don't come out, I'll let myself out.' But she followed him to make sure the door was double-locked. After listening at Franz's door, she went back into the living-room and stood against the window-frame, looking sideways down to the street. She knew he always crossed the road when leaving the house after an evening visit, so that they could be sure he had gone unmolested away. They never spoke of this habit. Julie knew it was the result of her anger over that note he pushed under the door on the day he discovered Franz to be in the apartment. Watching his tall, foreshortened form stride across the pavement now, pulling down his soft felt hat over his brow, she thought of Kerenyi's perceptiveness where Franz was concerned. If only he understood how I feel as he understands Franzl, she thought. But nobody does. Even Fina doesn't care about me. There is nobody who does care. She had an almost physical sensation of how it would feel to have those hard long arms hold her so that she could lean against him and close her eyes with confidence.

She was exhausted but wide awake. She took a book and opened it, reading one paragraph several times without taking in a word. She looked about the room. Then she got up and found her sleeping pills in the bathroom, and took one. She had not eaten, but felt no hunger. There was silence in the house. She picked up the book again, looking idly at the title on the spine which meant nothing to her. Then she wandered over to the window and stared out at the clear yellow glow of the gas-light in the street lamp. It wavered and swam a little under her fixed stare. She felt the welcome dizziness of the sedative working, and leaned against the window-frame. In a moment she would go to bed and sleep. A figure passed slowly along on the other side of the street, and as it passed she had the impression that the head was turned sideways and upwards towards her. Instantly she was wide awake. Moving away from the window, she laid down the book which she still held in her hand, and went to get ready for bed. As she lay down the dreamy dizziness came back. She relaxed her muscles deliberately, as she had been taught. The room swam gently away. The single figure turned its head. Chance, she said quickly to herself, and was wide awake. Whoever it was just saw the lighted windows. Of course. The events of the day, of the week-end, slid through her mind, half dream, half memory. Nando clung to her, dragging at her strength. Fina's eyes reproached her hardness, terrified for Franz and for herself. To be caught; final disaster; the scene pushed out of mind a thousand times became reality and she saw Fina dragged screaming away. Fina she could imagine, crying to her for help, expecting something from her. But not Franz. That she could never imagine. Sleep flooded over her nerves and she sank gratefully. Then she recalled with sharp clarity speaking to the doctor in the front hall, in hearing distance of the apartment door. Could one hear from its far side? Fina was sure it was impossible, but nobody knew better than Julie herself how her expert voice carried. She could whisper at the back of the Burgtheater stage and the last standing student in the upper gallery heard it ... 'Do not talk to me, Emilia; nor answer have I none ...' Something missed out there. 'Do not talk to me, Emilia; I cannot weep, nor answer have I none, but what should go by water.' Hansi wanted her to sob it, but the whisper was more effective, as Hansi admitted later. Had Pichler waited outside the door, after bringing up the doctor? She knew he must be curious. Curious as house porters always were and curious in a specific way about her and her affairs. Affairs. Pichler probably thought Kerenyi was her lover ... Good God, she had used Kerenyi's name to the doctor, as she heard his key in the door. Not 'Georgy!' but 'Kerenyi!' She reared up in the bed, clasping aching head in shaking hands. The doctor was afraid for his family; he would go to the police; he had not grasped the implication of the two different sets of prescriptions and as Kerenyi came, she had no time to force them on his mind. What was that? Yes, there was something. Half drugged, Julie swayed from the bed to the door, and heard the cistern of the hall lavatory flush and then Fina's thick shape, wrapped in her flannel dressing-gown, cross the hallway on her way back to bed.

I'm not going to sleep, thought Julie, closing her door again. She went, from habit, to the window to look down into the street where a little wind swayed the lights and nothing else moved. She had the feeling that she should kneel and try to pray, but could not. To what could she pray, and for what? She was enclosed in the desolate loneliness of the strong, and God was a fable of childhood. The nearest church struck the hour and was echoed from far and near by the clock towers of the old city. In the many bells Julie could not make sure how late or how early it was. But it did not matter. She lay down again. The night wore away until about five o'clock when she fell into a deathly slumber.

5

'Well, and how is everybody? I feel as if I had been on another planet for months.' Hella Schneider tripped up the staircase of Lehmann's pretty house, flipping at the painted ribbons and flowers of the wrought-iron balustrade with a long fan held in her gloved hand. When closed, as it was then, the fan looked like a riding switch or an exotic fish held by the head, with a curving, springy tail. Arrived at the main hall, Hella flipped the fan open, and then hung it by a loop from her wrist with a flourish that emphasised its ambivalent appearance.

'Unnecessary to underline your sexuality, my dear girl,' said Kerenyi behind her. 'We are out of the Wedekind age — we can take it for granted that women too are animals.'

Hella was already greeting Lehmann effusively. 'But Berlin!' she cried. 'This place is a backwater! I am determined to get back there — they have asked me tentatively for next season. I shall certainly accept.'

'So you enjoyed Berlin?' said Lehmann slowly: he evidently found this attitude bewildering, and had some difficulty in looking delighted at the compliment to the Reich capital. 'It is certainly very stimulating ...'

'Stimulating! It's overpowering! Nobody ever goes to sleep there! The audiences ... the parties! The Führer complimented me personally. I was asked to tea at the Chancellery, and the most wonderful man I ever met was there too!' She looked round at

Georgy. 'He remembered you. You know who I mean? I find this rule about not mentioning names a frightful bore. Do we have to keep it up among ourselves? I mean, even Party leaders have to relax sometimes, and why not?'

'Party rules!' said Lehmann, with playful sternness. 'The broad mass of the people would not understand.'

'They wouldn't understand the sort of parties Hella means, certainly.' Kerenyi switched smile and object. 'How are you, Maris? Perhaps you should visit Berlin? Hella seems to think we all should.'

'Oh, no,' said Maris quickly, 'I shall stay here. I think Berlin would be too much for me – don't you, Friedrich?' She looked up at Lehmann and Kerenyi, and though she smiled her lips quivered and there was something in the timid questioning look of her eyes that made Kerenyi feel sorry for her.

'How was the performance? I was kept by Party business and couldn't make it. I shall go the day after to-morrow, instead.'

'I don't know; I wasn't there either,' said Hella laughing. 'I've grown out of *Lear*. I had to go to a private showing of Riefenstahl's new movie ... it was terrible, of course.'

'One of the most presumptuous remarks I ever heard,' said Kerenyi with genuine pleasure. 'And a complete synopsis of your character, Hella.'

He turned to Lehmann, carefully including Maris, to whom Hella had not spoken. 'Jochen Thorn is a first-class Lear. I hope he'll stay.'

'Better than Willy Mundel?' asked Lehmann anxiously.

'Yes, I believe he is, at any rate for this part. He is hard and sharp, where Mundel had soft edges. There's none of the bewildered ancient out of his depth in Thorn's Lear – he fights all the time, and makes his age clear only by struggling with it.'

Lehmann took his elbow. 'I'm so relieved. Julie doesn't like the Goneril part I'm afraid. And little Silovsky as Cordelia? I had to fight to get her the part. Neither Schoenherr nor Ostrovsky thought she could make it.'

'Have you given Anita Silovsky Cordelia?' cried Hella, astonished. 'Why, only the other day she was playing bit parts as my

334

page! She was madly in love with me ... But she'll never make a Cordelia.'

'Mm. I'm still not sure she will.' Kerenyi screwed up his eyes and lifted his nose consideringly. 'She's got it in her, perhaps, but there's something inhibited about her ...'

'She's scared to death,' said Lehmann, grasping the excuse eagerly. 'She got the dresser to telephone and say she was too tired to come – scared to hear herself discussed. But give her time and she'll come through with it. Julie was marvellous to her, spent hours coaching her.'

'Julie was really fabulous to-night. She is the only actress on the German-speaking stage that one can think of using the word "genius" to. By the time she is fifty she'll be the greatest actress of her time.' Hella was about to interrupt him, but Kerenyi went on with a movement of his large hand that was almost rude. 'Her versatility alone is astounding. When I think, St Joan only a month or so ago ... and to-night this tigress of a Goneril!'

'I'm thinking of doing a Strindberg for her.' Lehmann took Georgy's elbow again. 'Do you think we could get away with it? Schoenherr is game, but I don't want to take too big a risk. We don't want to get ticked off for being decadent, when we're doing so nicely. What do you think, Kerenyi?'

He was going on, but Hella interrupted again, successfully this time.

'Really, I don't understand you, Friedrich,' she said sharply, and trying to sound as if she really did not understand. 'You sound almost – I was going to say almost disloyal, but that would be too strong ...'

'Much too strong,' agreed Kerenyi firmly. 'Hella, my dear, stop trying to be grown-up and go and talk to those lovely tall SS officers. We ask them especially to keep ourselves respectable, and since they don't understand a word we say, any of us, they are very useful.'

'We?' The clear blue eyes mustered Kerenyi slowly and then moved with a slow lowering of the eyelids to Lehmann. 'You two have become very cosy in the last month or so, haven't you?'

'Not more than usual,' Kerenyi saved Lehmann from replying.

'You've just forgotten in the heady atmosphere of Berlin what we are like in our backwater.'

'Yes, yes, Berlin's powerful air has elated you, my dear Hella,' cried Lehmann. 'You will do some splendid work after your tonic there. I'm quite adamant and so is Schoenherr, that you shan't do any more films for at least a year because we have a lot of plans for you ...' A whole chattering new group flooded up the stairs and among them the quartet was split. Kerenyi said in an undertone to Maris, 'But the tact of a camel, your Friedrich!'

'No, no,' said Maris, her trembling voice almost whispering. 'It will work with Hella. You'll see if you watch. She's really mortally ashamed of her own mercenariness. She loves to pretend that the public forces her to make these awful films of hers.'

Hella was glad to be divided from the other two and turned to Lehmann.

'Julie will be here in a minute, and then I can't ask you. But I must know ... Are she and that handsome Kasda still together? Is she really playing so well?'

'Kerenyi exaggerates a little perhaps but yes, Julie is playing wonderfully. Kasda will be with her.' He looked at his watch.

'Of course, it's a relationship that exactly suits Julie. She keeps him like a pet. I was asked about her in Berlin, you know. Twice. Why doesn't she marry again? People speculate, you know. It doesn't do her any good!'

'Marry? Who, Kasda? Oh, no, my dear. Why should she? He's a charming boy and adores her, but he's not up to her weight at all. She'd never marry him.'

'I see I've missed a lot while I was in Berlin,' said Hella laughing to cover her annoyance. Berlin, the world where power and ambition belonged, began at once to lose its appeal when a rival could be called the future greatest actress of her time in Vienna. 'You are right about the cinema, Friedrich. I belong to the theatre. And after all, backwaters produce surprises for the great world sometimes.' She tilted her head engagingly and repeated something she had heard at a Berlin party. 'Like Hahn discovering the atom, or whatever it was he did discover.'

'One could hardly call Göttingen a backwater — as far as

learning is concerned.' Lehmann shook his smooth blond head, smiling. 'But I see what you mean. Is that what they are talking about in Berlin?'

'Oh, you know, everyone is talking about new developments,' she said airily without the slightest idea of what she was saying. 'At this marvellous party where I met Heydrich everyone was talking about unmanned artillery. They'd all been looking at some model or other and were full of it. Of course, it's all frightfully secret, in the early stages. Only the most inside of Führer circles has even heard a whisper of it . . . '

'I don't think Hahn had anything to do with military matters,' said Lehmann dubiously, 'but all those war-games are boring, don't you agree?'

'Wouldn't quite call it boring,' drawled Hella. 'I heard of things I had no idea of before, in Berlin. For instance,' she dropped her voice to a murmur. 'The war is not over as everybody here thinks. Far from it.'

'Come and talk to the director. He has plans for you, as I said,' Lehmann led her, by holding playfully on to her fan, towards the old man, bowing over Maris's hand. Lehmann had learned a good deal in the last two years, but he still was not able to prevent indiscretions.

With his sure instinct for what was necessary, Schoenherr went straight towards Hella and Lehmann, towing, as if by chance the new German actor with him.

'Julie is looking well, I see,' said Hella, over Schoenherr's shoulder.

'As a matter of fact, I feel tired out,' said Julie in answer to the same remark but made in a very different tone, by Maris. 'I think the programmes have got a little out of hand; I seem to have too much to do suddenly. Don't you think so, Hansi?'

'You certainly have been overworked lately. We've been short of several people, but it will be better now that Hella is back and this new man Thorn is going to stay.'

'Little Anita Silovsky is going to be a help,' said Julie firmly. She knew that Hansi Ostrovsky had no confidence in the young girl. 'I think, and she thinks herself, that Lehmann pushed her above her ceiling with Cordelia. But she is growing up fast. It's a pity we aren't doing *Hamlet* – I'd like to see her as Ophelia.'

'My dear girl,' protested Hansi, nervously lighting a cigarette. 'You'll be imagining her as Desdemona next! She's not a Shakespearean and never will be. She should be kept to comedy, and light comedy at that.'

'The point is, Hansi, there isn't that much choice,' said Kerenyi. 'You need at least two more competent middle partners and you just haven't got them.'

'You're right, I know,' muttered Hansi gloomily. They all knew what Kerenyi meant. Five junior actresses had left the Burg in two years; two of them to New York, one to London, and two pure Aryans had since gone over to the film studios entirely. 'The public won't stand for the programmes being cut down, and the only alternative – and it isn't even an alternative because it will inevitably happen – is a drop in standards.'

No one answered. Poor old Hansi, thought Julie tiredly, he always has to say what everybody else avoids.

Kerenyi turned his tall shoulders a little to shield Maris and spoke in an undertone, while lighting a cigarette.

'Can you move Hansi and Kasda for a moment? I must talk to Julie.'

She gave him a covert, frightened look, a look that said, 'what, more trouble?' and at once slid past him, her tiny form in its filmy, dark, smoke-coloured dress like a ghost.

'Come and talk to Jochen Thorn, you two,' she said. 'He's still feeling that nobody in Vienna wants to know him . . .'

Reluctantly, the two men allowed themselves to be drawn away from their fixed star, and Kerenyi could reach her a glass of wine and bar the way for other guests for a few moments, between his tall figure and a half-column crowned by a hanging fern that stood a little way out from the wall.

'Can you get away early and come back with me?' he said without preamble. 'You always leave parties early, so it won't be unusual.'

Julie did not need evidence that he was serious. He would not have bothered her about a detail.

'I can't leave Nando,' she pointed out.

'Have to. You can't bring him. Think of a way.'

'Headache? No, that won't work. He knows first nights always overstimulate me ...' She glanced about her quickly, raising her eyebrows questioningly. 'Get me another glass of wine, Georgy.'

He gave her his glass. He knew she always drank about half a bottle of wine immediately after a performance.

'I haven't touched it,' he said. 'Have you eaten?'

'Yes, in the interval. Lotte always makes me something, bless her.'

'I shall just have to say I want to go straight home,' she said, after searching vainly for an excuse. 'I'll say good night and then wait inside my front door until you fetch me.'

They drifted easily, without anyone noticing, into the chattering throng.

It was nearly two hours later before they arrived in Kerenyi's taxi before his door.

'My goodness, it's cold already,' said Julie shuddering slightly in her evening coat as Kerenyi turned over his key-ring to find the key to the house door. 'Georgy, what is that car over there – there, look, by the corner? It looks like – it can't be – but it does look like Nando's old sports car.'

'You're getting jumpy, my dear. There are thousands of those cars, after all.'

'I suppose so,' she said uneasily, and followed Kerenyi into the low vaulted hallway of the old house. 'But I thought I heard a car come out of Schellinggasse just after we drove away. One doesn't hear many cars about nowadays after midnight ...'

Halfway up the curving stone staircase, between two floors, Georgy stopped Julie with a touch on her arm.

'You need to know, before we get into the flat,' he said in a low voice. 'This girl is quite hysterical, I can't do anything with her. She refuses to stay in the flat with me. So I had to say I'd bring you back, to reassure her.'

'But you got back yesterday – was she all right then?'

'On the contrary, she was in a state of collapse. Fortunately Fräulein Bracher was still with us, and I managed to slip her a sleeping pill for the girl. She slept until noon. When I got back this afternoon, to write something in peace out of the office, she was cruising round the rooms like a mad thing, weeping and tearing at herself with her hands.'

'Is she afraid of being shut up with a man, or is it the police?'

'Both, I think. I got Bracher over this evening again, but she has a frightful old nag of a mother to take care of – she can't do it constantly. Anyway, she's pretty scared herself.' He touched her arm again and they started up the stairs to the next floor.

'Fortunately my cleaning woman didn't come this morning. But she'll have to pull herself together before the morning, or the old girl will notice something.'

He opened his apartment door quietly. It was an old house, in which there had originally been water and lavatories only on the landings. Kerenyi had had plumbing installed in his own part of the lovely old building with its thick walls and stone floors. It was warm inside, and very quiet. Quiet as it only ever is in modern cities in houses with walls of the thick stonework of a former time. As Kerenyi turned the shaky electric switch and lit the hall a muffled sound made Julie whirl round.

Ruth was behind the door, so that its opening sheltered her. Her hands stretched out low on either side of her, she appeared to be attached to the whitewashed wall and Julie had the momentary picture of a long insect pinned to a board in a museum. The girl seemed to hang on the wall, flattened against it she seemed to be trying to force her thin body whole into it, into invisibility. The dark hair fell loose about her neck and shoulders and all there was of the tiny narrow-boned face was two enormous eyes, sightless with fear, with non-comprehension, in their shadowed cells. The family likeness to Franz hit Julie like a blow from a friend; but it was at once clear that that stout spiritual skin of Franz's which simply rejected an area of madness in the momentary world so that he could continue to believe in his own sanity was here totally lacking. This creature was like one let out of long solitary confinement; for her the whole world was unknown, unknowable, she had no apparatus for coming to terms with it. In that instant, and it was no more, Julie saw backwards as in a repeating mirror sequence, the whole upbringing of this lost girl, unreal, conventual, hardly teaching her more than her letters, deliberately keeping her in a state of dependence; for otherwise she might rebel against family, religion, the husband she would be delivered to. The upbringing that produced whole generations of suffragettes, dominating business women, brilliant talents, out of angry rebellion; here was its other side; one among millions of creatures without souls to call their own, delivered up to their fate. Everything she disliked about Jewishness, everything that was generally agreed to be backward and reactionary – 'Hebraic' – flared up in an instant of anger and took the form of angry disgust with the girl herself. She covered the flood of perceptions, as always, with a phrase to herself: it is sordid to be so scared.

She turned her head quickly to look at Kerenyi, perhaps for help, perhaps because of a vagrant thought that he might have scared the girl himself ... His face was like a skull. Greyish livid, the bones sharply outlined, the sandy hair suddenly reddish against the changed colour of his normally healthy skin, he watched the girl out of his deep-set secretive eyes as if she were some animal dangerous in its deadly panic. It was a traumatic moment of silence. The sharp move of Julie's head made him try to recover his self-command, and Kerenyi passed a bony hand over his brow to wipe away the cold sweaty feeling on it.

'What is it?' said Julie angrily, demanding normality from him.

'Nothing. I had the feeling ... Nothing.'

The girl made no move and no sound. Julie turned back to the stretched figure and moved her head with a stringent command, indicating that the girl was to go into the study, the main room of the flat. She was unable to speak to the girl, as if it were no use to use words to her; as if she would not understand human speech.

Degrading though it was, it proved to be the way to get a reaction from the terrified girl: at the silent, unquestionable authority of Julie's manner she slid slowly away from the wall, keeping her eyes fixed on the face known to her, the face that had told her what to do on that no longer remembered occasion that fixed her in childishness, and slipped sideways down the stone hall, over the uneven flags, round the open door and into the badly lighted, brown, tobacco-smelling, book-filled room. Moving as if she had been cramped for hours, Julie followed her, and Kerenyi followed Julie.

As she came into the room herself, Julie said to Kerenyi in an undertone, 'My God, if I'd known what we were letting ourselves into ...!' It was so typical of her pragmatic temperament that Kerenyi could have laughed with relief.

The girl's eyes flicked round the book-littered room; she retreated into a corner. Julie sat down in one of Kerenyi's old leather chairs.

'Ruth, come and sit here,' she said, pointing to a chair opposite her own. 'Come along.' With intense reluctance, the girl moved out from the wall and hesitated, fidgeting with her long thin fingers at the arm of the chair. Her eyes rolled sideways to cover Kerenyi, who went to a tall cupboard. He got out a bottle and glasses, shuffling the stubby cheap little tumblers together on to a stained old tray. They clanked gently together and the girl's eyes watched the tray — or Kerenyi's hand — was it? She seemed to shrink together as he passed by her, hunching her shoulders forward over her thin bosom, and the wandering fingers became quite still for a moment. Julie saw that the nails were uneven and coarse, the skin roughened. Kerenyi set down the tray on his writing-table, pushing aside a heap of typescript to do so, and sat down in his desk-chair, which creaked loudly. Julie did not look round at him.

'Have some *barack*?' he said, half behind her. 'I haven't anything else ...' His voice still sounded strange to Julie's ears. The girl jumped visibly at the sound of it and Julie thought — she's putting more than half of it on. She knew that this was not so, and that she herself was the last person to deal with anyone in this girl's state of mind. She knew too, with deadening finality, that it was a major error, bringing the girl back to Vienna. It's the first real mistake I've made, she thought.

'Sit down, Ruth,' she said again, and slowly the girl slid sideways round the chair and sat, obediently.

Julie stretched out a hand without looking round. 'Give me a drink, Georgy. I need it.' She drank the fiery spirit and choked on the gulp. This reminded her of something.

'Ruth, have you eaten anything to-day?'

The girl spoke for the first time, and Julie was startled at the deep, husky voice that seemed not to belong to the fragile body.

'My name's not Ruth any more,' she said, whispering.

'What do you mean, not Ruth any more?' asked Julie stupidly.

'Uncle and Auntie always called me Anna – for my saint's day in their church.'

'Of course, Ruth is so ...' Kerenyi did not finish. Uncle and Aunt were, of course, Julie's parents, where the girl had made her home for two years. I wonder how bad she was before, thought Julie: but it wouldn't be so noticeable in the country where they never see strangers and half the world is eccentric anyway.

'Listen to me, Ruth – Anna,' she began slowly. 'Do you remember me?'

The girl nodded, her eyes flickering.

'Do you think I would harm you?'

Silence – no move now of eyes or head.

'Do you, Ruth? Ruth, answer me.'

'N-no.' Very slowly, almost inaudibly, obviously insincerely.

'But you know almost everybody would harm you, don't you?'

She felt Kerenyi stir and his chair creaked but Julie took no notice. Some basis of comprehension must be established; and now, in this moment. 'Ruth? Did you understand what I said?'

The girl moved her head a little. 'They hate me,' she whispered. 'I could hear the things they said, sometimes ... the men, on the farm.'

'Do you know why you had to leave there – leave Auntie and Uncle?'

The girl's eyes lifted slowly, and fixed on Julie's; she made no answer. There was dead silence.

Kerenyi spoke quietly, sounding more normal now.

'She probably believes they just wanted to be rid of her, don't you think? I doubt if she'd take in the business about the passes?'

'Probably. Ruth, listen to me. I'm telling you the truth. We had

343

to get you away from there. It was dangerous for you. For *you* — you understand?'

The eyes did not move. The cringing figure was like a statue.

'You must believe me, Ruth. Uncle and Auntie didn't want you to go.' Was there a faint flicker of rejection there? Julie went on, cunningly: 'Why should they? You were very useful to them, weren't you? You worked hard, didn't you?'

Silence again. The idea seemed too complicated for the bewildered thoughts of the girl. Julie did not know what to say next. She was aware from the loaded atmosphere of hysteria that almost anything she could say might be dangerous. She turned slightly towards Kerenyi for help, with the feeling of being at the end of her tether. She was aware of being deeply tired and overwrought herself.

'You will be safe here for a time,' said Kerenyi, speaking very quietly and levelly. He used the formal 'you' and kept a neutral tone as if they were speaking in a shop about merchandise. 'If you just keep quiet and behave so that people don't notice you. You don't have to do anything, not talk to people or anything. Just try to behave normally when the cleaning woman comes in the morning, and not take any notice of visitors going in or out. You can stay in your own room and need never see them ...'

He stopped, distressed and almost frightened by the way the girl turned her enormous eyes towards the sound of his voice without moving her head. She still could not quite see him, but he could see the whites of her eyes straining, and the fear hit him that she was actually insane. When he stopped speaking the eyes slowly turned back again to Julie, and then dropped to her lap. The thin hands began to pick quickly at the stuff of her dress, as if it were covered with bits of fluff.

Julie made to say something, but she just did not know what to say and sat back again, completely at a loss. The girl stared again at her movement, and as the silence lengthened, she began to turn her head from side to side, her breath coming faster and faster. Suddenly she gave a low cry, a wail, almost a howl, and with one sudden movement flung herself out of the chair and towards the door of the room to flee.

'Oh God,' said Julie, and put her head in her hands. 'I can't stand this!'

Kerenyi was after the girl and caught her before she could reach the front door. It was locked, but he knew she would hammer on it with her thin, grimy fists, hammer until she bled. He caught her in his arms and she gave a muffled scream of horror. He forced himself to put a hand over her mouth, struggling, for she was much stronger than she looked. It was like trying to overcome a hungry animal; she slobbered on his hand; he could feel her bones and a sensation of nightmare disgust shook his mind at the secret thin, acid smell of the sweat of fear. She struggled her head away from his hand, and he saw over the writhing shoulders Julie's staring eyes, helpless, propping herself against the room door.

After a few moments the thin body seemed to slacken in his grip and as suddenly as she had sprung up to flee, the girl now began to weep wildly. The tears poured down her face, wetting Kerenyi's hands, matting the untidy mass of hair over her face and neck. He had never seen tears like it, it was like a flood, and through the stream the girl wailed and moaned as if demented, all the strength gone out of her. She ceased struggling; she could hardly stand, he had to support her. Terrified to move or speak and release another burst of hysteria, Kerenyi stood quite still, holding up the thin form with one arm under her shoulders. Gradually the girl stopped straining back against his arm. Her head fell forwards, hiding the stream of tears and muffling the moans of the half-opened mouth. She fell with her head against Kerenyi's breast as if against an inanimate tree, and he embraced the shuddering little form like a father with a weeping child.

Again Kerenyi had the dream-sensation he felt as they entered. He heard the scream of a taxi's tyres on gleaming dark asphalt; the clang and rattle of a tram wheeling past its window. And in the fogged lighted window of the tram, steaming with condensation from within, the thin shadowed face of a lost girl, framed in a dark hood, gazing out with unseeing eyes into the black night.

Presently the girl was quieter and he could lift her and carry her into the cold little spare room. Julie pulled back the thick quilt of down, and without attempting to undress the inert form, except to remove the clumping country shoes, they laid her in the bed and covered her. It was Kerenyi who remembered to push up the pillows so that the heavy head should not fall downwards and perhaps stifle in sleep. The crisis was over. The girl seemed to be unconscious, and when Julie crept back to put a little candle on the bedside table in case she should wake up, with a glass of water beside it, the form in the bed did not stir.

Julie leaned on her chair, in the study, and told Kerenyi to call the Westbahnhof for a taxi. Even in such a crisis, he marvelled, she remembered to order a taxi from the main station, where nobody would notice the order or the fare. A few minutes later, they heard a motor outside and Julie took the house key to let herself out.

'I'll ring up to-morrow,' she said and went.

Without waiting for an instant, Kerenyi turned and went back down the flagged hall, through to the spare room. He pushed at the door and it swung open. In the tiny light of the candle he saw the enormous eyes on him.

'It's all right,' he said softly, 'I'm not going to hurt you.'

He came in, and she shrank into herself; he crouched his tall form down and balanced with a hand upon the bed's wooden frame.

'Do you want something to eat?' he said.

She watched him for a moment, then her tongue came out and ran round her dry lips. She nodded, unable to speak. He nodded too, and got up from his uncomfortable crouch with a creak of his knees. He went away to the kitchen and searched about for food. There was a crock of buttermilk ready for his breakfast, a dark round of peasant bread cut across, cheesy yellow butter. Kerenyi did not like town food. He looked at a bowl of eggs and decided against the difficulties of cooking them; normally his cleaner made his breakfast. He poured out a glass of the thickened milk and spread butter a centimetre thick on a whole round of bread, cut it into four pieces and put them on an old blue plate. Holding the utensils carefully in his clumsy big hands, he turned to the door, but the girl was already there, watching him with those enormous eyes.

She came in on soft feet and he put the plate down on the

scrubbed wooden table. Without a word, not even looking at him, the girl grabbed one of the pieces of bread and butter and began to wolf it, half choking herself, pushing it in with unsteady, thin fingers. She looked round at him to see what he was at; he was standing still watching her. Then he went out of the kitchen and fetched his bottle of *barack*. He took a drink and they stood there, staring at each other with a nervousness that was no longer complete mistrust, he drinking the sharp spirit and she eating and smearing butter round her mouth. When she had finished she picked up the sturdy glass and sniffed at the contents. She drank the milk, and looked round for more to eat, wiping her fingers secretly on the side of her skirt. He began to laugh a little, quietly inside himself.

'More?'

She nodded, and he brought the loaf and cut a thick piece unevenly off it. He slapped a big pat of butter on to it and began to spread it awkwardly. She made no attempt to take it from him, but waited until he pushed the plate towards her, when she began to eat again, but now less ravenously.

'When did you last eat?' he asked. She frowned, and her eyes slid sideways at his face with that idiotic look that frightened him. Then she swallowed, made an effort and said hoarsely, 'Day when they told me I had to go.'

'It wasn't like that,' he said. 'You're imagining things.'

She just stared, eating still. Suddenly he had an idea. He took time to think that he must be a bit drunk, and then took another drink. Then he went out past her – she shrank away again – and went through to what had once been the maid's room next to the kitchen, and was now the bathroom. He began to feed the tall copper geyser with wood chips into its firebox, and lit them with a match. He piled in slivers and then a handful of small blocks of wood and left it crackling. She was staring still when he came in again, brushing wood-dust off his hands. He sat down by the table and poured another drink, this time lighting a cigarette.

Presently, rubbing one wool-stockinged foot against the other she began casting glances at the open door from where a soft roaring noise came. She must have known perfectly well what the noise was, but he was prepared to believe she was too estranged to place it.

'It's the hot water,' he said, drinking. 'You're going to have a bath.'

After a long pause, she said stubbornly, 'It isn't Saturday.'

'I know it isn't. But you stink. You're dirty. You're going to have a bath. People have baths without going to Mass, in Vienna.'

Finishing the glass of *barack*, Kerenyi went out to the spare room and opened her brown cardboard suitcase. He found a long night-dress with feather-stitching round the neck and wrists, and a set of clean underclothes of the sort peasant girls wear, as he remembered from his army days. He laid the clean underclothes on the chair and brought back the night-gown.

'Here,' he said. 'Can you manage the water?'

She shook her head, refusing the garment and the task at the same time. He went into the bathroom, and turned on both hot and cold taps for the geyser made boiling water. In a moment the bath was full of hot water and the little stone room full of steam. His own rough towel hung there and a cake of coarse soap. He smelled at the soap; he had never noticed its smell himself, but it didn't seem right for a girl; but then she was hardly a girl. His various women always seemed to have their own things.

To his surprise, she seemed to have accepted the idea of bathing, and when he gestured towards the door, from which a curl of steam, iridescent in the kitchen light, was escaping, she skirted round the other side of the kitchen table and disappeared into the little back-room.

Kerenyi sat at the kitchen table, drinking *barack* and smoking. He was quite aware of the ambivalence of his actions. Kerenyi was not a man who was ever unconscious of what he was doing, and he knew that the thin, dirty and frightened little creature, who seemed hardly human to him, had become a sexual object in his mind; he knew, too, that she was just nubile and that her hysterical fear was more than half her own unrecognised instinct to attach herself to a man who should become responsible for her protection. Her hysterical demands for Julie during the day might have been partly a need to be clear about Julie's position with him,

Kerenyi. Kerenyi dared to hope that the girl would continue to act half consciously in accordance with her needs, so that she would do nothing to cause him any trouble in the house here, or with his cleaner. The question in his mind was as to the worth of what was offered to him in terms of the long-lasting, complex and immediately dangerous price he would have to pay for it.

Sheltering her meant a ten-year sentence; having physical relations with her would be high treason and criminal miscegenation and her sentence — if caught — was death. Not being a sentimentalist, Kerenyi did not disguise these considerations under hypocritical disguises, but thought them over seriously. What was by no means clear was how strong and how far curable was the girl's neurotic, ignorant fear of the world. If she could not behave sensibly in her own interests, then they must get rid of her quickly and by any means — any means — before she involved Franz, Julie and himself in her incompetence. Kerenyi had no intention of dying for an unknown and useless human being. Fräulein Bracher had already told him that the risk was too great, pointing out that if the girl gave herself away or became unrestrainable, Kerenyi and Frau Homburg and Frau Homburg's parents for allowing her to leave her registered home, would suffer for it; had she known of Franz's presence in Vienna, her argument would have been the stronger. As Fräulein Bracher, with the hardness of a woman who has fended for herself since childhood said, the girl was never going to be worth much. She probably couldn't even cook.

As Kerenyi stretched and glanced at his watch, the figure of the girl crept out from the door behind him and slipped towards the door, enveloped in the floor-length folds of the thick night-gown. She had had the sense to wash her hair, and it stood out round her tiny face in a fluffy aureole now, the long ends lying still damp over her shoulders. She did not speak, only moved her eyes towards him, and then fled down the flagged hall. It was very late, half past two o'clock; Kerenyi emptied his glass and very deliberately went to bed.

At exactly one-thirty Julie put her key in the outside door of the house in the Schellinggasse as the taxi drove away with a clatter.

At the same moment something, she did not know what, made Julie look round and she saw Nando standing just behind her. He must have been waiting in the deep doorway of the next-door house.

'We can't talk here, Nando,' she said at once, without greeting him or pretending surprise.

'No, we can't,' he said with the false firmness of a weak man who has determined on a bold course. 'I'm coming up with you and we're going to have this whole thing out in the open.'

She looked at him with astonishment as if he knew quite well not only that he could not come up to her apartment, but knew why he could not. She did not argue, but looked down the street to find some other solution that would seem natural.

'The workmen's pub is still open,' she said as if surprised. 'Let's go there, shall we?' The cellar tavern almost next door was always open until four in the morning because of the printing works nearby that worked a night-shift on a small local newspaper. A shrouded yellow light showed mistily through its half-windows just above the pavement. She had never once been in there. As if nothing had happened Julie moved away towards the tavern door, set down three deep steps, and Nando followed her as she knew he would. She opened the heavy door herself and he hastily caught the iron grip to relieve her of it. She smiled backwards and went into the misty, smoky little room, half filled by the wide zinc counter and the huge cooking stove alongside it. A woman Julie had never seen before, of enormous girth, turned at the sound of the door, a long ladle in her thick red hand. When she saw who it was — Julie was known to the whole neighbourhood, by many people she had never herself been conscious of — she stared and set down the ladle in the soup-pot that simmered over the coal fire showing redly through the half-opened ring in the stove top. The host wiped his hands hastily on a greyish cloth and smoothed down his bulging apron to come forward. He was a tall man, with a long and bulbous nose, fat but not as fat as his wife. Julie knew him for he had often brought draught beer up to the apartment in the old days and she greeted him now with her quick, open smile and took his hand to shake, which he made to kiss in gratitude for this compliment.

'Shall we have some beer?' she said, going behind one of the bare wooden tables and seating herself on the bench behind it. She opened her evening coat. At the only other table occupied were seated four typesetters from the printing works, eating their late meal of soup with coarse sausage in it. They discussed a cut in the newsprint allowed to their paper, which would mean reducing its size.

'That soup smells good,' said Nando, typically pleased with the idea once Julie had forced it on him. 'May I have some please?' The fat woman hurried to serve him, smiling nervously at Julie the while.

'We shall speak English,' murmured Julie in that language. 'That is if you do wish to speak with me of going away with Georgy?' She smiled sideways at Nando, making fun of his jealousy and he had to smile back for she looked so lovely. Though she was very tired, she was prepared to take this trouble to pacify him and this knowledge filled him with a rush of love for her.

'Darling,' he said quietly in English. His English was much better than hers for he had spent two years at Magdalen. 'I love the way you say "wiz" instead of "with". It's sweet.'

'It is a nonsense that you follow me about,' she said, lifting her stoneware tankard of beer and considering it with her head on one side. 'I don't like beer but I have thirst.' She proved it by drinking half the beer at once. She was always thirsty after a first night.

'I had to talk with Georgy in private. About somebody who is in trouble. That is all. You must believe me.' She stopped and waited for a moment but he said nothing. His face was troubled again and he stared at his beer. Julie was conscious of a slight fear for she did not want to lose his companionship and the comfort of physical love. The knowledge that she used Nando had troubled her before, but never so strongly as now and she felt a genuine shame at using him, at manipulating him in a way that would hurt his pride if he became conscious of it. I ought to tell him the truth, she thought, or enough of the truth for him to make his own decision. But she knew she would not, because she could not trust his discretion. There was nothing she could do about it.

'Do you believe me?'

'I don't know,' he said, frowning at his beer. 'I've often wondered about you and Kerenyi.'

'Nando, I do not always tell you things; but I would not lie to you.'

'I shall have to believe you, shan't I?' said Nando almost under his breath. He raised his eyes and she saw that he was really suffering. Her eyes filled with tears. 'I love you,' she said in English. 'You know that, don't you?' Nando's dependence on her, instead of being burdensome, as it had threatened to be on their unlucky week-end, now seemed a necessity to her.

'If you love me,' he stubbornly said, 'then take me up to your flat with you. I know Kerenyi is allowed to come to see you there . . .'

She stared at him, startled at this logical extension of Kerenyi's almost weekly visits to Franz. She had thought Nando's distress was simply caused by her going off with Kerenyi on this one evening.

'How do you know that Kerenyi comes to my flat?' she asked, and that was a mistake. We shouldn't have come here, she thought uneasily, it is much more difficult to cope with him in this foreign language. I should have suggested going home with him.

Nando looked at her under his eyebrows and she saw that this determination was not of one day's growth.

'I've known for ages,' he said. 'You know he is watched. I see the reports occasionally.'

Julie had little notion of Kerenyi's Gestapo contact but she knew enough to know that if Nando saw agents' reports on Kerenyi it must be by asking for them in his official capacity. Her head swam with fear and anger; and that damned girl here too, she thought. She was silent, and drank some more beer. Her thirst was gone and she felt as if the unfamiliar drink would choke her. At last she said quietly, 'You should not have told me that, Nando. It was unwise of you.' I am going to lose him, she thought.

'Yes,' he said. 'But I am unwise.'

'You have now made it quite impossible for me to take you up with me. I am not going to be threatened. Besides, I now ask myself that you may all this time be watching me. If I would take you into my home now, I would think I am taking a police agent there. That is even worse than Fina seeing you with me.'

'You don't mean that?' he sounded shocked.

'I forgot for a long time how it was we met. Now I remember. And I remember also, how you came to me at Dirnhorn in the mountains. It was a long way to go to see a stranger. You were perhaps obeying orders, is it not so?'

She did not for an instant believe it herself; she had again the desolate feeling familiar from the time of her aloneness, of life draining out of her. How had she allowed them to get into this situation of cross-purposes? She should have given in at once and taken him upstairs. Both Fina and Franz had been asleep for hours. No, Franz often lay awake most of the night and sometimes Fina sat with him; sometimes now, since his illness, he had called her softly as she came in and she herself went to his little room and sat with him. She had begun again, after a gap of nearly two years, to tell him where she was when she was going to be late. He might easily be awake and waiting to hear about the party at Lehmann's house. There was no way out of this quarrel now but to pursue her attack on Nando.

'Kerenyi is my friend,' she said aloud, dropping back without noticing it into her own language. 'I can't allow myself to be cut off from the few friends I really have. There is nothing between us and never has been. That is all I have to say.'

'He is too close a friend: that's just it. I remember you saying his name, that night at home.'

Did she imagine it or were the host and his wife looking strangely at them? It was risky to talk in foreign languages, nowadays … Or were they showing their emotions? The tall man came over to them, smiling eagerly. His bulbous nose makes him look like an ant-eater. Whatever that may be, I must have seen a picture of one at some time. He removed Nando's soup-plate and asked if they wished for more beer.

'No, thank you, no more beer,' said Julie, smiling up at him. 'It is time to go home, I think.' The man hovered still and she felt she must say something to him, something pleasant and neutral. She glanced up and saw the vaulting of the low ceiling and a comment occurred to her. 'Was this part of the old cellars,' she asked the host. 'I mean, this vaulted ceiling is not part of the new buildings here? Were these houses built on the old foundations, do you think?'

'Oh, yes, gnae' Frau,' said the man eagerly, glad to demonstrate to the typesetters that he was on conversational terms with his exotic guest. 'All this row of houses. Have you never noticed in your own house? But there, gnae' Frau does not go into the cellars! That was in my father's time, when the old houses here were pulled down and the new ones built. Yes ...' He looked up and about at the lateral vaulting, the brickwork of which could be faintly seen under the whitewash. 'The upper cellars are built with these narrow arches and the underneath ones, deep down, with square vaulting. They must be very old.'

'Your family had the tavern here then?' asked Nando.

'Long before that, sir. I don't know how long, but certainly my great-grandfather was here. I remember him after my father took over the business. He used to sit over there by the stove, every day.' He looked quickly at Julie to make sure she was still interested in what he had to say and went on. 'The old cellars underneath here' – he struck the stone floor with his metalled heel and made a deep hollow ring – 'they are all connected with each other. Some of the ways are lost now, but there are still old people who know how to go from one cellar to another all over the inner city. That was how the people hid from the Turks, long ago.' This piece of folklore had a childhood ring for Julie and Nando. 'The Turks will get you' brought back a nursery threat to naughty children.

'Do you know the ways through the cellars?' asked Julie, but the man would not answer directly for his knowledge belonged to the underworld not only of the cellars but of the common people, wary of the sense of property of the wealthy who owned the houses and thought they owned the cellar keys.

'Ah, gnae' Frau, everything has changed nowadays,' he said, wagging his head from side to side regretfully, 'the old ways have gone and nobody knows them any more.'

'Yes, indeed,' sighed Julie. 'And I must go home.' She drew the edges of her silk coat together, and picked up her little handbag from the table, slowly, turning the narrow beaded bag over in her still-gloved hand. As she rose she looked up at the tavern-keeper whose eyes were fixed on her face and it came into her mind not as a supposition but as a definite fact, that he meant something by his remarks. This man had taken an opportunity to tell her something, assure her of something ...

'It's an honour,' said the man, hesitating slightly over the words, which like everything he said were spoken in an affected voice that attempted to rid itself of the Viennese dialect which he must have supposed Julie would not understand. She looked at his face again as he bowed, and smiled, and his smile confirmed her impression. He is trying to tell me something, she thought; no, trying to assure me of something.

'I am always at the service of gnädigen Frau,' said the man. 'I remember well as a boy, when the Herr Bankdirektor was building the houses along here. I was a small boy then and he used to give me a few heller every time he came to see the building and I opened his carriage door. He never lived in the house himself ...'

'No,' said Julie slowly, 'he never did live there himself.' She turned her head and nodded to the fat woman. 'Good night,' she said.

Outside, Nando asked her, 'What did he mean by all that?'

'He was talking about Franz's grandfather who built all these houses,' explained Julie. 'I suppose he meant to show me – what? That he is sorry how things have turned out? I don't know.'

She turned at her own house door.

'You must go now,' she said, 'it is too late to talk. And I have a rehearsal to-morrow. To-day, that is, now.'

'But we can't part like this,' said Nando in a tone of desperation.

'Let me go now,' she answered pleadingly. 'I must get some sleep. I'm quite stupid with tiredness. Please, Nando!'

And he was forced to let her go.

6

*F*or the next few days Julie had so much to do because of the overwork discussed by Kerenyi and Hansi Ostrovsky, that she was able to avoid seeing Nando, and the problems of Ruth's presence and his jealousy were only a nagging feeling in the back of her mind. As always, when working, work was more real to Julie than anything outside it; and since Franz was far from recovered she spent her spare time sitting with him. For those few days it seemed to Julie that work and his renewed companionship were enough for her.

He was still entirely confined to bed; the damaged liver seemed unable to resume its vital role, but fortunately the foods his diet needed were those still comparatively easy to come by. It was months before it became clear to Julie and Fina that his health was permanently undermined.

She was reminded of Ruth by Kerenyi himself. He had found an Italian cook in a restaurant who was willing to marry his dangerous charge. Julie was to transfer the sum demanded for this service to a post-office savings account by the simple means of drawing the money out of her account in cash and taking it to the nearest post office herself, so that no bank record should exist of the transfer.

The Italian would do as well as another, as Kerenyi said, though perhaps a Yugoslav might have been preferable since Italy was allied to the Reich. But the seasonal workers from Slovenia seemed to have migrated back to their homes earlier than usual this year — an ominous sign that did not strike Julie's unpolitical mind.

'I'm still not at all sure that we oughtn't to get Ruth out of Vienna altogether, Georgy,' said Julie dubiously. 'When the registrar asks for her papers, what then? She may be connected with her grandfather's murder, or with Franz …'

'I don't think so. Her papers from Graz are in order, and it will seem as if she came straight from there to this man — the registrar won't know she has been here for days. And luckily the Graz papers have her name misspelled.'

'I expect my stepfather did that on purpose,' said Julie thoughtfully. 'But this Italian — what is he like? He won't turn awkward?'

Kerenyi shrugged. 'How can we know … he seems all right. I've known him for some time. I often eat at his place. He wants to put money into the restaurant — become a partner. He has some savings, he says, but not enough. Your ten thousand Reichsmark cover the gap.'

'I suppose we should count ourselves lucky to find someone so quickly. But I'm not sure I like it. And Georgy — the registrar — suppose he is a Party member?'

'He isn't. I've found out about him. This Italian lives in the Hernals district and by chance the local registrar is the old one, been there for a generation. He's almost due for retirement and locally very popular; so the Party machine has rather left him alone. No doubt when he goes a Party man will get the job, but that won't be until next year.'

'You've gone into it all,' she commented, looking at his beaky face and deep-set eyes with a new sharpness. 'You're interested in this girl, then? You want to keep her with you, in Vienna?'

'I haven't made up my mind.' It was clear he meant to say no more than that.

'Franz doesn't know about her return. I haven't mentioned it. Georgy …' Kerenyi made an impatient movement but she stopped him with a hand on his sleeve. 'No, something important. I'm not going to interfere — you know your own business. But the other night Nando said something about this man — what was his name, this Gestapo man?'

'Blaschke? What about him?' Kerenyi's manner changed instantly.

'Nando is jealous of you. I know it's absurd, but it might be dangerous. He took the trouble to check on the reports from Blaschke's office and he knows you come here.'

'Why didn't you tell me this at once?' he said roughly. 'You'd better tell that young man of yours to mind his own business.' He got up and moved down the long room, scowling in front of him without seeing anything. 'No, on second thoughts, say nothing to Nando. Behave as if you'd forgotten it. Tell me, though, what did he say about Blaschke?'

'He said he saw the reports on you – I suppose in his own office.'

'No,' said Kerenyi, shaking his head slowly, 'it wouldn't be in his own office. Either he must have gone and asked to see them in his official capacity – or he works for the Gestapo.'

'Oh, no,' cried Julie, shocked. 'That he wouldn't do!'

'Be sensible, Julie. Nando would do anything to remain quietly in the civil service. He says so quite openly, as you know. And there is no reason at all to suppose that it is just a way of talking – though I know it's considered smart. It's quite the fashion lately I've noticed, to say it's all none of our business ... After all, one might say I say it myself in a way. I've kept my quiet corner safe – why shouldn't Nando?'

'But not working for the Gestapo, Georgy?'

Kerenyi looked at her, his eyes cold and secretive.

'Don't be a child, now, Julie. You are always so realistic. What does it mean to "work for the Gestapo"? When I see Blaschke once a month, do you suppose he asks me no questions? Or that I don't answer when he does?'

'Questions? Yes, I suppose he does – you do. But I thought – about the *Independent* – about the editor – that sort of thing ...'

Kerenyi laughed his short bark of a laugh.

'Yes, sometimes about the paper and Schmittgen, who as you know is a passionate Nazi. Sometimes about Lehmann too; sometimes about Maris, about Schoenherr; sometimes about you. I always answer.' Kerenyi was glad to be able to say these things, to this one human being in the world to whom it was safe to say them – Franz he did not count, Franz was the prize and, as the prize always must be, was outside the struggle.

'Of course,' she said softly, 'of course. If you didn't, somebody else would, somebody like Hella who would really talk.'

'I knew I hadn't misjudged you,' said Kerenyi. 'You will see, if you think about it, how dangerous young Nando could be – to everything.'

'I know, he is irresponsible. But then, he doesn't know – anything.'

'Krassny is the man who can control him. He listens to Krassny, not only as his boss, I have the impression. But of course I can't go to Krassny about this directly. Can you have a word with him? But you will have to make it quite clear you expect action. I asked his help once and never heard another word from him; though I have to admit that may be because he never had news for me. Which, I suppose, was good news.'

Julie did not ask to what he referred. She did not want to know too much of Georgy's contacts which she supposed to be immediately connected with the conversation about Blaschke.

'Krassny – dear me, we have hardly any contact ... but perhaps through Otto? I could try ...'

'Otto?'

'His son. The boy is coming to the University this semester. He must have arrived in the last few days. I'll telephone them. If I could manage, somehow, to ensure that the boy stays at the University ... they are all terrified he may be called up, or volunteer.'

'Then Krassny would be indebted to you, you mean? That could be very useful. The boy will have to take a technical or medical degree – you know that? Engineering, physics, medicine; they are absolutely safe. He ought to join the Party, too.'

Before they left the room Julie went to the writing-table and looked at her diary, open upon it.

'I'll find time to-morrow,' she murmured to herself and scrawled something on the already half-filled page.

Franz turned his head in the now familiar movement towards the door as the two friends entered his room; a movement so expressive of loving gentleness and dependence that it cut into both their hearts afresh. His eyes were fixed, as always when she was present, on Julie's face and she went at once to him and took his outstretched hand into hers. The chair that stood by his bed was in her way, and she pushed it aside with her foot and kneeled beside Franz so that he could see her without having to raise his head from his pillows. Kerenyi leaned over and kissed Franz on the forehead, moved the abandoned chair to the foot of the bed and prepared for his expected round-up of the news of the day.

In the kitchen they could hear Fina quietly moving about getting Franz's evening meal ready and humming an old song to herself as she worked. As Kerenyi talked in expert phrases of political affairs about which he was, in spite of his apparent banishment from political journalism, extremely well-informed on the highest professional level, a strange impression began to form in his mind of a quiet pool of purest spring-water welling up in a forest glade where human beings with their tormented incurable foulness rarely go and which is left to the service of innocent small beasts. This image rose without conscious thought; he did not form it as a literary concept afterwards to fit his feeling, the feeling itself formed in his mind. Presently Julie rose and left them without a word, only pressing Franz's delicate bony hand before she went.

Franz was lying quietly, hardly moving, listening, and absorbing what Kerenyi told him. His illness had taken the last barriers of egotism from his powers of reception, and he was able now, without interposing himself, to absorb and order what he read and heard into his former knowledge, so that nothing was lost by the operation upon it of his own 'opinions' or 'principles'. He knew now, it had become clear to him in the weeks he lay helplessly sick, that when he was able to begin work again, everything written up to now would simply be an introductory exploration. What he would write now would be no detailed historical account of certain events, but a short analysis from the events that would be a contribution to the thinking of scholars on the relations of peoples to their rulers.

Julie herself went to the theatre, where a message from Nando was lying on her dressing-table; after the performance he was waiting and they went to his flat for supper as they often did, and nothing was said by either of them about the conversation after Lehmann's party.

When Kerenyi left Franz, he went to the back courtyard of the big house and called upon the old French translator who was helping him with the translation of the diaries and papers of Napoleon's meeting with Czar Alexander. Then he went home.

For some reason the pretty garden in front of the Rathaus, where the dry leaves scattered and flew and the fountain was already turned off in expectation of the first frosts, reminded him of his impression while talking to Franz. He did not want to think about it; his mind touched upon some depth here that did not belong to everyday life, the image was the apprehension of a condition of purity or goodness that had nothing to do with the actual circumstances of living, but which existed somewhere and was able to comfort him in the shifts and deceits he lived in.

As he opened the door of his apartment, Kerenyi was at once aware of the presence of the girl. She was sitting primly on the same chair she occupied when Julie was there, but now she had a white blouse on with a dark skirt and this dress made her look at once more grown-up and more ordinary. The pathetic waif had disappeared – at least for the time being – and a young woman sat there who was clearly, from the way she turned her head as Kerenyi approached, aware of herself. But in fact the neutral blouse and skirt made her look commonplace, and Kerenyi said as he smiled at her in greeting:

'We must get you some new clothes!'

Ruth flushed and rose nervously, at once unsure of herself again.

'Isn't this all right?' she asked. 'I always wore it on Sundays.' She passed her long, thin fingers over the skirt and Kerenyi watched them move.

'Of course it's all right,' he recovered himself, 'I only mean we must get you some more nice things. All the girls in Vienna have lots of pretty clothes, not just one or two but dozens.'

'But then I would have to go out,' she said seriously.

'After we have you safely renamed, you can go out. I've thought it all out. We'll leave your permanent address registered at Graz

— it will be months before anyone notices that you aren't there any more and then Uncle can say you ran away.'

'You mean I can really go to a dressmaker, once my name is different?' She sighed. 'I've forgotten what to say to people like dressmakers.'

'You will soon get used to it again,' he said.

'I've done some cooking,' Ruth said, looking sideways at him. 'I don't think it's very good, though.'

In fact the food, ordered through his cleaning woman, was better than Kerenyi expected and he enjoyed the housewifely little airs Ruth gave herself as he always enjoyed the wooing tricks of women.

In the last few days he had even ceased to be astounded at the speed with which Ruth adapted herself to her new life. She was apparently so naturally dependent on others that adjustment to a new protection came easily to her, like a cat whose home changes and who adapts itself to new owners as soon as it finds them well disposed. And after their meal, while Kerenyi wrote a book review awaiting his attention for some days, he was aware of Ruth all the time, sitting in the same chair, that she seemed to have adopted as her own, and doing some kind of sewing.

The door-bell rang. Kerenyi looked up from his concentration and frowned at the interruption.

'Who on earth can that be?' he wondered abstractedly. For a moment it did not occur to him that Ruth must hide; until he turned and saw her wide dark stare, the eyes again as they were two weeks before, glaring in the pallid face and switching to and fro in panic fear.

'It's all right,' he said quietly. 'Go to your room while I see who it is.'

He could see that she mistrusted him again; the surface of adaptation was very thin. He raised one hand to warn her not to speak loudly, and went towards her. She was half risen from her chair and shuddered as he came near her, shrinking away from him. He had not touched her since the night after she came, but now he put out a hand and stroked her thin cheek.

'Take your mending,' he said softly. 'I'll get rid of them, whoever it is.'

She gazed at him, her large eyes welling full of tears, and put her hand up timidly to her face, to touch his. Then she seemed to flick out of the room, like a bat, silent and floating as it were through the air. This silent speed of movement was characteristic of her.

Outside the door stood Sturmbannführer Blaschke.

He said, almost bashfully, 'I was going by and I thought I might just call on you. Just say if you have guests . . . ?'

He had called before on several occasions. There was nothing sinister about it, Kerenyi assured himself.

'Not a bit,' he said quickly. 'I was writing a book review.'

'You're sure? I thought I heard a voice – inside?'

'My own,' said Kerenyi, standing aside for the policeman to enter. 'I said, "Who the hell can that be," when you rang the bell. Come in. Take your coat off and have a drink.'

'I won't say no,' said Blaschke, struggling out of his heavy uniform coat. 'I've been to a movie and that always makes me thirsty. I don't know why.'

'It's always so hot in the cinema,' suggested his host, struggling with a sudden desire to burst out laughing. 'Was the film good?'

'Not bad. A crime film. Of course, they always get the police parts wrong, but otherwise quite good.' Blaschke came after Kerenyi down the flagged hall, his metalled heel-tips making a pleasant clear ring on the stones. 'I don't know why, but your flat always reminds me of my childhood. Perhaps it's these flagstones?'

Kerenyi did not answer, he was busy getting the bottle of *barack* out of the corner cupboard, and could ignore this remark which produced an unpleasant effect in his mind.

'Though I was brought up in a house, not a flat – you wouldn't ever have heard of it – Gallinden in East Prussia. It's just a village.'

'Were your people farmers, then?'

'Peasants rather – too small to be called farmers. We were tenants – still are – on a big estate.'

They sat down and drank. Kerenyi refilled the glasses. He lit a cigarette and Blaschke brought out his pipe. By some, to Kerenyi quite meaningless point of police etiquette, or perhaps out of a streak of genuine decency, Blaschke never asked Kerenyi questions in his visits to his home. Now he did.

'You know the administrator at the Burgtheater, don't you – Lehmann?' He stopped, waiting for a lead but Kerenyi offered none, though he was tempted to, so that Blaschke should leave more quickly.

'A queer customer, Lehmann!' said Blaschke at last. 'Why do you suppose he intervened over Wedeker's property with the Emigration Board? I've had a complaint from the chief of the Board. They still maintain that the property should go to the Reich.'

'The reason Lehmann intervened is simple,' said Kerenyi coldly. 'And you have asked me about this before, by the way, just after it happened. Lehmann was faced with resignation by Julia Homburg, Wedeker's widow. The property legally belongs to her, as I suppose you know. Besides that, I gather – I was not present myself – there was something like a mutiny at the theatre about these disgusting scenes in the Riding School and elsewhere, in connection with the transportation. One quite famous actor did resign, but Lehmann and Schoenherr were able to prevent further trouble. I don't suppose they could have done so if they hadn't been able to show that they were able to protect Frau Homburg's property.'

'I notice you refer to Frau Homburg as a widow. In fact, she divorced Wedeker, and is not his widow.'

'I am assuming that Wedeker is dead, in fact. Doesn't everybody? She must have heard from him by some means if he were alive. It is quite out of the question that he should not have found some way of letting her know where he is in more than two years. I take that as proof that he is dead.'

'It's true she has never had any message from abroad through the post,' said Blaschke slowly. 'But for a lady with as many friends as Frau Homburg, the posts are not the only means of communication.'

'She would certainly tell me if she heard. I am sure of that.'

Blaschke smiled suddenly, the expression of amusement changing his knobbly face quite remarkably.

'It may surprise you to know that Frau Homburg is a subject on which I do not have complete confidence in you. I think you would risk a good deal for this beautiful lady ...'

Kerenyi was silent for a moment. He knew, of course, that it was widely believed among his acquaintances that Nando was not her only lover and that he himself occupied her bed from time to time. Then he filled up the glasses again.

'On that subject I am not prepared to speak – naturally. I will only point out to you, my dear Sturmbannführer, that if what you imply is the case, I am likely to have an interest in knowing what has happened to Wedeker. In any case, the property was signed over to Frau Homburg long before the divorce; the transfer can be inspected at any time at the Office of Landed Property of Vienna. The State Police ought to concern itself with the reasons the chief of the Emigration Board is so determined to get his claws on this Aryan property, rather than the perfectly obvious reason that moved Lehmann to protect its legal owner, or the even more obvious reason why Frau Homburg is interested in keeping her fortune. Since you know so much about all this, I expect you know the rumours current that there are those on the Emigration Board who do not always pass its confiscations on to the Reich Treasury ...'

'You are being naïve, my dear fellow,' said Blaschke, again with the disconcertingly pleasant grin. 'It is the Emigration Board I am concerned with. One or two of the staff have had rather sudden promotions lately. And been transferred.'

'In that case, I would be happy to be able to help you. I'm sorry I can't.'

'You don't think, for instance, that anyone is getting money out of Frau Homburg – in some improper fashion?'

'You mean one of these thugs is blackmailing her? Why would anyone be able to do that?' Kerenyi frowned angrily, his deep eyes almost disappearing for a second between the prominent nose and the heavy eyebrows. 'You think someone may be giving her the idea that if she pays up, the attempt to confiscate her – Wedeker's – property will be dropped?'

'Just that. She made a drawing from her current account

yesterday, of ten thousand Reichsmark, leaving it almost empty. That has not happened before.'

'I honestly don't think so,' said Kerenyi shaking his head. 'I saw her only this evening, before she went to the theatre, and she didn't seem worried or anything out of the ordinary. I think she would tell me if she were in trouble of that sort. And, by the way, I don't think she is the woman to pay hush-money. She'd go straight to Schoenherr or Lehmann.'

Blaschke drank his drink, and stood up. 'Perhaps she has bought some new clothes,' he said. 'I won't keep you from your work any longer.'

Kerenyi expected to find Ruth back in her chair when he returned from seeing Blaschke out, but she was not there. He opened the far door and found her just beyond it, hands flat against the wall in the now familiar attitude. She turned her head quickly as he came through the door, and stared at him in silence with those frightened and frightening eyes. He shook his head warningly, and went back to the window from which he could see down into the narrow street. He saw Blaschke's bulky figure off along the street and came back to Ruth who still stood against the wall. He smiled at her, and she moved from the wall very quickly. She flung her arms round Kerenyi's neck and clung to him with all her strength. He took her narrow little head into his large hands and began to kiss her face and throat. After a moment, he picked her up in his arms and carried her into his bedroom.

Kerenyi did not dare risk another visit the next day to the Schellinggasse so he dropped in at the theatre and managed to catch Julie by herself.

They had to keep their voices down in the dressing-room and this increased the sordid atmosphere of intrigue which was their world.

'The bank people told me a couple of years ago that they would have to answer questions about my money affairs,' she said. 'So I'm not surprised. I gave them formal permission then – I didn't want them to resent me if they had to go behind my back ... you know how people are if they feel they've done something mean.'

'But don't say anything to Schoenherr or Lehmann,' Kerenyi warned her. 'Blaschke was quite clear that the Emigration Board is what he is interested in. If you complain it will come out that you have been warned and then my contacts with Blaschke may be exposed – you see?'

'The things one has to think of! But that was a good hint of Blaschke's about clothes. In fact, I did have my sable wrap refashioned in the summer and I can wear it a lot. Nobody will notice it isn't new – except perhaps Hella.'

'If it were new, it would have cost enough to account for your heavy drawing?'

'Oh, much more even. I'll drop a hint to someone or other that I haven't paid my bills – they'll think I mean the wrap ... Ah, this lying! I lie to everybody, every word I speak I have to consider first; things do get about so. I use that – that people gossip – it's a great help, in fact. But, God, the dreariness of it. I feel as if a week's solid sleep wouldn't cure my weariness.'

Kerenyi glanced quickly at her, and away again so that she should not see the pity in his eyes.

'This crazy wedding is a week to-morrow,' he said at last. 'I shall not appear. Fräulein Bracher will take Ruth in a taxi and the man is bringing another Italian from the restaurant as second witness. Then we all meet at the restaurant and I give him the money. Bracher has been invaluable – done far more than I would ever dream of asking of her. I don't deserve it.'

Julie noticed that Fräulein Bracher's help was to Kerenyi a service to himself, a valuable personal help and not part of the complex intrigue of secrecy.

'You'll let me know, won't you, when it's over? I shall worry. From what you say about yesterday when Blaschke came, Ruth's nerves are still very rocky.'

'I hope she'll be all right. You'd have been terrified if you'd seen her last night, when the bell rang. But now ...'

Ah, now, she thought. So things are different – now. Aloud she said, 'I'm glad I didn't see her,' rather grimly. 'I had quite an evening myself, struggling with Frau Krassny who loathes me. She didn't want to accept any favours from me, and the boy is to study medicine in any case, it seems. But I managed to frighten her that Otto could still be called up. I spoke to Lehmann before I saw Frau Krassny and he will do as I ask; but the boy will have to put in an application to join the Party. Frau Krassny referred to that condition as a disgrace to the family name …' Julie looked up at Kerenyi and laughed suddenly. 'I was almost glad to force them to compromise – they're a self-righteous lot, the Krassnys. But they agreed. They'd do more than that to keep Otto out of the army. I told them it was only for a short while; when the war is over he can let his membership lapse again.'

'Lehmann must have been glad to do something for you. He ought to be. If this insane business of Fr— of your property came up again there would be trouble.'

'I told him if it did I should resign at once and there would be a scandal. He'll talk to his Party friends to-day and then I can deal with Krassny. I shall bring this business of Nando up quite openly as if I believed Nando was acting officially. Unless they keep their promise to leave me in peace I shall resign and get Otto called up as well – Krassny knows I can do it, too. Don't worry, Georgy. It will work.'

'It has to work.'

'It will work,' she repeated wearily. 'Then I shall be ready for the next crisis. It's the thought of the winter coming that depresses me. Food is getting more and more difficult – there are so many things he can't eat. And I'm not sleeping well. That makes everything seem such an effort, you can't imagine.'

'My dear, you worry me when you talk like that. You should see a doctor.'

'I can't go to Moller again, and I don't know anybody else I could trust – for why should I be so tired and … Georgy, just as soon as the war is over, I shall get him out to Switzerland, cost what it may. I've made my mind up about that.'

Kerenyi could not bring himself to contradict her stubborn belief that the war would soon be finished. There was a tap at the door and a voice outside called Julie to the telephone; they left the room together and Kerenyi went back to Ruth.

BOOK FOUR

October 1941–April 1942

1

*J*ulie proved right in her guess and her personal life was for some time easier. Even before Krassny gave Nando a quiet hint to cease interesting himself in Kerenyi, he had made up his mind to accept what he thought of vaguely as an intricate involvement which might well be of some other kind than personal; of a kind he had better know nothing about.

The comparative peace of their own lives was not matched in the outside world. The warnings Julie might have heard in Krassny's conversation with Nando about the Yugoslav border left her unimpressed; her preoccupation was entirely personal and concerned with Franz's safety, Ruth, her own mother. But the two men were right. Control over the war had slipped from the initiative of either Hitler or the High Command. Italy's unsuccessful actions in the Balkans forced German intervention and in April 1941 the army entered Yugoslavia, at first with the connivance of the royal government and then, after confused plots and counterplots, against the growing and ferocious resistance of the people. The appearance of warfare just across their own borders blinded the public view in Austria to other preparations and it was with a shock of horror that the news was received of 22nd June, 1941. The Wehrmacht had attacked Russia at dawn that day.

The 16th October, 1941, was a brilliantly sunny day with the sharp hint of coming winter in the frosty air. As always at this time of year, the Naschmarkt was an opulent mass of colour and movement. Though many foodstuffs were rationed, this did not affect the autumnal abundance of fruits and vegetables in the market from the surrounding countryside. Before the dark little wooden hutments with their open fronts on the narrow stone pathways were piled heaps of aubergines, green, yellow and red paprikas, apples, pears, maize heads, a whole scale of differing greens from the most delicate yellow-green of early endives to the black-green of winter cabbages and broccoli. Fresh trout and river langoustes swam in the brown water of wooden tubs, brought slopping in the early dawn through the quiet streets on neat little pony-carts by peasants half asleep behind the clop-clop of hooves. Hare and venison hung beside boiling fowls and the first of the winter's geese. Eggs were heaped in baskets, creamy and brown. In the sausage-maker's window, glassed for hygiene's sake, hung fifty kinds of smoked, preserved, pickled and cured meats: and in the alley reserved to potatoes were, as always, twenty different kinds of tuber for the variety of dishes, loved by the Viennese, each of which needs a particular kind of 'earth-apple'. The Italian booths displayed yellow polenta, boxes of long spaghetti, stout macaroni, and huge heaps of noodles only just made and cut, still slightly soft to the touch. Next door a flour-merchant was still able to advertise 'Hungarian Strudel Flour – finest quality' and the date on which it was milled to prove that it would not be too fresh and sticky for the delicate pastry that can only be perfectly successful with the highest-quality Hungarian wheat flour.

From the tram-stop alighted the early housewives carrying capacious baskets, chattering and pushing, joking with the conductor or frowning abstractedly or ill-temperedly about them, and clutching their worn black purses in the hollows of their hands. It was just before seven o'clock in the morning.

The women dispersed rapidly among the hundreds of stalls and huts. Young, graceful, or stolid and thickset with years of hard work and solid food, they flitted or lumbered about their business, preoccupied with the eternal concern of filling hungry stomachs. In the twin roadways bounding the market on either side heavy trucks and carts rumbled to and fro as they always did, the light pony-carts bouncing without load over the cobbles, the larger wagons drawn by draught horses shaking their blond manes and snorting among the petrol vans and trucks. If there were a few more closed trucks that morning than on every other morning, none of the preoccupied women noticed them.

Yet suddenly, from the unnoticed trucks, a stream of men began to drop over the back-boards into the bumpy roadway, where cabbage stalks lay in the deep gutters and it was easy to slip on a squashed tomato on the rounded stones. The men wore grey uniforms and sharply smart caps; they were young, vigorous, energetic; they carried small-arms and sheathed batons of black artificial rubber. Here and there a man carried a light machine pistol and remained by the side of the roadway. They laughed and shouted to each other as they let themselves down with athletic ease from the tail-boards and streamed across the road. One of them, a tall young man with a high blond head and long neck, slipped on a rotten fruit and almost fell. He pulled himself together with a self-conscious shout of mock alarm, and ran after his comrades; but the hard laugh of a market woman changed his grin to a frown of injured dignity and his brow showed a taut anger.

A sergeant with a hoarse voice roared an order and the main part of the groups lined up neatly across every outlet and alley-way of the market that gave on to the thoroughfare. The stall-keepers called to each other, tipping a warning signal with a thumb to those who had not yet noticed anything. The hurrying women, with here and there a man among them, began to look round irritably at what looked like being an interruption of their full morning's work. From the lines of uniformed men small groups detached themselves, and began systematically and quietly to work their way through the crowded market. After a few moments of silently scanning the identity cards offered to them by the marketing crowd without their having even to demand them, a group came upon one small old man with a shabby shopping bag of imitation leather. Without hesitation he produced his card and a young SS man, topping him by head and shoulders, opened it. Across the inside of the printed card was a broad stripe of yellow and a six-point star. The young man turned his head and shouted over his shoulder. Instantly two comrades appeared, and without the slightest fuss either from the crowd of people or the old man, who showed no sign of emotion of any kind, they led the old man away from the crowded alleyway and beyond the line of men at the entrance of the roadway.

The little group of uniformed men advanced a few steps, treading in their metalled boots with stiff pride. One fat housewife attempted to ignore them, and did not produce her identity card as all the others, including the stall-holders, were doing. She was a stout, stern-faced woman who had, it might be supposed, ruled a large family for years without argument. The same tall youngster demanded her pass in a taut phrase of command, and she reluctantly drew it out of her fat purse. She was the fifty-year-old wife of a skilled motor-mechanic, Catholic, five children, the eldest twenty-seven and the youngest just turned four years old. Her name was Hermine Weissberger, born Fiala. She was unable to prevent herself muttering some sarcastic comment on the youth of her interrogator though it was clear by the damp flush that rose into her well-fed face that she knew the unwisdom of what she did.

'What d'you mean by that?' snapped the youngster, his voice clipping the words in the current fashion among his kind, into a dog's yap.

The woman looked about her at the faces of her neighbours, apprehensive but not able to believe that a boy she could have put over her massive knee only a year or so ago would actually defy her personified domestic authority.

'Why di'n't yer let 'im go?' she growled in slurring dialect, and the tone of a mother who remonstrates with a disorderly urchin. 'Poor old feller. Lives alone, like as not.'

The young man stared at her red face for a moment, and suddenly his silky light hair looked yellow against a dusky flush that rose into his prominent cheekbones. Without a word, and with a smooth, sleep-walking movement of his right hand, he drew his service revolver from its black holster and with a crack-nailed thumb, pressed back the safety catch. The woman, and everyone within hearing distance stared entranced with unbelief at this extension of his hand. At that instant the sergeant with the hoarse voice pushed himself through the throng and stared about him under lowered brows, taking in the scene without any intervening thought-process as men long used to the handling of human beings do. Then, casually, not even contemptuously, he pushed aside the youngster's gun-hand and said, 'Get on with your job, and don't play the fool.'

There was a second of doubt and then the group, drawing the tall youngster with it, moved on about its business. After a moment of stunned silence, the fat woman gave a loud laugh of released tension. The backs of the young men walking sternly away seemed to stiffen, but none of them turned.

And that laugh, the sign of an old-fashioned human feeling of disbelief, of a natural cantankerousness, cost the lives of at least ten people. If the fat woman had not expressed her feelings, at once of relief and contempt in that audible fashion, the group to which the blond youngster belonged might not have felt bound to take their orders to their logical conclusions. Two half-Jewish women in the next few minutes who protested that they had come out without their passes, were moved away to the side of the road- way; and an 'Aryan' woman along with them, who was only able to prove her identity hours later. The group, with all the other groups, moved slowly on through the market alleys.

The round-up started at one end of the market, a narrow oblong bounded on the long sides by the twin roadways and cut across about in the middle by a third road and a tramline. The groups went steadily through the crowded market towards the intersecting road.

Frau Weissberger pushed past the men to continue her shop- ping and lumbered up to a stall near the cross-road where she had bought vegetables for thirty years.

'They are rounding up the Jews,' she muttered to the stallholder, so as not to be overheard. The man, elderly and slight-built, turned his bald head to stare past her, and Frau Weissberger did so too.

'No, you can't see 'em yet,' she said. 'They started at the other end.' A gasp beside her made both of them turn towards a young woman who stood beside Frau Weissberger. She was very young, hardly more than a girl, and was heavily pregnant. She wore a scarf over her dark smooth hair and her swollen belly strained against the buttons of her raincoat. Like all the other women, she carried a wide basket and a dark leather purse cuddled in the hollow of her hand.

She stared wildly from the face of the old man to Frau Weissberger, and neither needed telling why. The pale, delicate face had turned a whitish grey, and the great eyes, mournful and terrified, looked black as sloes against the pallor.

'Let me through the back of your shop,' whispered Ruth, putting out a shaking hand to touch the old man's arm. He glanced round apprehensively, but at the moment there was nobody else nearby. He made a quick gesture and Ruth slipped past him and through the dark little hutment to the far door that gave on to the cross-road for unloading. She rattled at the locked door, but the old man had remembered at the same moment and pushed the massive key into her trembling hand. The key rattled loudly in the lock, the handle was stiff, it seemed like minutes before the wooden door was open. Right up against it was the uniformed back of an enormously broad and tall man. Ruth pushed the door shut again, and leaned against it, gasping for breath. Then she pushed past the old man again, brushing against him without seeing anything, blind with terror and stumbling with the weight of the unborn child. The little hut was dark, the sunlight outside brilliant. She stood, paralysed, between heaps of purple aubergines and sharp red tomatoes; the group of men was already upon them. Ruth could smell the clean aromatic smell of the freshly gathered tomatoes and beyond them multicoloured paprikas. She saw nothing and heard around her only a confused babble; she stumbled forward in instinctive flight. The tall youngster put out a long arm, and to avoid his grasp Ruth flung herself against the mound of piled-up boxes. They slipped and a torrent of beautiful ripe fruits began to tumble about, all the fruits of rich autumn, the juices of a bountiful nature. In the momentary confusion, Ruth slipped between the crowded men and women, and ran for it. In her unseeing panic, she misjudged her distance from the next stall, and bumped heavily against its end support. She fell to her knees, clutching at her burden, trying to protect it with her arms, and gave a groan of anguish. A long arm caught her shoulder and pulled her to her feet, more dead than alive.

'Don't even need to see your identity card,' triumphed the blond boy. Ruth gave a loud tearing cry and her head fell back against his shoulder. It looked for an instant to the muttering crowd, as if he were protecting her. She tried to say 'I am a foreigner' but nothing louder than a harsh breath came from her throat.

'She's fainted,' cried someone from the crowd.

'You ought to be ashamed – in her condition.'

'Why don't you bully someone your own size?'

'Leave her there until she comes to,' shouted another man to the blond youngster harshly. But the sergeant pushed his way through the throng, saw the temper of the crowd, and made a gesture with one hand.

'Carry her out of here,' he shouted. 'And gently. Make way there. Make way, I say.'

Reluctantly, not knowing whether the pregnant girl was to be spared or not – which was just what the sergeant meant them to feel – the crowd gave way and one of the uniformed men carried Ruth bodily away to the far side of the road where a truck was waiting, already half filled with weeping and hysterically chattering people.

Frau Weissberger, overcome with an appalling sensation of frustrated rage and humiliation – for this was more than anybody ought to be asked to witness – burst into a flood of angry tears, sobbing harshly and crying over and over, 'It's wrong. It's wrong. What's going to happen to the baby? You can't do this. Somebody will have to pay for this.'

'Yes,' said one of the few men shoppers behind her, a well-dressed elderly member of the upper classes, his ascetic face drawn with fear and anger, 'You're right there, somebody will have to pay for all this.'

Frau Weissberger turned on him savagely.

'Call yourself a man?' she screamed. 'I hope the same thing happens to your daughter, one of these days!'

The sergeant, feeling the situation getting beyond him, roared suddenly into Frau Weissberger's face. He was beside himself with rage at the horror of what he was doing.

'Silence!' he yelled in his hoarse voice which cracked with the force of his shout. 'Silence or you go with them. You hear me?'

A stunned silence fell. There it was, quite simply, the choice.

Gradually the crowd began to back away, to disperse, each member of it looking, or trying to look, as if nothing to do with himself had been happening. At the back of every mind was that naked threat, always implied, and nearly always understood, but spoken that morning openly. What was one to do, faced by that threat? The girl was beyond saving; was one to suffer the same fate as hers for a total stranger, when the children would be coming home for their dinner in only an hour or so . . . ?

Scowling after the retreating crowd, the sergeant felt nothing but anger.

'Get on with it,' he ordered his men harshly, 'we don't want to be here all day. I want a drink, by God.'

That night the sergeant got blind drunk and the following day, in spite of the pleadings of his wife, he volunteered for the Russian front and was killed two weeks later.

None of the people rounded up at the market were ever seen again. It was known, much later, that the long locked train that left Vienna the next day took nearly ten days to make the journey to Lodz over the crowded and overworked railways. Many of the travellers were dead on arrival when the doors were unlocked and the clearing of the coaches was made difficult by the way they were built. After that time, cattle-trucks were used for similar transports.

Kerenyi was already sitting at his desk in a cloud of rank tobacco smoke when his cleaning woman arrived late, at half past eight. She peeped through the half-open door, saw the tall square back hunched forwards over the typewriter, heard the clatter of the keys and decided not to interrupt Herr Dr at his work. Instead, after taking off her shabby coat and head-scarf in the kitchen, she went down the passage and looked through the bedroom and spare room, and then into the bathroom. Then she looked from the kitchen window into the dark, tidy court below to see if anyone stood at the rubbish bins, the carpet-beating poles, or if perhaps steam was coming out of the communal wash-rooms.

She moved about quietly in the kitchen, gathering the dishes for washing up in a state of confused worry; she was an old woman who had worked for Kerenyi for many years. She had lived all her life in the 5th District and had come to work six mornings a week on the same tram for over twenty years, the tram that ran through the market intersection.

Presently something occurred to her mind; she went to the hall cupboard and looked within. Sure enough, raincoat and shopping basket were not there – she had known it all the time. She would have to interrupt Herr Dr, have to. Wiping her bony hands on a kitchen towel, she went to the door again, and rattled the handle experimentally. Kerenyi did not hear. She knocked then, first timidly, and then loudly. He swung round with his familiar scowl. She was so nervous of interrupting him – something absolutely understood was that his work was sacred – that she could hardly say anything, but came into the room, still holding the grey linen cloth in her hand.

For some reason Kerenyi looked at this cloth, a homespun greyish square, damp with dark marks, that had seen much service. Afterwards it seemed to him that he remembered only the bony old hands, work-worn, twisted with rheumatism, soft and wrinkled by a thousand pails of soap-suds. There was something that stopped him from shouting at her. He looked up into her familiar face, and as their eyes met with the intimate acquaintanceship of a generation together, her colourless eyes filled with tears.

'What is it?' he said, and his voice was a hoarse whisper for the look in her face told him that something terrible and unalterable, something that could never be undone, had happened.

'Where is she?' asked the old woman. It was the first time they had ever addressed each other without using the correct titles.

Kerenyi put a hand on the wooden arm of the desk-chair and half raised himself. Their eyes were locked together.

'She went – she went to market,' he whispered. He pushed

himself upright by pressure on the arm of the chair, as if he had no strength in him. 'What is it?' he said, still in that hoarse whisper.

'They were ... in the market, they were rounding up ... rounding up people ...'

'So early?' he said stupidly. Ruth always went very early to market when there were only working-class people about, just for this reason. 'But of course, they know that too,' he muttered and she understood what he meant.

Suddenly, Kerenyi seemed to realise that he must do something. He shoved the heavy chair violently away from him, so that it rocked on its legs. Knocking the old woman out of his path he rushed out of the room, and to the apartment door. It was only when the sash of his old working dressing-gown caught in the door as it slammed behind him, that he remembered he was not yet fully dressed. She was behind him, holding his jacket, and opened the door again before he could even knock or ring.

'You've forgotten ...' she began to stammer and then saw that he had come to his senses. He struggled his big shoulders into the jacket.

'Keys,' he said sharply. 'Money. I shall need ...'

He tore back into the flat, she following, wringing her hands.

His face was cramped into a stony grimace, the face of a man who has looked upon the Gorgon. She heard a crash as he upset something in the bedroom, and then he ran past her again, leaving the door swinging and was leaping down the winding stairway, four at a time, banging his shoulders against the curved white walls, his heels slamming on the worn stone steps.

It was several minutes' normal walk to the nearest taxi stand, but Kerenyi was there in under a minute and grasped the door of the first cab he came to. The cab driver was just about to say that the next cab was before him, but when he saw Kerenyi's face he changed his mind. The gears already connecting, he said a single word.

'Where?'

'Naschmarkt,' gasped the fare, and the sudden move of the old vehicle swung him violently on to the leather seat, where he half lay, gasping for breath. Through the back streets it was only a few minutes. As the cab came to the nearest of the twin roadways, a wholesaler's van blocked the roadway while loaders trundled their iron-wheeled lifters to and fro.

'Drive through them,' shouted Kerenyi, and pushing his head through the open window, he yelled at the workmen, 'Out of the way there!' The men turned their uncomprehending heads with infinite slowness. The nearest, seeing Kerenyi's distorted visage, cried out and the men scattered. The taxi mounted the pavement on two wheels to pass the obstructing van, and a second later they ground to a halt in the intersecting road. Flinging the door away from him as he ran, Kerenyi left the cab standing without a word and disappeared into the throng, shoving any who came in his way aside as if they were invisible.

'What's the matter with him?' asked a startled passer-by of the taxi man.

'Ask me another,' replied the man. 'I only hope he comes back – he hasn't paid me.'

He did not even know where she bought her foodstuffs, and ran past the stall where he could have heard what had happened. He was almost through the centre alleyway to the far end when he realised that he was achieving nothing, and stood still swaying on his feet, his head lowered like a maddened animal's, breathing harshly. There was nothing out of the ordinary happening, nothing at all. Everything had a nightmare normality and for an instant it occurred to Kerenyi that the old woman might have been mistaken. But he knew that she was not. Pulling himself together with a violent effort, he closed his eyes for a second, and then opened them and accosted the first person before him. The moving population of the market had changed in the intervening time, and was now filled with middle-class housewives, men choosing their own fruits for table and the maids of rich houses. The man Kerenyi addressed was a senior civil servant who always did his marketing before going to the office, for as he would have told Kerenyi if he had been given time, you can't trust women to take enough trouble over details.

'Has anything been happening?' asked Kerenyi.

The man stared at this wild stranger with cold impersonal disapproval and, lifting his eyebrows, simply walked past.

Kerenyi turned from him, a laming sensation of utter despair making his steps stumble. A stall-keeper caught his arm, a hugely fat woman in a flowered apron.

'Are you ill?' she said, holding on to him.

'Yes. No. I'm looking for somebody.' Kerenyi became conscious that he was incoherent and taking a deep breath, he started again. 'Tell me, has there been a round-up of some sort here this morning?'

The woman stared at his strained eyes, and the face in which every muscle seemed stretched against every other muscle. She looked frightened as far as her enormous fat allowed her face any expression at all. Two other stall-keepers came near, exchanging cautious glances.

The fat woman put her hand into the big leather money-bag that hung on a strap round her enormous waist under her bright apron, in case this madman was after her hard-earned money. She backed away a step and glanced round her to see who was listening. One of the other stall-keepers, a meagre little man, stepped forward.

'They were here, but over an hour ago,' he said, in a cautious undertone, not looking at Kerenyi. 'The SS. They took off a lot of people. In trucks.'

'In trucks,' repeated Kerenyi dazedly. 'Where? Where did they go?' He grabbed the little man's thin arm and shook him savagely. 'You must have seen something. Where did they go?' He glared round him at the group which had gathered. 'Didn't anybody see anything?' he pleaded, and inside himself he felt as if his heart must explode in his body with anguish and horror. 'Did anybody see a young girl — a dark young woman? She was pregnant. The baby would have come next month ...' With a new horror worse than the former, Kerenyi realised that he was already using the past tense.

They all shook their heads, ashamed of his grief, afraid of his violence, and afraid for themselves if the police should come up.

'Nothing of that,' said the meagre little man, rubbing his arm where Kerenyi's grip had hurt him. 'You couldn't see from here where they went. But they went that way, I could tell from the sound of the motors ...' He pointed towards the east.

A tall and elegant young woman pushed through the group and touched Kerenyi on the arm.

'They were rounding up people near my place this morning, too,' she said. 'And I live out in Hietzing. So it sounds like a big round-up. They probably took them to the Prater, don't you think?'

'You can't tell,' argued the meagre little man; his story being taken from him and changed in this way made him feel a personal interest in his version. 'They would go by side streets anyway. I reckon they'd go straight to a railway yard somewhere.'

'That's right, like as not,' chimed in the fat woman. 'Over beyond the Praterstrasse, in the goods yards, that's where they'll have took them.'

The tall woman looked anxiously into Kerenyi's eyes.

'They may be right,' she said. 'I have a car here, let me take you over there.'

The humanity of her look brought Kerenyi back to his senses, and he remembered that he would bring anyone who helped him into danger. He remembered his taxi as well, and shook his head, unable to smile or say anything civil.

'I have a taxi,' he muttered. 'I'd better try the police . . .' He turned to go, and turned back. 'I . . .' He made a helpless gesture and the tall woman's face twisted with pain. 'It's all right,' she said in a breaking voice and walked quickly away.

Kerenyi walked, more slowly now, back the way he had come. He stopped two or three times and asked people if they had seen a slight dark girl among the people arrested, a girl about to have a baby. Nobody had seen her, and he did not chance to ask at the stall where she would have been remembered. The colour and ripeness of the heaped fruits seemed to shimmer and sway before his eyes, swelling into monstrous distortions and retreating again into the distance, so that all he recalled afterwards was a blurred mass of colours.

The taxi man was waiting with some anxiety for him. He had had half a mind to lose his fare and drive off, but when Kerenyi appeared he moved towards him and took his arm. He had in the meantime heard of the morning's events and had no need now of an explanation of his fare's wild manner. But when Kerenyi told him to drive to the Gestapo building on the Kai his heart nearly failed him again. He stopped his cab some yards away from the correct entrance, and Kerenyi, on getting out, stared about him, hardly recognising where he was.

'Look here, are you sure you really want to go there?' said the driver. Kerenyi stared at him stupidly, and then grasped what the man meant.

'It's all right,' he said vaguely, putting his hand in his pocket for money. 'I know whom to ask for. You needn't wait for me.' He pushed the money into the man's hand and turned away without waiting for change.

He asked for Blaschke at the entrance desk and after a short wait was led by a uniformed porter to the familiar door. The porter knocked and at the growl from within, left the visitor there.

Blaschke stared at Kerenyi, without hat or coat, his hair in disorder, his face gaunt and stony. Kerenyi stood in the middle of the office and did not seem to know what he was doing there. As Blaschke, concerned, rose from his chair, he blinked twice and spoke rapidly, without greeting or explanation.

'There was somebody rounded up in this morning's action, somebody I have to get back. She's going to have a baby in a few weeks, and I have to get her back. It's all a mistake, she has a foreign passport. I have to get her back.'

'Sit down and tell me what you are talking about,' said Blaschke. 'I can't do anything unless I know what it is all about.'

'Sit down?' said Kerenyi slowly, looking about him. 'No, I can't stay. I have to go and look for her. Are they in the goods yards? Someone at the market seemed to think they would be taken there?'

'The market?' Blaschke seemed bewildered.

'She was out marketing,' explained Kerenyi impatiently. 'Don't pretend you don't know about this round-up. You must have been informed.'

'Christ,' said Blaschke, and sat down heavily. 'You mean the girl you were living with? She's been picked up?'

Kerenyi was searching through his pockets, but found no

cigarettes. Blaschke had none for he did not smoke except for his pipe.

'You knew then?'

'Yes. I knew.' Blaschke stared round the room. 'But I didn't know she was — I doubt if I can do anything without getting you and me arrested.'

'Wait a minute,' began Blaschke again after a pause. He picked up his telephone and dialled a number. Answered, he asked rapid questions for a few minutes and then put down the receiver. He stared heavily in front of him, his ugly face falling into deep creases. He pulled at his underlip and then he said in an under-tone, 'I could just try, perhaps ...' and reached for the outside telephone. Then he dropped it back again and said, 'No, I daren't risk it.'

'Who?' asked Kerenyi.

Blaschke shook his head without answering. Then he said slowly, 'They don't like me much at the moment, in any case. There is talk of transferring me.'

Kerenyi came over and leaned his hands on the sides of Blaschke's wide flat desk, bending over so that his reddened eyes stared into the policeman's.

'You bastard,' he said thickly. 'Do something! Do something! I've done things for you, and you knew perfectly well what the pay-off was. Now pay off.'

'You don't understand,' said Blaschke, not looking at Kerenyi. 'It isn't that I won't — I don't know that I would, or that I wouldn't. I mean I can't. There is nothing I can do from the security section except land myself in the same boat.'

Kerenyi seemed to sag together suddenly. He turned away blindly from the table and reeled to the wall. He put his forearm up against the wall with its ugly greenish wash, and leaned his head on it, his back to the room. There was a long silence.

Then Kerenyi pushed himself upright from the wall, walked out of the office, down the echoing corridor, down the wide stair-case and through the hall out into the street.

The sun was still shining.

For a little while Kerenyi stood in front of the office entrance, unaware that he was swaying on his feet. Then, as if suddenly galvanised, he set off at a stumbling half-run towards the Schwedenbrücke. It was not until he had been following the tram-lines for some time at the other side of the bridge, towards the Praterstern and the big shunting yards, that it occurred to him to stop and board the grinding red iron worm that was just coming to a stop beside him.

It was sheer chance that he boarded a tram that went to the goods yards. And chance again that he descended at the main gates, simply because nearly all the passengers got off there and he went with them, sleep-walking. It was, though Kerenyi did not know it, a shift-change time and most of the burly fellows on the tram were going inside the big gates, and he went with them, unchallenged. Noon whistles blew, the noon bell clanged from the nearest District House, a relic of old times when not every house-hold had a clock. Kerenyi was enough aware now of what he was doing to say nothing until he was well within the complex of roadways, rails, squat administration and switching buildings and standing trucks. He had no idea where he was, nor how he should go about finding her. Passing one of the squat buildings, he saw on the shelf of an open half-door a bundle of paper folders. Having given the dark interior a once-over and seen that there was no one inside, Kerenyi simply took the folders and tucked them under his left arm, as if about to consult them when he should reach his destination. He could guess from their printed headings that they had something to do with the making-up of goods trains, and walked along, circumspectly now, aware that he could not continue to be taken for a workman once he spoke. His shabby old tweeds would probably pass muster if only he had no tie; but he did not dare take off this bourgeois article of dress for fear that someone would notice him. He thought if he walked about enough he would perhaps see a train of 'hard' coaches among the many goods wagons and locomotives ranged about on various sidings which appeared to Kerenyi's uneducated eye quite chaotic. There were numbers of men about, workmen, minor officials and the like, but nobody took any notice of him for in such a large complex a strange figure was nothing odd. Once he crossed a shunting line and a man called a warning roughly, which reassured him for the tone was of one speaking to a workmate; a second later an old locomotive steamed slowly by and the fireman leaned out of his cab and shook his head at Kerenyi standing beside the line. The hiss of steam and the grinding of iron wheels, the banging of trucks, the whole music of the railway was comforting to him; it seemed that an organisation so useful and necessary could not be evil.

But after walking about for nearly an hour, Kerenyi still had as little idea as when he entered the yards, of where the transport might be. It did not occur to him that he might be in the wrong place; he *knew* the train was being made up here somewhere, if he could only find it. He must locate it and wait for the people to be brought in some unimaginable column attended by the dark-uniformed men with guns ... probably during the night.

A few yards away, across two diverging lines, a gang of workmen did something to the sleepers of a track. The ganger, identifiable by his jacket, walked off behind a small tool-hut. The gang instantly slacked work, and Kerenyi walked over to them. They were hollow-cheeked, stubble-bearded and dirty, dressed in a collection of dilapidated trousers and ragged shirts in which they had clearly been living for some time, day and night. They spoke, as Kerenyi could at once hear, Polish to each other.

'Any of you seen the transport?' he said brusquely in German, and then added in halting Polish which made them grin. 'I can't find the damn' thing.'

The men shook their heads, glancing sideways at each other. Then one of them said something in an undertone to the man next to him.

'I have to collect somebody off it,' said Kerenyi truthfully. 'She got picked up by mistake.'

'Oh, that transport, you mean,' said one of the men now, in accented German. 'Jerzy, you heard something, you said ...?'

The man who had spoken before now spoke again, but with such a thick Ruthenian accent Kerenyi could not follow his rapid speech. He shook his head impatiently, and the German-speaker translated for him.

'He says they were shunting hard passenger-coaches, long-distance ones, over on the far side. Down there ...' he pointed a ragged arm towards the north of the yards. 'That might be it. Don't see many passenger trains about here.'

'You'd better go,' said another man suddenly in Polish. 'The chief will be back in two minutes and we don't want to get into trouble.'

Kerenyi nodded and walked on, over the tracks. As he went the men started working again in a lacksadaisical fashion, one of them keeping a lookout for the absent ganger. Kerenyi realised that the Polish workmen did not believe for a moment that he had any official business with the transport, but out of their own half-outlaw existence they recognised his lawlessness. A roadway intercepted his path, running roughly north and south and he struck north, walking casually as if he came along here every day. No German would challenge him if he continued to behave normally, for they had not acquired the sixth sense of those foreign workers. He walked for a long way along the concrete roadway; once or twice motor-trucks passed.

At last he saw the siding the Pole meant. It was an old loading side-track with a raised platform on the far side from where he walked. At one end, a number of linked but engineless coaches were already ranged. They were passenger coaches dating from before the First War, paintless and rickety but still sound. As Kerenyi watched, a gang of ragged foreign workmen shoved by main force another coach towards the line and shouting rhythmically to each other, rolled it down the unnoticeable slope to the train. It clanged heavily against the next bumpers and one of the men ran, bent double, under the shivering irons to connect the hooks, encrusted with rust. Kerenyi walked along the train parallel with it. In the first three coaches there were about a hundred people and his heart and nerves gave a leap of hope and he crossed the lines hastily. But the people there were all very old and clad mostly in grey dressing-gowns. They sat about on the wooden seats listlessly. Two elderly nurses stood on the wooden loading ramp.

Kerenyi skirted the end of the coaches and went up to the nurses.

'Are these the ones from the Rothschild Hospital?' he asked. It was the first thing that occurred to him to say.

'No, these are from the Community Old People's Home,' answered one of the women, a stern-faced raw-boned amazon of fifty-odd. She meant the home belonging to the Vienna Jewish Community. 'Are the geriatric wards of the Rothschild being cleared as well, then?'

'That's just what I'm not sure of. They seem to have made the usual muddle. Can't see why the train had to be made up here, in any case.'

'Perhaps you can give us some information,' asked the second nurse. 'We were just told to come down with the bus from the Community Home, put the patients in the first coach and leave them there. We have to report back to the General Hospital, but there seems to be nobody here to take care of the patients. We can hardly just leave them here. They have no provisions with them, and we don't know where we should check on the arrangements?'

'Hm. You were just detailed to accompany them this far? They aren't your patients?'

'Oh, no. We were just sent because we happened to be changing wards this morning. The supervisor said we should do this extra duty and take up in the new wards this afternoon instead of this morning. Then the bus picked us up to go to the home, and that's all we know. The instructions were to put them only in the first coach, but of course, that must be a mistake. There are ninety-three of them and some of them are senile and incontinent. One coach isn't nearly enough.'

The nurse who had first spoken smoothed her gloves and turned the edge of her cape over one arm.

'What is bothering us is whether we should report the breakdown of the arrangements here – in the station – I mean, it isn't a station, but here somewhere. Or whether we should get back to our own hospital and report there?'

'I don't know whom you would report to here, Nurse, and that's a fact,' said Kerenyi, bringing out his folder of forms and frowning at them. 'My business is only with the train-shunting, and I don't know any more than you do. I should think the best thing

would be for you to get back to your hospital and report there.'
He looked round and up and down the loading ramp, as if he did
this every day. 'I tell you what. I shall have to come back myself
and by then there will be somebody here in charge. Bound to be.
If some attendants and food haven't shown up in an hour or so,
I'll find somebody. In the meantime, you get back and report
there. That way we have two means of reporting.'

'Yes, that sounds sensible. I feel we ought to stay until someone comes to take over. But on the other hand we are both on duty
at two-thirty this afternoon in our new wards. It will take us that
long to get back.'

'We have tidied them up after the bus ride,' said the first nurse,
looking anxiously into the coach window nearest her, where four
very old women, their white heads nodding, sat looking out at
them.

'Let's just go through again and see that they're comfortable,
and then we'll go back,' suggested the other. They thanked Kerenyi
politely and took their leave, and he walked away up the ramp
until he came to an open doorway into an echoing hall, long
empty and unused. It must have been a customs inspection hall at
one time from the heavy locks, some still with seals hanging from
them. Kerenyi found a small cubby-hole of an office with a standing desk and pigeon-holes marked with various numbers and
bureaucratic hieroglyphs of the old Imperial railways. It had a
small window on to the hall, but this was so covered with years of
accumulated dirt that he did not think anyone could see inside it
from the entrance. Still, for safety's sake, he sat down on the dirty
boards of the floor. He would wait for darkness. He heard the
voices of the two nurses as they went away, and then there was
silence inside the hall but for the distant shunting and clanging all
over the yards. He was glad he had got rid of the two nurses, for
he could not maintain his pretence of having business here in their
presence, since he might have to change his story if he used the
trick again.

Kerenyi did not think of the old souls waiting impatiently for
their customary midday meal and wondering what was to happen
next – if they were still able to think at all. He knew that the two

nurses in their innocence had simply been used to make the bus transport through the city look respectable and no further sick-attendants nor food of any kind would be forthcoming. What at any other time would have enraged him with disgust and pity did not even strike him now as extraordinary. He did not, in fact, even think much about Ruth, nor speculate as to how she was being treated – he knew nobody would be ill-treated within the city after the trouble caused by the first round-ups at the outbreak of the war. Kerenyi had only one thought in his mind, and that was less a thought than a return to brute instinct, to protect his unborn child.

The afternoon wore on, and Kerenyi did not notice his cramped discomfort, nor feel hunger or thirst though he had had nothing but a cup of coffee since the previous night. At a few minutes past three o'clock he could hear a sound of many people approaching. There were voices, a confusion of voices and the shuffling of an unorganised crowd moving. Now and then there were masculine shouts, and once a dog bayed deeply. Once or twice he distinguished single words from the murmur and the clang of further coaches being coupled to the train. The movement gradually settled, but the siding was no longer quiet, and Kerenyi knew that several hundred people must now have arrived at the train. A painful excitement began to fill him, his nerves screamed for action, to move about and see what was happening. He did not worry about the train being moved, because he guessed it would pull out in the night – perhaps just before dawn.

Later there was a further addition to the train's load, and from then on columns of people seemed to be almost continuously arriving.

With infinite slowness the sun set, and shadows filled the long hall through which Kerenyi could see nothing of the ramp, only the light falling through the still open door.

At last he thought it was safe to move. On the ramp hundreds of people moved, always in the same direction, and when he opened the office door, he could hear sharp orders and the clumping of top-boots going to and fro. Everything seemed to have a curious orderliness, there was no crying, no screams, no yells, no curses. How docile these people were, he thought, docile as Ruth was docile. They had a nightmare calm, a trustingness in what the authorities did, that it was somehow so ordered and must be so; and this began to anger Kerenyi, who could not attach it to any similar feeling in his own critical and non-comformist mind.

Kerenyi opened the door and waited. Now he moved quietly out into the hall and began to skirt the wooden wall to the back, keeping flat against the dark background. At the first window he came to he realised what he should have thought of before – that they were all barred and locked with old and rusty but still stout padlocks. And so were the doors. He would have to go out at the door he had come in by. He began to move quietly and swiftly round the walls and had almost reached the open door, standing diagonally open, when he heard new sounds without.

A group of men, walking together with disciplined strides, was approaching. He slid quickly into the triangle of deep shadow behind the open door, hearing the creaking of leather and the slight metallic clank of equipment. He waited, straining his ears to hear above the confused hubbub of the train's burden. About five minutes later he heard them again. Then he heard a voice, one used to command, speaking in the sharp clipped fashion that was by now a definite SS style.

'What is this door here doing open?' it snapped. 'I thought you told me this shed was no longer used?'

An obsequious voice replied, the voice of a minor official.

'No, sir, it hasn't been used since the new customs building was finished and that must be ...'

'I don't give a damn how long the new customs building has been built. I'm talking about this open shed. How long has it been open? Who opened it? And what for?'

'But, sir, I don't quite understand ... It was not opened according to any order of mine. I dare say it is used for storing tools when the gangs have to work far away from the proper tool sheds, like here. But we can close it quite easily. Wittmack, go and get my keys, will you?'

'You still have not understood me,' said the first voice, now silky with controlled rage. 'And how dare you come on an inspection with me without your keys? You seem to be less than capable of doing your job properly.'

'But, sir . . .'

'You poor oaf, how long have you been here in this cosy siding away from the world? Fifty people could have hidden themselves in this shed. Do you understand me now? Close it, can you, you fool? It has to be searched from top to bottom, and at once. Berthold, call up a Schlar and get the place cleared out. They had better get some more lights up, it is almost dark now.'

'At once, Herr Oberführer! You ordered no unnecessary lights to be shown near the train, Herr Oberführer. May I take it the order is changed?'

'You may take it the order is changed. And go quickly. I don't want any trouble here.'

The clap of heels indicated a salute and then the rapid steps of the adjutant's disappearance. The group shuffled uncomfortably about, once one of them stepped inside the long hall, and his heels rang on the cement floor.

'It seems to be empty,' he said in a slightly effeminate voice.

'If it is these bloody people really are sub-human,' replied the brigadier with savage irony. 'It's a positive invitation to them to slip away from the train.' There was a ripple of sycophantic laughter and the effeminate voice said, 'Of course, most of them are women.'

'I can't imagine what gives you the impression that women are less resourceful than men, my dear Fabian. That has not been my experience with the other sex, not in the slightest.'

'I don't suppose Fabian knows as much about women as you do, Herr Oberführer!' said a fresh voice, and there was another burst of laughter, this time louder, the relieved laughter of juniors who have succeeded in placating an annoyed senior.

'A nuisance that all these coaches don't have shutters,' said the Oberführer's voice. 'Are you sure the blinds have all been secured with boards, and nailed inside? We don't want this load of rubbish opening the blinds and attracting attention to themselves.'

'Oh, yes, Herr Oberführer,' the obsequious official hastened to answer. 'My men put up the shutters as far as they went this afternoon, and the other coaches are all nailed over the blinds. We would have shuttered all the coaches, but there are not many of these old coaches left with shutters. If I might suggest, though ...'

'What? What do you want to suggest? If you've got something sensible to say, say it, man!'

'Yes, sir. I was going to say. In future it might be a good thing – if we knew in time – to paste stout paper over the outside of the windows, beforehand ... It's only a suggestion ...'

'Not a bad idea – if we use this sort of coach again.' The group seemed to move about restlessly. Then the same voice said, 'We'll go and check the numbers over in the office, while we are waiting. No point wasting further time here ... No, don't you come. The Scharführer will need you to show him over these thrice-damned sheds when he comes. Wait for him here. Come on Fabian, let's go.'

'We shall be back in about half an hour,' said the effeminate voice, evidently addressing the unfortunate official of the railway. 'Mind the sheds are properly inspected.'

After a few moments Kerenyi thought he could hear the footsteps of the railwayman moving away with the hesitating step of a man hanging about waiting. He must be walking up and down, thought Kerenyi. He would have to take a chance or be found here by the SS men who must come up at any moment.

He slipped out of the tall doors. He had been wrong, the official had only walked as far as the edge of the ramp and was trying, his back to Kerenyi, to peer into the nearest coach, round the edge of the fastened blind. The train itself was in absolute darkness, and from it came the hum and stir of many hundreds of people close together. Now that he was out in the open, Kerenyi could hear that many voices wept and wailed in a curious rhythm, almost singing together in an undertone. This wailing murmur reminded Kerenyi, though it was not in the least like it, of the soft chanting of monks at the monastery of the Jesuits where he had been at school in his boyhood. Kerenyi was not an atheist, but a blasphemist who hated the church and God, and the sensation of enraged frustration connected with his schooldays and their discipline rose in him for the first time for many years. Kerenyi stepped cautiously sideways, keeping his face to the peering man.

He had moved several yards when the man turned suddenly, tired of his useless attempt at voyeurism. He saw Kerenyi at once, and Kerenyi moved forward quickly.

'I didn't see you there,' he said sharply. The man looked, in the dim light, to be about fifty, a little bent, with a lined face. He stiffened at Kerenyi's tone and then a look of stupid cunning crossed his face.

'Oh, no, you don't' he said. 'You don't belong to them.'

'I've come over from the Kai,' said Kerenyi, ignoring the man's suspicion. 'There's been a couple of mistakes and one or two people are on the transport that should not be. Foreign passports. Can you take me through the train? Or do I have to wait for the Oberführer to come back? He's such a bad-tempered devil – I'd rather get it over without him shouting at me.'

The railway official moved forward so that he could see Kerenyi's face clearly in one of the shaded lamps dimly burning over the ramp.

'Go through the train?' he said. 'You can't do that. Have you any idea how full it is? You'd never get through the corridors. There must be thousands of 'em.' He came closer and peered up into Kerenyi's stony face.

'You're not from the Kai,' he said angrily. 'You haven't even got a hat. If you are from there, show me your pass.'

'Come on, man,' said Kerenyi impatiently. 'Don't let's have any more trouble. He's been chivvying us for days already.' This last with a jerk of his head in the direction in which the SS officers had disappeared.

The man shook his head. He was quite sure now of his rightness. There was something in Kerenyi's face that convinced him that this stranger did not come from Gestapo headquarters.

'Now, what are you up to?' he asked reasonably. 'You don't belong with them, I can see that.' He now jerked his head towards the loaded train with its wailing burden. 'And you don't come from the Kai, either.'

Without knowing he was going to, Kerenyi told the truth.

'I've got to get somebody off that train,' he said. 'She has a for-eign passport, and ...' he could not get the words out. 'Give me

393

your keys,' he growled. He moved towards the smaller man, who withdrew sharply.

'Give me the keys, or I'll throttle you with my bare hands.'

The man was staring up at Kerenyi's rigid face. His look changed from fear and anger to a kind of understanding. Kerenyi thought, now I've got him. Then they both heard the approach of a squad of troops. Their heads turned together.

'Quick,' said the older man. 'If they see you we're both for it. Come with me. Quick.'

He caught Kerenyi's arm, and as if his will had left him, Kerenyi went with him. They ran softly down the ramp, jumped off its end and the man, pulling at Kerenyi's arm, turned round the end of the block and across an open space in the total darkness. They ducked past a line of empty trucks smelling of fish, across rails. Kerenyi stopped, hesitating, and tried to look about him.

'Come on,' whispered the man desperately. 'You'll be safe in my office and I'll come back when I can and get you.'

'But if they inspect all this area . . . ?'

'They won't. The gates have all been locked for hours and there is no night-shift. Only the dispatchers up there – see?' He raised his arm towards a lighted square some distance away, that seemed to hang up in the darkness. 'The nightwatchmen have all been sent away, in case they see anything.'

'I daren't go so far away,' said Kerenyi wildly. 'How can I trust you?'

'You can't,' said the older man with sudden shrewdness, 'but if they get you now, what do you think your chances are?'

'You're right,' muttered Kerenyi, and in a monotonous undertone he began to curse a cruel God and all His creation. They were beside a low wooden hut of several rooms, and the railwayman unlocked a door, and beckoned Kerenyi inside.

'Quick,' he hissed again. 'I've got to get back there.'

Kerenyi slipped inside the door and before he could recover his balance from an unexpected step, the door slammed shut behind him and he heard the key grind in the lock. He could see nothing in the total darkness. He stood still, feeling the thunder of his labouring heart, which had begun to hurt with a dull jab that ran up under his left arm. It seemed a long time before he could make out dimly what was around him. Then he knew that the railway-man had betrayed him, for this was no office. He made out shelves, and with his hand could feel large tins of some sort, per-haps paint. It was some kind of store-house for equipment. There must be light somewhere. Kerenyi began to explore the sides of the door for a switch. At last he found it, but when he turned it, nothing happened.

He moved cautiously away from the door. His hands out in front of him, he moved forwards. It seemed to be clear in the middle, and he took another, longer, step and slammed into a pile of crates. Kerenyi staggered as one of the crates hit his right arm, and clutched wildly to his left. He came up against another rack of shelves, and his flailing hand brushed against a large empty can that fell with a mad clatter. Something shifted and as Kerenyi tried again to right himself, a heavy object from a shelf above caught him on the temple. He fell instantly, knocked out for a moment, and before he could save himself, was among the crates on his hands and knees. One, unsteadily balanced, fell heavily and hit the back of his head.

When he came to himself Kerenyi had no idea what had hap-pened nor where he was in this black hole. As he cautiously moved a sharp pang of pain shot through his head, and a crate shifted scraping on the cement floor. The store shed came back, the slammed door, the fall. He did not know how long he had lain there.

He got slowly to his knees, and shook his head to clear it, but the sharp pain made him retch. Somehow he managed to get into a sitting posture and his head sank on to his doubled knees. The reason for his being there came back to him as the pain in his head receded, and he was assailed by a deadly weariness and despair that paralysed him, he did not know for how long. He could not think nor move; only the brute fact that he could do nothing was in his consciousness.

Ruth was not even married to him, but to an unknown Italian who had returned silently to his own country. If Kerenyi claimed the unborn child as his, its fate and the fate of its mother were even more totally certain, supposing that to be possible, than they were now. Not for the first time was Kerenyi's Austrian citizenship a drawback to him; he should have stayed Hungarian ... These were not thoughts, but memories, often gone over in his mind in the months since he knew that Ruth was pregnant. As a Hungarian he could have married her, taken her to Hungary, saved her.

After a long time he began to move his hands, trying to locate the fallen boxes and cans. Then, cautiously he got down on his knees again and began to crawl about, feeling his way before him with one hand raised. It took a long time to discover that the shelving went all round the enclosed space, except for the doorway. The door was of wood, he could feel that, but ironbound and very stout. The lock did not even rattle when he pushed on the door. He pulled himself to his feet against the door, and began to feel over its surface and over the framework round it. The wood smelled of creosote faintly, a coaly smell. There was not the smallest area of breaking or rotten timber in it. The idea of burning it came to him, but he had rushed out of the house without thinking of matches or cigarette lighter.

The pain in his heart began to frighten him; he was afraid of collapsing and this fear made the bruised and cut head unimportant. The black dark and closeness of the store seemed to be leaning in on him. He began to scratch with his nails, senselessly, at the wood of the door. Presently he began to shout and as his own voice echoed dully about his ears, to weep aloud.

'Oh, God,' he groaned aloud. 'Do you mean to kill the whole world and send me mad? I've got to get out of here. I've got to get out of here. Let me out! Let me out!'

When he paused in his shouting the deathly quiet drove him to begin again, and after a time his voice began to crack and weaken and he started to bang with his fists on the door and to try to shake it by pulling on the lock-handle.

Kerenyi was not a man of his hands and could not even change an electric fuse without help; it was a long time before it occurred to him that he might find, among the stores on the shelves, some instrument he could use as a lever against the stubborn lock. He began again, very slowly, his round of the store, feeling among the piled boxes and tins for an iron box-opener or a pair of pliers or grips such as he vaguely knew must be used by storemen. Whether such tools were there or not he never discovered, but he did not find them. Exhausted with his own despair, he moved back to the door and, pulling himself up again, leaned against it, no longer battering it, but crying weakly with his face against the unyielding wood.

Very slowly and faintly the black dark lessened, and at last he could see slight cracks round the rim of the door. It was dawn. Soon after that he heard footsteps approaching the hut, and then the grind of the key in the lock. No doubt afraid of Kerenyi, the railwayman had not come to open the door himself, but had sent one of the ragged Polish workmen. The heavy door swung outward, and Kerenyi was staring into the scared eyes of a thin, shivering boy. The boy said nothing; he gave one look at Kerenyi's face and began to back away. After a few steps he stumbled over an uneven stone and then turned and ran as fast as he could.

It was cold outside. Kerenyi shivered, blinking in the dawn light. The sun was just coming up. He began to stagger forwards, not knowing where he was going, and broke into a stumbling run. Somewhere he could hear the ring of iron hammers on metal; a voice called. Kerenyi turned towards the voice, but found himself in an alley between wooden huts that reminded him, in his half-conscious state, of the market stalls. Outside one of the huts, in a little free patch, some workman had sown a packet of flower seeds and in the slanting rays of the new sun, glinting with gossamer and the clouded dew of a slight frost, there grew a group of late asters. They flaunted their purposeless gaudy beauty of many colours like a living mockery. Kerenyi stood, swaying, and stared at them for a time, unable to harness his tired mind to his will. Then he set off again, and this time was able to remember roughly the direction in which he had been led the night before. He retraced his steps out of the alleyway and found an open space across which ran a diagonal side rail, and some way off he could see the long shape of the disused customs sheds. He shambled forward, but at the end of the sheds his courage failed and he had to stop and rest for a moment, leaning against the stone base of the sheds. Then he made his way slowly round the end of the building, where he could see the ramp and the rails glinting emptily in the morning light, the frosty rime already melting into drops of water in the grass roots between the unused and slightly rusted rails.

He had known the train would be gone, and now he wandered on, as if nothing urgent had brought him to this place. He never knew how he left the goods yards; hours later he found himself some miles away in a completely strange part of the city where he had never been before, surrounded on all sides by tall newish blocks of brick tenements. It was almost noon. He asked a passer-by, a woman with a shopping bag, where the nearest tram stop was, and did not notice that she was frightened by his look. Neither did he notice the way the tram conductor looked suspiciously at him, as if he might be drunk or mad.

There was nobody about in the entry or on the stairs. Kerenyi let himself into his flat and fell heavily on to his bed. It was not until the next morning, when his old charwoman came, that he regained consciousness. He came out into the passage, and found himself stumbling and swaying. The old woman turned, and a look of utter horror came into her face; she put up a trembling hand and crossed herself. Her eyes were red with weeping and she leaned for support against the hall cupboard where only the morning before she had searched for Ruth's raincoat and shopping basket. Kerenyi stared at her blankly for a moment, and then, stupidly, puzzled, turned to look in the discoloured glass of the hall mirror. His face seemed to have sunk into itself, making the big nose more prominent than ever, and his hair was streaked with grey.

2

They had been wrangling for over an hour in the rehearsal room, and the atmosphere was acrid with all the past and present disputes of everyone present.

'You are changing the entire balance of the play, my dear fellow,' said Walter Harich for the twentieth time, and took another cigarette.

'For God's sake stop smoking, Wally,' groaned Hansi. 'You know Julie has a cold.'

'Can't we get back to the point at issue and discuss it sensibly,' suggested Jochen Thorn. 'It seems to me ...'

'I don't recall asking how it seems to you,' snapped Hansi. 'You have only been here a month or so and haven't the least idea yet how we work.'

'I've been here over a year now,' replied Thorn equably. 'And since I am old enough to have been taught by Max Reinhardt himself, I don't feel that you have all that much to tell me about my trade, Ostrovsky.'

The name of Reinhardt made Hansi look swiftly over his shoulder.

'Let's leave Reinhardt out of it,' said Julie wearily. 'He isn't to the point. Let's go back to the author. The first time we played *Elisabeth von England*, Brückner himself was at the rehearsals, and the way he saw his play is the way we ought to play it. If we make her into a monster – Elisabeth I mean – the whole point of the play is lost.'

'Nobody cares about the play any more,' said Harich bitterly, and threw away his cigarette, still burning, into a waste-basket. 'What Hansi hasn't told us yet is that half the Party bosses from Berlin will be here at the opening night. That is the point.'

'The wastepaper-basket is on fire,' said Julie. 'You'll get arrested for sabotage if the theatre burns down, Wally.'

Harich stared moodily into the little flame curling up from the metal tub. He reached past Julie and took a mug half full of cold coffee from a stool and threw it with the mug into the basket, making a flurry of smoke and burnt paper scraps rise into the stuffy room. Hansi pushed himself off the edge of a table on which he had been leaning and took the round box to the door to put it outside. His long-suffering silence irritated the actors more than another outburst of temper would have done, and they looked at each other, assessing their own determination.

'The stage manager wants to set the stage to-morrow for this scene,' began Hansi again. 'Provisionally, of course. Have they finished with your skirts, Julie? We can at least get the positions right.'

'The frame went two days ago to be altered. It must be ready, I should think.' She sounded quite indifferent. Hansi made a motion of his head at his assistant, who stood silently to one side, and the youngster went quickly out. There was a gloomy silence.

'That noise!' said Julie suddenly. Through the half-open door came the sound of a piano thumping and the rhythmic tread of trainees rehearsing a dance.

'Dancing practice, that's all. They sound like cart-horses.' Thorn shut the door with a bang and Julie jumped, twitching her brows together.

'I didn't mean that. The wailing noise, I mean. Can't you hear it?'

They all listened. From a distance, outside the building, came a metallic wail of sirens, rising and falling.

'More practising,' said Hansi, trying a nervous joke. 'It's the air-raid sirens.'

'Are you sure they are practising?' asked a young actress who had not spoken for a long time. She sat with her long, silky hair falling over a high brow, which she raised now sharply from the support of her hand. The sirens faded into silence. There was no sound of aeroplanes, nor of gun-fire. The girl looked round the room at the faces of the others, all older than herself. Then she went back to studying her part as if they were not there.

Julie began to walk about the large, gauntly lighted room, holding her upper arms with her crossed hands and frowning. There had never yet been an attack on the city and it was generally agreed – in Vienna – that the ancient and beautiful town would be respected by all the combatants, but the thought of Franz on the fourth floor and unable to take shelter in the cellars with the other inhabitants if there should be an air-raid tugged at her nerves with a fresh fear. As her year-long habit now was, Julie changed internal fear almost instantly into a deceitful but practical matter of the moment. The three men, and in particular Hansi Ostrovsky who had known her longest, were unaware of what made the subtle change in Julie's manner; they were not even aware that they registered this change for it had grown gradually into the fabric of their companionship of work. But it produced, in its repetition whenever she thought of Franz, an inevitable thread of something mysterious and unspoken into their close friendship. This something was more obvious to Jochen Thorn who had known Julie for only a year, than it was to the other two men who had grown up with her.

She stopped abruptly with unconscious effectiveness, in front of the sloping skylight window and turned towards Hansi, staring moodily at the floor.

'All right,' she said. 'I'll play it the way you want it. No, Wally. We are letting ourselves into this nationalism by drawing the line with Brückner's play. We made no protests when *Merchant of Venice* was changed about. Nor when the Josefstadt put on *Three Sisters* as a bunch of cretins and made a circus act out of the play. We take up *Elisabeth* because it is a German play, not because it is being falsified. I'll make Elisabeth into a dirty old goat, if that's the way we see her now ... Why not, after all?'

Harich's handsome face flushed about the cheekbones and he stuck his jaw out.

'Neither of us was in the production of *Merchant*,' he said angrily. 'How was that any business of ours? And as for the Josefstadt – they are a bunch of clowns lately, anyhow ...'

'I'm tired,' said Julie, interrupting him. She turned away and stared out of the dirty window over roofs and browning trees already showing their winter bones. 'I'm too tired to care any more. I've hardly slept for days and the more sleeping tablets I take the worse it gets. I just dream more clearly, as if I weren't asleep, with the same things going on in my mind that go on when I'm awake.'

There was silence. Then Hansi shifted his feet, scraping them on the boarded floor.

'Have you seen him?' he asked abruptly, in an undertone.

'No. He won't answer the door or the telephone. I pushed a note under the door, but of course he hasn't answered it.'

The blonde girl lifted her head again from her text.

'Do you think he's dead?' she said with the brutality of youth.

'Georgy? Commit suicide? No, poor devil, he's not that sort.' Harich hunched his shoulders as if he were cold.

'Somebody will have to pay for all this,' said Hansi quietly. 'I cannot believe that anybody – any power – can get away with this sort of thing.'

'Pay? No, no, my boy!' Harich laughed loudly in his histrionic way. 'They'll get away with this too, you'll see. They are going to win – that is the fact we have never faced. The Wehrmacht is outside Moscow now. Leningrad is almost surrounded, and this morning's papers describe the drive towards the southern oilfields. This madman Hitler is a genius and he's going to rule the world. As soon as Moscow is taken, the Americans will start to negotiate with Berlin. They'll want to be in on the trade. Then the British will have to give in.'

'I suppose we shall all be rich, then,' said the blonde girl. 'At least that's what my father says. He's joined the Party.'

'We can't win,' said Hansi. 'Even if Moscow is taken, how can we hold those vast spaces ...'

'That's a fallacy, Hansi,' said Thorn, unfolding a short cigar from a paper wrapper which crackled. 'Austrians are always stunned by the Russians. Partly no doubt because Napoleon beat them but couldn't beat the Russians ... and partly because of the last War. In fact the Russians themselves invaded and colonised the spaces, and the Swedes owned large tracts of what is now Russia for generations. From what I hear from my brother, the Ukrainians and Russians in the occupied areas actually rush into the arms of the German troops when their towns are taken. They're so glad to get rid of the Bolsheviks they'd welcome the devil himself.'

He clipped the end of the cigar with a little pocket knife and threw the scrap of tobacco on the floor. 'I don't see why we can't hold western Russia,' he said, feeling for matches. 'If we treat the people only a little better than their late masters did. And, for God's sake, why not? The war would be over and we could all relax. Everybody would be better off, including the Russians and the Poles.'

'Everybody except ... ' Julie bit off the word. 'But even that would taper off, if the war were over ... Ah, God, if only it were over!' Her face, raised a little towards the window, did not alter by a muscle, but tears began to slide over it which she made no attempt to hide. The men looked away, ashamed; only the young actress stared with frightened curiosity as people stare at a street accident.

'If only it were over,' Julie whispered, 'and I could get him out.'

The silence was broken by the return of Ostrovsky's assistant, followed by the sewer and the dresser, Lotte, who carried a wide wire frame for Queen Elisabeth's farthingale. Julie took no notice of them. She stood with her feet apart like a man, her arms still folded, the stream of tears running over her cheeks.

'Go away,' whispered Hansi hastily, waving his stubby hand. 'We'll leave it until to-morrow.'

'No, no,' said Julie, turning. 'Give me a handkerchief, Hansi. Let's get it done with.' It was Lotte who gave her the handkerchief and Julie wiped her face and blew her nose. Then she pushed her hands through her untidy hair, forcing it back off her brow in a movement that showed the drawn tautness of the strained muscles.

Lotte looked from her to Hansi who gave an imperceptible

nod, and the woman began to open the metal fasteners in the front of the wire frame. They took it to Julie and folded it about her and the boy kneeled to do up the fasteners again. When they had finished they stood back, not looking at her face. Still holding the handkerchief in her palm, Julie shook herself, moved a few steps, bent to one side and the other and then sat down on the stool where the coffee mug had stood.

'Yes, it's better now,' she said calmly. 'But the waist bones still stick into me a little. Do you think you can pad them, Lotte? Or should they be cut shorter?'

'If we cut them the frame will slip down,' said the assistant, speaking for the first time.

'I'll pad them with tape at the ends,' said the tailor, bending down with a creak of her own heavy corseting to release Julie from the frame. 'And perhaps I can mount a soft leather belt inside, to hold your waist, gnae' Frau. It would sit easier then.'

'That's a good idea,' said Hansi quickly, 'why didn't we think of that before?'

'I went and had a look at the real ones in the Costume Museum,' explained the sewer. 'They have a sort of leather waistband to them.'

'I can't remember having this trouble with the frames before,' and Julie. 'Were they made differently last time, Lotte?'

'No, gnae' Frau,' said Lotte grimly. 'This is the same frame you used last time. But you've lost a lot of weight since then, and you feel the wires more. Then you wore it with just a slip-string through the waist bones.'

Julie left, and the young actress followed her out. Hansi said, 'Give me one of your cigars, Thorn? Let's go and have some beer, eh, Wally?'

'Good idea,' said Harich. Thorn picked up his text from the table, dropping loose papers out of the cover. He bent down to pick them up, and as he crouched towards the floor, he spoke, his voice slightly muffled.

'Strange woman, Julie. I don't quite understand how she feels about this Kerenyi business. You would think she'd have been jealous of this poor little wretch of a Jewess. Wouldn't you?'

'How do you know she wasn't jealous?' asked Walter Harich, striking a match for Hansi.

'Well, she can't be or she wouldn't be so broken up over Kerenyi's loss. Didn't you hear her say if the war were over she'd get him out of the country?'

He had his papers now and stood upright, his face a little flushed from bending.

The three men, two of them strikingly handsome, and Hansi with his thin bony face and untidy hair already thinning back from his forehead, stood looking cautiously at each other.

'Or do you think perhaps she wasn't speaking of Kerenyi?' said Thorn softly. 'I heard a rumour . . .'

Hansi moved jerkily, his eyes shifting swiftly to Harich. 'Let's go and have that beer,' he said, too loudly.

'And talk about something else,' said Harich turning towards the doorway. There was nobody there.

The taxi was nearly at her home when Julie changed her mind and told the man to go to the 8th District instead. She asked him to wait in the narrow street and went slowly up the winding stair to Kerenyi's door. This was the third time she had tried. There was another man standing outside the door, a man with a broad, ugly face and stocky solidity of figure. Like all big-city people, Julie had an instant classification system for strangers and knew at once that he was a policeman. The man turned and looked at her, his calculating look changing slightly as he recognised her. He spoke in an accent that Julie thought of as Berlin, though in fact Blaschke came from country far to the east of the Reichshauptstadt.

'I'm afraid there is no one there, gnädige Frau. I've rung the bell three times.'

'Perhaps he has gone away,' she said vaguely. It was half dark in the hallway. The feeling of weary dizziness that overcame Julie was so strong that she blinked swiftly to clear her head, and leaned with one hand on the door-frame of varnished wood. She was about to tap on the panel and call out to Kerenyi, in case he was inside and listening; her knuckles were almost on the wood when it occurred to her that she did not know what this man wanted.

'You had better go away,' she said loudly. 'If Dr Kerenyi is there he won't want to see a stranger.'

Then a new thought struck her tired mind labouring with its weariness.

'Have you come to arrest him?' she said.

'Arrest? No. There is no charge against him – that I know of.'

'Does that count nowadays?' said Julie contemptuously.

The man thought. 'That is treasonable,' he said at last. 'A most unwise thing to say.'

'You'd better go away,' said Julie again, hardly listening to him. Then, as he turned to go down the stair, she thought of something.

'Perhaps you have news? Is that why you came? Have you something to tell him?'

The man shook his head. 'I thought he might have some news for me,' he said. This penetrated to Julie's veiled consciousness as a piece of monstrous cynicism, but all Blaschke meant by it was the faint hope that Kerenyi had succeeded in tracing Ruth; he knew what Julie did not know, that Kerenyi had been trailing from one official to the next throughout the last days trying with increasing desperation to get someone to listen to his story of a foreigner wrongly rounded up, trying to find out where Ruth's lawful husband now was. Neither the Italian consulate nor anybody else was disposed to intervene; almost everyone was prepared to overlook the obvious reason for Kerenyi's despair but that pretence of naïveté was as much as anyone would risk.

'If you do see him,' said the man, his thick hand already holding the wooden rail clamped to the stair wall, 'try to persuade him to stop trying. He can't achieve anything and may get himself into trouble. And tell him – perhaps you will be so good? Tell him I am being transferred to Agram. He will know ...'

When the sound of the man's descent had quite gone, Julie began to tap quietly on the apartment door, leaning her shoulder against it, and acutely aware of the graining of the varnished wood. She stood on her toes and tried to look into a spy-hole set rather high in one panel; but the little round glass was covered. It was not like the one on her own door, a square cut in the panel masked by a curly pattern in pressed brass and covered by a tiny door that could be opened inside. This one was made like a lens so that from outside nothing could be seen even if the cover were open inside, except whether or not a light was burning in the hallway. She could not even tell if the cover was closed or whether the hallway was just dark. Kerenyi might be looking out at her from his shadowy fastness. This thought made her begin to cry again, and she wept helplessly and silently, leaning on the door, for quite a long time.

Even the sound of dragging footsteps on the stairs did not recall her to the need to behave conventionally in public which was so strong a strand in Julie's normal consciousness. It was not until he addressed her that she realised it was Kerenyi who stood behind her.

'Let's open the door,' he said, his voice muffled and hoarse as if he had a bad cold. It did not seem strange to Julie and she stood aside, wiping the tears off her face with her hands while Kerenyi unlocked the door and gave her a push on the elbow so that she went before him into the study where Kerenyi lowered himself carefully into his heavy writing-chair by its arm-rests. The leather seat creaked slightly. It was half dark in the room; one of the shutters was pulled over the window. Julie was scrabbling in her bag for a handkerchief. She found one, blew her nose and pushed her hands through her hair as she had done in the rehearsal room. Kerenyi sat still, his hands slack on the arm-rests, and his head bowed. She could see him now, properly, and the deadened shell of his head took away her power of speech. She moved very carefully, like one who finds himself suddenly in the presence of death. He was very dirty, it was clear that if he had slept at all in the last days it was in his clothes. When she found the strength to get up at last and go past him to the big cupboard, she could smell his sweat.

'That bottle is empty,' he said in the slow, hoarse voice, knowing what she was looking for. 'Get another, will you? In the kitchen.'

He got his *barack* direct from the distiller in Kecskemet. She found the case of bottles easily enough and brought one in, even remembering the corkscrew and glasses. When she pushed the glass into his hand he stared at it dully, having evidently forgotten what he had just said. But the rough apricot smell reminded him and he lifted the glass carefully, steadying one hand with the other. Julie drank and though the spirit was pungent on her throat and its powerful fumes rose into her nose, she felt her head clear after a moment.

'What are you going to do?' she said at last.

He lifted his head then, and looked at her. To see her he had to screw up his eyes and peer, but when she made a move to get up he said quickly, 'No, leave the shutter alone. The light bothers me.' He paused then as if to rest.

'A friend of mine – you wouldn't know him, he used to be one of the compositors at the *Independent* – suggested I should offer myself as an army reporter for the East Front. They can't get journalists to go, apparently. I could move about a good deal – it's quite a good idea. An old chum of his is in Poland now, working on one of the Wehrmacht report teams and he's going to get him on the army line to-night and find out the names to use. Then when I volunteer the unit chief can ask for me at once, and I can get into the General Gouvernement area.' He stopped and took another drink. 'What was I saying . . . ? Oh, yes. Extraordinary people, printers – always know how to get things done. This fellow still manages to keep in touch with trade unionists in England and America through Switzerland. He says the Wehrmacht reporters have a good deal of freedom of movement in practice – not officially, of course.'

'But what do you think . . . ? What can you do, Georgy?'

He stared for a moment, not understanding her ignorance. 'I might find her,' he explained.

After a while she left him sitting there. Franz had not been mentioned.

Julie had forgotten the taxi driver, but he was still waiting for her. He grumbled all the way back to the Schellinggasse, about the loss of earnings entailed in waiting hours for women fares who never knew what they wanted, and to appease him Julie doubled his fare with a large tip on top.

Fina was waiting, and had evidently been coming out into the hall every time she heard the lift, for some time.

'He knows about the arrests,' she whispered without preamble.

Julie stared at the round face, aghast.

'How did that happen?' she whispered back.

'Pichler was up here and I couldn't stop the old devil talking and Herr Doctor was standing behind the door.'

'What did Pichler want?' asked Julie sharply, the unreliability of the doorman piercing for a moment her misty estrangement.

'New air-raid precautions. He's left a paper – official. I put it on the desk for you to see. We're not allowed to store coal or coke any more and all sorts of other things.'

'To hell with that,' said Julie. 'You tell Pichler to-morrow to remember who pays his wages. If he doesn't want the job, my dresser's husband would like it very much.' Her voice returned to its cautious whisper. 'Where is he now?'

'He's gone to his room.'

Fina followed Julie down the hall on the pretext of showing her the new regulations, but in fact because she did not want to be left alone. Julie picked up the yellowish official form, glanced at the first words and threw it down again.

'Rubbish,' she said to herself. 'Of course we have to store coal.' Fina sighed heavily, but made no other answer. 'Sit down, my poor Fina. You look about as wretched as I feel.' She put her hand on Fina's thick shoulder, noticing how fat the once muscular body was getting, and the streaks of iron grey in the tight dark hair.

'You've been crying, gnae' Frau,' said Fina at last.

Julie put a hand up to her face. 'They caught Doctor Kerenyi's girl in the round-up. He is quite broken. You wouldn't recognise him.' Even at this moment Julie remembered not to mention who Kerenyi's girl was for she had never said a word at home about Ruth's return to Vienna.'

'You've seen him, then?' Fina glanced up. 'He hasn't been to see Herr Doctor for a week now. I thought it must be ... He used to talk to me about the baby coming, thinking it would shock me, you know.' Fina's sad round face showed a fugitive smile for a second. 'What do you think will happen to it, now?' It was clear she had no real idea of what the round-up meant.

'From the little I've heard, I should think they are both already dead,' answered Julie in that harsh, crude tone that she assumed more and more often lately. 'Kerenyi won't have it, of course. He thinks he can find her again.'

Fina's face took on a waxy pallor and she raised a trembling hand to cross herself and began to whisper prayers.

'What do they do to them? Where do they go?' she asked, breaking into the muttered prayer and then going on again with it.

'I don't know. Nobody seems to know. There is some kind of settlement in Poland where they are sent. But that's only a rumour.' She considered for a moment, then she added harshly, 'A ghetto, I suppose. Yes, a ghetto.'

Fina glanced sharply sideways at the door in the panelling that led to the dining-room. She always heard Franz long before Julie did, no matter how silently he moved. Now she gave a quick jerk of her head to indicate his approach, and got up from the chair where she had seated herself.

'I'm getting so rheumatic,' she said complainingly, 'my back hurts all the time.'

From his illness, over a year before, Franz had never recovered. He moved now only slowly, leaning his slight frame on a stout walking-stick with a heavily padded ferrule which appeared to give him a crooked gait, bent towards the right. He stepped only where carpets lay, to avoid making sounds loud enough to be heard from the apartment underneath and since he resisted with what little energy was left to him the slightest change in the layout of his home, this gave his progress an erratic and roundabout way-wardness. Fina and Julie had tried, long since, to alter the arrangement of carpets and furniture to give him more ease, but his uncomplaining distress quickly taught them not to interfere, and everything was moved back into the position it formerly occupied. Like all prisoners, he made of his life a minute routine in which every moment and every object was exactly regulated; and so refined had his nervous consciousness of his prison become that a clock left unwound one day over its time was audible to him from the slight irregularity of its tick. Fear seemed to have left him, its place taken by the infinite repetition of detailed habits that had come to have a magical quality; and not only for himself. So long as everything was done as it had been done before, all would be well. The breakage of an old crock used for milk in the kitchen was an event of menacing purport both to Franz and to Fina, and when some such small accident did occur Fina would for days spend her meagre free time searching for a replacement, in shops already showing shortages and lacks in their stocks, which should be exactly like the object broken or worn to uselessness.

Julie sat still as Franz came through the door in the panelling that led to the dining-room; he always came into the living-room by this way, avoiding the front hall. He did not like to be helped, maintaining little courtesies to Julie as they had always been and ignoring his own weakness. At the door he turned, leaning on the stick, and with his left hand closed the panelled door with delicate quietness and slowness, so that no sound was made. This matter of sounds had long since become part of the ritual of their lives and none of them noticed it any more, though it was carried to quite unnecessary lengths,

'How good to be home,' said Julie. 'Come and sit down and talk to me, Franzl ...'

She reached him her hand and he bent his bowed shoulders still further to kiss it, and then seated himself with great care in the big 'English' arm-chair which always stood by hers for his 'visits' as he called them.

'I heard you come in,' he said in his very quiet, delicate voice. 'It was a long rehearsal to-day. You must be tired, my dearest. You ought to have a rest, you aren't looking yourself.'

'I am very tired. But that doesn't matter. I've just seen Georgy and that upset me. His girl, you see ...' she gathered her voice together, for it had to come out. 'His girl, who was living with him, was in the round-up the other morning.'

'I heard Pichler talking to Fina about it,' he said as if the round-up had no possible connection with himself. 'And I wondered then about Georgy's girl ... but he explained to me some time ago that she had a foreign passport?'

The identity of Georgy's girl, having not been admitted when Ruth first returned to Vienna, had now become a taboo and Julie had almost forgotten, or persuaded herself she had forgotten, what their original relationship was.

'It all went so fast, Georgy couldn't find her in time. They had it very well organised, it seems. Before he could get through the red tape, the train pulled out.' She rested her aching head on one hand and sighed unconsciously. 'We found her an Italian husband, you see. I expect Georgy told you? But when it came to the point, we found he'd gone back to Milan some months ago. It's the sort of detail one just doesn't think of.' She raised her head and looked round the long room wearily.

'Where have they gone? Did Georgy manage to find out?'

'Somewhere in this Polish area – what is it called, I saw something in a headline ... ?'

'Poor Georgy,' Franz whispered. 'Is there nothing we can do for him?'

'He talks of joining up – in the army reporting teams, or something. I don't think they'll take him; he looks ... ' She got up restlessly, and went over to the window to stare out. She had to keep reminding herself that Franz was officially dead; nobody would come seeking him any more. His name was on no list, there was no record of his existence, his personal papers and passport had been burned by Julie after Lehmann had achieved his official death. He did not exist, and yet he was. His own uncanny detachment, as if the transportation were only a personal tragedy for Kerenyi, increased the unreality of the atmosphere, and for a short space Julie was seized by an intense irritation at his unjustified confidence, his estrangement from what might be happening to hundreds of his fellow beings. To hide her feelings, she turned to the window, telling herself that she should be grateful for his protective unworldliness.

She did not notice how closely Franz was looking at her nor at once hear the change in his voice when he spoke, after a silence.

'So Georgy will be going away, then?'

Julie was staring diagonally down from the window into the street, where the pearly shadows of a frosty late afternoon were gathering. In the street, opposite, stood an open coal truck drawn by two heavy Hanover horses and a coal heaver in his bucket hood went and pushed one of the bells outside the double house doors. Julie was unconscious of remembering, she felt only the return of some, as yet only threatening portent, that connected backwards through her unrecalled reveries of years before, with her father's illness and death. With a shudder of dark fear as if she had received a warning, she turned sharply from the window and was reassured by brilliant crimson dahlias standing in the Meissen vase.

'We aren't supposed to store coal,' she said vaguely, half aloud, 'but I suppose nobody keeps the regulations any more than we shall ...'

'They won't take Georgy in the army, Franzl,' she said as she came back to her chair. 'He looks suddenly like an old man.' Then she saw his eyes and it struck her that she must prevent Georgy going away from Franz. At once she said aloud, 'Krassny and Nando must do something. I'll get after them to-night. They must find out, at any rate where she is, and get hold of her husband in Milan. Make him do something.' She had no sooner seated herself than she got up again. 'I'll go and call Nando now, in the office.'

'Who is Nando?' asked Franz as she turned to go. 'Can he do something?'

'A friend,' she said from the doorway, 'in Krassny's department. He's a sort of cousin of poor Frau Pohaisky's.'

'Nando?' Julie said when his voice answered. 'What are you doing this evening? I want to talk to you. Oh, good, if you're eating at the Pohaiskys', I can come after for coffee. Will you let her know, or shall I ring up? Will there be many people? The brother-in-law — you mean that judge? That's a bore, can we get rid of him? ... Yes, I suppose they will.' Nando had said the former judge would probably leave early.

He was right. Julie was in the drawing-room, full of renaissance furniture that made it like a museum, for only half an hour when the retired judge and his wife began exchanging glances and a few

413

minutes later they left to walk home. Julie did not ask after Alois Pohaisky as long as they were present, but as she heard the maid close the outer door she at once did so.

'How is Doctor Alois?' she asked abruptly. Nando, gone to see the others out, returned to sit down by her and asked permission, by raising his eyebrows, to smoke.

'I went down to see him last week. His rheumatism is getting worse, but Isabella says it will improve when the real winter starts. It's quite true, it is always worst in spring and autumn.'

Isabella was Nando's mother, Frau Pohaisky's cousin.

'How are they all? I haven't been home for ages,' asked Nando.

'They seem well, but ... ' Frau Pohaisky glanced at Julie. 'Since two sons of a neighbour's family were killed – what, Nando – you hadn't heard?'

'Clothilde's brothers?' said Julie. 'Two of them?'

'Last week. One in Russia, somewhere near Moscow I gathered. And the other was in the Luftwaffe, he is missing over the English Channel. It has upset Lali very much. She's afraid Otto Krassny will insist on joining up now.'

'Otto?' said Julie sharply. 'He can't do that. He's studying medicine here.'

'I didn't know you knew them so well, Julie,' Frau Pohaisky sounded startled, as far as her breeding allowed her to show surprise.

'One sees the Krassnys now and again. I was able to help them about getting Otto reserved, a year ago.' Except over Franz, Julie had never needed to be cautious with Frau Pohaisky and was not now. 'And just at this moment, I can't afford to lose my goodwill with the Krassnys. Somebody was rounded up three days ago and I need Krassny's help to find her. And yours, Nando, too.'

'But, Julie! It's more than my life is worth to interfere in anything to do with the transportation! It's entirely an SS affair. You know that.'

Frau Pohaisky, like everyone else in Vienna society, had known of Julie's liaison with Nando for a long time, but they had never addressed each other so familiarly in front of her before, out of respect for her religious scruples.

414

'Just the same,' said Julie grimly, 'you're going to have to do something. But it isn't as bad as you think. The girl has an Italian passport.'

'But who is this girl, Julie?' asked Frau Pohaisky.

'She is a distant connection – by marriage.'

'Oh.' Frau Pohaisky's voice went blank. 'I see.'

'But she's more than that. She has been living with a friend of mine for a year. You don't know him, I think, Margarete – Kerenyi? No, I thought not. He's hardly your kind. He couldn't marry her, being a German citizen, and we found an Italian waiter to marry her. I paid the man, myself. Georgy had no money. We thought she would be safe, but the round-up was so sudden she was gone before anything could be done. Then Kerenyi found the Italian was gone. We'd got a bit careless, I suppose, in the last months when everything seemed so quiet, and forgot to keep an eye on him.'

'Perhaps you can reach him, Nando, without making too much fuss?' suggested Frau Pohaisky.

When Nando spoke at last his voice was sulky.

'It wouldn't do the slightest good if I did. And there are other drawbacks. It's dangerous to make oneself conspicuous about … in such cases.' His voice quickened, as a respectable excuse for inaction occurred to him from the foregoing conversation. 'It's not only oneself, either. I should put my whole family in danger if I got into trouble. And, to be quite frank, I'm not prepared to do that for a woman I've never seen … nor for Georg Kerenyi.'

'But she was just having a baby, Nando,' pleaded Julie helplessly. She put up a hand to her aching head, the little frown coming and going nervously between her brows. He did not answer. And the knowledge that the unborn child was not the real ground for her urgency seemed all at once disgusting to her; at least as much for her own sake as for Franz's did it seem essential to keep her husband's only friend within his reach and the pettiness of this real ground was, in comparison with two human lives, so unworthy that Julie was made doubly angry by Nando's franker egotism. A sensation of despair made her reckless and she said the very last thing that might induce Nando to help her.

'Kerenyi has got to stay in Vienna,' she said in that harsh tone neither Nando nor Frau Pohaisky had heard from her before. 'He is talking of going to find her and I've got to keep him here.'

Nando laughed angrily. 'He hasn't a chance of even getting into the General Gouvernement!'

'He says he can join one of the Wehrmacht reporting teams that go to the front.' Then she noticed what Nando had said. 'So you do know where they have gone – been sent?'

'The transport was directed to Lodz. And I'm not supposed to know that, so don't repeat it to anyone. I just happened to overhear that brute Obergruppenführer Tenius talking.'

'Tenius – who is he?' asked Julie, seizing on an authoritative rank.

'Tenius? He's a big shot from Berlin. Came to inspect the arrangements – for future modifications, I suppose. He's much too big a brass hat to have come just for this transport.'

He glanced at Julie, saw what she was thinking of and added hastily, 'He's gone back to Berlin – went yesterday.'

Julie groaned aloud. 'What am I going to do? I've got to keep Kerenyi here – got to!'

There was an uneasy silence. Then Nando rose from the heavy chair with gilded arms and brocaded velvet upholstery to match the brocade wall-covering of dark red and tarnished gilt. The feet of the chair scraped on the dark polished wood of the floor. His heels clipped sharply as he stepped to the side table where the decanters stood and helped himself to brandy without asking.

'So! Kerenyi is that important to you! Why?'

'Why?' she asked dully. 'Oh, no, Nando, not for any reason you may think of. But yes, he is important to me. And not only to me . . .'

'Julie, be careful!' said Frau Pohaisky quickly. The two women looked at each other. Then Julie said, very quietly and deliberately:

'He is important for something much more valuable than my life.' Frau Pohaisky seemed to have been holding her breath.

'I don't care for brandy, but I think we all need a drink. Nando . . . ?'

416

'It's getting terribly difficult to get,' said Julie irrelevantly as she took her glass without looking at Nando.

'We still have a few bottles in the cellar,' said her hostess, 'but I shan't even try to replace them when they are gone.'

'It won't be difficult to get from now on,' said Nando, replenishing his own glass. 'I was reading about the trade agreement with Vichy in the paper yesterday, and they seem to be keen on selling the Reich all the wine and brandy they can. I suppose the exports they used to make to England are all stacking up since last year's harvest.'

'It's an ill wind that blows nobody good, I suppose.' Julie drank her brandy and held out her glass again to Nando. 'Willy Mundel will be glad. He's taken to slivovitz lately and doesn't like it.'

'You see Mundel, then?' asked Nando. 'I thought he never came to town any more, holed up in his cottage out there in the Marchfeld all the time.'

'He was in the theatre yesterday to sign some papers. He gets a small pension, you know, and he manages quite nicely I think, what with the rents he gets from the oil company. He says the village is full of German engineers and nobody can understand a word they say.' She laughed unevenly, recalling Mundel's imitation of the local people and chattered on. 'They hate the Germans because they have to work faster since the oilfield was taken over, but nobody seems to mind the increased ground rents. Willy says the peasants are all getting rich. Hansi Ostrovsky was trying to persuade him to join a company to go to the troop theatres. But he wouldn't.'

'Will you go, Julie?' asked Frau Pohaisky.

'I may have to. There is a company going to Warsaw and Krakov in the spring, and I shall probably have to go with them. But it's only for ten days and will let me out of doing anything for some time afterwards. At least, so Hansi promises me. The whole thing is really Hella's fault. She's always promoting these trips to make herself popular with her wretched SS friends.'

'There's even talk of her marrying one of them,' interposed Nando unexpectedly. So that Julie should not revert to her questioning, he did not say that the possible bridegroom was Brigadier Tenius.

'She's almost bound to, I should think.'

Margarete Pohaisky looked up, her sad, plain face flushing with an embarrassed determination.

'Why don't you two marry?' she said. 'It would surely be better for both to have a settled home.'

The question hung in the air, while Nando looked at Julie who instantly abandoned her tone of febrile triviality.

'There is no chance of my marrying again,' she said at last with a definiteness intended to end the conversation. 'And it's a rather surprising thing for you to suggest, Margarete.'

'Ah, my dear! I can't believe that God concerns himself exclusively with our personal foibles in times such as these, the young and beautiful being killed every day. Any comfort we can give each other is a little less misery in the world, so long as it hurts nobody else. Besides – your former marriage was not quite valid, from a narrow religious point of view.'

'Neither is the divorce valid from a narrow legal point of view,' answered Julie sarcastically. It struck both of her hearers painfully for to their ears Julie spoke of a loss well over three years old which, for whatever reasons, she herself had made final. Not for the first time it struck Nando that Julie's continued bitterness was not only morbid but somewhat theatrical.

'The divorce is perfectly valid,' he said in a low voice. 'The reason we don't marry is that Julie does not want to.'

Julie allowed her silence to last so long that it became a tacit agreement with what Nando said. She was in fact so tired that it was difficult for her to concentrate on what was being said, and she had slipped into a reverie over the extraordinary chance that neither Franz nor Fina had ever discovered anything about the divorce. Even though it was not noted in any of the Vienna papers and only half a dozen people knew of it for certain, it was still strange. Hansi Ostrovsky had kept a careful watch on the press for some months after the five-minute hearing was finally over in a closed court-room but not a word had ever been printed about what might have been a scurrilous tidbit for the popular press. Julie knew, of course, that Schoenherr had warned his 'menagerie' in his roundabout way at the time, that frightful consequences might follow any injudicious gossip; but that Hella Schneider and her mother had never risked a hint to some intimate was extraordinary. The only mention of the affair ever made in public was in a French-language monthly devoted to the stage and published in Berne; the repetition of an unconfirmed rumour that raised no echo. The explanation of Frau Schneider's silence was the simplest possible; she knew that any gossip would be blamed instantly on herself and the result would be the loss of her living which she owed solely in Director Schoenherr's favour. For that good reason she had taken the safest course and never mentioned her knowledge even to her daughter.

Julie returned to consciousness of her companions as she heard Frau Pohaisky mention the name of Otto Krassny.

'What was that about Otto?' she asked, interrupting her friends' laboured effort to cover the silence with family gossip.

'He was there last week-end,' said Frau Pohaisky, 'that's all.'

The mention of the Krassnys reminded Julie of her purpose in coming there that evening but her weariness was so great that she was willing for the moment to accept Nando's obstinate unco-operativeness. She would go direct to Krassny, instead.

She swayed on her feet as she stood up and both her companions moved towards her. She smiled foolishly; she might almost have been drunk.

'I'm not sleeping,' she said, in explanation. 'This girl's disappearance has had such an effect on my nerves – I wouldn't have believed I could be so upset about somebody I hardly knew.' She sat down again, unable to stop herself talking, though she knew that expressing even indirectly the terrible danger dragged into consciousness by Ruth's fate would bring on again the weeping fit that signalled a near-breakdown of her nerves. The threatening disaster of a serious breakdown was as tempting in its promise of irresponsibility as a great height is to one who suffers from vertigo.

'Julie you need a much better doctor than Moller. He really isn't up to much. Let me ring up my man to-morrow and make an appointment for you to see him – will you?'

Julie looked up at Frau Pohaisky with dazed surprise.

'Oh, but I haven't been to Moller for ages,' she said. 'Not since he came ...' It was only habit that stopped her going on, sheer habit; all her tired mind wanted was to say the unrecoverable words that would free her of her sole responsibility by pulling these two human beings into her knowledge with her. She was silent for a moment, and then, by an effort frighteningly visible in her features, the danger was gone. She pushed at the arms of her chair to raise herself.

'Sit still for a minute,' said Frau Pohaisky. 'Just for a moment. I'll get you a glass of tea, it will quieten your nerves before you go out. Nando, come and help me, will you?'

The housekeeper was gone to bed and in the silent kitchen Frau Pohaisky put a kettle on the gas.

'Nando, she is completely overdriven. She needs a proper rest — at least a week without work. You must persuade her. If you want to take care of her as you say, it is your duty to make her rest.'

'She won't let me take care of her,' said Nando. 'When I try she pushes me away from her — I always have the feeling that she makes me keep my distance.'

'Yes, she would do that, I can see that. Because, Nando, Julie is living under some terrible strain — I recognise the signs of it from my own experience. I don't, of course, know what it is, but you must consider ... If there is something — something, we don't know what — and if Julie breaks down, there may be a disaster that will involve us all. I remember very well how her father's nerves collapsed suddenly. He just gave up and died. It's true, Julie has much more her mother's temperament — thank goodness. Still, inheritance is an odd thing. I am warning you for your own sake as well as hers. For all our sakes.'

In the meantime, Frau Pohaisky put tea-leaves with her fingers into a little *chinoiserie* teapot and poured over them the boiling water.

'What are you hinting at?' asked Nando. 'If you know something, tell me.'

'I know nothing,' said the older woman sternly, 'and I don't want to know anything. There is enough cause for Julie's condition in overwork and we need not know more than that. The Burg has been exploiting her loyalty and willingness for a long time. She has to have a rest.'

The tea was ready now, filtered into a glass with a slice of lemon swimming on top. They found Julie where they left her, sitting with her eyes closed, hands gripping the carved arm-rests of her chair. She opened her eyes at the sound of their entrance and drank the hot tea docilely. They could see that she had been weeping.

Having driven Julie to her own door, Nando made no attempt to go up to the apartment with her. He took her hand as they still sat in the car.

'You will see this doctor of Margarete's, won't you, Julie?'

'Well, no,' she hedged. 'I don't need a doctor. But Margarete did make me realise that I need a rest. I shall ask Hansi to rearrange the rehearsals for the Brückner play and someone else will have to take over my parts for this week. I'll go to the Semmering for a few days of fresh air.'

Julie had not wasted the few minutes' respite given her by the teamaking. She knew perfectly well that Nando and his cousin had been discussing her in the kitchen, and she knew too that any competent doctor would order her to bed for a week – her own bed. That meant doctor's visits, even perhaps an officious nurse. Like a parent bird who sees the approach of a stranger in the nest, she fluttered away from the dangerous ground to attract attention away from it. To keep strangers out of her home the simplest trick was to agree to go away herself.

'Wouldn't you be more comfortable here at home?' he objected. 'Here Fina can look after you. I don't think you are fit to travel.'

'No, not at home. And just because of Fina,' said Julie hastily, 'she fusses so. She'd drive me mad. I shouldn't rest at all. But I need not go as far as the Semmering. How would it be if I asked Willy Mundel to put me up for a week? That's near enough to Vienna for you to come and see me. It is very quiet there.'

She was cozening him, bamboozling him, and because she was too exhausted to do it with her usual artistry, Nando could feel it. There was a single overriding necessity not obvious before in spite of his jealousies and suspicions; simply, nobody was allowed to enter Julie's apartment with the single exception, known to

Nando, of Kerenyi. And it was no question of who went in. There was something *there* that must remain unseen.

Nando stood later, glooming out of the window of his little sitting-room with its anonymous hired furniture in the dark. All he could see through the dirty windows — like most bachelors he was diddled by his cleaning woman — was the faint outline of the old house opposite in the narrow street and the black sky, moonless and starless, heavily clouded. He tried ineffectually to persuade himself that his own nerves were playing tricks on him, that he imagined more in Julie's evasions than was really there. But he remembered her refusal, the night he followed her to Kerenyi's house and back again, to take him up to her flat. He knew, too, though coming into a situation already established he had taken it for granted, that none of Julie's friends and colleagues ever went to her home and vagrant remarks came back to him now, he hardly knew from what conversations, to the effect that this state of affairs was not always so. Once 'everyone' had gone there; it was once a hospitable place. Unbidden, the night returned to Nando when he and Julie talked by the open windows in the moonlight in his own home. He recalled his elusive feeling then that there was something known between them that could not be spoken. He recalled the other times he had suggested marriage, and how swiftly Julie had withdrawn from the subject. His feeling about her refusal to admit the divorce as valid had been mistaken; it was perhaps morbid but not affected; Julie had her own reason for her stubbornness.

With this, Nando reached a point in his thoughts beyond which he could formulate nothing clearly, even in his own mind. And this was not only the almost immeasurable capacity of normal human beings to reject what would be unbearable if it were admitted; he was quite unable to imagine a presence never known to him and never spoken of except as vanished for ever. Julie herself never mentioned her past marriage; the name of her husband never passed her lips when she was with Nando, or indeed anywhere else outside her home.

He turned hastily from the window, drew the blinds and switched all the lights on in the room.

3

Julie walked to the village post office every morning to speak to Hansi in Vienna, who had promised to telephone both Fina and Kerenyi's flat every day to hear if there were any news — of Kerenyi or Ruth, of course. This was her only activity. Otherwise she sat in an old arm-chair in the sun outside the kitchen door of Willy Mundel's low-built house which faced south and caught the last warmth of the year. There was no news, and after the first two days Julie recognised that there would be none.

Wherever Kerenyi had gone, he had gone at once after seeing Julie and without leaving any information behind him. His newspaper knew nothing, his charwoman had found a scrawled note and some money waiting for her; and the note said nothing more than that she should clean the flat and lock it up.

The longing to weep constantly had gone away. But she was glad to be alone. Every day Mundel went either fishing or shooting over the rough reedy land of his neighbours, tramping through the low growth of woodland, the boggy fields. He went out at dawn; Julie did not see him until late afternoon after his bag for the day was divided with his local friends and packed in a basket on the Post bus for the game dealer in Vienna where the shooting and fishing co-operative had a contract. It was the game season and every day pheasants, hares and an occasional wild piglet or venison were divided between the farmers, Mundel and the game dealer. For the fish they had a barrel-cart that clopped away in the dark with live crayfish or river fish slapping in its water; every afternoon the yellow bus ground into the single wide street of the hamlet with the post, parcels and peasants back from business in the city; it waited an hour while the driver ate at the only tavern, and then ground slowly back, thumping on loose springs on the dreadful road. The driver was the local source of news, nobody in the village read any Vienna newspaper; the telephone in the post office was reserved – except for Julie's calls – for birth, death and business. If the aged postman was seen after the midday meal hobbling up the street, that meant a telegram; and telegrams now meant either death or wounds in one or another of the low cottages where the women prayed openly for a wound bad enough to end some peasant lad's military career far, far away where, unbelievably, snow already fell.

Here in the Marchfeld plain no battle had been fought for many years; the Turkish wars were commemorated by a cannon shot stuck in the metre-thick stone and plaster of the tavern wall. The wide and thick wooden gates of its courtyard were the same as those battered on by Napoleon's stragglers, by the orthodox soldiery described by Tolstoy. War was an old commonplace, but there was stillness and silence to belie both past and present. The sun set slowly over the reedy lake and a little breeze crept over the lush grass, turning the thinned willow leaves silver in the hedges. In the next village oil-managers and engineers came and went, but here they were not seen. Only here and there in the harvested fields a slow and rhythmic arm rose and fell where the precious fluid of war was pumped from under the crops.

When the sun went, Julie went indoors carrying her chair and the rug full of dogs' hairs she wrapped round her knees. The sulky girl moved quietly about getting the evening meal ready; she hardly spoke to Julie for normally she lived in Mundel's house and shared his bed but had been sent home for the week Julie was there, to sleep with her mother in the village. The fire crackled in the big green stove set between the two main rooms. It was always warm in here, comfortably dirty, and smelled of log wood, apples and food. They ate well; the girl could cook and Mundel's neighbours kept him well supplied. He drank steadily, but less than formerly and was never now seen drunk. Julie had a third room, still on the ground floor, which was otherwise not used. There was a deep cellar, but no second storey. All the houses hereabouts were long and low and in the summer only their tall hooded chimneys, some of them crowned with storks' nests, could be seen above the fruit trees that surrounded them. The birds were gone now; it was a still, late autumn, but soon the driving rains that signalled winter would begin to fall.

There were some books, and Julie read idly with the inadequate electric lamp pulled down as far as its cord would let it, over the table in the stove corner. Among the books she found a couple of bound volumes of a court magazine that had long ceased publication. She never asked Mundel how he had come by them, but the accounts of formal occasions, weddings, military appointments, royal inspections of fifty years before amused her and she turned the pages when Mundel's stock of old novels and theatrical memoirs became boring.

Julie heard Mundel come in talking to his two cross-bred dogs and the girl in the kitchen. There was a bath-house with a wood fire out beyond the scullery, but the girl heated water from the pump on the side of the kitchen stove for her employer's perfunctory toilet.

Mundel came in, in leggings and leather jacket and breeches, but in stockinged feet, his hair still wet and flattened down. His slippers, patched bootees of soft leather, stood by his chair but he went straight to the big roughly carved cupboard for a wine bottle.

He put the two glasses brimming over with wine on the table without saying anything, greeting Julie with a silent jerk of his greying head as he raised his glass towards her and drank. Nando had sent a case of the newly arrived French brandy out on the bus, but that was for after the meal — who knew how long the supply would last?

Julie drank slowly. Mundel pushed his feet into the slippers and the door creaked as it was pushed slightly open by the old bitch who always claimed a place by the stove before the other dog, that was much her junior.

At last Mundel spoke, his actor's sonorous voice contrasting with his appearance and surroundings.

'Still no news, then?' he said.

'Nothing,' said Julie. 'Georgy must have talked to his printer friend and gone off straight away.' Julie knew the story was known to Mundel from his visit to the theatre the week before. He had not even asked why she wanted shelter for a week and she had not explained.

'You were wise to get out when you did,' said Julie after a silence.

'Yes.' They drank the green-gold wine, glinting in the big glasses. The girl came in to lay the table – Mundel ate his meal in the evening, unlike the peasant families – and they both moved away from the table to the other side of the stove.

'You look better than you did three days ago,' he said, refilling the glasses.

'It's peaceful here,' she answered.

They had already seated themselves to eat before either spoke again. A savoury mess of hare with dumplings and a green salad mixed with field herbs filled the room with its odour. For the first time in months Julie felt hungry and they set to with appetite. The earthenware pot in which the hare had been cooked smelled faintly of woodsmoke and so did the dark crust of the flat round loaf in the reed basket used here for baking bread.

'Hansi told me that it was you who introduced this girl to Kerenyi,' Mundel said presently, with his mouth full. He picked out a small shot from between the ribs of the meat on his plate and pushed it carefully to the side with his fork. The tableware had black wooden handles and was old and bent.

She took her time answering, but found she was able to do so without the tears rising.

'I suppose that was why it upset me so much.' She stopped eating and stared in front of her. 'She'd been at my mother's house and couldn't stay there any longer when they closed the frontier ...'

At his raised eyebrows, she explained. 'They live east of Graz near the Slovenian border.' He nodded, satisfied. 'I didn't mean her to stay long with Georgy — not even in Vienna. It was just until I could get her name changed, really. But in the meantime — you know how things are. Georgy evidently didn't want her to go, and then she was pregnant.'

'How did you manage to change her name?'

'God,' she said, 'that awful Italian waiter. When we — Georgy that is — went to find him he had gone back home. By that time the transport was gone.'

Eating salad, Mundel said, 'It's no good blaming yourself. Things just happen.'

'I remember thinking at the time, when she came to Vienna, that it was a mistake. I had a superstitious feeling that she would get us into trouble. But she didn't, as it turned out, only herself.'

'You could look at it the other way round and say you saved her life for a couple of years perhaps.'

Julie looked across at him. 'You wouldn't say that if you'd seen Georgy,' she said grimly.

'Georgy knew what he was at. You can't run other people's lives for them, any more than you can fight a private war with the Nazis. They are a bit too big for you and don't you forget it.'

They ate for a time in silence.

'You know what I thought when Ostrovsky told me?' She did not answer but he continued. 'I thought how typical of you and Kerenyi to think you could get away with such a scheme.'

'It wasn't as simple as that,' she said.

'Nothing ever is simple. I suppose you wanted to get the girl off your mother's hands at the time, and one thing just led to another. Ostrovsky didn't tell me she had been living in your mother's house, so I thought she was just some stray girl you wanted to help. A servant, or some dressmaker's assistant. All the same, you did what you could. More than ninety people out of a hundred would have done, even for their mother's sake. If you'd asked me to have her here, I should have refused. Kerenyi could have refused if he'd wanted to, couldn't he?'

Julie was silent again.

'You didn't refuse to have me here,' she said at last, 'and for all you know, I'm in trouble with them.'

Mundel grinned at her. 'You don't know yourself very well, do you?' he said. 'If you'd been in trouble with the police, you'd have told me before you came here.'

She thought about that. 'You mean I'm a romantic? I'm not, you know; the thing just happened. As you say, one thing led to another.'

'But you didn't try to deceive Kerenyi, did you, when you suggested he should take this stranger into his house?'

'No,' she agreed thoughtfully, 'no. I didn't try to deceive him. I couldn't have done.'

'Well, then. I suppose you are – both you and Kerenyi – romantics. One could put it like that. I would have said, rather, you have such a high opinion of yourself that you never do anything that doesn't fit with your picture of yourself.'

'You mean one does such things out of pride? Egotism, in fact?'

'Of course. I wouldn't have thought twice about this girl. Nor would I have worried about feeling guilty. I'd have thought of my own skin.'

'Yet you resigned from the Burg over the first transportations!'

'Look,' he said patiently, 'I was in trouble anyway. Lehmann and that bloody accountant of his were after me and I knew Schoenherr wouldn't protect me because I'd been warned several times. I took a chance at a moment when I knew they would be glad to pension me off to avoid a scandal.'

'You're lying, Willy,' she said calmly. 'I remember the afternoon it happened very well.'

'You remember very little about it. You were in such a state you actually fainted – you!'

'I didn't faint,' she said with indignation. 'I was perfectly conscious. I just wanted to change the subject – which was dangerous. The whole thing was an act.'

'Then why can't you believe that my whole scene was an act, too?'

They looked at each other and Julie laughed unexpectedly.

'It's nice here,' she said. 'Have an apple, fellow egotist!'

On the Thursday Mundel was shooting over a property almost next to his own holding, which he did not farm but leased to the peasant next door for pasture. In the afternoon Julie went out to join him as he stumped about in rubber boots, grunting now and then in dialect with the two other members of the co-operative. The little wind had turned colder and was now a steady piping breeze from the flat eastern plain, the border of Czechoslovakia for twenty years and now of the Ostmark with the Protectorate of Bohemia and Moravia. The border had not made much difference to the local people before and made even less now; they came and went from both sides. Julie was glad of the heavy woollens under her tweeds by the time the sun set in flamy streaks of yellow and red over the shallow lake waters. In the water the sky was mirrored, the colours ruffled by the breeze until the red with the pale greenish streak over it faded into the slow dusk. The men kept looking at the sky; the weather was changing. As darkness gathered they parted, making monosyllabic arrangements for the next day. It was the turn of Mundel's neighbour, a stocky old man with heavy grey moustaches stained yellow with tobacco, to meet the bus and to-night Mundel did not go with him to the tavern but, out of consideration for Julie, walked straight back with her to the house. Outside the kitchen door, the one that was always used though there was a front door to the house to proclaim its status of a gentleman's house, stood a gun-case and fishing tackle.

Nando's voice could be heard calling to them from the kitchen window. He had made himself at home already with the servant girl.

'This is really it!' he came out to meet them. 'You look like a different woman,' he said, kissing Julie's cold cheek. He held her with a long arm round her shoulders and they stood talking; Mundel whom he hardly knew was at once a friend. They talked of what they would do on the morrow as if Nando came here every week-end and indeed he was already planning to himself to come again, and frequently.

'It's almost impossible to believe that Vienna is only an hour from here.'

As the long yellow bus bumped over the road not remade since the previous war, Nando's night thoughts had returned to him and he felt confusedly that something must now be different between himself and Julie, that she must know in her sharp-witted way that something had happened. He was not a man of much insight – the desire to please and be pleased which was his dominating characteristic prevented that – and it did not occur to him that the 'something' had always been present to Julie and she was unlikely to recognise as new what she had lived with for years.

What Julie needed from Nando – and again Nando felt with that sensation of responsibility how great was her need of him – was the ease and comfort of their physical pleasure in each other and the lack of seriousness in their relation. So the relation fell back at once into its natural shape and content. Nando's jealousy and Julie's inability to explain her relationship with Kerenyi were pushed out of sight, gone over in silence; the necessity to retain comfort for each other was what mattered and they both instinctively clung to what mattered. The difference in their two situations made no difference in their equal determination to ignore what might disrupt their delicately balanced ease; each of them bore what to him was as much as he could bear.

So the week-end passed in delightful superficiality. On Sunday evening they talked of the theatre and Julie read to the two men an account of a first night in 1902 from one of the court chronicles she had discovered.

'Shall you go on the tour to Poland in the spring, Julie?' asked Nando. 'I ask because I may have to go there myself – some horrible chap is making himself a quiet little fortune. Not quite quietly enough, unfortunately for him. He was transferred from Vienna some time ago for just the same sort of racket and there is to be a Court of Inquiry. Someone will have to go and if you are going to be in Poland I can make sure it will be myself. Evidence of his past activities, you know?'

'If we can be together there, I'll certainly agree,' said Julie. 'I don't like to leave Vienna, as you know, but sooner or later I shall have to join one of these cultural groups – it's beginning to be obvious that I've never volunteered. There's one going in April for a short tour. Only ten days, that's why I thought of going then.'

'Good. I'll tell Krassny. The arrangements are in his hands and the court is waiting for our side of the evidence. We can easily drag it out until then and set the court for the same date as your tour.'

'Does anybody care, then, about racketeering in Poland, Nando?' asked Mundel.

'Lord, yes. The *Reichsheini* cares like mad. His bloody SS must be absolutely pure of any desire for personal gain, you know. This is by no means the first case where officers have been tried for privately confiscating property, or for bribery. Sometimes they even get shot!'

'Incredible!'

'Not at all. You clearly don't understand the principle of the New Race of Supermen. They may not do anything for a reason – any reason; they have no personal feelings about anything. Obedience to the Führer and the cause; absolute exclusive eternal obedience and devotion – family life is only excepted because they must breed.' He glanced across at Mundel and grinned cynically. '"My Honour is Loyalty". Everything is contained in those words. Everything is covered by loyalty – obedience that is. "Theirs not to reason why: theirs but to do and die".'

Early the next morning a car arrived, sent by Lehmann to take Julie back into the city, and Nando went with her.

'Come again,' called Mundel as they shut the doors. He had come to see them off and even removed his battered headgear with a bunch of pheasant feathers at the side. 'The room is always there – I don't use it.'

'We must take him up on his invitation,' said Nando, leaning back in Lehmann's luxuriously upholstered motor car. 'It's a perfectly splendid place. And Mundel is the perfect host.'

'We must certainly come again – when we have time,' agreed Julie.

4

*F*ranz remembered Willy Mundel well from the past and did not fail to feel a gratitude he could not openly express — except to Julie and Fina — for the hospitality which had restored Julie's balance. The moment of Kerenyi's disappearance from his own life was connected in his mind with the dread aroused by Julie's near-breakdown and the little he knew of the reasons for Kerenyi leaving Vienna so suddenly for the army reporting service increased this dread by its covert threat to himself. Julie's work, and that meant Julie's health, were the fundament on which his life literally depended and Franz, if not Fina, was well aware of that with a gratitude and guilt all the stronger for his utter helplessness to support her in any practical way. All he could give her was understanding.

He was now cut finally off from the outside world, as he knew he must be by Kerenyi's departure. Neither of the two women were able to keep intact the slender lifeline his friend had held to public events and when Julie recounted tales of her own life they seemed like news from another world, for the scraps of gossip picked up from influential friends could no longer be attached to any coherent knowledge of what was happening. He lived like a monk in a cell, in the inner world of his mind. His mental food came from books which Julie ordered for him or borrowed from libraries and collections to which her profession gave her the entry. A constant flow of books and historical papers went to and fro through the theatre unnoticed, for producers and actors frequently read such scholarly records when studying the backgrounds of plays. The unknown Lehmann was particularly useful to Franz; his pedantic concern with every small detail of social and sociological derivation for the productions under his general responsibility made it possible to get records from the old State Archives not available to the public, without remark. The newspapers and periodicals subscribed to for years continued to arrive, as if for Julie, but after the end of 1941 the last foreign publications to be imported, those from Switzerland, stopped coming. And no matter how carefully he read German publications they failed to give any picture of the world and above all, of the war itself, for during that winter the censorship changed. Negative censorship had always been modified by a fictional positive presentation; after the autumn of 1941 the suppression of news gave place to imaginative reconstruction and even invention of false news.

The source of this change was the terrible condition of the troops in Russia, the losses of thousands of men from the climate as well as the enemy. Throughout the autumn and winter the immense battles became a holding action decimating the army; in the centre of the front a regiment of the 7th Division was commanded by a 1st Lieutenant and whole battalions were left by the death of all their senior officers in the hands of raw boys of twenty. The overdriven railway stock, engines and personnel could not bring up winter supplies for the men, even if they had existed for a winter campaign never planned for; ammunition and food were all they could tackle and not always those essentials.

Only the few with military experience could deduce anything of these immense events from the spare inverted news of von Rundstedt's demotion, the names of newly appointed army commanders, the out of date positions to be compared on maps. A couple of Hitler Youth boys came to beg for winter clothing and Fina, feeling a pleasure she did not recognise, gave them all Franz's coats and hunting clothes stored in the dressing-room wardrobes in a fog of mothballs. Civilian rations became suddenly stringent; Julie and Fina ate margarine for the first time and although Franz did not know it, the veal and chicken Fina wheedled out of avaricious shopkeepers by using Julie's name went all to him.

In their almost silent life together Franz and Fina grew into an intense, compact interdependence and if Franz could not survive for a week without Fina's services, neither of them could have survived the loss of the simple presence of the other. There was nothing Fina did that was not devoted to the comfort of the one human being she had ever loved. Even Mass became the opportunity to pray for Franz; his health to be restored, his safety to be protected, the rare luxury of food he could enjoy to be increased; with humility and intense pride, for his work. Fina did not pray for Julie, Julie could take care of that herself, she felt. And with Julie she was more and more irritable and cantankerous while for Franz she found an eternal undemanding gentleness; Fina became a mother, jealous of her daughter and thinking of nothing but her son. They were a family; all trace of the original relationship was gone and Fina's wages, paid into a savings account month by month, accumulated into a modest prosperity untouched.

Fina's best times were Julie's rare absences from Vienna; then she had Franz entirely to herself and there was no breeze of oxygen from the real world to disturb the stifling density of their communion. She began to look forward to Julie's tour to the base troops in Poland as soon as she heard of it, in November.

Although it was April, the weather was still winter, bitter cold and with constant lashing rain. The truck journey from the Luftwaffe air base, though uncomfortable, did not last long on the new military road. Soon their vehicle began to stop and start frequently for traffic, and then they reached the centre of the medieval city in a few minutes. Krakov is not a big town. They heard the driver and the sergeant jump down and begin to open the sheltering — or confining — canvas from the back of the truck. One by one the company struggled down, cramped, travel-worn and exhausted, scrambling in the dim light for hand cases and bags. It was still raining, though the gale that had driven their two aircraft off course had dropped. The houses of the narrow alley were dark, sparsely lighted from behind curtains, almost closing together over an alleyway just wide enough for the truck to pass. A faint light from the entrance of the hotel hardly showed the low steps of its entry. A corporal in uniform stood inside the glass doors but, of course, made no move to help them.

In the small lobby a junior officer of a service unit, the military manager, moved nervously forward, mindful of the telephoned instructions he had received a few moments before from the adjutant at the airfield. The hotel, requisitioned as the only decent one in the city for the military, had rooms booked for the company for a week hence when they would be back in Krakov; they could use these rooms for the hour or so that remained before the night-train left for Warsaw. While this information was being given to Hansi Ostrovsky, Julie and the other actors went farther, in search of warmth, into the inner hall of the hotel. The old building, last renovated in the 1860s, was furnished with dark red carpets and dusty crimson hangings. In a shadowy pier-glass, greenish black with age, Julie caught sight of herself and hastily averted her eyes. She turned instead to the wide steps of the stairway, flanked by two marble urns upon the ornamental ends of the balustrade, which contained unhappy ferns. The stairs ran up to a bay of heavily curtained windows on the low landing, and divided there into two curved arms to the upper stories.

There were no visible servants. Julie went out again into the outer hall and accosted the military manager, discussing a bundle of questionnaire forms with Hansi.

'Look, Hansi, can't all this red tape wait? I want to have a bath and some sort of a meal before the train leaves.' She turned impatiently to the manager, a pallid, unhealthy-looking man of about fifty, obviously unfit for any more active duty.

'You can collect all our passports, and then get us shown up to our rooms,' she suggested. The man smiled nervously.

'These transit orders have to be all filled up and signed,' he objected in a thin, nasal voice. 'I don't think—'

'Well, don't think then,' interrupted Julie in the brutal tone that more and more frequently seemed to be the only one that got anything done. 'Fill the forms from our passports and we can sign them when we go to the dining-room. In the meantime, where are some servants?'

The manager-officer showed his resentment at her tone with a flush that spread from his forehead down; he was accustomed to this kind of speech from officers coming through from the fronts, but no woman had ever spoken to him in such a way in his twenty-two years of service. He was about to object, but the civilian manager of the hotel now appeared at his elbow and with servile speed waved forward two elderly porters to carry bags and show the way upstairs. The moment he appeared servants appeared too as if from nowhere, and it was clear that this fat short man with his lilting Polish accent and vigorous gestures of obsequious busyness was in actual charge. This was the first time Julie had seen the occupation atmosphere, and she was aware of it at once as a multiple structure of corruption. From the manner of the official manager, the way he at once busied himself with ostentatious concern at the hotel desk with his forms, and the sharp tone he used to his Polish employee — who had in fact been managing this hotel since the late twenties — it was clear that their relationship was one of mutual dependence in what is known under one name or another to all armies as 'fiddling'.

In a few moments a woman in long black skirts and white linen apron was showing Julie into a first-floor room full of dark furniture and lit by a mean ceiling light. The maid ran forward and switched on a still weaker lamp on the bedside table to the right of a wide and high bed, and then busied herself turning taps and arranging towels in a bathroom nearly as big as the bedroom.

Julie took the private bathroom for granted, but she was in fact in a room reserved for General officers. The woman was showing her the bell-push by the door and bowing deeply. Her face was half covered by a clean white cloth bound tightly under the chin and covering her forehead, and looking at her for the first time Julie saw that she was old and wrinkled. When she smiled and made some murmur of thanks, the woman smiled too, a smile frightened at her own determination. She hesitated and then spoke softly in halting German with a strong Galician accent.

'Gnae' Frau is from Vienna, is she not?'

'Yes, we all are,' said Julie surprised. 'Why do you ask? Do you know Vienna?'

'I have never been there, gnae' Frau. But my husband was there once, long ago. He was in the Imperial Army then.' The pale old eyes looked curiously at the strange tall guest, testing for sympathy.

Julie laughed to herself, nodding at the old woman.

'Those were better times than these, you mean, eh?'

The old woman nodded and came close to Julie, fingering with worn fingers the pocket of her apron.

'The Austrians — they were quite different,' she said softly, tipping her sheathed head sideways to indicate some unspoken ending to the remark. Then, scared at her own temerity, she bowed again and caught Julie's dirty hand to kiss it before she almost ran out of the room.

'A bit cracked,' said Julie aloud as she closed the bathroom door. It took her half an hour to bathe and clean herself up and then she rang the bell to tell the old servant that the bathroom was free for someone else to use.

'I'm sorry it's German money,' she said as she slipped a substantial tip into the apron pocket. The old woman looked up at her, her face suddenly terrified.

'But what is it?' she asked.

'Gnae' Frau, I didn't mean anything — just now? You won't tell anyone?'

'I don't understand . . . oh, I see. I didn't mean anything either, only that I am sorry I have no Polish money. Of course I shan't tell on you — what is there to tell?'

That the old woman kissed her hand again was not so very strange, though it was a gesture gone almost completely out of fashion, but there was something about her scared manner that now disturbed Julie, restored to normality by the application of warm water and a hairbrush.

'I shall go out and get a breath of air,' said Julie, finding Harich and Hansi with several others in the hall with drinks in front of them on a marble table. 'I'll be back by the time dinner is ready.' No one seemed disposed to accompany her so she went out alone, into the damp dark where slow drops still dripped from the wide eaves into the street though it no longer rained. It was cold and Julie pulled her coat tighter and pushed her hands into the pockets. She had no idea where she was or what the shape of the city might be, but took the next turning to the right into a slightly wider street which led in a few metres into a wide open square. The lighting was so bad that little was visible, but when her eyes were accustomed to the gloom Julie could make out a low massive building in the centre of the square which seemed to have a gallery running round it. She walked across the square, watching her step on the uneven paving stones and glad of her comparatively sensible travelling shoes. On its far side stood a tiny church, very, very old, and beyond that the roadway that ran round the square. Only as she looked to each side before crossing the road did it occur to Julie that the square and its surrounding road were almost completely deserted. Then in the dim light, she saw a heavily wrapped figure, a man, who crossed to the other pavement as she approached him. When, on the next street corner, this happened again Julie saw that people were out at night in this town but they avoided each other with care. She turned and walked back towards the square, not wishing to lose herself in the labyrinth of streets left as they were since the middle ages. Some way away the sharp smack of metalled heels could be heard on the empty paving. Two soldiers approached on the far side of the road, and a passer-by, his head bent and turned away from them, moved off the pavement to walk in the gutter as they passed. From a slight movement in the doorway of a house, Julie was aware that several people stood there whom she had not seen. She came nearly level with the deep doorway and the shadows melted into the dark, only the pale glimmer of a face confirming her impression.

As she reached the ancient chapel again she could hear the cautious pad of footsteps behind her, and turning saw two shadowy forms melt into the deeper shadow under the church wall. They did not move again while she was in the wide expanse of the dark square, but she was aware that she was watched. On the far side she waited at the sound of a motor car approaching, and stepped back a little so that the wet roadway should not throw mud over her ankles. In the swish of the car's passing she heard quite distinctly the soft rush of footsteps behind her and for the first time a faint fear ran over her nerves. She glanced over her shoulder; there was nobody to be seen but she guessed correctly that several people had run across from the shelter of the chapel into the shadow of the low and massive building she had first been impressed with. She crossed the road quickly and under the faint light of a street lamp on the other side, looked back at the totally empty square. As she watched a small figure detached itself from the dark, and ran, slightly bent, across the road towards her. She could hear a whining murmur of Polish and realised that the figure was a boy of perhaps eleven, with a pallid, filthy face, and unkempt wet hair in streaks on his forehead. He huddled in his soaked ragged coat, both arms wrapped about himself, and sidled up to her, pale face lifted imploringly. In the meagre light she could see that he was half starved and as his eyes shifted at some vagrant sound of the wind, there was a flash of something wild and dangerous in their look, at once veiled again as the child bent its head and whined its beggar's tale.

A grimy little paw caught at the wide sleeve of the beaver coat she wore. Julie became aware that she had no money on her, not even a few groschen loose in her pocket. She said this in German, but the ragged boy did not cease his plaint; it was obvious that he did not understand her. Two much taller figures detached themselves from the shadows of the big building, moving hesitatingly towards herself and the boy, who intensified his efforts to extract money from this obviously rich passer-by. Julie said, 'But I have no money!' and to prove it she pulled off her gloves and turned the pockets of her coat inside out. A voice behind her shoulder startled her, speaking softly in German.

'You came from the hotel, didn't you? You could get him some money from there!'

Julie turned, perhaps a little too quickly and found herself staring straight into the face of a young man of about nineteen or twenty, as far as she could tell. His wide hat was pulled well down and by hunching his shoulders he almost joined the turned up collar of his overcoat to his hat brim. The face was of the Slav cut, the prominent cheekbones and wide jaw of a heavy-set and naturally fleshy face framing in outline what was no more than skin stretched over the promontories of bone. In the faint light a stubble of dark beard and a lock of unkempt hair over the shadowed brow made him look dirtier than he certainly was; his eyes stared out, abnormally large but sunken in the fleshless mask with a look of cold and threatening insolence. They at any rate were very much alive, those eyes; the eyes of a man with quite literally nothing but his life to lose.

At this moment the sound of another car approaching could be heard. The hand scrabbling at Julie's coat fell away and in the instant that she glanced down at the boy, with astounding suddenness and silence they all faded into shadows and were gone from sight. Instantly Julie turned and walked quickly towards the hotel. At the turning stood another weak street lamp and in its light Julie saw a small baroque church which she only noticed now that she walked towards it. Its door was well above street level, and a short flight of stone steps, or rather two flights, one from the left and one from the right ran up in a typical device to a little podest before the church door, edged by a stone balustrade. As Julie turned the corner left, from which the hotel door was not more than ten metres distant, the ragged figure of the boy ran down the church steps towards her. How he could come to be there was unbelievable to one who walked only paths laid out for walking; he had slipped through the warren of back ways known to the lower depths of every old city. Running to Julie he walked backwards before her, softly wailing his begging plaint; at every second step he glanced back for the sign of any activity at the door of the hotel.

The voice she had heard before said softly behind Julie in German, 'He will be beaten half to death if he doesn't get something out of you!' Having seen the young man's eyes, Julie could well believe this. She said sternly but quietly to the boy, 'Stay here,' and hurried into the lobby of the hotel. When she came out again five minutes later the alley was empty, nothing but the dark houses, and the street lamp dimly lessening the dark at the turning by the church. She stepped forward a couple of paces along the pavement. Something touched her hand, what she held in it was gone and with nothing more than a whisper of footsteps she was alone again.

'What is the town like?' asked Hansi. 'Or could you see nothing in the black-out?'

'The little I saw was most interesting,' said Julie and looked at him coolly. 'Is our meal ready yet?'

As they went into the brightly lit dining-room Julie was aware of the Polish manager watching her face. As she passed by him at the door she stopped.

'Tell me,' she said to him, 'is there a curfew in Krakov?'

'Yes, Madame. A permanent curfew from dusk to dawn.' He lifted his eyes cautiously, to take her mood. 'I expect Madame found the streets deserted?'

'Very deserted,' she agreed, looking into his hooded eyes. 'But I was passed by two military cars; I should have thought they would stop and ask me for my papers, if there is a curfew?'

'They probably did not see Madame,' he suggested. Then, casually, 'Military personnel mostly tend to remain in their vehicles after dark in the city. There are many outlaws and criminals about. If I had known Madame wished to go out, I should have ventured to suggest some protection.'

'I see,' she said, and went in to join the others.

They were in the middle of a discussion conducted with the complicated acrimony usual to theatrical administration. It was reassuring to be back to her normal atmosphere and Julie nibbled thoughtfully at the mushrooms sizzling in a little copper dish as a first course, musing vaguely about what must be the real condition of this city in which such incidents were taken for granted under the occupation surface of military control.

'What were you talking to the manager about?' asked Thorn suddenly, bored with the subject of who should have the sleepers available on the train that night.

'Apparently there is a curfew here,' Julie answered. 'I asked him about it; but we were rather at cross-purposes. There are, actually, quite a number of people about out of doors. Not, I suppose, nearly as many as there would be in normal times, but still —

people about. What I noticed was how cautious they were of strangers — or perhaps just of anyone else being about. He thought I noticed how deserted the streets were; in fact, rather the contrary. I had the feeling there were a lot more people than I saw, but they have developed terrific skill at not being seen or heard. That was how I guessed there must be a curfew.'

'You never know with the Poles,' said Thorn, as he helped Julie to chicken. 'They are a surly lot — and damned devious. That manager for instance — sly as a cartload of monkeys, I shouldn't wonder.'

Thorn was far from being a Nazi, Julie knew; but naturally he adopted what was not only the current official attitude to the Poles but an attitude based on long scorn of eastern peoples whose social and administrative methods were, to a central European view, slack and incompetent. She stopped herself pointing out that being occupied was probably enough to make the Poles surly, as he put it, with the thought that this remark would expose to Thorn the immense difference between her attitude and his own — that is, the one generally accepted.

'Chicken!' she commented instead. 'I haven't eaten chicken for months. The army seems to do itself well.'

'I believe they do — behind the front,' he said sarcastically.

They were interrupted by the approach to their table of a masterman of many years standing and the head theatrical electrician of the Burg. Hansi greeted him and asked him to draw up a chair, pouring at the same time a glass of wine for him.

'Thank you, Herr Ostrovsky,' said the man, and pushed the glass slightly away from him to make it clear that he came on business. 'The others have asked me to have a word with you. We hear that there will only be five double sleepers available on the train. That is, only ten of us can sleep properly. Do you know if that is correct?'

'I'm afraid so,' said Hansi, at once nervous of what he knew was going to be a protest by the technicians and dressers. 'I have done what I could, but apparently this train is always full and we are lucky to get any sleepers at all.'

'In that case,' said the man with quiet firmness, 'I am of the opinion that the whole company should draw lots for sleepers.' He always spoke in this formal manner when discussing theatrical business, which the technicians took much more seriously than the artists.

'We decided,' began Hansi, and corrected himself hastily at this hint of a cabal of the privileged actors. 'I mean, I decided, that the sleepers should go to the people who are acting to-morrow night. That is ...' He pulled a crumpled paper out of his jacket pocket.

'Herr Ostrovsky, we have to work every night.' The technician's face was stolid and his voice assured.

'That is true, of course. But it is important that the cast for to-morrow should be fresh. There will have to be a rehearsal to-morrow afternoon, after all.'

'I have no intention of giving up my sleeper,' announced Hella Schneider.

'Please, Hella!' Hansi waved an imploring hand. 'Herr Brenner, it is not a matter of any member of the company getting privileges of rank. It is simply a matter of who has the brunt to bear without a rest to-morrow afternoon. I'm afraid there is no question of all the company drawing lots because some of us will be able to rest in the daytime to-morrow.'

This meant that the dressers were not to be considered as eligible for sleepers, which was reasonable, but seemed like the reflection of a lower status to people always extremely conscious of their essential but inferior services.

'That does not apply to any of the three of us,' pointed out Brenner, meaning himself, the head scene shifter and the stage manager. The reason the stage manager had not undertaken this argument was, it now occurred to Hansi, that they had decided to make a union matter of it; the electrician was the union representative. That their union had been radically altered in structure and powers over three years before made no difference to its activities which continued as they always had and were carried out by the same persons; the difference was that a quite useless superstructure of Party officials now headed the union and were paid out of theatre budgets and general taxes. In theory Hansi or Schoenherr could have recourse to this committee in the constant, the almost continuous, disputes between the artistic management and the technicians; in theory Herr Brenner was not even a union official. But the theatre could not be run without his co-operation.

'I rather agree with Herr Brenner,' volunteered Walter Harich to Hansi's intense irritation. 'It is more difficult for the stage-people to manage in a strange and probably badly run theatre than it is for ourselves.'

If Herr Brenner was grateful for this unexpected support, he did not show it.

'The dressers are not my concern,' he said primly, 'but I feel it my duty to let you know, Herr Producer – they will not agree to a draw that does not include themselves. At least, that was the sense of what was said to me.'

This move put the possibility of drawing lots out of the question. 'What you mean, Herr Brenner, is that you three technicians want sleepers. Isn't it?' Hella put the matter into a nutshell. She caused more trouble with the theatre staff than anyone else in their community.

'Then what is to be done?' Hansi tried to ignore her. But Brenner had taken her point. It was indeed precisely what he intended but it was against an unspoken rule for him to admit it or for anyone else to mention the fact that the senior technicians were concerned only with their own position and had even less regard for their inferiors than the artists had for them, while the actors cared a good deal for the comfort of their dressers, with whom they were in close personal contact.

The whole table was now listening, and all other conversation had ceased.

'I am quite prepared to give up my place,' offered Thorn with a shrug, and reached for the wine flask across the table.

'That's out, Jochen,' snapped Hansi. 'You have the longest part of all to-morrow night!'

'I can never sleep in trains in any case,' said Thorn. 'Why waste a sleeper?'

Nobody seconded this idea with other offers; there was silence.

'Let us give up all the sleepers,' suggested Julie contemptuously at last. 'Then we're all in the same discomfort, since we can't all be in the same comfort.' Jochen Thorn and Harich laughed at this, and Anita Silovsky joined her treble giggle to their loud demonstration.

Herr Brenner's look had darkened to a solemn anger. Two yellowish patches appeared on Hansi's tired, bony face. His stomach, already upset, always reacted to difficulties and Julie could see he was in pain and was sorry for her joke.

'I only meant to warn you, Herr Producer, about the dressers. They are not my concern, as you know, even if some people appear not to know it. In fact, I am being very reasonable. The technicians are very much upset at the whole conduct of the tour so far. While we do not, of course, blame you for the weather, we do feel that better arrangements should have been made for transport. None of us had ever flown before to-day and it was disgraceful that we should be forced to fly in such a storm. We were all sick and if you really want to know how the others feel, they are threatening to call off the entire tour unless we have some assurance of better arrangements.'

'There was a fighter wing on transfer due at Tulln for the East Front, just an hour after we were scheduled to take off. It was impossible to change the programme, as the station commander told you all, because as soon as the military planes were signalled every other machine would be grounded in the whole Vienna command area for two days. Neither I nor anybody else is able to influence military orders and I really don't see any ground for your complaint at all. After all, we were all sick, too.'

'Yes, that may be, but we could have gone by train in the first place and avoided this terrible flight.'

'Train passes were impossible to get,' interrupted Thorn. 'I was there when Herr Lehmann tried to get them out of the railway authorities. Civilian travellers are allowed only to fly; the order came out months ago apparently.'

'But we are going by train now to Warsaw. That can hardly be so,' interjected Hella.

'Only because of this emergency. We were supposed to fly direct to Warsaw from Tulln. You don't appear to appreciate, Herr Brenner, that we have very little say in anything once we are in a military area. When our pilots landed at the airfield here we were within an ace of being arrested for security reasons. Perhaps you don't know it, but the hours you spent waiting there after the emergency landing, I was arguing with the Luftwaffe officers to release us *at all!*'

'I could hardly know anything about it, Herr Producer, since I was not included in the discussion,' said Brenner stiffly.

'Discussion! There was no discussion. I tell you, we were threatened with arrest. The security officer was all against our being allowed off the station. There's obviously something big going on. I was told there is an absolute stop on movements of military personnel, let alone civilians.'

'We should never have been released at all if I hadn't mention Gruppenführer Tenius,' claimed Hella scornfully.

'Be that as it may, we were brought here under armed guard from the airfield, in case none of you noticed it. And it may be as well to mention it since we are rather inexperienced in such matters, that we are technically under military orders as long as we are in Poland. And that applies to union members.' Herr Brenner began to rise, mortally offended at this, but before he could express his outrage Hansi's attention was taken by the military manager who appeared at his elbow nervously coughing.

'Yes, what is it?' he demanded furiously.

'The bus is ready for the station, Herr Director. If the hand baggage is ready, can I get it brought out?'

'I am not a Herr Director,' snapped Hansi. 'Yes, yes, let's get the stuff taken out.'

The table emptied as everyone busied himself with his baggage. Hansi turned again to Herr Brenner.

'You can see for yourself,' he said, 'that there's nothing to be done. We have to get to the station.'

Herr Brenner compressed his lips and stood his ground, clearly not finished yet.

'Herr Brenner, this is not Vienna,' Hansi's voice rose with nervous exasperation. 'Military trains do not wait for civilians and unless you want to remain here alone, you must come now.'

Further discussion was prevented by the appearance in the doorway of the sergeant from the airfield,

'The bus is leaving — sir,' he said loudly.

'Coming,' said Hansi, looking about for his briefcase. 'Oh, the passports?'

'I have them,' said the sergeant patiently.

In the blue-lit station, its glass roof much broken, there was a subdued and orderly bustle about a long train at the main platform. The sergeant led his party to the door of a dark carriage and handed the bundle of their papers to a military orderly who waited at the top of its entry steps. They were counted as they entered and the door then closed and, as they suspected, locked. Only then did Harich make the discovery that there were no sleepers in their carriage and the orderly knew nothing about them having been reserved.

'I dare say they were changed over. There's a whole lot of senior brass on the train to-night,' he opined with unconcern.

'This is absurd,' cried Hella. 'I must see the train officer at once. Please go and fetch him!'

The orderly seemed to find her imperious tone amusing. He simply walked away down the corridor. Hella stared after him for a moment, and then turned into the nearest compartment and seated herself, provisionally, while the others were making themselves comfortable. Julie pushed a make-up box with some difficulty on to the rack above the corner seat she had annexed.

'We'd better make up our minds to it, Anita,' she said, 'we are getting no sleepers.'

'Serve Herr Brenner right, too,' muttered Anita Silovsky. 'I'm so exhausted I shall sleep anyway.' She shrugged off her musquash coat and tucked up her feet, wrapping the coat round her like a blanket. Julie went to close the door and, looking up the corridor, saw her dresser standing with a bewildered air at the door of another compartment.

'There's room in here, Lotte,' she called.

'Oh really, Julie!' objected Hella. 'We can't have anyone else in here.'

'It won't affect you, my dear,' said Julie good-humouredly.

'You'll get a sleeper as soon as the train man comes through. Come in and shut the door, Lotte. Have you got my travelling-rug still? You wrap that round you. I'll use my coat, and put my feet up on your side and you'll keep them warm for me.' She copied Anita Silovsky and took off her coat to wrap it round herself.

The train gave a series of uneven jerks and then rolled slowly out of the station. At once, Hella rose to her feet and they could hear her arguing with the orderly in the corridor. Presently the man himself appeared, collected Hella's hand baggage without a word and took it away. After a while, Julie stretched herself out along the now empty seat and gradually fell into a kind of doze, as the train rattled and swayed along the old track. At every lurch of the train she felt the sensation of falling though her back was lodged against the dusty cushions of the seat back. The cushions smelled of age-old soot, reminding Julie of train journeys in her childhood; she had had the foresight to lay a silk scarf under her head. The train stopped for signals twice; once it was shunted to a siding for quite a long time and hooters heralded the rush of an immensely long and slow train clattering past in the same direction. In the grey foredawn Julie woke. The train had stopped again. Outside was total silence; there was no sound of wind, not even the twitter of a waking bird. On the other seat, Anita Silovsky slept like a child, curled almost into a ball on the narrow ledge of her seat. Lotte slumped in the other corner; her greying hair, come undone, fell over her face and hunched shoulder. She breathed steadily through her mouth with a low, groaning sound. Julie rolled unsteadily to her feet. She was cold and felt stiff in every muscle as she stretched her legs and arms cautiously, making no sound. She raked her shoes out from under the seat and slid into them, and then tiptoed to the door, opening it inch by inch with her head turned to see if she disturbed the sleepers but they slumbered in exhausted depths. Through the uncurtained dirty window of the corridor she could see a wooden platform, a tiny hut at one end with one lamp over the door. There was no house visible; whatever village this stop served was well off the railway line. There was nothing to be seen beyond the platform but a dark mass that could be forest. All was misty and looked very cold. Julie stood there for several minutes, yawning and rubbing her eyes, which felt inflamed as if they were full of sandy dust. Then, from some way off, she heard the horn of a large motor car, and the bobbing sweep of its headlamps appeared, rising and falling over what must have been an unmade road with deep ruts and holes in it. The train engine gave a short blast on its hooter; the approaching passenger was awaited, then. The shrill signal from the train caused a low stir of movement in the carriages, but no one else came out into the corridor. At last the car stopped by the hut and two men got out, turning to call something to the driver. The boots of the newcomers sounded briskly on the boards of the platform. A valise dropped with a thud. From somewhere up the train a door was opened and a soldier hurried down the platform, picked up the valise and pointed with a raised arm. The two men, both clad in long black greatcoats almost to their ankles, and with peaked black caps with silver badges, followed the soldier. The second SS officer carried his own bag. A door slammed heavily and immediately the train shuffled into motion. The car was still being turned laboriously behind the hut, its lights flashing up and down. They were no longer needed; it was getting light.

The outskirts of Warsaw were dark, beginning with strings of low hut-like dwellings scattered along the line, and thickening into industrial suburbs with the backs of tall tenement houses crowding each other in unrelieved poverty and wretchedness. The buildings showed signs of damage here and there, but not as much as Julie had expected. The battle had been a short one outside the city and since then some patching had been done with boards and sheets of rusty corrugated iron that made the aspect of the houses more miserable even than the occasional pile of ruins that was visible. As the train ran quietly into the central station Julie noticed that the signs read WARSCHAU HBF instead of WARSZAWA and for some reason this struck her as a misuse of the German language; as if in such a foreign and un-German city as this clearly was, seen even so superficially from a train, some other and less cultured language should be used. If she had not been so tired this trace of Viennese superiority in herself might have amused her. There was no sign on the clean and tidy platform of any but German military figures. This section of the station was clearly reserved to the Wehrmacht, though a group of uniformed porters appeared as the train doors began to open who were directed by a German corporal in a simplified form of his own language which again struck Julie as offensive. Even if the porters had not looked different she would have known they were Poles because they neither looked at nor spoke to any of the passengers they served, but scurried about with heads bent and eyes averted in what was, as Julie recognised uneasily, only an acted servility. That impression, as Julie told herself repeatedly in the next few days, was the hypersensitivity of an almost sleepless night; but it remained her fixed impression of Warsaw, only increased by exiguous contacts with people about her. They did not dare to turn their heads away, or not usually, but they were inwardly turning their heads away from the occupiers, of which she was one. She had, several times in the days she spent in the city, the feeling that she must say to one or other of the people she saw – 'Look, I am not one of these people.' Which was absurd because she was one of those people, the Germans. She avoided – she noticed this herself – occasions for speaking to the hotel servants and the theatre staff where they played, for every time she had to speak to one of them the feeling deepened that they did not want to answer her.

The big hotel was reserved for German officers and officials. Julie's room was large and luxurious in the nineteenth-century style and looked over the wide street where overcrowded trams ran on the far side and there was a constant throng of slowly moving people but a lack of motor traffic. She could see from her window the towers and cupolas of what was obviously the old city of Warsaw diagonally to the right and she several times wanted to take a walk and see something of this old town which she had heard of as charming; but she did not do so and never did see the churches and patrician houses and the medieval walls.

The suitcases had arrived, and Lotte came in to unpack as Julie's telephone rang by the bed. It was Hansi, suggesting a leisurely breakfast before they went to the theatre. He had a bundle of envelopes before him on the table and sorted them methodically as the others arrived, giving two to each of the company as they joined this or the next of the two long tables reserved for them. Their places were neatly marked as if for a banquet, and Julie noticed that they were carefully arranged in order of their rank in the company.

'Isn't it funny?' said Hansi as he handed her two invitations. 'True German orderliness.'

'Hansi, we can't go to this luncheon to-morrow, can we?' she objected at once. 'Surely we keep to the normal rule of no parties on tours?' She examined the other card, an impressive embossed affair in a heavy hand-made envelope with an official seal on it. 'This I suppose we can't avoid, as it's late evening — Monday we have free in any case before going to Krakov.'

'It's a bit awkward to refuse, you know.' Hansi hesitated. He looked better this morning, in spite of a *nuit blanche*.

'Of course we have to go,' said Hella briskly. 'We can't possibly refuse an invitation from the commandant. Anyway, I know him. I shall certainly accept.'

'Then we shall all have to,' decided Hansi. 'And don't forget — Frank is coming specially to Warsaw to see the Sunday performance and give this reception for us.'

'I thought we should see him in Krakov,' said Julie resignedly. She always had disliked official parties. 'Doesn't he live there?'

'He does, yes, but apparently he's keen on the theatre and wants to see us twice.'

'So do several other people,' said Hella smiling to herself and showing her dimples. 'My general has come on special leave to see us.'

As if at a signal, a waiter hastened forward and pointed out to her an army clerk standing at the door, looking for someone in the large, glass-ceilinged room. Hella rose and went out and Hansi and Julie looked at each other with slight grins.

'When are your admirers arriving?' asked Hansi, emphasising the 'your' with a slightly sarcastic tone.

'Nando's at Lodz, doing some inquiry or other,' she answered. 'If it finishes, he should be here to-morrow.' She glanced round the room, admiring its white panelling and huge looking-glasses, everything picked out with shining brass-work and one whole wall a great window that looked on an inner court with a dry fountain. 'Very grand,' she decided. 'It looks French, don't you agree, Hansi?'

'Very. Paris, *fin de siècle*. I'd expect a magnificent creature in a huge hat and dragging miles of ruffles to enter, followed by several men not half her size in cutaway coats.'

'Not at eleven in the morning, Hansi,' protested Julie. 'Your magnificent creature would not be up until noon at the earliest.'

'I don't know about that. The only magnificent creature I know has been up all night, though one would never know it.'

'Dear Hansi. I did get some sleep, in fact. Did you?'

'Not much. I was with Harich and he snores. This tour has been pretty terrible so far.'

Julie laughed. 'Wait a bit. It will get worse.'

'You've noticed it, too, have you?' Hansi was fiddling with a cigarette, and managed to break it. He threw it into the ashtray with a gesture of irritation out of all proportion to its cause. 'Where does it come from, I'd like to know – because nothing has happened.'

'It seems to be simply there – everywhere. Let's go to the theatre. How do we get there, do you know?'

There was an official car waiting, one of several as they later found.

'Drive us about a bit,' said Hansi to the soldier, as they closed the doors. 'We're in no hurry and I'd like to have a look at Warsaw.'

The moment they left the army-run hotel, they found themselves staring out of the protecting windows of the big car at an entirely different world. It was the first time either of the passengers had seen the effects of large-scale bombing, and in the more modern parts of the city through which the corporal drove them they could see everywhere traces of heavy air-raids from the short campaign of 1939, left just as they were except where the roadway or pavements had been cleared of rubble. It was a dark day, windy, damp and cold. The hurrying crowds afoot were clothed in an extraordinary variety of what was obviously anything that would keep them warm.

'It's so bombed, I wonder where they all live?' ventured Julie after a silence, in a cautiously neutral tone.

'They seem desperately poverty-stricken,' said Hansi. 'Can they always have been so poor?'

'I was here before the war,' volunteered their driver and they now noticed that his voice was the voice of an educated man, neither in tone nor pronunciation the voice of a common soldier. 'Poland was always a poor country, but you never saw poverty in the centre of Warsaw.' He shrugged slightly and they saw that he was eyeing them in his rear mirror. 'Any more than you see poverty in the centre of Paris – or Vienna.'

They were both aware of being sounded out. It was Hansi, with his tactless honesty, who declared himself.

'Well, then, how do they come to be suddenly a slum-population, if what you say is so?'

'Well, you see, a lot of people have moved about in the last two years. Most of the Poles from Warthegau, Silesia, the Corridor area, have been transported into the General Gouvernement. Naturally, townspeople, especially the Jews, came here to Warsaw. As a matter of fact, if you went to Bydgosc or somewhere you'd find the new German population not much better off. You can imagine the Poles smashed a lot of stuff when they knew they were being transported.'

'But didn't they get punished if they did that?' asked Julie fearfully.

'Of course,' agreed the driver briskly. 'But they couldn't be caught!'

'They stick together, then?' asked Hansi.

'And how they stick together! The whole population is one huge nest of partisans and bandits,' answered the driver cheerfully, quoting a familiar phrase from radio reports without the flicker of an eyelid.

'You're rather a subversive young man, I think,' said Hansi, pretending sternness.

'Oh, no sir. Everybody here will tell you the same thing. It's like this. The Germans brought from Russia were living under Bolshevism for twenty years so their standards are pretty low. And there's a lot of people in Warsaw without proper papers, so they get no rations; that's why they look so poor, some of them.'

'What people do you mean,' asked Julie. 'I don't understand.'

'A lot of Poles come from the Russian-occupied area, they get across somehow. And, of course, most of the Jews from there came here in 1939.'

'But that's absurd, that can't be true,' protested Hansi. 'They'd be putting themselves in the ghetto.'

'Well, now,' said the driver with his air of patient cheerfulness that was beginning to get on their nerves for they could see that he was forcing all this on them for some reason of his own. 'They always did live in ghettoes – special districts, they are called. When they come here they go straight to the "district". Where else could they go? It's a lot safer than the open country or towns without ghettoes – there they are free game for any stray peasant. Here they even have their own administration and people with a bit of money or something to sell are much better off than anywhere else. Even when they can't buy themselves out of the labour units they get some sort of food – not much, it's true – and two marks a day wages. And their employers try to protect them for their own sakes; there are a lot of highly skilled work-people here in Lodz – Litzmannstadt, I mean. The cutters and stitchers in the clothing factories are all Jews, so are the jewellers and fur-workers; that's highly skilled work for two marks a day – you couldn't get it anywhere else.'

'This is disgusting,' interrupted Julie. 'Let's get to the theatre.'

'Didn't you know about it, gnae' Frau,' asked the driver innocently. 'But then, I don't suppose you would, in Vienna.' His tone now had a cool edge of contempt. But by now it was impossible to treat his familiarity as impudence.

Julie said in a low, shaking voice. 'You misunderstand me. My own husband was Jewish – is Jewish ...'

'Ah,' said the man. 'He emigrated then? Lucky for him, you'll agree, gnae' Frau ... Or is he here in Poland?'

'He emigrated,' she said tightly.

'We shall see the walls of the Jewish quarter in a moment now,' said the driver, as if changing the subject. 'There – you see, on our right? Where the houses stood on the edge, they could just be bricked up on this side and where there was an open space or a

454

street, the wall was built across. We're coming to one of the gates now. Where the police are standing — you see?'

'We don't want to see,' protested Hansi. 'This is horrible. Take us to the theatre at once.'

'This road runs right through the quarter, you see,' said the man blandly, taking no notice of what Hansi said as if he had not heard. 'It's the main road to Posen and Berlin, so they couldn't close it. So that's what we call the little ghetto on the other side of the road down here. Lots of factories in that part. Well now, are you sure you haven't time? I should like to show you where the Polish underground meets. They have a restaurant and a café on Mazowiecga.'

'You mean, you know where they meet?' Hansi asked with an amazement that made him swallow his anger.

'Of course,' said the driver. 'Lots of us know. The police are waiting for them to do something really awful, so that the places can be closed down. Though in fact it's better for the police to know where they meet. But they are pretty stupid, policemen, everywhere! I go there occasionally, myself, when I have an all-night pass.'

'Why do you need an all-night pass — the curfew doesn't affect you, does it?'

'No, no, we can move about as we like — even corporals. But you don't want to be seen by a patrol coming out of a suspect Polish restaurant late one evening. They might not be so easy to persuade as my own friends are that I'm just doing a little snoop-ing for the Gestapo.'

'That's what you say, is it, when you go out at night?'

'That's what we all say. It has the great advantage as an excuse that nobody tries to check on it. And for some of us — no doubt, it's true!'

'You're a real tricky one, aren't you?' said Hansi, half forced to laugh and half in disgust. 'Or is it true for you — is that what you mean? Do you work for the Gestapo?'

'Well, there you are, you see. Nobody really knows, but nobody can check up very easily, either.' The car turned a corner, and drove up to a building with an eighteenth-century façade only slightly damaged by an artillery shell. There were large notice boards in front of the steps, announcing that the theatre was requisitioned by an SS unit and trespassers would be dealt with according to military law. Over the centre doors was the legend cut in the stone, TEATR POLSKI.

The corporal got out and opened Julie's door for her.

'I'll wait for you,' he said to Hansi over his shoulder. 'Those are my instructions. When you need me, I shall be in the men's canteen at the back there.' And he pointed.

'Just a moment,' said Julie, and put out her hand to touch his arm. 'What is your name?'

The driver looked at her and she saw that his eyes were clever and sharp.

'Corporal Luders,' he said. 'Just ask for Berthold. They all know me here.'

'You mix with the SS too, then, as well as the Polish underground?'

'Naturally, Frau Homburg. I mix with everybody. Everyone knows me. In the ghetto, too,' he added, looking with an effect of suddenness straight into her eyes.

'You are mistaken if you think I wanted to stay behind when I could have gone – then, in 1938, when my – my husband emigrated. It was quite different – quite different from what you evidently think.'

For a moment they stared into each other's eyes.

'I am sure it was, gnädige Frau,' said the man equably, with a courteous gesture as he closed the car door. As they went up the steps, broad and low, to the centre door, they heard his voice say quietly but very distinctly behind them:

'It always is different.'

Hansi's face was showing pale patches and he turned furiously on Julie.

'This is abominable! You shouldn't have said anything to him about – about . . . ' He turned back to the car, but the driver had put it into gear and was already moving off to the car park. 'I shall report him!'

'No you won't,' said Julie quietly. She had gone rather pale and now her face showed the sleepless night. 'What would you say? Any more than I could explain that ...' She stopped. They stared at each other for a moment, bleakly.

'Why should he believe me?' said Julie and went up the steps to the door. 'And why should I feel I have to defend myself?'

There was an SS sentry at the door who examined their passes, the same ones hastily made out in the Krakov hotel, which now, Julie saw, had an endorsement with a blurred official stamp that made them valid for Warsaw.

There was an administrative office in the theatre devoted to its occasional use for its real purpose and apparently only loosely connected with the unit that used the building for offices and stores. The theatre was in use several evenings a week as a cinema for the SS troops, although its gallery was filled with large packages and crates of some kind of military stores.

Some of the company were already in the office when Hansi entered with Julie following, discussing with a young officer the arrangements for the night's performance. The room was crowded and full of smoke and Julie did not at once see who the officer was for he had his back to the door as he searched for something in a tall filing-cabinet. When he turned she saw that it was the same young man who had forced his way into her apartment during the autumn of two years before. She was faintly surprised to find that she remembered his name.

'Untersturmführer Schultze!' she said, 'don't you remember me?'

It was clear that he did for he flushed vividly at her greeting; but shaking hands with him she saw that this was the only evidence of extreme youth left to him. The tall fair boy was changed; his open and naïve look had given place to a sullen and troubled glance and he averted his eyes when anyone looked directly at him.

A woman was telephoning by the office desk and while Schultze began to explain to Hansi the difficulties of getting together the scattered theatre staff for their tour he listened all the time with half an ear to the conversation in Polish.

'Well, that makes five, Lieutenant,' said the Polish woman, as she laid down the receiver. Her German was good, she spoke it

457

with a French accent and pronounced the title in French, obviously to avoid having to pronounce the SS rank.

'Thank you, Frau Malczewska.' The lieutenant turned to Hansi. 'The staff is so scattered, it is hard to get hold of anybody,' he continued his explanation, 'and it's doubtful if we can get them passes to go with you to Krakov, in any case.'

'We could help there, perhaps,' suggested Harich. 'We've got to have lunch with Fischer to-morrow, so we may as well make use of him, eh, Hansi?'

'Commandant Fischer — certainly he could order passes for them ...' Schultze hesitated. 'Trouble is, all these people have to work and if they give up their jobs they'll find themselves in difficulties afterwards.'

'Won't their theatres just lend them to us for a week?' suggested Julie.

Both Schultze and the Polish woman turned to look at Julie, again with that testing look, and it was clear that they thought to hear sarcasm in her remark. Schultze hesitated once more and the woman answered for him, not looking at Julie and speaking in a flat and neutral tone.

'If they were working in theatres, you could simply requisition them for the week,' she said, 'but after the theatres were closed down the staffs took whatever work they could find. Like myself.'

'You are an actress yourself?' asked Hansi.

'No. I was a producer,' she replied in the same tone. 'Here.'

'Frau Malczewska works as my secretary,' explained Schultze in a constrained voice, giving the woman an anxious look.

'How awful for you,' said Harich sympathetically. 'Oh, Lieutenant, nothing personal meant to you, my dear fellow.'

'On the contrary,' replied the woman, looking at Harich, at any one of them, directly for the first time, 'I am very lucky.'

'The best actress in Poland is working as a waitress,' explained Schultze, not able to hide his anger at this fact.

Hansi glanced sideways at Julie in the silence that followed this unwise remark.

'We are not the only two being indiscreet this morning,' he said. For once he weighed his words carefully before speaking, and the answer was at once an expression of sympathies shared and a warning. As if to point the warning the door opened and Hella Schneider danced in, attended by a tall and broad-shouldered officer in SS uniform, carrying his cap under his arm.

'Here they all are,' cried Hella. 'I can introduce you to them all at once!'

The Polish woman had already faded through the doorway into an adjoining room. Schultze jumped to attention.

'Ah, Schultze,' said the SS Gruppenführer in a loud, jovial voice, and with a stride forward he clapped the young lieutenant familiarly on the shoulder. 'How's the wound in this horrible weather, eh?'

'Not too bad, sir, thank you,' Schultze answered as heartily as he could, and stepped back towards the wall to remove himself from attention.

'Schultze was on my staff in Vinnitsa last year,' said the newcomer to Hella. 'We were wounded by the same shell. Ha, ha! I got promotion and he got this cushy job. It's all a matter of luck — the luck of what part of the body you get wounded in, in this case. And now, my dear, introduce me to everybody before I carry you off again!'

When the formalities had been performed with much loud gusto on the part of Gruppenführer Tenius and much flirtatious condescension on the part of Hella, Tenius clapped Jochen Thorn on the shoulder just as he had done Lieutenant Schultze.

'Saw you in Berlin, once,' he claimed, 'before this rotten war took up all my time. I'm looking forward to seeing you again. Will you be acting to-morrow night? Can't come to-night — we've got other plans for this evening, haven't we Hella? Ha, ha, yes — other plans!'

'We're playing together to-morrow, aren't we, Jochen?' answered Hella, already a little disappointed at the impression her admirer was making. 'They have to rehearse for to-night, so we'd better go now, Teni. I can see Hansi looking sideways at us already!'

'Not a bit of it!' cried her companion loudly. 'He's a very good fellow — anyone can see that, even an idiot like me. See you at lunch to-morrow, Hansi — you won't mind me calling you Hansi, will you? I always do, you know.' His rather red face, which could easily in a few years become either choleric or sentimentally engorged with wine, beamed round at them all like a sun rising in mist. He had a wide, loose mouth and startlingly thick black eye-brows.

'God, what a horrible stinker,' muttered Thorn as soon as the door closed – slammed – on the visitors.

'Not a bit of it!' mimicked Julie. 'I thought he was rather sweet. Better than some of Hella's men, anyway.'

'Yes, my boy, you should have known her first husband.' Harich put an arm round Julie's shoulders, who replied, 'Teni must be the SS officer I watched get on the train at a wayside stop in the dawn. He was coming to see Hella act.'

'Seeing her act is incidental to his main purpose in coming, I rather fancy,' suggested Thorn, and they all laughed. They had not noticed the Polish woman return to the office, but Julie looked at her now and stopped laughing. It was not that the woman's look was angry or contemptuous; it was a wondering, detached look, the look of one who glimpses another world; a world once known, but now far distant. Just so does someone suffering a great grief look at carefree passers-by who laugh and talk as if nothing had happened.

5

There was a housemaid in her room when the next day Julie came in to make up and change for luncheon with the District Commissioner. The girl pulled the bed cover straight and looked round to see that all was in order before leaving. Her sullen look met Julie's in the dressing-table glass and for a second, before the girl averted her face, they considered each other. She then, without speaking, left the room.

What was it? Not hostility, nothing as sharp as that, something more negative. Julie stared at herself in the mirror. The word rejection occurred of itself. Unsuitable, but she found no better one; rejection was incapable of summing up the real relation between the Warsaw people and their conquerors, yet it was the word she meant and it stuck in her mind. Inevitably Julie's view of Warsaw was that of her own world, that the Poles were backward, superstitious, disorganised, especially so here where the benefits of Austrian administration had never been felt. Even superficially in the big hotel, it was clear that this was a less advanced society than her own; door handles came off in the hand to nobody's surprise, the plug in the bath was missing and this too was quite ordinary to the servant who went to find it and brought back one that was obviously, visibly, too small but was nonetheless thought to be adequate. Under the surface of pretentious decorations and furnishings was the dirt and inefficiency of the 'East', where minute and detailed instructions must be given to get the simplest thing done and where the gap between the noble and educated classes and the people was a crevasse unbridged by the influence of popular education.

Certainly they were now cruelly oppressed; the driver for whatever reason of his own, had driven that much home in a way impossible to ignore. But not so much more oppressed than they were before by their own ruling classes, surely, that she should feel here a totally strange and new situation between rulers and oppressed? Julie knew enough from Franz to know that military defeat alone could not account for the all-pervading atmosphere, for Germans and Slavs had lived together in these lands for hundreds of years and must have means of getting to personal terms with each other; the people brought up and educated in the Polish-German society – there is no ethnological difference, only differences of social organisation – had always dominated the towns and much of commerce except land tenure. Even on the land, as she knew from acquaintance with Polish landowners who lived permanently in Vienna, the Polish owners depended normally on German or Jewish estate-factors and saw the local people only on hunting trips. Yet she could not be mistaken about the atmosphere – Hansi had noticed it, too. She was conscious of being totally rejected as a human being, let alone as a privileged person. Franz could explain it to me, she thought, putting on her rings. The naturalness of the thought shocked her as if she had expressed it aloud. Yes, that must be it; I know the people deported from Vienna were sent somewhere in this country and I connect that with Franz in my mind; that is why I feel so strange here. For the moment this satisfied her. I must be careful not to show it or somebody will notice that I feel differently from the others – or perhaps they feel it too, not only Hansi and myself?

The governor lived in a beautiful and palatial villa well outside Warsaw. The streaming rains of late winter made the day dark and the whole house was lighted as if it were evening as their trail of cars approached it by the winding drive.

The hall was full of huge vases of hot-house flowers and very warm. In the brilliant lights the scented banks of roses, carnations, azaleas, lilies seemed to shimmer in the air like the heat shimmer of blazing summer. At the first glass of champagne, before they even had their coats off, an extraordinary elation seized on the half-exhausted actors and everybody began to laugh and talk at once in a mixture of relief at the sudden change from the dark, rainy, comfortless outdoors and amusement at the over-elaborate show of hospitality and wealth produced for their entertainment. Hella could be seen in a salon that showed through open doors a long dining-room swarming with servants and blazing with tall candles. She wore a dress of silver tissue and blazed like the chandeliers with diamonds; necklace, bracelets and ear-rings of large baguettes and pear-drop pendants. As she turned her head which had just been expertly coiffed, a semicir-cle of diamonds glittered across its back. She looked stunningly beautiful, but absurd.

'Thank heavens I didn't put much on,' murmured Julie to Hansi. She was wearing a black coat and skirt of fine wool, in her lapel the twist of goldwork and alexandrines designed for her by Franz before the war. On her long hands the beautiful rings of pearls and emeralds she always wore disappeared in the general blaze. Dress uniforms, the elegance of perfectly cut black tunics, silver badges of rank, sleek heads bending, it seemed, in rows over the few feminine hands available; it was the very picture of an assembly of the great world.

'So,' said Jochen Thorn quietly behind Julie's shoulder. 'So. This is victory, is it?'

'Shut up, Jochen,' said Hansi, equally quietly. 'They wouldn't understand your brand of irony here.'

'Just the same, I wish I'd brought my wife. She'd have loved to see Hella looking like this. She always said Hella was a vulgarian.'

'Where did she get those rocks, I'd like to know?' asked Harich.

'Teni,' answered Julie and they all began to laugh again.

'What was that? Did I hear my name?' boomed the voice of the Gruppenführer from behind them.

'We were asking where you were,' explained Julie. 'So many strangers, you know. I wanted to see a familiar face ...'

'And here I am, dear lady, entirely at your disposal. Come and be introduced to Commissioner Fischer for a start.'

The Governor of Warsaw District was a man so little noticeable that only his splendid and close cut uniform was really visible with its Party and Italian orders. Undistinguished in face and manner, his uniform was himself. There are many statesmen and generals whose reputations rest on a prominent nose and chin or on commanding height, on the manner of power taken for granted; only in crisis or to those who know them well is it clear that a habit of saying little and a talent for obeying orders has saved them from making fools of themselves. Fischer was appointed, like many more impressive men, because he did as he was told and knew the useful politicians; but in Fischer's case his mediocrity was obvious to any onlooker. Two minutes after his greeting to her Julie would not have recognised Fischer again, but for his orders and the group of aides-de-camp that moved with him wherever he went. His colourless, softly unformed features, balding head and solid, shortish figure could equally well have been those of any tradesman, any town clerk of a small town. He did not seem even to enjoy his position, but to be the captive of the trappings of his power. As indeed he was; his surrounding subordinates 'ran' him so that even the dubious pleasures of his office, which were many, went, as far as enjoyment was concerned, to others. It was not Fischer who engaged the dozens of lively small gypsies who formed his household staff; neither did he go much to bed with the female members, nor derive any pleasure from the music made by the male members among them. It became a legend that the Warsaw Governor rescued gypsies for the pleasures of their services; but to what obscure subaltern the credit for saving these people really went is for ever unknown.

Any gypsy who could cook, sing, dance, make love or play the fiddle was a possible member of Fischer's staff and there was no lack of candidates for the honour. At all the Governor's festivities the gypsies produced their own pervasive idiom of pleasure, contemptuous cynicism, sensuous enjoyment of the moment and the warm lymph in which everyone present floated, of their own intoxicated music.

Directed by an unseen major-domo, the gypsies stormed the long salon and filled its temporary inhabitants with their own joy, the splendour of their expanding elastic world that dimmed the glitter of lights, flowers and jewels into second place. The music stunned the ear, and raised the assembly to a heightened realisation of being, quite simply, alive. Few of those present were conscious that to be alive, of itself alone, was a supreme blessing. To introduce such absurd, outlandish ideas to unthinking strangers, is the quality of gypsy music.

The arrival of the musicians allowed the guests an interval in which there was no need to talk. This was a mercy for most of them were still tired and the champagne made them dizzy in the hot salon. When Julie looked across the room and saw a familiar figure entering by the double doors from the hall, it had the effect of an hallucination; it was Kerenyi but for a moment Julie did not believe he was really there and it seemed as if the thoughts before her mirror had conjured up his face as part of her secret life.

'I say, there's Georgy!' said Hansi quickly and she felt grateful to him for readjusting reality. 'What can he be doing here?'

The unknown man they were standing with looked over his shoulder at the newcomer and seemed to find nothing strange about his arrival; he was no stranger there, then.

'You know Kerenyi?' asked the man. 'Of course, he is Viennese, isn't he?' In a pause of the music they could hear Harich's baritone and watched Hella as she greeted Kerenyi with gushing condescension. He must have asked some question for Hella said loudly, ducking her head prettily in the gesture of one who blushes, Yes, it was her engagement party.

His ironical congratulations were lost in a fresh outburst of music, and Julie watched him as he detached himself neatly and began to make his way across the crowded room towards herself and Hansi. He stopped to speak to everyone in his way and appeared, as always, to be completely at home. Except for the actors he was the only man not in uniform.

His approach had the effect of lounging; but to Julie who knew him so well the casual glance of his deep-set eyes and the cool way he moved, threading his way by turning his big shoulders and nodding as he greeted and was greeted, were obviously assumed.

'My dear fellow,' cried Hansi, stretching out his hand as Kerenyi reached them, and clapping, as his own hand was grasped, his free hand over the clasped ones. 'My dear Georgy, how are you? What brings you here? Splendid surprise for us, to see you!'

'I've been looking forward to it for weeks – ever since I heard the Burg was sending a company,' said Kerenyi and put a long arm for a moment round Hansi's slight shoulders. As he turned to Julie and took her hand she saw that he had recovered from the shock of his loss and though the almost white hair changed him he did not seem older. She stood on tiptoe to kiss his cheek and felt that his old energy had returned with all its force; the big nose still probed the air, the eyes were as sharp and reserved as ever; yet he had changed. She felt tears prick sharply in her eyes and laughed to cover them but said nothing and neither did he. After a moment, in which he stood lounging and looking about him, he said quietly, 'Well, how are you all?' and she knew that he too had needed a moment to recover.

'We're all very well,' she answered, knowing what he meant to ask. 'The others would have sent their love if they'd known we should see you.'

'The others?' asked Hansi.

'Lehmann, Maris, everybody – Fina too, I know. She always had a soft spot for you, Georgy.'

'And I have for her – especially for her cooking,' answered Georgy. 'Does she still go to Mass properly?'

'Of course. Even more than she did, I think.'

He began to tell them about his job, which kept him travelling most of the time. He had the rank of sergeant, he informed them and seemed proud of this implicit explanation of his coming in civilian dress to the party.

'How absurd for you to be a sergeant,' laughed Hansi. 'Why on earth don't you get a commission?'

'The official army commentators are mostly sergeants. Only the office chaps who run the PR set-up are commissioned. And I wouldn't want to be tied up in an office job, doing paper work all the time.' He looked casually about him, one hand in his trousers pocket. 'Besides, there will be a lot of men about when this is all over who would be glad to have been "only" sergeants.'

It was said so calmly that at first they did not understand him and when they did, they looked at each other quickly, saying nothing. Involuntarily, Hansi glanced first to one side and then to the other. In the chatter no one seemed to have heard. The music began again and the fiddler who led the musicians left the bay window where their stands were set up and began to move about the room, his bright red jacket and striped cummerbund marking his passage as he leaned towards the more distinguished of the guests and played for them. He came near their group and Kerenyi nodded familiarly to him.

'Hallo, Paul,' he said, and the man bowed to Julie and began to serenade her, with his bright black eyes fixed on her face. After a moment he changed his tune and played a familiar air to which Kerenyi sang the first phrase in his tuneless flat voice ...

'Es muss' was wunderbares sein, von dir geliebt zu werden ...'

Julie heard her own laugh as strained. 'Are you flirting with me, Georgy?' she asked. He looked directly at her.

'No, never, Julie. That would be presumption with a woman as beautiful and as powerful as you.' He seemed to be quite serious.

As the gypsy moved away the major-domo gave a signal from the doors of the dining-room and the music ceased. A general movement began towards the long table and Julie found an aide-de-camp at her elbow to lead her to her seat. She was on the Governor's left while Hella had the place of honour at his right hand. Georgy and Hansi were both well down the table where men sat together for there were only a half a dozen women present and about thirty men.

'It really seemed to go on for ever,' said Julie later when she could speak again to Kerenyi. 'I thought the speeches would never end. All those heavy compliments and gallantry!'

'But Hella enjoyed it,' Harich comforted her.

Julie was watching past him as Hansi said something to Hella, and appeared to be urging something on her, to which she shook her head and they could hear her tinkling laughter.

'I shall go back to the hotel as soon as the Governor goes, Georgy,' said Julie. 'We've had an awful couple of days and nights and I'm going to sleep until to-morrow morning. I'm not playing to-night, thank God. But I must see you again, we must have a talk.'

He looked at his watch. 'I have to leave for Krakov in a couple of hours,' he answered. 'But I shall be there while you are there and we'll have time then.'

'Can we give you a lift back to the town?' asked Harich. 'We've got official cars. The number one treatment – nothing too good for us.'

'I have a car here, thanks,' replied Kerenyi. 'See you in Krakov, Julie. Ah, before I forget – I believe your driver is Berthold Luders, isn't he? He's a very good chap; if you want anything just tell him and mention me.'

'You know him, then?' Julie was startled.

'Certainly. We non-coms stick together, you know. I must get along now.' He lifted one hand negligently and strolled away. Hansi was coming towards them as the bustle of the Governor's departure began. He waited only as long as Fischer took to kiss Julie's hand again, which he did with the awkwardness of a man not used to social niceties.

'I shall have to stay with Hella,' said Hansi. 'She insists on staying on and if I don't stick with her she'll never get on stage to-night. She seems to have taken leave of her senses,' he added, frowning anxiously past Julie.

'I'm going back. I'll see that Julie gets to the hotel all right,' Harich assured him.

Julie was just about to protest that she was quite capable of returning to her hotel without an escort, when it struck her that Harich too must have felt something in the atmosphere if he knew at once that Hansi did not want her to be left alone even in her official car. So she smiled instead of protesting.

'All right, Wally. We can leave now,' she said.

Out of doors the lashing rain still poured down as if it would never stop. She was so tired and the massive meal and wines, the heat, the brilliant lights and the scents had so dazed her that she almost slept in the big car while Harich, equally overcome, dozed in the opposite corner. Only when the car stopped and the driver's cheerful voice announced the hotel, did she pull herself together with a start.

As the driver held the door for her she turned her head and saw he was looking into her face with that direct, challenging stare she had noticed before.

In her room, she lay down and at once fell asleep. It was late in the evening when she awoke and remembered that Nando had still not arrived from Lodz.

Julie lay for a little while, listening to the small noises of the hotel; she became aware that she was hungry, and still more, thirsty; that she would not go back to sleep.

The dining-room was full of people, mainly men in uniform, and beyond it could be heard music from the bar. Julie retired from the door and crossed the hall, looking for the café. In the outer hall, drivers and military messengers stood about talking and waiting, among them Corporal Luders. There was a gloomy lounge, half lighted, and clearly little used. By the lift cage a black and gold glass sign pointed a finger with the legend CAFÉ to a side stair. Julie went up to the mezzanine and turned corners, coming then into the gallery of a café on the ground floor of which a number of groups sat at the little tables in a haze of smoke. The outer doors to the street were – Julie had seen them from the outside of the hotel – locked and barred by steel expanding gates. From the inside, these public doors were shrouded by heavy frieze curtains.

There was only one couple in the little gallery, and Julie seated herself at the table farthest from them. A German in uniform came by and asked her civilly if she were staying in the hotel; the gallery was reserved for hotel guests, and Julie gave him her room number. Going out again, the man nodded to the officer sitting at the far table with a woman whose back was towards Julie. Only then did Julie see that this was Lieutenant Schultze.

Presently he came over and bowed to her, commenting on her not being at the theatre so that she found herself explaining the programmes. It was clear that Schultze wondered at her being there alone. Quite against her real wishes Julie found herself suggesting that the two should join her; the habit of sociability was

469

too strong for her, she was unused to being alone in public. Lieutenant Schultze looked across at the back of his companion with his anxious and careful expression and murmured something about that being difficult, but perhaps Julie would not mind joining their table instead? Having finished her eggs, she did so.

The woman with Schultze was Malczewska. As Julie came up to the table, she glanced down into the café and moved her chair still farther into the corner to make room for Julie. There was a screen of white-painted wrought iron jutting from the wall in the corner and this almost cut them off from the vision of anyone in the downstairs room. Julie became aware that Malczewska was not supposed to be in the café; like the hotel it was reserved for Germans.

'I saw you last night,' said Malczewska. 'You are very good. It is a fine production of a rather bad play, and your Elisabeth makes it.'

'I'm glad it was not noticeable that I was half asleep most of the time,' replied Julie. Malczewska was watching her face with a candid professional eye.

'Have you ever played Hamlet?' she asked suddenly. At Julie's surprised shake of the head, she explained. 'I produced *Hamlet* in 1937 with a woman — she was rather like you to look at.'

Schultze was pouring out a second glass of tea for her; in his protective, anxious manner the relationship between them was clearly expressed. She gave him a quick half-smile and lit a cigarette which she smoked quickly, pulling on the harsh black tobacco as if she needed it. She was at least twenty years older than Schultze and Julie found herself examining her face. A long angular face with the dark, flat hair pulled back carelessly and tied with what looked like a shoelace and probably was one. There were heavy pouches under the eyes, discoloured by illness or lack of sleep, and the mouth was set with a look of permanent irritation; it was the mouth of one consumed by a controlled anger. The nose was long, irregular, deeply rooted, a masculine nose surmounted by two deep vertical grooves that cut the forehead. The face was so totally without grace or charm that it interested Julie to look for its attraction; for attraction it certainly had. A group of junior officers was noisily leaving downstairs; they went out through a narrow side door.

'Why is the main door closed all the time?' she asked Schultze.

'It's always been closed, ever since I've been here – I don't know why.'

'A bomb was thrown in at the door one evening,' Malczewska said laconically. She glanced at Schultze. 'That was in 1940, before you came here. The same day Igo Sym was assassinated.'

'Igo Sym – haven't I heard the name somewhere?' Julie asked.

'You may have done; he was quite well known as a film actor and I suppose his name may have reached Vienna ... Or perhaps you read of his death?'

Julie shook her head. 'I don't think so,' she said.

'He worked for the Gestapo, even before the war, so they say. Certainly after it started. The Armiya Kraiyowa knocked him off as a sort of throwing down of the gauntlet. After that things began to get really bad. The theatres were closed down and then all the newspapers stopped publishing. Except the one issued by the Germans in Polish. One side would kill somebody and the other side answered. It became a running battle – still is. Every time the Gestapo makes a raid, the Home Army men shoot a couple of policemen. That causes a fresh raid and the dilemma has become a sort of madness now. Both sides kill for the sake of killing.' She smiled at Julie. 'We think of nothing but death here. You will find that out while you are here.'

'There is no meaning in it any more,' said Schultze in a low voice.

'Just death for death's sake. Every day, every night. Innocent and guilty alike. Not that one can any longer say there are any innocents. We are all involved now, even the children. A pity you can't talk to my son. You would see what I mean.'

'I feel it,' answered Julie. 'The atmosphere is terrible here. We all feel it ...'

A bell shrilled somewhere.

'Ten o'clock,' said Malczewska, 'I must go.'

'How will you get home?'

471

'My sister works in the hotel, and I am sharing her room tonight.'

She went quickly away through the gallery door; Schultz and Julie followed more slowly.

'People who work for the army get special passes,' he said, as if he felt some explanation to be needed. 'It is easier for them to get about.'

'Even at night? I thought, from what the driver said . . .'

'At night it is dangerous, yes. Sometimes the police shoot on sight. And the Poles nearly always. They assume anyone who is out at night without their knowledge is a Gestapo spy. The Home Army network is very tight.'

They were waiting for the lift which did not come down.

'I shall walk up,' said Julie, and said good night. Schultze watched her go but did not follow; he turned, hands in pockets and head bent, moodily, towards the noisy music in the bar. From two closed doors, as she walked down the corridor to her room, Julie could hear laughter and dance music from radio sets. Clearly Malczewska was not the only woman from outside who sometimes spent the night in the hotel.

She pulled back the curtains in her dark room. It had stopped raining for a few hours. The wide street was silent and empty. Nothing stirred, not even windows were lighted as far as she could see, up and down the blank stretch of dark only faintly lessened by the occasional, shrouded, street lamp. She stood by the window for some time, waiting to see the shadows of people moving close to the house walls, as they had in Krakov. But here nothing moved. Twice large cars swept up to the hotel entrance, headlamps full on. They were the only sign of life. If people in the houses opposite were still up, they had their windows heavily curtained. Presently Julie drew the curtains again and then went downstairs to wait for the company from the theatre, rather than stay alone in her room. She would have telephoned Nando in Lodz, but had no idea of where he was to be found.

The next morning when she and Hansi arrived at the Teatr Polski, Lieutenant Schultze was standing by the main door, talking to a civilian, and they both greeted him as they went in. The

472

rehearsal went well; after a late luncheon they could get a rest in the afternoon.

'Weird how we sleep at all hours in this place,' said Julie in the car on the way back to the hotel. 'I seem to be turning night and day round for the last week.'

'Everybody does, here,' said the driver from his front seat, without being consulted. 'Excuse me asking, but do you know Lieutenant Schultze well?'

'What on earth has that to do with you?' interrupted Hansi irritably.

Julie put out a placating hand.

'No, I don't,' she answered. 'I met him once while he was stationed in Vienna — what, two years ago, I suppose. Then we found him here in the entertainments office. Why?'

'Oh, nothing,' said Luders in his off-hand fashion. 'It's just that he's a bit dangerous to talk to. That girl-friend of his has turned his head and he talks too much. I'd be careful with him, if I were you. He'll end in trouble.'

'Look here, Corporal, suppose you mind your own business,' snapped Hansi.

'Yes, sir,' said the man coolly.

'As a matter of fact, I think he's right, Hansi. Schultze seems a little unbalanced to me, too.'

'It is still none of Luders's business.'

Julie decided not to answer and glanced at Luders's reflection in his driving mirror to make sure he understood. Apparently he did, for no more was said.

'I don't like that driver,' said Hansi as they sat down to table. 'And I shall ask for him to be changed. We've all got enough on our minds without being exposed to his impertinences.'

'Please don't get him into trouble, Hansi,' begged Julie. 'I agree with you,' she went on quickly, as he turned his irritable thin face to her to protest. 'But it could be done without getting him into trouble, couldn't it? I mean — we could just change drivers with Jochen and Wally? They have a car to themselves, too?'

'I don't see why they should have to put up with his conceit, either.'

'But he won't be the same with them — don't you think it was just because of me being a woman?'

'I suppose they would just shut him up the first time he opened his mouth,' Hansi was grudging. 'Or just not answer him at all.' He gave the soup just being served to him a bilious look and pushed the plate away. 'The food here is as bad as everything else. I have the feeling here — ever since we got out of the train — that something is going on. Hella not telling us about her engagement; and why did this bounder of a driver pick on you in that way? It's positively uncanny.'

'He's a good psychologist, I suppose.' Julie too put down her spoon and left the soup almost untasted. 'Or perhaps he's heard something?'

'Heard something? What should he have heard? What are you talking about, Julie? You're getting as bad as the others.'

'I meant,' she said in a low voice, 'he might have heard about the divorce. That was what occurred to me at the time, you know.'

Hansi stared at her, and the whitish patches appeared sharply under his cheekbones.

'Do you *still* think of that business?' he demanded. 'I thought that was all over and done with years ago!'

'It is difficult not to think of such things,' she admitted miserably. 'Here, I mean. Seeing Georgy Kerenyi reminded me — you know?'

For a moment he did not know what she meant; then he said slowly, 'I didn't ask if he'd heard anything of her — did you?'

'No. Not there. I couldn't.'

They were silent while the soup was removed and chicken cutlets with tinned peas placed between them. Julie refused wine and poured out some water from a bottle the label of which claimed that the contents alleviated liver troubles of every kind. Neither of them touched the large dish of potatoes.

'Our eating habits must please the staff,' Hansi tried to joke. 'We leave enough food to feed the whole kitchen.'

She did not answer; after a pause he broke out suddenly.

'You'll never forgive me for forcing that business on you, will you?'

474

She looked at him carefully.

'Let's not have a scene, Hansi,' she said at last. 'I never thought of it as being your doing. If you feel yourself to blame, it is quite unnecessary, really and truly it is. I went into it quite deliberately out of my own will – I won't say my own free will – but I made up my own mind. It was the alternative to giving up my career, and that's all there is to it.

'I was trying to remember,' she went on presently. 'But I can't. There must have been a moment when everything could have been changed, but I'm damned if I know when it was.' It was so rare for her to use a vulgarism of speech that Hansi looked at her sharply. She shook her head at the bottled plums the waiter had put down in place of her half-eaten chicken. 'You know there just was never a moment when I could have acted differently. There was no time before it happened to get used to the idea for me just to go – that never occurred to me in the few hours after you warned me. Well, yes, it did occur to me; I remember thinking about it, but it wasn't real, if you know what I mean. Then, afterwards, it was just one thing that led to another.'

'It seems a long, long time ago,' he said. 'Much more than four years.'

6

Nando had still not arrived by Saturday morning.

'It's odd he hasn't let you know, Julie,' said Harich. 'I suppose he's all right, is he?'

'He would have let me know if anything was wrong. He knew the Court of Inquiry might take the whole week, that was understood. He'll be at Krakov on Monday if he doesn't arrive to-morrow.'

'Shall we just leave his invitation open, then? For the reception? Nobody is ever going to notice.'

'I don't think we can do that,' said Hansi. 'I did ask for an invitation for him as a favour ...'

'My dear boy, these barbarians here have no idea of the decencies of life. They'll never know the difference. Just leave it.'

'You're wrong there, Wally,' said Jochen Thorn. 'Just because these ghastly philistines have no idea, they're very strict about what they call protocol. Frank holds court – as he believes – like a king in Krakov with every sort of etiquette and precedence worked out by a special staff.'

'That was my impression, too. I shall get the receptionist to telephone and say Nando has not yet arrived. That leaves it neutral.'

'The whole affair is going to be the most dreary bore,' said Julie rising from the table. 'And that reminds me – I must get Lotte to press my dress.'

'I wonder what Hella will wear this time?' said Harich, chuckling. Except during performances Hella had hardly been seen by the others and her dresser had mentioned to Lotte that she was not sleeping in the hotel. 'That was a typical ploy of hers over her engagement, wasn't it?'

'You found out what happened, then?' asked Hansi, idling with a cigarette.

'I asked her, straight out, why she hadn't told us. She said Tenius felt his chief – Fischer, she meant – ought to be the first to be told. I knew by the way she put on that eye-fluttering act of hers that it was all her own idea. They told Fischer the day before his lunch party so that he was practically forced to declare it an engagement party.'

'She didn't tell you that!' cried Hansi. 'You're inventing, Wally.'

'Well, she didn't put it like that, of course. She said, they were having dinner with Fischer the night after we arrived – you remember Tenius said when she introduced him that he had plans for the evening – and how delighted Fischer was and what a fuss he made and how he insisted and so on, until I thought I should slap her face.'

'She'll be more impossible than ever married to this satrap,' said Thorn. 'You can hardly get her on to the stage now, Hansi.'

'She used to be a good actress,' said Harich. 'But films spoiled Hella, long before she got notions of being the wife of one of the rulers of the Reich.'

'Perhaps Hella will retire now she is to marry such a big shot?'

Hansi stared at Thorn's question and laughed. 'My dear chap, you don't understand Hella at all, if you think that. She'd sooner not marry again. She wouldn't marry Göring himself if it meant giving up her career. No, no. She wants to have everything, and everything of the best and most expensive. She's no more interested in her Teni than she is in – in Herr Brenner, the electrician. Hella is the most complete example of the egocentric I have ever known. You will see, once she is back in Vienna, she will go back to working hard. She's got her fortune now. There won't be any more film-making that conflicts with the stage. But she will want to go to Berlin, of course.'

'That was all just money-making, all those awful films, then? As Wally says?'

'Of course,' said Harich, yawning and stretching. 'I never seem to get enough sleep in this weird town.'

'It's getting late. I must go to the theatre. I've still got some paperwork there to do. We've managed to get together some sort of team to go with us to Krakov and I must see that their passes are all in order or they will have trouble with the military authorities.'

'Damn it, Hansi, it's Saturday. You don't have to do everything yourself. Take a day off and let that queer entertainment officer worry about all that.'

'I can't quite do that,' said Hansi uneasily. 'I must make sure they will be all right. Tenius promised he would have a word with the town major and get him to telephone the offices concerned. It ought all to have been finished yesterday, but Tenius is never to be found and when he is, he's only half sober, if that. Besides, Julie would skin me alive if she thought I hadn't done everything I could for these people. She's asked me twice about getting their jobs back. That's why we only engaged people who are working for the occupation authorities – so that we could fix it.'

'I should have thought it would be easier to arrange it with civilian employers?' hazarded Harich.

'So did I until that queer entertainment officer, as you call him, put me straight. He says any Polish employer would as soon sack anybody who does us a favour as not. And jobs are hard to come by, it seems. Civilian jobs, that is.'

'You think feeling is that strong, Hansi?' asked Thorn. 'One does have a nasty feeling in these parts, I have to agree. But I think that fellow – what's his name, Schultze – exaggerates a bit. And still more that vampire of a secretary of his.'

'She's working for the Home Army, if you ask me,' said Harich lazily, 'I mean, of course, the partisan bandits.'

'I suppose she is,' agreed Hansi. 'I just hope Schultze isn't working for them as well. I don't like that impertinent driver of ours, but he's right about Schultze. He'll come to a sticky end if he isn't careful.'

'I find Corporal Luders quite an amusing chap, Hansi. Can't think why you changed over with our driver. Luders is very knowledgeable.'

'Yes. Too knowledgeable for my taste. In any case, he was saucy to Julie and I can't have that.'

'He's got some nerve if he was familiar to Julie. She's not exactly the come-hither type.'

'I don't mean in that way,' said Hansi hastily. 'He just kept on about the filthy ghetto. Seemed to think it's his duty to make us thoroughly ashamed of ourselves.'

'Hm,' was all Harich or Thorn said to this. Harich, who had not been working the previous evening, had in fact spent it with Luders in a small cellar bar in the Jewish quarter but did not feel that his companions were obliged to know of his outing.

'I must go,' said Hansi again and rose to his feet, with determination this time. They did not again try to dissuade him and he left them sitting there. It was by now after eleven o'clock.

'Let's order some vodka, Jochen,' said Harich suddenly. 'There's something about this place that makes me want to drink all the time.'

'You're not the only one,' said Thorn gloomily, and raised his arm to signal the waiter.

Hansi could have saved himself his concern with the details of etiquette; in the late afternoon, while the company was scattered in its rooms, bathing, drinking coffee, or resting before the evening performance, an official message was brought by military courier. The reception for the following evening was cancelled because of an indisposition of the host, Governor-General Frank. He would, however, the message ran, certainly be well again in a day or so and looked forward with the greatest pleasure to entertaining the company at his official residence in Krakov.

Julie was not quite ready when her telephone buzzed and Hansi's voice asked her how long she would be. Their official cars had been cut down, he said, and Harich and Thorn would take them to the theatre. An hour later, Lotte was putting Julie's wig on, both women staring closely into the big looking-glass in the dressing-room at the mask-like vision of a face that no longer bore any resemblance to Julie's own, concentrated entirely on the fit and firmness of the elaborately curled fox-red hair on which a head-dress was already fixed. There was a tap at the door.

'No one can come in,' called Lotte.

'Julie, it's Hansi,' said the voice.

'All right, Lotte. Let Herr Ostrovsky in. Oh, Lotte – you've left the wig-stand uncovered. Put something over it, quickly, first.'

Lotte hastily threw a silk scarf, the one used by Julie in the train to protect her head from the dirty seat, over the blank head-shape of the wig-stand, and grumbling under her breath, went to open the door. It was one of Julie's few tricks of temperament that she could never bear to see the wig-stand naked; its facelessness gave her a superstitious feeling of transference as if the shape of canvas and horsehair were something to do with herself.

She saw at once that something was wrong, for Hansi was smoking a cigarette, a serious breach of rules before a perform-ance in the dressing-rooms. Looking at Hansi in the glass she saw Lotte's shocked gesture and Hansi irritably stubbed out the offending cigarette on the side of the wash-basin and threw it into the waste-box.

'What is it?' she asked his reflection, surprised. Then, 'It's firmly on, Lotte. But I've smudged my forehead.' The make-up woman began, from behind Julie's shoulder, to powder over the shadow of Julie's real eyebrow which had appeared from under its painting-out where Julie had brushed the heavy greasepaint with the side of her hand. 'Mind the eyebrow,' said Julie, watching her in the glass and meaning the thin line of eyebrow painted on higher than her own. The woman did not answer, but went on stolidly powdering up over the flesh-coloured rim of the wig where it simulated a much higher forehead than Julie's, traced with the dark lines that from the auditorium would look like a lined and elderly high brow.

'It's a beautiful job of make-up,' said Hansi, watching closely. 'I'm glad you didn't pluck your own eyebrows this time – it does so spoil your own face.'

'They were still too low, in any case,' answered Julie, narrowing

480

her eyes to get the effect, 'even with all the underpart plucked. This way is much better – but more trouble, of course. It's all right now. Lotte, the petticoats now.' She looked out of the glass and down at her watch lying on the cluttered table. 'God, I'm late. Only five minutes.'

'I came in to tell you, Hella has called off to-morrow's performance,' said Hansi. Julie got up from her stool and turned facing him, to go behind the shoulder-high screen. She was only half attending to what he said.

From the corridor the call-boy could be heard intoning the call, five minutes before curtain time.

'Why?' Both women were bent behind the screen, pulling at the stiff petticoats which caught on the wire farthingale frame. Then Julie's disguised head popped up over the screen and she said angrily, 'That means I shall have to play again?'

'I'm afraid it does,' he hesitated nervously.

'And suppose Nando arrives? You promised me Sunday free.'

'I know. But if you don't play we shall have to cancel.'

'It's a disgrace,' said Lotte's voice from behind the screen.

'Hansi, I'm tired out. Can't you make her play? I really don't feel like killing myself so that Hella can go to bed once more – without any warning, at that. It's impossible. One can't work like this!'

'The trouble is, she just sent me a message and I don't even know where she is.'

'How like Hella! But I shall complain to Schoenherr as soon as we get back. I shall insist on an official reprimand.'

'Hm. Yes, I wish you would, but I doubt if Schoenherr will agree, once she is married to Tenius ... that is, if what that know-all of a driver says is true.'

'Luders? What has he to do with it?'

'Nothing at all. He was just standing about at the stage entrance when the message came – he's always standing about somewhere I notice. He volunteered the information which he said was top secret, that all leave has been cancelled and a High Command order threatens all officers who took French leave to come to Warsaw, with disciplinary inquiries.'

'What on earth does disciplinary inquiry mean?'

'Something like a court martial, I imagine.' Lotte was fastening Julie's overskirts now and Hansi handed her one after the other the pieces of stage jewellery laid out on a side table ready. She looked so strange and unrecognisable that Hansi had the feeling of talking to some gaudy waxwork figure in spite of Julie's clear, sharp voice which remained her own. 'According to Luders, Tenius and Hella are being married first thing in the morning because he has to go back on duty. I dare say he knows what he's talking about, too.'

'I'm quite sure he does. I have the feeling that if that young man said the Führer himself had telephoned, I should believe it.'

'I gather it was almost as bad as that!'

'But what can be happening to cause such a to-do? Or do they recall people from leave all the time? Everything is so crazy here, it may just be the way they do things in the army?'

'No,' he said. 'No, I don't think so, quite. I can hear the auditorium bell. Are you ready?'

'My fan, Lotte! Let's go.'

They were in the wings before the call-boy tapped on the dressing-room door, and found Harich, costumed and made up as Leicester, crossing himself nervously; he was nervous every evening for a few minutes. They heard the trundling sounds of the curtain-lifters. Hansi watched for a moment and then turned away to find Luders. In spite of his irritable resentment of the driver's manner the man had achieved a position of importance for himself which Hansi had to recognise while still finding it both annoying and ridiculous.

He found him in the canteen, which, for the first time in the week the company had been in the theatre, was empty.

'Where is everybody?' he asked, and nodded at Luders's beer glass to indicate his wishes to the soldier behind the counter.

'Recalled to units,' said Luders laconically. If he was either amused or gratified by Hansi seeking him out, he showed no change in his cheerfully insolent manner. 'There's going to be a big opening attack on two fronts in less than a month from now and it's occurred to somebody that a little discipline might come in handy in the circumstances.'

'How on earth do you know that?' asked Hansi, appalled at this breach of security. The constant official reminders to civilians that the enemy was always listening to pick up military information made him far more conscious of security than any of the military personnel he had lately met seemed to be.

'Oh, everybody knows. They've been arguing it to and fro ever since the generals were sacked just before last Christmas. Obergruppenführer Tenius was chatting about his orders to Lieutenant Schultze this morning and I heard him. He thinks Schultze is a chum of his! Just because they were wounded by the same shell . . .'

'And who is "they" who have been arguing?'

'The High Command, of course. Commander-in-Chief of the Forces, if you know what I mean.' Involuntarily, Hansi glanced over his shoulder. 'It's all right, the canteen chaps are friends of mine: we do business together. The Führer knows just what to do and how to do it, and we're going to get the oilfields and Moscow and even Leningrad in a month or two, now that he's taken command into his own hands. We're just waiting for the snow to melt because of the shortage of winter boots, that's all.'

'But the communiqués? I thought we had been advancing all the winter . . . ?'

'Oh, we have. In a manner of speaking. Look, you don't understand military language, that's all, Herr Producer. Don't you let it trouble you; everything is under control.'

'You're a subversive young bastard,' said Hansi laughing suddenly. 'I can't tell when you're joking and when you're serious.'

'I only joke with people I'm sure of,' said Luders coolly.

'And you are confident of your own judgment? Don't you ever make mistakes about people?'

'I haven't done yet, or I wouldn't be here. Take you, for instance; I know you're all right because of the way you look at Frau Homburg. I'd as soon talk like this to Schultze as cut off my hand. Not because he's a bad lot – he's just unreliable, hopelessly unstable.'

'What do you mean, the way I look at Frau Homburg?'

'Why, no more than I say. The way you treat her is the sort of man you are. I can't explain it better than that. But I know I'm right.' Luders looked sideways at Hansi and grinned.

'Now look here, this is interesting. If the way I treat Frau Homburg is a measure of my character, you must judge her to be a remarkable person, in some way entitled to special consideration. How do you know it isn't simply that we are very old friends and colleagues?'

'Oh, I know that too. Heard that from a friend of mine. And isn't Frau Homburg a remarkable person? She's a famous actress, after all?'

'I didn't mean professionally. You know that quite well.'

'No, I don't know what you meant, Herr Producer. You don't understand how these things work any more than I understand how your mind works. I haven't any intellect, you know, I don't work things out; I just know them — or not, of course. If I feel I don't know, then I leave somebody or something alone, strictly alone. But I couldn't explain how I know.'

'Well, I wish you knew where Frau Schneider is now. I suppose you don't happen to know that too?'

'No, I don't know that. Frau Schneider is the beautiful blonde, isn't she? But I can find out if you like?' Luders glanced sideways at Hansi again. 'On the other hand, if I may give you a tip, I wouldn't do anything to annoy the Obergruppenführer, if I were you. He isn't always such a jolly fellow as he seems.'

'That I can well believe,' said Hansi, suddenly serious. 'Perhaps you're right. Better leave well enough alone.'

'That's right, leave sleeping dogs lie. Or sleeping wolves, you might say, since he's off to the Wolf's Lair to-morrow!'

'Is he!'

'Yes, he's got a new job. He's rising very fast, is the Obergruppenführer.'

'Doesn't the order about — what was it — disciplinary inquiries? — apply to him, then?'

'Ah, no, he had official leave. Even now he's so senior, he's much too clever to clear off without his papers! I say, I'm afraid I must clear off too. I have to report to my sergeant some time during the evening. I'll be back before you need me again.'

Luders picked up his cap from the next stool and was gone before Hansi had time to answer him. Of Hella nothing was seen or heard until the company assembled on Monday evening on the platform for their night-train to Krakov; this time with sleepers for all of them.

I've never been so glad to leave a town before, thought Julie, staring out through the blank in the dark reflecting window made by the shadow of her own head, into the pitch dark of the night as the train ran through the tall tenements and then, only to be seen as humps and masses, the suburbs of those hut-like shanty groups in the sandy, sordid landscape. She was glad to have a sleeper to herself, not to have to talk or consider someone else's wishes. She seemed for weeks never to have been alone. Now she was free to relax and to wonder with the beginnings of unease that she had still heard nothing from Nando. It was warm in the sleeper; the heating made a soft hissing noise nearer than the rumble and clatter of the wheels over the rail joints coinciding hypnotically with the sway of the carriage. She had pulled up the blind in the carriage, turning the main light off in deference to the military regulations about showing no lights, and stared out over the draught protector looped across the bottom of the window; heavy coarse frieze with a braid edging and the embroidered initials RB. Nando would be in Krakov.

It seemed much longer than a week, that she had been away. A slight tap at the locked compartment door; Hella's voice called to her but she did not answer. She did not want to hear about Hella's wedding or accept her apologies for burdening Julie with her own work without even speaking of it beforehand. She watched the door in the dim light until Hella went away and then turned again to the dark window through which, now, rolling through the countryside, nothing at all could be seen.

Warsaw had tired her, in spite of her great physical energy, the fundament of a sanguine, equable temperament; so that she now felt slack and depressed. Gazing out at nothingness in the dark was about all she could manage although it was hardly ten o'clock and no prospect of sleeping for some time – used as she was to late hours. A drink would be good, she thought, but she had nothing to drink with her and supposed correctly that a military train would have no service. Wally Harich would certainly have something to drink, but that would mean conversation; she stayed where she was, leaning against the window corner of the made-up bunk.

There was a message in the hotel, which appeared familiar although not seen in daylight before, because the building was so enclosed in the narrow, high-built street that it was lighted both day and night as if it were always evening there. Nando had arrived, but had business in Krakov during the day and would see her after that evening's performance. That he had not arranged to be there when the company arrived at breakfast-time was a slight shock. It was no longer possible to pretend that nothing was wrong.

Instead of going in to supper with the others, including a now rather subdued Hella, Julie went straight upstairs to Nando's room. She tapped to make sure he was there and his voice answered, quietly.

At first she did not see him. The room was small and full of large pieces of furniture with a high-gloss polish which reflected everything. The curtains and the covers of the two chairs were in bright prints of a 'modernistic' design, so that the room was stuffed with ugly and restless objects. Nando rose to his feet; he had been lying full-length on the narrow bed. She had never seen him in uniform before and that was a shock, the dark tunic and breeches. She did not know why, but she did not move quickly to embrace him, but stood there, wondering what it was that was so wrong. It occurred to her stupidly that he must in the past have gone to quite a lot of trouble never to wear uniform; here he must conform.

They exchanged some kind of greeting, afterwards she had no idea what had been said. She sat in one of the hard, crude uphol-stered chairs, he leaned back with his handsome head against the backboard of the bed with its glassy sheen of walnut veneer. She saw he had been drinking and that too was a shock. There was a silence and she watched in detail his long, muscular man's hand which lay with the lassitude of a sick child's over the edge of the bed, on the little finger a gold signet with the hollowed inverted crest of his family.

'What is it, Nando?' she asked at last. He turned his head towards her and stared away again at the wallpaper opposite. That too was sharply patterned and ugly. There was a very bad painting of some pine trees and a mountain peak in the middle of the wall. The peak had snow on it.

'I've volunteered for the front,' he said at last.

The feeling of a blow inside came later; she did not at once take it in. 'Why?' she said. 'Tell me why.'

'I don't know, I just have. I've asked to be transferred to the Wehrmacht.'

'But what has happened? Obviously something dreadful has happened. Tell me, Nando.'

'Nothing has happened.' He thought it over for a moment and then added, 'I've just seen Poland, that's all. I suppose it's that.'

'It is something to do with the Court of Inquiry – that man who has been embezzling. Is that it?'

'Oh, him!' Nando gave a short laugh. 'Ulrich Benda! He's got away with it. Nasty creature. It's all been hushed up – for the time being. He'll come to a bad end, that one, but not just yet. Even the SS will have to get rid of *him* eventually.'

It was the word 'even' that told her his motive.

'You have to get out of that uniform – that's it, isn't it?'

'Precisely,' he said with assumed briskness. 'You're a clever woman, Julie. But don't ask me any more questions because I can't answer them. Even if I could explain, there are things one can't discuss with a woman, and absolutely not with you. What we need is a drink – not to talk. I've done it now, and now that you are here I realise just what I've done. But it's done now.'

'The drink is easy.' There was a bottle of vodka on the curved fat-fronted dressing-table and though it was no longer very cold, it would do, and she poured out drinks in the two tumblers, adding water to hers. She watched her face for a moment, wavering and greenish in the bad glass and saw that a trace of make-up remained quite clearly to be seen down one cheek in front of the ear. Round the ears one always misses, she thought for the hundredth time after a hasty face-cleaning. She went into the tiny bathroom and took one of the hand towels to clean the make-up away. There was a notice by the bathroom glass forbidding the use of face towels to clean razors or make-up.

When Nando had disposed of his vodka he got up from the bed and turned round in the crowded space, looking at the room.

'Isn't it horrible?' he said. 'I've been alone here nearly a week with this furniture.' He stopped and then went on, forcing himself. 'You've been at home, so you'll know what I'm talking about. You would anyway, but it's easier that you've been at home with me. My father was stationed here, and my grandfather. We always had seasonal workers from this district when we had a lot more land than we have now and they came year after year, the same people by arrangements my father made when he was stationed here – long before he was wounded, before he married my mother. I dare say my grandfather made the arrangements originally. They came until 1917, I remember quite clearly. Nineteen-eighteen, they didn't come. After 1920 when we sold a lot of land we didn't need them any more. It was all long before I had any hand in running the place, of course, but I remember them.' In a slightly tipsy way it had become important to him that she should grasp his memory of the harvest-workers. 'I used to watch the younger boys, boys about my own age. They would bring messages that they were the younger brother or the son of somebody else, married, moved to the town; they recommended each other. Girls came too. The first girl I ever lay down with came from here.'

He stopped speaking and after a while she realised he would say no more.

'I'm pretty drunk,' he said at last. 'Can we still get something to eat? You must be hungry.'

'Let's go down,' said Julie. 'The others are there, though.' He shrugged at her interrogative remark and they went down and sat with the others as if nothing had happened. Julie was amazed to see by the dining-room clock that she had only been gone for about twenty minutes. There was an empty seat at the table next to Hansi and she was, on the other hand, not at all surprised when

Kerenyi came in and reclaimed the place, explaining he had been telephoning. His appearance seemed perfectly natural, not only because she knew he was in Krakov, but because she connected him in her mind with disaster, with loss and danger.

It was late when Nando at last entered Julie's room and they could be alone. She was cleaning her teeth, as he could hear, in the bathroom, and came out to find him pulling off his boots by the boot-jack.

They stood silent for a moment and then knowledge of coming loss overcame them and they grasped for each other with an urgency near desperation.

BOOK FIVE

July 1944–May 1945

1

*J*uly sun blazed through the windows of the reserved carriage
closed against the dust; the door to the corridor was open to
the outer draught which incessantly flapped the dirty window-
curtains to and fro so that they afforded little protection against
the blaze of light. The wind of the train's passage was hotter than
the exhausted drought of the still countryside. At St Pölten three
soldiers, ignoring the FIRST CLASS signs and the reservation label,
tumbled in with long and bulky canvas bags. The aura of sweaty
wool and leather and the oily smell of side-arms filled the carriage;
they laughed much and talked loudly in the assumed coarse tone
of very young conscripts, claiming a right to seats that nobody
denied them. The corridor was full of passengers struggling past
those already sitting on cases, in the search for seats, swaying and
bumping with the rapid swing of the train and cursing the weather
and each other. Frau Pohaisky and Julie sat in corners, silent, each
enclosed in her own inner concerns, grateful at least to each other
that they need not make the effort to talk. Between St Pölten and
Vienna neither said a single word.

The train slackened speed for the curve and ran into the station
which rang and clanged with furious activity. The heavy doors
slammed, a stampede of passengers poured lumpily through the
corridor from the neighbouring carriages. Outside, the stunning
heat increased the noise of rattling luggage trolleys, ringing of bells,
shouts, banging of doors, hundreds of voices calling, nagging,

demanding, questioning, answering; it was bedlam. The two women waited until the corridor emptied itself and then stood stiffly up, collected in silence their hand baggage, pulled on thin gloves; Julie let down the wide window and looked out purposefully into the racketing mob. After a moment's frowning search she drew in her head again, brushing the brim of her straw hat on the frame so that she touched it with one hand to adjust it.

'The driver is there,' she said. 'Are you ready?'

The theatre now provided officially for the convenience and segregation of its members and so did every organisation that could claim a place in the ever stiffening hierarchy of a society losing its contact with traditional customs. One no longer simply took a taxi to the station and bought a ticket; instead, arrangements were made. The accountant's office, enlarged to ten clerks from two in the last years, reserved carriages, booked official motors, noted length of journey and time of absence. Because members of the company could not rely on getting seats in trains and therefore could never forecast exactly on arrival or return or the strain on nerves and temper the journey might involve, these arrangements began to be made – at first casually and then more formally. It was known where Julie went and for how long, that Nando von Kasda had leave for the first time in his two years of service and had been at his home. Even the smallest privacy in the most intimate matters had given way to record. Since air-raids had unbelievably at last begun anyone leaving his home reported his absence at least to the house caretaker and left a message as to where he could be reached if the house should be damaged; for their own sakes and in their own interest everyone did this and would have done it even if it were not demanded by regulations. What would have seemed even a couple of years before cumbersome, unnecessary, an intolerable interference, now appeared an advantage and was claimed as such; in the pathological state of society it was an advantage and the last little corners of privacy and freedom of choice were given up to gain order. Very few people were still sane enough anywhere in the areas touched by the war to recognise that the organisation, the administration of order, had become necessary because all was in disorder.

So a driver now collected Julie from the train and when the man offered her over his thick shoulder a clipboard with a ruled form on it on the last used line of which was her name and the place she was met and the time, Julie signed at the right, closing the record of the drive with her admission that she it was indeed who had been driven. In the widest, centre space of the divided page in the column headed 'remarks' was entered the information that another passenger was to be dropped off. This was Frau Pohaisky who shared the privilege of the car.

'Idiotic, isn't it?' Julie said to Margarete Pohaisky with a shrug and the sharp little frown showed between her brows. 'But one can never be sure nowadays of getting a taxi; and, as soon as we started to run cars of our own, people began using them for all sorts of things that had nothing to do with business. So now we all have to sign these forms.'

'It is better than taking the bus,' was all her companion answered.

'What a racket these loud-speakers make!' complained Julie after a moment. 'And one can't hear a word they say!' The car had stopped at a police signal at the top of Mariahilferstrasse and a raucous voice echoed, crackled and boomed from ill-adjusted amplifiers.

'You haven't heard the news, then, gnae' Frau?' asked the driver, staring stolidly before him at the people moving across the crossing. He moved into first gear and slowly allowed the clutch to engage.

'No – what news?' Sharply, for all news was bad.

'There's been an assassination attempt on the life of the Führer!' intoned the man, pulling left to pass a bus about to stop. 'A clique of irresponsible, aristocratic officers. The attempt failed. The Führer is unhurt. A miracle, no less.'

'Indeed, a miracle,' said Julie automatically agreeing. 'We'd better stop at the Ring and buy a newspaper. There's a kiosk there, where we turn left.'

Over the still sticky black headlines the women looked at each other without words, behind the driver's back. In a few minutes they were outside the house where the Pohaiskys' apartment was.

The driver got out to lift Frau Pohaisky's light suitcase out of the boot and she bent to the window to thank Julie for bringing her home.

'That's all right, my dear,' said Julie, shaking her aching head. 'Keep in touch, won't you?'

'Of course,' said Frau Pohaisky and nodded and went with her neat, quick step into the house where, for what reason she never knew, the police awaited her. Someone at some time had reported something she said – or not said when she should have said something, such as Julie's 'Indeed, a miracle' a few minutes before. It was one of thousands of arrests. When, days later, it leaked out that Margarete Pohaisky had disappeared, it was assumed that her arrest had something to do with the old story of her husband; in fact there was no connection, and Alois Pohaisky was left untouched in his country retreat.

Julie leaned back in the corner of the car, holding on to the greasy strap with a clenched fist. The headache, hanging about somewhere in her head all day, pounded now in her forehead like a slowly swinging weight.

Somewhere behind that loaded weight still existed the five days with Nando. She held them in her mind knowing they would have to feed her for a long, long time.

There was no one in the caretaker's lodge to carry her bag and the driver brought it as far as the lift with an air of doing something not only immensely difficult but something he was not supposed to do, that he could be reprimanded for doing. Frau Pichler had volunteered for afternoon shift-work in a factory over the Danube Canal in the spring for which she got extra rations as well as wages, and Pichler was now responsible for the houses on either side of their own, so that he was rarely to be seen. There were mud tracks visible on the black and white stone flags of the hall floor. It had evidently rained heavily in one of those summer storms that relieved for an hour or so the Vienna heat. Julie could hear the rattle of locks as the lift moaned to a stop; Fina's head appeared cautiously and then, as she saw Julie, she came out to take the bag.

'There you are at last. The train must have been late.'

'Of course,' said Julie, taking off her hat and dropping it into the carved hall arm-chair. 'How are you?' Her voice dropped. 'Where is ...?'

'Waiting in the living-room. Gnae' Frau, we shall have to do something about Pichler.'

'Yes, later, Fina.'

'We have no coffee this week.'

'Franz shouldn't drink too much coffee in any case. Tea is better for his liver.'

'Tea!' said Fina. 'It's nothing but dust we get now.'

Julie was down the hall already and did not answer. In spite of the oppressive heat all the windows were closed and Franz sat with a light rug over his knees, in a high-backed chair with its back to the door.

'Fina?' he said softly, as he heard the door.

'Franzl! It's Julie.' She could see from the movement of the rug that he tried to rise and moved quickly to prevent him. She crouched on the footstool, holding his hands closely.

'You are back? I didn't hear ...' Relieved that he need no longer move, that she was already there in front of him, he sank his head back against the chair. 'My lovely girl. I was afraid the train might be stopped. You have heard the news?'

'The driver told us on the way from the station.'

'Us?'

'Margarete Pohaisky was with me – you remember I told you she would be there?'

'Yes, yes. I'd forgotten. Could you see anything of the streets from the taxi? Is there any sign of disorder?'

'None at all – what disorder could there be? There is only the bombed building opposite the station – that's still not cleared up since I went away. The pavement is still roped off.'

'No, I expected nothing,' his voice was fainter. 'They will do nothing. What would you expect from the Viennese?'

'Franzl, I don't understand. What sort of disorder are you talking about?'

'A rising! Some sign that the people would rise against their tyrants, now the signal has been given.'

'Ah, my dear, what could they do?' she asked. It filled her with terror even to consider it, and she was ashamed of her fear; but she would have felt nothing but anger for such an idea if anyone but Franz suggested it.

'The rebels broadcast an hour or so ago, on Vienna Radio,' explained Franz. 'The Gestapo and SS units are being disarmed all over Vienna it seems. But if they are not supported – the rebels – by the people, they can do nothing.'

'But the driver said the attack had failed.'

'Naturally that is what the official report says. But the rebels broadcast that Stauffenberg got away to Berlin at once after the explosion – he had a service plane. Everything depends on the Bendlerstrasse. If the War Office does its part the army will follow. If only we knew what is happening! If only I could do something!'

'The army?' she cried in horror. 'What can the army do – they are retreating and fighting rearguard actions every foot of the way. That I do know for certain. I heard nothing else all the time I was away. If the army stops fighting for even a day it means letting the Russians in.'

'Even the Russians can't be worse than the Gestapo,' he began when a crackle from the wireless set in the book-case reminded him. 'Fina turned the radio down,' he said. 'Perhaps there is some more news?'

The loud crackling filled the room when Julie turned the knob; after a moment a hasty, violent voice shouted something unintelligible and there was a break filled with the rushing of background noise. The room was suddenly flooded with martial music and Julie quickly turned the knob back to reduce the volume of noise. She stared at the little box for a while, then looked at her watch and went out to telephone.

No, Herr Ostrovsky had left the theatre; the performance for that evening was cancelled. The agitated secretarial voice knew nothing further.

She reached him at home. Had she not postponed her return? Why should she have? Well, for God's sake hadn't she heard the news? Nobody had any idea what was happening and would she for everybody's sake please this time have a little sense and stay where she was. The angry, anxious voice increased the sense of crisis, infected her with its own anxiety. They were mad, whoever they were, these adventurers. Did they really believe it would be the western Allies who would hasten in over the Rhine? And if they did – or could – how could that help them in Vienna, where the Russian armies were a thousand miles nearer?

The Russians, she thought bewildered, the Bolsheviks, while the nagging voice sawed at her nerves. Was it really possible . . . ? The mysterious vast hinterland to the east loomed out of the shadows of history, blundering into the present; the hordes of Ghenghis Khan, the armies of the Turks, the imminent threat of Asia against civilised Europe . . . Hansi was demanding something of her, and without having heard him she knew what it was and assured him stammering, that she would stay at home and do nothing, commit herself to nothing, wait for Hansi to let her know what she should believe.

She shook her head at Franz as she came back to his chair and then sat there not speaking as the stream of *Hoch und Deutschmeister* washed through the room. Whoever was in the broadcasting station now was taking no chances. They could not turn the noise off; there might be news. But the music tramped on; there was no announcement.

When the long gasping shrill of the telephone aroused her from her thoughts of Nando, she ran out into the hall, where Fina had already lifted the receiver.

'It's the telegraph office,' she said, her sagging, ageing face making a knot of lines leading inward to the mouth set sullenly.

The girl's indifferent voice read so rapidly that Julie had to interrupt to ask her to read more slowly. When at last she got it down she sat staring at her scrawl, so carefully formulated that she had wearisomely to work out what the message meant.

'Transferred immediately stop one six five army post office number two two three three seven will try write but uncertain stop everything Nando.'

Everything, she thought, everything, Nando. That at least she could understand. He had been stationed in Italy, comparatively

497

safe; this could only mean the East Front. His journey must have been interrupted for he only left the house yesterday afternoon.

The yellow house, basking in the heat, wood-doves bubbling, the rooks cawing in the beeches, farmyard sounds at dawn; the dusty tickling odour of ripening wheat as they walked, pulling the long-stemmed daisies and cornflowers of high summer idly as they went. Everything, Nando. She did not think of his mother, but suddenly, of Lali. Lali on the terrace after breakfast, tilting her brown face to the sun and closing her shining eyes, saying she felt sick. At Julie's startled 'what?' she laughed and added casually, yes, she had missed once and hoped she might be pregnant. Julie looked down, unseeing, at the scrawl on the message pad; this crisis might mean that Otto now would not get leave to marry? She reached for the telephone to call Krassny but he was not in his office. At the home number a boy's clear voice answered. His father had gone to the country, he said. Should he rouse his mother, who was lying down – she did not feel well, he added. No, said Julie slowly, no, his mother should not be disturbed. Was his father at the house near Enns? The boy's voice, unnaturally cautious, did not know. A telegram had arrived – that was the cause of his mother not feeling well – saying that Otto was transferred to the East Front.

Otto transferred to the East. Nando too. Krassny 'gone to the country ...' From the endless tirades Julie knew how little their kind of people were liked by the Nazis; from their point of view with reason, for this plot was made by 'aristocratic officers', evidently. From Nando's talk she knew how men not liked were sent to dangerous posts.

For some reason she recalled the screaming voices announcing the loss of Stalingrad; the curses against the officers mixed with judicious praise of the soldiers. They had all fought, starved and died together, but the officers reaped only unworthy accusations of treachery. The mourning bands in the newspapers, the trumpet calls, the popularised music of *Götterdämmerung* on the radio, choirs singing '*Ich hatt' einen Kameraden ...*' Kerenyi had written to them about Stalingrad, a report that could not be published, pushed by some soldiers passing through into the letter-box. That made her picture of the East Front. Howling winds beating the exhausted men with endless snowstorms while they starved in the holes of cellars waiting for help that could never reach them; the endless columns reeling out of the smoking ruins into the snowy wastes of captivity carrying or supporting their wounded, already starving, frost-bitten. They could be seen winding black on the white ground eastwards as the last planes staggered into the air overloaded with wounded, buffeted senseless by anti-aircraft fire and the winds. Among them Kerenyi, sent back with his second wound.

Nando and Otto. She tried to imagine what it was like in heat, without the snow, which had become, for Julie as for millions of other women, the symbol of wilderness, of vast, empty stretching space over which the armies struggled. Nando, and Otto, facing the tremendous onslaught of vengeful fury. Mutiny – she thought of mutiny as a sudden comprehensive act, not of men's wills but as if of nature, such as perhaps, a great storm, which would disrupt organisation and expose its victims unarmed to the forward roll of the Russian armies. She had already unconsciously adopted the official version to some extent, that of huge masses of loyal men betrayed by a small number of selfish mutineers; there was some reality in this view for those behind the fronts as for the armies and this confusion with the view she had held for years that the real betrayers were the Party 'Bonzen' oppressed her with its contradiction. She could not, it was impossible to feel, that the mutiny had any validity for it weakened her own actual physical defence.

'My God,' she said aloud to herself, 'what have we come to!' At the sound of her voice, Fina came out of her room and looked along the passage.

'What was it you wanted to tell me about Pichler, Fina?' Julie said, getting up slowly and going towards her.

'You've been crying,' said Fina accusingly. Julie shook her head, but not in denial.

'It's the news,' she said, 'everything seems to be falling to bits.'

'I know. You can't help feeling, if senior officers are mutinying, then there must be something terribly wrong somewhere. And yet ... where's it going to end?'

They stood staring at each other for a moment. Fina leaned her shoulder against the door-frame as if she were very tired; she was too well trained from girlhood to lean on doors, cross her arms, fidget. So that this sign of weakness or weariness, like Julie's tears, was one more sign of 'everything falling to bits'.

'Yes, Pichler,' Fina sighed with the effort of pulling herself together. 'He's been up here twice, on at me to go down to the cellar when the air-raid alarm goes. If I keep on refusing, he'll get suspicious. Him and his air-raid regulations!'

'He will get suspicious, you're quite right. He's afraid for himself if everyone doesn't keep the rules. The block-leaders are very active lately. Pichler told me weeks ago that they go round regularly asking people in the houses what everyone else is doing — everybody is too scared to lie to them even if they want to. And they don't even want to, because they know we have no power any more. People are all the more resentful now of anyone who used to be top-dog, they feel the house doesn't belong to us any more.' She stopped, losing the thread of what she wanted to say, her thoughts going back with a sad, hardly rebellious pang of loss to Nando again, and her eyes wandered over the scratched and worn paintwork, rubbed down to the wood near the door handle. 'We have to be very careful,' she finished vaguely.

She wanted to warn Fina specifically not to exacerbate the nerves of the other people in the house whom Julie rarely saw but to whom Fina was the representative of the owners and showed she knew it. In the small matters that irritate women, priority in the laundry-rooms, the custom that one whole rubbish bin was for the use of the owner's family alone; things always insisted on by Fina which procured respect from the other servants and from the women in the back-house. These things were now a danger to them and Julie knew that the conspiracy must increase class-resentments; for it never for an instant occurred to her, in spite of what Franz had said, that the plot could have succeeded. And the very people who had always been more obsequious were now likely to be the most malicious, most eager to tattle to the block-leader when he came with his talk of equality, of everyone being the same to the Party so long as they were loyal to the Führer in his titanic struggle against the godless, Bolshevik Russians.

And they were equal – in their powerlessness, the privileged as well now as the poor and servile. Party propaganda was clever and the mutiny would make it more effective in its denigration of those who had position, privilege, money or attainment; this had always appealed strongly to the baser feelings of ordinary people, feelings they hid even from themselves. The envies and resentments which the Party made respectable disguised from people the truth that their old rights were gone, in the satisfaction they felt at the greater rights of others being destroyed. They did not see their own increased impotence, for they had always felt – wrongly – that they were powerless before authority.

Julie was too tired to express such abstracts, and her quite conscious knowledge of the need to express them to Fina and to warn her was not strong enough to overcome her weariness and grief.

'But what am I to do when Pichler comes up again?'

'I don't see what you can do. You'll have to go down to the cellar with the others.'

'Couldn't you get me an exemption – you know, a bit of paper that I have so much to do for you ...?'

'You mean from the theatre? I don't think that would be allowed.' Julie frowned at the headache pounding behind her forehead. 'If you go down once or twice perhaps they'll forget about it.'

'I don't like to leave him ... it frightens me that something might ...'

'I know. I know. I'll be at home whenever I can be. Nobody will know whether I'm here or not, since I'm out so much. I can always stay up here. But you will have to go down. We daren't take the risk of you getting into trouble.'

Unnoticed, it had grown almost dark in the narrow passage. It was getting late. Julie went into the living-room, drew the heavy curtains and switched on the lamps. Franz stirred in his chair, opening his eyes. His drawn face, worn to a pale mask of his former self, pierced her with a fresh grief. The five days of absence gave her eyes a new and frightening power; he is wasting away, she thought. Somewhere she recalled seeing a face of that gaunt shadowy kind; a painting she supposed. A moment later the association moved back in time and she remembered the taut, fleshless face of the menacing young man in the dark square of Krakov.

'There is no news,' he said. His frail hand moved over the back of the book that lay on the rug over his knees. 'I was sitting here thinking of Georgy.'

'So was I.' They looked in each other's eyes, not needing to say more. So that when the bell rang from downstairs, it was as if they had known.

'Is it the police?' asked Fina, keys already in her hand. Julie took them.

'I'd better go,' she said. 'They won't do anything to me. Get him into his room. And make sure there is nothing lying about in the living-room. Just in case.'

She let herself out of the door and locked it again behind her. Just in case. But she was not afraid, because she was fairly sure it was not the police.

It was Kerenyi and she was not surprised. He was in uniform, with the tabs of an official military reporter and a senior sergeant's badges. The familiar face looked odd with the uniform. He was thinner, hard and brown, his big nose more prominent than ever. There was no nervousness or fear in his look but she could see at once, even in the dusk, that the thought she and Franz had not needed to speak was correct. She locked the door after him and pressed the time-switch before they spoke.

'It's all right,' he said. 'My travel papers are in order.' Then he smiled. 'How good to see you. Though I'm sorry to have brought you downstairs.' He put his arm round her shoulders for a second of time.

'It wasn't fear of *that*,' she said, shaking her head. 'But the regulations about showing lights are being strictly enforced now. Since we had some air-raids. I'm always forgetting, needless to say – but Fina and I were just talking about her having to go down to the shelter.'

'How is Fina?' he asked as they closed the lift on the landing.

'Her rheumatism bothers her. You'll see. It's lack of exercise, I think, but I can't get her to go out.'

She was unlocking the door now and could feel a small inward tremble of excitement and impatience to bring Kerenyi to Franz. Fina, tidying papers, turned and gave a little wail of pleasure at the sight of Kerenyi. She was grasping his hands in greeting when her face changed so quickly from joy to suspicion that she looked like a different woman.

'Herr Doctor!' she asked sharply. You're not in trouble?'

'Not yet,' he said and laughed his bark of a laugh. Julie thought, it must be worse than I thought. Fina was already out of the room to fetch Franz from his hiding-place.

Kerenyi turned to Julie, lifted his chin and glanced meaningly up and down the room.

'It's all right,' she said. She was pouring him a drink. 'Brandy, I've no *barack*, I'm afraid.'

'Amazing you can still get it,' he said, drinking.

'That we can still get, but food is awkward. I eat out as much as I can.'

She heard Franz before the side door in the panelling opened, but Kerenyi heard nothing. He saw her hand tighten on her glass; looked round and instantly sprang across the room to embrace Franz, who stood trembling on the support of his stick. Fina hovered behind him, watchful but not daring to try to help him. Both men wept a little, without shame; Kerenyi practically carried Franz to his chair.

They sat staring at each other.

'We are both quite grey,' said Franz at last. Kerenyi put up a hand and rubbed it over his thick, almost white hair.

'I'd forgotten that. I've been white for years now.'

Then Franz remembered. 'I'm sorry, my dear,' he said humbly. 'Clumsy fool, to remind you.'

'You knew, then?'

'Julie told me, at the time. And you heard nothing? Nothing at all?'

Kerenyi stared at his large, bony hands in silence. Then he said quietly, 'Nothing. It was as if she simply disappeared from the face of the earth. And she did, of course. Simply disappeared as if she had never been.'

He looked up at Julie. 'I've never spoken about it from that day when you came to my place, to this. Never even realised what a relief it would be to say it. But, of course, there was nobody but you I could have said it to.'

After a little while, Julie said, 'And now?'

'Now?' Kerenyi shook his shoulders. 'I have to get myself posted to another front. I thought I would look up my old friend Blaschke, who is in Agram.'

'Are you deeply involved, Georgy?' asked Franz. 'Do you know what is happening – or what has happened?'

'You know yourself – or you wouldn't ask like that. Of course, they have failed. By the time Stauffenberg reached Berlin, the Gestapo were waiting for him.' He glanced down at his wrist to see the time. It was almost ten-thirty. 'I guess he's dead by now. Lucky for me I was in Rumania.'

Kerenyi got up restlessly and moved down the room, shoving his hands down into his trousers pockets with that suppressed violence in the small act so familiar to them both.

'You were in touch with each other on the telephone, then?' said Franz.

'Oh, yes. For months now. I was useful to them because I could move about constantly and carry messages.'

'The radio station was in their hands this afternoon ...'

'I dare say it was, in several towns. But, you see, in modern conditions and in war conditions at that, it's either instant success or total failure. And they weren't even certain of the men on duty at the signals centre at GHQ! They thought the few they could be sure of were enough. The signals-staff rota changes every week almost. They needed complete control of the signals officers. It's the romantic attitude to the officer-class; people like signallers, corps troops, messengers are not real soldiers and only real soldiers from military families are to be trusted. I see their point of view – I do, honestly – but it is just not the way a modern army functions. The nineteen-year-old boy actually sitting at the signals controls is as important to a closely organised thing like this as the solemn old men who propose to take over the government.'

'You have pretty well thought this all out, I see,' said Julie.

'By God,' he said. 'I've lived with nothing else for nearly three years.'

'Are you in danger yourself?'

'I think they have nothing to go on as far as I'm concerned. But they may have. Somebody may have kept my name in an address book. I know what I've done, but I can't know what others did – or neglected to do.' Kerenyi walked back down the room and took another brandy. 'I thought of staying where I was because the front in Rumania may break up at any time and I could disappear in the chaos. But I couldn't trust the news officer where I was.'

'Did you say the Rumanian front is in danger, Georgy?' Julie's voice shook. 'Surely that can't be true?'

'It is not only true; the Russians can also cross the *Hungarian* border in the next week or so.'

Julie got up and walked to the window; she remembered just in time that she must not pull back the curtain and turned back, the edge of fringed velvet still in her hand.

'What is to become of us, then?'

Nobody answered.

'How long, Georgy?' asked Franz at last.

'A year perhaps. I can't tell. The Russian advance may gather momentum suddenly. Beaten troops suddenly lose heart, you know; something happens to the resolve of the men. No matter how the communiqués lie, they know the truth and then the battle is a rout. I saw it happen to Russian troops, often, and to us at Stalingrad. But one can't tell when ... Everyone in Rumania, except apparently the High Command, knows that the Russians are building up for a big attack on the Prut. Then the Rumanians will surrender. They have been plotting to for months. That will signal the breakthrough ...'

'But I just can't believe it. You're saying that the Russians will be here – here?' Julie stopped and gulped down something that filled her throat. 'It will be as bad as the Turks!'

'It will be worse than the Turks,' he answered her grimly, not looking at her. 'Imagine the Turks with modern aeroplanes and artillery. And you have no idea what we have done to their country – civilised as we are. I couldn't describe to you what this war has been like and if I could you wouldn't believe me. What they will do to these fat, rich lands when they get them, there's just no way to imagine it. You've got to grasp it, they are barbarians, their own officers often have to threaten them with revolvers to maintain discipline. They're like a horde of children gone wild through neglect. Not bad or wicked, but simply wild, and corrupted to their souls by the total cynicism and lack of personal responsibility they live in. I've seen them burn a whole store of blankets to make a fire where there was a forest of trees nearby, and then freeze to death in the night for lack of blankets. And the slaughter ... As we pull out of a village, time after time, you can hear them fusillading an hour later everyone who stayed behind there – they assume that everybody worked for us. It's just senseless horror, horror ...' Kerenyi brought his heavy fist down, once, with a crash on the corner of the writing-table, making Julie jump violently. She felt a crazy, dazed sensation in her head, as if she were drunk. Kerenyi made an effort to control himself that stretched the muscles of his face into a scowling mask. His hands flexed and unflexed themselves; he forced himself to sit down, overcoming the need to make violent and useless gestures of rage.

'The important thing now is for me to get hold of Obergruppenführer Tenius. He's in Vienna at the moment, on leave.'

'Hella's husband!' cried Julie. 'What on earth ... I thought he was in Poland?'

'He was. I need backing from him; I can put pressure on him to get it. I have some written evidence of what has been going on in his district. Very hard it was to get, too. They keep such things, as far as they can, from the general troops, so an army reporter is the last person likely to get near them. We shall make a little bargain, Tenius and I, to-morrow.'

'You will stay here to-night, then, with us?'

'Can I? I want to talk to Franz. There may not be another chance.'

'So long as nobody knows you are here — of course. You're sure your papers are in order?'

'Made them out myself,' he said laconically. 'All stamped and signed.'

When Julie was gone to arrange for Kerenyi to sleep in the spare room, Franz began to question his friend.

'Millions of people have been murdered,' Kerenyi answered him. 'The moment the Party took over the occupation they began to behave in such a way that almost everybody in the occupied areas was turned into an enemy. It was absolutely unnecessary, certainly in Ukraine where the people were only too glad to have the chance of a change of rulers. Franz, it is an outbreak of madness. The army didn't conduct itself like a bunch of angels — you know what soldiers are like, anywhere. But the occupation is something quite different. It's a lust for destruction, a disease. It looks so reasonable — I mean in Party terms reasonable; they pick on certain groups of people; commissars, whatever that may mean, Jews, gypsies, partisans. But that's only the habit of orderliness, the last mental barrier from the civilised past of law. The real condition of east Europe is chaos, insanity. It's a disease spreading from east to west, west to east, every man who catches the infection reinfects every other man. Look, I can even prove it to be mad. The transports and the administration of the occupation constantly hold up military planning. The army is short of everything it needs, even reinforcements get held up on the railways — they are hopelessly overburdened in any case — by trucks carrying thousands of absolutely useless and pointless bodies from one place to another to kill them off — I've often been held up for hours, even days, in troop trains while these transports rattle to and fro using trucks that should be used for tanks and ammunition ... We might even have won the war if it hadn't been for this madness ...' He stopped, defeated by the vast meaninglessness of what he was trying to say.

'And the Russians ...?'

'The Russians! There the disease has reached an acute form. I've thought about this a lot in the three years I've been going in and out of Russia. You see, we were always blinded by the idea that the revolution was necessary, had its good aspects — even those with no sympathy for socialist ideas. I suppose we accepted that view by a historical transfer that connected the Russian revolution with the French one. Because we admire the French revolution and connect it in our minds with the ideas of personal liberty.

'But the condition of Russia, even without any intervention from the Germans, is in reality a state of near chaos. Whatever social fabric existed there before the First War, the civil war destroyed it and left nothing organic for a new society to form itself out of. The police apparatus covers a chaotic disorder, it has nothing to do with order. The most stringent ferocity is needed to maintain a mere appearance of order. This is one of the factors in the occupation — there is no doubt that the actual condition of Russia affected the Germans — us. The disease of destruction, you see? I know the *Promi* uses the figures as propaganda, but they are more or less correct, in spite of that; the 1939 census showed twenty-five million missing Russians, and even allowing for their inefficiency and the fact that a number of those listed as missing had in fact just cleared off and changed their names in another district to avoid arrest, twenty-five million missing persons means that at the very least fifty million Russians had their normal lives broken up. At the very least. That is about a third of the total population. And this process was still going on as the war broke out. Even if the purges stopped and even in peace, it would take several generations for any kind of stable society to re-establish itself. What this means to us here, all over central Europe, is that a horde of armed wild children is going to roll over us. A Red Army man of twenty typically saw at least one member of his family die of starvation, at least one more disappeared never to be seen again. What sort of people do you suppose they are?'

'What sort of people — what can they be but as you say, a horde of wild children?'

'They are — fragmented. Even if one speaks their language, there is no means of communicating in any real sense. The rule they live under is so totally arbitrary, so beyond normal understanding in its demands, and so built on the one premise — that everyone must be afraid of every other one – that Russians are bound to disbelieve and distrust themselves, everyone about them, everything that attempts to deal with them. The fragmentation going on here in the last year or so – arbitrary regulation – has been taken there to its logical end. We are just in a less universal stage of the same process; here some groups are outlawed but the rest, unless they are connected in some way with an outlaw, are comparatively safe. There every single human being is constantly threatened with outlawry without in the least understanding why or how it comes upon him.'

'Is it the same disease, then, your insanity, your moral chaos?'

'No question in my mind, none at all. And I've seen the two things from close up.'

'It's very interesting Georgy. You've put in a different form something of what I've been thinking myself, shut up here all these years. Wait, I'll give you the manuscript.' Franz struggled up from his chair and went to the desk, where he took an untidy bundle of manuscript from the middle drawer.

Julie came back into the room without the two men noticing her, until she spoke.

'If what you say is true, Georgy, it seems to me to make the men who planned to kill Hitler even more irresponsible than they seem ...'

'They hoped to save something from the wreck. No, they were not irresponsible. But they were amateurs. What they really wanted to do – had to do – was make a gesture of morality.'

'But how can you talk like that?' she cried impatiently. 'In that theoretical way! How can mutiny be a moral gesture if it lets in the Russians? And the men actually fighting? While the High Command wastes time playing at politics, they are deprived of direction, supplies; it's betrayal! It's as bad as Hitler, destroying the army!'

'The idea was to be able to fight the Russians better ...'

'The idea! You and your ideas. If they wanted to kill Hitler it could have been done much more simply by getting hold of some of those pills he's supposed to take all the time and putting something in them ...'

She could see that she was interrupting their thoughts by what seemed to them irrelevancies, and went away again, forgetting to tell Kerenyi what she had come to say, that his bed was ready. She left them talking and they talked most of the night. She lay for a long time, trying to imagine what the East Front must be like; but all she saw was an infinite multiplication of Nando, a mass of men struggling with some pressure she could give no form to, without any more say in their own destiny than the pack animals in their armies.

2

'*I* should try Maris first, Georgy,' she proposed at breakfast, discussing his plans. 'Don't try to influence Hella directly because she won't be frightened of anything Tenius has been up to – she believes absolutely in the victory of the Führer. Especially just now when she is back from a guest visit to Berlin; she's always more Nazi than usual when she gets back. Maris owes you something, after all, and she has Lehmann in her pocket.'

'All right,' Kerenyi agreed equably, and he yawned and blinked with sleeplessness. He and Franz had talked until five o'clock. 'I'll try to call Krassny again, and then perhaps you would get hold of Maris for me, could you?'

'It's no use trying to get hold of Krassny,' she said, 'I tried yesterday and was told he was in the country. I suppose he was your contact here, was he?'

Kerenyi looked up, suddenly sharp-eyed and wide awake.

'One of them,' he agreed. 'And you'd better forget that. In the country, is he? I wonder what that means. What did you want with Krassny yesterday? I thought from what Franz said that you'd been away nearly a week.'

'I was, and when I got back I thought I'd ask Krassny what the news was. Oh heavens, no, it wasn't that – queer slips of memory one has when one is tired. It was Hansi I asked for news. I wanted Krassny to tell me what . . .' She felt in the pocket of her dressing-gown and passed the scrawled message slip across the table. 'What this telegram meant. You will know, better than Krassny.'

Kerenyi scanned her scribble.

'This army post office number is the 6th Army, deployed across the Prut river. Or they were ten days ago, when I was last at their front line, which was pretty stable then. But they may have moved back since. Yes, the 165th Regiment is with the 6th Army. I just missed seeing Nando if he went through Bucharest a day or so ago.'

'He can't have been in Bucharest before last night,' said Julie, taking back her message. 'He didn't leave Enns until the afternoon before yesterday and was going back to Italy as far as he knew then.'

'The orders would have been at the depot in Linz,' Kerenyi explained. 'He would be given them when he picked up his travel orders and probably left at once for Bucharest.'

'I gather from what you said last night that the transfer is bad news?' asked Julie carefully. He looked at her for a moment before going back to his imitation coffee.

'It could hardly be worse. I am paying you the compliment of telling you the truth, as you see.'

'Thank you,' she said coldly and ironically, and rose from the table as the telephone began to ring in the hall.

Hansi had news. The plot had failed completely and all the conspirators were, or soon would be, in the hands of the secret police. Of course Hansi gave Julie this news as if it were nothing but indignation at the wickedness of the plot and relief at its overthrow that moved him; and these feelings were genuine to both of them for reasons which had little to do with joy at the Führer's escape from death and much to do with their own situation in Vienna, but these undertones neither of them expressed then or later. While the three of them had been talking the night before, there had been a series of personal broadcasts by the Führer and the service chiefs so that there was no doubt of the truth of the news. There was, said Hansi, still some confusion here in Vienna and the theatres would remain closed to-night but would take up their normal programmes to-morrow. In the meantime the greatest care should be exercised not to exacerbate the situation in any way or to make the restoration of order more difficult by unnecessary gossip. Docilely, Julie agreed at the same time as she was deciding in her own mind that she had better go to see Maris Pantic and not attempt to telephone her. The indiscretion of some of Hansi's remarks on the telephone the previous day was now noticeably corrected; it was clear that he had recovered himself and remembered that telephone lines can be listened to. And when Julie said she was proposing to go out for various commitments he agreed that she should do so since, as he put it, there was no reason to suppose that the forces of law and order did not have the situation in hand. But, he added, if there was any sign of confusion she should return home at once in order not to make the task of the authorities more difficult.

'The difficulty is,' Julie said after relaying the news to Kerenyi and to Franz who had now joined him at breakfast, 'I don't think it wise to make a number of telephone calls so, if it's all right, Georgy, we had better go over to Lehmann's house and call on Maris. I can ring up for a car from the theatre – there's no reason why I shouldn't be going there – and you had better take a taxi.'

'Maris will be there, will she?'

'Well, she's more likely to be there than anywhere; we'll try there and find out where she is if she's not at home.'

'Can I telephone for a taxi?' asked Kerenyi. 'No, better not since you will have to order your car by telephone. Just in case your phone is tapped. But I don't want to walk about in the streets any more than I have to.'

'I'll stop the car at the cab-rank when I go out, and send a taxi back here,' said Julie.

They themselves were later at breakfast than was normal, but Maris was still sitting in her little sitting-room upstairs, not yet dressed, when Julie entered. Lehmann had gone already to his office; everyone was concerned to show dutifulness and loyalty in any way that offered itself, for the most part quite useless ways such as being present in offices where as in Lehmann's case, there was no business to transact. In Maris this showing of loyalty had taken the form of wearing her Party badge on the collar of her gauzy blue garments, a piece of extravagance that would normally have delighted Julie.

'You and Hella will both get decorations, I am sure,' she said as Maris poured coffee. 'When are you going on your tour to Berlin?'

'It's been called off,' answered Maris, with a suspicious look at Julie's eyes, which reassured her with their dark expressionlessness. 'The tour is to go to evacuation areas in Pomerania instead because of the terror-bombing attacks on the capital. I understand from Hella that Berlin is being terribly bombed, day and night, so I must admit I'm not altogether sorry. Though it will be rather uncomfortable in those little country towns – playing in local cinemas and all that.'

'Still, important work for the war-effort. Even more important than your work on the home front.'

'You mean on the bedroom front I suppose,' said Maris sharply.

'Yes,' replied Julie simply.

'You always were a complete egotist, Julie.' Maris lit a cigarette with an assurance in her manner that had recently grown from week to week. 'Has it ever occurred to you when you make remarks about my private life that your own is not entirely in order? Not that it matters, nowadays.'

'Of course it occurs to me. Though there is the slight difference that Nando is not married with several children. However, don't let's quarrel just because we are overtired and nervous.'

'Of course not. That's just what I mean about your egotism; you may say what you like and then when it suits you the subject can be dropped with no hard feelings. And as for Nando not being married. Neither are you, and that is a matter I have heard a number of comments upon lately. The reason for your not marrying, I mean.'

'That old story! People have been gossiping about that for years now. Is there a new version of it?'

'Oh, yes. It used to be that you can't have children so that Nando will have to marry some wretched girl some time to have sons. But Hella has a new story now. That you know where your former husband is and he doesn't know you have divorced him, so that you can't really marry again.'

'That seems a little elaborate. If that were so and I were still in touch with my former husband without having told him I'd divorced him, I surely wouldn't hesitate to go further and marry Nando? If I wanted to, I mean. The simple fact is I don't want to marry but that is too simple.'

'Oh, they go further than that. They think your former husband is here.' Maris drank coffee, real coffee, secure in the knowledge of her bombshell having its effect. Julie, however, was silent and after a long pause Maris was obliged to go on.

'Hella gave a little party last week, when she got back from Berlin. Of course, everybody was there – except you; you were in the country at Nando's place. So Hella naturally asked after you, and then someone remarked that nobody ever went to your apartment any more. Of course Hansi Ostrovsky tried to stop the conversation – he always protects you – and old Frau Schneider for some odd reason. But really, nobody we know has been in your house for years now. Interesting, isn't it?'

'I wonder it hadn't occurred to any of you before this,' said Julie and took a rare cigarette. 'People living alone don't entertain, as I hardly need to tell *you*.'

'True, but it wasn't quite like that. Hella and her mother have two evacuated children living with them now, did you know? Orphans whose parents were killed in Berlin. Hella wondered how you managed to get away with that great big flat of yours, with only you and your housekeeper living there.'

'I imagine the housing authorities leave me alone because of the theatre,' said Julie and she could now hear a slight tremor in her voice which Maris seemed not to notice.

'Besides,' she went on slowly, 'Hella's gorgeous villa is right outside the town. There wouldn't be much point evacuating people into the centre of Vienna, now that we are being bombed ourselves.'

'I don't think the air-raids we have had here are taken a bit seriously by anybody who has seen the bombing in Germany.'

The conversation was mercifully interrupted here by the

announcement that Kerenyi was below. It had been agreed that no explanations should be embarked upon by either Julie or Kerenyi about their coincidental arrival to see Maris, and Maris herself, in her eagerness to show Julie a quite new malice, unconsciously assisted in this deception by assuming that Julie had called to catch up on news she might have missed in her absence.

'Kerenyi!' cried Maris as the servant withdrew. 'What can he be doing here? But I shan't see him.' She stopped, considered with a thoughtful look at her cigarette and added, 'No, perhaps I'd better see what he wants. I'll go and put on some clothes.'

'I'll wait for you here,' said Julie calmly.

Maris greeted Kerenyi without pleasure and with surprise intended to show him how little he was welcome in this house. Julie and Kerenyi merely nodded and Maris glanced quickly from one to the other.

'You don't seem surprised to see Kerenyi so far from the front,' she said suspiciously to Julie.

'Oh, no. He came to call last night. At home.'

This answer to the preceding conversation Maris registered by raising her eyebrows. Her air of confidence, almost of condescension, had lessened in Kerenyi's presence. He came at once to the point.

'I'm on my way to Laibach – Lyublyana, to you, Maris. Any introductions you can give me I'd be more than grateful for.'

'That town is not Lyublyana to me, its name is Laibach,' she said stiffly. 'And it is years since I knew anybody there, years.'

'But my dear, you must have dozens of relations in that neighbourhood!'

'I haven't seen any of them for over ten years. I don't know even if any of them are still in the district.'

'Have they sold their holdings, then?' he asked smoothly. 'I thought since they were *loyal* they'd be all right?'

'What do you know about my family?' Maris cried sharply, and the cry was of fear and hatred. In an instant her face had lost the whole veneer of prosperity, confidence, even its increased roundness. She was again the sad little waif with her way to make in the big city that she had been when Kerenyi first knew her, looking for work and living mainly on odd meals offered by admirers of her frail prettiness. Her shadowed eyes became as big and starved, in the pale triangle of her face, the lips trembled together as they had when hunger and eagerness made her vulnerable, desirable and docile, at first to many men and later to Kerenyi, then powerful and secure.

Julie watched her, perfectly conscious of Kerenyi's brutality and caring nothing for it; she was curious, only curious, to know what Kerenyi had against Maris's family. It could hardly be anything to do with a non-Aryan background for Maris had had plenty of time to arrange the disappearance of any parish records that might threaten her position. That had been done by thousands of people without the influence of Friedrich Lehmann behind them, and nothing was more simple to do for those who came from regions through which the tides of war had passed. It could only be one other thing.

'I've known for two years,' answered Kerenyi, watching her expressionlessly. There was silence. The sound of a bell ringing somewhere at the back of the house and a servant's voice calling to 'Aderl' to answer it, it must be the baker's boy, could faintly be heard.

Maris threw Julie an imploring look but she could see that there was no help to be expected from that quarter.

'It's a plot,' she wailed and burst into tears. 'You've cooked this blackmail up between you. Why should this happen to me? Oh, why, why? Haven't I suffered enough? They are nothing to me, I don't know anything about them, they might as well be dead!' Her husky voice broke on her tears. 'I wish to God they were dead!'

'If they aren't dead now, they probably soon will be,' said Kerenyi taking no notice of her tears. 'The SS has the district surrounded where their group was last heard of.'

How much of this Kerenyi really knew was unclear to Julie. Like his assertion that he was going to Laibach, when he was in fact bound for Agram further south, it might be mostly fiction; but Maris could not know that. She looked up, hope showing at once in her eyes at his last remark.

'If they will soon be dead,' she said viciously, 'you can go to the devil with your threats. They can't be killed soon enough for me.'

'But they never changed their names,' he pointed out reasonably. 'Unlike so many of the Partisans. And, you know, in the state of mind the Gestapo must be in at the moment, right after this abominable attack on the Führer, I wouldn't want to be in your shoes if the SS circulates their names; as they often do, I don't have to tell you.'

Maris groaned and put her head in her hands. Kerenyi remembered those hands very well. 'If that happens, I am lost,' she wailed; then she lifted her head, shaking the hair from her eyes and wiping the tears with the palms of her hands. 'So why should I do whatever it is you want of me?'

'Because I am going there, to that region,' he said patiently. 'You are slow this morning, Maris. You've got too used to safety, my dear. Wits getting slack.' He grinned at her with all the hateful irony he was capable of.

'You brute,' she said, with bitter hatred.

'You ought to understand well enough. I am in danger – like you, and like you I don't have much time for the civilities of life when I am threatened. Now, are you prepared to listen to me, or not?'

Maris pushed herself upright with one hand on the arm of her chair and went waveringly across the room to the bell-push by the door. It was a pretty room, the oval drawing-room that Kerenyi had once admired with its owner, when Lehmann's ownership of the house and of Maris were new.

'I've got to have a drink,' she said. 'Ask them to bring some brandy when they come, will you? I don't want anyone to see me like this.' She moved towards the door of the connecting room.

Kerenyi glanced quickly at Julie. The same thought was in both their minds, and he rose and followed Maris to the doorway, where he could watch what she did: it was Julie who spoke to the servant.

'What is it you want?' asked Maris drearily. 'Or is it you, Julie, who wants something?'

Julie shook her head but said nothing.

'I have to see Hella and her husband. I know Tenius is here ` for a day or so. You have to see them and prepare them to back

518

me if there are any inquiries about me. I've left my posting — transferred myself. The papers are all in order; my fool of a news officer signed them without even looking to see what they were. But it is just possible that the Gestapo may be after me. Tenius has to stand up for me, even before that happens. He has to get in touch with the Prinz Albrechtstrasse and let them know that I was in touch with him, secretly, ever since I met him. That was about three years ago, in Lodz, in case he has forgotten. Otherwise, and you can tell him this just as I am saying it to you, otherwise he will be in trouble at the end of the war. I have papers signed by him that will get him hanged by the Allies — by the way, we are talking rather freely; I hope this house is safe?'

'So do I,' said Maris wearily. 'As far as I know, it is. But God only knows where one is safe, nowadays.'

'You can drop the self-pity, Maris,' Kerenyi said harshly. 'And if you're sensible I'll do what I can to make sure you don't lose what you've done for yourself. And you'd better not take too much of that stuff, while we are on the subject of being sensible.' He gestured to the glass of neat brandy, none too securely held in Maris's trembling hand.

She said with contempt, 'I drink a bottle and a half a day and have done for years. Nobody has ever noticed anything of it yet. So you can mind your own business. I know what I'm doing.'

'Have you understood what to say to Hella and Tenius? How soon can you see them — at their home, of course.'

'But look here, Georgy, it's absolute nonsense for me to talk like that to Tenius. You must be out of your mind. He is completely confident — as we all are — that the new weapons the Führer is about to put into action will drive the enemy back both east and west. I heard only the other day that they are ready. I've no doubt now, after the news of the last few days, that they have been held up by this group of traitors and saboteurs. But now that that has all been cleared up we shall see changes and very quickly. If I repeat what you just said to me about Tenius to his face, he would simply have me arrested at once. You just don't know what has been going on, you've been out of touch so long.'

'I know far better than you do what has been going on; it is you who are out of touch, I assure you. Fed on lies as you have been, you know nothing about the real situation. The Russians' summer offensive has gone forward like a flood of lava. They took Lublin a week ago and broadcasts have been picked up in the last few days about what they found there. The world press will be full of it in a day or so. If he tries to bluster, just say one word to him. Birkenau. Can you remember that? Birkenau. Since he's in charge of the commission trying to clear up the mess there, he knows just what the word means. And Maris. Another thing. There are no new weapons that could win this war for us. None. The war is lost.'

Maris twisted her hands, looking fearfully about her as if, after all, she was not sure of the safeness of the house if such things were said in it.

'My God, be careful,' she whispered. 'The servants may hear. Even if there isn't a telephone in here, we can't be sure ...' She turned to Julie. 'Do you believe what he says?'

'Of course,' said Julie briefly. 'And so do you. You know perfectly well that everything told us is lies, and you've always known it, just as I have and everybody else has.' Suddenly she felt anger rise in her throat like bile. She went on rapidly. 'We've all been lying to ourselves and each other, pretending to believe everything we are told, for years. We're in a great sea of lies, drowning in them, like that terrible mud in Galicia when I was there, with the rain pouring down eternally. And that atmosphere of everybody knowing that every word they say and that is said to them is not meant to be believed, is meant to mean something else. The whole vast conspiracy is based on the assumption that we believe everything and anything on the understanding that we don't really have to believe anything. We're all rotten with lying, soaked through with falseness. Why don't you admit it for once? It might make you feel a bit better — inside anyway since we all have to go on lying outwardly. If you believed that rubbish you were telling me upstairs about Hella, you might think how dangerous it could be for you, too. But you don't believe it, you just adopt it as one more possible lie to cover all the other lies. It's because you know it is all lies that you turn on me as you did just now. I was something you could take it out on, your own knowledge that the war is lost, that we are defeated, defeated, ruined. You hang on to your lies as a shield to stop you knowing what is really happening. What is going to happen. Look at a map, you fool. Listen to the names in the army communiqué to-night on the wireless for once and then look at a map. Nobody listens to them – they're so dull! That is the only part of the news that has any relation to reality, the place names!'

'I had no idea you were such a military expert, Julie.' Maris hung on to the last shreds of her confidence with frightened sarcasm. 'Since when have you been listening to the communiqués?'

'Since Nando was in the army,' replied Julie simply. Her anger was gone and she felt a dry exhaustion. There was a long silence while Maris tried to make up her mind what to believe and what would be the least risk for her to take.

'No, I can't go to Tenius, Georgy,' she said at last, reaching for another drink and then walking hastily about the room with the full glass slopping in her shaking hand. 'It's madness. He would have me arrested for defeatism. Why, you can get shot for that!'

Kerenyi rose to his feet.

'All right,' he said. 'I shall have to do it direct, myself. But before I go out to Hietzing I shall go to Gestapo HQ on the Kai and report you as a spy for the Jugoslav Partisans. That too will come in handy as evidence of my loyalty to the Führer!' He turned as if to go, pretending not to notice the gasp of horror from Maris. She blundered against a little table which fell sideways with a small crash. A round ashtray and a small box rattled across the shining parquet floor. The glass fell from Maris's hand and tinkled into pieces, spreading a splash of cognac and a strong aroma with it. Maris broke out again into noisy tears, sobbing and gasping.

'Tears are so useful!' said Julie slowly, 'I often wish I had the talent for crying at the right moment.'

At that moment the servant tapped on the door and entered with a scared look at Maris; something of the altercation had been heard outside the room.

'Frau Schneider-Tenius is here, gnae' Frau,' she wavered. 'What shall I say to her?'

Her mistress gaped at the girl, hardly understanding what she said and still sobbing noisily.

'Maris, what on earth is going on here?' cried Hella's clear high voice, and she entered the room, staring about her at the confusion. 'Kerenyi! Julie! What are you both doing here? I thought you were miles away!'

'I came to see you and your husband, as a matter of fact,' said Kerenyi, staring baldly into Hella's astonished face. 'I thought Maris might prepare the way for me, but, as you can see, she is not in favour of the idea.'

The servant made a move towards the overturned table but was prevented by a frantic gesture from Maris and hastily left the room again.

'What can you want to see Teni about?' asked Hella, staring at him and from him to Julie and Maris and then at the table and the objects scattered on the floor. 'You look as if you'd all been brawling in here.' She stopped, frowned and turned back to Kerenyi. 'How did you know Teni was in Vienna? I thought nobody was supposed to know.'

'I called his staff from Bucharest and they told me he had gone away for a few days on private business. Since I knew you had just come back from Berlin, I guessed he would be here with you. Rightly, as you see.'

'But how did you know I was in Berlin? And why should you guess that he would be here to see me after I came back? You seem to know altogether too much — you always did, as I remember.'

'Nothing mysterious about it, my dear. Since I am in a news team I see the Berlin papers, where your guest performances were enthusiastically reported as the greatest acting of the century. I knew your husband wasn't in Berlin with you for the simple reason that I knew where he was until this week, and what he was doing. I also knew his immediate task was over for the moment and therefore that he would be going to report. Since he missed you in Berlin it was obvious he would come through here on a little detour.'

'You know a hell of a lot more than I do then,' she said suspiciously. 'All I know is he turned up in a filthy temper and nobody was supposed to know he was here.' Hella turned to Julie. 'What's been going on in here, will somebody please tell me? You're unusually silent, Julie.'

'I have nothing much to say,' said Julie coldly, and walked away to the window, stepping over the broken glass as she went.

'In a foul temper is he?' asked Kerenyi thoughtfully. 'That, after all, is to be expected. Well, we must see what can be done to better his temper. Hella, I take it you just dropped in casually to gossip with Maris? Unless you have important things on hand, I suggest we might go back to your place straight away.'

'As a matter of fact, I have some important business – with my dressmaker. The saucy bitch just told me I'd have to wait half an hour. Her girls are all playing the fool and she isn't ready to fit me. I thought I'd take a cup of coffee off Maris to pass the time.'

'And what is the matter with the seamstresses, may one ask?'

'One may indeed ask. Just what I asked myself. It seems one of them has been picked up by the police. Her young man is under suspicion – something to do with this horrible attack on the Führer's life. The whole workroom was in a hysterical uproar I gathered. As you appear to be here, I may add.'

'Oh, we're not hysterical. Not a bit. Maris's tears were purely tactical as you might say. Look, why don't you call your dressmaker and say you'll come to-morrow? Then I can drive back with you in your car and talk to Teni.'

'Hmm ... not a bad idea. But only if you'll tell me what you were rowing about!'

'I shall tell you everything. Teni, too. You may rely upon it!'

'I shall go on to the theatre,' said Julie, turning round from the window. 'I'm supposed to be playing to-morrow so I suppose I'd better see what is happening – the programme may have been changed ...' She looked over her shoulder out of the window again. 'I was standing here remembering that housewarming party, all those years ago. I wonder if the nightingale still sings?'

'A charmingly romantic thought!' interjected Maris savagely. 'One would never guess how you were talking a few minutes ago. Yes, the nightingale does still sing – though not any more this summer, after the turn of the year.'

Julie looked at her thoughtfully. 'I don't remember that I said much just now, did I?' she asked. 'It seems to me you said a good deal more than I did – upstairs, before Georgy came. D'you expect me to rush to your defence against Georgy when you say such things to me?' She looked again out of the window. 'A pity the nightingales stop singing after the longest day. It's an odd thought that I may never hear them sing again, in this garden.'

'Why shouldn't you?' said Hella. 'Have you quarrelled so hope-lessly with Maris?'

Julie laughed a little. 'No, no, not that. But by next summer we shan't be listening for nightingales, I think.'

'Just what do you mean by that?' cried Hella. 'That sounds like defeatism to me! Where do you think we shall be next summer?'

'Heaven knows.' She glanced across at Hella, standing in the centre of the room in a dress of flowing red silk, without a hat, a picture of beautiful health and confidence; and from her to Maris, her perfect foil, dark loose hair to Hella's smooth corn-coloured curls, small and pale to Hella's opulent pink beauty, delphinium-blue, soft wispy dress to Hella's bold scarlet. Tense and frightened to Hella's infinite self-assurance. 'One thing I'm sure of, though, and that's that you two will be well away from it, when it comes.'

'You've taken leave of your senses,' answered Hella brusquely. 'The strain of your life is too much for you, that's clear!'

'You never said a truer word,' agreed Julie. 'Georgy, will you be coming back to Schellinggasse?'

'No,' he said, watching her closely. 'Better not. I'll stay at a hotel to-night. But if you're playing to-morrow, I'll come to the theatre. Will there be a seat for me?'

'Of course, my dear. The house is always sold out, but that doesn't mean it is always full. You can have one of the seats always reserved for the Party.'

'Julie in her most histrionic mood! It would be just too suitable if you were playing Lady Macbeth to-morrow, Julie!'

Julie measured Hella, as she pulled on a glove.

'No,' she said, smiling to herself. 'Unless the programme has been changed, it is *The Death of Wallenstein.*'

'Clever!' snapped Hella as the door closed on Julie. 'Somehow she always manages to get the last word.'

'So you do know what she was hinting at just now?' Kerenyi laughed his sudden bark. 'You've given yourself away, Hella.'

'Not at all,' said Hella coolly. 'She was always a defeatist. She'll get in trouble for it, yet, you'll see! I expect Julie to say things like that; I know what she means by them — always have known — but that doesn't mean I agree with her. As a matter of fact I know perfectly well how wrong she is. Long before next summer the war will be won!'

'I am glad to hear you say so,' said Kerenyi. 'Shall we go and put your Teni in a better temper now? I'm sure Maris will let you telephone your dressmaker, won't you, Maris?'

'Of course,' said Maris hastily. 'But I'm coming with you, Georgy, don't forget.'

'Ah,' he pointed his big nose at her. You are coming, then? Good. When you are ready, Hella, we can all go.'

'We can go now. The dressmaker can work it out for herself, silly bitch. I want to know what all this mysterious talk means.'

Tenius, like Maris, had been drinking early. He sat on the terrace, incongruously surrounded by climbing roses and honeysuckle trained over mock-Greek pilasters in a carefully designed state of ruin. The red and white stripes of the sun-awning threw an even more flushed light on his broad, sweating face than its natural engorgement accounted for. Tenius was one of those men who appear to have too much blood in their bodies, and normally, when he was able to spend most of his time in the open air, he seemed to burst with heartiness and health. This morning, however, he came from a period of confinement to offices and barracks that did not suit his temperament; or perhaps he had received some shock, for his purplish face had a spongy look as if the red skin were stretched over a soft mass confined by a pallid inner skin. Disordered newspapers were strewn about the feet of his rough-hewn terrace chair but his attention was confined to a tall glass half empty, of beer and the small schnapps glass beside it. He looked sideways at the sound of their approach by the garden side and then emptied the little glass of clear colourless corn spirit as if he needed it. He frowned at the sight of a man in sergeant's uniform, but then as he looked at Kerenyi's face both surprise and relief showed in his somewhat bloodshot eyes.

'I know you, don't I?' he said. 'Thought for a moment you were some message I should have to cope with.' His voice was thick and congested as if he had a cold and in fact Tenius did suffer from hayfever. He took no notice of his wife or Maris, who moved towards the tall open doors of the drawing-room behind him, seeing at once that neither of them could usefully intervene.

'My God,' sighed Hella. 'Men!' She went to a small cupboard and brought out bottles. The sound of a child's voice called from upstairs somewhere, and as a servant looked in at the door to see if he were wanted, Hella turned and shouted at him.

'Keep those damned kids quiet, can't you? I've told you before to keep them out of the way when my husband is at home!' With a curious glance at once servile and familiar the man nodded, but Hella beckoned with a hand, looking towards the terrace door for a second. 'Tell my mother she must take them for a picnic or something, keep them out of the house,' she instructed in a low-ered voice. 'It's going to be one of those days.' The man withdrew without a word. Both women were listening at the same time to the men talking outside on the terrace.

Kerenyi introduced himself and reminded Tenius of where they had met before, in Warsaw and before that in Lodz and Lublin. It was clear to him that the introductory shock he wanted Maris to give this man had already occurred without their agency. Tenius raised his voice to a bellow and the manservant appeared quickly, with a tray of beer bottles, fresh ice for the schnapps bottle stand-ing in an ice bucket, and glasses for the visitor.

'Sit down,' said Tenius thickly, waving a big hand, on its back dark hairs showing from the cuff of his shirt which were damp with sweat. 'Help yourself. Damn' daft you should be a sergeant. Why don't you get commissioned?' He stared gloomily at his beer glass after this piece of advice as if he did not think much of it himself.

Kerenyi took beer and waited. He could see that Tenius wanted to talk to anyone who would listen and whom he dared to talk to.

It was not the first time recently, that Kerenyi had seen men in this state of confusion.

'You have heard the news about Lublin?' he asked cautiously.

'Lublin? All the news is about those filthy bastards in Berlin being hanged. Too good for them. What about Lublin?'

'You know quite well what about Lublin,' said Kerenyi coolly.

Tenius stared at him, his eyes becoming intelligent and careful.

'You managed to get yourself transferred from the General Gouvernement, I suppose?' he asked, his voice rumbling as he lowered it. 'I don't recall seeing you for some time. Take off that bloody cap, will you? And if you take off your tunic you'll look less an enlisted man. Can't be too careful, you know, in a world full of traitors.' Kerenyi did as the General suggested, hanging his tunic folded over the back of his chair so that it was inconspicuous, simply the drab field-grey of uniform.

'Listen,' he went on after a pause for drinking beer and pouring out more schnapps. 'The new weapons must be coming into action any day now. If we can drive the Russians back we can deny all their filthy propaganda reports. Why aren't they put into action? That's what I don't grasp. What is the Führer waiting for?'

'Perhaps until the conspiracy was dealt with?' suggested Kerenyi. Tenius looked at him out of the corners of his eyes. He shook his head, not in denial but as if to shake off flies.

'I believe the conspiracy came as a complete surprise,' he admitted. He was feeling his way with the unknown quantity of Kerenyi as much as Kerenyi was with himself.

'But I thought the Führer was waiting to draw them into a trap – like the Russian armies?'

'If he was, it was a pretty close call; they nearly got him. And *where* is the trap for the Russians? I know all that territory. There aren't any mountains, no big rivers. The marshes? Yes, but the Red Army is over the marshlands already.' He stopped, looking again sideways at Kerenyi mistrustfully.

'The question is, does the Führer know what the Russians found in Lublin? I mean, did he know before they took the town? I sometimes fear that a lot of things are kept from the Führer that he ought to know about. Such as Lublin. And other places in the

General Gouvernement ... If the new rockets really are going to drive the Russians back out of the area, well, all right. But if they are going to be held until later, there are some places that ought to be cleaned up before any more propaganda use is made of them. You know what I mean, sir. I don't want to talk too plainly, but I know you were heading this commission of inquiry ...?'

'Oh, you do, do you?' Tenius growled and shifted in his chair. 'You news fellows know everything. Let me tell you, it's not so easy to get anything done over these things. Everyone is trying to play his own hand, you can't be sure of anyone. I've put in one report already – in the spring – to the Reichsführer SS. It just disappeared as far as I can tell. It's more than my job is worth to try to by-pass the *Reichsheini*. Even if I knew whom to go to.' He glowered at a spray of pink roses and brushed his head as a bee buzzed round it, with his heavily ringed hand. 'You get about everywhere. You're a clever chap – I know, Hella has told me about you. What am I to do? If I stick my neck out now and next week, the whole front begins to roll back under a tremendous rocket attack – what do I do then? I'm suspect for ever.'

'These rockets. It's true I have been in Rumania for some months. But I still have contacts in Poland. A big onslaught that could change the direction of the front as a whole there – that would need large firing installations, wouldn't it? You see, I went on one of the news trips to the experimental station at Peenemünde a year ago just before it was bombed. Those are very big installations, General Tenius. They require large forces of labour, big concrete works, a lot of machinery. Where are these launching bases – that's what worries me?'

'They are far back from the fronts – well back out of danger. You wouldn't ever have heard of them even.'

'Yes, I dare say. But where? Do you know where they are?' Kerenyi paused to light a cigarette and leaned forward, his elbows on his bony knees. 'Do you know they exist?' he asked very quietly.

'You've just said yourself they exist and you've seen them.' Tenius brought out his handkerchief and wiped his streaming neck. He was sweating with more than the heat and the beer.

'Yes, proving grounds. I've seen the things being built; unmanned aircraft. Nasty looking objects. But I've seen no installations for firing them towards the east. Of course, I don't know what their range is — are rather, for there seem to be various types. But it's in the two—three-hundred kilometre range as far as one could tell — you know how it is, they tell you a lot of stuff on these inspection trips but by no means everything.'

'If you've actually seen the rocket weapons, you know a good deal more about them than I do,' said Tenius. As the meaning of his own admission dawned on his confused brain, he looked round over his shoulder. Then, as if something fresh had occurred to him, he got up out of his chair, and with blundering movements turned it round so that it faced the house. He scowled at the crowded table with dissatisfaction, for it was now behind his chair.

'Wait a moment. I'll carry the table.' Kerenyi lifted the light thing easily and set it down again in the same relation to Tenius in which it had stood before. Tenius viewed the new arrangement with increased satisfaction, and, kicking the clutter of newsprint out of his way, sat down again so that he could now watch the house. Kerenyi moved his own chair nearer to the SS General, but still facing the garden.

'Why do you ask me about these installations? I'm just the general of a police area, I know nothing about military affairs.'

'That's what I mean. You know better than I do that there are a few matters in the area of your command that ought to be cleared up if the Russians are going to see them. Now look here, General Tenius, I'm going to be frank with you. I don't care about you, but I do care about Hella and the theatre. This war isn't my career as it is yours, and I belong here.'

'Yes, you Viennese stick together. A funny lot, you are. I never can understand how you all tick. Sometimes I wonder how I came to get mixed up with all you artistic lot. And that's not the only thing I wonder about ... You know, I've been sitting on this terrace since yesterday evening, trying to puzzle out what to do ...'

Kerenyi made no attempt to enlighten Tenius, either about the very dubious loyalty of the Viennese to each other or as to how he came to be involved with the theatrical world of the city. If he did not know why Hella picked him as a husband, so much the better for his peace of mind, if there was any part of his mind that was still at rest. Tenius stared morosely before him at the paving of the terrace.

'This house,' he maundered, 'it isn't so well built as a Berlin house, but it has something about it. I like its little curlicues, all those funny-shaped rooms ... Listen, Kerenyi, can I trust you? I don't know what the hell to do and there's nobody I can talk to – not my own lot, they're all intriguing bastards. And the army people – they don't like police officers. You know how it is. You're an outsider, don't really belong to anything, do you? I could talk to you, if I could trust you.'

'You don't need to trust me, General. I know already what's on your mind. I haven't been there, but I've heard enough. They don't take news teams to places like Birkenau, but one hears things, you know. I know about the places in your police area that you have been inspecting. If you report that the whole – undertaking, shall we call it? – should be blown into rubble, you get in trouble with Kaltenbrunner; if you recommend it should be left alone you fall foul of the Reichsführer SS who sent you on inspection there. Right? Not to mention falling foul of the Allies after the war is over.'

He had said it. The murder was out. Tenius drank a glass of schnapps with a quick flick of his wrist, and choked hoarsely. Kerenyi took a mouthful of his beer and emptied the rest of it into a large tub of hanging geraniums that stood handy to his chair. He reached over and helped himself to a fresh bottle of beer and the opener as if he had drunk the last one.

'So you don't believe in the new weapons?' asked Tenius at last. 'You know you can be shot for saying that, I suppose?'

'I believe in them as much as you do, Obergruppenführer Tenius.'

Tenius laughed suddenly, a loud bellow of anything but amusement, which made Hella inside the drawing-room run to the window.

'He shouts like that when his gout is bad,' she explained to

Maris, 'it's always a bad sign. What on earth can be going on? Do you know what it's all about? Georgy said he'd tell me, but he won't say a word. I know him. Crafty beast. Teni has been drinking steadily since yesterday afternoon and I don't believe he even went to bed at all last night. I went up alone and left him there – he said he'd slept in the guest-room so as not to disturb me. And that's not like him – not to disturb me. Usually when we can meet he pesters me all the time – it's absolutely exhausting. But that's better than this drinking and staring in front of him.'

'You don't think – it couldn't be anything to do with ... You know – the news from Berlin ...?'

'Teni?' said Hella, and her mouth fell open with astonishment. 'Why he's loyal to the death to the Führer! How can you even think such a thing.' She stared at Maris, her pretty face suddenly blank with fear. 'It couldn't be anything like that! It couldn't!'

Maris came closer and whispered. 'Then why is he talking to Kerenyi so intimately? He's only a sergeant. Generals don't discuss their souls with enlisted men, do they? Georgy is disloyal, you've always known that as well as I do.' She would have continued, but Hella interrupted.

'Teni doesn't give a damn for rank. He has lots of odd friends. It's part of his job to know all sorts of people. He used to go drinking with the drivers when I first knew him. Not in his own area headquarters, of course, but when he was off duty. That doesn't mean a thing. No, there is something serious on his mind; he's worried to death about something. But it isn't anything to do with that terrible plot.'

'I'm sure Georgy was mixed up in it,' persisted Maris. 'He practically said so this morning. That's what we were arguing about when you came!'

'You mean Georgy is in trouble?' cried Hella, 'and he has the nerve to come here ...?' She started for the open windows, but as she came in sight of the two men on the terrace, she hesitated and then drew back into the shelter of the long yellow silk curtains. They were sitting almost head to head, murmuring, the very picture of conspiracy.

'Good God, there is something,' she muttered.

'He said this morning that the new weapons don't exist. That the war is lost. Julie agreed with him.'

'Ah, Julie! Of course, she talks like that. But I won't have you saying such things in my house! There's no defeatism here, and if you want to talk like that, you'd better go! I'll report you!'

Maris drew near and stood staring out of the window. 'You won't report me,' she said softly. 'There's something going on. Kerenyi said he had something on Teni that would get him hanged after the war. Something about a place called Birkenau he said. I didn't believe him, but now I see Teni takes him seriously, I do. He – Kerenyi – is in trouble but so is Teni and that means you. You won't report me or anybody else, Hella. You'll do just what I'm going to do.' She walked over to the table where she had left her handbag, drained her cognac glass, picked up the bag and her gloves and walked out of the room, through the front hall and let herself out of the house door quietly. She walked down the sun-baked suburban street, flicking in and out of the shade of flowering trees, until she came to the turning and a tram stop. When a tram came, Maris mounted and, for the first time for years, rode into the town on the tram.

Left alone, Hella wandered about the luxurious but slightly untidy room for a few minutes; she pulled at her lower lip with hasty fingers smudging her made-up mouth. Once she passed a hand across the shining surface of a baroque console of gilded carving with a marble top between the long windows, on which an ornate lamp stood, and frowned at the smear of dust on her hand. But she did not ring the bell to complain to the servants that they were not doing their work. She went slowly to the door, looking back once at the terrace and then went up the curving stairway to her bedroom where she opened the wall safe and took out a folder of papers. She sat for some time at the absurd little secretaire, studying the varied contents of the folder. Some of the papers seemed to please her; others not. Once she put out a plump hand with beautifully polished red nails that matched her dress, to pick up the new telephone, but laid it down again without dialling a number. Once her mother put her head in at the door and began to say something in her whispering voice but

Hella merely said abruptly, 'leave me alone,' and took no further notice of her parent.

It was almost time for the long luncheon pause of the Viennese by the time Hella made up her mind, but this did not trouble her; she rang and ordered the car round and went into the city to the home of her banker. It was better not to go to his office; he would be at home for his midday meal. Hella's money affairs were kept quite separate from those of her husband, and Tenius was unaware that Hella was in her own right a fairly rich woman. It took only a few minutes to instruct her confidant that she wanted some of her investments altered; he at least could be trusted. He telephoned for her to a colleague in the real estate business and in the same private fashion Hella drove then to this second man's house and discussed the purchase of a small property in the country near Salzburg, where as the real estate manager informed her, a number of persons were buying properties which had stood empty for some years now. There were, however, several desirable small estates in the lake district which, with a little discreet rebuilding – it was always possible to get such work done by local men, even nowadays – would be habitable and secluded. A journey of inspection was arranged for the following week.

By the time Hella reached her house in Hietzing again, Kerenyi was long since gone about his business. Tenius, the manservant told her, had taken a long cold shower and eaten a large meal; he was now sleeping, as Hella could hear as soon as she went upstairs for his raucous snores echoed as far as the wide landing. Hella ordered a cold meal for the evening and instructed the servants to take the children to the cinema and to take her mother with them.

She pulled the napkins from the food laid out on the sideboard, and poured champagne for them both. The house was silent, warm and scented airs moved from the windows; they were quite alone. Hella had dressed herself with great care; they dined by candlelight.

The shower, food and sleep had restored Tenius to something like normality, but the first glass of champagne made him slightly tipsy again. Hella had no trouble interrogating him, even though she began from the wrong premise.

'Now Teni is going to tell his little Hella all about the horrible conspirators in Berlin, isn't he?' she wheedled.

'Baby doesn't need to bother her pretty head over things like that,' Teni assured her largely, stretching out his thick legs under the table. Like many couples whose private life is soaked in insincerity, they usually talked in the third person and in terms of childish loveplay.

'But Baby wants to know everything. Hella can't do what is right for her big bear's career if she doesn't know what goes on, now can she?'

Teni laughed, anticipating pleasures to come. 'Suspicious little devil, aren't you? You think that news fellow was talking about the plot, don't you? No, no, nothing like that, my pet. That story is all over and the filthy traitors already hanged or shot. If that is what my little girl was worrying about, she can forget it. We were talking about something much more important than that affair. A great task, an immense sacrificial task we have taken upon ourselves, that can never be talked about.' Tenius began to speak in the style of his exemplar and master when addressing his faithful SS officers in private. Even his broad red face and black hair seemed to fade a little towards the pasty skin and formless features, the flat mousy hair of the Reichsführer SS; except for the spectacles he looked almost like the great man for a moment. 'Much has been achieved in clearing up the vermin that infested Europe, and what remains to be done is only postponed a few months. What your friend Kerenyi and I were speaking of is a little detail in that great task, to ensure that it shall not be endangered.'

Hella sighed inside herself. What this rubbish meant she knew quite well, but she was not intended to know and therefore could not say briskly, as she longed to do, that he should stop hedging with her and tell her what Kerenyi and he had agreed upon. Maris had been quite wrong – of course, she would be – but Hella knew now what Tenius was talking about.

'Tell Hella, Teni, tell Baby so that she knows what to do if anything happens when big bear isn't here to help her out.' She poured him more champagne. 'You know how mean and jealous people are of your Baby; they can be very unkind and Teni isn't always about to protect her.'

'And no wonder,' agreed Teni, making a move towards her across the crowded small table. 'Who wouldn't be jealous of you – and of me? Come on, Baby, come and sit by Teni.'

'No. No. No lovemaking until you've told me. Baby wants to know what was worrying her bear and what that cunning brute Kerenyi has to do with it.'

'Now Baby, you know I can't tell you those things. They aren't fit for your pretty ears. Come along now, and be kind to Teni.'

She leaned back in her chair with a shrug, her opulent charms more visible than ever. 'No,' she said pouting sweetly, 'no, if you don't trust me then I shan't love you any more.' He reached over and tried to put his big fist into the low neck of her dress but she shook him off without effort and coolly helped herself to more cold chicken in aspic. Teni subsided sulkily into his chair and filled his glass again. In his befuddled mind it was difficult to separate the various advantages and disadvantages of any third person knowing what the day's business had achieved. But, as Hella had known it would, the threat of deprivation decided the answer.

'All right, I'll tell you about it.' His tone was now almost businesslike and the drunken slur had gone. 'Perhaps it's better if you know. You don't seem to trust this man Kerenyi and I don't want you doing anything to direct any unmerited suspicions to him. But you must promise me never to mention it to anybody – starting with your old crow of a mother. Promise?'

Hella, of course, nodded and leaned over the table so that he could drop his voice. He had to avert his eyes from her bosom so that he could concentrate on what he was saying.

'There are certain – installations, Auschwitz I and II, for instance – in the district where my headquarters are. Not directly under my command, but run by a different branch of the service. There has been a certain group for some months now who hold the opinion that these – installations – should be removed, liquidated, cleared up. Another group, near the Führer, is not of this opinion. They know that the new weapons about to be used for the first time in history will make any changes unnecessary. The question is whether they can effect the change in time to prevent the Bolshevik hordes overrunning further terrain in the General Gouvernement and so discovering these – installations – and using them for propaganda purposes with the Roosevelt–Churchill clique of world Jewry that caused the war and began the whole trouble for us.' If Hella had not already had a quite clear idea what her husband was talking about, she could hardly have understood more from this rigmarole, but in fact she knew and understood. From the way he said with emphasis that the second group of opinion near the Führer *knew* that the new weapons would change the course of the war, she knew that Teni had no confidence in these weapons.

'Of course, you must get transferred at once,' she said, forgetting to use her baby voice and speaking as if she were talking to her dresser. 'It will be best if you transfer to the Wehrmacht, and I'll go to Berlin and see if I can't get you sent to Italy where it's safe.' She did not mean safe from wounds or capture, but safe from complicity in the installations Teni had just, for the first time, spoken of.

'My rank is too high for a transfer,' he complained. 'No, I have a better idea than that. I shall see if I can't get back to the police in the old Reich – after this foul plot they need some vigorous officers I should think. I have friends who could help me there. But in the meantime, your friend Kerenyi is going to arrange for my reports on these – installations – to be saved for the future. Just in case they are needed. Of course, they won't be quite the same reports that I wrote for the Reichsführer SS. I shall have to rewrite whole parts of them and I'll be glad if you'll help me with them, to-morrow.'

'And what is Kerenyi getting from you in return? He's not doing this for nothing, I'll be bound!' So Maris had been at least partly right!

Teni screwed up his face into a leer of conspiratorial cunning and tapped his gleaming forehead with his forefinger.

'Don't you worry about that,' he said. 'I shall arrange that Prinz Albrechtstrasse knows I have been in touch with Kerenyi for the last two years. That covers him. Or so he thinks. In fact, I shall see to it that his transfer to Agram is reversed and he will be sent back to the front in the east. The Carpathians will be the best place, where the big attack is expected. The chance that he will ever be able to claim anything from me will be pretty remote. All I have to do is to telephone a chum of mine. At the same time my protection of him is on record and he will see to it that the rewritten report recommending the destruction of installations in my district gets into the right hands. See? Your Teni is no fool when it comes to the push, is he?'

'I don't understand why you should do anything at all about the Prinz Albrechtstrasse,' objected Hella. 'Why should you cover Kerenyi for whatever he's been up to in the last two years – and it isn't hard to guess what that was!'

'You women! You will interfere in men's business and then you can't understand it! I cover Kerenyi for the moment with the Prinz Albrechtstrasse – that is, that he has been reporting to me on the plotters for two years. If he has any trouble with the Gestapo at once, I shall never get my own protection, don't you see? Then, in about a month's time, he will be transferred back to the East Front where his future will be taken care of by the Bolsheviks. At the same time, *if* the new weapons ... if they don't prove as decisive as we all believe, than I have an alibi. Now do you see?'

What Hella saw was that the whole idea had come from Kerenyi, but she had some confidence that Tenius would really be able to dispose of Kerenyi after using him; she knew he had not made his career to general from second lieutenant in three years without having the threads of manifold intrigue in his apparently clumsy hands. But the thought foremost in Hella's sharp mind was a kind of wondering gratitude at her own perspicacity. Even in his own house, the renewed electric wiring of which he had personally attended to, Tenius was not saying openly what he meant about the new weapons. But he had said enough for Hella to draw her own conclusions and to know that her activities that afternoon had been the right and sensible ones.

'I shall have to go into town in the morning,' went on her husband. 'And make a couple of long-distance calls from the Kai. In the meantime you could read through my report draft and see where it needs amending for the new copy. It has to be made much stronger in its recommendation to destroy these installations and we have to give the impression that on this second tour of inspection I was even more shocked by what I found than on my first tour – I can't find out what happened to that first report so I can't get it back – but it has to be quite clear now that I am prepared to risk my neck to tell the facts to the Führer in this report. Facts which have been kept from the Führer by people close to him whom he trusts. Do you see? I tried to draft the report in general terms without going into much detail and we'll keep it that way – only change the emphasis. You'll see what I mean when you read it. Where I talk about the danger of typhus to the German population in dealing with the suggestion that some of the prisoners should be transferred to industrial districts in the Reich as labour, we can expand that a bit to include the health of the prisoners as such and perhaps suggest an improvement in their feeding or something of that sort. And the parts about tightening up discipline among the administration staff and the hygiene of the whole camp – that can be strengthened too. Individual excesses must cease – that sort of stuff. You'll see when you read it. Then I can rewrite this version of the report for Kerenyi and he can take it with him when he leaves the day after to-morrow for Agram.'

'Take it with him?' cried Hella, alarmed. 'Is that safe?'

'He knows what he's doing, don't worry about him. If he didn't, I have a shrewd suspicion he'd be hanging on a meat hook in the Prinz Albrechtstrasse at this very moment.'

Teni was right in his near certainty as to Kerenyi's recent activities but wrong in the supposition that the hangings reported on the radio in the last twenty-four hours had taken place at SS and Gestapo headquarters in Berlin. Tenius was by no means the only senior officer confused about the events of the last two days and from this time on confusion about what was happening, both at the fronts and in civil life became a kind of growing epidemic of uncertainty. Nobody, certainly not the Führer's headquarters far from Berlin, knew exactly what was going on anywhere but in its own immediate neighbourhood.

The efforts of the Gestapo and criminal police to discover every last soul who might have had, or whose relatives might have had, anything to do with the plot of 20th July, and the resulting terror and deceit among the general public, combined with the chaotic state of communications under the massive bombing attacks which had, by this time, reached a new depth of horror in almost all the major towns of central Europe, made civilian life more like a state of civil war than any condition of administration – even by secret police – that existed up to then. The confusion in people's minds was added to greatly by the knowledge, now general, though unadmitted, that the army communiqués from the fronts were works of fiction in which, as Julie had long discovered for the same reason that millions of other women had secretly discovered it, only the place names had any relation to reality and even this tenuous hold on reality was normally days, or even weeks, out of date.

The effects of these conflicting and multi-crossing confusions was endemic confusion in the relations and arrangements of everyday life, but even more than these confusions, a state of mental confusion existed and grew in people's minds so that gradually nobody knew what was real and what unreal; what was lie and what was true; what they themselves had said to cover some minor or imagined misdemeanour and what had actually happened. Above all, the constant bombing made it impossible for individuals or administrative bodies to keep in touch with each other, or to recall what had happened a few days before. Everyone was gradually unhinged by the after-effects of sleeplessness and appalling noise and danger, by the loss of home and familiar objects, by removal to other towns, by distress in their own hearts for themselves and distress of uncertainty for any who were dear to them or upon whom they were dependent. The truly extraordinary part of this growing chaos was that water and electricity and gas, and telephone wires continued to be repaired at all; the population clung tenaciously to jobs as a last resort from total disorder, so that post office mechanics would laboriously rejoin broken wires, working in open bomb-holes, that were broken again the following night in a further bomb attack. Engineers from town waterworks would set groups of workmen mending sewage and water pipes, emergency electricity was somehow or other produced for at least a few hours every day, even after attacks that killed unknown numbers of people and destroyed whole town centres of big cities. To the terror of police and neighbour and the fears of the war itself were added the terror of what would happen to them all if they were finally defeated by the enemies who were mercilessly destroying people and their homes, but not industry and transport; this fact people could see for themselves in every town and they believed the evidence of their eyes that their enemies wanted to destroy them totally.

As the couple at their dinner table finished the bottle of champagne, the air-raid warnings could be heard, echoing their universal wail of misery from far and near. Rather than close the windows Hella blew out the candles on the table and in the wall-holders, and the two of them went out on to the terrace whence they could see from their sloping garden towards Klosterneuburg where circling shafts of light illuminated in flashes the great monastery on its hillock and from where they could hear the banging and plangent slamming of anti-aircraft guns protecting the approach to the city. The oddly disoriented drumming of heavy bombers passing overhead awoke a sensual lust for survival and after watching and listening for a few minutes, they turned by mutual consent and went up to Hella's bedroom where the only answer to the death bringers was possible. They did not hear sticks of bombs fall in the far outskirts of the city, and their ritual movements were very different from the frantic running and falling in the long rows of tenements sliding with huge crashes into rubble, where the bombs sprang their tremendous surprises.

Maris had managed to waylay Kerenyi in Director Schoenherr's office where he was paying one of many calls, and Schoenherr passed the telephone to his visitor. Kerenyi noticed how the padded soft hand trembled holding the black receiver; Schoenherr's blood pressure was evidently worse than when Kerenyi last saw him.

'You can stay at my little flat to-night,' said the shivery deep voice into his ear. 'I have left the keys with the doorman at the theatre addressed to you. It's better for you than going ...' She did not finish the sentence. But Kerenyi knew the ending and if he was amused at the new concern for his welfare, he showed nothing, but thanked her civilly and rang off.

By the time Kerenyi left Franz in the Schellinggasse and took a taxi to the single-roomed but self-contained apartment near his own apartment which was sub-let, it was dark. He remembered the layout of the little hall, the bed-sitting room and its old-fashioned bathroom, and explored them in the dark, making sure curtains were drawn and shutters closed. The only thing he did not find to his comfort when he could switch on the light, was something to drink; evidently on the rare occasions when Maris used the flat — she had to occupy it once or twice a month in order not to come into conflict with the laws on empty apartments — she did not drink there. He was still looking in the cupboard that did duty for a kitchen when he heard keys in the outer door and went to listen. Was it the Gestapo? Could it be that he had simply walked into a trap? He leaned against the wall where the door must open on to him and waited; then he saw that he had left the keys Maris had given to him, in the lock. The key from the outside was tried again. Again. Then a pause. He waited for the bell to ring or for fists to pound on the door. He could feel the old shot of pain descend from his armpit down his arm, but felt no conscious fear.

Then, disembodied, he heard her voice, whispering into the keyhole.

'Take the keys out. Let me in.'

He bent his tall back level with the keys and whispered back.

'Are you alone?' Not that she would say anything else but that she was, he knew.

'Of course,' she whispered impatiently back.

Cursing himself for a fool, he turned the key backwards and slipped it out of its resting place and instantly the slight form of Maris slipped through the door.

'I didn't think you would leave the keys in the door,' she murmured, once the door was again closed and locked. 'Didn't you realise I meant to come?'

'How could I? The last words we spoke were hardly indicative of a night-visit.'

'Don't let's stand here.' Maris walked into her room, where light burned by the narrow bed. She went at once to the tiled stove and reached into the firebox, making a little clicking sound with her tongue at the smudge of soot on her wrist when she withdrew it with a cognac bottle.

'I have to hide it,' she explained with a little laugh. 'The caretaker who cleans up once a week steals it.'

She poured large drinks for them both, standing close to his tall body by the only table. She smelled of brandy but he could also smell the old-remembered odour of her springy loose hair for her head was almost under his chin. The almost palpable sensation of her body that this odour aroused made him, without attempting to overcome the impulse, feel with his hand in her loose short sleeve of some soft stuff, and touch her damp, silky armpit which she never shaved. He remembered that even in evening dress she always wore some kind of sleeves, for that reason. He drank, the glass in his right hand, and set it down half empty on the table behind him. Then he moved his left hand and put it into the neck of her dress. She wore no underclothes, and this too he remembered. The familiar sensation that the under-fleshed body would break in his hands returned to him. There was not an ounce of fat on her so that where she was muscled her flesh was hard and almost stringy, the muscle just under the smooth downy skin. This hardness was the oddest contrast to her appearance when she dressed in her always loose and soft clothes.

He gave her a little push on her shoulder and she backed to the bed. She jumped under him like a trout – like a trout if it were warm, he thought quite clearly, his mind taking no part in the lust of his body.

When he awoke the light was still burning but she was no longer there, so that he rose to his feet in one movement, the thought that it was, after all, a trap, coming back to him. But he heard water running and after a moment she came in from the bathroom pulling a dark silk robe about her. She went to the cupboard and drew out a man's dressing-gown which she threw towards him. It fell on the rug by the bed and he bent down to pick it up, and it was somehow familiar, though old and worn. It was days later that he grasped that it was an old dressing-gown of his own that he must have left there at some time years before, and he startled the other men in the mess with him when he suddenly burst out into his barking laugh at the thought that the frugal Maris had kept his old dressing-gown to lend to her various lovers.

Now she went to her large handbag and brought out brioche and a packet of butter and eggs.

'I brought them for breakfast, but I'm starving. We'll eat them now,' she said, speaking for the first time. He too was suddenly very hungry and when she had cooked the eggs they ate them eagerly, sitting opposite each other at the table. The brioche was stale, from yesterday, but still quite edible.

'You've knocked me about,' she said after a time, looking with curiosity at a blue bruise on her exposed forearm. 'I shall have to keep away from Lehmann for a day or so.'

'What's he like?'

'Big soft creature. Always sorry for himself.'

'Matches you, then,' he said and laughed, pushing the plate away from him. He got up and went to his uniform tunic to find cigarettes.

'He has nothing to be sorry for himself about, I have.'

'He will have, soon,' he said brutally.

She looked at him sideways and took a cigarette. This was what she had come for. Then she poured out some brandy, to which he added water for himself. She drank hers neat, as always.

'Listen,' she said. 'Is that true, what you said this morning? Be careful how you answer. I'm not too sure of the neighbours here.'

'Nobody will be listening at this time of night,' he said, but he kept his voice down. 'Of course, it's true. You know it yourself, only you won't admit it.'

'And you will try to get the names lost – if you find them – where you're going?'

'The names?' he asked, forgetting what she meant. 'Ah, yes, the names. Well, I'll try, but I don't know people down there as I do in Poland and Rumania. I have one contact though, and I will try with him. You ought to have married years ago, if only to change your name ...'

Without warning the phrase reminded him of Ruth. The comparison had been under the surface of his mind in the last hours, with that other delicate dark body, as thin and frail as Maris but so different, so virginal, loving, docile; so lacking in the sensual skills of experienced flesh. He felt a stab of agony as if it had happened yesterday and the thought of the curled body of the unborn child that had lived on inside him since its death was like a knife turning in his own flesh.

'What is the matter?' she whispered with fear in her deep voice.

He stared at her unseeing, with a hatred he was unable to hide.

'Nothing,' he said at last, forcing himself to speak in case she should scream. He got up from the table and moved with his explosive energy to the window and back, three steps, and then gripped the back of his chair with a violence that lifted it off the floor. 'I'm just sick to death of survivors,' he muttered through his teeth. He made a harsh sound that could have been a laugh. 'Including myself.'

She sat stunned with lack of understanding, having no idea of what was in his mind. The words were meaningless, and she thought for a moment that he was suddenly unhinged. During the time he had been living, an open secret, with Ruth, Maris had been completely engaged with Lehmann and did not even recall the existence of the girl whose meaning for Kerenyi would in any case have been lost on her.

He would have given anything then to be able to dress and leave, to walk the streets for hours as he had done in Lodz and Warsaw for months of dead nights during the winter after she was lost and in Lublin during the summer that followed. With the longing to walk, the smells of Lublin came back to him, as if the summer heat had brought them back. Smells of overcrowding and poverty; nauseating odours of sewage, bugs, unwashed masses of human animals with their rags, foul breath of starving mouths, sick smells of typhus and dysentery; the revolting smells of hatred and despair from which he would never again be free.

Here he could not even walk the streets, for fear a military police patrol examining passes, or searching for a name on one of the endless new lists of suspects might pick him up and find that he should be in Agram. He had walked obsessively then, staring into faces, asking questions, pushing into the broken down warrens in the fearful hope of finding some trace of the child. Being shut in was new to him and he knew suddenly what life had been for years to Franz. He sat down again, put his crossed arms on the table and laid his head on them, remaining so until Maris touched his elbow and offered him brandy, which he drank gratefully. He spilled some and drops ran down into the curled, greying hair of his chest. He rubbed himself with his open palm and reached the glass for more. The summer dawn, hot before the sun rose, crept past the shutters but they went on drinking steadily in the enclosed room.

Yet he went, apparently normal, to the theatre the following evening at seven; to the play.

3

Kerenyi walked, in the interval, up and down the wide gang-ways of the theatre, promenading with the audience which in spite of many uniforms still looked normal. Or perhaps, car-ried normality about with it, collectively, with obstinacy. It was no surprise to find himself face to face, at a lower level, with Fräulein Bracher, who towed her fusty old mother with her, grumbling and fidgeting with her hearing aid. His former secretary, he knew, had an inherited subscription to the theatre, about the only thing her father had been able to leave; this she faithfully renewed every year and rarely missed a performance she was entitled to.

They chatted casually, ignoring the old woman who mumbled crossly by their side. He was on his way to Agram, he said, and she asked if he meant to break his journey at Graz to call upon Frau Homburg's mother and stepfather. It surprised him to hear that she had visited the manor farm which was their home sev-eral times, since the occasion he had taken her there; he had forgotten that short episode of his life, wiped out by later events. But now he recalled the car journey, the conversation with Julie's mother — it was hard to connect her with the Julie he knew, somehow — and the return journey with the half-hysterical child both younger and older than her sixteen — or was it seventeen? — years.

'It seems long ago,' he said, and they stood silent in the chat-tering throng. The bell rang for the return to the tragedy. Bracher put a nervous bony hand for a moment on his arm, as they all moved to go.

'We did what we could, Herr Chefredakteur,' she said quietly. 'Nobody can do more.' He watched her under-set figure, the unwieldy hips, the meagre upper body and the greying, dusty hair, pulled back into a tidy net, of her rear view. He felt ashamed of himself. She had risked her job and her freedom to help him and the girl ... he doubted whether he had ever thanked her. As soon as she was out of his view he could hardly recall her features. He had not even asked whether she was still the editor's secretary.

The Death of Wallenstein is probably the most sublime piece of dramatic art since Shakespeare, and the scene in which the Countess Terzky persuades the great general into treason is its high point. Kerenyi had not seen Julie act for more than three years and never in this part. As her voice rose in vibrant metallic hardness into the calculated scorn of 'Must I remind you how, at Regensburg ...' he knew he was witness to a rare occasion of greatness. Schiller's poetry, the moral quandaries of the play, the meanness of the motives for which men risk their lives and their whole achievement, the greatness of their self-realisation at the moment of their lowest baseness and the immediate connection of the play with the events of the outside world that brought Schiller's creation into an unbreakable connection of realism here and now, these he knew were unique. As Walter Harich's beautiful baritone rang out, tormented, 'I never saw it in that light before ...' there was a discreet hissing from the back of the gallery where eager Party members underlined the moment to prove their loyalty. But the sycophancy sank at once into the hush of comprehension in which the whole auditorium was gripped so that many people present that night could afterwards not remember whether the hissing had actually happened or whether it was so utterly appropriate in its toadying stupidity that it had grown out of the commitment of the audience as counterpoint to its meaning.

As people at last began to pull themselves together and think of collecting whatever parcels or books had been left in the cloak-rooms, for there were few coats at that season of summer glory,

Kerenyi made his way round the outside of the theatre to the stage door and was admitted to wait for Julie. They were to go to supper with Hansi Ostrovsky and Harich and then on to the Schellinggasse for Kerenyi to make his farewells to Franz.

The part of Gräfin Terzky required no complicated 'building' make-up; Julie would not be long, Lotte assured him. He hardly recognised her, she had aged so much since her nephew was lost at Stalingrad. Her solid fullness of body, once comfortable, was now loose fat, and her features had a sad, complaining air under the white hair.

'How are you, Frau Lotte?' he asked and she answered, with a shrug, 'Ah, one keeps on, one keeps on.'

Hansi had not been present at the performance, but he did not need to ask about it, the atmosphere was still full of its tension. He always knew how a performance had gone as soon as he passed the door-keeper though if anyone had asked him how he could tell he could not have answered.

'The town is depressing,' Kerenyi answered Hansi's question as to how he found Vienna after his long absence. Hansi passed an awkward hand over his thinning hair which had once been soft and full, with a lock falling forward on his forehead.

'We are all getting older,' he said as if in apology. 'How long is it? Three years, I suppose, though we did meet in Krakov that time – when, two years ago.'

'A bit more than two years. When Nando joined the army during your tour. I don't like to ask Julie questions about him – did you see him on this leave? How is he?'

'I didn't see him – he didn't come to Vienna. Julie went to his mother's place near Enns. Poor Julie, it is a tragedy for her. I don't know how she stands her life, I really don't. Come to that, I don't know quite how any of us stand it!'

Kerenyi looked at him under his brows. They were standing in the corridor so that he could light a cigarette, strictly forbidden by fire regulations. Hansi really means it, he thought; he really believes they are suffering here in Vienna.

'Another air-raid last night. Some workers' blocks hit over the river. Did it disturb you much?'

'I didn't even hear the alarm!' answered Kerenyi surprised. It must have happened during the short time he slept.

'God, I wish I slept like that,' rejoined Hansi, and greeted Harich absently.

'Yes, they are getting more frequent,' said Harich, hearing their remarks. 'I've decided to leave my wife and the children in the country for good. She's looking for a house.'

'Ah, here you are, Julie. You were very quick.'

Kerenyi said nothing in greeting, but took her hand and kissed it. She wore a dress of black and white silk with a bold pattern which he remembered from years before, and carried a sable wrap over one arm.

Seated opposite her in the bad light of the little restaurant that was their standing supper-place, he studied her face. She too has aged, he thought, not as much as Hansi but more than a few years. The hardness which had threatened at one time to turn her beauty rigid had been tempered by steady and ignored suffering. The brow, the wide, dark eyes and above all, the set of the mouth showed now an acceptance that could degenerate into sullen patience but would no longer become icy. Nando saved her from coldness, he thought, and for some reason he did not examine, felt a slight surprise that there was no jealousy in the thought.

'I'm vastly hungry,' she said, intent on practical affairs as usual. 'Lotte is finding it more and more difficult to get things to eat in the intervals.'

'Couldn't you get something to bring from home?' asked Hansi. 'Hella always seems to have plenty of everything.'

Julie made no answer. Harich looked at Hansi and frowned. Hansi busied himself with the menu card, which he had already read once and laid aside. They know, thought Kerenyi, and Julie knows they know. It has all, at some point been taken for granted, some point I missed.

They began to eat smoked trout, a delicacy kept for special customers.

'Well, Georgy, when are you off? Julie says you are going down to the Partisan country? You'd better watch your step down there. These Tito brigands are said to be utterly ferocious.'

'So I hear,' Kerenyi answered Harich. 'But I dare say no worse than the Russian front.'

'Not so much danger from artillery or bombs,' agreed Harich, his mouth full. 'But trickier I imagine. Every man's hand against you, eh? The knife between the ribs in the night. No clearly defined front.'

'I shall survive the knives too, I expect,' Kerenyi's mouth twisted sardonically. 'I've come to the conclusion I am a survivor. More wine, Julie?'

She nodded abstractedly, feeling for a trout bone with her tongue and then, with an air of satisfaction, picked it from between her lips with a long finger and thumb.

'Even picking fishbones out of your teeth you are the most beautiful woman I know,' he said, laughing with genuine pleasure.

'It wasn't in my teeth,' she objected and laid down her fork. 'That's better, now I can take an interest in you all. Now I've had something to eat.'

The fat waitress removed their plates and brought warm ones. She made no remark, but brought a large platter of roast pork instead of the goulasch they had chosen from the bill of fare.

'Meat!' cried Hansi in a joyful undertone. 'Must be "black".'

'Just tell the entire restaurant!' Harich reproved him. 'It's for me, as a matter of fact. I spend a lot of time and trouble flirting with the proprietress so that you can get proper food, I'll have you know.'

'We eat better here than any of the grand places,' agreed Julie. 'I can't see why Hella says it is so mucky here. I've always liked it.'

'Oh, you know how Hella is – never goes anywhere without a *maître d'hôtel* to pull out her chair. She hasn't been here for years.' Hansi glanced across to Kerenyi. 'So I hope you were not expecting to see her this evening?'

'I saw her yesterday – at home. That was enough,' answered Kerenyi. 'But unless my memory fails me the table over there in the corner is reserved for Lehmann, isn't it?'

Julie looked at her watch. 'They'll be in in a minute. They come almost every night, like us but for different reasons. We come for the food and Lehmann comes because he knows it's the thing to do.'

And sure enough, after a few minutes Lehmann entered followed by Maris and a stranger. The three were still standing up, arranging themselves with that fussiness that accompanied everything Lehmann did, about the small table enclosed in high settles — as most of the tables were — when two police officials in the familiar uniform entered. Julie hardly glanced over her shoulder and said at once to Hansi in an undertone, 'We shall put our passes all together on the table when they come — Georgy's is out of date.'

'This is the third time this week,' complained Harich. Fortunately they had by now finished the meat and the fat waitress flew by and picked up the dish, leaving only the remainder of potatoes and salads on the table among the wine glasses and the litre glass jug, now almost empty.

'More Nussberger please, Fräulein Leni,' called Hansi after her back. She did not stop to answer, only called, 'Coming,' as she went. In the flagged kitchen the sweating cooks were putting the rest of the roast pork into a wooden tub which, a moment later, appeared only to contain sauerkraut. The police officials guessed this — they drank a glass of wine regularly with the proprietress — and were glad to ignore it. It was not an illegally slaughtered pig they were after this evening.

Lehmann's guest, like Kerenyi and a number of other eaters, was in uniform; the black of the SS. The policemen went first to him and he produced a pass that made them salute him. Lehmann said something to them and nodded across the table where the friends sat. The senior of the policemen saluted again. As they went round the room, the policemen bowed to Julie and Harich, whose faces were familiar, and made no demand for Kerenyi's pass. Since he was by chance the only soldier there whose papers were not in order, the police left again without anything further happening. One man had a folder of photographs to which they referred twice when examining the passes of army officers. After they left, it took a little while for the hum of talk to rise once more above the rattle of cutlery.

This intervention made them cautious when they left and as Hansi and Harich walked off together Julie, instead of walking the few hundred metres to the Schellinggasse as she would normally have done, signalled to the taxi standing opposite.

'I'm glad Georgy could come,' said Harich as the two men walked towards the Kaerntnerstrasse. 'Nice for Julie not to be alone for a few days.'

Hansi sighed absently. His liver was troubling him after eating roast pork in the heat.

'You think it's like that?' he asked. 'I hope you're right, but I'm rather afraid not.'

'Oh surely,' said Harich. 'Why wouldn't they?'

'I've never been sure they were lovers — ever,' answered Hansi. 'That was an idea of Jochen Thorn's, you know, when he didn't know us very well. But for Julie's sake, I hope you're right.'

'I've always taken it for granted, myself,' said Harich idly and they changed the subject.

Franz was waiting. The previous afternoon and evening Kerenyi had spent reading the manuscript of the book Franz had almost completed. The two men began at once to discuss this work while Julie went to take a shower and get into a dressing-gown. She was very tired. More tired than the familiar letdown after a successful performance. Kerenyi reminded her inevitably of Nando, and her body, stimulated by the interval with Nando, had not yet returned to its dullness of deprivation. She was both exhausted and irritable at the same time, and went through the old argument in her mind as to whether she should take a sleeping pill and risk being fast asleep 'if anything happened' or whether to suffer a sleepless night. The search in the restaurant decided her not to drug herself.

'You've taken the things I wanted to say so much further than I can do,' Kerenyi was saying as she came into the living-room, 'that I'm not a bit surprised at your impatience with my crude efforts to put my thoughts into words the other night.' He half rose as Julie came in and made a gesture towards the decanter. She shook her head.

'Fina usually leaves me a herbal infusion ready to drink at night,' she said, going towards the hall door. 'I'd better not drink any more alcohol to-night.'

'If you really want my advice, Franzl, just on the technical matter ... I think you should leave the discourse on the Turkish wars in the shortened form you suggest. Don't drop it altogether because it's a good general example of one of your main points. But I'd shorten it drastically as you suggest and use it as a preface to the main argument, as an indication of how your mind began to work on the problem – a concrete example of sociological change in a society. I think that solves the technical problem of where to include the passage. It's too long for one chapter since the entire book will not be much more than twice the length of this passage. D'you see what I mean?'

They were sorting sections of unbound manuscript on the flat writing desk, completely absorbed.

'Now the other technical problem of typing. I ran into my former secretary this evening at the theatre and that gave me an idea. I'm sure she would type it for you and she could get it into the hands of my old friends the printing trades unionists as well, more easily than anybody else can. As you know, they still have a quite good communications network of their own – goodness knows how they maintain it, but they do – to Switzerland, and even to Sweden. That way you could be sure that one copy was in safe hands, anyway.'

'But your secretary would know then that Franz is here,' objected Julie, interrupting the two men.

'Fräulein Bracher doesn't have to know anything. All you have to do is inquire if she has time to do a private typing job for you, and mention me.'

'I see. You mean, I am to undertake the business?'

'Well, I can't. I shan't be here.'

'Georgy,' she said, putting down the big breakfast cup from which she was drinking some aromatic herbal tea, and making a visible effort to control her irritation, 'Georgy, we've been through this before and even for you I'm not going to do anything that could get me – all of us – into trouble. Not to mention this unfortunate typist. If you want to carry on this sort of danger-ous game, you must do it yourself.'

'Look, Julie, do understand.' He tried to explain, glancing

quickly from her to Franz and back again. 'This isn't for me, it's not a conspiracy. It's for Franz. He's spent years working on this book, you know that; he began it in the Lungau. But even that doesn't matter – the time Franz spent on it. It's a new, a major contribution to sociology and the art of government. His analysis of the forms of administrative power – their possible control by means of other organised interest groups – this is something quite new on the great political problem of our time because it gives concrete, organisational answers. Proposals as to how organic, genuine social life can survive and be encouraged in the conditions we have to live in of hugely enlarged industrial populations. It's of vital importance that at least one copy should exist in safety ...'

'Georgy, I don't want to persuade Julie. She has enough of danger and trouble as it is. She knows what is possible and what not – after all, God knows, she's had enough experience! She's an expert in what can be got away with.'

'No, that won't do,' cried Kerenyi, getting hot. 'Julie, this is Franzl's life-work. It's quite different, much greater than anything he wrote before the war – it goes so far past his former opinions that they don't even exist any more. They were just that, opinions; he's moved out in this work, to the universal question of society living or dying. This is something much more important than any ordinary question of safety.'

'There are no ordinary questions of safety!' she said, her voice rising and trembling with nervous anger. 'You talk about society living or dying, but society is people, and it's a question of life and death for us here and now. Even if I would do it myself, I couldn't possibly put Fina into such danger, and then – what about Fräulein Bracher? – she has a life too, remember.'

'She will be willing. Listen to me, Julie; this work makes sense of Franz's suffering all these years. He's used his own tragedy, not submitted to it; this work that my hand lies on is what gives meaning to his life. This is what he has made of his own fate. Don't you see how overriding that importance is?'

'No,' she said stubbornly; she looked away from Franz, who had bent his head on his hand. 'No, I see Fina's life, mine, his, Fräulein

Bracher's. We can hide the manuscript here — we've hidden things before.'

'If you think that,' he said savagely, the tension of years breaking out, 'then you know nothing of what the sack of this city is going to be like. The book will be burned, and if it survives to fall into the hands of the Russians, they will destroy it. This is the absolute word, the contained meaning of everything the Gestapo and the MVD exist to destroy.'

'Then, do it yourself,' Julie cried, frantically. 'You find a typist; you take the responsibility.' A cracking gasp made her voice break and she automatically put a hand to her throat. 'You've been plotting all these three years with other men's lives. Now you're off to Agram where you'll be safe. If you want it typed, find someone to do it!'

'It's nothing to do with all that!' He was shouting now. 'Do you want me to stay here and get you all into trouble, since you're so concerned suddenly for your safety? You know I have to go, and at once. If you don't care about Franzl's work, why did you devote yourself to saving his life all these years?'

'Georgy! For God's sake, how can you say such a terrible thing.'

Franz rose shaking to his feet and reached out an imploring hand to Kerenyi.

Julie stood looking at him with an expression of such bitterness and disillusion that Kerenyi lost his anger in a second and stood silent, a handful of manuscript paper still in his hand. She said nothing, however, and after a moment turned, and putting out a hand to support herself on the back of her chair, made to leave the room.

Before she reached the door, Kerenyi leaped after and caught her round her shoulders, roughly, like an older brother clumsy with painful emotions.

'Julie! Forgive me for God's sake. I can't think how I came to say such a thing. I must have been mad. Julie, don't go away like this! At least say you will try to forgive me.' His voice broke, and as she tried to free herself, still without speaking, the bundle of papers in his clenched fist crackled protestingly.

'Julie!' cried Franz, stumbling hastily towards them. 'My beautiful girl ... wait ...' He sank, gasping with weakness, into Julie's own chair. She ran to him with a cry and fell on her knees, pushing wildly at his shoulders with trembling hands.

'It's all right, dearest one,' he whispered. 'I'm all right. I just can't bear to think of you being so wounded ...'

She sank her head on to his knees and gave way to a storm of weeping. Franz stroked her hair and murmured endearments, letting her weep. Kerenyi came slowly back to the desk, and slumped into a chair where he sat trying stupidly to smooth out the crumpled papers with the ball of his hand without being able to see what he was doing.

'What have I done?' he muttered to himself.

Presently, Julie raised her head without turning it, and stretched out a hand behind her so that Kerenyi could take it, wet with her tears. She tried to speak, her voice muffled with despairing sobs.

'I will do what you want,' she brought out at last. 'I shall never understand – never – but if it is so important to Franz I'll do whatever you say.'

'No, no, I won't allow it,' whispered Franz, pulling her head against his bosom. 'Nothing is worth a moment's sorrow for you that I can prevent.'

She did not argue any more; she knew that she would take the manuscript and it would be typed, just as if it had already been done. When she had had time to compose herself a little, she rose and went away without any more being said. And presently the two men began to talk again of the manuscript.

They sat there most of the night until, at about five o'clock, Kerenyi had to go to catch his train from the South Station. His meagre luggage was already there and when the transport officer took him up on the date of his travel pass, Kerenyi told him that his family had been involved in the air-raid of the night before last which in fact he had spent with Maris, not even hearing the warning sirens. The transport officer shrugged his shoulders; it was happening every day and would take longer to prove or disprove than it was worth. He said perfunctorily that the overstaying of transit leave was a serious offence and would have to be reported to the proper authority at Kerenyi's new posting.

To Kerenyi's disgust he found that his old acquaintance Blaschke had been transferred to an anti-Partisan special unit some weeks before. It therefore took him longer than he had expected to get the Tenius report safely into the hands of friends. Only a few days after he completed this task and sent a signal to that effect to police headquarters at Breslau he was himself transferred without warning to the Carpathian front. On the same night that he left Agram again, Blaschke was surprised in a night attack and ambushed by a Partisan column. The whole police group was wiped out and Blaschke had the good fortune to get a bullet in the brain; not all of his group were so lucky and some of them, the Croatian Ustashe members, took a long time to die. The Partisans were not accustomed to take prisoners.

By the time Kerenyi reached his eastern destination, brigade headquarters had been overrun by the Russian tanks; there was no longer any question of reporting anything and Kerenyi was summarily redrafted on the spot into a broken infantry company, of which he was commissioned the lieutenant later after its last officer and warrant officer were killed.

It was a hot and dry autumn. Blinding and suffocating dust storms hampered every movement of the retreating and disordered armies. Up to regimental strength they broke up, were re-formed, broke up again in the next day or night. Men changed the name and number of their company so often that none had any clear idea of what unit they belonged to. Rations came or did not come up. Ammunition and weapons, transport, uniforms changed hands by the oldest and simplest means; whoever got it first took it. In the weary heat the smashed roads led back from one ruined village to the next, already wrecked by the artillery over the heads of the retreating, routed soldiers. The hourly attacks by swift aircraft that appeared instantaneously out of the hell of other noise with a scream and a racket of cannon-fire, scattered columns to the roadside ditches where the dry grass lay white with dust. This happened so often that time was only a repetition of dazing, bruising, running and cursing dust-filled light or darkness that had no end and no beginning. Men prayed for death and were so stunned with noise and sleeplessness that it was sometimes hours before a man who had been there for days or weeks was missed.

When the rain came at last it was infinite relief and pleasure just to be rid of the dust. It rained for two days and nights and then cleared up again. Kerenyi had a long scouring flesh wound, in those circumstances not much more than a graze, along one upper arm. On an evening suddenly still and quiet – the pursuers were waiting for stores to catch up with their headlong forward rush – he bumped a 'box' Volkswagen which had been his for two days into yet another ruined village. Birds sang in the clear air of dripping sunset after long rain. The ditch by the ploughed up roadway gurgled with thick yellow-white water. An ambulance a few metres ahead caught by a cannon shot had slumped over, half in the ditch. Its crew stood by it. There were four badly wounded men inside the vehicle and their moaning could be heard. Neither the driver nor the orderly was hurt. The orderly dressed Kerenyi's arm for him. He dragged his summer tunic over his arm again, wincing and gritting his teeth, and the orderly offered a sling but Kerenyi shook his head. With a sling he could not drive. He would wait a little for whatever of his company or another company should come up with him. They had been blasted apart by a fighter attack from the air two hours before.

On a rough bench before a low, whitewashed cottage he sat down and rested. It was quite still. Slowly it grew darker. There seemed to be nobody about; the villagers had fled as usual, before the onslaught. When he heard voices he could not believe for a moment that he heard Magyar spoken.

We must have crossed the border, he thought numbly. He had seen no signs of a border on the road, no barrier, no customs hutment; but then, both eyesight and the power to register its evidence were so much affected by the noise, heat, dust and constantly moving danger that he might easily have passed a red and white turnpike, if it stood open, without noticing anything. No frontier formalities here at any rate, he thought grimly.

The voices were quite near him. He called out in Magyar, his native tongue which he had not spoken much in the last years.

An old man incongruously wrapped in a long overcoat wavered towards him cautiously, keeping to the house wall.

'It's all right. We shan't hurt you,' Kerenyi reassured him, although he could only speak for himself; even men who would normally be horrified at the shooting of a civilian were so over-wrought that shots were fired at the slightest suspicion of danger.

The man was standing by the bench now and Kerenyi saw he was not old, but in his middle years; he only moved as if he were old.

'When will the Russians be back?' he asked without preamble.

'Back? Have they been here already, then?'

'Two days ago for a few hours,' the overcoated man seated himself gingerly on the very end of the bench, ready to flee again. He groaned and rubbed at his ankle. 'I don't know what I've done to it,' he muttered. And suddenly garrulous, he raised his voice. 'They shot the mayor. Said he was a *bourzhui* and corrupt; dragged off all the women that hadn't managed to hide themselves. There weren't many, which is just as well, I suppose.'

'Is the road clear down here, do you know?' asked Kerenyi. He pointed with his good arm. The road ran roughly south-west.

'Of course not. They are in the next village. Valea. Well, a real town it is really. Bit more than this dump.'

'Are you from there?'

'Of course. Just come from there. We're mostly Hungarians there.'

'Are we on the border or over it?'

'Border ... it's a few kilometres down the road. How far are they up here, where you came from?'

'About ten kilometres. They stopped moving suddenly an hour or so ago. Waiting for their stuff to come up, probably.'

The ambulance driver was standing nearby, smoking his last cigarette. Gradually a group of other men had reached the village street and were searching the wrecked cottages for something to eat or drink.

'Do you know another road?'

'Ah. There's a field-path just out of here, left of this road. I could show you, if you'll take me with you. You'll never find it by yourself now it's dark.'

'You can't bum a ride with us,' said the ambulance driver suddenly. 'The two wounded that can sit up will have to go in the VW.' He added a recommendation as to what the old man should do with himself; in general, the soldiers rarely spoke without including meaningless filth in every phrase. It was by now the only relief they had from their misery.

'He can ride on the running-board,' said Kerenyi, and shifted his wounded arm uneasily. It hurt much more since it had been cleaned.

'How long have they been lying there, tipped sideways?' The driver did not answer and Kerenyi shouted impatiently, 'The wounded. How long have they been there?'

'Dawn yesterday,' muttered the driver indifferently. 'They stink already,' he added. 'We might just as well leave 'em here. They're for it, anyway.'

Kerenyi tugged at the lanyard of his whistle. It was, as always, stuck, and he cursed, almost weeping with exhaustion. The scattered men answered his signal slowly.

'I need a strap. Somebody find a harness and get me a strap.'

One of the men produced from somewhere part of a harness, after a long search, and with its aid they secured their guide to the door of the Volkswagen so that he should not be thrown off by the bumping and swaying of the vehicle. (Later he would tell the Russians that he had been shackled to the transport and abducted by force by the Fascist beasts.)

Even where the roadway was not ripped up by tank and heavy gun tracks, the wretched transport rocked and bumped, for one of its tyres was gone and hung in ribbons that accompanied their passage with slapping sounds on the wet mud. The two other wounded were loaded into a medium truck with the men whose feet were too bad for them to keep up with the group. They had finished their rations that midday and not a crumb had been found in any of the cottages. Everything was smashed or scattered. Kerenyi winced as he laid his bad arm on the rim of the wooden car body and grasped the wheel. Two men chosen for their small stature crammed themselves into the narrow space next the driver's seat. The two wounded huddled in their filthy rags of uniform, cut about by the orderly to get at their wounds, reeking of ordure and urine and vomit. Above this reek Kerenyi could presently distinguish the filthy sweetish smell of gangrene.

'What did you say the name of the next town was?' he asked the guide when they stopped to allow the straggling men to catch them up. 'Valea, was it?'

The man was moaning to himself about his damaged ankle, and Kerenyi told him savagely to shut up – he was riding wasn't he?

'We may not have much time,' he called to the dozen or so men now catching up. 'Get yourselves on to the two vehicles. Throw everything except ammo out of the truck. Christ, not the two wounded, you bloody fools!' A howl of agony had betrayed the purpose of one of the able-bodied men. 'And hang on. The lane is getting worse all the time.'

After some confusion, they finally set off again at a crawl. Valea, the word went numbly round in Kerenyi's mind. At last he recalled where he heard it, years before. It was the town Julie's mother came from. Weird tricks one's memory plays – can't remember things that happened yesterday, why should I think of that ...? It seemed to him he was in the theatre again, watching Julie. He knew every move and change of expression by which she got her effects. Not a finger moved but to contribute to the characterisation and the voice was an instrument of the most delicate subtlety, handled by a true master of her craft. If only the audience didn't stink so ... he came to with a crashing bump and found the overloaded car almost in the ditch.

'One of you two had better take over the driving,' he muttered. 'I seem to be passing out.' His long and solid body was too large to cram into the side seat with his companion. He fitted himself somehow in between the two reeking wounded, whose faces he never saw and who moaned incessantly, and groaned through gritted teeth as his arm pressed against one of the stacked M.Pi. guns. He was drowning in the foul smells of war.

4

*I*t was cold, an early winter; iron frost gripped trees and
earth, and anything hung out in the courtyard froze stiff in
a few minutes. When Fina insisted on keeping the living-room
windows open during air-raids the cold invaded the house through
the secured shutters and the heavy curtains. Fina had heard from
one of the neighbours that blast would not break open windows
and she lived in a special terror that Franz would be injured by
flying glass. Unwisely, Julie had told her that Lehmann's house had
received a hit in the garden and every single window on the back
of the house, to which all the major rooms looked out, was
smashed. One of the servants was terribly cut about and Maris
escaped by a miracle; she had left her bedroom to go down to the
hall a few moments before the bomb exploded and at the very
moment opened the front door to go out to the car. The force of
the blast wrenched the door out of her hand and slightly sprained
her wrist. The detail of the opened door had confirmed Fina in
what was an almost superstitious belief. So they were condemned
to sit muffled in coats and blankets for hours at a time until the
high whine of the all-clear siren brought relief. If Julie had not
been clever enough to have thought of a trick to save Fina from
going to the cellar, they could have closed the windows after she
went. But Julie had suggested that Fina might tell old Pichler she
was going into the tavern cellar next door, which was deeper — the
foundations were older and went further down into the earth.

Since Pichler and the fat tavern owner quarrelled months ago over a special issue of flour to public eating-places of which Pichler had failed to get his usual cut, he was unlikely to discover that Fina did not go next door when the sirens sounded. So Franz lay on the flat sofa and Fina sat beside him whispering prayers at intervals of calling down every curse on the heads of the enemy bomb-crews that she could think of without using foul language. She was not imaginative and the repetition of her wish that the hands of the young men swaying in their frail, threatening craft above her head in the buffeting of the anti-aircraft guns should wither and drop off was almost as irritating to Julie as the horrible crash and whine of noise outside.

'Fina, be quiet, for goodness' sake. You are disturbing Doctor Franz.'

Fina was silent for a few minutes. Then she began again to whisper '*Ave* Maria ...' She had reached '... and in the hour of our death ...' when a howling whine of unbelievable energy struck her dumb. They froze, all three into images of themselves. The sensation of primeval savage force, irresistible and inhuman, with which heavy bombs plummet into the earth lasted only an instant and then a crash greater than all the noises ever heard together threw them to the floor which bounced up towards their stiffened bodies. Julie's head, without her knowing, hit the arm of her chair and she was dazed with a splitting blaze of light inside her brain. A pause like silence; then a slow slipping and crashing of brick-work sliding into rubble, the cracking of beams, the wild tinkle of glass, a stunning uproar. The walls seemed to be folding in on them and it was incredible that only chunks of plaster fell. The long room was filled with a rolling fog of stifling dust. Then they faintly heard screams.

'It's across the street,' gasped Fina. She was stretched across Franz on the sofa. He was silent and they did not realise at once that he had lost consciousness.

'No, the windows haven't gone. It must be the back-house.'

Julie ran out and through to the kitchen with its window on the courtyard. The floor was covered with glass and in the flicker of the first flames Julie saw with staring unbelief that great jagged splinters were embedded in the doors of the wooden cupboards opposite the window. She could see two or three jumping flames in the black fog of night and dust, she was not sure how many; they wavered and danced before her eyes. Into the wails and screams came the howling of the fire engines and she could hear their thundering engines tearing up the street past what had once been the back-house which no longer offered any resistance to the sound. She knew when she saw their blue-shaded lights flickering and the torches of the first rescue party jumping their round blobs of feeble light that the back-house was gone. What had been a five-storey house, not counting cellars or attics, a minute before, was now a heap of nothing. As she watched, half unconscious with shock, a shout of warning and screams made her strain her eyes across the choking fog of brickdust. The central chimney block, just visible against a lighter background, folded slowly as if it were tired and hung for a second, bent over before it fell into the crowded courtyard. Its fall made a rushing, slithering roar and after the crash she could hear bricks bouncing. There were further cries, a wild scream of some poor soul pinned under the mass of masonry, shouts, whistles blown, one after another the wail of ambulance sirens.

I ought to go down. Perhaps I can do something. No. I am not supposed to be in the house. And if I show myself they will think of bringing the wounded, the homeless up here. Nausea and weakness overcame her and as she swayed away from the window to reach the hall she put out a hand and cut it on a three-cornered sliver of glass. The blood brought her back to her senses and she reached the hall and stood swaying. The dust was choking her and she began to cough. She stared at the blood dripping from the fleshy edge of her hand and heard Fina calling her. In passing she fumbled the door of the big closet in the hall open and pulled out the first piece of linen her hand found, to bind round the running blood.

Fina was trying to force brandy between Franz's clenched teeth. It ran over his chin and into the cushions. He breathed with a groaning sound.

'He's wounded,' she wailed. 'He'll die. What shall I do!'

Julie slipped her good hand, the left one, under the old dressing-gown.

'It's all right. His heart is beating,' she muttered to herself. Then aloud. 'Where are the drops he takes?'

'In his room,' Fina struggled to her feet, shaking a clutter of plaster off the foot of the couch.

'I'll go. I know where they are.' When she saw the wreck of the secret room by the flickering light of what by now were considerable fires Julie was struck by the terror of a new thought. The emergency repair squads would have to come in here and into the kitchen next door. She had no light and ran out again into the hall where they kept a torch in a drawer for just such an emergency. At first her clumsy fingers could not get the little beam of light to show, but then the switch clicked and shielding the light with her hand, although nobody was likely at this moment to be taking any notice of her, she tried the book-shelves where the phial always stood. Plaster, wood chips, glass, dust, ripped books, broken lamp, torn paper, but no phial. She went down on her knees, feeling to and fro; then the cupboard where his toilet things were kept. Other bottles, tubes of tablets, but no phial with the rubber capsule for measuring the drops met her frantic searching fingers.

'That damned doctor,' she sobbed, over and over again. Dr Moller had refused a fresh prescription and she knew there was no spare phial, only the one precious tiny object. She had to bribe the chemist every time to renew its contents on the years-old prescription and risk his reporting the sale; he had a thin, sharp look, that chemist, and she supposed he was a Party member. Finally, frantic with haste, she tried to turn on the electric light in spite of the regulations. The switch clicked and clicked again but no light came. 'It's no good, I just can't find it,' she admitted aloud to herself at last and dragged herself back into the hall and the living-room.

Fina kneeled by the sofa, stroking Franz's hand.

'It's all right, he's come round now,' she whispered over her shoulder. 'You'd better go and see how many windows are gone. I'll stay with him.'

'That can wait till morning. I'm going to lie down.'

'Don't go to bed,' cried Fina sharply, accusingly. 'We must stay together at least until the all-clear sounds.' She dragged her eyes from Franz's face to turn and rail at Julie but caught her breath in a gasp.

'Your face!' she wailed. 'What have you done to it?'

Julie put up a hand, wonderingly. There was a large bump over her left eyebrow and when she touched it, it throbbed heavily. There was no mirror in the living-room. She went through to the bathroom and examined her face in the glass there. There was no doubt, a huge bruise was spreading and her eye was already swollen and red. In a few minutes it would be purple.

'A black eye,' she said aloud and the absurdity was so incongruous that she began to laugh weakly, until she heard her own voice rising and pulled herself sharply together. Her hand was still bleeding a little. It was a narrow deep stab but nothing serious. She held it under the cold tap until the blood was only a squirming streak of pale red, and then dropped the white pillow-case she had wrapped it in and bound it tightly with a face towel, pulling the smooth huckaback as close as she could, awkwardly with her left hand.

The window there was intact, it was set crookedly across the corner and by a trick of blast had not caught the blow of explosion directly. That's something, she thought, at least it will be warm in here. She went back into the living-room and deliberately closed the three windows. Then she got herself a large brandy. Fina began to expostulate, but saw Julie's face and decided not to say any more. Instead she struggled heavily to her feet from her kneeling posture by Franz.

'I'll go and look for his drops,' she muttered.

'You won't find anything. The kitchen and his room are wrecked.'

But Fina would not believe this and went out to look for herself. She came back in a few minutes, staring at Julie with a dismay and unbelief that made Julie want to start laughing again.

'The kitchen is smashed to bits,' she said incredulously. 'How am I going to cook? The stove is all crooked and the gas pipe pulled out from the wall.'

'Gas?' said Julie sharply. 'We'd better turn off the main.'

'I have. But it didn't smell. I think the gas main must be cut.'

'Probably. The electricity on that side is off. I wonder if the water is, too?'

'It may be. There's water in the bathroom but that may be a different pipe.'

They stared at each other.

'Workmen,' said Fina at last and they both looked across at Franz who lay watching them.

'Are you hurt, Julie?' he asked faintly.

'No, no, I only bumped my head when the bomb knocked me off my feet. It's nothing.' She went to him. 'His hands are cold as ice,' she whispered to Fina.

Fina struggled with the firebox door in the stove. The shock had pulled it crooked and the fire-cement round it was loose and cracking. All about the stove was dark brown dust, soft and thick. The fire, when she got the iron door open, was out, and laboriously Fina set about lighting it again. Smoke filtered out of cracks between the tiles, sprung by the explosion.

'I suppose they will all be like that,' she said, watching the thin twist of smoke rise wavering in the light.

Over their heads they could hear the howl of an aircraft out of control as it rapidly lost height.

'I hope it's the one that dropped that bomb,' said Fina viciously.

'It will probably come down on another house,' said Julie looking fearfully upward.

'We have been lucky once again,' said Franz in his quiet, gentle voice. 'Another millimetre on that fellow's instruments before he pulled the switch, and that bomb would have fallen direct on us.'

'You would have to think of something like that,' answered Fina with loving scorn.

That was the beginning of December, and after that they all lived most of their time in the living-room where Julie managed to persuade the emergency repair men to set up the old fire cooking-stove from the wrecked kitchen. Fina could cook on it and it warmed the room a little for the stove burned sullenly for a few days after the bomb and then stopped drawing air through its flue and refused to burn at all. They supposed a block of brick-work had shifted somewhere in the chimney above them but could not investigate because the people in the upper apartment had left the city and their home was locked and deserted. The cooking-stove flue was connected to the neighbouring stove in the next room by an iron pipe which cracked and rustled when it was hot and which was obviously dangerous; neither the workmen who were disobeying orders nor Julie and Fina cared about that for the pipe added to what warmth there was in the freezing room. When it had been fitted the two women moved the flat couch as near as they could get it to the pipe and Franz was installed there.

It was while the emergency squad was actually in the kitchen, nailing sheets of stout cardboard over the shredded window-frames to keep out some of the weather, that Hansi Ostrovsky walked in through the open door through which a boy of twelve had just carried one of the sheets of cardboard.

'Is that boy old enough to be working?' he said abstractedly, looking after the youngster.

'His mother took him out of school – his brother was called up and he's only fifteen, so the mother thought the kid was safer work-ing.' It was Fina who answered, without either greeting the Herr Producer or showing any sign of surprise at his unexpected arrival.

'Where is Frau Homburg? I must speak to her at once.'

He was already on his way down the hall before Fina could col-lect her wits, but Julie came out at the sound of his voice. Her black eye was much better, but the discoloration still showed and Hansi frowned and clicked his tongue against his teeth at the sight of it.

'It still looks terrible,' he said. 'But that wasn't what ... I'm so frantic, I hardly know what I'm saying, Hella was the only clever one among us – she managed to get a health permit at last. She's gone off to the Salzkammergut; it seems she bought a house there last summer. Listen, what was it I wanted to ...?'

Since all the theatres had been closed in August, they had all been scattered to strange and in the main useless jobs, and saw each other less regularly than formerly.

He stared blankly at Julie who leaned against the door of the living-room, hugging herself with her folded arms. Franz was lying in the dressing-room while the men were in the flat. He jerked his head to indicate the workmen.

'Let's go in,' he said and she let him into the disordered living-room where evidences of Franz lay about on tables and chairs. He seemed to notice nothing. Then he saw the botched pipe of the cooking-stove stuck into a raw hole hammered through the connecting wall.

'What on earth is going on here?' he asked.

'You know quite well we were bombed, Hansi,' she said irritably. 'What are you putting on this innocent act for?'

He sat down and she saw with indifference that he was both ill and frightened. For a little while he sat still, fidgeting with an open book that lay on the table beside his hand with pencilled notes by Franz in its margins.

'Yes, that was it. Do you know a woman named Bracher?'

'Bracher? No. Oh, wait, yes I do – Fräulein Bracher, she used to be Georgy Kerenyi's secretary. Why?'

He looked up at her. 'Have you got a drink anywhere?' he asked. With the glass in his hand he seemed to feel more sure of himself.

'She and one of the printers at the *Independent* have been shot in the courtyard there while trying to escape from arrest,' he said, not brutally but in a quiet, reasonable tone. 'The point is, she had your name and address in her pocket book when she was arrested. The police have been with Lehmann and Schoenherr all morning.'

Julie sat down slowly. She said nothing.

'Well, aren't you going to say anything? You might at least ask what it's all about?'

After a time she spoke quietly. 'I don't need to ask. I know what it's about.'

'Then you won't be surprised when the police start asking you what has happened to the manuscript.'

'Manuscript?' She shook her head, not able to focus.

'The manuscript they sent to Zürich in galley-slips. The manuscript that arrived safely and that its recipient wrote to acknowledge the arrival of. That's how they were caught.'

'You wouldn't believe anybody could be so stupid, nowadays,' she said as if they were discussing a colleague who had suddenly forgotten his lines.

'Julie, for God's sake, what are you going to tell them? You have to come with me, now, to Lehmann's office. And that's an enormous concession. Schoenherr and Lehmann practically went down on their knees to them.'

She stared past him at the ragged hole in the wall with the dark, unpainted pipe disappearing through it. She frowned and pressed her lips together, thinking how quickly the pipe would rust.

'I don't know anything about a manuscript,' she said coldly and decisively. 'This Fräulein Bracher went to see my mother a couple of times and once she brought me a few eggs back from the farm. That is all I know about her.' She glanced at him sharply to judge the effectiveness of this. 'Will that do?' she asked. 'You said they'd shot – them – already, did you?'

'A Sturmführer and five men went to arrest them. She confessed on the spot but the man tried to run for it and they were both killed.'

'Not very bright of the Sturmführer,' she said and actually smiled.

Fina put her head in at the door.

'They've finished,' she said. 'Have you any small change for them? I haven't as much as a groschen on me.'

'Hansi, give Fina some money, will you? I'll give it you back later.' He did so and Fina went out again.

'I shall have to tell her. But wait until the workmen are gone.'

When they heard the front door shut, Julie went to the door and called Fina.

'I have to go out with Herr Ostrovsky, Fina,' she said, watching Fina's face closely. 'Try not to be frightened. Just remember – if I don't come back, don't try to find me. Do you understand?'

'Don't try to find you,' repeated Fina stupidly. She looked at Hansi. 'Is it the police?'

'Yes. I managed to arrange for them not to come here. At least, not yet. It will probably be all right.'

'You just say that,' said Fina expressionlessly.

'Get me a handbag, Fina please, and my heavy coat. And bring my chequebook with you – it's in one of my bags.'

'Aren't you going to – to …?'

'No. Better not.' She looked up at Hansi, standing over her with his hands in his coat pockets. 'I won't take anything with me – might look as if I expected trouble if I did.'

His face twisted.

'My liver is killing me,' he said.

'Listen,' she said to Fina, ignoring him, 'I'll write out a big cheque. If this bombing goes on we may again not get to the bank and really run out of money. So when you've cashed this, keep some of it as a reserve.'

'I can always draw on my own money,' said Fina sullenly.

'You won't need to do that, I hope. Fina, I'm going now. Be careful. Especially of Pichler.'

'You ought to …' Fina looked towards the closed door that led to the bedroom and dressing-room.

'No. Better not.' At the door she turned. 'I'd better leave my keys with you too.'

'You think of everything,' said Hansi bitterly.

'If the police keep me, they will take the keys off me,' she pointed out reasonably.

'If it goes that far, we are all lost,' he said.

As they got out of the car he noticed her face.

'You didn't make up,' he said.

'Oh, Hansi, what does that matter?'

One of the plain-clothes men was familiar, but she could not place the known face. Besides Lehmann and Schoenherr, both of whom got up as she entered, there were three other men in the elegant office.

'I was sorry to hear about your house, Friedrich,' she said as Lehmann kissed her hand. 'Is it very badly damaged?'

'It's a pretty good mess,' he said shrugging. 'But you've been having trouble too. How is the eye now?'

'It doesn't hurt any more,' she said, putting a hand to it. 'Now, let's get this over. I understand the police have found my name and address on Fräulein Bracher? Is that right?' She looked quickly at the familiar policeman.

'Yes. Now. We have reason to believe—' began one of the men pompously. Julie cut in on him.

'It's perfectly simple. Fräulein Bracher was formerly the secretary of an old friend, and through him she met my mother and stepfather. She went to visit them several times, and a month or so ago she brought me back some eggs from their farm. I suppose that is technically illegal, but I'm sure it is the only crime she ever committed in her life.'

'I'm afraid it is not so simple as that,' one of them began again.

One by one, perfectly civilly, they began to question her about the manuscript. They went on and on, picking up questions from each other in a trained routine, but since they were asking questions to which she really did not know the answers she was able to give them convincingly bewildered answers. As policemen so often do, they started at the wrong point; not a point at which they could be sure Julie knew something about Fräulein Bracher, but at the point they wished to understand. But they were not, of course, convinced by anything she said.

'I don't understand why you should suppose I know anything about a manuscript,' she said once again, hours later. 'I've never written anything longer than a letter in my life. Fräulein Bracher was the secretary of the editor of a large newspaper, as you know. She must have handled thousands of manuscripts. But what has that to do with me?'

They began again, testing her on addresses in Zürich, addresses she had never heard of. Twice they telephoned and asked whether the other end of the line had any information yet. The answer seemed to be disappointing. Other people were being questioned too.

At intervals one or the other of the policemen suggested she should eat or drink something; or that the gentlemen must have other business and could perhaps be excused if they wished to leave. Both Schoenherr and Lehmann left the room separately for a few minutes, but they never left her all alone with the policemen. After some hours Schoenherr was clearly exhausted and Lehmann suggested quietly to him that he should go and rest.

'No, no,' said the old man rather loudly. 'I shall stay until these gentlemen are finished.'

'I am afraid you may not be well, Herr Director,' apologised the pompous man. This was only too clearly true; Schoenherr's heavy face was sinking downwards as if formed of melting wax and his tremor was now a coarse tremble that made the table shiver on which his folded hands lay. His skin had a livid, purplish mottled look.

Later again, the telephone rang and one of the policemen, the one familiar to Julie, picked the receiver up quickly before Lehmann could get to it.

'Really, Herr Luther,' said Lehmann, affronted. 'Be good - enough to allow me to answer my own telephone, if you please.'

'Now I remember where I've seen you before,' said Julie, unaware that her voice dragged sleepily.

Luther was listening, but not to them.

'Leave the old girl, then,' he said at last, 'and concentrate on the typesetter.' He put down the telephone. 'The mother seems to know nothing about her daughter's business affairs. She's senile, anyway. But one of the typesetters seems to be softening.'

The pompous man made a note.

Hansi was staring insistently at her; he wanted her to know something but she could not guess what it was. On and on they went, speaking calmly and civilly, one by one. It would never end. But it did end.

When the telephone at last rang again Lehmann made no attempt to touch it and Luther answered it. A nerve was jumping in Hansi's cheek and this troubled Julie. Lehmann kept looking at his gold wrist-watch.

'He's singing now,' said Luther. 'We've got him.'

'Has he confessed?' asked Hansi hoarsely. Nobody answered. The three policemen were gathering papers, ignoring the others. Julie saw that Hansi's face was shining with sweat. They were in a great hurry suddenly, to be gone. If Lehmann had not hurried out with them they would have gone without telling anyone that all was well. Hansi bent over Schoenherr's chair.

'Ring for a doctor, Julie,' he said. 'The old boy's in a bad way.'

She was amazed that the offices were empty, the switchboard unmanned, that it was almost ten o'clock at night. The words of the emergency list in the directory jumped before her eyes. Finally she got the nearest doctor on the duty list for emergencies. She looked over her shoulder.

'You'd better order an ambulance, I think, Doctor,' she said.

'It's a miracle,' muttered Hansi. 'That he didn't remember you, I mean.' Schoenherr was trying to say something. His lips puffed in and out but no sound came except his harsh groaning breath.

'They've killed him,' whispered Julie under her breath, without emotion. It was an histrionic gesture; this was replaced after a moment by the clear thought that it was she who had killed the old man, if he died. This idea she pushed out of her mind. Lehmann reappeared, nervously smoothing his sleek blond hair. He looked at Schoenherr, seemed about to say something, and then sat down in his own desk-chair which had been occupied for hours by one of the policemen. He put his elbow on the desk and rested his forehead in his hand. Julie became aware that he was weeping silently. She was interested by the brass moulding that bordered the rococo writing-table. I wonder where Lehmann knocked that off, she thought, it's a nice piece. Up to the time the doctor came hastily in, already opening his bag, nobody had spoken again. He was followed by two sturdy, elderly bearers with a stretcher carried downwards. The doctor picked up the inert hand, and felt the pulse. Then he carefully opened his bag, took out a pair of spectacles and put them on; slowly he brought out then a small white napkin, on which he laid, on the edge of Lehmann's table, a hypodermic syringe, a little file and, after searching for it, a phial out of a flat packet. As he assembled the syringe and its needle with finicky care, one of the bearers came forward and taking the tiny phial delicately between thumb and finger, filed off its narrowed head, squinting at it myopically the while. After a few moments doing something with the old man's jacket sleeve, there was a ripping sound as the bearer tore up the fine linen shirt. Julie could not see what they were doing, and it seemed somehow that they must be going to drug the director and take him to the police who had left. She knew that this was not so and struggled with the notion. Only a few seconds after the injection, Schoenherr's breathing eased. She was then aware that the sound of his groaning breath had filled the room. From outside the shuttered room – when had somebody closed shutters and curtains? – the wail of sirens filtered in.

'Good Christ. Again,' said Hansi. The doctor looked round crossly.

Without knowing she was going to speak Julie said hastily, 'I must get home. Can you take me in the ambulance, Doctor, and drop me off – anywhere near the Schwarzenbergplatz will do?'

He stared. He was a small, dried man.

'We are going to the General Hospital in the opposite direction. In any case it is against the rules. Good night.' He gave no instructions to the bearers. Very carefully and gently, they loaded the heavy old man, now breathing slowly and quietly, on the stretcher flat on the floor, covered him with a dark grey blanket and with some effort lifted the burden and walked steadily and carefully out of the door. The doctor put up his glasses, packed his equipment and closed his bag with a loud snap. He left the room without looking at any of its occupants again.

'This is impossible,' said Julie. 'Friedrich, pull yourself together!' She turned to Hansi. 'Ring up for a car, Hansi. I've got to get home.'

'You're staying here until the all-clear sounds. We don't want any more trouble.' His voice rose suddenly. 'How many miracles do you think you're entitled to? Are you mad?'

There was nobody in the elaborately appointed shelter in the basement, except for the nightwatchman who was at the same time the air-raid warden for the building. After a time Julie half slept, knowing she slept, and dreamed that she was arguing with Luther in front of the house in the 2nd District, not seen since 1938; there was something urgent she must convince him about, but could not express it so that he could understand. She was being shaken in a hard grip and Hansi's voice woke her telling her not to mutter; the all-clear had sounded. But they could raise no answer from the car-pool. Amid the protests of the watchman, Julie rose and struggled into her beaver coat. She had no hat.

Hansi sat with his knees drawn up on the mattress next to the one she had been lying on.

'Let her go,' he said to the watchman. 'The raid is over.'

The night was bitter cold, a wet raw wind from the east with snow in it blew against her steps. She had not thought that the park gates would be closed. It was a long way round the Ring. She stopped once to lean against the tall wrought-iron railing and found she was outside the Burggarten.

At the Opera crossing she was stopped by a police patrol and had trouble getting her pass out of her bag with her frozen fingers. She was aware of the men staring after her with wonder; though there were several other people straggling about, held up most of the night by the raid. She had heard no bombs, but there was a billowing smoky glow from the direction of the Danube Canal when she looked down the Kaerntnerstrasse as she crossed, bent against the wind. At the next crossing for some reason, the rectangular blocks of the roadway were very uneven; she stumbled but was not aware of having fallen until she found herself getting slowly to her feet. She stood, trying to focus in the pitch dark, and at last saw that she was on the tram lines in the Schwarzenbergstrasse. Farther on towards the square she could see a large group of hurrying, crouching men. Or she thought she saw them. Then something lurched against her and she heard a rough voice say, 'Careful now.' And then, 'Frau Homburg, what are you doing out here?' An ant-eater's nose and a curve of stomach; ah, Nando, she thought, the night we quarrelled. She began to laugh to herself.

'It's only just occurred to me that I can't ring my bell at this time of night,' she said. 'I should frighten Fina out of her wits. She'd think it was the po—' The tall fat man had caught her wrist in a hard grip.

'You'd better come into my place, gnae' Frau,' he said and turned her smartly in the direction of her own home. 'It's right next door to you and you can have a rest until it's light.'

He almost carried her down the sunk steps to the cellar tavern. Not until she smelled the soup did she remember that she had eaten nothing since morning. 'You don't want to go about saying things like that, now,' he chided her, stoking the dying fire with split wood. 'Talking like that about our friends and helpers the police, that's no sense, now is it?'

The enormously fat woman was nowhere to be seen, nor indeed anyone else. When the soup was hot the tall big man gave her a bowl of it, and took some for himself. It was goulasch soup, sharply spiced. She began to talk after a bit.

'Has anything happened in the square? I thought I saw a crowd there? Were you damaged here when our bomb came down? Can't think why people always say bombs fall. They don't fall at all. You see, I fell and blacked my eye. I mean, the bomb threw me off my balance. Fortunate it was late in the evening, wasn't it? Otherwise Fina would have been killed, playing about in the kitchen as she always does. To-night? (The man had said something.) No, it wasn't the raid that kept me out all night. At least I mean, I couldn't go home because of the raid, but I was out. I was in the office with the police. I thought they would never let us go, and I suppose they wouldn't have done, quite literally never, only some poor devil of a printer confessed somewhere else, nothing to do with us, and they forgot all about us. They were all in a muddle, I see that now, because this stupid SS man had shot the only people who really knew what they wanted to know, shot them on the spot, so they had to ask everybody they could think of and that was me, too, because she had my name and address on her when she was caught.' She stopped speaking and stared about her at the smoky low room with its vaulted ceiling that she remembered but no longer knew from where she remembered it. 'Is there any more of that wonderful soup? I could use a drink, too? Schnapps, yes, that would be best. I must pull myself together, mustn't I? I ought not to talk like this, I shall get you into trouble. Or you'll get me into trouble. No, you won't do that. I didn't mean that. The police always seem to get hold of the wrong end of the stick, don't they, but it was nearly the right end this time, if they had only known it. If they had only kept on at me about her – Fräulein Bracher, I mean – I should probably, certainly, have made some mistake after an hour or so, but they kept on about the manuscript and the printer and these people in Zürich that I've never even heard of. They thought I suppose that she was unimportant since it's the manuscript's getting out of the country that is important to them, even if they don't know what was in it and I don't suppose they do. Certainly I don't, I never read it, it's much too clever for me, I just asked Fräulein Bracher to get it typed out and send it away and she must have got the printers to run it off because they kept talking about galley-slips. You know what galleys are, don't you, because there were printers in here last time I was here and you said then they came every night. It would have been all right still, only the man — people — in Zürich that the printer sent it to — Georgy said printers still have contacts abroad — and he was quite right, you see — were mad enough to let Fräulein Bracher know that the galleys arrived safely. Of course, it seems mad to us, here and now, that anybody should be so casual about such a thing, but to them, I suppose they don't know what it's like. I mean, they read things and they think they know I expect, but it's not the same kind of knowing. So the police intercepted this letter, I suppose they must open the post coming from abroad, yes, of course they do, and it was addressed to Fräulein Bracher, poor old girl, and they assumed she was the go-between, that's what they kept calling her, and she was, of course, but they'd got hold of the wrong end of the stick and were worrying about the manuscript getting to Zürich and if they had kept on to me about how the manuscript got into Fräulein Bracher's hands they'd have caught me out sooner or later. But of course they couldn't know I gave it to her because they must have believed the reason I gave them for her having my address. I expect it was convincing — not that they were convinced, I don't suppose they ever are convinced of anything — but it happened to be true that she had been to see my mother several times but not that she brought me eggs; I wish she had. Isn't it strange that I say that so calmly, only a short time ago I'd have been prostrated at the thought of anybody I knew — anybody at all, being shot. Shot!—'

The man managed to interrupt her at last.

'The police,' he asked slowly, 'will they be coming back? Here, I mean?'

That stopped her hysteria.

'I don't know.' She spoke now in her usual tone as if suddenly sobered up. 'That's what I just don't know. If they do – come here, that is – I suppose they will shoot us in our own courtyard, too.'

'Yes, if they come back they will make a job of it, this time. Find everything.'

'Everything . . . ? You know, then?'

'I've always known. Ever since you sacked – or Fräulein Fina sacked – your charwoman, years ago. She came in here, afterwards, talking about it and saying she meant to take this story to the newspapers, that you had a man there. I knew she'd never have the guts to do that, but I didn't forget it, either.'

'Did you tell anyone else?' she asked after a time.

'Nobody. Not even the wife. Not that she would have repeated anything. But she's gone in any case. You didn't know? No, I dare say you wouldn't hear. She had something in her stomach, like a stone it was. No, I didn't say anything because I was pretty sure I knew who it was, you see.'

'How could you know? It might have been anyone – just for a night.'

He shook a ponderous head. 'You learn about people in this trade. Everybody about here knew he was gone away, and you were alone so long. Where he was, that was what nobody knew. And you, you mustn't mind me saying it, you aren't the type to change and start having men in the house. Some do and some don't and what is sure about people is that they don't change their ways. What they do once, they go on doing, one way or another. Of course, I didn't know. But I knew.'

She thought.

'But the man I was with the night I came here before?'

'That was just it, you see, gnae' Frau. I'd seen him before, once or twice. He brought you back to your door and said good night, but you never took him in with you. Did you? The only one that ever went in alone that I heard of was the big sandy man with the nose; the one that was here last summer. He came sometimes, but I saw him off and on when you were at the theatre.'

'You seem to know everything,' she said slowly.

'I'm always here, you see, gnae' Frau. I tried to say something once, but I didn't know if you'd got my meaning. That time you were in here. And as long as I knew the Pichlers knew nothing, I just kept my own counsel.'

'If you know so much, it seems incredible that the Pichlers never saw or heard anything.'

'They aren't well liked about here,' he said darkly.

'If you know, several other people in the street may know?'

'Maybe they do, or think they do. But nobody knows that would report it, or you'd have been caught long since. Mostly the people who would go to the police or the block-leader would go to you first and try to make something out of it. But I don't think anybody does know. It's a remarkable thing how little people notice of what goes on around them. Mostly they are too busy with their own family affairs, and the rich folks don't bother themselves with other people.'

'Don't the police ever ask you things?'

'Not for years now. I never had anything to do with politics, not one way or the other. They came sniffing about years ago once or twice; but they must reckon I'm dumb so they leave me alone.'

'And I suppose I was protected by the theatre, so they left me alone, too.'

'They don't want any more scandals. They've got enough trouble without famous people getting in the papers.'

'Just lately they haven't cared much about scandals, though.'

'You mean since last summer? Yes, a lot of people have been in trouble, but that was mostly the military sort or politicals. You can see for yourself, gnae' Frau, how careful they are with anybody in the public eye. Just look at the way they treated you to-day – yesterday, I mean. Like cats walking round hot broth. Just so long as you stay out of politics, you're all right.' He stopped, then he got up heavily and went to the stove, where he shovelled coals on the fire, and set the water urn on for coffee. 'It's morning,' he said over his shoulder. 'Be light soon.' He went to the locked door and opened it, reaching outside for a large oval basket covered with a clean cloth and full of warm rolls of bread. It was still quite dark, as she could see through the cracks of the opened door which let in an icy current of wind.

'We don't open until eleven, being a late-night place,' he said. 'But the cook and the girl will be coming soon after six.' He came back to the table and leaned his great fists on it. The rustle of flames was joined by a threat of sound from the urn as the heating water turned.

'It won't be long now,' he said and something in his voice made her look up into the old leathery face where the colourless eyes were shrewd. 'And I don't mean the coffee. Why don't you get away like all the other rich people? It won't be pretty here when it comes to the end.'

'I can't do that,' she said flatly. 'I can't go away.'

'Don't say afterwards you weren't warned,' he said very quietly. 'I know what the Russians are like. I was a prisoner there after the last war. Can't you and Fräulein Fina get him away somehow?'

'He is too ill. Even if he were fit to be moved, we should be caught.'

'Then go yourself. At least get yourself somewhere to go and be sure you can get there when it comes.'

'I can't do that,' she repeated, staring at him hypnotised by what he was not saying. He watched her for a little while and then seemed to shelve the whole matter; he went and measured coffee.

Presently she left and he would not allow her to pay him, saying they would arrange that some other time. Light was already burning in the lodge window on to the hall, when Pichler shuffled to the door to open at her ring.

She said something about the raid, and about the fires reflected on the night sky towards the Danube Canal. He was concerned, however, only with the apartment abandoned above her own.

She unlocked the lift door which once he would have rushed to open for her, and stood half in and half out of the cage, holding the sprung inner sliding barrier open with one foot.

'There is nothing I can do, Herr Pichler, if the housing authorities mean to bring in bombed-out people. The flat is certainly empty and I don't know any more than you do where the owners have gone.' She was quite sure that he himself had reported the empty flat to the block-leader.

'We'll have scum from the slums in here,' Pichler muttered. 'Like as not with a dozen kids.'

She found, when Fina opened the door, that she could not face either Fina or Franz. She shook her head when Fina tried to question her.

'I don't know,' she said. 'It's no good asking me because I just don't know.'

She went to her room and lay down but she could not sleep. The words to Fina, she knew, were understood to mean that she did not know whether the police were satisfied; but that was not what she had meant. To tell Franz that Fräulein Bracher had been shot for his manuscript, that was impossible; equally impossible to talk to him and not tell him. She was aware that to Franz himself as to Kerenyi, the man was his work and she was aware that too, Fräulein Bracher who had worked in the newspaper business all her life, must have known quite well what risks she ran and the printers knew them equally well, which was proved as she wearily told herself, by the fact that they had kept open their secret line of communication. Some newcomer, full of eagerness to help but without the experience to know how, had unwittingly betrayed them from the safety of Zürich? Or a traitor, a Nazi sympathiser? Possibly even a communist trying only too effectually to destroy the solidarity of the old socialists? From Franz she knew that such things happened often. But to herself, the manuscript meant little; only the disgusting personal fact that her actions, weakly doing what others assured her was the right thing to do, had caused more death, more fear and hatred, had lessened the strength of the living by a few – one would never even know by how many – notches on the sickening, meaningless, nameless toll of death. Perhaps she should not even have come back home? She should have gone to a hotel and told the police so – that man Luther who might even yet recall – unbelievable that he had not recalled – seeing her years ago on that Saturday in March. No, her instinct to return simply home had been right. If the police wanted her again, a new address would arouse immediate suspicion. And did she even care any more what happened? She supposed she must do, since she continued to act as if she did, but there was nothing of feeling any more and she was aware that this was no new fact in her mind. If only it would all stop, stop as it did in the theatre, a curtain cutting off action and thought neatly so that audience and actors alike could go away, go away. The time spent in the tavern had restored her and she was conscious and rational. I know what the Russians are like, he said. She did not know what he meant, it was a dark cloud of threat, but she was aware with deep fear that he meant something worse than she had yet contemplated. Why had she not listened when Georgy talked last July? Why had she not read all those books she would now certainly never read from Franz's shelves about the revolution? And to-morrow she must work again. Nando, she thought, if only you could get back somehow and help me. As you helped me long, long ago when we could still dance in the tiny living-room and drink champagne and cover the telephone in a caution that was still half a joke for you, Nando.

The longing for an end, which struggled with terror of the dark forces coming from the eternally threatening east, was like the longing for unconsciousness that torments a suicidal mind. An end, any end, better a frightful end than a fear that never ends, as the simple people had already begun to say secretly to themselves and each other.

5

'*I* know you would have let me know if you had heard anything, yet I must write and ask you. It is like a disease, wanting to hear news and never being satisfied, you must know what I mean, one listens or reads what is supposed to be happening though nobody seems to know exactly. Every day we put on the wireless for the news but there is never anything about the troops that were on the Rumanian front before it broke and the Rumanians got out of the war. Lali and I have decided he must be a prisoner for surely we must have heard if he were wounded or killed? It is a strange judgment of God that Otto was killed before he could get back to marry Lali – she refused a proxy wedding for some reason of her own that she says nothing about. So there will still be a von Kasda when the child is born next month. We are sure it must be a boy. I know you would let us know if you heard from Nando. Really this letter is to send you Christmas greetings, but we are not thinking much of Christmas. Lali took the blow very well about Otto's death; he fell on 13th November, but his mother got the news only ten days ago and is still prostrated with grief. He was just twenty-one. Christian, her younger boy, is all she has left now, for still nothing has been heard of poor Peter Krassny, though Alois Pohaisky heard that Margarete has been taken to the old Reich. I think Lali knew before she heard. She'd been very still and quiet for some weeks and I feared it was the child causing her pain but thank God she is perfectly healthy

584

and does not cry or seem frightened. I would try to keep the news of the Russian advances from her, but that is impossible because we must listen to the damned radio for news of Nando's regiment. Everything is otherwise in order here, we manage somehow and I am able to send food packets to Margarete Pohaisky though we do not know where she is, only a post-office number and we are nervous of trying to find out, in case we make matters worse. Christian is bringing this letter to you, he moves between their house here and Vienna so that neither authority will be able to call him into the Volkssturm. He is very cut up over Otto's death, they were very close and Christian felt that his place was with Otto in the army but he deferred to his mother's wishes as he always does, poor boy. He has no talent at all for his engineering studies – he is here with us a good deal and he and Lali sit and talk for hours together – and I try to encourage him, but he knows that it is all just to keep him out of the army and feels guilty but I tell him that somebody must survive, if it is God's will. Here I just run on about our own affairs and do not ask how you are. Vienna must be terrible, with the bombing constantly. Lali asked only the other day if the theatres are still open. I think of you constantly because my Nando loved you. Dr Alois sends his blessing to you, and Lali says to tell you that you are to be the child's godmother ... '

The letter from Enns and a shaky postcard written from his hospital bed by Director Schoenherr were the only signs of Christmas. The police, every day more active, were also every day less feared as the knowledge of the coming catastrophe spread through the city, from the lower depths upwards. Huddled in cellar shelters, dozens of families spent their nights and half their days below each block of proletarian dwellings, and formed forcing houses of rumour and sedition that grew in tropical abundance and spread rapidly to other layers of the populace. Every man on leave for a funeral after a fresh raid had tall tales to whisper, warnings to spread. The city began slowly to empty itself, the people following the example of the bourgeoisie who had begun their flight after the events of the previous July. Whoever had relations in the country, went to them, whether they were welcome or not.

Vienna is a small city and bombs in numbers that could hardly mark a vast spread like Berlin damaged the tight-knit fabric of city life irreparably. In a large city there is always an alternative route for wheeled traffic, water pipes, electricity and telephone cables, but in the eighteenth-century boundary of Vienna's centre and especially where the medieval foundations supported modern buildings, one gaping hole could tear apart communications for which there were no alternatives possible in the overcrowding, noise, material shortage and lack of will.

Refugees from Budapest brought fear, like a plague, and it grew to panic force. Their stories, the evidence they brought with them in their persons welled in waves through the city, whispered, leaking like gas from long queues at the hospitals waiting for first aid, the rare drugs, the surgeon who would mercifully abort; and from the shopkeepers who accepted bits of jewellery for sale, bartered clothing or small valuables for foodstuffs. The stories of the crash and flame of cities these refugees brought with them could be heard and felt in every shock and crash of bombs so that disbelief was impossible; the overture to final catastrophe was already to be heard by everyone.

Some time in January, the water was cut off by police order after a bomb broke into a main pipe and the dead bodies of those who had been sleeping uneasily above it were irrecoverably smashed into the dark wet mass. After that, water had to be fetched in pails from a standpipe on the corner. Noise, endless crashing howling noise, dominated a dazed nightmare of struggling for water, heat, food. Time ceased; continuity of noise and a weariness long past exhaustion took over from hours and days, days and nights.

Until 12th March, they managed to eat, for Julie ate every evening at the little restaurant where she had last seen Kerenyi, and could sometimes bring back part of her food in her handbag. These slices of meat, spoonfuls of potato were heated up for Franz by Fina. But he ate hardly anything. The date was the only clear one in Julie's mind because it was a Monday – she went shopping on Monday – and she discovered that one of their precious ration cards was gone after standing nearly two hours in line.

Franz was so ill that Fina could never leave him, and for weeks the shopping had been left to Julie. She fared worse than Fina ever had, for she was unused to using her elbows and her familiar face and aristocratic manners aroused the resentment of the other women and the shopkeepers. What was she doing, they wanted to know, only half under their breath, playing at housekeeping as if she only now discovered what they all knew for years. Let her see how she should manage! Any of the other women in the queue would have got rations even without the precious document, but Julie was forced to stick to the rules when she failed to produce the dog-eared card. Even worse, it was her own privileged special card that was lost – or stolen – and on Fina's ordinary card there was little to be had.

The rise and fall of sirens hardly affected the dark shop where there had been no proper lighting for a week; housewives went on buying, haggling and quarrelling and it seemed that the squadrons of planes heard in that quiet that always followed the sirens' dreary wailing, were on their way past the city. Even as Julie discovered her loss and the overdriven girl behind the counter was telling her in the crudest terms that there was nothing she could do about people who were stupid enough to lose their papers, the planes, with their curious broken rhythm, firmly believed by the populace to be a device of the flyers to prevent accurate anti-aircraft fire, could be heard thundering back again. The rumble was joined by fresh flights roaring up from the south and in a few moments the whole building was jumping and cracking as if it must burst apart in splinters. How she came to be in the cellar Julie never knew, but crammed into a struggling mass of bodies between the tall racks and shelves she stood for endless hours, until the air seemed totally used up. It became very hot down there, children wailed and howled, were sick and their mothers were sick with them. Fainting with fear and lack of oxygen they did not fall, for the whole street seemed to have rushed with the customers into the cellar as the appalling crash and whine began and they were too closely packed together to fall, and lolled against the shelves and each other as if drunk.

After an eternity of noise and shock an elderly man of

considerable girth lost consciousness near her and somehow was pushed and dragged along the floor to a clearer space, so that she could now move a little. Only then did she see that the shelves were crammed with packets and tins of food, stocks to last for months of everything people lacked. Here and there women were removing a tin or a bag of flour or rice; whatever came near to their hands in the intervals of mortal terror when the noise and rocking and shaking eased. Immediately in front of Julie's face when she managed to turn away from a group of wailing and dribbling small children who seemed to be motherless, was a stack of bottles of good Rheingau wine. Across the labels was stamped the legend SS STOCKS FOR OFFICIAL USE ONLY, and she realised that a panic rush from the street had forced the mass of people down into secret cellars reserved for special customers of which all these years neither she nor the rest of the populace had known anything. So this was where the stores for those parties came from! She could have laughed aloud at the thought of Lehmann's parties and felt about on the shelf nearest to her for some implement that would either remove the cork or smash the neck of one of the bottles so that she could drink. But she found nothing except more bottles.

At that moment a crash of maniacal force flung shelves and contents flying into the crowd and an uproar of screams and shouts prophesied that they would all be buried alive; the building over them must be gone, at any second the masonry would descend on them. Every living soul not stunned by some edible or drinkable missile was struggling wildly in every direction, nobody any longer conscious of where an exit might be found but frantically tearing himself away from where he was. A shelf descended cross-wise past Julie's body and cut her off from the mob. Her last wish was fulfilled; a large can of olive oil – unknown for months – crashed into the row of bottles nearest to her and neatly decapitated three of them, the rest being hurled to the stone floor where they crashed, causing some splinter cuts among the struggling children she had only a moment before turned away from. She was not only isolated, she also had something now to drink, and drink she did the most delicious wine of her life; she could even sit on a cross-shelf emptied of its contents and shorn of upper structure, and stretch her cramped limbs. That was enough for the moment.

Not until the all-clear sounded hours later was it discovered that the building was only badly damaged from a direct hit next door and the crowd could at any time have left it by clambering painfully over the great heaps of bricks and mortar piled before the smashed door. When she came out Julie thought the raid had lasted into the night, it was so dark. But the dark was smoke and dust and this cloud of filth hung about for days over the centre of the city. Julie was completely unhurt, only drunk with shock and Rhine wine, but when she at last struggled out into what was left of the square she could not find her bearings and found herself presently walking in the wrong direction, stumbling about among great beams and blocks of masonry. She recognised her whereabouts by seeing the spire of the cathedral, which should have been at her back. It was raggedly illuminated by reflection from a great sheet of fire-shot smoke but she could not go back in her tracks for as she turned to do so a long sliding crash a few metres ahead brought a fresh mountain of rubble into the road-way and she struggled on towards the cathedral square simply because she could see it and must get away from the howls and screams behind her from the collapsed building.

Much later, as it seemed, she was behind the great church with its damaged sacristy, the wall of smoke and flame to her right now, she could feel its gusts of heat.

There was a fresh billow of flame, as far as she could judge just past the Archbishop's Palace. Here there was a strong stink of roasting flesh. But a narrow medieval street seemed to be clear and she could turn towards home at last. Even the smoke was less here, the narrow street miraculously not touched. She stumbled for a long way parallel to the main street, and came out at last into a new holocaust of smoke, flames and flying sparks and cinders. At a discreet distance from the centre of the fire a great crowd lined the smashed square and she heard from the hum of talk that the fire brigade was just letting the Opera burn. The expert men had all been called up for military duty and the forced-labour

Ukrainians who replaced them had neither skill nor interest to defend the rigging lofts, to save which would have saved the building. Julie heard someone say in a cultured voice that the great house would burn for weeks and wondered how he could know, but whoever he was proved right and the Opera was still smouldering three weeks later.

Now the street was full of a struggling mob of people, smoke-blackened, their clothing torn and filthy. Every one of them seemed to be carrying or dragging some bundles, of bedding, of household goods, of food. From somewhere they had numbers of small wheeled objects; children's scooters with boxes bound to them, perambulators, hand-barrows. A tall old man in a long black overcoat with a fresh cut on his forehead that dripped blood into his eyes, stood on the edge of the pavement. In his arms he held a bundle of large and heavy books which appeared to be important to him. She saw that he was weeping and the tears ran down mingled with blood into his straggling little white beard and moustache. She stopped pushing and struggling a moment beside him to catch her breath, and a hand-cart loaded with a feather bed, two small children howling at the top of their lungs and a number of cooking pots held together with a rope through their handles caught her sideways and threw her off an unsure balance. She fell against the old man who, in unwittingly catching her fall was flung down, and fell into the gutter, where he lay. The cooking pots rolled with a hardly heard clangour off the hand-cart, and its owner, a burly man of about thirty with a villainous squint shouted curses at her which she could not understand. Still clutching the small parcel of foodstuffs she had bought hours before, and holding it against her breast with both folded arms, she pushed her way backwards towards the shelter of the house walls. A woman was there before her, breathing heavily and resting one emaciated arm, visible through her sleeve ripped down from the shoulder and hanging loosely as she propped herself against the wall with a hand wrapped in a filthy and blood-stained cloth. They faced each other. After some time Julie accepted the wandering illusion that she knew the woman's face. A long angular face, the hair bound back in a dark scarf; a face discoloured by illness or lack of sleep, but this state belonged to it when Julie first saw it and was not the stigma of the strain they all now bore. A long irregular nose, masculine, a mouth set with controlled anger for years, habitually.

'Where did you come from?' she muttered, without having placed the memory of the face. The woman seemed hardly to see her and did not answer. But she spoke at last in a strange accent and dragging her words with exhaustion.

'I remember you,' she said.

'Warsaw,' said Julie, remembering.

'Schultze got me away, just after the uprising. Now I have to move on again out of here, before the Russians come.'

'Schultze?' asked Julie stupidly.

'I heard they shot him, after I'd gone. He got forged papers for several of us. He was bound to be caught at last ...' Her face changed as her eyes managed to focus on Julie's face and its ugliness was increased by a savage sneer. 'It's worth everything I've been through to see you suffer too.' She changed the arm she leaned upon, shifting her feet in men's boots and pushing away the bundle between them to ease her weariness. 'Now you know what we suffered. A valuable lesson, is it not?'

She began to speak again, but a fresh crowd of refugees eddied round them and she was pulled along with them, only grabbing up her bundle tied in a jacket by the sleeves, just in time to save herself from being trampled underfoot in the rush that pushed Julie roughly back into a doorway. There she waited for some time, she did not know how long, until the stream of fleeing people had exhausted itself; but presently she could edge along – she now found she could not walk properly and needed the support of the houses which irritated her with their constantly changing contours, here a deep-set doorway, there a railing sticking out into the pavement to protect a basement entrance, then the long smooth expanse of shop window. She did not know where she was going, but a deeper knowledge of her whereabouts had taken over from consciousness and she found herself at last without surprise outside her own house doors. Which were firmly locked.

At last her continued ringing at the bell brought a slatternly woman she had never seen before to open a crack.

'Pichler's gone off somewhere,' she excused herself, 'and we locked the doors in case that mob got in here.'

As Julie reached the lift doors, the woman's snivelling voice behind her said resentfully, 'It isn't working.' Julie turned to look at her, shook her head and began to make her way up the winding stair that enclosed the lift shaft. It was quite dark for all the windows on this side were covered now with cardboard sheets already bent and stained with wet and in some places torn.

They were where they always were, Franz lying on the flat sofa near the primitively installed cooking stove, and Fina half lying, half kneeling across him, holding his hands. Since the front window of the chemist's shop had been smashed some weeks before, the owner had cleared off and the bribed refilling of Franz's old prescription had become impossible. Julie sank into a chair. She took as little notice of the other two as they of her; Franz was half unconscious. Without the drugs, the condition of his heart and liver reduced him to an inert daze most of the time.

After a time Julie managed to bend down and get out of her shoes; they were cut to pieces on the rubble, filthy, the soles badly burned. She had not been conscious of walking on anything burning. She examined her hands – gloves and hat had disappeared – and her coat, but it was only the soles of her shoes that showed burns; her hands looked like a coal-heaver's with soot and some nails were broken, but there was nothing else wrong with them and a three-cornered tear in the filthy fur of her beaver coat detracted from its looks but not its usefulness. There was no water in the two pails in the bathroom. The lavatory smelled foul; it had for weeks, since the water was cut off, and they had become used to it, but she noticed it now. She took one of the pails and began the downstairs journey. From the porter's lodge the slatternly woman appeared, holding her hand under her sacking apron. Julie reached her hand through the hall window to the board where the big house keys hung without speaking to the woman.

At the door she thought of something which had been on her mind since she came in, but she had forgotten.

'Where *is* Pichler?' she called to the woman, now hovering in the shadowy back of the long hall.

'He went next door before the raid started. I don't know where he is. He can't be hurt. There wasn't anything in this street at all.' The woman was trying to be ingratiating. She even came forward and made to take the pail out of Julie's filthy hand. But Julie shook her head, and went out, her mind now working with something like normality. The standpipe on the corner was running only with a trickle, but nobody except Julie was interested in getting water, so she set down the pail and the tap slowly dribbled it full. She could hardly carry its weight back to the door. God, she thought, the stairs. The woman with the sacking apron was nowhere to be seen, and this was a relief.

When she finally got the pail of water into the apartment without spilling very much of it, Julie called Fina. She called three times before Fina came to the door of the living-room and stood looking without saying anything.

'We've got to get him down to the cellar,' said Julie. 'Pichler is not about. We can carry a mattress down and blankets, and arrange everything else afterwards. I'll go down and bolt the house door from the inside so that Pichler can't get back in until we've got him down. You fetch the mattress from the spare bed – it's narrower to carry – and get it out on the landing.'

They were lucky, once again, as they always had been lucky. Pichler was still not there and Julie pulled the heavy iron bolts, not oiled for years, on the main doors. She then pulled down the sash-window of the porter's lodge from the inside and bolted it in place. Then she locked the lodge door from the outside and put the key in her coat pocket. Nobody would notice for a time that the outer doors were bolted, it was too dark in the unlighted hall-way; and the woman with a hand under her apron would account for locking up the lodge, so that no one could get at the keys.

It took what seemed a long time to shift enough of the trunks and old junk in their cellar to make room on two steamer trunks with a crate between them for the mattress. It was not quite even, but it would do. They had a separate cellar for coals, and would not have to share the cellar with their fuel supply. The store cellar even had an air vent which let in a thin draught of shudderingly cold damp air. All the other cellars already had mattresses and the most essential of needs in them belonging to the other families, but none was occupied at the moment; they were always empty just after air-raids as Julie realised now for the first time. It was not until they were finished and back in the apartment that the two women recognised that they could not get Franz down the stairs without help. They edged him slowly to the flat door, his hands, which now seemed much larger than formerly, since he had become so emaciated, hanging slackly over their shoulders. His feet in carpet slippers dragged very slowly after their hauling, gasping bodies, bent over with the effort of dragging him. But they knew before they were even on the landing that they would never get him down the stairs. He tried feebly to help them but that only made matters worse.

'It's no good,' said Julie, gasping for air. 'We have to have help.'

'Not Pichler!' said Fina. They moved backwards and let Franz sink into a hall chair. Fina wiped his grey face lovingly with a soiled handkerchief.

'The man from the little pub next door,' said Julie at last. She pulled herself upright from the closed door on which she was leaning, and went off again down the curving stairs. She could hear Fina calling her and took no notice. It was quite a business getting the door open; the bolts were rusted. She locked it after her again and ran, or scrambled, the few steps to the sunken entrance. Luck again. There were people in the smoky tavern, but all talking and taking no notice of anything but their own disasters, and the owner was there.

He began to protest when he saw Julie's state, but she cut him short, holding on to his arm.

'You have to help us,' she said rapidly. 'We've got to get him down to the cellar now while nobody else is about. Pichler is away and it's a perfect chance. But at once — can you come right away? We've tried and tried, but we can't hope to get him down the stairs and the lift is gone.'

'Of course,' he said reasonably, 'the electricity's off altogether.' He untied his coarse linen apron and came immediately, only calling to the woman by the stove that he would be right back. She did not have to explain that in a few hours the cellars would be full for the night; she did not have to explain anything. This man knew.

He kneeled down with his back to Franz without a word, not even seeming to look at the exhausted face. Fina folded Franz's hands at the front of the tavern keeper's chest, he picked up the long legs and rose unevenly to his feet again. The two women supported his burden on either side. The weight that seemed so terrible in its inert helplessness only a few minutes before was now perfectly manageable. Very slowly, feeling for the dark steps in front of him, pausing on every landing, they guiding him and holding Franz upright, he descended the stairs. He began to breathe heavily through his mouth and the sweat broke out all over his big body in streams so that Julie could smell it; he gritted his teeth and muttered something to himself over and over. Franz was murmuring something in a painful undertone, but there was no time to take notice of anything but the business in hand. As they reached the mezzanine they could already hear the door-bell shrilling, and a knocking at the door. They took no notice. A door of one of the apartments on that floor, the office of an attorney, opened a crack and a woman peeped out but thought better of it and let the door-bell ring on. Another woman stood in the cellar passage at right-angles to their direction; she stared but said nothing. She may have thought it was someone injured in the raid whom they carried. Such scenes were too frequent nowadays to arouse interest. Franz rolled on to the mattress and the big man straightened himself, stretching his neck and catching breath in hoarse gulps.

'Heavier than he looks,' he grunted at last, as if in absurd apology.

'I must open the doors,' said Julie. 'Someone will suspect something.'

'You go on,' said the man, wiping his head with a dark blue cloth out of his pocket. 'I'll slip out when nobody's looking in case Pichler is back.'

The candle flame flickered wildly in the draught from the air vent.

'I can't thank you,' muttered Julie helplessly. She was holding on to his thick arm, and became aware of weeping. He shook his head, unwilling or unable to say anything.

Later, upstairs in the flat, after she had washed herself, she opened the windows and shutters to get, as she thought, a breath of air into the stuffy and foul-smelling room where they had lived together for weeks. She had to close them again directly, for the billows of smoke and dust only made matters worse. She leaned out to catch the last shutter to fasten it. The noise in the city had abated now; here where there was no damage to-day, the crackle and rumble of fires could not be heard and the mob of people had streamed away. Far, far distant, on the wind blowing cold and steady from the east, Julie heard a faint thumping. She supposed a fresh air-raid was going on somewhere in the suburbs.

Incredibly, the telephone began to ring. She let it ring, but it went on and on, so at last she went and picked it up.

'Isn't it unbelievable that it's still working?' said Maris's voice. 'Listen, Julie. I can hear the guns. Have you heard them? Are you there? Why don't you answer me?'

Julie mumbled something, not knowing what Maris was talking about or why she should telephone her; they had not seen each other for some time and Julie had almost forgotten her existence.

'Can you hear? This line is so bad. It's the guns, the Russians, can you hear me? Lehmann just had a message that they will break through the front at any moment. From some friend of his. They're fighting at Odenburg, and that's only just over the border. I am leaving at once. Friedrich will follow in a few days, as soon as he can. Julie, why don't you come too? I'm a bit scared at going alone, the West Station is a hopeless mess and God knows when I can get on a train. They are being shunted about all over the place it seems ...'

'I can't leave,' said Julie flatly.

'What do you mean? Are you mad – you can't stay here ...'

Julie put down the receiver.

There were still mattresses and blankets for themselves to carry down the everlasting stairs. A packet of food, a bottle of water, wine and brandy. A case filled with clothes in case of a near direct hit. They discovered in an hour or so what other people in the house had done weeks before. The possession above price was candles for now the electricity, even when there was any, was turned on for a few hours each day only, and there was no shimmer of daylight in the cellars. They had plenty of candles, pre-war ones of fine tapered shape not used for dinner or supper parties after Franz first went away. The tins and glasses on the storage-shelves began to disappear at a frightening rate for Julie's attempts through the theatre administration to get a fresh ration card remained unsuccessful. Or rather, the usage of the stored food would have been frightening if either of them had thought about it seriously. But it was five minutes before twelve o'clock, and what was to happen when the food was gone was no longer of any importance. Chaos was due long before that time. This was now universally known. Even the swinging bodies of the two deserters from the Volkssturm that hung, so they were told, in the Stadtpark as a warning to defeatists could no longer prevent everybody knowing that the end was here. The rumbling of the guns swelled all in one day to a slamming and booming, the *whing* and *pang* of rocket shells, the low whistle of artillery and looping mortar missiles were now familiar but almost unconsidered. Those who live in a battle are concerned, as Julie discovered, more with the immediate problem of eating and keeping at least partially clean, than with life and death. The smells in the cellars were not noticed except on coming in from the outside or from upstairs, cooking some mess of rice, beans, potatoes. Gradually, too, the cellars were emptying; there were fewer people there on the night after the great raid, the next night fewer still. Those who remained talked only of local shell-hits, and of the choice which did not exist between terror of the Russians and longing for the end. As if the end would make an end. But of that nobody thought, it seemed. There would be a blank, the curtain Julie had often longed for would come down and the long play would be over.

Noise. Shuddering, clanging, booming, howling, whistling, wailing noise had become the condition of existence. There was never quiet for more than a few minutes. Even in the cellars, for there noise was distorted and amplified by the hollow spaces, and short interims were filled with febrile voices and the crying of children and one or two old people who had come in from nowhere.

Nothing was, afterwards – the end was not an end and afterwards came – remembered about these days. There were noise and confusion. At one point there was a row with Pichler. Fina assured Julie afterwards that Julie told the caretaker to go to the block-leader and see where that would get him; afterwards Fina herself slipped up the stairs to the porter's lodge and assured Pichler that she would kill him personally with her own hands if 'anything happened'. Nothing did happen, from Pichler's doing; this was not remembered, but disappeared in the whirlpool of noise like everything else. Including the appearance of Hansi Ostrovsky in the cellar, with a revolver he had found from somewhere and a box of ammunition for it. He said there were bands of escaped foreign workers all over the city, seeking booty and revenge. Julie and Fina did not even laugh but sent him away again with his protective toy, but they laughed afterwards, sitting beside Franz; they seemed to be laughing a good deal, somehow. At what, they did not examine. They spent hours sitting beside Franz and holding each a hand. Life as Julie had known it receded to an unmeasurable distance.

Hansi was the last visitor from the old world; the telephone call from Maris was forgotten. They went out of the cellar only to trail up the endless winding stairs to wash or cook. Outside the building was another world, nothing to do with their familiar city street and that world they penetrated by turns for water. A small calibre shell churned up the asphalt of the roadway, but this did not prevent the straggle of refugees using it for their carts and hand-barrows; in the first few days the trail of dirty, scared, hungry people spoke their rattling Magyar. After that, the lilting German of the Burgenland followed them. Sometimes the roadway was empty, sometimes filled by a stream of carts, a herd of lowing cattle, bellowing for rest and milking, sheep, pigs, fowls in baskets on hand-carts, straggling children wailing for their mothers. Old women sat down for rest on the kerb, hugging bundles, a baby, a useless cooking pot, wagging their heads and muttering to themselves their unbelief. Members of families found each other or more often asked unsuccessfully for each other at the standpipe, stopping to drink and resented by the people who lived there, for the trickle of water often stopped altogether now.

Julie was up in the apartment at least once when the telephone, again incredibly alive, rang for a long time but she did not answer it. There was nobody who could have been at its other end who had anything to do with her. Once or twice, she did not really know how often, she had hallucinations. It seemed to her one night, dozing uneasily on the thin pallet on the cellar floor – for months, even before they were in the cellar, nobody really slept – that she was awake and heard Nando's voice quite clear near her asking quietly, anxiously, how his sister was.

'Lali,' said the voice, 'Julie, how is Lali, how is the child?'

In answer to this, Julie went out, so she seemed to remember, and trudged over to the house where the Krassnys' flat was, and the house still stood and their name was still over their bell-push, but no one answered. She pushed a slip of paper under their door asking Christian Krassny to try to come to see her, but he did not come and she supposed she might have dreamed it. The outing, if it occurred, took a great deal of time and it was hard to get back; this quarter of the city was now under direct artillery-fire and a storm of steel opened up during her real or imagined trek back to Schellinggasse. She was not afraid; it meant nothing. But a nuisance, dodging here and there, and very dirty in what was by now dry spring weather. The stink from the bombed and ruined houses was bad, Julie held a handkerchief to her face but it did not help and somehow in the dream it got into her mind that nothing she ever read or heard about had told her what foul smells were connected with war. This, it seemed in the dream, was a betrayal, and it got into her mind that this lie about smells was part of a greater lie that disguised until it was too late the reality of the nightmare in which she moved; or did she move? The smells became an obsession. When the constant air-raid alarm wailed she smelled vomit and excrement and did not know in the end whether the vomit was actually vomited, whether the cellar inmates dirtied their already dirty clothes and bedding or whether she was dreaming it. The dead people under the ruins of the back-house stank abominably and the corruption was in the cellars, impregnating everything, blending with more immediate and temporary smells. A special smell was the dry, sweetish reek of rubble and burned wood soused with water; house bugs added to this reek, crawling from the old twice-used bricks of bombed buildings into the whole houses and taking their curious filthy smell with them where it had never before been known. The poor revenge themselves sometimes on the rich; the travelling bugs took dysentery and skin ailments with them.

At some point Fina wept with an anger at physical humiliation she was still able to feel, because she was constantly scratching and though they agreed that it was no good minding and she must try not to scratch, she could not help scratching and Franz began feebly scratching with her. They did not discover why.

They found too, that they had to hide or lock up anything to eat and even more, to drink, so the trail up and down the winding stairs became habitual for in the flat they could still be sure that none of the strangers with children who cried and for whom it was permissible to steal could get at their precious supplies. Wine and the remaining stock of brandy became increasingly important. There had not been, or not noticeably, children in the house before; at some moment the presence of children puzzled Julie and she failed to understand why it seemed — even to herself — important that they should be there. Absurd, she vaguely thought, but it reminded her and without remembering to say anything to Fina or Franz she struggled into her beaver coat and went out into the street. It took some time to get to the post office and it was strangely hot, the air dark with hanging dust. When she found it the post office was closed, with a steel shutter over its entrance. She stood, leaning on the dirty door post and turning a button of fur in useless fingers, and it seeped into consciousness that it was too warm for a fur coat; somewhere in limbo the winter was over.

She pushed herself upright with a shove of her shoulder and started off again. She had no idea from where and when she knew where the next post office was but she was right and after a time, some time, there it was and open. Only one old clerk, but he accepted her telegram and promised it could 'still' be sent. Still.

There was trouble deciphering her handwriting and she printed the words out a second time on the back of the form. I have no news but let me know about Lali: Julie. Yes, that would do. There was a crowd in the post office pushing and complaining and smelling. One had to wait a long time, but time did not matter. Time was not any more. She was halfway back to her cellar before it occurred to her with absolute certainty that when she heard the telephone ring and ring and had not answered, it was Nando's mother. Perhaps it still works and I could telephone Enns, she thought, but it was a vague and unreal thought. Any immediate contact was out of the question.

She pulled into a deep doorway for a trail of SS troops that filled the narrow street. Blackened faces, drawn, grey; dead eyes of sleep-walkers only just alive. She heard the word 'bridge', which like everything else meant nothing. A cackling laugh, not like a man's laugh; she found herself sliding slowly against the doorway towards the ground and pulled herself upright with a strength she no longer possessed. The filthy uniforms looked worse in ruin than the drab uniforms of soldiers; I suppose that's why soldiers wear that greenish grey. They had been a mistake, a last romantic spasm intended only for victory. That was where the word defeat came in; she still thought in words from training and habit, but the words meant nothing or meant something unknown that she had not explored. If you would only shut up for a moment, she said inside her head, I could remember what I was going to do; and the roadway being clear now she began cautiously to trail along under the house walls back to the cellar. Cautiously because she had to catch hold of things now and then. This was absurd, of course, and she had the feeling she was showing off to herself.

Corner of the street. The house door visible. Only now and suddenly she was aware with menace that it was quiet. She stopped, one hand on the wall. Yes, quiet, almost silence. The battering and whining of the guns had stopped. This is the end, then, she thought, and was proud of that quite artistic phrase which appeared whole in her mind. Listen, she said in her head, would you please be quiet a minute, I have to concentrate. She was still trying.

They all knew, it seemed. Faces turned in the flickering lights of candles and paraffin lamps and said the same thing she had said in her head. How did they know the quiet meant the end; she had thought it but how did others know. Someone said they were over the bridges. You're guessing, she said, but nobody answered. The quiet answered.

Everything flickered. Fina's voice, not heard, apprehended, complained and asked her where she had been and she said to the bridge and was not aware that this was 'untrue'. If this goes on much longer we shall run out of candles, said Fina's voice and from his pallet where she sought a skeleton hand, Franz murmured that she should sit down and rest. Rest.

Over. It should just be over. That was the only thing. When they came they would take care of Franz and value him. He was the living, the still living opposition. We have saved him, Fina and myself; she was perfectly well aware that this new thought was madness. Saved him and they will take care of him. Then I can rest, as he says. But yes, they really will save him and value him, and it will be over and this idea gripped her with a terrible euphoria from the darkness of a thousand years of fear. The immeasurable value of his life, the obsession of years, was suddenly clear in the value they would put on it.

She lay down on the thin mattress and slept, her hand sliding out of Franz's hand; Fina was curled in the curious posture she had adopted, leaning half on her mattress and half against the raised mattress where Franz lay, so that she could always touch him.

In the quiet the whirling dust clouds settled slowly, so that the air outside when they went to get water at the standpipe was a fog. The dust of battle was settling; the phrase so often read meant now exactly what it said. A man at the standpipe reported that they were camped in the Landstrasse with their small ponies and panje-carts. The Landstrasse was perhaps a kilometre, direct, from where they stood at the pipe, waiting drearily, patiently, for buckets to fill. The man who told her this lifted his bucket and set off across the street, one arm stretched out sideways to balance the weight and his shoulders bent forward as if he were running, although he walked quite slowly forward into the middle of the street. There was a crack like a whiplash from nowhere. The man with the bucket jumped in the air. The bucket flew out of his hand and the precious water ran over the surface of the dry broken roadway making a large dark patch which Julie watched as it spread. Then she was aware that the man had collapsed and now lay in a shapeless bundle of useless clothing. From somewhere far, far away, Julie seemed to look down from a height and see a scattered group running, foreshortened by the angle of height, scattering and joining up again and then backing off down the street, the fringes of the group fraying off in single figures but the centre a struggling knot of yells and shaken fists. Then a high shout and the clatter of horses' hooves on the cobbles and from a horseman in uniform, suddenly on the scene, a single shot followed after a pause by a volley of rifle-fire; and a woman in long full skirts of dark cloth keeling slowly round and over, her shawl falling first so that she afterwards lay across it. There are no cobbles in this street, Julie pointed out stupidly to herself, and no hussar officer riding ahead of a troop of cavalrymen. Her bucket was still only half full. She looked backwards; it was three steps from the kerb where the standpipe stood to the house wall. She knew this from counting her steps when carrying heavy buckets. On the other hand she was sheltered from everywhere by a curve in the street, except from directly opposite. This was quite clear, but she did not know where the shot had come from except, she thought, from the street and the right, not from a house. Just the same, she lifted the half-filled bucket, remembering even to turn off the trickle of water, and backed quickly with it to the house wall. Three houses down from their own house. She kept her back to the house walls so that she could see what, if anything, was happening. Inside the house door was a knot of curious bystanders come to see what the shot was and she pushed her way through them. She was across the hall before something occurred to her and she set down the bucket and went back to the doorway.

She said something about either coming inside or going away; she was going to lock the door and bolt it.

'You're not allowed to,' said a voice, at once frightened and excited. 'They keep on broadcasting that everything has to be left open. Haven't you heard?'

She must have stared because whoever it was, a man in shabby overalls, raised his voice as if to an idiot and repeated, 'Haven't you heard?'

'I can shut the door of my own house if I want to,' she said slowly.

'Oh no, you can't,' shouted the man, enraged. 'They say everything is to be left open. Anyone who resists them will be shot out of hand.'

'Is it true?' she asked the group in general. Mutters were the only answer. Evidently she was the only one who had not heard the orders. She did not believe it but there was something in the atmosphere that gave her a new unease. These people would turn on her; the overalled man had more than fear and anger in his voice. He was enjoying something too. Julie went back to her bucket and retreated with it down the cellar steps feeling her way in the dark.

Halfway down the curving steps she stumbled and spilled most of the water. She felt a febrile anger at this mishap. Water became precious when it was so heavy to carry, and one hand was needed to trace the curve of the cold stone wall. At the foot of the stair there was the flicker of several candles in the constant draught. Pichler was there and for the first time in a long while, his wife, too. They turned their heads together and their faces, scored by uncertain glimmers, were puffy and drawn with a pasty dirtiness. She supposed she looked like that, too; they all did. It had never struck her before how alike were the faces of the two Pichlers.

He was addressing a group of cellar-dwellers, telling them about the new regulations. She did not wait to listen, but he saw her, and having finished he came to the cellar door and knocked.

'You are not allowed to lock the door,' he instructed in a hectoring tone. 'Water will be fetched in turns, and I am drawing up a list.'

'Then put your own name at the head of it,' said Julie.

'I have to report at the district administration offices. All the caretakers have been ordered to report themselves there to give lists

of the people in the houses. I shall have to report the presence of
the man in your cellar.'

'If you mean my husband, do. The Russians will be interested
to know that he is still alive and here.'

This had not occurred to Pichler and he tried to ignore it.

'All house property will be nationalised now,' he said but his
voice took on an uncertain note. From his former point of view
it was hard for him to grasp that what had been a potential means
of blackmail against Julie and Fina had reversed its meaning. In
the last weeks his wife had said that having sheltered a Jew and a
Socialist might be a good thing for the future, but he was still not
quite able to believe the new situation.

'Go away and leave me in peace,' said Julie. 'Go and crawl to
your new masters. I hope they arrest you, you Nazi.'

'I've never been a Nazi,' his voice rose to a whine ridiculously
like its former obsequiousness so that Julie wanted to laugh aloud.
'I've known for years that Doctor Wedeker was in the house. I
never betrayed you, did I?'

'Oh you have, have you?' Fina screamed. 'Then why did you
refer to him just now as that man? And you needn't trouble to tell
your district administration anything about it. We shall go there
ourselves as soon as the shooting stops. So be careful what lies you
tell them.'

'They won't listen to you,' he cried in a beseeching voice.
'Everything has to be done officially.' He cast about for something
that would mollify them. 'I will see that you get water brought down
to you,' he offered, glancing quickly sideways at his wife for approval.
A couple of strangers approached the corner of the cellar corridor
to listen, and they began muttering among themselves. Julie heard
a woman's voice saying that she certainly was not going to carry
water for any conceited bitches who thought themselves too good
for ordinary people. You'd think the whole house belonged to her,
the way she talked. It was the woman Julie had seen the day of the
great air-raid wearing a sacking apron. A stocky man never seen
before pushed himself forward from the group by a curious alter-
nate shoving motion of his shoulders, which looked to be
immensely thick and strong although he was short in stature.

'You don't have to truckle to her or anyone,' he told Pichler in a loud hoarse voice that echoed in the hollow corridor. 'Now Vienna is liberated all property belongs to the people and everyone will have to work. Even the likes of you,' he added addressing Julie directly.

'The things that crawl out from the woodwork!' muttered Fina at Julie's shoulder.

'Then you'll go back to coal-heaving, since you seem to have escaped the army,' cried Julie, beside herself. 'And I'll go back to the Burgtheater where I've worked all my life. Only your friends the Russians have wrecked it!' She turned on Pichler who had laid a hand on her arm, and shook him off. 'You hold your tongue, Pichler. You and this rabble were all screaming for the Führer a year ago or so, and now you'll all claim to be socialists – communists, even, I shouldn't be surprised. Yes, I've waited for years to say this. You'll carry on just the same, ratting on your neighbours, taking bribes and creeping to the authorities. But just you be careful, because you're not the only one who knows Franz Wedeker is down here. The theatre people will be in touch with the Russians before you, remember.'

She intended to say more, much more, but at that moment there was a great crash upstairs of something very heavy thrown down on the stone tiling. Every head turned fearfully towards the cellar entrance. In the wavering lights their faces showed deep shadowy lines and the first crash was followed shortly by a series of heavy thumps and a medley of cries and shouts, coarse laughter, a yell of protest and more laughter.

Without saying anything everyone in the threatening little group near Julie's cellar door was sidling away. In a moment there was nobody to be seen.

'Sounds as if they've got hold of drink,' she heard someone say and the harsh man's voice shouted, 'Hide the women. They'll be down here!'

'Put the candle out,' whispered Julie to Fina. 'No, wait. Let's pull the trunks a bit away from the wall. We can hide behind them.' They had found a disused door leaning against a wall somewhere in the cellar corridor, taken out of one of the apartments upstairs at some time, and this they had laid across the two trunks and the crate between them so that the unevenness under Franz's mattress was alleviated. Now they hauled and pulled desperately at the big trunks until they could squeeze behind them to push them a little away from the wall. The door with the mattress still on it then covered a narrow black corner of space into which they crouched while Franz managed to raise himself on to his mattress again without their help. They were now in total darkness. So was the rest of the cellar.

For a long time, they had no means of knowing how long, the thumps and crashes from above could be heard, accompanied by shouting and laughter. Then gradually the sounds faded and at last there was silence, a thick, smothering, dark silence. The silence and darkness went on for a long, unknown time.

She dozed uneasily, but suddenly was horribly awake; Fina was gripping her hand so that it hurt. It was at once cold with the cellar damp and stifling in their narrow hiding-place, and her knees, doubled up for she knew not how long, ached miserably. Outside there was a noise of heavy objects being dragged along the stone floor, then a scream and men's voices in a strange mono-syllabic talk that sounded like a series of barks and grunts. The woman screamed again, sobbing wildly, begging for mercy. Then a moment's silence and the screams began again, continuously now for a long time, a long time, and gradually the screams slid down the scale of sound until they were only a low moaning. They became aware that there was a flickering light, perhaps coming from outside their cellar opening, and the smell of burn-ing paper. Julie could feel the door with its mattress shaking over her crouched head. The cramping pain in her knees and the back of her neck was unbearable. She could hear her own heart pound-ing. Then she felt above her Franz moving, heard the scrape of his slippered feet as he searched for the floor in the dark, heard him whispering something she could not understand, and remembered with a sensation of horror that he spoke some Russian. Fina too heard him moving. She started to scramble wildly backwards out of the narrow slot, whispering to him to keep still, and as he still struggled with something – it was his dressing-gown caught on a corner of the flat door – she cried aloud to him.

Not all the men were concerning themselves with the woman outside who now moaned with a snuffling, bubbling sound and could hardly be heard. The half-open door of their cellar crashed open against the wall with great force and now the smoky flame of a burning paper torch impaled on a bayonet, illuminated the small crowded space of their refuge. Fina had released herself, she was on her knees still, trying to rise from her cramped crouch, Julie could see her face. She could hear Franz's gentle, feeble voice in the strange tongue but nobody listened. She began to creep out, and then hesitated. Something pushed Franz and he fell against the uneasily balanced door, which fell forwards, throwing him to the floor. Julie began to push herself up against the wall. They were several short stocky figures, she could not see how many, for they milled about and the dim flicker of paper was burning down.

In the uproar there was no way of knowing what happened. There was Fina being pushed backwards and Julie heard ripping sounds of cloth and wild screams and curses. Franz, struggling to his feet, flung himself forward and the grunting barks of the short men rose to a babel of shouts. There was a flare from the dying paper torch and she saw distinctly a man in stained uniform pulling himself free and struggling to release the short stubby gun slung over his shoulder. The flare-up of the paper died and as shots deafeningly filled the tiny cellar with acrid smoke and ear-splitting shocks that were no longer noise, there was total dark in which the flashes of the gun blazed. She could hear and see nothing, and was stifled by the explosive smoke.

There were hands, feet, knees, elbows, shoving and scrambling. She felt hands, many hands, and felt cloth tearing and heard shouts and screams in the muffled stupor of bursting eardrums. She felt her throat straining and splitting, felt what were left of fingernails fighting with the strength of desperation, felt herself falling and smothering in a new stench until her head burst with a tremendous crack inside it, a burst of lights and nothing.

Darkness. Complete darkness. For a moment she thought she must be still alive but blackness from inside her rolled up again to meet the outer dark. This sensation came several times, at unknown intervals. A falling into endless black. There were sounds and voices, a flicker of light perhaps. Dreams. Once a voice said from a great distance but clearly, I think she's dead and a woman's voice answered, Well, she's down in the muck now, all right, with the rest of us. Blackness consumed the voices and when the sensation of being there again came she felt it was after a long interval.

She could hear a voice again, Pichler's, blubbering, My poor old woman, My poor old woman, My poor old woman ... She knew it was Pichler's voice so she knew she was alive. She felt she should move but was unable to. Pain began, diffused everywhere, not inside her but outside, enfolding her completely. Darkness again, rushing upon her from inside and outside. She came to and longed for water but could not move; when she tried to she found that the worst of the pain was somewhere near her head and with the slightest movement overwhelmed her so that the black came back, in a wave of nausea, swooping up.

In the blackness there was a tramp of feet somewhere, voices that swelled and receded, a clatter. She felt herself lifted, groaned, and opened her eyes long enough to see a cuff of white coat and a hand feeling about her wrist. She was being swayed, rocking like a boat rocking on water and for a second failed to focus on something with dark lines that swayed over her. A voice said, Be careful on the stairs, and the black came up again.

It was a white crispness, clean, soft; the most delicious sensation she had ever known was the white cleanness; this faded, returned, faded again. Later people moved about, spoke softly, a huge winged white something threw a faint shadow over her face, approached and was removed at once. A low gentle voice said, She is conscious, Herr Doctor, I believe. There was a space where the white cleanness was brighter; when she woke again it was all dark, but a luminous dark with a glow somewhere and the winged shape threw this time a huge flickering shadow and the soft voice said, Don't try to move. Your head is injured and you must not move.

Smells of medicaments or disinfectants at last gave the clue to the white winged something which she gradually realised without ever being aware of understanding it, was a nun's winged cap. The space of lighter light was a window and she could now see that outside it there was a light green moving mass, too much light that hurt so that she closed her eyes again. Then she was aware of being fed some liquid and heard voices again. She opened her eyes, but saw nothing of the voices, only the edge of the winged cap as it turned away and fell into a dream of birds' wings in mountain sunlight, like the winged cap.

'You need not worry about penicillin. There is plenty.' This was a voice with a strong, outlandish accent. A voice in correct German murmured something she did not hear and the voices moved farther away and then one came back and said so that she could hear, in the correct German, 'No, Sister, you must keep visitors away a few more days. He will have to wait.'

She was aware of being moved about on a rolling bench, being eased over, a sharp prick in her upper arm. Then the white winged cap was back.

An oldish face, she could see it now, pale, fine skinned and round with a distinct moustache of white hairs on the upper lip, the lips moved and she heard a new voice, higher than the other one but gentle, too, saying, 'You'll soon feel better now. Everything is all right now.' This was nothing to do with her and she was not interested, any more than she had been interested in the other voices.

At some point she discovered that her hair had been cut very short which puzzled her. Still later she found that on one side there was a pack or pad on her head.

She opened her eyes to see a face above her that she had once known but it was not until later that she remembered it was Hansi Ostrovsky's face. She was hungry. The voices irritated her, speaking where she could not see and she tried to wave them away with her hand which moved on the white coverlet of itself. This seemed interesting but she wished they would bring something to eat and waited impatiently for the winged white cap.

'We are unlikely ever to know,' said the correct voice in German, with a severe tone and she knew he was saying something he knew was not true. 'Frau Homburg will certainly never be able to tell us anything about it; she will remember nothing. Indeed, it is almost a miracle she survived that crack on the head. She must have a wonderful constitution.'

It puzzled her, a little later, after the winged cap with the moustache had carefully spooned some kind of broth into her mouth, to think what it was they would never know and who had wanted to know it. It was something he was not supposed to inquire about, that much was clear, but it faded into mistiness before she thought it out.

Sometime, after it had become light again, she heard herself speak.

'You mustn't think about anything,' said the soft voice, but now with a disciplinary tone. 'Just try to concentrate on getting strong again.'

It was a room she could now see, entirely painted white and a while later she found herself propped up so that she could really look about her and lie fascinated by the tree in spring finery outside the closed windows which flicked its fresh green about gaily in the glitter of sunlight beyond which she could now see blue, pale but intense blue. Now she could look at it for a little while before her eyes began to dazzle and ache, but it was somehow painful to her and slow tears rolled down on to the white sheets. She was worried by this, knowing by now that everything must remain perfectly clean and neat all the time, and she brushed them feebly away before they sank into the weave of the linen. Her hand seemed very long and thin. She turned it over with interest as if she had not seen it before this moment.

Something struggled inside to get into her mind and she began to shift about and fidget. Presently a tall man in a white coat leaned over her and said to someone out of sight, 'Yes, you are right, Sister. A slight sedative, I think.'

'It's quite untrue that I don't remember,' she protested angrily. 'I remember distinctly up to the moment the paper burned out.'

'Yes, yes,' he murmured and made a gesture but not to her. He reached backwards with his far hand and a second later – he kept that hand covered by the other one – she felt the slight prick in her arm.

But in the night she woke and was conscious and remembered.

The nun was not in her room all night any more. Every now and again she looked in at the door but Julie was careful to keep quite still. In the morning she tried to hold the bowl with milk and coffee for herself but the nun did not trust her not to spill it. She was pleased and praised Julie for trying, like a child.

She waited impatiently until the doctor came. He spoke to her now, but very quietly as if she were a deranged infant, even more like a child than the nuns did, but he did speak to her.

It took her a little while to determine to speak. They might give her some more sedatives. At last, as he was already turning to go, she moved her hand.

'Herr Doctor ... I want to see Fina.' She was quite aware that this was a stupid thing to say to begin with. He would not know Fina. She must make an introduction. She tried again. 'I want to see my husband and Fina who were in the cellar,' she said distinctly. He appeared not to hear.

'She can start on solids now,' he said and clearing his throat, he retreated to the door and disappeared.

'It's no good trying to hide them from me,' she called after him and began to weep helplessly. The nun, it was the moustached one on duty again now, wiped her face and made her blow her nose.

'I'm sorry, Doctor, but I don't agree,' said Hansi's voice outside, later, much later. 'She has to know and we can't go on deceiving her. You don't know her as I do. I *am* being quiet—' the correct German voice had said something in an undertone – 'but it is better for her to be told now, before she recovers completely. Can't you see how she would hold it against us if we tried to deceive her?'

'Hansi,' she called. 'Hansi!'

'There,' his voice said triumphantly. 'You see?'

He was sitting by the bed; he looked much older, grey folds in his face and his hair a kind of dusty grey too. She recognised who he was now, but as a stranger.

'They are dead, aren't they,' she said flatly. 'Don't lie. They are dead.'

'Yes,' he said, gulping. 'They are dead.'

She did not put out her hand, but he took it and after a moment he laid his face on it on the coverlet, bent right over, and she could feel hot tears running between her fingers which he held tightly.

She began to cry too, and this annoyed her because she could not explain that it was not grief that made her tears run off her cheeks, but simply that she was so weak and helpless. Grief did not come later, either. She felt no grief, but she began to think of the waste.

The consuming feeling of waste obsessed her and she could not eat the milky slops or sleep. The doctor wanted to give her sedative injections again but now she was quite conscious and refused them.

'But you must have sleeping draughts at night,' he protested. 'You will have a relapse if you don't get some sleep.'

'Ah,' she said, 'you are talking to me like a human being. This is a great step forward.'

She was aware of having said something wounding but did not care. If she was alive, very well, she would be alive. But she was unable to explain this feeling to the doctor or the white-capped nuns. Things were constantly done, fiddling with the pad on the side of her head and every day injections. She asked sharply what those injections were and the doctor promised they were not sedatives, but penicillin. Since she had never heard of penicillin it told her nothing much. But she was no longer treated like an idiot child so she began to trust them, especially as she did not go to sleep after the injection but became irritable and only slept much later when she had tired herself out.

Then hints began that she ought to go to some place to recover her strength; she would soon be quite better, but needed care and special food with gentle exercise. The man with the strong accent came back and explained this, as well as the tall doctor in his correct German.

'Yes, I would like to go,' she said. 'Could I go to Dirnhorn?'

This needed explanation and vague remarks passed which she did not understand after she had explained about the Gasthof Pfaundler near Meran. They sent for Hansi. When Hansi came, the man with the strong accent remained in the white room with them, in spite of Hansi's frowning hints.

'It would be difficult for you to go abroad,' he tried to convince her, but she knew from the way his eyes wandered sideways that he would not say what he meant while the man with the accent was there. 'Somewhere near Vienna. There are several good clinics – on the Semmering for instance ... ?'

'I've always disliked that touristy place,' she said fretfully.

'Your jacket is slipping,' he said too loudly. 'Let me help you up a bit.' As he lifted her awkwardly she felt his bony fingers shove something into the fold of the sheet, something that crackled slightly.

They went on talking until she became irritable and at last they left without any decision having been reached. Then Julie fished out the scrap of paper.

'They won't let you go anywhere outside their own jurisdiction, in case you clear off. Agree with them. It is the best thing. They are mad about starting up the theatre again and will give you anything you want so long as you stay here.'

Very well, she said next day, she would stay in Vienna. She didn't want any dreary convalescent clinics, she would go back to her own home. The nuns and the tall doctor were dismayed by this attitude; but to their surprise, though not to Julie's, the man with the accent agreed at once.

Another week, they said, and now she was able to measure time again and counted the days. She began to worry about how she would manage, for she was conscious of being very weak, unable to do more than move about with her limbs, which, reassembling herself, she found to be all there. There was a chair by the window, and she took steps to and fro; but when she thought of fetching water and struggling up those stairs, her courage failed her. But she said nothing. Anything to be alone.

She felt excited. There was the chair they carried her downstairs in, and the ambulance and astoundingly, if anything could still surprise, Pichler and a group of bedraggled people at the door. She saw everything with a clearness that surprised her a little too. The glass of the outside door was all gone, some of the wrought-iron bars twisted. In the hall, as she was swiftly carried by, the black and white flags were cracked and broken. But the lift was working again. The apartment was hardly recognisable. But that was a good thing, she did not want to recognise, only to be in her own place, and her bedroom was – more or less – as it had been. The lamp by the bed looked strange, but she accepted it almost at once. There was a fat tall girl, red cheeked, with a jutting bosom, and the nuns were to come each day.

'Where did that girl come from?' she asked. 'She's nothing to do with me!'

'We allowed ourselves the liberty,' they said absurdly, 'of engaging you a servant, most gracious lady,' and the incredible unsuitability of their language was so delightful to her that she had to swallow hard and the tears of suppressed laughter rose to her eyes, which pleased everyone very much.

There was a whole group of them, with Pichler and other hangers-on in their tow. They wore uniforms of a warm dark beige with various caps; that is, caps with various bands and badges though all the same in shape and size. They left and a nun put her into her own bed and she could hear complicated instructions being given in her hallway to the fat, tall girl.

She stretched out. This was nice.

When she woke the lamp, being a different one from her own bedside lamp with an alabaster base, began to trouble her; she rang the bell of which the cord was frayed and without its tassel.

'Where is my lamp?' she asked when the massively built girl appeared. 'This isn't mine – where did it come from?'

'Doesn't it belong here, gnae' Frau? It was here when I came, lying on the floor. The bulb was broken, so I took a bulb from one of the lamps in the beautiful salon. They hadn't touched the ceiling lamps there – too high, I dare say.'

'Was the whole place ransacked, then?' she asked.

'Well, it wasn't too bad up here – it's high for them, four floors up. They don't like stairs, thank God, but anyway we have a guard on the house now, so they won't come up here again. I went into the lawyer's place on the mezzanine, though – you should see it, there isn't a thing left whole in the place. They'd taken the filing-cabinets, big steel things, and thrown them down the stairs into the hall. There was paper everywhere, you waded through papers and folders when I came.'

'And here?' insisted Julie. She began to fidget and move about. 'I think I'd better get up and see what is damaged.'

'Ah,' said the girl, 'don't trouble yourself. I tell you they didn't do much up here – tired out by the time they got this far, I expect.'

Will-less, Julie lay back again. Some other time would do.

'Where did you come from?' she asked instead. 'Did they bring you with them?'

'From Raab,' said the girl simply. 'We pretended we weren't Germans, but bless you, that didn't make any difference, we could have saved our breath. They were just as bad with the Hungarians. Worse, if anything. And they can't tell the difference in the language, you know. They took me with them to cook, so I was all right. You have to learn fast with that lot, and once I'd got fire and hot water to threaten them with they began to behave themselves. At first it was bad, but they say they weren't so bad by the time they got to us in Raab. We had a lady in our cellar, she'd trekked from Szeged, and she told us at first when they were just over the border they were shooting every living soul that had electricity in the house or even a water closet. *Bourzhuis*, they call them. Some people must have had a bit of a shock, because the rich folks had all left long before and most of their houses were taken over, as you might put it, by peasants and refugees. They began to move out pretty fast, you can just imagine. But by the time they got to us, they were used to seeing lavatories and baths. Not that they used them, of course. They're used to going outside, you know, but in the towns where they can't find somewhere, they use the corners of the rooms. But that was the first wave; they have all gone now. They say they're near to Linz now and will be fighting the Americans any day. Sooner the better. They keep saying on the wireless that the war is over, but it can't last long. As soon as the Americans see what they are like, the fighting will start again. I was—'

A loud knocking at the apartment door interrupted the girl, whose name Julie still did not know.

'That will be the workmen to finish mending the door,' she announced and disappeared.

So they had broken the door in. She could hear rough voices, then hammering and the hiss of hand welders; evidently the iron bars and framework of the door had been damaged. It was only then she remembered that the windows in here, in her bedroom, had been broken by shell-splinters the last time she had come up to wash and change clothes (she found nothing clean to change into and remained as she was), and now she could see that the panes of glass in the inside windows were whole. The separate upper casements were covered with cardboard. She began to push off the bed covers. When she managed to reach the windows she saw that new panes had been solidly though clumsily, puttied into place. From this evidence she grasped that she was of great value to them. Window-glass had been non-existent for months. She let herself down into her dresssing-table chair, which was whole except for a slit in the silk covering. Then she saw that the doors of the long wardrobe were only loosely closed, the locks and handles all broken. This was also the state of every other fastening she could see, now that she noticed it; later she found that the cupboards and drawers were in fact full of her things; in disorder, but a good deal of her clothing was there.

These unimportant things were most important; she concerned herself entirely with them until exhaustion drove her back into bed. Outside she could hear a different voice, a tone, in the strange language she reacted to with a long fit of shuddering. But nothing happened, and presently the big girl came back with a tray of food. The food was unfamiliar, coarsely prepared but appetising. She recognised *kasha* and some kind of pork stewed with cabbage.

'The rations man comes every day,' explained the girl. 'I just have to heat it up. You're the only one in the house that gets their ration.'

'What about you, then?' Julie stopped eating.

'I get the issue. We don't have ration cards any more, they issue stuff. Bread, that's the same as usual, only damper than it used to be – they say they use more water to make it heavier. And dried peas we get, but they aren't much good without salt.'

'We had salt left. You'll find it in the store cupboard in the kitchen passage.'

The girl laughed at her innocence. She had rather a pleasant laugh, softer than her voice would lead you to expect. 'There's nothing left in the cupboards,' she said without resentment. 'They scattered everything all over the floor, jars and all. Nothing left.'

'Here, you can finish this. No, I can't eat it all. The thought of their food makes me sick, in any case, now I know it's their food.'

'It's all food,' said the girl. 'There is even an apple for you.' She added shrewdly, 'You must have known it was theirs. It's different from what you're used to, I'll be bound.'

'I didn't think of it. And then, the food in hospital was different too. Like everything else, for that matter.'

'Yes,' said the girl, frankly staring, 'you must be very famous and great, I suppose – gnae' Frau? Or they wouldn't have taken you off to hospital, that's all reserved for their own wounded. And there wouldn't be a guard on the house and I wouldn't be here and they wouldn't be repairing your apartment in the great hurry they're in.'

'Ye-es,' agreed Julie slowly, and her brows creased in the sudden frown which was not familiar to the girl so that she stiffened slightly, afraid she had said something wrong. 'I see what you mean. We must make the best use we can of that. When the man with the accent comes I shall tell him we must have some stores delivered and you must get rations.'

'You learn fast, like me,' said the girl. 'You mustn't mind me, you know. I'm not used to your city manners and I talk a bit rough, I expect.'

She took the tray with the half-eaten food cooling upon it and as she went she said over her shoulder, 'They're coming to-morrow to clear up the mess on the kitchen side where the bomb damaged the house.'

The next day a whole squad of workmen, Viennese, but with a Russian corporal – as the girl told her – to watch them work, took over the back part of the flat and worked noisily all day. The doctor came with the nuns, two of them, but not the one with the foreign accent; the one that spoke the very correct German.

'You are not an Austrian, Herr Doctor?' she asked him. He was looking sideways at the coffee pot on the tray. 'Will you have some coffee? The girl will heat it for you.' One of the nuns disappeared at once with the tray.

'I am from East Prussia,' he said stiffly. 'From Königsberg, in fact.'

'Did they bring you with them from there?'

He stared. 'These troops have not come from that direction,' he explained, thinking her confused over military organisation, not knowing it was her geographical sense that was hopelessly vague. 'But no, I was captured two years ago, in Russia itself.'

'Ah, you are working for them, then?' she questioned.

His face stiffened and when he replied his voice was hard.

'Yes, I am working for them. As I believe you will be, when you are quite recovered.'

'I hadn't thought of it like that,' she said slowly. 'But obviously you are right. I had only thought of my going back to the theatre – to my own work.'

'You will find,' he said coldly, 'that nothing is quite your own now. Nothing is as it was before.'

Evidently the time when she was treated as a child was very much past and it occurred to her that she had been expected to die.

'Is my head all right now?' she asked, refusing to consider what he had said.

'Your head?' he seemed surprised. 'Ah, that was not too bad. You have a terrific skull, made of steel. A bad concussion, laceration, extensive bruising, nothing more. We feared a fractured skull, but it is quite all right. But you know, you had been lying there for days – we don't know how long – and you had lost a lot of blood before they came to find you. Through the man from the theatre, as I understand . . . ?'

'Hansi? Was it Hansi who brought you there?'

'I wasn't there. But it was someone from the Burgtheater who told the Kommandatura where to find you when they began to round up the company and technicians. You know they have the-atres open again? Oh yes, for a week or so now . . .'

'But not the Burg?' she said sharply. 'That's ruined.'

'A complete wreck, unfortunately. But the Burg company is playing at the Ronacher, just near you here. It will be convenient for you when you return to work.'

'Ronacher!' she wondered. 'But that's a variety theatre.'

'It was almost intact.' The coffee – real not ersatz coffee – had been brought back by the nun and he drank it, but did not sit down. Neither did he thank her for it; and after all, it was not hers, why should he.

When they had gone she recalled his phrase. 'Nothing is quite your own now, nothing is as it was before.' This brought her closer than she could bear to be to thinking clearly. 'As it was before.' Instinctively, she busied herself with details again. All the various dressings were gone now, she could move more easily, and she got as far as the open door to the living-room before she tired so that she had to sit and rest.

Presently she got up and went into the living-room, driven by the need to know, to probe – to know what, she did not ask herself. The books struck her first; many were missing and in the gaps the dark woodwork showed gloomily in the long rows. Those on the shelves were in unfamiliar places, many were upside down. About the useless stove were piled others, some that belonged here and some that did not; from their titles she supposed they had been collected from all over the house, including the attorney's office for some of them were law books. At the windows, intact here for the shell had glanced off the outer wall between the salon and her own room, were clean curtains of her own coarse linen net although the velvet over-curtains were missing. All had been carefully cleaned, a long rent in the old carpet mended with long, cobbling stitches; the rugs bought one after another to cover shabby patches were now laid in unfamiliar places at odd angles and one of them was not hers. This no longer puzzled her as the bedside lamp had done; she knew now that things had been gathered together, the place put in order as well as it could be by people who had never before seen it. The door in the panelling to the dining-room hung loose with a hinge missing, the lock forced. She did not remember locking the dining-room but it was so long since it had been used that it could well have been locked for months; the months spent waking and sleeping here before going to the cellar. The clumsy iron cooker, its enamel covering chipped and scarred, still stood in the corner and its pipe, already rusting, disappeared botched into the discoloured wall. At the stove end the wall was papered, there were no book-shelves there, and the whole area was blotched and stained with unidentifiable stains as if whole buckets of heaven knew what had been flung against it. The room still smelled of antiseptics from its hasty cleaning. There were no flowers, of course, and the Meissen vase had lost one snake handle; there was a long crack winding across its upper curve. The pictures from between the windows were gone.

On the big flat desk there was nothing left. Its scratched, much-used surface gleamed dully, quite blank. Not even the inkwells and pen-rack of green marble, never used, were there. All the locks were broken. The drawers were empty. Every single piece of paper, every notebook was gone. Even unused paper was gone, even the pencils and fountain pens, the copy pencils, the stapler with a lion on its grip, the folders, the files of letters. Here there had been no attempt to put anything back in place; the desk had been totally cleared. The chair was intact and she sat down in it and rested her elbows on the arm-rests, her clasped hands lying before her on the surface of the empty desk. I wonder what happened to my rings, she thought indifferently.

All this no longer belonged to her, just as the glittering rings were no longer hers. This empty desk was not what was left of lives or objects that once had content and meaning. It had no relation to anything and might have been a piece of furniture in a hired furnished room.

She tried to push her thoughts back to her rings. Where had she last had them, remembered having them? The unconscious tricks she had been playing no longer worked. She looked at the unbelievable fact now, and could not avoid it. Not only the desk was empty, it had all gone for nothing. The shifts, the struggle, the sacrifice of Fina who had been nothing else but victim, even though the victim of her own female self-sacrifice; the deceit, the responsibility, were all nothing. There was nothing left of Franz; she was alone in a new life and world, as she was alone in this apartment. A world so strange that it had as yet not even a form; and certainly, all content being gone into nothingness, no content.

As the doctor said, nothing was her own any more and nothing would be as it had been before. There was only one question left in the void of meaning: how could it happen that she had been forced to survive?

Meaning, reality, retreated from its containing form backwards into the primitive dark of a cave underground and, in an instant of mindless uproar, was gone. And those who finalised the breakdown into chaos, its unknowing and unmeaning agents who now inherited the empty space, attempted by filling shelves with books turned upside down to refill the monstrous emptiness. Chaos claimed meaning and destroyed it; immediately the unknowable content was to be replaced by objects put into what might seem like their proper order. The bloody tattered flesh was sewn together, cosseted and serviced back into a semblance of meaning so that it could be exposed in public as incontrovertible evidence of the survival of what had been destroyed.

She became aware that if there was no meaning there was still sensation. As healed wounds do, the long scar on her head began to itch and, remembering the nuns' warnings not to scratch, she rubbed it gently with her fingertips. She had not yet seen this scar and wondered vaguely whether she would carry a visible mark; but she was too exhausted to get up and trail back into the bedroom where there was a looking-glass that would show her what she looked like.